MW00816540

A CLASH OF FATES

THE ECHOES SAGA: BOOK NINE

PHILIP C. QUAINTRELL

This is a work of fiction. Names, characters, places, and incidents either are the product of the author's imagination or are used fictitiously. Any resemblance to actual persons, living or dead, events, or locales is entirely coincidental.

Copyright © 2021 by Philip C. Quaintrell
First edition published 2021.

All rights reserved. No part of this book may be reproduced or used in any manner without written permission of the copyright owner except for the use of quotations in a book review.

Cover Illustration by Chris McGrath
Book design by BodiDog Design
Edited by David Bradley

ISBN: 978-1-916610-17-0 (hardback)
ASIN: B095LFLK2S (ebook)

Published by Quaintrell Publishings

For John and Wendy, thank you for always being there...

ALSO BY
PHILIP C. QUAINTRELL

THE
NIGHT
SEA

KHAI

THE
DREAD
WOOD

SILVYR
HALL

STORM'S REACH

HYNDAERN

THE RUINS OF
THE VALAN

THE BROKEN MOUNTAINS

NIMDUHN

THE VENGOR

WHITE
TOWER

THE WATCHTOWERS
OF ABODNOHUN

DRAKANAN

THE DRAGON VALE

BRENDALMUS' CAVE

THE FOREST
OF RUIN

SNOWFELL

DRAYSHON

THE RED FIELDS OF DUNMAR

THE KINGDOM ROAD

SUNHOLD

CARSTANE

FREYGARD

THE DEEP

THE VERGS OF ARNAGUN

THE RUINS OF
ULLANUM

MOUNT
KALIBAN

ELRADOR

RIVERWATCH

GRAVED
WOOD

THE STABLES OF KANE

THE SUNKEN ROAD

VANGALA

THE TOWER
OF JAIN

THE RED
HOLD

ELDERHALL

CASTLE
HOLD

HEMON

THE
HOX

FARNFOSS

THEDARIA

WARTH

LAKE
CELARA

TORINN

ALLISANDER

CARTHAN

HABAN'S
TOWN

SECOND
FOREST

BROADCASTLE

QALANQATH

OLD DRIFT

DRAMATIS PERSONAE

Adan'Karth (Adan)
A Drake

Adilandra Sevari
The late elven queen of Elandril and mother of Reyna Galfrey

Alijah Galfrey
Half-elf and self-proclaimed king of Verda

Asher
Human ranger

Athis
Red dragon, bonded with Inara

Doran Heavybelly
Dwarven Ranger/Prince and War Mason of clan Heavybelly

Ellöria Sevari
The late Lady of Ilythyra

DRAMATIS PERSONAE

Faylen Haldör
An elf and High Guardian of Elandril

Galanör Reveeri
Elven ranger

Gideon Thorn
Master Dragorn

Gondrith
Reaver - bonded with the dragon *Yillir.*

Ilargo
Green dragon, bonded with Gideon

Inara Galfrey
Half-elf Dragorn/Guardian of the Realm

Lord Kraiden
Late Reaver - bonded with the dragon *Morgorth.*

Kassian Kantaris
A previous Keeper of Valatos

Nathaniel Galfrey
An ambassador and previous knight of the Graycoats

Reyna Galfrey
Elven princess of Elandril and Illian ambassador

Rengyr
Late Reaver - bonded with the dragon *Karsak.*

Sir Ruban Dardaris
Captain of the King's Guard

The Crow (Sarkas)
Late Leader of The Black Hand

Veda Malmagol
The Father of Nightfall

Vighon Draqaro
The usurped king of Illian

Vilyra
Reaver - bonded with the dragon *Godrad.*

PROLOGUE

This is the end.

How could it not be? The world had been set alight, the sky blackened with ash, and the earth torn asunder. Civilisation was falling into ruin. Dragons, bereft of their murdered Riders, melted the stone with their righteous fire, torching the streets of Ak-Tor, Illian's doomed capital.

Sarkas watched it all like a god, removed from the carnage and death. The winds of time battered him, threatening to hurl him into the bleak future he now witnessed. With bloodshot eyes, he willed himself to keep watching, to observe the world to come.

Despite those ethereal winds, tearing at his clothes and pummelling his pale body, Sarkas wore the grin of a very satisfied man. For all the madness and sheer terror of such destruction, it was indescribably beautiful.

And all it took was a handful of dragons. Mage knights, cloaked in red, launched all manner of spells into the air. For all their effort, they only succeeded in adding some colour to an otherwise bleak vista. Ballistas hurled bolts, hoping to reinforce the knights' magic, and some even struck true, bringing down a dragon here and there.

Ultimately, and inevitably, there was nothing to be done in the face of such raw power. If the dragons of Verda wanted to raze humanity to the ground, there was no one, no thing, and no spell to stop them.

Doomed indeed.

To the west, Atilan's palace succumbed to the wrath of Garganafan, a dragon famed for his hulking size. Sarkas had heard of Garganafan, his name carried in the tales that breezed through The Citadel. Sarkas, however, had never seen the dragon before and attributed the knowledge he now possessed to the magic coursing through every fibre of his being - it whispered the truth into his mind.

Without turning to look, Sarkas's sight found another dragon to the south, clawing his way through one building after another. Just as he had known Garganafan when he saw him, Sarkas just *knew* that the black behemoth destroying Ak-Tor's southern district was Malliath the voiceless.

The black dragon rammed his way through an entire street of houses, his horns flinging people and debris high into the air. His tail always followed him through the chaos, swinging one way then the other to flatten anything that had survived.

When Malliath finally unleashed his breath, the jet of fire engulfed half a battalion of mage knights standing their ground on the district boundary. The smoke would have blinded any who witnessed such a massacre, but Sarkas was granted a view of it all.

The front four rows of mage knights had either failed to erect a shield or their magic had simply failed to hold up to Malliath's might. Now, the scorched bodies formed a black line in the street, separating the surviving mage knights from the dragon.

Sarkas fought against the winds of time to widen his vision, but the spell had a life of its own, as if it was showing him only what *it* wanted him to see.

Apparently, it wanted him to see death.

The mage knights resisted with spells, poking holes in Malliath's wings and chipping his armour-like scales. It only served to anger the beast all the more. His tail, lined with spikes, swung around in a wave of dirt and debris - a force no man could deny. Half lost their lives to the devastating retaliation, many of whom were thrown, like rag dolls, into the air. More spells followed, bombarding the black dragon until he staggered into the side of a building.

Under a shower of falling bricks and tiles, Malliath inhaled a sharp breath. Sarkas knew what would follow. Another jet of dragon fire spread out amongst the mage knights, weakening any shields they might build. Then, with great savagery, Malliath leapt from the shattered building and used his gargantuan size to crush the remaining humans. His claws lashed out, raking those lucky enough to have avoided his sheer weight.

None survived.

Sarkas wanted to follow the dragon and watch the city's ruination to its glorious end, but the magic he had conjured grew beyond his control. The young wizard, as he liked to consider himself, was violently pulled and pushed through the currents of time once more.

The world around him blurred into streams of colour as Ak-Tor's sharp edges vanished altogether. Stars shone through the myriad of colours, dazzling Sarkas into a disorientated state.

When, at last, his vision calmed and the end of days was behind him, Sarkas found himself standing on a beach bathing in golden sunlight. Standing before him, oblivious to the wizard who watched from eons past, was a young man draped in a green cloak and tired leathers.

As soon as Sarkas asked himself who this man was, a single name came to him with perfect clarity.

Alijah Galfrey.

He was treading through the soft sands of The Shining Coast, Sarkas knew, even though he had never visited Illian's coastline or even laid eyes on The Adean.

Alijah wasn't alone. Not far behind him was another young man whose name was suddenly emblazoned in the wizard's mind.

Vighon Draqaro.

The two were friends. No. Closer than friends. They were

brothers in bond, if not blood. It felt familiar to Sarkas, who had considered the slaves in The Citadel his brothers.

Through a halo of light, cast over Vighon by the sun, Sarkas caught glimpses of a crown on the northman's head. His hair had lost some of its colour and, like the crown, it came and went with the vision, lending the man a beard before quickly returning to stubble.

Then came another, behind the king-to-be. Her dark hair succumbed to the sea breeze and took off over her left shoulder. She was a vision of beauty and strength, a combination the young wizard had never come across before.

Inara Galfrey.

Her name hit Sarkas, adding a wave of heat to the ethereal winds that constantly blasted him. She was important to the world, just like the two men who had preceded her.

Inara looked right through him with her startlingly blue eyes, the same shade as Alijah's. Sarkas watched them ascend the cliffs and return to the green fields of Alborn. The wizard could see that all three of them were entwined, their destinies tied to the realm itself.

It occurred to Sarkas that he didn't know *when* he was. There was nothing around him to help distinguish the year and certainly no one to ask. As with everything else, he plucked the knowledge from nowhere and knew he was witnessing events ten thousand years from what he considered to be the present day.

The winds began to change again as time twisted and lurched. Illian's coast was torn away, replaced by a nauseating swirl of colours and stars. Sarkas could feel his strength waning. For all the secrets he had unlocked from the forbidden books of the Jainus, he simply didn't have experience or training on his side - just his will.

He continued to defy those powerful winds and ride the spell to its conclusion. He needed to see what was to come. The future *had* to be better.

The heat of Illian's coastal sun was replaced by the icy cold of winter. Sarkas took in his new surroundings, desperate to grasp his environment as quickly as possible. He was in the woods, The Wild

Moores to be exact. Snow coated everything and it was deathly still but for the sound of feet crunching through undisturbed powder.

The young wizard turned to see Alijah Galfrey again, only this time he was older and more rugged in his appearance. He was ploughing through the snow, bow in hand, searching for something. Sarkas wanted to reach out and touch him but the winds kept his hands at bay.

Then he was gone, flung forward in time again. The pain increased but it was nothing Sarkas hadn't experienced at the cruel hands of his master. His will endured.

Now, he stood in a damp cave beneath the school known as Korkanath. He looked up at the wet rock aware, without having witnessed the event, that the school above was naught but a charred husk.

Growing comfortable with the nature of the Jainus's magic, Sarkas stopped marvelling at his knowledge and focused on whatever significant moment was occurring around him before it was too late.

Alijah Galfrey was once again standing before him inside the cave. He was looking up at something, though it was obscured by the torrent of ethereal winds. How long did he have left before he couldn't see anything at all?

Any question Sarkas might have attempted to answer was forgotten in the wake of the splitting headache that ripped through his mind. He closed his eyes but it made no difference to his vision.

To his left, Alijah remained inside the cave beneath Korkanath but, to his right, was an entirely different environment.

And an entirely different time...

The contrast of both environment and time was difficult to comprehend for a mind so fragile as a human's, but Sarkas did his best to piece it together without losing too much of his sanity.

Scrutinising the new vision on his right, the young wizard laid weathered eyes on a single dragon egg. The shell was rough and easily mistaken for a lump of ancient stone. Deep purple in colour, it was set apart from the lush green vines and grey rock that surrounded it. Scattered around the egg, Sarkas discovered numerous scorch marks where other dragon hatchlings had been born.

Sarkas's eyes flittered between the two scenes, each more thousands of years apart than he could count, for the egg resided in the time of the great Leviathans, before man roamed the world.

Alijah moved, snatching at Sarkas's attention. "Things will be different now," he promised, his voice reverberating throughout Sarkas's mind. "Balance is the reason you and I have been brought together. But first, we must find harmony."

Who was he talking to? Displaying a will of its own again, the spell kept the answer from Sarkas.

Instead, he looked back at the egg, his focus stolen by the cracks that began to appear up and down the shell.

"I will take on your suffering as my own," Alijah continued, his hand outstretched as if he could see the egg. "You don't have to be alone anymore."

Unknown to Alijah, so far removed from events of ancient history, the egg was disintegrated by a furnace from within. A small dragon head emerged from the smoke and revealed its purple eyes and black scales.

Sarkas couldn't believe what was happening, and happening because of *him*. Whether he had meant to or not, his spell had bridged the timelines. Phenomenal as it was, a single tear escaped each eye and ran back across his temples under the pressure of the spell.

These two beings were bonding across the ages, born into the world with only half of who they were meant to be. Sarkas felt a profound sadness for Malliath, who would be forced to endure eons without the one who coaxed him from his egg as the Dragon Riders did. The wizard already knew that the dragon would never speak to another soul until he met Alijah in Paldora's Fall.

Just thinking of that event collapsed the two worlds into nothingness. The blinding colours were brief, propelling Sarkas into yet another time and place beyond his control.

All was quiet now, but for the sound of licking flames.

The young wizard was suddenly spared the buffeting winds and the constant pain. He looked around, confused. This moment of clarity was unexpected with no mention of it in the Jainus's spell book. It had spoken of the repercussions, the sacrifices that came with pushing against time, but not this.

Turning on his heel, he was encircled by the sandy rock of The Undying Mountains, deep into Illian's south. It was dark except for the torches that illuminated the elevated dais that had been carved out of the rock. A new sound reached his ears and Sarkas looked up to see the shattered remains of Paldora's Star.

The magic that radiated from the heavenly rocks kept the pieces afloat, there to collide for evermore.

A sharp squawk turned the young wizard to the dais. There, perched on the edge, was a crow, its feathers a deep black. Again, the knowledge of what was happening escaped him, as if the spell was refusing to reveal the truth of the event.

Sarkas cautiously approached the dais, his sight drawn to the crow's dark eyes. The bird watched him intently, never flinching. A few steps from the dais, his feet rooted him to the spot. Slowly, but surely, the world around him faded from his vision, leaving only those bottomless orbs.

A horrible feeling crept over Sarkas, opening a pit in his stomach. The crow pulled him in until the darkness swallowed him whole.

The winds of time returned with a blasting vengeance. Sarkas screamed but the sound of it was lost, drowned out by the wind in his ears. Nameless colours imprinted on his mind, keeping his eyelids from closing.

The future assaulted him like the crack of a whip, the power of it threatening to undo him.

He saw himself standing in the middle of The Wild Moores, surrounded by his brothers of The Black Hand, a cult of his own making. He could feel that this particular place, hidden deep in the heart of the woods, was drenched in old and powerful magic. Sarkas winced when the older version of himself plunged a dagger into his own heart, dropping him dead into the snow.

Time swept in and ravaged the landscape. The young wizard saw people flit in and out of the site where he had been buried but they were naught but blurs, specks in the canvas of time. Sarkas could only watch, sure that his skin was soon to be stripped from his body by the savage winds.

The same landscape returned to him with clarity and he knew he had just watched the world move on ten thousand years. Now, his long dead corpse was surrounded by men in black robes - The Black Hand. Following the instructions he would leave, they used the magic of the Jainus to resurrect him so that he might continue his work.

The winds of time increased and he could no longer hold on to the moment. Dragged away, he gritted his teeth and let the currents take him where they would. What bombarded him was difficult to comprehend. Images, sounds, and even smells washed over him as he was thrown from one moment in time to another.

He saw pale monsters, crowned with horns, rising from The Under-Realm to greet him: orcs, beasts still unknown in Sarkas's time. They were cruel and barbaric but they served their purpose he saw. Illian would fall to their wrath, only to rise up, stronger than before. The kingdoms, long fractured, would be brought together under one banner, though Sarkas saw two competing for the throne.

The Fated War. The house of Galfrey pitted against the house of Draqaro. The dragon and the flaming sword.

The outcome of this war would reshape the realm forever, changing not only the way people lived but also the way they thought. It was true peace. Reaching this point would be arduous, leaving a trail of death and blood in history's wake. But the peace he observed was shatteringly beautiful and worth all the sacrifices.

It all hinged on one single event in the Third Age: the birth of a boy and a girl, twins. Their fates would clash and determine the world that would rise from the ashes of the war.

Great turmoil was added to Sarkas's pain when he saw the events that would lead to their birth; events *he* would orchestrate. The War for the Realm would claim thousands of lives over thousands of years, but it would bring a princess and a knight together. The love between Reyna Sevari and Nathaniel Galfrey would change all of Verda.

The pain intensified.

Sarkas would have fallen to his knees but he wasn't really standing on anything; simply existing. He saw western armies marching on the east as Erador's ancient warriors were raised from their graves and set to the task of restoring order in Illian. He saw dwarves, the mysterious children of the Vengoran mountains, flattened by Reavers and undead dragons. He saw an elven fleet burning on Adean waves, though he had never heard of or seen such fair creatures.

Malliath reigned above it all.

The fire beneath him grew until the dragon and the ocean itself disappeared. Sarkas was drawn back from the blaze by unseen forces until he was granted the image of a burning tree. It was mountainous. The white bark was slowly being charred black by the ravenous inferno. Its magnificent red leaves were reduced to ash on the breeze. With every inch it lost, the world lost a modicum of its magic.

What came next was heartbreaking, bringing more tears to Sarkas's eyes.

Then, like a child discarding a toy, time rejected its observer and spat the young wizard out. His eyes opened to the real world and he immediately lurched to the side and expelled the contents of his stomach. His heart was pounding in his chest and his muscles ached from the tension.

Seated on the floor, he collapsed back against the wall and let his head loll to the side. In the quiet of a long-abandoned storage room, Sarkas wept, his emotions scattered. There was a way, however convoluted, that he could create a future where the strong held up the weak. It was a contrasting world to the one he knew. But to get there, to bring peace and prosperity for endless generations, he would have to become something far worse than anything that had come out of The Echoes order or even their predecessors, the Jainus.

He would have to become a monster...

Sarkas shut his eyes but he could still see all the things he was going to do to that poor boy. But Alijah Galfrey would unite the world - he had seen it.

Feeling warm steel in his hand, the young wizard looked down to see a knife clutched in his fingers. It was red with blood.

Lying beside Sarkas was a man, perhaps his own age. He had recently been initiated into The Echoes priesthood, along with hundreds of others. No one would miss the wretch, destined with the rest of his order to achieve nothing with his life. His blood, however, had served the entire realm.

Sarkas looked to his right, where the book of the Jainus lay with its pages open. His eyes ran along the title, translating the older language.

The Winds of Time.

It was the most powerful spell in the whole book, in *all* the books. Sarkas wiped his mouth before ripping the page out and stuffing it into his robes. Thinking of everything he had just witnessed, he could already feel particular events fading, their edges losing their details. He would need to use the spell again: and then again and again if he had to. He would get every piece of the tapestry right in his mind.

He would see it done.

PART ONE

CHAPTER I
HOME

Darkness. That was all that awaited Alijah Galfrey. Beyond that, the unknown. Such was the fate of any who fell into a portal, a pitch-black maw hungry to consume him like quicksand. There was nothing he could do. In the same moment he heard the crystal shatter at his feet, the magic therein tore through the fabric of reality with terrifying ease.

The shock of it instantly robbed the half-elf of his rage. There was barely time to think, but he still managed to consider what awaited him on the other side and wondered if it was death.

Adilandra, his grandmother, watched his descent into the abyss. Disappointment and heartbreak ruined her fair features. One more step and he would have brought his wrath down upon her, striking at the betrayal that broke his own heart.

But all that rage was gone, taken by surprise and fear of the unknown. Had she doomed him? Had he doomed himself with such rash action? His questions fled with all haste when the world returned to him with despairing clarity.

Emerging from the portal, he could see The Hox churning as he plummeted towards it: an ancient beast of a sea that took no prisoners. Turning inward, Alijah sought to erect what he could of a shield, anything to soften the blow. He could feel the magic swelling inside of him, but he was still exhausted from the Jainus's spell.

The shield flickered, its strength fluctuating in harmony with Alijah's faltering will.

I'm coming for you!

Malliath's voice was the only thread of comfort before the ocean accepted the king into its icy embrace. There was pain, but there was also peace. The shield saved his life if not all of his bones, leaving Alijah to drift deep beneath the surface. Had he claimed victory? Had he done what the Jainus had failed to do so long ago? These questions, and many more, faded away.

He sank into the icy depths, weighed down by his scale mail. Somewhere between life and death, he saw a monster gliding towards him. The Hox itself birthed the dark creature as it grew in size, encompassing his vision.

What remained of his mind wondered, without fear, if it was the fabled Leviathan that stalked these cold waters. There was no fight left in him. Even now he could feel himself succumbing to the call of death.

Hold on... Malliath beckoned, his voice strained with pain.

That dark creature, the Leviathan that had come to consume him, revealed itself to be a creature of beauty and hope. Malliath scooped up Alijah in his front claws and made for the surface. The waves gave way to the dragon and he flapped his powerful wings, clearing The Hox altogether.

It was only seconds before their flight came to an end.

Alijah felt wet sand beneath him as Malliath's claws released him onto the beach. He turned his head as much as his fatigue would allow and laid eyes on his eternal companion. The dragon appeared just as exhausted as he did, his purple eyes struggling to stay open.

Malliath... he called across their bond. ***Take us home.***

~

Alijah opened his eyes and awoke with a start. Dream and reality bled into one, colliding with dizzying effect.

There were memories, just beyond his reach, that beckoned his attention. He could hear clashing steel in the passages of his mind, then the staccato of devastating spells. Galanör Reveeri's voice called out to him, though his exact words escaped Alijah's grasp.

It all felt so surreal.

Before sitting up, his fingers investigated the ground beneath him - wet sand. He could smell the ocean, hear its crashing waves. He lay within a cavern of stalactites, each glistening like the stars.

Alijah knew instantly where he was. Sanctuary. The king sat up, aware that his surroundings were a construct of his mind, a place where his bond to Malliath was given physical form. As always, it was beneath the ruins of Korkanath, in the cave where ancient mages had forced Malliath to dwell while he guarded their island. It had also been the first place Alijah had made real contact with the dragon, beyond the machinations of The Crow.

Something darker than the shadows stirred in his periphery and he knew it to be Malliath. Alijah picked himself up, ignoring the sand that clung to him - it wasn't real after all. On his feet, the king glanced at the cave entrance where The Adean leapt at the island with an incessant rhythm. He paid the view no heed, instead turning his attention to the dark corners of the cavern.

Two purple eyes looked back at him.

I have no memory of coming here, Alijah confessed.

That is because I brought you here, Malliath answered, his voice the perfect resonance inside the king's mind. Just the sound of it slowed his beating heart and steadied his breath.

Alijah inspected his fist before clenching it. *I am hurt,* he deduced in a softer tone.

Yes... You nearly died, Alijah. Malliath's tone took the king back to his youth, reminding him of the way his father would speak to him after doing something foolish or dangerous.

But you saved me, Alijah replied with a swelling heart. *As always,* he added.

You weren't prepared enough, the dragon chastised. *It nearly cost you your life.* Malliath drew in on himself, his thoughts and feelings his own for a moment. *I could not live without you,* he finally declared.

Alijah welcomed the words and the emotions that accompanied them. Even after seventeen years, he knew Malliath still found it difficult to voice his deepest feelings, preferring to convey them without words.

I can feel you protecting me, Alijah commented, tapping the side of his head. **Whatever condition I am in, I can handle it. Show me.**

Malliath tilted his horned head and it all came back to Alijah then with clarity. Adilandra had opened a portal at his feet and dropped him into The Hox. That certainly explained why he was hurt. Another flash cut through his mind and he saw that final bolt of lightning before it struck him... and Galanör. Putting the elven ranger aside for the moment, the king turned to his companion with the most important question of all.

Did it work? Alijah asked, almost afraid of the answer.

Malliath didn't respond straight away. *I believe so. The magic I see in you appears different, just as I feel different.*

How so? Alijah pressed.

Magic moves like the currents in a river, Malliath explained. *It flows through us, coursing from the source, through the realms.*

The Tree, Alijah added.

Yes. But I can no longer sense those currents. The magic that resides in us is that of a spring now, flowing in and out of our bones.

Unlike dragons, Alijah had no way of detecting that for himself, though he trusted Malliath implicitly. He only wished there was a way to test it, before he destroyed magic and put his companion's life at risk. He didn't even want to entertain the idea of ruling Verda without him.

There is more you should know, Malliath continued, *before you wake to the harshness of the world.*

I told you - I can handle it. Show me everything.

Sorting through all of his memories, and combining them with Malliath's, Alijah quickly relived the events on Qamnaran. Seconds after Alijah had hit the water, the dragon had witnessed the tower of silvyr fall into the sea, taking some of the island with it. Though the king couldn't say for certain, he knew in his heart that his grandmother could never have escaped the tower before it collapsed.

The queen of elves is dead, Malliath announced confidently, having already come to the logical conclusion.

Alijah could feel the dragon probing his thoughts and emotions then, searching for any sign of remorse or sadness. The king didn't want to disappoint his companion with a show of such weakness, not after all they had gone through to rise above the drudgery of an ordinary life. Aware of his desire, Malliath assisted him in quashing any regret or guilt, burying it deep beneath an over-whelming sense of righteousness.

Moving on from the loss of his grandmother, the king focused on something else he had lost, something of great value.

The book of the Jainus, he lamented, his head hung low. **It was inside the tower.**

It shares a grave with Adilandra Sevari, Malliath stated without a hint of emotion. *Good riddance,* the dragon added.

Alijah didn't share his companion's feelings on the matter. **That book possessed the knowledge of the Jainus! There were spells inside those pages that hadn't been seen for thousands of years. They predated Atilan!**

Calm yourself, Malliath instructed. *We have no need of the book nor the knowledge of the Jainus and their magic. We will open a doorway to the realm of magic without spells. And when magic itself is but a memory, so too will be the notion of mages and their wretched ways. In the balance that follows, peace will reign.*

Alijah let his head roll back beneath the jagged stalactites. As always, Malliath was right. With or without the book, they could still change the world - The Crow had seen it after all.

The book is not all we lost, Malliath continued, releasing more memory.

Alijah was instantly looking through the eyes of Lord Kraiden in his final moments. The Dragon Rider had been slain by Doran

Heavybelly, and his dragon, Morgorth, had succumbed to the power of the elves. The king cursed magic, mimicking the venom that Malliath held for it. Yet again, it had tipped the scales and taken a valuable tool in the war for peace. Of the five Riders he had taken Illian with, he was now down to three.

Two, Malliath corrected, reading his thoughts like a book.

His awareness returned to the sanctuary, and Alijah met his companion's reptilian eyes. ***Two?*** he repeated, knowing only of Kraiden's death to Doran and Col-vok's death to Inara, two years previously. ***What are you holding back?*** the king demanded.

Your mind needs time to embrace memories that are not your own.

My mind has never been stronger. Show me!

Malliath adjusted his position in the shadows, revealing a glimpse of his deadly teeth. *As you wish.*

The dragon brought down the walls that had been protecting Alijah's mind from a flood of foreign memories. Again, he was transported from the sanctuary and into the passages of Malliath's mind. It was a labyrinth. There were hundreds of Reavers constantly witnessing and hearing events across the realm, but Malliath helped him to focus on just one - a lowly warrior in Namdhor. At great speed, the scene played over and over in his mind.

Ensuring his comprehension, Malliath simply stated, *Namdhor has been taken.*

Alijah's jaw clenched when he took on the memory of Vighon jumping from the keep's walls with the sword of the north blazing in his hands. Karsak's death was instantaneous, its rotten skull no match for burning silvyr.

Then there was Rengyr, his Dragon Rider.

Alijah opened his eyes, returning to the sanctuary, after seeing his mother take Rengyr's head with her enchanted bow.

"YOU WILL NOT TOUCH HIM!" Reyna had shouted. Her words echoed in his mind. The betrayal stung, piercing his heart.

Yes... Malliath purred, nurturing his rage. *You have been discarded, replaced. They have a new son now.*

Alijah rubbed his face, distorting his features. A storm was taking shape inside of him, preventing the half-elf from grasping any single emotion.

They believe you are weak, Malliath provoked. *Your parents. Your sister. They rally behind the northman and his false promises. He cannot deliver peace to the people, just as he cannot defend the realm from threat.*

Alijah's mind was filled with violent images, though none more so than Vighon impaled on a green Vi'tari blade while all of Namdhor watched. The imagery became all the more gruesome when Malliath ate his corpse, wiping the house of Draqaro from history. The king blinked hard, regaining his grip on the sanctuary's reality.

Malliath raised his head, his muscles tensed beneath his scales. *For the crime of his defiance, Vighon Draqaro has but one fate! You should embrace it.*

Vighon was indeed his enemy, and a powerful one at that given his claim to the throne, but he was not the gravest threat to Alijah's plans.

What of my sister? Alijah's choice of words was met by a sense of disappointment from Malliath. **What of Inara?** he asked instead. **With Athis by her side she poses a greater threat than Vighon.**

Malliath slowly dipped his head to bring his gaze in line with Alijah. It was unnerving. The king's stomach lurched when he processed the information that passed between them.

Inara was in Erador.

Alijah reached out and leaned against the rock as he considered the potential repercussions of her presence there. Taking his time, and assisted by Malliath, he relived events from within Valgala's walls. His fears only worsened when he saw Asher in Inara's company, both fighting in the foyer of his personal chambers.

One detail especially caught Alijah's eye: Mournblade. He had mounted it in his study, yet now he was looking at it slung over Inara's shoulder.

So they're looking for Gideon, he concluded.

They were *looking for Gideon,* Malliath responded. *This was days ago. The last time they were seen was on The Spoken Road.*

Again, Alijah pushed through the memories of dead Reavers until he found the right one. Indeed, the companions, including a Drake of all creatures, had last been seen fleeing the capital on the road to the Tower of Jain. Thanks to Athis, the memory was burned away.

Alijah could sense Malliath's unease. *If they find Gideon,* the dragon reasoned, *they will come to know everything including the importance of our work in The Moonlit Plains.*

Alijah could feel every ounce of his companion's quiet fury. **We should assume they have discovered him by now.**

Malliath's thick claws dug deep into the rock as his purple eyes pulled the king in.

I will eat your sister, he promised. *But not before she watches me rip out Athis's heart. Gideon Thorn, however, will die by your hand. You wished for him to remain alive - his interference will be on your hands.*

Alijah turned away from his companion, haunted for the moment by the image of his sister disappearing down Malliath's throat.

How long have I been asleep? he asked, changing the subject.

Two days, Malliath answered flatly.

I want to wake up, Alijah said with the hint of a demand in his tone.

You are still healing. The Jainus's spell took its toll on you in more ways than one.

"I want to wake up!" he barked out loud. "As you've shown me, the realm is in danger of falling into ruin. It needs its king."

Looking down on him, Malliath exhaled a long breath from his nostrils. With it came a cloud that stole away the details of their sanctuary.

Alijah opened his real eyes and sat up, barely aware of the comfortable bed on which he resided. He looked around the room, assessing every detail to determine his surroundings. Alijah didn't need to be told he was inside The Bastion, high in The Vrost Mountains. There was something about the black stone that would never leave the king, nor he it.

Comfortable in his environment, Alijah's mind began to settle somewhat. Even now he was becoming aware of the Reavers working on the fortress in a bid to restore it to its ancient grandeur. They were like ants in his mind, busy toiling away without complaint.

Only it wasn't *his* mind that was pulling the strings.

Malliath had them under his command, ensuring they continued the work they had begun nearly two years ago. Wondering why, of all places, he was inside The Bastion, Alijah recalled his last words to the dragon.

Home. The word and its meaning tried to steal Alijah's attention, but he didn't want to dwell on his attachment to the dreadful place. Besides, it was *time* that eluded him.

Closing his eyes, Alijah reached out, drawing comfort from the bond he had with Malliath. He could feel the dragon, feel his power and magnificence. It was, as ever, intoxicating for the half-elf.

The king swung his legs over the side of the bed and made a quick inspection of himself. Though he could see no cuts, he could feel the itch of where the skin had recently healed. The muscle beneath was tender, yet to knit fully back together. His bones harboured an ache where The Hox had broken them, but they were strong enough to support his every movement.

He spared a second to marvel at the speed with which he could heal himself and survive without food or water. For all the potency he was to acquire during his life as king, he knew none would make him more powerful than his bond to Malliath.

Taking a breath, Alijah stood up. A sharp pain shot through his left knee, forcing him to reach out and use the end of the bed as support. With a flushed face and gritted teeth, he exhaled and straightened himself. His back and shoulders forced a groan from his lips. Pinching his fingers together, he quickly discovered that they were partially numb.

So he wasn't entirely healed.

Fighting through the pain, he waved his hand through the air and conjured a mirror image of himself. The image moved exactly as he did, giving the king a good view of his body. A large and discoloured bruise ran up his left leg and touched his hip. He also caught sight of a fresh scar, under his ribs, that ran up and around his torso before splitting into three strands across his back. Neither hurt to touch, but his knee was more than aware of his weight when pressure was applied.

He was about to dismiss the image when he discovered the wound on his face. Alijah leaned forward and the conjured twin did the same, mirroring his fingers as they traced the jagged cut that split his left eyebrow and reached for his hairline. The king had never considered himself a vain person, but he instantly hated his disfigurement. He was indomitable, unyielding, invincible. He shouldn't be seen to bleed.

The people should see you bleed for them, Malliath argued from afar. *Rising to defend them will be what defines you. They will see that you put their lives before your own. In return, you will have their loyalty and with that you can forge a real and lasting peace.*

Alijah was picked up by every word, his resolve given new life. He waved his hand again, reducing his mirror image to a cloud of coloured smoke to be carried away in the draught.

Enduring the pain in his knee, Alijah limped away from the roaring fire beside his bed, his naked skin left to fend for itself against the mountain chill. Pausing in front of the arched window, he gave no care to the icy breeze that penetrated his chamber. How long had The Crow kept him chained to a freezing wall, exposed to The Vrost Mountains? Only now did he appreciate the strength it had given him.

Outside, he could see Reavers, all immune to the blasting winds, hauling stone, fitting glass, and installing new doors and furniture, all of which had been transported up the treacherous mountain path.

Testing the potency of his bond to every Reaver, Alijah silently commanded those outside his chamber to enter. He knew that they had been waiting there, per Malliath's command, with his clothes, armour, and cloak. It satisfied him to see the knights of Erador react immediately to *his* command.

Given the pain in his knee, he allowed the Reavers to assist in dressing him and fastening his armour in place. It was with irritation that he noted the dragon scales were chipped where Galanör's spells had impacted them.

Alijah accepted his Vi'tari blade from the last Reaver, thankful that Malliath had retrieved it from The Hox. He studied its emerald edge before sheathing it on his hip. The extra weight didn't help his knee and his hand wrapped around the hilt, squeaking against the leather strap.

He dismissed the knights with a thought before leaving the chamber himself. Without real awareness, he wandered through the ancient halls. The Bastion would always be his retreat, somewhere he could rest and quieten his mind. It was within these walls that he had been remade, forged into something that truly mattered. The Crow's lessons were never closer to his heart than when he resided herein. He promised himself, when the realm had been set on course, he would spend more time here, where he could renew his vows to himself.

Inevitably, he found himself on the highest platform in The Bastion, exposed to the elements. Circular in shape, though time had ravaged its edges, the platform overlooked much of the fortress and offered a magnificent view of The Vrost Mountains.

It was very likely, once upon a time, that King Atilan himself had stood on this platform and stared at the same mountains. Try as he might, Alijah couldn't hold on to that thought, his mind snatched by dark memories. It had been here, on this very stone, where he had tried to kill himself, to prevent The Crow from turning him into a monster. How wrong he had been. How naive.

Limping to the jagged edge, he looked over the side. There was nothing but a stomach-churning drop and sharp rocks: a sure death had The Crow not intervened.

You dwell on the past when you should be thinking about the future.

Malliath's voice washed away all memory, honing Alijah's thoughts. He stepped back from the edge and made his way to the centre, his eyes searching the mountain tops for the dragon. Malliath wasn't hard to find against the pale dawn, gliding between the snow-capped peaks. Alijah studied his companion in the distance for there was something different about the way he was flying. He was certainly slower than usual. He decided the recent spell, burnt into the dragon's hide by himself no less, was responsible for his apparent fatigue and, possibly, the hint of pain the king detected, though it could easily have been his own wounded leg muddying their bond.

The dragon glided round, banking towards the fortress. It wasn't long before he was grappling the side of the mountain, beside the platform. His claws easily found purchase, digging into the rock face and allowing his head to dip over the hewn stone.

I sense reproach in you, Malliath observed.

Alijah experienced a wave of nausea rise up in him, his vision blurring around the edges. With his wounded knee, he staggered away from Malliath's gaze to take in the mountains.

We have but enemies now. There is no bond, blood or otherwise, that is stronger than ours. Vighon, Inara, your parents... they must be sacrificed for the good of the realm, for the good of the millions yet to be born. Remember where your heart lies. It is the people we serve. We must love them above all others. Anything else would lower us to the standards of those who came before us.

Alijah felt an icy wind pick up his cloak and blow out his hair before it knocked loose a tear from his left eye. The path before him was laden with familial bodies.

Heroes die, Malliath announced, reciting The Crow's second lesson. *We will lay low the enemies of our kingdom and rise to fight again and again because we are not heroes, Alijah. We are kings. Only we can redefine what that means.*

Alijah cast his eyes to the cold stone and saw his parents lying bloodied side by side. They were dead, along with Vighon and Inara beside them.

Then, Malliath's breath washed over him from behind like a cleansing vapour. His vision cleared and his stomach settled. He was the king of Verda, not the brother of Inara Galfrey nor the son of Reyna and Nathaniel Galfrey. He was everlasting. He was the pillar on which the realm would reside. Any who tried to break him would die - it was that simple.

"Sacrifice without hesitation," he muttered under his breath. *Gideon will die,* he vowed, turning back to Malliath. *And Ilargo with him.*

Malliath's head inched closer. *Good,* he hissed. *We should move quickly,* he insisted. *Inara and her ilk will move to undo our work in The Moonlit Plains.*

They cannot stop us now, Alijah opined. *The Moonlit Plains have been prepared. There are already reports of unusual activity at the lowest depths.*

If there is even a single doorway down there, Malliath urged, *you should take it now. With magic gone, we have but to wait until its death claims Ilargo and Athis. Without them, Gideon and Inara will fall and there will be none to protect the usurper. With him gone, The Rebellion dies.*

Alijah nodded his head, but mention of Vighon ignited a seething rage in his veins. *He sits on my throne! That cannot go unchallenged. It could have lasting consequences for my reign, even generations from now. Every second The Rebellion occupies Namdhor the weaker I look. I want his head.* The king looked away as a strategy began to form in his mind though, admittedly, he couldn't tell whether it originated from himself or Malliath, their thoughts so entwined on the matter.

Malliath tilted his head. *You propose abandoning our work in the plains.*

No, Alijah said definitively. He paused, reaching out to his Reavers across the realm. With thought alone, he redirected them from their current tasks and stations.

Malliath could sense and interpret his every action. *You would move so many of our forces to defend the doorway?*

Of course, Alijah replied with half a grin taking shape. *Let Athis and Ilargo descend upon it with all their might. It will do them no good against our army.*

Any confrontation jeopardises the doorway, Malliath protested.

I want his head! Alijah fumed, giving in to the spring of hatred that swelled from nowhere. *We will go to Namdhor and take it. We have no other choice. To hold the capital is to hold the realm itself. I cannot let that ripple through my kingdom.*

Our kingdom, Malliath corrected.

Of course, Alijah conceded, taking a breath. *You know, as well as I, that The Moonlit Plains cannot be taken by two dragons. The ballistas alone would tear them to shreds. Besides that, the longer we leave the doorway to form the more stable it will be. I fully intend to succeed, Malliath. And when I do, I don't want to emerge into a world that heralds Vighon as king again.*

Malliath slowly shifted his position. *Then we shall take his head.*

Alijah grinned for nothing felt better than when they were in harmony. *First,* he exacted, *I would take his courage and, with it, the backbone of this tiresome rebellion.* Reaching into the minds of the Reavers still positioned outside Namdhor, the king gave them one simple command.

Malliath emanated a sense of pride, raising the hairs on the back of Alijah's neck. All he wanted was to be worthy of the dragon, a sentiment he couldn't hide.

Malliath extended one of his front claws onto the platform, inviting Alijah onto his back. *We are equal to one another, each a half of the whole. Our fates are bound, destined for greatness.*

Greatness sounded good to Alijah but, with someone else sitting on his throne and threatening his kingdom, he would settle for wrath.

CHAPTER 2

NORTHMAN

Winter was upon Namdhor and, with it, the black city was adorned with white roof tops and lined with powdered streets. Vighon Draqaro walked those streets, his boots crunching through the snow. Though the city's towering cathedrals and spires lifted the gaze of most, the northman's sight was cast low, for there were the bodies.

The majority had been claimed by loved ones, but there were still numerous corpses up and down the main slope, draped in cloth. They had fallen two days past, having risen up to fight beside their king and repel the Reavers.

Vighon stopped by one of the bodies and crouched down. With care, he pulled back the material to see the face of a man, perhaps a little younger than himself. He wasn't attired in the clothes of Kassian's Keepers but the simple garb of an ordinary man. To Vighon, however, he had been anything but ordinary. Without armour or sword, he had stood up to his enemy and given his life for the people around him, for the realm itself.

He was a hero.

The king looked over his shoulder at the small group who had accompanied him everywhere since they took back the city. Two of

27

Kassian's Keepers stood tall beside a pair of servants from the keep. Despite his best efforts, Vighon had been unable to walk freely without any of them - Nathaniel's doing.

"If this man has a family, I want him returned to them. He deserves a pyre."

One of the Keepers nodded his chin down the road. "Your Grace..."

Vighon turned back to see a woman and a young boy approaching. The mother was holding the child tight to her side, her hands wrapped around his shoulders and head. Even before they reached the king, the woman's expression fell into despair as she laid eyes on the body. Together, they fell to their knees as tears ran freely down their pale cheeks. The boy cried out softly for his father while the woman gripped her husband's frozen hand, her jaw set in anguish.

His heart breaking, Vighon made to stand up and leave them to their grief. There was another part of him, however, desperate to leave before the wife turned her anger on him, blaming the northman for her husband's death. And she would be right to, he thought. He had raised his flaming sword and rallied Namdhor's bravest to fight with naught but shovels and whatever else they could find.

Before he could stand, the wife threw herself at the king and wrapped her arms around him. Vighon heard the Keepers reaching for their wands as he himself was tempted to reach for a weapon. But the wife simply held him in place, her face pressed to his chest, as her shoulders bobbed with her crying.

"What are we to do, my Lord?" she wept.

Still somewhat surprised, Vighon tensed his arms and hugged her close. "I'm so sorry," he choked. "Your husband met a hero's end."

The wife pulled her head back to lay eyes on the king. "Braden didn't want to be a hero, my Lord." Her arm outstretched, she pulled her son into their embrace. "And there's no sorry to be heard," she continued. "My Braden looked up to you - always said we had the luck of the gods to live under your kingship. He was there when you stood up to The Ironsworn you know. And the orcs too. He wanted to be just like you." Her gaze fell over her husband's body. "He just wanted to protect us."

"That he did," Vighon replied softly. He held them both, offering what comfort he could. The moment brought a recent memory to the surface, reminding the king of Inara's last words to him before she left for Erador.

"*Those men and women you called upon,*" she had said, "*the ones who fought and died beside you - they weren't there for you. They weren't even there for the realm. They were fighting for their families. They still are. They died fighting for their loved ones, so that they might live in a world under your reign. Their lives have always been their own, and each and every one of them wanted to fight for what they held in their heart.*"

Braden had died fighting for what he held in his heart; the very two people currently in Vighon's arms. Instead of crushing guilt, the northman felt pride. He was proud of Braden and all who had fallen defending their families and homes. Though his death would leave a sting for some time, he was sure his wife would come to share his pride.

"He may not have wished to be a hero," Vighon said, "but he will be honoured as one all the same." The king turned to his servants. "See that they are taken care of - winter will not bother them."

One of the servants nodded his head. "Your Grace," he affirmed.

Vighon finally stood up and left mother and son in each other's arms. "See to it that *every* family who has lost a husband or a father is honoured with coin and supplies to see them through the frost."

The same servant hesitated, his eyes darting from the mother to the king. "Your Grace... That is a *lot* of supplies."

The king locked eyes on the man. "See it done," he commanded. "And give them all a pyre each."

The servant bowed his head despite the reluctance that spread across his face. "It will be done, your Grace." Vighon almost groaned when only one of the servants left his side.

"Your Grace..." The older Keeper, Quaid, was looking up the main slope, towards The Dragon Keep. "Looks to be something going on."

Vighon moved to see for himself. A small crowd was beginning to gather not far from the keep's main gates. The sight wouldn't have concerned the king too much, but the gathering appeared to be focused around the enormous dragon corpse.

"Now what?" Vighon muttered.

With the Keepers and his remaining servant, the northman trekked up the slope to investigate. The people parted for him just as they had prior to Alijah's invasion. Something in Vighon still didn't feel like he had earned his return as king.

The smell of Karsak's rotten body hit Vighon like a club to the face. He winced and turned his head to the side, though it made no difference. Flies had taken to the beast like crows on a bloodied battlefield, while rats scurried in and out of ragged holes that had been poked through its ancient hide.

"What's going on?" he asked before noticing Nathaniel and Reyna.

The Galfreys approached from the head of the dragon, both similarly distressed by the powerful odour. Despite the gruesome scene, the pair were a vision of strength and resilience. In their late seventies, the couple appeared no older than thirty years - in fact, younger than Vighon looked in his early forties.

Reyna came to stand beside the king, her bow in hand. "Something stirs inside the beast," she informed.

Vighon looked at her in disbelief, noting then that Nathaniel was holding his sword. The two Keepers who had accompanied the king removed their wands and began to usher the people back from the dragon.

Something snapped inside the bowel of the monster.

"What new evil is this?" the northman questioned, drawing the sword of the north. The flames blew wild in the wind, forcing him to lower the blade to the ground.

Nathaniel nodded at the headless corpse beside Karsak. "Well we know it isn't Rengyr."

More bones were broken inside Karsak and the hide itself moved to some unseen pressure. Distressed murmurs broke out amongst the people and they no longer required the Keepers to usher them back.

Grotesque innards were suddenly pushed out of various wounds in the dragon's side. The rats displayed the most wisdom when they turned tail and fled.

If Vighon had blinked, he would have missed Reyna nocking an arrow. "Whatever it is, kill it quickly," he urged.

Reyna pulled taut the string of her bow. "As you say, your Grace."

Vighon was almost distracted by her words when Karsak's hide was torn apart from the inside. A hulking form emerged from the dragon, its wide-set frame coated in gore and death.

"Wait!" the northman blurted, halting Reyna from releasing her arrow.

Standing taller than everyone else, Sir Borin the Dread awaited his master's command.

Nathaniel lowered his sword. "I hate to think how he got in there."

Vighon had no problem imagining Karsak swallowing the Golem in their bid to escape the cascading slopes that wiped away the eastern Watcher. In fact, he could easily imagine Sir Borin clawing his way out of the mud and stone to challenge the dragon and its Rider.

Realising that the surrounding crowd had become deathly silent, the king glanced around to see the horror on their faces. Sir Borin was the stuff of nightmares, and that was before he had lost his armour and helmet. Now, his demonic features were there for all to see and made all the worse by Karsak's remains plastered to his pale flesh.

They needed to get him out of sight.

"You." Vighon turned to the servant, though the man's eyes were caught by the horror of the Golem. The northman clicked his fingers in front of the servant's face, snatching his attention. "He won't hurt you," he said plainly. "Take him inside the keep and clean him up. Then find something to cover... *everything*."

The servant only swallowed in response.

Vighon turned back to the Golem. "Sir Borin, go with this man and do exactly as he says. I will remain close by."

The servant required an extra nudge to get moving, though the company of Keepers offered some reassurance. Vighon would have enjoyed the moment, free of an entourage, if he wasn't so caught up in the fact that Queen Skalaf's monster had returned to haunt him.

The king watched the wall of muscle that Sir Borin called a back disappear into the keep. "Will I ever be free of that thing?" he asked aloud.

"Doubtful," Nathaniel replied, sheathing his sword. "If he can survive a mountain dropping on his head and a dragon swallowing him whole, what can stop him?"

Vighon sighed and sheathed the sword of the north, extinguishing the flames. "I suppose we need all the help we can get if we're going to hold the city."

A shadow overcame Nathaniel's face as he too considered the hardship ahead of them. "Ravens have been sent to The Black Wood. A rider should be here in a few days with a diviner we can use to reach Ruban Dardaris. His forces in the south are sizeable."

Vighon wasn't convinced. "A few days could spell the end of our occupation. And regardless of Ruban's numbers, they still need to travel the length of the country if they're to defend Namdhor."

Nathaniel tried to offer a balm to the king's concerns. "I have no doubt the rider from The Black Wood will be in the company of a dwarven force. Doran didn't take every warrior to Qamnaran. And we have allies in Lirian. In fact, the last I heard they were using The Pick-Axe as a base."

Reyna stepped closer to the northman, her features set. "We *will* hold this city, your Grace."

Though his title sounded familiar, it still grated in his ear. "We've taken back a city by the skin of our teeth," Vighon began. "The realm is still firmly in the hands of Alijah."

Reyna gave the northman a warm smile and placed a loving hand on his arm. "This city is home to us all. We will not give it up." She squeezed his arm affectionately. "And you will always be a king to these people, whether you win a battle or the war itself."

Vighon nodded his appreciation and hoped that they saw his love for them in his eyes. "Has there been any word from Qamnaran?" he asked, almost afraid of the answer.

"No," Nathaniel said definitively. "But we shouldn't expect one. They have no idea we've taken Namdhor back. The last they heard, we were still looking for Asher in the hope of tracking *you* down."

"Hopefully," Reyna added with a lighter tone, "either Doran or my mother has sent word back to The Black Wood and we will receive news with the rider."

"I dare not keep a hope," Vighon uttered, always one to trust the strength in his arm over all else.

Nathaniel planted a heavy hand on the king's shoulder. "Keep the hope alive," he beseeched.

Vighon narrowed his eyes at the knight. "Those sound like Inara's words."

Nathaniel beamed with pride. "That's because they are."

The quip on the end of Vighon's tongue was held back under the barrage of thundering hooves. A single rider brought his mount to a halt at the tip of Karsak's tail. The man could have held any number of professions by his garb, but his build suggested he had once served in Namdhor's army.

"Your Grace!" he called from atop his horse.

Vighon frowned. "What now?" he mumbled as he made his way towards the rider. "Why the haste?" he asked.

"It's *them*, your Grace. They're... They're doing something."

The king opened his mouth to reply but, instead, turned to Nathaniel and hissed, "Horses!" Reyna though was already running back to the keep to retrieve them from the stables. Within minutes, Vighon had mounted beside the Galfreys, and the trio set off down the slope at a gallop.

From top to bottom there were signs of battle. The Keepers had called on every destructive spell in their repertoire to fight the

Reavers stationed in Namdhor. Numerous buildings had lost their windows and brickwork while others had lost portions of their roofs. Thankfully, there were no more scattered remains of their foe, having been collected and burned outside the city.

Here and there, outside their homes or shops, Namdhorians stopped upon seeing the king. They raised their fists into the air or bowed their heads in respect. Vighon would have slowed to offer his own respect, but it was their safety he now feared for... *again*.

Reaching flat ground, they navigated the lower town that sprawled around the capital's base and made for the snow-covered plains of The White Vale. There, Vighon's eyes quickly found Kassian Kantaris. The ragged mage knight was resting on a barrel with a pipe hanging out of the corner of his mouth. His torn coat draped over the sides, the man looked right at home among his Keepers. Surrounding them was a larger group of Namdhorian soldiers who had raided the barracks and reclaimed their armour, cloaks, and weapons.

Vighon felt his spirits lift at the sight of the flaming sword emblazoned on their shields. It gave him hope. It was, however, tested by the sound that came from beyond them.

Jumping down from their horses, the trio were given a clear path to the vale and Kassian's perch. Vighon didn't pause to greet the Keeper, his attention entirely stolen by the clamour before him.

"What are they doing?" the king asked aloud to anyone who might have the answer.

Kassian shrugged. "Your guess is as good as mine... your Grace."

Vighon scrutinised the three hundred Reavers who had withdrawn from the city. They still couldn't say why the fiends had retreated to the snows in the first place, for Reavers weren't known for giving up. Since then, they had stood as sentinels, unmoved by winter's sweeping hand.

Now, however, they were beating their gauntlets into their armoured chests. It reminded Vighon of orcish war drums.

"When did this start?" he pressed.

"Oh they've been like this all day," Kassian quipped, exhaling a breath of smoke.

Vighon resisted the urge to roll his eyes.

Nathaniel cleared his throat and shot the Keeper a look before saying, "They've been standing here since they withdrew and not made a sound. Why would they do this now?"

Slowly, but surely, the answer came to Vighon, and with it the icy hand of Fate gripped his insides. He turned to see Reyna, whose expression suggested she had arrived at the same conclusion.

"He's coming," the king declared, turning more than a few heads in his direction.

Kassian looked at Vighon and let his pipe hang loose in his mouth. "*Finally,*" he said with determination.

Nathaniel's response to the Keeper sounded harsh, but Vighon failed to take in a single word of it. Alijah was coming. His minions were beating their chests in anticipation. Such a command could only have been received from Alijah himself. Of course, if The Crow's protégé was indeed coming to Namdhor, he would be coming on the wings of Death itself.

Vighon could hear the screams of dying men across dozens of battlefields, their bodies being ravaged by dragon fire. Behind it all was Alijah's booming voice.

"ANYONE WHO SIDES WITH YOU WILL BURN! AND, VIGHON, YOU WILL BEAR WITNESS TO IT ALL! YOU WILL WATCH THEM ALL DIE CLINGING TO YOUR BANNER!"

Backing his way out of the group, Vighon turned around to see all of Namdhor rising before him. The entire city had rebelled against Alijah's reign and sided with him. Now they would all burn for it.

Vighon's throat felt as if it was constricting and the only cure was a strong drink. His eyes scanned the lower town and discovered more than one tavern, but all were closed. Then his sight landed on his horse and a new desire rose to the surface. Perhaps if he fled, Alijah would spare them all and hunt him instead.

A voice, sweet to the ears, called out to Vighon. Ensnared by fear as he was, the king mistook Reyna's voice for Inara's. Without meaning to, he clenched his fist as if he was grasping on to that which he truly fought for - what was in his heart. That was all he could ever do, what any of them could ever do.

Defiance quickly dominated his fear, reminding the king that, above all else, he was a stubborn northman. Fighting was in his bones.

Turning on his heel, Vighon faced Reyna's expectant face before taking in the others. "I want anyone too old or too young to hold a sword inside The Dragon Keep!" he yelled over the Reavers' cacophony. "Everyone else needs to prepare for battle! I want those catapults loaded and manned at all times," he added, pointing to one of the mighty weapons situated inside Namdhor's first tier. He paused, catching the eyes of a few Keepers and soldiers. "Make no mistake, our enemy is coming! They are coming for our homes, our way of life, our blood! But I say let them try! I am a northman! I will fight till the snow turns to sand, till the heavens rain fire, and I will fight till the very end of Verda! Are you with me?"

A chorus of cheers met the king's speech, lending grit to his bones. If there was to be one final stand, he would be honoured to have such company.

Kassian was the first to break free of the warriors and approach the king. "We're going to need more than encouragement and old catapults if we're going to survive this. We should put a proper strategy together. I know where *my* people are best placed."

"Agreed," Vighon replied. "Though I would not listen to *that* a moment longer."

Kassian glanced back at the Reavers before nodding his head up the main rise, to The Dragon Keep. "I believe the big house is yours."

With the Galfreys and Kassian in tow, the king rode back to the keep with his head held high. By appearance alone, he informed the people of the north that he would stand up to anything that threatened them. Now and for evermore.

Only a few steps into the keep, Vighon felt a strange pressure against his right hip. He dismounted and placed a palm over the pouch on his belt, feeling the subtle vibrations of the diviner Inara had given him.

Reyna was the first among the others to notice. "Inara," she said with some intensity. "You must speak with her!" Those five words came out as one.

"Your chamber," Nathaniel suggested. "We will make sure you aren't disturbed."

"Perhaps we should all speak with her," Reyna countered, clearly eager to commune with her daughter after so much time.

Nathaniel squeezed her wrist affectionately. "She gave Gideon's diviner to Vighon - they must speak." Reyna replied with the slightest bow of her head and made an effort to relax her muscles.

Vighon offered her a warm smile reserved for very few in his life. "I will relay every word," he promised.

Rushing into his chamber, which was still cluttered with Alijah's sundries, the king seated himself at his desk and placed the diviner on the wooden surface. He wasn't accustomed to using the ancient form of communication, but this wasn't his first time either. Cupping the black orb in both hands, he did his best to relax and allow the sphere to pull his mind inside.

It was there, on that ethereal bridge, that he saw the one who held his heart.

CHAPTER 3
INSTINCTS

As she waited in the quiet void between realities, Inara Galfrey felt her mind drifting, her focus untethered. This was, perhaps, the first moment of real silence she had experienced in some time and her uncaged thoughts were taking advantage.

Only minutes ago, she had stepped foot in another realm. That thought alone was nearly enough to numb the rest and hold her in awe. The mountainous tree. A starry sky of stalactites. Soil rich with crystals. It was like nothing she had ever seen nor could ever have imagined.

Naturally, that thought soured when she considered her brother's intentions toward it. If Gideon was right, Alijah was going to bring down the world of magic and all the dragons with it. It was enough to send her thoughts spiralling.

Inara considered the multitude of paths that potentially lay before her and saw naught but violence, bloodshed, and death. One death in particular opened a new realm of nightmares for the Guardian. In her mind, she witnessed Athis dying over and over again, his soul burned with the tree.

Trapped in that dark place, Inara drew on that part of herself that was undoubtedly dragon in nature. She had often called on it in battle, though now she called on it to bring some form of cohesion to her wild thoughts. With the wisdom of a dragon and the calm of a predator that knew it was always at the top of the food chain, she banished the chaotic web of fears that had attempted to rule her.

The road to victory was hidden from her, but she believed it *was* victory that awaited her.

Her worst fears under control, Inara remembered where she was, her consciousness residing on the bridge between diviners. Unfortunately, that brought Vighon Draqaro to the forefront of her mind.

Vighon had always clawed at the human side of her, a side that had been dampened beneath her Dragornian bond but, now that she was her whole self, just thinking of the northman was guaranteed to bring out the reckless human in her. It didn't help that she still failed to understand or know how to process all of her emotions.

And now, her attempt at control was ruined. As the seconds and minutes ticked by, she began to fear the worst. After all, Vighon had taken on a dangerous quest of his own in the north. Had he reclaimed the silvyr sword of Tyberius Gray? Had they failed and retreated? If so, at what cost? Her father was among their party, only adding to her fears.

All this and more fell on the shoulders of the Guardian of the Realm. She didn't dare focus on whatever was transpiring on Qamnaran, where her grandmother, Galanör, and Doran fought to free the dwarves and face Alijah himself. Inara suspected that any battles to be fought on that wretched island had already taken place. Being in the dark about it all was agonising.

But it was the darkness now that began to offer hope, as shadow and mist came together, coalescing into a familiar shape. There was a flutter in her stomach as a ghostly image of Vighon Draqaro came into being. Ethereal as he was, it was impossible to discern his current condition but, wounded or not, he was *alive*.

"Inara." His voice, long known to the Guardian, was a comfort she hadn't realised she needed. It was also somewhat hoarse, suggesting that he had been shouting a lot - alarming given the secretive nature of their errand in Namdhor.

"Vighon," she replied, enjoying the sound of his name on her lips.

A silence was held between them as they absorbed the other, regardless of the real distance between them. Inara longed to reach out and embrace him in her arms and, judging by his body language, Vighon was eager to do the same.

"So much has happened," he said.

"You won't believe what's happened," she said at the same time. Inara quickly replaced her faint smile with a serious expression. "Do you have it?" she pressed. "Do you have the sword of the north?"

"I do," Vighon answered, though the weapon seemed the last thing on his mind. "It's not all I have," he continued. "We took the city, Inara - the capital is *ours*."

For all the turmoil her human emotions put her through, there was no getting in the way of joy, and Namdhor once again flying the banners of house Draqaro was certainly joyous. It was also an incredible and unbelievable victory that filled the half-elf with hope and dread all at once.

"Tell me everything," Inara demanded with no lack of intensity. "Wait," she added, taking a breath - she had to know. "Are they alive?"

Ever in tune, Vighon knew exactly who the Guardian was referring to. "Yes," he stated with clarity. "In fact, both of them are only a few feet away from me."

Inara's heart swelled, causing her eyes in the real world to fill with tears. "They're together," she reasoned, adoring the image of her parents side by side.

"Very much so," Vighon reported happily.

Inara nodded along, unable to contain her smile. "I dared not entertain the dream in these dark days," she confessed. "Vighon, tell me everything."

The northman was no storyteller, but the tale that followed

gripped Inara from start to finish. Even their journey to Namdhor was fraught with the kind of terrors that would make even the strongest of warriors give up. Though she disliked the sight of Sir Borin, Inara was thankful the Golem had been at Vighon's side when it mattered most.

She hadn't been able to hold back a smug grin upon hearing the events inside the keep's garden. What else but his intended destiny could have brought both Vighon and the sword together in such an unlikely place? Whatever the future held, Inara truly believed that Vighon was fated to be the king.

A swelling sense of pride took hold of her when she imagined her mother saving his life, a moment described in great detail by the northman. His own feat, slaying the dragon Karsak, was humbly lacking in detail, however. Inara decided that she would have to inquire of others, sure that his leap from the keep's walls was far more dramatic and heroic than he let on.

What followed, however, sounded like a bloody battle to retake the entire city. A day and night of pitched fighting with only a score of Keepers and any and all who could wield a weapon. Inara wished she could have seen Namdhor rally to their king.

Finally, Inara blew out a long breath. "You were only supposed to retake the sword," she jested.

Vighon shrugged his ethereal shoulders. "Things got a little out of hand."

That particular phrase made Inara think of Kassian and his missing finger, but she refrained from commenting. "So the Reavers just retreated?"

Vighon's features creased into a forced wince. "That brings me to the end of my story. They remain just beyond the lower town. There aren't enough that I'm concerned about losing the city, but..."

Inara narrowed her eyes at him. "But what?"

"They've started beating their chests like drums." Vighon gave her a hard look. "I think Alijah's coming."

Inara immediately wanted to cast doubt on that scenario, but who else could have given them the command? "He always did like a dramatic entrance," she noted.

"It's a fear tactic," Vighon commented. "I don't exactly have an army on my side and he knows it."

Inara agreed. "Alijah's most likely expecting the city to submit to him when he arrives. He will want to execute you publicly." Just saying that out loud placed a new weight on her shoulders, not to mention the strain on her heart. "I'm coming to you," she declared as a matter of fact.

Vighon stumbled over his response. "I don't even know where you are. Have you returned to Illian? Did you find Gideon and Ilargo?"

Inara considered her own tale, wondering if its complexity and implications were, in fact, greater than Vighon's. Besides Erador itself, and the manner in which they had found Gideon and Ilargo, there was all they had learned about Alijah's true goals, even before they arrived at Drakanan - a place that held a story all of its own. How could she convey the sight of so many dragon eggs and the feelings that accompanied it? It was too much given the limited time they had.

"I will tell you everything, I promise, but I cannot sit here and regale you while my brother is on his way to kill you and everyone else in Namdhor. Gideon and Ilargo are with us - that's what matters. We're coming." Inara closed her ethereal eyes, preparing to depart from the shadowy realm and make haste.

"Wait!" Vighon pleaded, drawing her back. "I... I just need to..." The northman tripped over his words, though Inara could guess at some of what he intended to say.

"I know," she replied, her tone speaking volumes. "We will see each other soon." The Guardian offered him a warm smile that told him to hold on.

When next Inara opened her eyes, she was in a place almost as dark as the ethereal world her mind had inhabited. Drakanan's ancient halls loomed around her, supported by pillars thicker than any tree.

Almost any tree.

There was no escaping the images left imprinted on her mind after crossing over to the realm of magic. That tree, with its bark as white as snow, was gargantuan, its size mirroring its importance. It required their attention in The Moonlit Plains, where Alijah and Malliath had set plans in motion to open a doorway. That was where her real duty lay.

Namdhor is our destination, Athis spoke into her mind. *There can be no other path. We must protect the king and your parents.*

Your life is tied to that of the tree, Inara pointed out. **Undoing whatever Alijah has done in The Moonlit Plains could save you and every dragon in the realm.**

Alijah's presence in the north would suggest there is still time. We must protect that which lies in our heart, whatever the cost.

Inara placed one hand to the cold stone of the eastern wall, wishing there was nothing between her and Athis.

Set to action, she made her way back to the entrance to the bonding chamber, easily found by the warm light spilling into the antechamber. When she had left the first time, Gideon had been lying on the ground while Adan'Karth saw to his wounds, inflicted by The Red Guards' inquisitor. Now, her old mentor was on his feet with one hand resting against his ribs while Adan, seated on the lip of a step, inspected one of the exquisite eggs.

Inara glanced at the darkness behind her. "How long have I been gone?" she enquired, sure that it must have been quite some time given Gideon's appearance.

"Not as long as you think," the old master replied, wincing as he stretched his back. "It would appear Adan's abilities know no bounds," he remarked.

The Drake lazily waved a hand. "Appearances can be deceiving," he said, a phrase he had no doubt learned from Asher. "I would sit here a while and recover."

Gideon reached out and placed a comforting hand on Adan's shoulder. "I am most grateful for your efforts. That's twice you have put me on my feet."

Inara scrutinised the Drake, seeing the physical consequences of that effort. "After all you've done for us, Adan, I would have you rest in a palace, but we must leave this place *right now.*"

Gideon turned to her with a frown creasing his brow. "You have spoken with Vighon," he stated, easily detecting her distress.

"Yes," she answered gravely. "He has taken Namdhor, and with a small force no less."

"Alijah," Gideon interjected, his mind always a step ahead. "He won't stand for the capital, of all places, to fall into the hands of his enemies; it shows weakness."

Inara agreed wholeheartedly with the assessment of her brother. "He's likely travelling there as we speak."

Gideon took in the hundreds of dragon eggs, obviously reluctant to abandon them. "Then we should be there to greet him," he still declared boldly.

Inara hesitated as she imagined confronting her brother. They hadn't come face to face since that fateful day in the throne room of The Dragon Keep. Since then, she had come to see Alijah's true face after experiencing, first-hand, his malevolence. He was powerful, ruthless, and unwavering in his vision of domination. But he was also her twin brother.

There was no running from the inevitable clash. A part of her even craved it. He was her blood, her kin. Alijah needed stopping at all costs and who else but the Guardian of the Realm could face him? Athis poured his conviction into their bond and she soaked it up until her jaw was firm.

"To Namdhor," she concluded.

Adan'Karth sighed with the effort required to stand. "I would not hold you back. And I would never give up the opportunity to fly with a dragon," he added with half a smile. "Though I would not leave without Asher."

Inara scanned the elevated tiers that rose up within the cavern. "He hasn't returned?"

Gideon shook his head. "We thought he was out there with you."

The Guardian experienced a sinking feeling in her stomach.

"He talked of food and water," she said, making for the antechamber.

"There might still be Red Guards lurking in this place," Gideon warned, pausing to avoid one of the floating shards that passed in front of him.

Leading the way, Inara lifted her palm to the ceiling and called forth an orb of pure light to accompany them. Gideon looked tempted to do the same but, instead, used his limited magic for another purpose.

"Wait," he commanded, halting the companions in the antechamber. "I would not leave them to harm."

In the stark shadows of the orb, he raised both of his hands and slotted the four heavy columns of stone back into place, securing the bonding chamber behind them. The entrance blocked, it once again looked like nothing more than a large wall that boasted an intricate mural.

The eggs safe and Adan protected between them, they took cautious steps back into the maze of Drakanan. At every turn its ancient history jumped out at them, be it in the murals and statues or the signs of battles long forgotten.

With a destructive spell at the forefront of her mind and Firefly in hand, Inara felt confident calling out the ranger's name. As much concern as she held for Asher, she was reminded by memories, old and new, that he was easily the most dangerous person in all of Drakanan. If anything, they were likely to come across a pile of bloodied Red Guards.

"Wait," Adan breathed, his reptilian eyes turning down the passage on their left. His pale skin possessed a soft glow in the white light of Inara's orb, his shaven horns dull by comparison.

"What is it, Adan?" the Guardian asked.

The Drake, clearly recovering, tilted his head. "I can see the magic from his bones."

Inara didn't question Adan's observation, his supernatural sight proven time and time again. Instead, she moved in front of him and led by his directions and the point of her Vi'tari blade. Like all the previous passages, this one offered multiple avenues, daring to tempt wayward explorers further into the maze. Adan guided them left and right, reassuring Inara and Gideon that they weren't going in circles.

"Stop," Adan bade, his tone soft. "His aura goes no further."

Inara turned back to the Drake with a question to match her confusion, but it was Asher himself who provided the answer. Dropping down from above, his legs having braced him between the walls, the ranger landed amongst them like a feral beast. The only thing separating his movements from those of an animal were his precise and effective actions, chief among which was an unorthodox twist that launched Adan into Gideon. Before either hit the floor, he planted a boot in Inara's gut, throwing her further down the passage.

By the time any had recovered enough to assess the situation, Asher was dashing away and disappearing around a corner. "Why would he do that?" Inara managed, picking herself up.

Gideon rose to his feet and steadied Adan in his hands. "Let's ask him."

Together, they sprinted back the way they had come until Adan picked up his trail again. Here and there, they caught glimpses of his green cloak before he vanished behind another wall. Their chase continued through the dark but it soon became apparent that Asher wasn't one to be captured.

Adan drew to a halt and looked in every direction. "I think he must be doubling back on himself. His aura is more intense, but it is beginning to mix with both of yours. I'm losing him."

Gideon slowly shook his head. "He's spent decades evading some of the best hunters in the world. We're not going to find him in here, not in the dark."

Inara couldn't reconcile the ranger's actions. "Why would he attack us?"

"He didn't attack us," Gideon countered. "We've all seen what happens when Asher goes on the attack. I think he was defending himself."

"From us?" Inara questioned incredulously.

Inara! Athis's call turned the Guardian to the east. *We have him!*

Having heard something similar from Ilargo, Gideon reacted first and darted for the next passage. It wasn't long before they were exposed to Erador's northern chill. Leaving the cover of the grand entrance, the three companions ran out into the light fall of snow as twilight beset the realm, casting Drakanan in a cold gloom. Carved out of the mountains, its high walls loomed either side, as did many of the statues that lined the central path.

For all its grandeur, nothing could take away from the spectacle of two living dragons. Ilargo and Athis, green and red, dominated the path, their wings spread out beside them. Both predators were angling their horned heads like spears at the ranger, who found himself with nowhere to run.

Inara's orb of light pushed ahead and remained at an elevated position above them all. Getting a better look at Asher, the Guardian wondered if he was better compared to an animal after all. There was a wild look in his eyes, a desperation that bordered on violence.

"Asher!" she called, being sure to stop before entering the swing of his arm. "What are you doing?"

The ranger gave no reply but to tug on his old satchel, shoving it further around his hip. His other hand, however, began to creep up towards the hilt on his belt.

Ilargo lowered his head even further and loosed a threatening rumble from his throat. Athis refrained from doing the same, but Inara could feel his muscles tensing around his front claws. A single swipe from either would kill the ranger.

"Asher," Gideon began, taking one step towards him.

The ranger altered his stance in the blink of an eye. He was shorter now, his knees tensed, with hunched shoulders, and a confident grip on his broadsword. Ilargo's claws dug into the ground.

"Don't do it, Asher," Inara warned.

"He is not himself," Adan surmised. "Even fools can see the folly in confronting two dragons."

Athis silently lowered his head towards Asher's back and sniffed the air. The dragon immediately pulled his head back and turned to Ilargo, though their conversation escaped Inara. Despite the situation, she couldn't help but think of all the times she had shut Athis out while carrying on a conversation with others. Irritating as it was, the Guardian kept her focus on Asher, who looked like he could explode into action any second.

Without warning, Ilargo lifted his head into the air and unleashed an ear-piercing roar. So close was the ranger that he bowed his head, instinctively covered his ears, and shut his eyes. In the silence that followed, Asher slowly lifted his head and took in his surroundings. That wild look had left his blue eyes, replaced now with startled surprise. Turning one way then the next, the ranger orientated himself to the environment and those that encircled him.

"Asher?" Inara called softly.

He stood up straight with one hand gripped to the strap of his satchel. "I don't know... I don't know what's happening to me."

Gideon sheathed Mournblade on his hip. "I do," he said, briefly meeting Ilargo's eyes. He took a step towards Asher, who immediately took a step back before catching himself.

"What's wrong with me?" Asher muttered.

Inara harboured the same question and looked to Athis. His facial expressions were impossible for all but her to read, and so she followed his subtle cues to the satchel on Asher's hip. The mystery then unravelled in her mind until the Guardian's jaw dropped.

"Do you remember what I told you?" Gideon asked. "About the Dragon Riders? They were *called* to the eggs. Their bond first began with the Rider protecting the youngling. It made them instinctively defensive. Of course, they knew what was happening to them having been brought here for that very reason. Asher," he said delicately, "you know what you have. But you don't know why you have it. I can't imagine what's going through your mind right now."

Asher let his vision slowly drop to the satchel. With one hand, he reached in and removed the largest item. A bronze dragon egg, layered in scales. "I need to protect it," he announced absently.

Inara moved to close the gap but Gideon held out a hand, cautioning her. "Give him space," he instructed quietly. "Of course you need to protect it," he continued, his focus returned to the ranger. "You are bound together now. You are beholden to each other... forever."

Whether Asher registered what Gideon was truly saying or not, he refused to take his eyes off the bronze egg.

"Is this really happening?" Inara asked aloud.

"It makes sense," Gideon mused. "Those eggs would only respond to one with a dragon's heart," he explained gesturing to Asher. "He's the first warrior to enter that chamber in countless millennia."

Inara did her best to fight against the surprise of it all, hoping to make some kind of sense of the revelation. "Asher's a Dragon Rider?" she posed in her need to say it out loud.

"No," the ranger replied definitively. "I'm done fighting on behalf of some order, whatever their motivations. I'm not a Dragon Rider and I'm not a Dragorn." He looked back down at the egg. "I don't know what I am."

Gideon held both of his hands out to calm the situation. "None of that matters right now. This is... It's *wonderful*. That egg has waited for *you*, Asher. For thousands of years it's just remained here, dormant, until you found each other."

Inara agreed with every word, but her sharp eyes had spent the moment inspecting what she could of the egg. "It's already started to crack," she observed with a hint of excitement.

It was hard to say what was going through Asher's mind, but he was clearly uncomfortable with the attention the egg was receiving. He quickly placed it back inside his satchel before taking a breath and facing them all. "I'm sorry if I hurt you," the ranger said gruffly.

"Your apology is unnecessary in light of Master Thorn's explanation," Adan offered, the curl of a smile pulling at his cheeks.

Appearing a little awkward, Asher adjusted his stance. "What do I do now?" he asked, revealing something of a vulnerable side to himself.

Indeed, Inara was unaccustomed to the ranger's uncertainty. "You do what you've always done," she replied. "Trust your instincts. Whatever the future holds, good or bad, your bond with that dragon will bring a new kind of hope to the world."

"But trust *us*, if you can," Gideon added more practically, ever the master. "The dragon inside that egg is connected to you now. When you feel threatened, so too will it. But it doesn't have your experience or training, Asher. It doesn't know how to control its emotions, which *will* manifest in the form of instincts while it's so young. You're going to feel all that and want to act on it."

Athis moved to the side of them, bringing his bulk into the ranger's eye line. Where most would tense in the presence of such a predator, Asher visibly relaxed.

"Being around other dragons will help," Inara relayed straight from Athis. "The hatchling will find their presence soothing."

Asher considered her words. "I think I can feel that."

Still maintaining his distance, Gideon jumped back in. "Though the Jainus considered the Dragon Riders to be rivals at best, they documented all they learned about them. I have read much on what to expect next. I will guide as you permit."

Asher nodded once in acceptance. "Thank you."

As momentous as the event was, Inara could feel the pressure building inside her, the need to return home before it was too late. "I'm sorry," she began. "There is so much to discuss and I know you must have a lot of questions. I know *I* did and I had Athis to help me through it all. But I have spoken with Vighon," she added, her tone conveying the dire situation.

Asher looked to understand. "There's always a storm," he remarked. "Are the rest of the eggs safe?"

"Yes," Gideon answered. "We're the only ones who know where the door is. And only those who wield magic can open it; something we don't need to fear in Erador."

Again, Asher simply nodded his acceptance of the situation. "Then let's get in the middle of it," he said, referring to the brewing storm back east.

"You don't need to come," Inara pointed out, sharing some of the concern for the egg's safety. "It's going to be hard to protect it in Illian. There's only war there. You could stay here. Erador is a big place."

Appearing more himself again, Asher didn't falter in his response. "The egg didn't call to me because I walk away from the fight. Besides, if Alijah succeeds in destroying that tree..." The ranger looked down at the egg-shaped bulge in the satchel, unable to say the words.

"That's what we're all fighting for now," Gideon agreed. "Let's go home."

CHAPTER 4
HEAVY IS THE HEAD...

Two days had passed since the tower fell. Two days since Grarfath and Yamnomora had welcomed so many more children of the mountain into their halls. Among them was King Gaerhard, ruler of the Brightbeards. He would not be the only king to dine at the Father's table.

Dakmund...

The name brought Doran Heavybelly to his knees. Surrounded by the trees of Ilythyra, at the foot of a snaking stream, he tore off his eyepatch and lowered his face into the water. His agonised roar barely escaped past the bubbling surface.

When his lungs began to burn, the dwarf pulled his head back. As the water settled, he looked hard at the rippling reflection that greeted him. He didn't see the War Mason of Grimwhal or the prince of clan Heavybelly looking back at him. Instead, he saw his failures as a brother and a son.

His face and beard dripping, the dwarf hammered his fist into the stream until he struck the bottom. Dakmund, the last king of Dhenaheim, had but one fate and it had been Doran who had sealed it. Lord Kraiden's sword was gone forever, lost to The Hox, and with it any hope of a cure.

He beat the water again and again as his rage and despair demanded their time. Feral was the cry that burst from his lips and foul were the threats he laid at Grarfath's feet should Dakmund pass into shadow. Only when his chest was heaving and his tears had run dry did he finally stop.

For the moment his fist was numb, but he knew there was pain to come. He would welcome it, a distraction from the pain that split his heart, for his brother's inevitable demise was only one of the troubles that plagued him.

He shut his eye tight and relived the tower's collapse and with it... the death of Adilandra Sevari.

Had the world ever known a better queen? A better *ruler*? Though her final moments would remain a mystery to all but Alijah, her death had ensured their victory on Qamnaran. All had witnessed the portal from which he fell and all had agreed that one so powerful as the half-elf would never have opened a portal above the crashing waves of The Hox. Had the queen not dealt with him so, he would likely have delivered destruction upon the survivors astride his terrible mount.

If only *their* demise had been so apparent. Doran could still see the black dragon diving from the heavens to retrieve his wicked companion, saving him from those murky depths. Time would tell of his retaliation, though the dwarf had no doubt that it would be swift and brutal.

"That's going to hurt."

Doran didn't need to turn his head to know that Russell Maybury was standing there. He had been listening to that voice for decades, heeding the counsel that always accompanied it. Like so many times before, the old wolf was right - his knuckles were already beginning to sting.

Russell crunched through the fallen twigs and flattened the small stones into the dirt as he brought his considerable size to its knees. "Let me see," he bade, his tone softer than normal.

Doran replaced his eye patch before relenting and offering his hand. Blood mixed with the water and ran between his fingers until it dripped onto the soil. Despite the strength in

Russell's meaty hands, he inspected the cuts with a delicate touch.

"How many times have I patched you up?" he asked rhetorically. "Can you close your fist?"

Doran clenched his hand and refrained from wincing at the sting of it.

"Does it hurt?" Russell enquired, while one hand retrieved a roll of bandage from his belt.

"Everythin' hurts," Doran croaked, having become well aware of his injuries over their two day trek from The Narrows to the ruins of Ilythyra. He had never been more thankful for Pig than when they had crossed the western lands of The Moonlit Plains.

"Adding to your wounds isn't going to help," Russell pointed out.

Doran had a biting response on the end of his tongue but he kept his mouth shut when he realised Russell's hands were trembling. The old wolf had bandaged him up more times than he could count, his movements fluid with experience. But now, he applied the bandage with all the coordination of a small child.

"I'm sorry," he said, clearing his throat. "It seems my hands aren't good for much but swinging an axe."

Doran sighed, expelling some of his grief and anger for the moment. "The apology is mine, old friend. Me mind has been cast adrift an' me eyes with it. I cannot see what's right in front o' me." The dwarf reached out and gripped Russell's hand, feeling the tremor through to his bones. "It's gettin' harder, isn' it?"

Russell took his hand back and massaged it in the other. "You carry the troubles of more than yourself these days. You need not take mine."

Doran craned his neck and looked up at the starry sky that peeked through the canopy. "How long?" he asked.

"She swells every day," the old wolf replied, glancing up at the night. "She will be full in days."

Doran could see the despair that gripped his friend and he wanted to dispel it with strong words, but he could see all the signs of a losing battle. The thumb nail on Russell's left hand was dark and half an inch longer than the rest, its end sharpened to a point. His cheek bones and jaw line were more prominent than ever and his yellow eyes were sunk within dark pits.

"We'll get through it, lad," he promised. "We always do."

A shadow of doubt crossed Russell's face. "Not this time, Heavybelly." He examined his hand in the gloom. "It feels different this time. I fear it will never give up its hold on me."

"I'll hear none o' that!" Doran waved the notion away. "The wolf will rear its ugly head an' then it will be gone again. It..." He nearly choked on his words. "It always goes."

"We both know that isn't the truth of it. Willing otherwise isn't going to change anything, Doran. It's called a *curse* for a reason."

Doran's jaw quivered as he tried to put his words together and, for once, he didn't care it was unbecoming of a dwarf. "I'll not be losin' ye too," he uttered. "This damned war has taken too many an' I know there's still more to lose before the end. Ye're goin' to fight that monster, ye hear?"

Russell's mouth turned up into a sad smile. "I think I'm all out of that fight. What I've got left, I'll give to The Rebellion. After that, when the time comes, I want you to—"

"I know exactly what ye want!" Doran interjected. "I'll not be hearin' it! Ye're jus' goin' to 'ave to toughen up an' that's the end o' it!"

"Don't you get it, you stubborn dwarf? That's exactly what I want - the end of it! I want to be done with it and there's only one way!"

"Bah!" Doran snorted.

Russell sat back, his heels touching the edge of the stream. He didn't say anything, which only aggravated the dwarf all the more.

"Well, aren' ye goin' to say anythin'? Ye want me to sully Andaljor's steel with yer cursed blood don' ye? Give me a reason!"

The old wolf took a breath, his sight lost to the thick woods beyond the stream. His silence began to infuriate Doran more, but the fool squeezed his injured fist and the fresh cuts made him wince. It took some of the ire out of his thinking and he too remained seated in silence for a time.

"I'm sorry, lad," he managed. "I'm jus' an angry old fool lookin' for a fight."

"Is that why you were punching the stream?" Russell queried with a look of amusement brightening his features. "You always did pick the losing fight."

The banter brought some cheer to the son of Dorain, but his heart was too heavy to laugh. Instead, he nodded along and sought to change the subject. "How goes it?" he asked, nodding over his shoulder.

"Everyone's made camp, though we're going to have to stick to the fringes. Malliath didn't leave much of Ilythyra intact. I believe Thaligg has seen to your tent, if it can be called that. Faylen has set her kin to the task of patrolling the perimeter. I'd say we're safe here... for now."

A good helping of guilt was added to Doran's grief. "I should 'ave taken charge when we arrived," he acknowledged. "There's too many clans in the same camp, and the Brightbeards among 'em 'ave witnessed their king bein' cut down. It'll be chaos."

Russell looked back at the forest behind them. "That's not been my observation," he replied. "There's a good amount of uncertainty among them but, mostly, they've all been brought together by the same thing - *loss*. There isn't a dwarf out there who hasn't lost a loved one, not to mention their home, their country. You should be among them, Doran. Let them pick you up."

The son of Dorain shook his head. "It's supposed to be the other way around. *I* should be the one givin' 'em hope."

Russell raised a curious eyebrow. "Is that what War Masons do? Offer hope?"

"Well, *no*. Not exactly." In truth, Doran didn't want to describe the violent role of the War Mason in his culture.

"It seems you can't get away from who you are," Russell remarked, though Doran didn't miss the irony in his words. "A time is coming when you will have to be rid of that title. Are you ready for your next one?"

Doran hadn't wanted to think about it, for that particular title only came with the death of Dakmund. "I'm just a ranger," he muttered with little conviction.

"You're a prince of Grimwhal," Russell corrected. "That makes you a natural leader to these people." The old wolf turned to face him, pausing before he spoke. "Let us stay in the here and now. The present is where you find yourself, not the future. And right now, you're still just a dwarf, flesh and blood like the rest of us. Walk among them. There's courage in abundance in your kin. Grieve with them. And then rise *with* them."

Doran succeeded in breaking a smile, however brief. "Ye're a good man, Rus, if a little soft in the head."

Russell mirrored what he could of the smile. "And you'll always be a stubborn bone-headed ranger to me. Come."

Together, they walked away from the stream and made their way to the outskirts of Ilythyra. Even here, the trees were thicker and taller than anywhere else in the realm. There were some that still possessed the spacious bowers in their trunks, places where the elves felt more at home. From the ground, Doran could see the soft glow of their magical orbs and even a few elves crossing the wooden bridges that connected the tree tops.

Numerous as they were, many elves had made camp on the forest floor, side by side with the dwarves. Indeed, there appeared no division between the two races, including those who had recently been freed from Qamnaran. To the west, those who had been injured in the recent battle were being seen to by their respective kin since the children of the mountain were less receptive to the healing touch of magic.

Doran broke away from Russell to visit the wounded. He walked between their cots, offering elf and dwarf alike his prayers as well as his thanks for their bravery. The War Mason took some extra time to sit with the youngest dwarf among them and listen to his story. He wasn't even a quarter of Doran's age yet he had displayed the mettle of a hardened warrior and fought with the heart of a lion.

When he grew tired, the son of Dorain left him to rest and drifted back into the main camp. He accepted a pitcher of water from a Hammerkeg and a strip of meat from a Brightbeard, both of whom offered their thanks for his efforts on Qamnaran. Again, he stopped for a while and listened to their dreadful tales of slavery and abuse. Doran gave them his full attention, though he was occasionally distracted by the mere sight of the two dwarves sitting side by side like friends.

Later still, the War Mason gave what comfort he could to a Battleborn mother, who still wept for her two sons, both lost in Alijah's invasion of Dhenaheim. Doran's heart broke for all of them as a tapestry of grief was woven between the clans.

He would have spent all night if that's what it required to speak with everyone, but his duties were ever present. That much was obvious when Faylen herself approached, beckoning the War Mason away from the small group of Heavybellys.

"It's Galanör," she said.

"Finally," Doran replied with relief. "Take me to 'im."

They crossed most of the camp, heading further into Ilythyra. It was here that Doran discovered some of the debris and destruction caused by Malliath and Alijah when they killed Lady Ellöria. More than one of the gargantuan trees lay across the forest floor, barring the way, while others remained standing with charred bark, their trunks shattered in parts.

Their journey came to an end at the base of one of the intact trees, where the trunk had been partially hollowed out and its interior carved into the shape of a large chamber. Yellow-tinted orbs floated around, illuminating Galanör and Aenwyn, the only two elves inside. Galanör was leaning against the wooden table in the middle of the chamber, one hand running through his thick mane of chestnut hair. His distress was just as apparent as his fatigue.

"There was nothing you could have done," Aenwyn was protesting.

"I could have killed him!" Galanör fired back. "Then she would..." He hesitated, his breath ragged. "Then Adilandra would still be alive."

"The blame does not lie with you," Faylen stated, stepping into the light. "Adilandra died as her sister did - defending us all."

"I should have beaten him," Galanör continued in vain. "I had him, right there! I had no intention of letting him live. I was prepared to kill him."

"He has the power of Malliath running through him," Faylen countered. "There is no greater foe, even for one of your skill."

Aenwyn half raised her hand to halt any further conversation. "Galanör, you need to rest. You haven't so much as stirred in two days. Eat, drink, sit a while."

"Listen to her, lad," Doran pleaded. "Whatever happened inside that tower, it were damned unnatural, an' I'd bet Andaljor ye were right in the middle o' it."

Galanör let his head hang low so that his hair shielded his face. "It wasn't supposed to end like this."

Aenwyn moved to his side and guided him to the chair at the head of the table.

Faylen glanced at Doran before stepping closer to the elven ranger. "What happened in there, Galanör? Did Alijah succeed in whatever he was planning?"

Aenwyn met the High Guardian's eyes across the table. "Faylen," she said softly with an edge of caution. "He needs to rest."

"We're in the fight for our lives," Faylen retorted. "Resting is a luxury our enemy will not afford us. We need to know what happened inside that tower. What was the purpose of his spell? Is Alijah recovering too? If he's vulnerable, now is the time to attack."

From the outside looking in, Doran could see Aenwyn struggling with the hierarchy that existed between them while the one she loved was caught in the crossfire. Doing what he could, the son of Dorain caught Faylen's eye and gestured for her to take a moment.

"We're all reelin' from the cost o' victory," he began. "An' aye, there's a fight comin', but if we don' rest now we've already lost."

Faylen slammed her fist into the table, her expression one of stone. There was a well of grief behind her eyes, desperate to be unleashed upon the world in the form of vengeance and wrath. She slowly brought her hand back to her side, leaving an impression of cracked wood behind.

"Victory you say," she whispered. "This doesn't feel like victory."

Doran dwelt on the countless skirmishes, battles, and wars he had fought in Grimwhal's name. "It rarely does," he lamented. "But I've jus' come from a camp o' dwarves, more than a thousand strong, who wouldn' know freedom if it weren' for our actions on that wretched island. Ye knew Adilandra better than all o' us. Wouldn' she 'ave given her life for even one o' 'em?"

With glassy eyes, Faylen stared hard at the damage she had caused to the table. "Yes," she breathed. The High Guardian shut her eyes, breaking the barrier for a single tear to streak down her face.

"She will be honoured among me kin for all time," Doran promised. "Ever will the name Adilandra be sung in Grarfath's Hall as well as me own. She will be the first elven hero o' the dwarves."

Faylen nodded her appreciation, though the elf was clearly in need of something more substantial to see her through the grief. Unfortunately, Doran had nothing to offer her, their quarry miles away.

"I know that feeling," Galanör said, watching Faylen. "You need to strike out at something, anything."

Aenwyn placed her hands on his arm, motioning for him to focus on naught but the food and water on the table.

The elven ranger reassured her with a squeeze of the hand. "Adilandra's sacrifice will be honoured," he continued, "and her death will be answered for. And you're both right. We need information if we're to renew the fight. But we also need to rest and regroup if we are to even glimpse victory. So tell me everything that happened on Qamnaran."

Doran pulled out a chair not far from the ranger and did his best to unfold the events that took place outside the tower. He made sure to mention Aenwyn's efforts slaying the dragon Morgorth as well as Russell's contribution in their defeat of Lord

Kraiden. It was far harder to detail the loss of the Dragon Rider's poisoned blade, though he left the obvious consequences unsaid. Faylen assumed command of the tale from there, informing Galanör of Alijah's expulsion from the tower as well as the increasing lightning storm that bombarded the silvyr tower. When, at last, she spoke of that final bolt, their stories came together.

"That was the last thing I saw," Galanör told them. "It must have struck us both," he concluded.

"Did he explain the reason for any of it?" Faylen pursued.

"No, but I would say he succeeded, otherwise that bolt would have killed us. And there were the glyphs etched into the walls. They were definitely responding to whatever spells he gleaned from that book."

"Book?" Aenwyn questioned.

"It was on the floor - ancient by the look of it."

Faylen sighed in frustration. "The truth of it all eludes us."

"What abou' *ye*, lad?" Doran asked. "Ye were hit by the same spell as Alijah. Do ye feel any... different?"

Galanör clenched his fist and examined his knuckles. "No," he answered. "I feel stretched out but no different."

Doran shrugged his heavy pauldrons. "Maybe he failed then," the dwarf posed.

Galanör didn't look convinced. "As Faylen said, I fear the truth of the matter continues to elude us." The elven ranger perked up, as if remembering something. "What of the others? Has there been word from The Black Wood or The Arid Lands?"

Faylen subconsciously touched the diviner on her belt. "I have spoken with our allies in The Black Wood, though even they were in need of answers. It seems Nathaniel and Kassian returned with both Asher *and* Vighon shortly before Inara and Athis returned—"

"With Gideon?" Galanör blurted, a dash of hope in his eyes.

"It appears not," Faylen reported on a sombre note. "Unfortunately, they all left again soon after arriving."

Doran was already shaking his head, aware of the reasons for their swift departure.

"Where did they go?" Galanör pressed.

Faylen acknowledged Doran's response but made no comment on it. "Vighon accompanied Nathaniel and Kassian and journeyed to Namdhor. Apparently they went in search of the sword of the north. Inara and Asher left with the Drake, Adan'Karth. They were seen flying west, but I'm afraid no one knew where they were going."

Now Galanör was shaking his head. "They went to the most dangerous city in the realm to find Vighon's sword?" His tone suggested he was in agreement with Doran.

"The exact reasons for their separate errands remain a mystery to us," Faylen went on. "That said, I have had them dispatch a rider to Namdhor disguised as a merchant. They will seek them out and hopefully deliver the diviner so that we might coordinate our efforts."

"We could 'ave used every one o' 'em on Qamnaran," Doran complained. "They better 'ave damn good answers for dallyin' abou'."

Galanör rested his back against the chair, his sight lost to seemingly nothing at all. "Whatever their task, I trust they had The Rebellion's cause at heart. Each of them has the capacity to deliver a terrible blow to our enemy." The elf stopped himself and rubbed his eyes, his fatigue shining through. "What of Sir Ruban and our allies in the south?" he asked, pushing on.

"Sir Ruban has had better luck than all of us," Faylen began with a lighter tone. "He has amassed quite the force in The Arid Lands, both natives and those of Vighon's army who fled south. As of two days ago, he was posted just outside Calmardra having combined his forces with the remains of our fleet."

"They made it?" Galanör looked to have found a new reserve of energy.

"Yes," Faylen beamed. "My husband, Nemir, is among them."

"Now that *is* great news," Galanör replied.

"Besides the Reavers under Alijah's command," the High Guardian continued, "I would say Sir Ruban Dardaris is in charge of the largest force in Illian right now."

"Their orders?" Galanör asked.

"Sit on their arse!" Doran growled.

Faylen's eyes shifted to the dwarf and back. "They are to remain where they are until we can speak to Vighon or Inara," she specified. "We know Alijah and Malliath survived the events of Qamnaran, but we have no idea where they are. There's also Vilyra and Gondrith to account for. Both have dragons and neither have been seen for days. I don't want our largest force to be moving aimlessly across the country with undead Dragon Riders somewhere in the sky."

"I told ye in The Narrows an' I'll tell ye again, we need to attack the dig site in The Moonlit Plains! It's not even that far north o' 'ere!"

The High Guardian straightened her shoulders. "We have discussed this, Doran—"

"There are even more dwarves in chains there than there were on Qamnaran!" he cut in. "Listen," he continued, raising his hands into the air. "I'm glad Vighon's back in the fight, but we were makin' battle plans after he disappeared. This is no different! Ye command the elves, Faylen. If they march for the plains, Sir Ruban an' his men will accompany 'em."

Faylen turned her whole body to face the War Mason. "Doran," she began. "I want to free all those dwarves just as you do and, for what it's worth, I think attacking the dig site is the right course of action. But the realm is a big place and right now we have no idea what's going on out there. Vighon is king of these lands and Inara is its proclaimed guardian. It would be folly to make our move without speaking to either of them."

Doran wanted to fume but he could see the truth in her words. Faylen was eager to free his kin and undo whatever evil Alijah was scheming in the plains. He could also see the wisdom in her strategy.

"Faylen is right," Galanör added. "We don't know what's going on out there. And what we do know troubles me. Alijah's first act as king was to have your kin begin digging that hole - he values it. If we are to attack it, we should do so with a coordinated effort."

Doran dropped his head and rubbed his brow. "I'm not good at waitin'," he confessed. "But damned if I don' agree with ye both." He looked up and met each of their eyes in turn. "We wait."

"We rest," Aenwyn corrected, directing their attention to Galanör.

Faylen stood up first and paused to squeeze Galanör's hand. "It is good to have you back with us," she said sincerely. Whatever she said next was in their elvish tongue and entirely lost on Doran, though Galanör seemed to appreciate her words.

"Aye, lad, I never thought I would miss the sight o' an elf." Doran knew there was more to his sentiment than that, but the dwarf in him couldn't find the words after having spent so much emotion already that night. "Get some rest," he commanded. "The next time I pick a fight with a Reaver, I expect ye an' yer blades to be at me side."

"You can count on it," Galanör replied.

With that, the son of Dorain returned to the towering trees of Ilythyra and left the elf to his rest. He didn' get very far, however, before Faylen called out his name.

"I'm sorry," he said before she could speak. "I shouldn' 'ave picked a fight with ye. I know yer reasonin' to be right. I jus'…"

Faylen placed a hand on his shoulder, directing his eye to her face. "I cannot imagine the weight pressing upon you," she said gently. "You hold up all of dwarf-kind now. I know that isn't the life you wanted. But we both know what awaits you in The Black Wood, and it breaks my heart to know what you will have to go through after so much strife. I just want you to know that I, and so many others, believe that you have the strength to carry that burden."

Doran knew the word burden translated to *crown*. "Dak's not gone yet. There's still hope," he added while shaking his head.

"It is hard to hold a hope without rest to lend you the strength," Faylen observed. "When was the last time you slept?"

Doran couldn't say with any certainty. "Before the battle," he guessed.

The High Guardian reached out and guided the dwarf with

both hands. "Then come," she bade. "I know the recipe for a soothing tea - you will be asleep in no time."

Doran looked up at her with a frown creasing his already harsh features. "Tea?" he exclaimed. "Do I look like I drink tea?"

Faylen smiled with great amusement. "You will," she promised.

CHAPTER 5
WHAT DEFINES US

Under a new dawn, as the world slipped by beneath Athis's red wings, Asher tried to make sense of the profound change taking place within him. The incessant whispers that had plagued his mind in Drakanan were now quietening to that of a single voice. So soft was it, though, that the ranger was yet to understand a word of it. For now, he was settling for naught but impressions as they impacted his own emotions.

The hatchling felt safe.

That made sense to Asher, given their height above the world. How the hatchling knew they were among the heavens escaped him, but it deeply comforted the ranger to know there was contentment.

There was another part of his mind, a part that had kept him alive for decades in a realm that had worked hard to kill him, that found the whole experience absurd. He had never cared for a baby or a child before, and he certainly hadn't harboured paternal feelings for one. Surely he wasn't fit to protect something as precious as a dragon egg.

Yet here he was, ready to die for it. There was a nudge in his mind, almost as if someone had tapped him on the side of his head. For just a moment, he was sure the hatchling was trying to tell him something. Perhaps, he considered, referring to the creature as an *it* was a mistake. He probed that feeling further still, wondering if he might glean the dragon's sex.

Nothing. Just a gentle whisper in the back of his mind.

Without warning to the ranger, Athis tilted his body and banked northward as he began to descend. That gentle whisper quickened and increased an octave, speaking of concern. As a result, Asher's muscles tensed and the warrior in him prepared for action, despite the lack of any real threat.

"Why are we going down?" he grumbled behind Inara's ear.

The half-elf turned to look over her shoulder. "We're halfway to Namdhor," she explained. "Ilargo and Athis need to rest before we face Alijah and Malliath."

The ranger couldn't argue their reasoning, but he didn't like the look of the terrain below. Peering out from either side of Athis, the forest beneath them had no end, its tall snow-capped pines stretching so far to the north that they faded from view. There was something about it, however, that didn't sit right with Asher, and his gut was never wrong. Even the golden dawn that washed the forest in a welcoming glow couldn't take away from its menacing feel.

The dragons glided down, settling on a wide strip of snow that separated the forest from a long line of mountains in the east. Back on solid ground, Asher walked around Athis and scrutinised his new surroundings. There had always been a side to the ranger that loved coming across new places and discovering more to the world but, now, with such a precious thing on his person, he found it too disorientating, too dangerous.

"Where are we?" he asked, casting suspicious eyes on the dark forest to the west.

Inara shared a look with her dragon before answering. "We're on the border of Dhenaheim and Erador." The Guardian pointed to the east. "Those are The Whispering Mountains - dwarven territory."

Gideon walked over, blowing warm air into his hands. "Once

we get over these mountains, it should be a straight shot east from here."

"All the way to Namdhor," Inara agreed.

Asher absorbed the information, but his attention was quickly turned back to the ominous forest. "And what's that?"

Both Riders turned to look upon the forbidding wall of trees. "That," Gideon told them, his tone already suggesting Asher's suspicions were correct, "is The Dread Wood."

"I have a feeling it's aptly named," Inara opined.

"I have read a great deal about Erador and its history," Gideon continued. "There is nothing good said about that forest. Think of every monster you have ever encountered in this world. None of them would survive in there."

Asher tightened his grip on the base of the satchel strap. "Then why are we here?" he demanded with a hint of frustration.

Gideon considered his response but Inara beat him to it. "Everything on the other side of those mountains is now the domain of Alijah. We have no idea what might be waiting for us. It could be nothing. Or it could be Dragon Riders."

Gideon was nodding in agreement. "Inara's right. We will rest here for the day. Ilargo and Athis have no trouble flying at night. We will reach Namdhor by late morning."

Inara pressed a reassuring hand into Asher's arm. "You have nothing to fear. No creature will threaten us in the company of Ilargo and Athis."

"I have embraced fear all my life," the ranger began, his response surprising the Guardian. "Fear makes you stop and *think*. It keeps us alive." He paused, glancing down at the satchel. "I am accustomed to fearing for myself, but fearing for another is... *crippling*."

"You feel vulnerable," Gideon surmised, smiling with understanding. "It is to be expected. And, in truth, it may never pass. Even when your dragon is fully grown, seated at the top of the food chain, you will still fear for them. Such is our bond."

Asher held any further reply when he spotted Adan in the

distance, not far from the trees. Leaving Inara and Gideon to organise some kind of perimeter - using the dragons' bodies as the walls of their camp - the ranger approached the Drake from behind.

The closer he got, the quieter the world seemed to get. There wasn't so much as a creak from the forest nor a branch blowing in the wind. Every sense at Asher's disposal told him that certain death lay beyond.

"The trees have grown bitter," Adan observed, his reptilian eyes angled up at the pines. "They do not welcome us."

Asher knew better than to question the strangeness of the Drake's comments. "Is that because they know I'm about to take some wood for the fire?" he quipped, reaching for his sword.

Adan's hand whipped out and gripped the ranger's arm. "I would not take anything from this wood. To disturb the trees is to disturb its inhabitants."

Asher let go of his hilt. "The world doesn't get much colder than this, Adan. We need fire."

"I have strength enough to sustain a fire," the Drake confided, suggesting they turn away from The Dread Wood.

Situated between the two dragons, both of whom had curled their bodies around to form a protective circle, Adan created flames from nothing. His hands crafted the fire, building it to a size that would offer comfort to them all as well as melt some of the snow away.

"Are you sure you can maintain it?" Gideon enquired. "It wasn't that long ago you were healing me."

"You measure magic differently to us Drakes," Adan said. "You always take into account your potential need of destructive spells. No matter what happens here *or* in Namdhor, I know I will not require such taxing magic. And so, I have more than enough to keep you all warm for a while."

Gideon shrugged as he seated himself on the ground. "I hadn't thought of it like that," he admitted. "I suppose we always do take a certain amount of violence into account where our magic is concerned. You are a credit to your race, Adan. After spending so long at Asher's side," he suggested with a coy grin, "I would have expected you to be wielding a sword by now."

"Don't think I haven't tried," the ranger interjected, as he prepared food by the fire.

Adan regarded Asher for a moment. "I must confess, I see no attraction to that of a ranger's profession. Though, I would enjoy seeing the world. Perhaps one day," he added.

While the dragons slept the morning away, the four companions ate and drank what they needed to replenish themselves. It was a mostly silent affair given their general level of fatigue. Adan entered some form of meditation that allowed him to rest while simultaneously keeping the fire alive. Inara stared hard at The Whispering Mountains, clearly frustrated with the distance that still remained between them and Namdhor. Gideon, the most sensible among them, sought actual sleep beside the comfort of Ilargo's neck.

Under normal circumstances, Asher would have appreciated the time to himself and his thoughts, but they were no longer just *his* thoughts. Try as he might to focus on the conflicts that lay ahead, as well as his friends in Illian, the dragon's young mind kept him grounded to the here and now, where The Dread Wood offered constant threat. It was enough to keep any decent rest at bay and the ranger on edge.

By midday, Gideon was on his feet again. He left Ilargo to his slumber and approached the companions around the fire, his hand resting on Mournblade. In a flash of steel, the Vi'tari scimitar was pulled from its scabbard and out for all to see. The sound of its reveal sent Asher's hand to his own sword, though he managed to refrain from drawing it.

"I would test myself," Gideon announced, looking to Inara.

"Now?" she questioned incredulously.

"Time is not on our side," he replied. "It's now or never. Besides, the way of the sword is a perishable skill."

Asher perked up. "You were killing Red Guards *yesterday*," he pointed out.

Gideon walked a little further away from the fire in search of a better space. "Red Guards do not wield Vi'tari blades," he finally countered. "Alijah fights with the cursed blade of Thallan Tassariön, one of Valanis's generals."

"I know who he was," Asher cut in. "I was fighting him at Velia when you first arrived with Ilargo. *You* killed him if I recall."

"Quite so," Gideon agreed, twisting his sword in his hand. "And you did better than most fighting against one so experienced as Thallan. That cursed blade of his once belonged to a Dragorn, until Valanis twisted its enchantment. Now it will obey any who wield it, whether they serve the light or the dark."

"I saw Alijah wield it on The White Vale," Asher replied. "He cut down legions of orcs that day. I also saw him use it in Ikirith... up close. It's a viper of a sword. I'm not sure I would have survived were it not for Adan."

Inara sighed. "Fine," she said, rising from the ground. "Alijah's dangerous - understood." The Guardian of the Realm removed Firefly from its scabbard in one smooth motion.

Asher watched her approach Gideon, noting the absence of any real expression on her face. To most it might appear that she was focusing herself before combat, but the ranger could see right through her facade. Beneath that stony surface, a storming sea churned within her, brought on by the mention of her brother.

It bothered Asher, but he kept his thoughts to himself for now.

Instead, he watched two of the world's greatest fighters collide in a clash of steel and a spectacular explosion of colour. It gripped the ranger. He had never seen two Vi'tari blades pitted against each other and it was proving quite the display. The scimitars would strike high then low, every blow showering sparks of every colour.

Adan'Karth opened his eyes briefly, but appeared wholly passive about the match. Similarly, the dragons each opened a lazy eye before returning to their much-needed sleep.

For Asher, it was pleasant to have something familiar to him to focus on besides the foreign voice in his head. He watched them flow through their forms, ancient in their design, as each combatant danced around the other. It was beautiful to watch.

Though, after several minutes analysing their efforts, Asher came to the conclusion that Inara was holding back.

So too did Gideon. "You're holding back," he accused, his breath laboured.

Having barely broken a sweat, Inara maintained her rigid fighting stance. "Of course I am," she replied. "I don't want to kill you."

"I need you to try," Gideon said. "You need to pour those intentions into the blade - Alijah will."

Inara's stance faltered and Gideon renewed his attack. It only took him seconds to bring his scimitar to bear across her neck, where he held it steady. Again, Asher saw her brother's name take its toll on her emotions and again she tried to bury them beneath the facade of a warrior. Tempting as it was, the ranger had spent enough time around Inara Galfrey to know when it was not a good time to make an observation regarding her capabilities. And so he remained seated, content to watch as she dashed forward, pushing Gideon's blade away.

Their fight endured a while longer, each taking turns to claim victory. Indeed, the ranger found it hard to discern the better fighter between them, though he knew such a thing was typical when the old master sparred with the experienced student. How many times had he tested Nasta Nal-Aket in combat only for them to draw? He could certainly see the similarities in their chosen fighting styles.

It was Gideon, however, who asked for the breaks between matches, never Inara. Adan might have healed him physically, but the old master still harboured wounds of the mind. Every time Inara bested him, Asher had seen it coming; evident in the hesitation Gideon displayed. He was doubting himself.

"You're too evenly matched," he remarked, catching both fighters' attention. "You win, then you win. Over and over again. You both adhere to the... that *mag* thing."

"The Mag'dereth," Inara instructed.

Asher nodded once. "You're able to interpret each other's

attacks and defences because you both know them so well. Was Alijah ever trained in the Mag'dereth?"

"No," Gideon answered flatly. "His training has been rather varied. His mother and father taught him more than just the basics, then there's whatever he picked up from Vighon."

"And the Arakesh," Asher added ominously. "In The Bastion, he was pitted against them repeatedly."

Appearing exasperated with all the talk of her brother, Inara let the tip of her Vi'tari blade drop unceremoniously into the snow. "What exactly are you suggesting?"

The ranger rose to his feet and drew his broadsword from its scabbard. The action spoke of his intentions far better than any words could have achieved.

Inara twisted Firefly in a loop before deftly slotting it back onto her hip. "You cannot fight with the egg. It will rob you of your discipline."

Asher watched Inara stretch out an arm where her hand then offered to take the satchel. Already the ranger could feel his control slipping away. His instincts demanded that he bat her hand away, if not remove it altogether.

"Asher..." Inara's voice found its way past the haze clouding his mind, allowing him to focus on her eyes. "You can trust me," she said softly.

The ranger required another moment to consider his options, though really he was stalling in the hope that her words would have time to sink in and quieten his instincts. He did, after all, trust Inara Galfrey with his life. But the contents of the egg were far more precious than his own life.

With one hand, Asher carefully lifted the satchel over his head. Inara's fingers wrapped around the strap and he felt the pressure as she tried to take it. Finally, after a few seconds of resistance, he let go of the satchel.

"I would die before harm came to this egg," the Guardian declared earnestly.

Asher gave a short nod of understanding, but he couldn't move until he saw Inara sit down beside the fire with the satchel over her lap.

"That was a big step," Gideon complimented. "You did well."

Asher didn't want to think about it. He knew the absurdity of his emotions and he hated that they were out there on display for all to see.

"Defend yourself," the ranger commanded, raising his two-handed sword into an attacking position.

Whether Gideon's reactions were up to the task or not, his Vi'tari blade interpreted the incoming attack and forced the old master into a defensive stance. Asher's cleaving blade came down across the enchanted steel only inches from Gideon's face. Trained to give no quarter, the ranger used his forward momentum to barge into his opponent, shoving him off balance.

Again, Mournblade flicked up and deflected the next attack before parrying left and right. Asher had seen all he needed to understand the nature of the weapon. Feigning his next attack, the ranger suddenly dropped into a roll and grasped a handful of snow before finding his feet again. A flick of the wrist sent that heap of snow directly into Gideon's face, blinding him.

As suspected, the Vi'tari blade was useless if its wielder couldn't see. Asher swatted Mournblade aside with the flat of his sword and planted a forceful boot into Gideon's chest. The old master left the ground with a yelp of surprise and pain. Only seconds after he impacted the snow, the ranger speared the tip of his blade into the ground beside Gideon's head, avoiding the obvious killing blow.

"Again," Asher grunted.

Gideon wiped the snow from his face and collected Mournblade on his way back up.

"I've seen you fight," the ranger said. "I've seen you on the battlefield against hordes. I've seen you defeat all manner of evil. Hell, I've fought you myself more than once. I can still see it in you - the boy who returned from Dragons' Reach a bold warrior. But you're hesitating now. You're relying on that fancy blade instead of what's up here," he added, tapping the side of his head.

"I know," Gideon admitted, catching his breath. "I'm not blind to the doubt that haunts me."

"He beat you," Asher stated simply. "You challenged Alijah and he beat you. Don't be defined by *his* victory. The Gideon Thorn I know has always got back up. *That's* what makes you more dangerous than everyone else. And that will be what Alijah fears the most."

The old master was overcome with a reflective expression as he absorbed the ranger's words. "You are wiser than you look," he replied bemusedly. "Perhaps you are beginning to..."

Gideon's words lost their definition in Asher's ears. He could see the old master talking to him, but the world was drawing in on itself, losing its sharp edges. His broadsword fell from his limp grip, though he was entirely ignorant of it hitting the ground. Instead, he found himself on his knees, his vision directed towards Inara. Gideon was suddenly by his side but the ranger took no heed of his actions.

The egg was out of the satchel.

Inara held it out for all to see as a new crack tore a jagged line across the egg's scaly surface. As the egg was cracked, so too was Asher's mind. There was an instance of pain. Then nothing. The world was snatched from him, taking any sense of orientation with it.

With no power to deny them, images, sounds, and smells were forced upon the ranger from a time and place that was not his own. He saw men and women adorned in the garb of warriors. Some were talking while others demonstrated their use of magic or sparred with exquisite blades. Then there were the dragons. They dominated the sky in a variety of sizes and colours, displaying their magnificent beauty. It was Drakanan.

The ancient home of the Dragon Riders rose up around Asher's vision in all its glory. Then, he himself rose, leaving the mountainous fort behind. The ranger flapped his wings and soared above all the dragons until Erador was laid bare beneath him. It was freedom.

His vision splintered, taking with it the open sky. Now, he was looking down at a bronze egg in the low firelight of Drakanan's main entrance. Asher watched through reptilian eyes as a Dragon Rider accepted the egg with a bow of the head before disappearing into shadow.

That shadow engulfed his sight until he was looking at the inside of his own eyelids. The ranger opened them to see Inara, Gideon, and Adan'Karth crouched over him. He was returned to the edges of The Dread Wood and its terrible cold. Then Ilargo's horned head loomed over them all, shortly followed by Athis and his piercing blue eyes.

"What happened?" Asher croaked, sitting himself up.

"You passed out for a few seconds," Inara explained.

"What did you see?" Gideon enquired with a hint of excitement.

Asher looked at the old master, wondering if he had pried inside his mind. "I saw..." He took a moment to compile everything he had seen and heard. "I was in Drakanan. A long time ago."

Gideon glanced up at Ilargo while nodding eagerly. "It was a memory."

The ranger was shaking his head. "How can I see *anything*?" he asked, gesturing to the hard shell that protected his dragon.

"There's a reason dragons are known for their wisdom," Gideon replied. "They have the ability to pass on memory if they choose to. Tell us. What did you see?"

"I was... I was flying."

"That's quite typical," Inara said enthusiastically. "You see through their eyes."

Asher rubbed his forehead. "I gave an egg. No. I gave *that* egg to a Rider."

"He was likely taking it to the bonding chamber," Gideon reasoned. "You were seeing through the mother's eyes, Asher. That will have been the last memory she passed on."

The ranger declined their help to stand and brushed the excess snow off his leathers. He accepted the egg and the satchel back from Inara but paused to inspect the egg in greater detail. For all the cracks that marred the shell, there remained another layer beneath, smooth in appearance, that was yet to show any signs of distress.

"What else can I expect?" he asked gruffly.

Gideon responded with a light shrug of his shoulders. "More memories. It's a good thing though. It means the dragon inside is experiencing it all."

"What does that mean?"

"It means that when they finally hatch, they will enter the world with some knowledge of it. Though, the world you're both seeing *is* long past. Hopefully, your hatchling will begin to absorb some of *your* memories and bridge the gap."

Asher failed to hide some of his distress. "My memories are no place to wander," he cautioned. "And... I'm not alone in there."

Gideon nodded his understanding. "You still possess some of Malliath's memories." The old master took a breath. "I'm afraid there is little you can do at this point. Until they hatch, everything is instinct and a little messy. And your bond is immature, meaning there is little to no filter between you."

"How long until they hatch?" Asher questioned, both eager and nervous to meet the being inside.

Gideon looked down at the scaled shell. "Once the outer layer has begun to crack, it can be anywhere from hours to days."

Inara ran a delicate finger over one of the cracks. "Has she told you the name yet? The mother?"

Asher was so focused on not pulling the egg away that he didn't grasp her question for another second. "Told me the name?"

Inara flashed a warm smile. "*We* may not know what lies within, but every dragon mother knows whether she has laid the egg of a son or daughter. Athis and Ilargo were both named by their mothers before they hatched. Of course, they were able to tell us themselves by the time we met."

"Inara's right," Gideon agreed. "At some point that memory will be passed on to the hatchling. You will either experience it yourself or they will tell you."

It all sounded so surreal to the ranger, as if he was hearing about someone else's life. "I don't know any name," he admitted quietly, his eyes fixed on the bronze egg.

"There will be time," Gideon reassured. "Come," he bade, gesturing to the fire. "Let us rest some more before we take flight tonight. Tomorrow will bring tests of its own."

Asher didn't argue. His head felt heavy, as if he could feel his mind altering to make room for more memories that were not his own. He decided, however, that he would accept these new ones willingly. He cradled the egg by the fire and closed his eyes. Whatever was happening to him, the ranger knew he wouldn't emerge the same.

And he was fine with that.

CHAPTER 6

THE DAWN OF A NEW DAY

Like every morning since that fateful night, Kassian Kantaris awoke with one thing on his mind: Clara. Waking up without the feel of her warm body beside him was agony, but he couldn't deny the sting had lessened over the last two years.

It was said that time healed all and the Keeper hated it. He didn't want to get used to life without his wife. He didn't want the fury to seep from his veins. Yet here he was, perched on the edge of his bed with an old feeling returned to his heart.

Hope...

He hadn't seen so much as a flicker of hope since his days in Valatos, with Clara in his life. But he could feel it, growing bit by bit as the days stretched on. Hope that they would defeat their enemy, and not just because that enemy was Alijah Galfrey, but because there was evil holding reign over the land. Hope that Vighon would be king again and bring a new age of peace to the realm. Hope that Inara and Asher would return with Gideon and Ilargo. Hope that their allies had claimed victory on Qamnaran because the world *needed* dwarves and elves.

And then there was the hope he held deep down for his fellow Keepers. Besides those who accompanied him, they were scattered across Illian, each possessing the knowledge and experience of a seasoned mage. Their talents were being wasted in hiding and there were potentially hundreds, if not thousands, of people out there with a sensitivity to magic who needed guidance.

That last hope meant a lot to him, its origins from a place in his heart where Clara still existed. More and more, in fact, he found himself wondering what she would think of his day-to-day actions. He knew his wife wouldn't have condoned half the things he did, but the world was broken - at least that's what he told himself.

Already exhausted by his first thoughts of the day, Kassian pressed his hands into the bed and pushed himself up. He winced and chastised himself, forgetting that his hand was still injured. He inspected the bandage, dismayed to see flecks of blood that had come through. He knew he needed to set time aside to heal the stump where his little finger had been, as well as garner the magic to perform the spell.

But there was a constant reminder that every ounce of his magic would be required soon.

Opening the window, the sound of Reavers beating their armour flooded his room. Kassian sighed. He wondered if the morning would ever come when he could get up, enjoy his pipe, and drink a hot cup of Velian tea. He hoped not. That all sounded rather dull, in truth. The Keeper had no plans on resting until his bones demanded it.

That in mind, he dressed in his usual attire, including his long coat, enchanted sword and bracer, and his wand holster. He held the wand itself in his hand for a moment. The texture and weight felt wrong, even down to the quantity of Demetrium in its core. It had, obviously, been perfect for young Fin, who had wielded it with honour until his dying breath outside The Dragon Keep. And so he holstered it on his right thigh and made to leave the inn that had been kind enough to give him free lodging.

Stepping out into the lower town, he was greeted by the pervasive chill of the north. Having grown up in Velia, Kassian preferred a warmer climate where one's breath didn't attempt to cloud the view every few seconds. The people, however, he found to be far more hospitable than the rest of the world gave them credit for. Approaching his fellow Keepers, several Namdhorians reached out to thank him for his efforts in the recent battle, as well as offer him supplies. He refused them all and ushered them up the city slope, there to join the rest of the lower town inside the keep.

Pleasant as the interactions were, the undercurrent of Reavers spoiled the atmosphere. Joining the mages by the edge of the lower town, he looked out on the several hundred fiends that beat their chests like drums.

Something wasn't right.

"Is it just me," he began, "or are they—"

"Getting faster," Aphira confirmed. Though not the smallest among the Keepers, she was easily a whole head shorter than Kassian. He looked down at her and was reminded by the tone of her skin that she heralded from The Arid Lands. Namdhor must feel like hell to her.

"When did this start?" he asked, feeling for the edges of the pipe in his pocket.

"A few hours ago," Aphira reported.

Kassian held the pipe in his hands and between his lips. "Why would they get faster?" he pondered aloud.

Aphira gestured down the line of Keepers. "Ayden thinks it's some kind of countdown," she remarked sceptically.

"It *is*," Ayden chirped up, defending his theory. "Why else would they do it?"

Kassian paused with the tip of his wand resting on the rim of the pipe. Instead of igniting it, he removed it from his mouth altogether and stared at the Reavers. It *was* a countdown. The faster they beat the closer Alijah and Malliath approached.

"I need to warn Vighon," he concluded, searching for the nearest horse.

"Wait!" came a call from farther down the line. "A rider from the east!"

Kassian walked out onto the vale and squinted his eyes against the glare of the white snow. Indeed there was a rider, a single man on horseback, his saddle laden with goods. The Keeper turned to his right to watch the Reavers, concerned that they might attack the rider, but they appeared content to beat their chests and stare at the city.

"Intercept him," Kassian ordered.

Two Keepers, Sadvik and Jorn, broke away and jogged out to meet the rider. He wasn't the first to arrive at the city since it had been liberated, but he was the first to arrive on his own, from the east where The Black Wood resided.

Once they were close enough for Kassian to take in the details of the rider, weary by the look of him, Sadvik called out in his thick Grey Stone accent, "He hails from The Black Wood!"

From atop his mount, the traveller looked out on the Reavers with no lack of trepidation. "I don't... I don't understand," he confessed.

"The city's ours now," Kassian told him boldly.

The rider's eyebrows slowly rose into his head. "Truly?"

"You come with news for The Rebellion?" Kassian probed, drawing his eyes down to the Keeper.

"I come with more than that," the rider divulged, revealing a black orb within his cloak. "Queen Drelda instructed me to give it to Vighon Draqaro himself."

Mentioning Doran's mother robbed Kassian of any suspicion he might have been harbouring for the rider. "Come with me," he instructed.

Out on her balcony, a cold dawn greeted the pale skin of Reyna Galfrey. The elf pulled on the blanket around her shoulders, determined to withstand the chilling wind and watch the sunrise. She had done just that for nearly two years, hoping each day that it would be the day she unearthed her son and freed him from the clutches of Malliath.

It was crushing to know that it would not be this day nor any other. That which she dreamt her every waking moment would never come to pass.

There was to be but one outcome.

A blast of icy wind swept her golden hair across her shoulders and dragged a solitary tear from her left eye. She wiped it away before Nathaniel's warm arms wrapped around her and his chest pressed against her back. He buried his face into her neck and she welcomed the heat of his breath. That, and so much more, she had missed in his absence.

"I don't have to see your face to know you suffer," he whispered.

"I failed," she uttered, her words almost snatched away by the breeze. "I could not save him."

Nathaniel squeezed her a little tighter. "It was never up to you to save him," he told her. "Nor me. We're his parents. We were only to love him."

"It wasn't enough," Reyna replied, her vision lost to the expanse of the north.

"Do you regret your choice?" Nathaniel asked softly.

Reyna didn't answer straight away, though she had already given that very question much thought while the moon still held sway. "No," she said firmly. "I made my choice. I stand beside Vighon. I will see this through to whatever end."

"We will see it through *together*," Nathaniel articulated. "From now on, nothing comes between us."

Reyna finally turned around to see her husband's face. He looked just as he did when she had met him, nearly fifty years ago. She knew every line in his skin, the feel of his lips, and every speck of colour in his eyes. He was the most extraordinary man she knew. Their roots went deep.

"Together, my love," she promised.

Nathaniel flashed her one of his confident smiles and she couldn't help but feel uplifted by it, as if everything was going to be alright. She responded by crushing him in her embrace and he kissed her on the head, where he paused to inhale her perfume.

"What's that?" he asked from over her shoulder.

Reyna pulled away and followed his gaze into the keep's court-yard below. It was packed with people from the lower town and their numerous supplies, but her elven eyes caught two servants guiding a pair of horses away while Kassian Kantaris escorted a stranger through the main doors.

"A messenger?" Reyna pondered.

Nathaniel frowned. "Surely it is too soon. The raven we sent to The Black Wood should still be in flight."

"It could be news from Qamnaran, from my mother!" Reyna concluded with her first dose of enthusiasm. "Get dressed!"

The Galfreys hurried about their chamber in a bid to collect their clothes, though Nathaniel's haste only seemed to slow him down. Reyna rolled her eyes, always amused by the clumsiness of humans. Finally attired, they made their way through the passages and ancient halls of The Dragon Keep, careful to weave through the makeshift camps of those that had taken refuge there.

Reyna bowed her head to the two guards standing outside the double doors of the throne room. They only possessed half the armour of a typical Namdhorian soldier and they had no promise of coin for their service, yet they still manned their positions to protect their king.

Inside, the throne room was a hub of activity. Servants were in the process of placing a long table between the pillars with its head in line with the throne. Kassian was off to the side, conversing with two of his Keepers and the stranger he had escorted inside. Despite the activity, Reyna was drawn to the throne itself, where Vighon was seated with his eyes closed.

He was holding a diviner.

Kassian caught their entrance in the corner of his eye and broke away to greet them. "A rider from The Black Wood," he quickly explained. "Queen Drelda sent him after speaking with Faylen."

"What news?" Reyna blurted, her eyes shifting back to Vighon.

"That's all he knows," Kassian replied.

"He came alone?" Nathaniel enquired wearily.

"Disguised as a merchant," Kassian confirmed. "The Rebellion has no idea we've taken the city."

Reyna shared some of her husband's dismay, hoping, as he had, that whoever came from The Black Wood would do so in the company of battle-hardened dwarves.

"That's not all," Kassian continued. "The Reavers outside the city - they're beating their chests even faster now."

"He's getting closer," Nathaniel reasoned.

"It would seem so."

Reyna was inclined to agree, though her attention was held by potential news from Qamnaran. "What's all this?" she asked, observing the table and chairs being put into place.

"Vighon wants to—"

"His Grace," Nathaniel corrected. "Or the king," he suggested. "I know they're just words but they hold weight for those around us."

Kassian shifted on the spot, struggling with the need to roll his eyes. "*The king* wants to set up a meeting between us, Sir Ruban, and the contingent on Qamnaran. My Keepers here can link the new diviner to theirs."

Reyna displayed her confusion. "Then why is the king speaking alone?"

"That was the message that accompanied the rider. Faylen wanted to speak with the king alone before we link all three diviners."

Reyna's stomach turned to quick-sand. "Why would she do that?" she said aloud without meaning to.

Kassian pulled a face that always preceded his usual sarcasm. "I would say it isn't for us mere mortals to understand... but look who I'm talking to."

Vighon stood up from his throne, ending every conversation in the chamber. "Empty the room," he commanded.

There was a brief pause before the servants turned to leave and the Keepers gestured for the rider to accompany them. Kassian, however, made no move to follow them. "Vig... Your Grace, my Keepers are required to connect our diviner to the others."

"The meeting will wait," Vighon told him. "Faylen wishes to

speak privately with Reyna and I would not deny her. Clear the room."

Kassian held back any remark he might have had and simply departed the throne room. Nathaniel, on the other hand, remained as grounded as a statue, a stance the king did not protest.

"Please." Vighon gestured to his throne, inviting Reyna to take a seat as well as the diviner.

The elven ambassador was brimming with questions but she dared not voice a single one. Instead, she walked towards the throne and ascended the few steps to meet Vighon. Only then did she notice Sir Borin the Dread, previously hidden by one of the pillars. They were, perhaps, the only things large enough to conceal the Golem and his wide frame. Thankfully, his grotesque features were also concealed by a cumbersome bucket-like helmet and a mis-match of armour and leathers.

"Here," Vighon said, presenting her with the diviner.

Reyna accepted the black orb and seated herself on the furs that lined the throne. Cupping the diviner in both hands, the elf gave her husband one last look before closing her eyes and allowing the orb to pull her mind therein.

Faylen's familiar features were there to greet her among the shadows and liquid-like smoke. How long had it been since they spoke?

"*It's been too long*," Reyna said in her native tongue.

"*Indeed*," Faylen agreed. "*I do not like to measure your absence in years.*"

"*How do you fair?*" Reyna asked. "*Do you suffer any injuries?*"

"*Nothing I cannot overcome*," the High Guardian replied.

A heavy silence hung between them, fuelling Reyna's fears, of which there were many. "*I know Alijah still lives*," she finally said. "*There are Reavers here.*"

"*Yes, Vighon informed me of your situation.*" The fact that Faylen didn't go on to make any comment on their miraculous taking of Namdhor spoke volumes to Reyna.

"*Faylen*," she said softly. "*Tell me.*"

Though her ethereal form made it impossible to tell, it

appeared the High Guardian wiped a tear from her cheek. "*Your mother faced Alijah alone, inside the tower. Whatever magic was wrought upon it, the island could not bear it. The tower fell into the sea... with Adilandra inside. She's gone, Reyna. I'm so sorry. She's gone.*"

Reyna remained perfectly still, numb almost, as Faylen informed her of the events surrounding her mother's death. The fact that so many survived because of her mother's efforts didn't pass her by, but she was unable to make comment on it. One of the hardest parts to come to terms with was the absence of any body to recover.

"*I will never see her again,*" Reyna grieved.

"*I'm so sorry,*" Faylen said again, her voice saturated with sorrow. "*I should have... I should have been by her side. That was my duty.*"

Another silence filled the space between them, a dark depression that threatened to rob the world of all light. Reyna didn't know what else to say. It hurt. She wanted to lay waste to everything. The pain made her want to lash out. She wanted to scold Faylen for failing to protect her mother and she wanted to throttle her son for causing her death in the first place.

But where would that get her? There would be more pain, more hurting, and heartache. Reyna wasn't sure she could take any more. Alijah would reap what he had sown, but Faylen deserved no blame, for who could deny Queen Adilandra? She had been a demon on any battlefield and it was no surprise her last act aided the survival of thousands.

But, right now, in the most painful of moments, Reyna wasn't sure she could have sacrificed her mother even for thousands of others.

"*You did as she commanded,*" Reyna stated, her tone even. "*That was your duty.*" Just saying the words helped her to get past the gnawing anger.

Faylen adjusted herself, taking on a more rigid form. "*This isn't how I wanted to do this. I never imagined I would have to,*" she added sombrely. "*Time and menace are against us, however, and it is still the future we must consider.*"

Reyna relinquished some of her grip on the pain and rage that simmered beneath the surface, allowing her to find a tether with which to pull back her focus. "*What are you talking about?*" she asked gently.

"*Elandril - all of Ayda - is absent its queen. That burden falls to you now, Reyna.*"

In and of itself, Faylen's decree was entirely logical and not at all a surprise. But Reyna was speechless. The obvious conclusion had escaped her and, even now, after it had been said aloud, the elven princess faltered to grasp its true meaning.

"*You know our ways,*" Faylen continued. "*There need not be any ceremony, nor grand announcement, to bestow the title upon you. Our people will bow to you now,* my Queen."

Reyna swallowed in the absence of any real reply. She wasn't meant to be queen - her mother was immortal! She had never had any qualms about being a princess for eternity, not when the alternative came with such tragic consequences.

"*As you say,*" she croaked, "*time and menace are against us. We will discuss this later. Right now we have to coordinate The Rebellion's efforts.*"

"*Reyna.*" Faylen reached out, sensing her imminent departure.

"*I have to go,*" Reyna insisted.

She closed her eyes and opened them again to The Dragon Keep's throne room. Vighon was standing beside Nathaniel at the head of the table, both deep in discussion. Noticing her return, Nathaniel looked upon her with sympathy and tears of his own, having heard the news of Adilandra from the king.

"My love..." he began, offering his hand.

Reyna didn't move for a moment. The fact that she was seated on a throne was suddenly a distraction she had never anticipated. Something tickled both of her cheeks and she realised there were tears streaking down her face. After wiping them away, she stood up and accepted the comfort of her husband's embrace. She felt Vighon's hand rest on her back and she turned to see his dark eyes sharing her pain.

At last, Reyna detached herself from Nathaniel and stood back.

"There are two things we must now accept so that we might take our next step with efficiency. Adilandra, my *mother*, is gone." Saying the words placed a weight on her chest, giving her pause.

"And the other?" Vighon wondered.

Reyna looked up at her husband. "We are now the king and queen of the elves."

CHAPTER 7
A ROYAL GATHERING

Descending beneath the clouds, The White Vale of Illian's north dominated the horizon with a blanket of snow. Alijah sat up in his saddle, astride Malliath, and took it all in as his cloak and hair were swept out behind him. It was all so peaceful from their lofty vantage. It would have been easy to think that the realm enjoyed the same tranquility.

But it didn't.

Unlike thousands of others who had worn the crown before him, Alijah was determined to keep his objectivity. No matter the vantage or luxury he enjoyed as king, he would never forget that there was a world beyond his view. A world of people.

Narrowing his eyes, he could just make out the faded line of The Vengoran Mountains. Tracking them west would take any traveller to Namdhor and The King's Lake. Of course, Malliath did not require such landmarks to know where he was flying. His bones were almost as ancient as those mountains.

Banking slightly to the left, turning westward, the dragon's wing twitched. Alijah patted his companion's scales. They were both dealing with injuries but Malliath had shown unparalleled strength during their flight. And Alijah couldn't say he hadn't enjoyed the slower pace - the last two years had been relentless.

Are you ready to do what must be done? Malliath's voice was the perfect pitch inside his mind, a soothing melody compared to the barraging winds.

With your power flowing through my veins, Alijah responded, **I'm ready for everything.**

Tell me, Malliath purred.

I will demand Vighon's head. Any who defend him will share his fate.

You will see, Malliath told him, *that the people love you. They will gladly give him up.*

Alijah rubbed Malliath's black scales. **I don't know if it will be their love for me or their fear of you.**

A wave of satisfaction rolled off Malliath. *Both will be needed to rule all of Verda.*

Though Alijah agreed, it wasn't the future he had always envisioned. **There will be turmoil for some time, many years even. But, in generations to come, you will be loved not feared. Can you imagine that, old friend? There will be peace in every corner of the realm. Without magic there will be equality like never before and every man, woman, and child will look up at you with thanks. They will see you and know they are safe.**

Malliath's muscles rippled beneath Alijah, telling of his anticipation. *Our forces have almost converged on The Moonlit Plains,* the dragon explained, moving the subject away from his feelings. *It will be well defended by day's end.*

Very good, Alijah noted, aware that Malliath's mind was better suited to monitoring so many Reavers with little effort.

Malliath continued his flight in silence for another mile. *What will you do with Reyna and Nathaniel Galfrey?* he finally probed.

Alijah could feel the dragon pressing images upon him, each more grotesque than the last. The king shut his eyes, searching for his own feelings on the matter.

You will not execute them? Malliath exclaimed.

The king sharpened his focus, wondering what gap he had left for the dragon to see into his mind. *They are assets we should not discard. With Adilandra dead, my parents will take command of the elves and all of Ayda with them.*

You would allow them to rule the east? There can only be one throne!

And there will be! Alijah pushed back. *But elves are immortal - they do not forget easily. Nor can we be everywhere at once. It will aid us to have them kept under better control while we see to Illian and Ayda. And without magic, they will pose no real threat.*

And what of the threat of your parents? Magic or not, they have a history we would be fools to ignore. They are more likely to lead a new rebellion against us than maintain peace in Ayda.

If they step out of line I will—

They have already chosen their side, Malliath argued, cutting Alijah short. *They will be executed with the rest of The Rebellion. We do not need them to curb the elves.*

Alijah wanted to reinforce his opinion but he knew the dragon was right - they had abandoned him, disowned him, and replaced him. How could they come back from that? And how could Alijah find the heart for them when his love was for the entire realm?

It will be hard, Malliath admitted, his tone soothing now. *But we will do it together. And we will get through it together.*

The king sighed, and with it his worries were taken by the wind, leaving him with one thought.

They will all die.

Seated at the head of the table, his chair like any other, Vighon watched friends and allies materialise around him. Thanks to the diviner, in the centre of the table, and the Keeper, standing off to the side, Doran, Galanör, Faylen, and Sir Ruban Dardaris were given form in the empty chairs.

As engrossing as it was to watch their ethereal bodies take shape, Vighon took the moment to glance at Reyna and Nathaniel, seated to his right. Both appeared to be in shock, though it was more likely, in Reyna's case, that she was numb. Nathaniel's expression had yet to change since he had been informed of his new station as king of the elves.

Vighon felt for them both, wishing more than anything that he could take it all away for them. He knew the immense pressure of a crown being placed on one's head as well as the suffering that accompanied the death of a mother. But he also knew there were no words that would make a difference.

He had urged them to return to their chambers and take some time, but both had rebuffed the suggestion, stating that the meeting was too important.

Turning to Kassian, seated on his left, the king noticed the Keeper's attention was similarly on the Galfreys. Vighon had found a brief moment, before everyone took their seats, to inform him of Adilandra's demise and the consequences for Reyna and Nathaniel. Of course, Kassian's feelings on the pair becoming king and queen were impossible to read, even if it was clearly on his mind.

And now, with the council at last assembled, Vighon was drawn immediately to Ruban, who was seated at the other end of the table. The northman hadn't seen the knight since the battle on The Carpel Slopes - since he had walked away.

Of all those seated around the table, Vighon could quite confidently say that Sir Ruban Dardaris, the captain of his King's Guard and once squire, was his most loyal ally and friend. And still the king had walked away from him, leaving the knight to continue the good fight in his stead.

The men held each other's gaze for the moment. Vighon was expecting some venom from Ruban, who was well within his rights to speak so. In fact, he was hoping the captain would have something to say on the matter; it was the least he deserved.

"Is it true?" Doran broadcast from across the table. "Ye've taken Namdhor?" he added with a hearty laugh.

Vighon tore his eyes from Ruban to address the dwarf. "We sit in the throne room as we speak, Doran."

The son of Dorain turned his head to better see the northman.

"Aye, I knew it would be good to see ye, an' it is, lad! 'ave ye got yer head sorted?" he asked more seriously. "Do ye know who ye are?"

Vighon looked back at Ruban before answering. "I am the king of Illian," he said evenly.

The captain bowed his head. "On that we agree, your Grace. Namdhor is where you belong."

"Before we begin," Vighon continued, "I would give you all my thanks and my apologies. I walked away and you kept fighting, every one of you. I thought I was doing the right thing for The Rebellion, but I see now that walking away was never going to help. We're in a fight where every sword counts and every ally makes us stronger. Our enemy would see us divided and conquered. My heart breaks with apology knowing that I aided in that endeavour.

"I can never thank you all enough for not only welcoming me back, but searching me out. I deserved neither. I again pledge myself to the crown and the realm, serving both until my last breath. I have nothing else to give."

"And I would serve no other king," Sir Ruban announced sincerely. "You earned that crown once before. I have no doubt you will do it again. I am glad you know who you are now. But when we next meet, your Grace, I *will* put you on your back."

Vighon stifled his laugh. "That seems fair."

"Hugs and kisses for everyone!" Kassian interjected. "Can we get back to the end of the world now?"

"Is that scoundrel still breathin'?" Doran spat.

"This scoundrel," Kassian countered, "helped to take the capital city with a handful of mages and a couple of spells!"

Doran waved the achievement away. "I was gettin' round to it."

Faylen raised her ethereal hand, bringing a halt to the bickering. "There is another who should be among us. One whose voice carried the weight of a queen and the wisdom of a thousand years." The High Guardian looked across the table at Reyna. "Queen Adilandra's death deserves acknowledging, her life given not only for The Rebellion but goodness itself."

All heads were bowed, though Vighon noticed Reyna maintained her posture, her stare piercing the stone beyond.

"She stood the line between the light and the dark time and time again," Faylen continued. "Her past deeds are the only reason any of us are here today."

Vighon would never argue that fact. Though he was born years later, he knew well of Adilandra's efforts during The War for the Realm. Had she not convinced Rainael the emerald star to lead her kin against Valanis and the Darkakin, the world would be a darker place.

Galanör straightened his back and looked directly at Reyna. "I offer my condolences and deepest regrets. It was my actions that led to your mother's..." The elven ranger almost choked on his words. "I have wandered the realm for many years now, allied to neither Illian nor Ayda. By way of debt, I offer you my services, Queen Rey—"

"Don't say it," Reyna cut in, speaking for the first time. "Your actions, nor those of any other, have ever swayed my mother. She was responsible for every step she took stretching back a millennium. So you see, Galanör of house Reveeri, you have no debt to pay."

The elven ranger looked to disagree but Nathaniel raised his fingers from the table top and gave a subtle shake of the head, dissuading him from extending his proposal. "Adilandra wouldn't have wanted us to dwell on the past while there's still a war to fight," the old knight said artfully. "We will carry our grief until such a time it can be given its day. What news of the campaign?"

Faylen nodded her overall agreement. "We suffered losses on Qamnaran," she reported, forging through, "but we gained thousands more dwarves to our cause. Sadly, King Gaerhard was slain on the battlefield, leaving the Brightbeards in disarray."

"King Gaerhard?" Nathaniel questioned, his focus now well and truly returned to the present. "Besides King Dakmund, was he not the last king of Dhenaheim?"

All eyes fell on the son of Dorain, their thoughts likely aligned.

Vighon had to wonder how many kings and queens were seated around his table.

"He was," Doran confirmed in a perpetually tired voice. "Lord Kraiden saw to his end, right before *I* saw to *his*."

"Lord Kraiden is dead?" Vighon asked incredulously.

"And Morgorth, his dragon," Faylen replied happily. "The battle was a victory for The Rebellion."

"Aye, we left no Reavers on their feet," Doran added.

"And what of this tower?" Vighon pressed. "Do we know why Alijah had it constructed?"

"No," Galanör answered. "Nor can we say whether he achieved his goal," he stressed. "If he did, the same has been done to me for I was there when the spell took effect."

This was enough to turn Reyna's head. "Do you feel different?"

"No," the ranger said, shaking his head.

Vighon waved a dismissive hand. "His intentions aside, the dwarves being held on that island enjoy freedom now - a great victory for The Rebellion. We too have seen victory here in the north. The capital is ours and Alijah has lost another Dragon Rider and his mount."

Doran slammed an enthusiastic fist into whatever table was actually in front of him. "Good on ye! Who did ye slay?"

"Reyna took the head of Rengyr," Vighon was pleased to inform. "She saved my life at the same time."

"You would have done the same for me," Reyna replied, "were you not recovering from killing Karsak moments earlier."

"Dragon slayer, eh?" Doran cheered. "It seems ye've returned to us with some thunder in ye veins, lad!"

Faylen turned to Vighon as if she had just recalled something. "Where is Inara?"

"We know she returned to The Black Wood without the Dragorn," Galanör added.

Vighon took a breath, his fingers drumming against the table. "We cannot rely on the Dragorn, in this fight or any other. They have turned from the path of their predecessors, choosing now to live in peace among the older dragons."

Despite the finer features being robbed in their ethereal images, all four from distant lands expressed visible concern and surprise at the news.

"It cannot be so," Faylen pleaded.

Galanör looked almost angry. "Gideon would not abandon the realm like this."

"Gideon was not in Dragons' Reach," Nathaniel expanded. "He journeyed to Erador to investigate Alijah some eight years ago. That is where Inara has gone, with Asher and Adan'Karth."

"Eight years ago!" Doran exclaimed.

Vighon could see a flurry of questions inbound from all sides of the table. "I have spoken to her recently," he interjected quickly. "Before Athis flew them west, Inara gave me Gideon's diviner, the twin of her own."

"And what of Gideon?" Galanör demanded.

"They found him - alive. Ilargo too, though I can say no more. After hearing of Alijah's potential arrival, they are making haste to return."

Slumped in his chair, a wand slowly spinning between his fingers, Kassian said, "Adding two dragons to our defences could ensure our continued occupation. But if those Reavers are anything to go by, Alijah is almost upon us. I fear we will not last the day as we stand."

"He's right," Vighon concurred. "We have evacuated the lower town and prepared what catapults we can, but our numbers are too few to hold back Malliath, not to mention the Reavers and Alijah himself."

"We cannot offer aid," Faylen said by way of apology. "We have taken shelter in what remains of Ilythyra. It would take us days to reach you."

"And we are further still," Ruban echoed.

Vighon sat back against his chair and braced his arms against the table. "I care little for holding this city," he declared, rousing surprise from many. "But I cannot leave the people to Alijah's tyranny. Not again." The northman tilted his head to regard the silvyr sword propped up against the table, its lion head pommel roaring for eternity. "We will hold Alijah and Malliath here for as long as we can. You should use the diversion to your advantage and attack the dig site in The Moonlit Plains. Together you have the numbers and you might never get another opportunity."

Faylen looked from Vighon to Reyna and back. "You will die if you stay in Namdhor!"

"Thanks for the confidence," Kassian quipped.

Faylen ignored the Keeper's comment. "I am the High Guardian of Elandril's army, captain to the royal guard, and I will not allow my queen to die for the sake of a diversion!"

Reyna's emerald eyes flashed over her old guardian. "Faylen," she said softly, if firmly. "*As* your queen, I command you to rally my army and free those dwarves."

Faylen quavered with no one to turn to. "If Inara does not return in time you—"

"I know," Reyna stated, cutting her off. "But Vighon is right. These people need defending and it is likely Alijah will take retribution upon them for fighting with us. We are all where we're meant to be."

Bells. Bells were ringing outside the keep.

Vighon whipped his head around to the open dragon gate but it was Kassian who jumped up first and dashed to the platform.

"What's happenin'?" Doran huffed.

Kassian stopped in the morning air and looked out across the city and The White Vale beyond. Turning back to the council, a grim shadow had overcome his features. "He's here."

Vighon hadn't noticed his own hand reach out and grip the hilt of his sword, but he looked at it now with a single thought: he was going to kill his oldest friend with it.

There was a part of him that still recoiled from the image.

"What's happenin'?" Doran growled again, unable to hear Kassian.

"Alijah and Malliath are here," Nathaniel informed them.

Galanör appeared on the verge of jumping out of his chair. "Is there no sign of Athis or Ilargo?"

Reyna stood up from her chair. "Do not be concerned for us," she told them. "March on The Moonlit Plains, free the dwarves, and destroy whatever Alijah is doing out there."

"This is folly," Galanör remarked, shaking his head.

Vighon joined the others on their feet and gave their ethereal allies his last word. "Keep the hope alive, keep The Rebellion alive." With that he signalled the mage to disconnect the diviner, leaving four empty chairs in their place.

~

Keep the hope alive.

Vighon's last words echoed through Galanör's mind but he couldn't quite grasp them. What hope was there to hold on to knowing that Alijah and Malliath were at Namdhor's gates? All the while, he was haunted by Reyna's face. Her personal loss made Adilandra's death sting all the more, if that were possible.

Rising quickly from the table, Doran scraped his chair out before turning to boot it away. He swore in his native tongue and slammed his palms down onto the wooden surface.

"We need to be there *now!*" he growled.

Faylen remained very still in her chair, her expression hardened to stone. Galanör could see clearly what plagued her - Reyna and Nathaniel would likely die in the coming hours. Them and so many more.

"Why are ye both jus' sat there?" Doran grumbled. "We need to—"

"What?" Faylen interjected. "What can we do, Doran? Namdhor is hundreds of miles from here!"

The dwarf shook his head and shrugged his shoulders. "I don' know! Use yer crystals! Open a portal!"

Faylen's head dropped in despair. "What few we have do not possess the magic to reach so far. And even if we did, there are none among us who possess the power to reach Namdhor." She looked up and met Galanör's eyes.

"They are on their own," he concluded.

"Bah!" Doran spat, kicking another chair. "I'll not sit 'ere while me friends die in the cold! Open a portal as far as ye can an' I'll ride up there meself with Andaljor!"

"I could maybe get you as far as Lirian," Faylen replied. "You would still face days of hard riding before you reached Namdhor. By then, Alijah will have left nothing but graves."

Doran's anger was building to a crescendo but he had nowhere to vent it. His chest puffed out before quickly deflating, along with his spirits. He was left hunched over the table with one glassy eye and ragged breath.

"I'm tired o' prayin' to the Mother an' Father for a miracle that ain' comin'," he uttered. "Grarfath gave me two hands an' a stubborn head an' he expects me to use 'em apparently. I can't do that stuck in these woods. The fate o' those in Namdhor might be out o' our control, but those who dwell in torment in The Moonlit Plains ain'. I'm takin' me forces north an' layin' waste to anythin' that tries to stop us. Are ye with me?"

Galanör paused, waiting for Doran to look at him. "We should wait," he counselled.

Doran's mouth fell open. "Did ye not jus' hear what I said, lad?"

"You heard the king: Inara and Gideon are on their way to Namdhor."

The dwarf's face screwed up in frustration. "There's bein' on yer way to somewhere an' actually bein' there! How long would it take Malliath to torch the city? Minutes? Maybe an hour if he took his time!"

Employing as much patience as he could, Galanör expounded in a calming voice, "If Inara and Gideon reach Namdhor in time their presence might just be enough to save them all. Then we could get back to coordinating an attack that will have two dragons behind it and a better chance at victory."

"So ye don' want me to go to Namdhor an' ye don' want me to go to the dig site. Ye'd 'ave me jus' sit 'ere an' wait. Wait while the dig site is absent Malliath's watch! Wait while me friends an' me kin are put to death! Sounds like elf talk to me! We don' all walk the road o' immortality, Galanör."

"But *you* do walk the road of faith," Galanör countered. "I beg of you, Doran, turn to your gods and pray. Just until midday," he added. "If we haven't heard back from them, and your gods can settle for letting your stubborn head lead the way, I will join you in attacking the dig site."

The son of Dorain grumbled and muttered under his breath. "Fine," he snapped. "In the meantime, I'm havin' me boys prepare to march."

Galanör bowed his head. "That's fair."

Doran stormed off, leaving the elven ranger alone with a stoical Faylen. She had yet to turn her head and visibly acknowledge anyone else since the diviner cut out. Galanör feared losing Reyna and Nathaniel would be enough to break the High Guardian, and at a time when their nation and, indeed, The Rebellion needed her most.

"The Galfreys have survived more than most," he offered. "Vighon too. Keep the—"

"If you say *keep the hope alive* I'm going to feed you both of your swords."

Without speaking a word to each other, a queen, two kings, and a mage strode from the throne room and made for the southern ramparts with a hulking Golem in tow. From there, they could see what felt like the entire world laid out before them. In the streets below, hundreds were racing up the main road to take refuge inside the cathedrals, emptying the city's nooks and crannies.

In the distance, against a pale sky, a black dragon glided in lazy circles. A cold dread tried to steal Vighon's spirit and grip his bones in terror - such was the malice that accompanied Malliath the voiceless.

"Why isn't he just attacking?" Kassian mused.

"I can't pretend to know him anymore," Vighon confessed, his knuckles paling around the hilt of his sword.

"Perhaps he is waiting to see who is loyal to him," Nathaniel opined.

The northman hoped that wasn't the case, as every person in Namdhor was fleeing the very sight of their immortal king. They would be made to suffer for that betrayal, Vighon was sure. He couldn't allow that to happen.

"It's fear," Reyna specified.

Vighon was inclined to agree. "The catapults?" he questioned, looking to Kassian.

"They're loaded," the Keeper replied, "but the men we have manning them aren't experienced. There's a good chance we'll destroy half of the lower town trying to take out those Reavers."

The king shrugged off the consequences. "Walls can be rebuilt. Those Reavers cannot be allowed to enter the city."

"He's landing," Nathaniel observed.

Vighon cast his gaze back to the view and watched Malliath glide down and disappear behind the furthest buildings of the lower town, where his Reavers were stationed. "What is he doing?" he uttered, mostly to himself.

Kassian was braced against the stone. "My Keepers are still down there. If they were in a fight, we'd see it from here."

An idea occurred to Vighon. He stepped back from the rampart and directed his voice over the courtyard. "Fetch me a horse!" he bellowed.

"You aren't going down there," Nathaniel warned.

"If he wanted blood," Vighon pointed out, "we'd be fighting already. I'd say he wants to talk first."

"Yes," Kassian chipped in. "Talk first, *then* roast you where you stand!"

The king almost smiled at the thought that came to him. "Alijah enjoys nothing more than the sound of his own voice. I will keep him talking and buy us some time," he added, his eyes shifting to The Vengoran Mountains in the west.

"We will accompany you," Reyna insisted.

Vighon halted at the top of the steps that led down to the

courtyard. "No," he said sternly. "I fear just the sight of you both might enrage him. We need him talking for as long as possible."

"Well I'm going down there," Kassian said. "Those are my mages holding the line."

Vighon didn't argue with the Keeper. "Very well." He looked up at Sir Borin. "He's going to need a big horse."

CHAPTER 8
FACE TO FACE

Leaving Reyna and Nathaniel on the ramparts, Vighon set his horse to a gallop down the main road with Kassian and Sir Borin either side. By the time they were halfway down the city, the streets and alleys were clear of people, freeing them of any obstacles.

Charging through the lower town, they soon came upon the Keepers guarding the furthest boundary. Beyond them, the Reavers had ceased their incessant percussion and returned to sentinels once more. Between the two groups, Malliath stood as a colossus, a mass of muscle and scales, even with his wings tucked in. His purple eyes contrasted with the black of his face like jewels on stone. A crown of horns projected back at an angle, each displaying centuries of violence.

Then there was Alijah.

The half-elf maintained a regal stance with his thumbs hooked into his belt and his dark cloak billowing out beside him, revealing flashes of its red interior. His Vi'tari blade hung casually from his hip, its green steel hidden within the scabbard. He stood proud, with his chin up, as if he was simply enjoying the northern air, immune to the cold in his armour of dragon scales.

Vighon dismounted and made his way through the Keepers, sure to instruct Sir Borin to stay among them. He had no idea how the Golem would react to any threats from Alijah or Malliath.

"Vighon," Kassian hissed, his tone full of warning.

The northman held out a hand to calm the mage. "Stay here."

His feet crunched in the snow as he put himself between Namdhor and his enemy. Alijah looked him up and down as he approached, though whether assessing him for weaknesses or simply judging his appearance was impossible to tell. Alijah had always been good at cards, his Galant face a shield against any tells. Arrogant as he looked, however, his wounded face and damaged armour spoke of a recent defeat.

Malliath expelled a sharp breath from his nostrils and Vighon came to a stop with twenty feet remaining between them. His hand was aching from the grip on his hilt. The last time he had seen either of these monsters, they had torched a field of his men at The Carpel Slopes. That part of Vighon that recoiled from the thought of killing Alijah was quickly slipping away.

"Hello, old friend," Alijah called, glancing over the northman's shoulder. "I was hoping to see my people bring you down the hill in irons, but a surrender will suffice I suppose." His words drifted apart as he narrowed his vision. "Is that Sir Borin the Dread I see? What on Verda's green earth are you doing with Skalaf's wretched Golem? Scraping the barrel aren't you?"

Vighon was sure to keep his attention on Alijah, lest those purple eyes stole his courage. "Like every man, woman, and child in this country," he replied, "Sir Borin knows who his king is."

Alijah clamped his jaw and sighed a jet of hot vapour from his nostrils. "It just isn't meant to be, Vighon," he began. "You had your time as king and I'm sorry it had to come to an end the way it did. But neither of us can deny Fate - nor should we. Not when the world to come is perfect! That's what I'm here to accomplish, Vighon; a perfect world. You and your lot have branded yourselves as rebels but you're not resisting *evil*. You're just short-sighted children who don't know what's good for the world." Alijah laughed to himself. "You wouldn't even know where to begin changing the world for the better."

Vighon kept his mouth shut for the monologue, satisfied to let Alijah indulge himself with the sound of his own voice.

"Look at you," he continued. "Even now, in the face of the inevitable, you have no idea what to say. What could you say?" he pondered. "I have considered your death over and over. You could beg on your hands and knees, Vighon, but today is your last day." Alijah's face creased into a depiction of wrath and his tone lowered to a menacing pitch. "You should have stayed lost."

"I *was* lost," Vighon admitted. "I took on a burden no man could bear. A burden you tried to lay at my feet. I saw them all dying again and again. Dying in the fields. Dying in the ruins. Dying in *fire*. But I know who I am now. I know what I'm fighting for. But, more importantly," he added, half turning to the city, "I know what all of them are fighting for. They don't fight for me and they certainly don't fight for you. They're fighting for the privilege of living free in the land their ancestors called home. And they're fighting so their children can do the same."

Over Alijah's shoulder, Malliath let loose a low and threatening rumble from his throat.

Alijah's jaw clenched all the tighter. "I suppose that all sounds rather poetic to you, doesn't it? Fighting for their loved ones, for *freedom*. They're stuck, like you, in a broken world that churns them up and spits them out." He looked beyond Vighon and took in the capital. "That's what *I'm* fighting for. I'm here to fix the world, to banish the shadows, and weed out the corrupt. When I'm finished, Vighon, there will be no threat I cannot face. There will be peace from Erador to Ayda."

The half-elf paused to take a breath and survey Namdhor. "I fear, however, that you have already corrupted the people of this once proud city. Your banner misguides them. All who stray from the dragon are led to torment and doom. That's all you've done here, Vighon - led these people to their death."

Vighon felt every muscle in his arm tense, eager to draw his fiery sword and strike Alijah down. "You would slaughter every person in this city?"

"By aligning with you, they have shown their true colours. There is no place in my kingdom for those who do not wish to live in peace. You've made rebels of them all and sealed their fate."

The northman imagined the families, the children that would succumb to Malliath's fiery breath and the cold steel of the Reavers. He pulled the blade free. With every inch, the flames came alive until the sword of the north was blazing for all to see.

Alijah was captivated by it, his eyes tracking the blade in Vighon's hand. "Is she watching?" he asked, his attention flitting to the distant keep. "She always loved you, my mother. I think she detected the resentment your own mother had for you. I know I did."

Vighon pointed his sword at the usurper. "You don't know what you're talking about," he spat.

"I know she tried to flee in the night," Alijah said provokingly. "To get away from the burden of you I suspect. My mother convinced her to stay, reminded her of her duty. I never told you for obvious reasons," he added casually.

Vighon lowered his weapon. "Am I supposed to start weeping now? Did you imagine I would drop to my knees and sob into the snow?" He brandished the flaming sword of the north again. "You stand before the king of Illian. You will need more than words to bring *me* down."

A wicked grin pulled at Alijah's cheeks. "You would be surprised what I can do with a few words."

"She *is* up there," Vighon quickly revealed, wondering if it would put Alijah off balance. "Both of them in fact. Will you burn your parents with the rest? Or will you spare them so they might remember your deeds here for all time?"

Indeed, Alijah's eyes appeared to glaze over for a moment, his focus left to wander. Malliath's, however, did not. His predatory eyes never drifted from Vighon, his gruesome jaws set slightly apart to reveal his razored teeth.

"Like I said," the half-elf finally replied, "you've led these people to their death. I have no parents here nor anywhere else. In choosing you they have disowned me. Now you all get to die together."

Vighon refrained from casting an eye over the western mountains, but he wasn't sure how much longer he could stall for. Perhaps it was futile. For all his efforts, Inara and her companions could still be a day away or more. He had no real idea how far away they had been. Coming to terms with the fact that this was most likely his last stand and these were, in fact, his last words, he decided to make them memorable.

"Alijah," he began, gripping the sword of the north in both hands, "I loved you like a brother once. But if you stay, I'm going to cut you down and chop off *his* ugly head and toss it into the lake for the fish."

Malliath bared his teeth and a plume of smoke escaped his nostrils. All he had to do was exhale and Vighon would be reduced to a charred husk with naught but ash for veins. Yet the northman stood his ground, the sword of the north braced in his hands for combat. He wasn't going down before drawing blood from at least one of them.

Alijah wrapped his fingers around the Vi'tari blade on his hip. "Out of respect for the friendship we had and your service to the realm as king, I will grant you a swift death. But it is you who will be dropped to the bottom of The King's Lake, there to be forgotten."

The half-elf took a step towards him, his arm beginning to raise the green steel into the light of day. But he did not take another step. Instead, Alijah's gaze lifted up and beyond Vighon to the very top of Namdhor. There was something in his eyes. It was only there for a moment but, however brief, the northman knew exactly what it was.

Fear.

Vighon looked back over his shoulder to the most spectacular sight. Two dragons, red and green, crested the keep and glided low over the buildings, bringing them swiftly to the lower town. Mesmerised, the northman watched Ilargo thunder into the ground not thirty feet away, his green scales sparkling with golden specks. Landing on his hind legs, Athis reared up with his wings flared before crashing into the snow with a steaming breath.

Inara was the first to jump down. Firefly was in her grasp before she even looked at Vighon. Her red cloak flapped out behind her as she strode through the snow to stand beside the true king. The northman could see that there was so much she wanted to say, but now was far from the time, as ever.

Asher was close behind her. Like Nathaniel, he appeared a man frozen in time with his favoured green cloak billowing in the morning breeze. He crossed the snow with his piercing blue eyes fixed on Alijah and Malliath. Indeed, it seemed the black dragon was fixed on him too.

Lighter on foot, Adan'Karth dropped down from Ilargo but did not join them opposing Alijah. Instead, the Drake walked back towards the Keepers where he might simply observe events.

The last to descend a dragon, Gideon Thorn stepped onto Illian soil for the first time in nearly twenty years. Though he hadn't aged a day since Vighon had said farewell on this very spot, the old master was not as he had once been. He looked haunted, as if he had seen and experienced things no man should come to know. He approached the king with a strong frame, however, his hand braced around Mournblade in its scabbard. The fact that his beard and hair could do with some attention was an observation Vighon kept to himself.

Gideon bowed his head. "Your Grace," he said by way of a greeting.

"You still have quite the timing, Master Thorn," Vighon remarked quietly.

Gideon acknowledged the comment before turning to their enemy. "Alijah," he called evenly.

The necromancer took a long breath before slotting those few inches of his blade back into its scabbard. "You look pale, Gideon," he provoked. "Have you been getting enough sun?"

Inara stormed forward, putting herself between them and Alijah. "You will not speak!" she seethed. "You have done the unthinkable at every turn! And not just to Gideon but to so many more I cannot count them all. You do not have the right nor the honour to speak to him *or* the king. From now on, I will be every-where you turn. It will be *me* you face."

Alijah levelled his gaze at her as a gust of wind picked up his hair and revealed the fresh scar above his eye. "You *were* always better at everything," he recalled, "but those years are behind us now. I have been remade," he exclaimed, opening his arms.

"You haven't been remade," Inara spat. "You've been *twisted*. Do you know what The Crow said to me? Just before he died. You might remember the moment yourself. He had just declared himself a monster for his own perverted reason. He looked me in the eyes and told me that monsters only beget monsters." Inara pointed Firefly directly at her brother. "And that's what you are, a *monster's* creation."

It was subtle, but delicate muscles could be seen to twitch beneath Alijah's face. "I have no patience for your lies. My path is set. I will not be unbalanced now." He took a moment, his eyes glassy. "You know this isn't what I wanted for you. I would have welcomed you in my hall. There would have been a place for you in my kingdom."

"Was that to be before or after you murder Athis?" Inara countered. "I know what you intend to do in The Moonlit Plains. You have to know that destroying magic is a death sentence for every dragon."

Vighon frowned and looked from Gideon to Asher, though neither offered anything useful to explain Inara's statement.

Alijah too looked at Gideon, though his was not with curiosity but rather a degree of wrath. "You have crossed that threshold," the necromancer continued, his attention returned to Inara. "Your bond has been irrevocably altered now. You would survive in the new world."

"You think I would want to live in a world built on the graves of every dragon? Brother, you have lost yourself to a darkness from which there is no return. That's why *I'm* here," she stated boldly. "I'm going to stop you before you undo the entire realm."

Alijah puffed out his chest. "If you directly challenge me, Sister, you *will* perish."

Inara didn't move, her muscles tensed. "I came into this world with you. If I have to leave it with you, so be it." Athis raised his mighty jaw and exhaled a sharp breath, expressing his agreement.

The air became thick with tension. If just one of them was to suddenly move, the battle would begin and the snow would quickly turn red with blood.

"Just leave," Asher called, turning all eyes to him. "There will be no fighting today. He's a *survivor*. He knows when the odds aren't in his favour."

"I can't tell if you're complimenting me or not," Alijah responded.

"I wasn't talking about you," Asher replied gruffly, his gaze shifting to Malliath. "You're facing two dragons and their Riders, with twenty mages at their back. You'd probably kill most of us," the ranger accepted, "but you've lived too long to die here, like this. So just leave."

Alijah looked to respond with harsh words but his ear was turned back to Malliath for a moment, their conversation their own. "Some diplomacy from the Outlander," he said instead with a tone of surprise. "I suppose all the deaths can wait. Enjoy the reprieve. Until the next time." The half-elf looked briefly at each of them before returning to Malliath's side.

His ascent to the saddle lacked the grace expected of one with elven blood in their veins. Vighon scrutinised him again, wondering if there were unseen injuries plaguing his foe. The answer would continue to elude him, for Malliath beat his wings and took to the sky in a maelstrom of snow. Shortly thereafter, the Reavers turned on their heels and began marching, taking The Selk Road south.

Vighon took what felt like his first breath since mounting his horse outside the keep. He sheathed the sword of the north, extinguishing its flames, and acknowledged those beside him. Gideon followed Malliath's flight intently with the look of profound thought.

"What is it?" the northman asked.

Gideon maintained his distant watch. "I'm not sure."

Leaving the old master to his thoughts, the king turned to Asher. "That was a hell of a hunch," he remarked.

Asher's response was more guttural than any recognisable language.

Satisfied with the ranger's disinterest in any conversation, and eager to greet Inara, he faced the Guardian of the Realm. "Your timing will be worthy of history's note, I'm sure. You certainly have *my* thanks."

"What exactly were you going to do?" Inara questioned. "Try and kill both of them with just your sword?"

"It seemed like a good idea at the time." Vighon was pleased to see Inara's judgmental expression soften to mirror his grin.

Despite the onlookers, both came together in a tight embrace. As always, her superior strength was made apparent and he did his best to squeeze her with all his strength. "I missed you," he whispered in her ear.

Inara pulled back and offered him a warm smile. "We have much to discuss," she announced, taking the others in and bringing Gideon back to the present.

Vighon reassumed his role as king, straightening his stance. "You mean like the destruction of magic?" he posed.

Inara fixed his dark eyes with some intensity. "That and more," she promised cryptically.

"We should return to the keep then," Vighon decided. "We cut off our diviner to Faylen and the others when Alijah arrived. They will be deeply concerned."

"They survived Qamnaran!" Inara reasoned with glee. "I would hear of my grandmother's prowess on the battlefield."

The king called for horses, instantly torn by the knowledge he held. "Inara..."

Gideon stepped forward, concern etched across his face. "Inara," he intoned. The Guardian of the Realm followed her old master's gaze to Asher, who appeared to be on the verge of fainting.

"What's wrong with him?" Vighon questioned. He instinctively reached out to help steady the ranger, but Adan'Karth beat him to it, as if the Drake had sensed his distress from afar.

"It's complicated," Gideon said, before peering inside Asher's satchel. "It's nearly time," he added, looking to Inara.

She nodded her understanding, which was more than Vighon could do. "We should get him somewhere warm and dry," Inara stated quickly.

"And somewhere they will feel safe," Gideon specified.

"*They?*" Kassian echoed, towing a horse.

"We need to get Asher to the keep," Inara ordered, helping the ranger towards Athis. "We can get there quicker."

Vighon watched Asher stagger away, clearly in need of assistance from Inara and Adan. "What in all the hells is going on?" he demanded.

"I will explain everything," Gideon promised. "Let us make for the keep and with haste."

The king noted Kassian's raised eyebrow and simply shrugged as he mounted his horse. "There's always something."

As Inara and Adan escorted Asher through the courtyard of The Dragon Keep, the majority of its inhabitants were turned to the sky, transfixed by the sight of Athis's return to the heavens. It suited the Guardian, pleased to simply weave through the crowd and enter the keep without a fuss.

It had been some time since her last visit, but she remembered the halls well and led the trio to the guest quarters in the west wing. Whenever she could, Inara scrutinised Asher, partially held up between herself and Adan. The ranger was already sweating, matting his hair to his stubbled cheeks. Whatever strength remained in him was focused on gripping the satchel and keeping his feet moving.

"What's happening to him?" Adan enquired as they reached the first quarters.

Though Inara had never experienced the birth of her companion, she was receiving information from Ilargo and Gideon via Athis. "Breaking the egg is stressful for the hatchling," she explained, relaying the words of others. "With their bond being so immature, that stress manifests physically in the Rider. It's the only time they share pain."

Entering the first guest room they came across, Inara closed the door behind them and Asher broke away, gesturing for them to leave him alone. The ranger absently grabbed the blanket from the bed and took himself off to the corner, where there was little space and two walls to his back. His breath was ragged as he rested his head against the cold stone.

"It's all instinct at this point," Inara remarked. "We shouldn't interfere."

Asher removed the bronze egg from his satchel and wrapped it up with himself inside the blanket. Inara nudged Adan to accompany her but the Drake resisted.

"I will stay with him."

Inara wanted to offer caution, but she could see the Drake was not to be moved. "Stay out of sight," she instructed, hearing Gideon's voice echo through the minds of two dragons. "Best he feels alone."

Adan nodded his understanding and slowly took himself off to another corner where he could wait unseen and unheard.

As always, duty demanded that Inara be elsewhere. She would have loved to see a baby dragon come into the world, especially one that had waited thousands of years for its Rider, but the world was far from safe. Carefully and quietly, she left the chamber and closed the door behind her.

There, she touched her head to the wood, closed her eyes, and sighed with relief. They had made it. For all their flight, she had harboured the sickening concern that they would be too late. She had half expected to top The Vengoran Mountains and discover a flaming monument in the place of Namdhor.

But they had made it.

Vighon was alive. Alijah had retreated. Asher and the egg were safe. Gideon was among them. Now she could breathe.

We will be ready for whatever comes next, Athis promised. Inara willingly accepted the dragon's boost to her morale, letting his confidence fill her with strength to continue.

Turning from the door, Inara was not ready for what came next.

"Hello," her mother greeted softly, tears in her eyes. Standing beside her, Inara's father was already wiping a solitary tear from his cheek.

There was no stopping the Galfreys from crashing into each other. As one, the three crushed together in a tight embrace of kisses and tears. Inara hadn't seen her mother since she took an arrow on the ramparts nearly two years ago, and it had been months prior to that. There were no words for a time as they each took the other in.

Reyna's hands were firm around Inara's face. "Only the sight of you could fix my heart," she whispered.

Inara gripped her mother's wrists. "I have missed you so much." She broke from her mother's eyes and looked to her father. "I have missed you both."

Nathaniel stroked his daughter's cheek before giving her one last kiss on the head. "We are together again. That's all that matters now."

Reyna couldn't help herself and pulled Inara in for another breath-taking embrace that no human could have sustained. "We saw you enter the keep with Asher," she finally said, looking at the door over Inara's shoulder. "Is he wounded?"

"We saw Alijah and Malliath retreat," Nathaniel added in a questioning tone.

Inara confirmed her father's observation with an affirmative nod. "There was no fighting," she reassured. "And Asher will be fine." Inara took a breath and used the moment to consider her explanation for everything transpiring behind the door.

"I think our tale deserves a bigger audience," Gideon announced from further down the hall.

Inara turned with her parents to lay eyes on the old master, though there was a great deal more emotion behind those of her parents.

"Gideon," Reyna said his name with the same affection mirrored in Nathaniel's smile.

"It's been far too long," the old knight told him.

Gideon closed the gap between them and happily wrapped each in his arms. It dawned on Inara that her old mentor hadn't experienced the joy of a friendly embrace in years. The thought brought her spirits down. Though it was certainly uplifting to see these three people together again.

Before their reunion could go any further, Gideon pulled away from Nathaniel. "Vighon and the others are preparing another council in the throne room," he shared before turning specifically to Inara. "Perhaps we should leave Asher for now and inform The Rebellion of our time in Erador. Our news will impact the next step."

Reyna reached out and lightly gripped Gideon's arm. "Before we rejoin the others," she said, looking at her daughter, "there is something I would tell you myself."

By her expression alone, Inara could tell there was naught but sorrow to follow.

CHAPTER 9

I AM RANGER

Asher pressed his head into the smooth stone, but there was no pain in all the world that could distract him from the storm that wracked his mind. He was drenched in a cold sweat, shivering from head to toe, and his throat was so dry it hurt to breathe - all of which were caused by the exertion of another.

Her exertion.

That knowledge was the only safe harbour he could cling to. It had come to him as the inner-most layer of the egg began to crack. The whispers that had burrowed into every part of his brain had finally focused into a single voice and it was most definitely that of a female.

He already loved her unconditionally. Her birth into the world felt like his own; only he had experienced the death of his older-self first. This dragon would bring with it more than a brave heart and a fierce spirit. She would bring a regality and honour that gave one a sense of duty and purpose that surpassed the transaction of coin or the need of praise. This dragon was a warrior in its purest form.

There was a part of the ranger that knew the dragon would not come into the world until her companion was in harmony with this way of life, the life of a Dragon Rider. But Asher was nothing if not stubborn. He told himself that a great deal of the hatchling's feelings had come from her mother, a dragon of a different age.

"No," he uttered through clenched teeth. He hugged the egg between the blanket, protecting himself from the intense heat that emanated from it in waves. "No," he hissed again.

Asher refused to accept the way of the Rider. He had wasted too many years in the service of an order. Orders came with rules and punishments. Never again would he be slave to one. There was but one life that he believed in, whether it came with coin or not.

"I... am... a... *ranger*!" he growled.

Claws raked the inside of his head, straining every muscle in his body. The dragon was scouring through images and sounds from his life, passing judgement on *The Ranger*. At the same time, the hatchling was imparting more memories from her mother. Every one flash-burned the parts of his mind where Malliath still dwelled.

The black dragon's experiences and thoughts remained like an echo, but his torment faded to nothingness. In the place of such horrors, Asher lived through the eyes of his hatchling's mother, a dragon who had led a very different life. She had fought the Red Worms of The Glimmer Lands, rooted out pirates on The Old Rift, hunted ridged-back whales in The Dawning Isles, and tracked Andaren horned-eagles through The Spine of Erador. Hers was a noble and ancient line of revered dragons and Riders.

Thessaleia! The mother's name was suddenly seared into his mind as if he had always known it.

Asher's knuckles paled as he squeezed the blanket. He was being hollowed out and filled back up again. All the while, the egg was giving off more and more heat. The outer shell of scales was entirely gone now, leaving a silky-smooth egg of copper in its stead. To touch it with his bare skin, however, was to burn himself.

The ranger dared to look down, but just the sight of it struck him with more visions of Thessaleia's past. Gone was the chamber in which he sat, replaced by sights that only a dragon could enjoy. He witnessed the rise and fall of kingdoms in the blink of an eye.

He saw armoured dragons fall from the sky, their hides pierced by giant spears. He felt the hum of magic from a massive congregation gliding over The High Plains of Erador, east of Lake Kundrun.

It was all so glorious and violent at the same time.

Flying over The Silver Trees of Akmar, an eclipsing shadow covered Asher's body. Cutting low in front of him, a colossal dragon dived down to glide over the tops of the trees. Trapped as a passenger behind Thessaleia's eyes, Asher watched as he followed the hulking dragon down to a clearing that could take the two of them. On the ground, the pair brought their heads together in what dragons considered an affectionate manner.

Taking in the male dragon and his scales of dull gold, a name came to Asher that he hadn't heard since The War for the Realm. Before him now was revered *Garganafan*. A distant memory of his own recalled Gideon referring to the dragon as the king of their kind, his life given to trap Valanis in the Amber Spell over a thousand years past.

Garganafan was the father.

Asher took that as an explanation for the hatchling's regal propensity, even if they themselves didn't know exactly why yet.

The memory ejected the ranger, sending him back to his personal hell inside The Dragon Keep. His head was pounding as if an orcish war drummer was beating his skull. His muscles were wound so tight they felt close to tearing through his skin. Through it all, his heart thundered in time with the hatchling's.

Asher.

His own name resounded inside his mind, threatening to rob him of consciousness. The voice that said his name, however, was sweet to his ears and somehow familiar, as if he had known that voice all his life.

After a wave of nausea passed, he listened to his instincts and quickly rolled the egg off the blanket, before throwing it away. Had he waited a few extra seconds to do so, the whole blanket would have gone up in flames, threatening the integrity of the chamber. Instead, the stone floor took the brunt of the heat being expelled. Soon after, smoke began to envelop the egg as the floor was charred black. Small flames broke through the egg, licking at the air.

At last, Asher's muscles were able to relax, allowing some of his focus to return. He wiped the hair from his face and stared at the egg, but he couldn't see through the fire and smoke. Taking a much-needed breath, he lurched forward on his hands and knees and cautiously approached the egg. His mind was beginning to settle now, having weathered the storm. Clear thoughts rang true and he knew not to reach out - dragons were fireproof, not their Riders.

Somewhere between shaking with excitement and trembling with raw nerves, the ranger waited for something, anything. There was no voice in his head, and no memories or impressions to be glimpsed. Yet he wasn't alone.

Confirming that, a noise came from within the smoke. Asher held his breath, listening for it again. It was between the hiss of a snake and the low squawk of a bird. It was her voice. With glassy eyes, the ranger wafted what he could of the smoke and saw that the floor was so badly damaged by the heat that it had left a well in the stone. Inhaling a deep breath, he blew through the remaining smoke just as two small wings fanned out, batting most of it away.

The sight of her left Asher in a silent daze.

She was beauty and strength given form. Her scales were a deep bronze with flecks of gold and silver throughout. Two horns curved over her head and sloped up into sharp points. Small claws tapped lightly against the charred stone and an armoured tail swished through the remnants of smoke. But her eyes, golden orbs cut with a single reptilian slit, drew the ranger in and held him there.

Without looking, Asher grabbed the blanket he had discarded and bundled it up. The dragon leapt forward in a failed attempt to fly and landed in the midst of the soft pile. He scooped the whole thing up and brought her into his chest. From end to end, she was nearly as long as his arm. More than anything, he knew he needed to keep her safe.

Movement in the corner of his eye set his heart racing. Upon realising it was none other than Adan'Karth, an extra moment was required to calm down. He trusted the Drake implicitly.

Adan approached with slow and steady steps, his form slightly hunched to make himself smaller. His eyes, not dissimilar to hers, examined every inch of the dragon with a wonder usually seen only in children.

"*Exquisite,*" he whispered in elvish.

Asher quite agreed, though he did not voice it. Instead, he listened. A contented smile, rarely seen on the ranger, consumed his expression. He looked at Adan.

"I know her name."

CHAPTER 10

TOGETHER AGAIN

G ideon Thorn was lost to his own thoughts. He barely registered Vighon's account to The Rebellion's council. He knew what he had seen, out there on the vale, but he couldn't straighten it out in his mind. If he was right, it would change everything.

You saw it too, Ilargo said into his mind.

Yes. Could it be possible?

It would require a degree of influence I do not possess. But I am not Malliath.

Finally, he was brought back to the present by a familiar sound: the hearty laugh of a dwarf. Indeed, Doran's laugh carried all the elation, relief and, indeed, disbelief of those camped far from Namdhor. And it was music to Gideon's ears. Even in their ethereal form, he was most pleased to see the son of Dorain, Faylen Haldör, and, his oldest friend, Galanör seated around the table. Ruban Dardaris also joined them, though Gideon couldn't claim to know the knight very well. Still, they were all friends and allies, both of which were hard to hold on to in such dark times.

"I can' believe what I'm seein'!" Doran cheered after Vighon's recounting. "I was this close to marchin' on The Moonlit Plains!"

he added, pinching his finger and thumb together. "I'd say Grar-fath's adopted all o' ye!"

"We dared not hope," Faylen commented quietly, glancing at Galanör.

"The Rebellion would have lost too much to ever recover," the elven ranger remarked. "I am thankful for your timely arrival," he said, looking from Inara to Gideon. "And it is good to see you again," he expressed sincerely.

"And you," Gideon replied with a warm smile. "It is good to see all of you again," he said a little louder, addressing the table. "Forgive my absence in your time of great need. Had I been able, I would have returned sooner."

There were some around the table who looked to Inara for some answers then, but she was still held in grief by the news of her grandmother. Gideon himself had felt a pang in his heart upon hearing of Adilandra's demise. His memories of her, fighting the Darkakin, were still so vivid in his mind. Whether Inara had or not, the old master also considered the ramifications for Reyna and Nathaniel. The responsibility that now lay on their shoulders was beyond immense. He felt for them all.

"Perhaps, Gideon," Vighon began, "you could inform us of your time in Erador?"

Gideon knew the best place to start was always the beginning, but there was so much to explain and so little time to act. Still, The Rebellion needed to make informed choices if they were to do what had to be done. But first there was one thing the old master would know.

"On Qamnaran," he said, glancing between ethereal images, "did Alijah complete his spell, inside the tower?"

"How do you know of that?" Faylen asked.

"The tower fell into The Hox," Doran replied unhelpfully, waving the whole event away.

"We believe he did," Galanör answered. "I was with him when the spell reached its end. What do you know of it, Gideon?"

"If Alijah succeeded on Qamnaran then he has already accomplished half of his plan. It also means we don't have much time."

"Until what?" Reyna enquired gravely.

Gideon took a breath and started at the beginning.

A stunned and palpable silence had settled over the throne room. Whether they were ethereal or flesh and blood, every member of the council looked around the table at each other. Only Inara remained indifferent, her mind elsewhere.

Gideon gave them all some time to absorb the revelations of his tale, consequential as they were. The old master looked over each of them, wondering who would be the first to speak and which particular part they would focus on. He had covered a lot.

"Asher's got a dragon?" Doran muttered.

"He's going to destroy magic?" Reyna mulled at the same time.

Kassian turned to Inara. "You crossed to another world?"

Galanör said nothing. Instead, he inspected his closed fist questioning, no doubt, whether his magic was shielded from the death of the tree.

Nathaniel was the first to actually address Gideon. "Is that what's happening to Asher right now?"

Gideon smiled. "I believe his dragon's arrival is imminent."

The old knight drew in on himself, his thoughts his own, though Gideon could imagine the surprise of it all. Was the need not so great, Gideon knew *he* would be hovering outside Asher's chamber right now.

For the first time since seeing her again, Faylen wore an expression of satisfaction and contentment. "I am glad for him," she announced softly.

"And I thought he couldn't get any more dangerous," Vighon remarked.

Kassian was shaking his head as his hands lifted from the table. "I'm sorry," he began. "It's great that the ranger has himself a dragon and I'm pleased you found so many eggs. But shouldn't we focus on the part where our enemy knows how to wipe out all magic? He would be unstoppable if we couldn't wield magic."

"Not to mention the loss of dragons," Ruban added.

Reyna looked down the table at Gideon. "Alijah truly believes this is right?"

"He believes the source of all evil," the old master replied, "in whatever form it takes, stems from the misuse of magic. He wants to make us all equal."

"Except for him," Kassian pointed out. "He wants to retain his magic to keep him in power. How can he not see that *he* is the form evil has taken?"

That question almost sent Gideon's thoughts spiralling again, but he put the issue aside and concentrated on what was in front of him. "If he succeeds, his victory is assured. Having completed the spell on Qamnaran, Alijah no longer relies on the tree for magic. That means he's only one step away from entering the realm of magic and finishing his work."

Faylen's ethereal form dispelled wisps of smoke as she turned to Gideon. "And you believe there is a... *doorway* at the bottom of that dig site?"

"It's the only thing that explains the work being done there," Gideon answered.

"But how's he openin' it?" Doran enquired. "He's not got any dragon eggs an' me kin can do nothin' but dig."

"He never discussed that part of his plan with me," Gideon lamented. "But he hasn't come this far just to possess a hole in the ground. We have to assume he's found a way."

"Perhaps it is simply the plains themselves," Galanör spoke up. "They were enchanted centuries past - the ground must hold some magic."

"It's a possibility," Gideon agreed. "But if the power existed in the ground alone I believe we would have seen multiple doorways by now."

"Gideon's right," Vighon said, drawing all to him. "We have to assume Alijah has already found a way to create a doorway. So I put to you: how do we stop him?"

"We should be there right now for a start!" Doran stated. "I bet me only eye that's where Alijah has gone!"

"How quickly can you rally your forces to the site?" the king asked.

"It's a day's march," the son of Dorain promised.

"It's closer to three for us," Sir Ruban said. "Maybe four. Though I'm sure the elves could cross the distance in half that time."

Nathaniel looked from the captain to the king. "We too could reach The Moonlit Plains in three days if we could muster what forces we have here and started marching this very day."

Vighon sat back in his chair, absorbing all the information. "We risk everything if we attack the site with only part of our force. And we risk everything by giving Alijah the time if we wait to attack together."

"He could destroy that tree thing this very day!" Doran argued. "We should set off now an' attack. Ye can all join us when ye get 'ere."

"Malliath is fast," Gideon interjected, "but he won't get there today."

"He's injured," Inara said quietly, emerging from her grief.

Gideon paused to see if she would say more. "Inara's right. Malliath bears wounds that slow his flight."

Kassian frowned. "I didn't see any wounds."

"You wouldn't," the old master told him evenly. "You would have to know dragon physiology to have spotted it. Your description of his dive into The Hox matches the damage I saw on his wings."

"He will need to rest," Inara concluded. "His flight to Namdhor will have exhausted him already."

"So... what?" Doran pressed. "We 'ave two days at the most then? That's still more than enough time to cut down some tree!"

Gideon resisted the urge to inform the dwarf that the tree was closer in size to a mountain.

The son of Dorain pushed himself up and leaned over the table. "I agree with ye good king. A unified attack from north an' south would increase the odds o' defeatin' our enemy an' maybe even endin' this war. But I haven' come this far to stop takin' risks now.

Were it anythin' else ye'd 'ave me word that I would wait. But news o' this damned tree has me stirred. I'm not for carin' abou' magic, but I know the world would be a darker place without it." Doran paused and took a breath. "Me an' mine could attack the site an' keep Alijah an' his lot busy until ye can reinforce us."

Nathaniel shook his head. "That's suicide, Doran. You would be fighting for at least a day, maybe a day and half before the elves from the coast could reinforce you."

"He's right," Vighon compounded. "By the time we joined you from the north and those with Sir Ruban marched up from the south there would be nothing left but a feast for crows. You - your people - are too valuable to lose by throwing yourself at the enemy like this."

"They would not be alone," Galanör declared.

Vighon cast his eyes down the table. "A better swordsman there is not, Galanör, but you alone cannot turn the tide of a battle. We don't even know what numbers Alijah possesses in the plains."

"We should assume a lot given the importance of the site," Sir Ruban theorised.

"We would fight beside them," Faylen made known. "Like the Alliance of old."

"As would I," Inara put forth, turning heads. "Athis and I will fly south and join you as soon as we can."

A flicker of concern for the younger Galfrey hindered Gideon's immediate response. He was terribly proud of his former student - already a far more accomplished and experienced warrior than he - but he wasn't going to let her fight alone. Not again.

"Ilargo and I will accompany you," he proposed. "We would be foolish to think the site is guarded by foot soldiers alone."

Doran wrapped his knuckles against the table. "Now ye're talkin'!"

Vighon dropped his head, though his worries were no mystery. "This isn't how I wanted it to end. We were to face him, *them*, together."

Inara reached out and gripped the king's hand, her features softening for the first time. "This is the only way. Stalling him until you arrive might save the tree. That has to be our priority now, even more so than freeing the realm."

Scrutinising the northman's reaction, Gideon could see that such a statement was hard to swallow. "Dwarves and elves from the south," the old master surmised, "and dragons from the north. We can hold them until the rest of you arrive."

Vighon sighed and retrieved his hand from Inara's. "Sir Ruban: begin marching your men to the plains. Make no delay."

The captain of the king's guard bowed his head. "We will leave immediately, your Grace."

The king acknowledged his response before regarding his ethereal allies. "Doran, Faylen: I will leave you to rally your forces and make tracks."

"With respect, your Grace," Faylen cut in. "As the High Guardian of Elandril's forces, I have made my intentions clear, but only the sovereign can give the order to advance."

Gideon could feel the tension filling the space between them all as every gaze slowly turned to the senior Galfreys. Eventually, even Nathaniel looked to his wife, the blood heir to all of Ayda.

"Queen Reyna," Vighon said, the first to use her official title. "Will you commit your forces to this attack?"

Reyna didn't move, a testament to her elven nature. When, at last, she lifted her eyes from the table, she looked from Faylen to Inara. Gideon could only imagine what was going through her head. She was being asked to commit her people to likely death in a battle that also pitched her children against each other. And it wasn't that long ago such a burden would have fallen to her mother.

Perhaps sensing some of the same apprehension, Inara said, "You can't make your decision based on your fear for my life. I'm in this fight, Mother."

"You're my child," Reyna countered. "I will always fear for your life and it will always inform my decisions, regardless of your abilities." She turned to Doran gravely. "But as you said, we haven't come this far to stop taking risks now. Sir Ruban - inform Captain Nemir that he is to lead my forces to the dig site with all haste, though I'm afraid they will inevitably leave you and your men behind."

The knight bowed his head. "Your Grace."

"High Guardian," Reyna continued, finding Faylen across the table. "March those who survived Qamnaran alongside Doran's army. Keep Alijah from his task at all costs."

"It will be done, my Queen," Faylen promised, her vision lingering over the elf.

Reyna, however, returned her attention to Inara. "The world needs the light you carry more than any of *us*. Make sure you survive."

"I will perish before Inara does," Gideon reassured.

"My fate is my own," Inara asserted. "Just like my grandmother's was."

No more was said between mother and daughter and Gideon made no further attempt to come between them. Even Nathaniel knew better than to do so, though he was gripping the arms of his chair with enough force to pale his knuckles.

Vighon stood up at the end of the table. "It seems this is the last time The Rebellion's council will convene. I hope that when we next meet it is on a victorious battlefield, and we might all share a drink. Until then; fight hard. Fight for what's in your heart and it will give you strength. We will join you soon."

Those of an ethereal nature bowed their heads to the various royals and faded from view.

"I'll prepare my Keepers for the journey," Kassian said, making to leave the throne room.

"I'll rouse every fighter we have," Nathaniel added. "We should be able to leave within a few hours."

Vighon looked down at Inara, but the Guardian was holding the gaze of her mother. "I will accompany you," he offered Nathaniel. "When will you leave?" he asked Gideon.

The old master, however, found his mind wandering back to the morning's events. Had he really seen it? Or was his mind playing tricks on him, giving him false hope. Impossible - Ilargo had noticed the same thing.

"Gideon?" Vighon prompted, drawing his attention. "When will you be leaving?"

"Ideally now," he replied, "but when we reach the plains we will face Malliath and, I suspect, Alijah's Dragon Riders. Ilargo and Athis need to rest before we enter that fight. I would leave them to eat and sleep for a few hours before we go."

"What of Asher?" Nathaniel enquired.

"Yes," Gideon acknowledged, "I would also like to be here when the hatchling arrives. Asher is going to need some guidance."

"Perhaps you should go to him now," Nathaniel suggested, his eyes shifting between his wife and daughter.

Gideon could see no part for him in the conversation to come. "That's an excellent idea."

Inara waited for the doors to close. "You can't do that," she instructed firmly.

"Do what?" Reyna asked with little curiosity in her voice.

"I know the circumstances of becoming an elven sovereign are always painful - I share some of that pain with you. But you *are* the queen of Ayda now. You cannot let your concern for me interfere with the decisions you make. You have responsibilities."

"I have responsibilities as a mother," Reyna interrupted.

Inara was shaking her head. "They cannot supersede your responsibilities as queen!"

"You're all I have left!" Reyna snapped, her tears on the verge of spilling out. "Whatever Alijah's fate, we both know he will not find redemption now. Ask Asher. Redemption takes *time*: time no one is willing to give him. I have already lost my son. Now I have to watch my daughter fly off into battle against the same enemy that just took my mother. This war is pulling us apart."

Seeing her mother sob, Inara rose from the chair and moved to crouch down beside her. She offered comfort with an embrace as she rested her head against Reyna's arm. She didn't know what to say. Their world had unravelled and there were no words that could put it back together.

"If there's any part of our Alijah left in there," Inara said, "he wouldn't want to live with the memories of what he's done."

Reyna looked down at her daughter. "If there is, if you see it in him - would you spare him?"

Inara felt her mother's tears splash across her hand. She turned her head to let Reyna see the sincerity behind her eyes. "No," she whispered.

Reyna scrunched her eyes tight and nodded some semblance of understanding.

"I would give him rest," Inara continued. "And then I would cling to those memories of golden days on the beaches of Alborn. I would remember him as he was."

Reyna cupped Inara's face. "I don't want to lose you too."

"You won't," Inara promised.

A smile broke through her mother's grief. "Oh to have your courage and strength," she praised.

"Gifts from you," Inara pointed out.

Reyna spilled more tears and brought their heads together. "Not from me," she wept softly. "I never got to say goodbye to her."

Inara recalled her last words with Adilandra, before she flew to Erador. "I parted ways with her in The Black Wood. She was so *strong*. She told me there would be victory for us both. And then, together, we would come here and take you away. She was so sure."

Reyna pulled back. "Adilandra Sevari was nothing if not sure of her path. Who else would leave Elandril and trek south to Dark-akin lands in search of dragons? Her legacy will always be the courage and strength that lives within you."

"Within us both," Inara corrected.

Reyna took a steadying breath. "Within us both," she echoed.

"When this is all over," Inara promised, "we will make sense of all this together. We'll forge what future we can."

Reyna shrugged helplessly. "I don't even know where to begin making sense of being queen."

Inara appeared to ponder over that. "Perhaps I should start calling you, your Grace."

Her mother waved the notion away. "Come then," she bade. "I would like to spend some time with you before you leave again. I would know all about this *alteration* to your bond with Athis. Your father was telling me but I would much rather hear it from you."

"There will be time for that," Inara reassured. "Have you ever seen a dragon hatchling?" she enquired instead, guiding her mother with a hooked arm.

"I can't say I have," Reyna replied.

"They're adorable," Inara remarked. "If a little dangerous," she added, thinking of Athis's excited descriptions.

CHAPTER II
THE MARCH TO WAR

Doran Heavybelly strode through the camp with purpose, clapping his meaty hands together. "Get yer arses movin'!" he bellowed at the laziest of his kin. "Get yer tents down, pack up yer gear, an' make sure yer bellies are full. We're goin' to war!"

He spotted Aenwyn in the distance, reassuring those that cared for the wounded they would be staying in the camp. The War Mason was glad Aenwyn and her bow would be counted among their army. He had never been envious of an elf before - and he told himself he still wasn't - but watching her navigate a battle and fire an arrow into Morgorth's eye at a hundred paces put her skill on a par with Reyna's.

Killing from a distance, however, was not the dwarven way. He was reminded of this when he finally arrived at the remnants of his tent, where Pig snuffled at the ground. His saddle was already laden with gear and supplies, seen to by Thaligg or Thraal no doubt. Lying on the ground, however, tethered to the back of the saddle, was Lord Kraiden's head - right where he had promised it would be. Since lopping it off, he had bolted the spiked crown to the wretch's skull so all would recognise it.

The sight of it tempted the dwarf's mind to spiral into dark places. Busying himself, Doran spat on the skull and stepped over the tether to inspect his gear. Andaljor was strapped horizontally across the back, both hammer and axe in need of a good clean. He had full water skins and even a skin of what smelled like Hobgobbers Ale. He reminded himself to thank the brothers when he could.

The sound of dwarven war songs carried on the breeze, drifting between the trees of Ilythyra. There were already hundreds of his kin making their way to the edge of the forest, where the northern tip met the green pastures of The Moonlit Plains. Most of them, he knew, were simply eager to put the trees behind them and see mountains again.

Lighter on their feet and swifter of action, the elves marched out of Ilythyra in neat rows of two abreast. Though many had taken what time they had to clean their armour, every one of them showed evidence of recent battle.

"They're quite the sight, aren't they?"

Doran turned to see Russell who was struggling to tow a horse. "They're good at walkin', I'll give 'em that."

The old wolf chuckled to himself. "Still can't bring yourself to compliment them, I see." His smile disappeared when the horse tried to get away from him again.

Doran shrugged. "It's in me blood. Are ye ready to go?" he asked with one bushy eyebrow rising into his head.

Russell applied both hands to the reins and tried to calm the horse, though what came out of his mouth was closer to a growl. "I'm ready," he answered through gritted teeth.

The horse finally lost its nerve and reared back on its hind legs. Russell lost his grip on the reins and staggered back, his arms out ready to tackle the distressed mount. Doran sidestepped and took a hold of Pig's reins, hoping to restrain the Warhog from responding with his tusks.

Like an angel descending from the heavens, Galanör dropped from the nearest tree and came down on the horse's saddle. It naturally bucked back and forth but the elven ranger could not be dismounted, his muscles adjusting constantly to maintain his balance. With some physical negotiation, he succeeded in placing his head beside the horse's, where he could whisper sweet elvish words.

Doran watched in amazement as the mount began to calm down. It wasn't long before Galanör was seated comfortably in the saddle, patting the animal's neck. After climbing down, he whispered something further into its ear and handed the reins over to Russell. Though somewhat skittish, it didn't lash out or try to flee.

"Thank you," Russell said quietly.

Galanör glanced up at the sky by way of gesture. "The full moon approaches," he observed.

Russell nodded at the horse. "It senses the wolf."

Galanör stroked the horse while shifting his eyes down to Doran. The dwarf could see the caution behind those sharp eyes but he dismissed it.

"Is this the last o' yer people?" he asked the elf, gesturing to the marching lines.

"There are still a few patrols out there," Galanör replied, easily looking over the dwarf's shoulders at the trees. "Another hour and we will all be on the plains."

Russell tentatively strapped his gear to the horse's saddle. "Do we have a strategy?"

"Bloody chaos," Doran quipped, in response to which Russell turned to Galanör.

"He's right," the elf sighed. "The Moonlit Plains are full of rolling hills, but the dig site is located on flat land. There will be no surprising them, and splitting our forces to attack from different angles would take days and make little difference." Galanör looked briefly at the War Mason. "We will meet them head on."

Doran leaned in. "Wait until they hear the sound o' dwarven boots - *thousands* o' 'em - thunderin' towards their line. On that day, even the dead will tremble, ye 'ave me word." The son of Dorain clicked his fingers. "That reminds me!" he exclaimed, looking up at Russell. "Come with me, lad; I've somethin' for ye." The dwarf paused before leading the way. "We'll see ye on the plains, Galanör."

The elven ranger let his gaze linger over Doran for a moment longer than was comfortable. "Good riding, both of you." With a grace unbefitting of one so ruggedly dressed, Galanör disappeared into the trees.

"Follow me," Doran instructed.

"Galanör doesn't think I should accompany you," Russell said.

"Bah!" Doran snorted. "Don' try an' get into the head o' an elf, Rus! There's not much in there but foliage an' hedgerows."

With so much of the camp packed down, the dwarf was able to reach his intended destination swiftly. The makeshift smithy was in disarray after so many weapons, shields, and pieces of armour had passed through it, and the variety of tools that accompanied every dwarven band were strewn across the benches and ground. Only the smith himself remained, the last to abandon any camp.

"Glain!" Doran hollered, aware that the old smith was partially deaf from centuries of hammering.

"War Mason!" Glain replied with a welcoming smile. "I'd o' thought ye would be gone by now!"

"Someone's got to make sure this lot clear out!" The son of Dorain thumbed over his shoulder at the stragglers. "Where we're goin' every arm counts!" he stated, before looking up at Russell. "Glain 'ere has been makin' all manner o' weapons an' armour for Grimwhal since he were a pup! Knew me father he did, back when ol' Dorain had some colour in his hair. An' some life in his bones," he added under his breath.

"What can I do ye for?" Glain asked, as he continued to pack up his cart. "I've got nothin' that'll compare to Andaljor, ye know!"

Doran scowled, his eye shifting from the smith to Russell and back. "Ye know," he said, gesturing heavily. "The thing I requested o' ye!"

Glain scratched his balding head and frowned. "I've had a lot o' requests come through here in the last day or so."

"The request came from me, ye dolt! Yer *War Mason*! Doran Heavybelly! Me name is the very clan ye belong to! Ringin' any bells?"

Russell bowed his head. "How old is *old* Glain exactly?"

Quite exasperated, Doran shrugged and rolled his eye. "Even Grarfath probably doesn' remember makin' 'im."

"I remember!" Glain exclaimed with a stubby finger in the air. "Now where did I put it?" he asked aloud, searching his wares. "I had jus' the thing I did! Fit yer requirements perfectly!" The ancient-looking dwarf rummaged through the weapons and tools poking out at the end of his cart. "'ere it is!"

A smile of satisfaction spread Doran's blond beard. "That'll do," he said, taking the war hammer from the smith. It was heavy, even to his strong arms. The head of the hammer offered two sides of attack, branching off into a flat piece of steel, ideal for breaking all manner of things, and a thick claw for everything else.

Russell accepted the weapon, taking it in both hands. The way he hefted it suggested the war hammer was just as light as a common sword. He twisted it this way and that, inspecting the head with a critical eye.

"It's no pick-axe," Doran remarked, "but it's a damn sight sharper! An' with yer strength, lad, ye can crush Reaver skulls with the hammer."

"Thank you, old friend," Russell said, his own fears and doubts resting visibly on his large shoulders.

"Ye jus' keep yer fingers wrapped around that hammer, ye hear. When the wolf comes callin', ye grip it all the tighter an' keep swingin'. We're seein' this through ye an' I."

Russell said nothing, preferring to simply nod his understanding. Doran wished he could rid his friend of the burden that coursed through his veins, just as he wished he could save his brother from the poison that ran through his. But Fate, it seemed, had chosen to render him helpless to both.

"What was that?" Glain called, his pitch suggesting there was considerable distance between them.

Doran turned back to see the smith only a few feet away. "Pack yer tools an' be on yer way, Glain!" the War Mason told him. "It's more than likely yer skills are to be needed again before we see real battle!"

"As ye command!" Glain shouted back.

Returning to their mounts, Doran and Russell took to their respective saddles and began making for the northern edge of the forest. "If ye lot don' get a move on," the son of Dorain berated the stragglers, "ye'll be chargin' into battle from the back an' Grarfath won' even see ye! Ye'll be sleepin' in the Father's stables for all eternity!"

They left the clearing to the sound of dwarves clumsily falling over each other to catch up. Weaving through the forest, they easily followed the trail left by the thousands that had preceded them, though Doran struggled to spot the tracks left by the elves. The forest obviously favoured the woodland folk - another reason to prefer mountains.

Under a clear blue sky and battered by winter's cold winds, the old rangers left the forest behind and rode out onto the plains. Thaligg and Thraal were charging up and down on their Warhogs bellowing orders. They were attempting to organise the dwarves into companies and battalions that suited their choice of weapons and expertise. Judging by the chaos, they were struggling.

To Doran's eye, the problem was simple: too many clans. Thaligg and Thraal were trying to coordinate Heavybellys with the remains of Battleborns, Hammerkegs, Goldhorns, and Bright-beards, all of whom had spent centuries fighting each other rather than side by side.

"Grarfath's beard, this is maddenin'," he cursed.

The sound of thundering hooves turned the son of Dorain to the west. Faylen brought her horse alongside him, though he didn't miss her eyes moving to compare the ranked elves to the rabble of dwarves.

"We will need to camp one more time before we can attack the dig site," she informed him needlessly. "We need to get *moving*, Doran."

"I hear ye," he grumbled. "I'll have 'em organised before we attack."

Riding away from Russell and the High Guardian, he charged Pig up and down the front line of dwarves and barked orders to get marching. He instructed his captains to keep the horde moving and begin to consider who should go where for the final attack.

"For now," he finished, "jus' get 'em north!"

A great clatter accompanied the progression of the dwarves. It reminded Doran of his days in Dhenaheim, leading his army across the icy plains to meet another clan. *That* Doran would never have believed the sight before him now. It almost made the son of Dorain believe that anything was possible.

Watching them advance from the east, Russell rode up to meet him again. "Doran," he warned, his yellow eyes flashing further east still.

The War Mason followed his friend's direction and cast his only eye over the distant hills. They were small given the gap between them, but Doran knew Centaurs when he saw them. They were a distinctive shape among the creatures that lived outside of civilisation.

"How many do ye count?"

Russell narrowed his eyes. "At least a dozen," he observed.

Doran's face screwed up as he tried to recall the name of any one of the Centaurs he had met, but it had been nearly fifty years since he had been welcomed into their home. The memory itself was fond, filled with merriment and old friends, but the individual names escaped him. He was sure the leader's name had an exotic sound to it.

Then again, he realised, the Centaurs watching them could be from any number of tribes that called The Moonlit Plains their home.

"What do you think they want?" Russell pondered.

"They're likely jus' watchin' us," Doran assumed. "Makin' sure we aren' 'ere to cause trouble for 'em. They're no threat to our numbers."

Russell raised an eyebrow. "It's been years since *any* Centaur posed a threat. The elves of Ilythyra saw to that."

"That were before a half-elf an' his dragon took over the realm. Now we're all a little wild."

Content to leave the Centaurs to their hill, Doran turned Pig to the north... and to war.

CHAPTER 12
INTRODUCTIONS

Asher waited for Adan's magic to extinguish the flames before he tore down what remained of the burnt curtains. He coughed through the smoke and added them to the pile of charred sheets, blankets, and even a broken chair.

"Your cloak!" the Drake warned, pointing at one corner of the fabric.

Asher quickly lifted the right side of his cloak and began roughly patting it down until the small flame was reduced to sparks, leaving the material singed. The most recent fire dealt with, the ranger turned back to finally greet his friends.

None of them had noticed a thing.

All three of the Galfreys, along with Gideon and the king himself, were staring in wonderment at a bronze dragon chasing her own tail. Asher couldn't blame them - she was beautiful. Every time her scales caught the afternoon light, she sparkled with silver and gold. The little noises she made didn't compare to that of a fully grown dragon yet, which only endeared her to them all the more.

Just looking at the hatchling, already running, jumping, and setting fire to things, brought up a sense of pride in the ranger. It was all dizzyingly new for him. Right now, he imagined his feelings for her were comparable to that of a parent, though he couldn't say for sure having never sired a child.

"Ilargo is already jealous of her beauty," Gideon declared with a beaming smile.

Reyna crouched down and offered a hand out to the hatchling. "Hello," she crooned.

Asher took a cautioning step towards her. "I wouldn't," he advised, concerned for her fingers.

Quite surprisingly, Reyna was able to run her hand over the dragon's scales. In fact, the hatchling leaned in to her palm and rubbed her horned head against the elf's skin.

"Dragons are notoriously good judges of character," Gideon informed.

"But she will also have your memories and feelings," Inara added.

Reyna smiled up at the ranger. "It's good to know how you feel about me."

There was barely a tap of claws on stone as the hatchling dashed across the chamber and ascended Asher's leg and chest. Coming to rest, the dragon perched comfortably in the crook of his arm with her head pressed to his leathers.

All eyes fell on the ranger and the dragon.

"Have you given her a name?" Vighon asked, perhaps the only one among them unaccustomed to the way of dragons.

"Hatchlings are given their name by their mother," Inara explained for him. "They carry it with them in their memories." The half-elf turned to Asher expectantly. "Do you know it? Her name?"

Just thinking of it brought a warm smile to Asher's face. "Her name is *Avandriell*."

Saying it out loud was like breathing new life into the world. The realm needed her, even if it didn't know it yet. To think how the world had coped without her baffled Asher. How had *he* coped without her? There was an argument to be had there but he was too consumed with the needs of his new companion to give it any further thought.

"Avandriell!" Inara repeated with a beaming grin. "A powerful name if ever there was."

Nathaniel put an affectionate hand on the ranger's shoulder and looked from him to the dragon. "Asher and Avandriell," he announced, listening to the sound of their names together. "I like it."

"*I* still can't believe it," Reyna admitted, with a tone of happiness.

"I found the timing of it all suspicious myself," Gideon confessed. "But it all makes perfect sense. You've been a warrior more years than any of us and your connection to the realm of magic would make bonding to a dragon all the easier."

"My connection?" Asher questioned.

"Well, you spent a thousand years trapped in the Amber Spell with Paldora's Gem around your neck. And then..." Gideon hesitated with his choice of words. "And then your resurrection was, in itself, an act of powerful magic. It's those kinds of tethers that draw a dragon and Rider together. The fact that you fit the description of a Rider... I'd say Fate has spent millennia ensuring you found yourself in Drakanan when you did."

Asher was used to feeling like Fate's puppet, though it had spent most of his life dragging him over the hot coals again and again.

"It makes perfect sense," Reyna agreed. "But I still can't believe it."

"You're going to make quite the pair," Vighon commented.

"Avandriell," Gideon muttered to himself.

"What is it?" Inara asked.

The old master tilted his head as if hearing something from Ilargo. "Yes," he said with some satisfaction. "That's where I've seen it."

"Seen what?" Nathaniel enquired.

Gideon looked directly at the hatchling. "Avandriell. I've seen it written down."

"Where?" Asher tried to suppress the interest in his voice but he was quite sure he failed.

"In Drakanan, back when I was searching for the doorway with Alijah. There are libraries of ancient tomes in there. The one containing any mention of Avandriell was among the oldest."

"What did it say?" Inara pressed, just as pulled in as Asher.

"There was only one mention of her, but it's not a name you forget. Avandriell was Garganafan's *mother* and one of the earliest recorded dragons. With a few others, she flew to unknown lands not long after the Dragon Riders were established."

"Garganafan?" Vighon mused. "Like the mountain in Ayda?"

"Like the *king of dragons*," Inara corrected. "The mountain was named after him when the elves sailed to Ayda."

"He gave his life to capture Valanis," Reyna added.

Gideon examined Asher's expression. "This doesn't come as a surprise to you," he observed.

"Before she hatched," the ranger explained, "I saw Thessaleia's - her *mother's* - memories. I think Garganafan is her father." Asher ran his finger over the dragon's soft wings. "You're named after your grandmother," he told her.

"Incredible," Gideon uttered, his amazement entirely renewed.

"She's of royal blood?" Nathaniel proposed.

"Not exactly," Inara said. "Dragons choose their kings and queens. Their offspring rarely replace them."

"Proof of that lies in Dragons' Reach," Gideon pointed out.

"Yes," Inara agreed. "You might be interested to know, Asher: Avandriell has a brother. Vorgraf the mountain child was sired by Garganafan too. Though, of course, Rainael is their chosen queen."

Asher had only a moment's notice - a flicker of emotion in his mind - before Avandriell leapt from his arm. Her wings fanned out, giving her some lift, and she came to land in Inara's waiting arms. The hatchling ran up her leathers and over her shoulders until she came to rest with her head hanging down beside the Guardian's jaw.

Avandriell felt safe and contented, emotions that the ranger was unfamiliar with. It was relaxing. Asher could feel the tension leaving his muscles and he wondered how many years they had been wound so tight.

"I think she has family enough right here," he replied.

Vighon slowly reached out, presenting Avandriell with the back of his hand. Only after she nuzzled between his fingers did he proceed to stroke her. "At last," he said, "a dragon is born inside The *Dragon* Keep. This will make for a much better namesake."

Asher wholeheartedly agreed, though he was growing curious as to why Adan'Karth was so reserved. "You're unusually quiet," he remarked.

Adan took in the sight of both Asher and Avandriell as he considered his response. "My journey with you has come to an end. It fills me with joy to know that end is not what I feared in my heart. You are no longer alone, nor will you ever die alone, if at all."

Reyna covered her mouth. "You're immortal," she whispered, as if it had only just occurred to her.

"Don't remind me," Asher grumbled. "A never ending horizon of sunrises and sunsets. It sounds exhausting."

The majority of the room shared a laugh at his description. "You're still thinking like a man," Gideon said. "I did for a while, before our bond matured. Soon you will begin to feel the energy of a dragon. It is the greatest of gifts. You will feel stronger, faster, wiser even. You won't need sleep like you do now. Your senses will retune to the world, lending it a vibrancy you couldn't imagine. It's a ranger's dream."

Asher's expression didn't change. "Like I said: exhausting."

Gideon quietly laughed to himself. "Take it from a man approaching his seventieth birthday; feeling like you're twenty every day is outstanding."

"I could do with some of that," Vighon commented.

Avandriell pounced onto the floor and scurried across the chamber on her claws. Asher held out his arm and she used it like a frame to climb up onto his shoulder. "I suppose you'll make it all the more interesting," he praised. "And thank you," he added, turning to Adan'Karth. "Had you not journeyed with me, I would have been undone long before we flew to Erador. And you certainly helped bring us together."

"It was the least I could do for the one who made me," the Drake replied, bowing his head.

Painfully aware of those who had just observed his moment of vulnerability, Asher puffed out his chest and addressed them all. "What did I miss?"

Nathaniel gestured at the old master. "Gideon told a rather unbelievable tale about the first wizards and a magical tree. Some of us were still stumbling over the revelation regarding yourself, but Gideon was kind enough to repeat it all for us."

"We need to stop Alijah from opening a doorway," Asher asserted, his own fate now tied to it.

"That was the conclusion we all came to," Reyna reassured. "As we speak, Doran, Faylen, and Galanör are marching their forces onto The Moonlit Plains. The rest of my army are advancing from the coast, along with Sir Ruban and his soldiers. They are to keep Alijah and his Reavers occupied until we can reinforce them from the north."

"Gideon and I will be leaving shortly to aid them," Inara informed.

Asher took it all in, his mind trained to absorb multiple sources of information at once, but his focus remained on Reyna and one particular phrase he had never heard her say before. "*Your* army?" he echoed.

Even if he were blind, the ranger could still have sensed the pall that overcame the chamber. Reyna straightened up, composing herself. "My mother fell on Qamnaran. I am the queen now."

Asher's emotions were instantly torn between condolences and congratulations. He also knew that Reyna had never been interested in ruling a nation, nor Nathaniel for that matter.

"I'm so sorry," he offered. His emotions crossed over to Avandriell, who stretched her maw and whined with sorrow.

Reyna held up her hand. "This is a moment of joy," she managed, her smile conflicting with the tears in her eyes. "I would focus on Avandriell and her beauty."

Asher nodded solemnly. His own memories of Adilandra Sevari were decades old, taking him back to the end of The War for the Realm. The woman he had met was strong and compassionate, explaining much of where Reyna had attained her own characteristics. Her passing was, indeed, the extinguishing of a powerful light in the world.

"And with Avandriell in mind," Reyna continued, "there is no expectation on you to accompany us, Asher."

"We will be leaving soon," Vighon confirmed. "The snows are only going to get worse. We have already rallied those who can journey south to fight and Kassian is convincing his Keepers to join us as we speak." The northman paused, considering those around him. "Your skill with a sword has historically made a difference in every battle you've been a part of. The king in me would press for you to fight with us, given what is at stake. But Reyna is correct: there is no expectation. Avandriell is as a child. She needs protecting, not thrusting into a war."

Asher met his companion's golden eyes. Her thoughts and emotions continued to bombard him with impressions rather than direct words. Still, he understood her and she understood him.

"Avandriell didn't choose me because I walk away from the fight."

"Asher," Reyna warned, her eyes flashing to the young dragon.

"No, he's right," Inara spoke up. "Avandriell was born of another age, an age of warriors and war."

"An age of heroes," Gideon added with half a smile.

"Neither of them can deny who they are," Inara continued. "Nor the consequences."

Asher took a breath, assessing his options. There was only one viable choice to his reckoning, though he hated to consider it. But Inara was right, he could not deny who he was.

"I have just as much at stake in this fight as the rest of you," he told them. "If Alijah succeeds and destroys the tree, Avandriell..." He almost choked just thinking of the word. "She dies," he finally managed. "I will journey south with you, if you would have me."

"If I would have you?" Vighon repeated incredulously. "I would grant you the title of general if I thought you would accept it."

Asher put his hand up. "I already have a title and I'm sticking with it."

"You're not to be a Dragon Rider then?" Nathaniel posed.

"No," Asher stated firmly. "Avandriell and I have come to... an *agreement*. Our life is long. For now, we're content to be rangers together."

"Well there goes Illian's monster problem," Vighon joked.

Asher acknowledged the king's remark with an amused grin, but he turned serious again when facing Adan'Karth. "You have already given so much and I never had to ask for it. But I have to ask you now; will you accompany me one last time? I cannot take Avandriell into battle, but I don't think I can be far from her either. I know a battlefield is the last place a Drake would want to be, but she already feels safe with you and you can handle the... *fires*."

Compounding his words, Avandriell jumped across to Adan, whose quick reflexes easily caught her and guided the dragon onto his shoulders. "It would be my honour to keep Avandriell company. And should we face violence, I will take us both into the wild and lose our quarry."

"I have no doubt," Asher replied, having seen the Drake move through The Evermoore. "And thank you."

"You have the thanks of us all," Vighon added, patting Adan's arm. "Victory is within our reach."

"I'm starving," Asher blurted without intending to.

Inara stifled her laugh. "I think Avandriell needs her first meal."

Asher turned to see the dragon staring at him, her intentions never clearer. "I'd say so," he concluded.

"The kitchens are yours to plunder," Vighon offered. "I would join you but there is still much to be done before we depart."

"I will accompany you," Gideon said to the ranger. "There is more you should know before we part ways."

Asher watched Vighon and Adan flinch when Avandriell belched a small cloud of fire. "I would agree."

CHAPTER 13

FINDING HARBOUR IN THE STORM

Leaving Asher and Avandriell, Vighon was happy to discover a strong note of hope in himself. As awe-inspiring as it was to see a baby dragon and to know that the ranger had finally received some kind of gift for all his suffering and toil, the king was simply happy to know that Verda's future had a new line of dragons in it. Their species had long brought peace and prosperity to the realm and, whatever that looked like, Asher and Avandriell were proof that one day that time would come again in some way.

Some of that hope was dashed when he listened to the report from one of Kassian's Keepers. He had been waiting for the king further down the hall and was quick to catch him. Though Vighon and Nathaniel had successfully rallied all those who would journey south with them, Kassian had taken over the hunt for supplies where armour and weapons were concerned.

"We checked the barracks twice, your Grace," the Keeper reported. "The only usable armour and swords have already been taken by those who currently guard the keep but, in truth, that's all that was left. The rest looks to have been melted down."

Vighon swore under his breath. "Do we have swords and shields for every man accompanying us?"

"Swords yes, though their condition isn't great. Shields, no, your Grace. Kassian himself is going from house to house to see if anyone has usable armour."

"They're likely to be antiques," Vighon remarked. "Do we at least have furs enough to travel through the snow?"

"Furs are the one thing this city has in abundance, your Grace," the Keeper answered with half a smile.

Vighon opened his mouth to reply but he caught Inara's eye, outside Asher's chamber. She was talking to her parents, but her attention appeared to be distracted by him.

Gathering his wits, the king managed to say, "Furs and old swords will have to do. The fate of the realm is in the balance and we will fight with tooth and nail if we must. At least you have your magic," he added, glancing down at the wand holstered on the Keeper's thigh.

The Keeper nodded his appreciation before being dismissed. Vighon turned back to Inara and discovered she was parting ways with her parents. Before she disappeared down the next passage, the Guardian looked back and locked eyes with the northman. Whether she was telling Vighon to follow her or not, the king felt compelled to go after her.

By the time he reached the next passage, her red cloak was just vanishing through a door that led down to the back of the keep. Vighon couldn't think of any reason why Inara would be heading towards the back of the keep, so she must be expecting him to follow. If she didn't, the king had no idea what he was going to say when he caught up with her.

It wasn't long before he was outside and walking down to the main courtyard. His black furs and thick cloak helped to keep winter's touch at bay, but there was no protection from the mob of Namdhorians yet to vacate the keep. People of every age tried to reach out and touch him, offering their thanks and loyalty. It was overwhelming, as noted by a few of his guards. They jostled their way through and tried to give the king some space, but it was ultimately Sir Borin's towering presence that parted the crowd.

Irritated by the enormous and forbidding shadow that refused to give him peace, Vighon commanded the Golem to the ramparts, reminding Sir Borin that he could watch his master from afar.

Free of the walking nightmare, the king took the time to shake several hands, greeting his people, as well as crouching to talk to some of the children, reassuring them all that they had nothing to be concerned about. He encouraged them all to return to their homes and help source supplies where they could. Most, it seemed, didn't feel it was safe enough to leave the keep yet. There was a degree of terror in the eyes of them all. They feared for their elderly parents and their young children.

Having done all he could with words, Vighon turned away and made for the north gate. It was the only place Inara could have gone, he reasoned. The guards remained stationed at the gate, ensuring the king wasn't followed by any of the crowd. He wanted to do so much more for them, but he couldn't give them anything but hope without an actual victory to claim.

Navigating the outer walls of the keep, Vighon walked round the cliff edge until he spotted Inara. She was standing on the most northern outcropping of rock, where Namdhor's mountainous slope extended another hundred feet beyond the keep. Her red cloak was billowing in the wind as she looked out on The King's Lake.

The northman approached, his feet crunching through the snow. He did his best to ignore the unnerving feeling that crept into his hands and feet when he took in the severe drop either side of the pointed bluff. When finally he reached her side, there was just enough room to stand shoulder to shoulder.

This wasn't the first time they had shared this particular ground.

"Do you remember the last time we were here together?" he asked.

Inara maintained her distant gaze. "You kissed me if I recall."

Vighon chortled. "*If* you recall? Was it not memorable?"

Inara smiled. "Have you come to kiss me again?" she replied evenly.

The king hesitated, taken aback by the direct question. "I wanted to offer my condolences," he began. "We haven't had any time since you arrived. I would have told you about Adilandra myself, but..."

Inara was already shrugging off any apology or condolences. "My grandmother had a warrior's heart... and a warrior's death. I expect we will all meet a similar end, if we're lucky."

Vighon couldn't help his look of surprise. "Expect? You're expecting us all to die?"

"Why not?" Inara countered. "The best of us already have."

"You have ever been a beacon of hope, Inara, for *all* of us. Don't lose that now," he beseeched.

"I have carried hope for others for so long," she replied wearily. "Where do *I* get it from?"

Vighon extended his hand and squeezed Inara's fingers. The lines between them had blurred of late, tempting him to offer a part of himself as hope, but he feared she would reject him again. To hear those words would open a scar that had never truly healed.

"I only wish this war hadn't made me so numb," Inara continued. "It's getting harder to feel anything anymore. Especially when your own brother can take everything you love away from you."

Indeed, Vighon could hear the difference in her voice now. Before hearing of her grandmother's death, Inara had sounded her hopeful self. Now, however, she had lost her softer edges in the wake of yet more grief.

"It was here that you told me of your love," he said. "For the realm and the people. For Alijah."

Inara cast her eyes down at the lake. "There is nothing left of my brother to love. The Crow hollowed him out."

Vighon was inclined to agree. There was nothing in his old friend he recognised anymore - just an insatiable hunger to conquer the world.

"Do not let it hollow *you* out," he warned. "Your love for the people is displayed in your bravery *every day*."

"What about my love for *you?*" she posed quietly, taking the king by surprise. "What display of that is there?"

Vighon swallowed hard, hoping the butterflies in his stomach would settle down. He still relived their recent conversation in The Black Wood, in which Inara had spoken of a kiss she might have given him. He had hoped, more than anything, that he was seeing something of *his* Inara in that moment, but he didn't dare cling to something that could shatter his heart.

"I do love you," Inara whispered, turning her glassy blue eyes on the king.

Vighon looked back at her, barely catching her words in the breeze. "I know," he uttered. "You told me as much the last time we were here. You told me you couldn't love in the way I wanted you to - in the way I love you."

"I was wrong." Inara maintained her intense gaze. "I never stopped loving you, even after I left for The Lifeless Isles. My bond with Athis quietened those feelings and kept me focused on my duty to the order. But they were still there, under the surface. Now, I struggle from day to day to fully grasp my own emotions. It's like sailing in a storm. But every time I think of you, every time I hear your name or see your face, it's everything else that quietens. That's how I know I love you. That's how I know I've *always* loved you."

Vighon could feel his eyes filling with tears. For so many years, the king had made every effort not to dwell on his loneliness, but hearing those words from Inara brought it all up from the depths of his heart.

"I have tried, for so long, *not* to love you," he confessed with an unsteady breath. "But it was like trying to rid the world of colour." Turning his whole body towards her, he waited for Inara to do the same before gently touching her cheek. "I am *desperately, hopelessly,* in love with you."

"Are we fools to give in to this now?" Inara asked. "We would only be giving Alijah so much more to take from us."

"You fear our love would doom us?" Vighon reasoned.

Inara tilted her head as their cloaks flapped around them. "I fear what losing you would do to me."

"I think it's too late for that," he countered, feeling Inara's hand on the side of his neck. "Since you left for The Lifeless Isles, all those years ago, I have woken up every day feeling like I had already lost you. For whatever time I have left, before whatever doom might await us, I would see it through with you by my side."

Inara cupped his face in both hands and brought their lips together in an embrace that both had waited a lifetime for. Vighon pulled her in as close as he could, his arms wrapped around her. It wasn't like the last time they had kissed with a moment of reservation from Inara. Now it felt like they were sixteen again, kissing in the shade of the trees on her parents' land.

When, finally, they parted again, the pair held each other in their arms as well as their gaze. Vighon would have given anything to stay in this moment, a moment he had dreamt of more times than he could recall.

"What do we do now?" he asked.

"Now we try not to die," Inara replied, with some hope, at last, returning to her tone.

"I've got pretty good at that," Vighon quipped, with a coy grin.

"Only because I've been watching your back," Inara informed him.

Vighon mirrored her smile and kissed her again, only this time he had no intention of parting.

CHAPTER 14
NOT FORGOTTEN

Having raided the kitchens for raw meat, Asher, Gideon, and Avandriell made for the ramparts of the keep. The old master guided them towards the northern walls, where the view offered a jagged vista of snow-capped mountains surrounding The King's Lake. The water's surface would begin to freeze over soon, signalling winter's hold.

Asher tried to take it all in, but his concerns constantly returned to Avandriell, who was dragging a raw steak across the ramparts. She battled with it, rolling over herself while shaking the meat in her jaws. More than once he had to correct her wildness and prevent her from falling into the small courtyard below. Then he feared she would leap over the walls of the rampart and fall on the rocky shelf that loomed over the lake.

"I feel for you," Gideon said. "Young dragons are quite the handful, prone to impulses. I never had to experience it myself."

Asher caught sight of Ilargo gliding over the lake, his green scales glistening in the sunlight. "How long will it be before she possesses the wisdom of her mother?"

Gideon leaned into the wall before turning to rest his back against it. "Thessaleia you said," the old master mused. "She was likely very old and her lineage older still. It could take years, decades even, before Avandriell absorbs all the memories. She also has yours to contend with and you have more than most."

Asher felt sorry for her in that regard. "I can't see Malliath anymore," he revealed.

Gideon looked at him. "You no longer carry his memories?"

"I found a way to keep them down, but they were always there. Now, after Avandriell... they're *gone*. It's as if she's purged them."

The old master cast a warm smile over the hatchling. "I think this is going to be the best thing that ever happened to you."

Asher couldn't argue as he watched Avandriell tear off a chunk of meat and devour it whole. She was the thing his life had been missing. "It makes me feel sick," he confessed, "the idea of leaving her to go and fight. But I can't let Alijah harm that tree."

"I know that sense of vulnerability must be crushing," Gideon sympathised. "She won't be defenceless for long though," he promised. "I'd say she's pretty dangerous right now in fact."

Avandriell exhaled a jet of fire and enveloped the last chunk of meat in flames before picking it apart with her sharp fangs.

"I can't imagine what it's like," the master continued. "I read what I could in Drakanan but I'm sure the descriptions don't do it justice."

"What did they say? The Riders."

Gideon looked out over the land, his memory casting back. "They describe an evolving bond, not dissimilar to that of a parent and child. It's nothing like what Ilargo and I had when we met. In the beginning they said it was like becoming a mother or father - you care for your child. Then, in some ways, you become a master of sorts while you guide them in the ways of the world. Then the bond changes again and you become friends before, finally, you're left with something akin to a brother or sister. They all said it gets easier though, once the hatchling takes on the wisdom of their parents."

That sounded like a long way off to the ranger. "What should I expect next then?"

"She's going to surprise you," Gideon answered with some amusement.

"How so?" the ranger pressed, never one for surprises.

"A fundamental fact you need to know about all dragons: they're magical in nature. In their eggs, they possess a portion of this magic, but it simply resides within them, dormant mostly. But, once they hatch, they begin to absorb magic from the other realm at a rapid rate. That abundance of energy has to go somewhere."

Asher looked expectantly from Avandriell to Gideon. "Where does it go?" he demanded.

"Some of it will be siphoned off to you - which reminds me; you're going to need some lessons in magic."

The ranger resisted the urge to sigh. "And what about the rest of it?"

Gideon turned back to Avandriell. "She's going to get *big*. *Fast*."

Asher raised an eyebrow. "How big and how fast?"

"That's hard to say. Her egg was sitting in Drakanan for more millennia than I can count, which might suggest there's an awful lot of magic already flooding her bones. My physical experience with hatchlings is limited I'm afraid. Some of this you'll have to learn as you go."

Now that was a concept Asher was familiar with. "I've adapted to new situations in the past, but my life was the only thing in the balance. I don't know any of this," he complained, gesturing to Avandriell. "I don't know how to help her."

"Like Inara said: listen to your instincts."

"My instincts have no idea what's going on," he confessed. "When will she fly? When can we speak to each other? Is she going to influence my thoughts?" The ranger groaned. "I'm too old for something this new."

Gideon held up his hands to calm the situation. "You're never too old for anything; words you should live by now that you're immortal." Asher threw him a look and Gideon stopped himself from laughing too much. "When will she fly?" he echoed. "*Very* soon. It's instinctual, like their breath. Try not to be overly concerned with her attempts either. They have strong bones designed to take impacts. As for speaking to each other..." Gideon shrugged. "Her voice will mature the bigger she gets, but every dragon is different. Avandriell can hear your thoughts but, right now, your emotions will be communicating more than words."

The old master paused to watch Ilargo glide past the keep. Even after all their years together, he still looked at the dragon with wonder, his devotion easy to see.

"You don't need to worry about her influencing your thoughts," he continued. "Avandriell is not from the line of dragons that filled the ranks of the Dragorn, so there is no elder to instruct her to do so and Ilargo certainly won't. Your bond will be pure, just as it was meant to be. That's not to say, however, that you won't both influence each other as your bond grows. You will both come to share the same temperament, but always remember; Avandriell can breathe fire. That's not to say *you* aren't dangerous. But you will have to find ways to calm each other when needed."

Asher sighed. "It all sounds so... *messy*."

"That's because it is," Gideon confirmed. "Two minds, two souls, coming together in perfect harmony. It's a strange way to live but, once you do, you will wonder how you ever lived any other way."

"Will we share pain?" Asher had to ask, despite Gideon's recent description of their bond.

"No. That kind of bond is a consequence of the influence. It was just another way to make the Dragorn feel like they were one person with their dragon. No," he repeated. "Whatever sanctuary you form between your minds will be a construct of you both. No hidden doors."

The ranger let himself relax a little, happy to know that Avandriell would not suffer the inevitable injuries coming his way. "You still carry the shame," Asher observed, having detected it in his voice.

Gideon tilted his head, mulling over the comment. "Some of it belongs to Ilargo, though I do feel the weight of my guilt. I kept it a secret from them all. None of them were whole. They still aren't."

Asher, who had long seen the world in a simpler way to most, had a different outlook on the whole affair. "You have read a lot about the Dragon Riders. How many of them turned from their order and caused chaos in Erador?"

Gideon looked away for a moment. "There were several accounts of rogue Riders, scattered throughout their history. Some brought down entire cities."

"And how many Dragorn did the same?" Asher posed.

The answer came to the old master much quicker. "None," he replied.

"Unnatural or not," the ranger concluded, "a degree of influence over the Rider has proven a good way to protect the realm. Ilargo was only doing as he was taught and you were only doing what you thought was right. That's all there is to it. Those in Dragons' Reach are happy and safe. That's more than the rest of us can say."

Gideon took a long breath and patted Asher on the shoulder. "Perhaps some of that wisdom is already taking hold," he suggested.

Asher shrugged. "I've always been wise."

Gideon laughed. "And humble too I believe."

"Of course," the ranger jested. "In Nightfall, humility was taught right after the art of decapitation."

Both men shared a laugh in the cold air of the north before Gideon turned to Asher. "That second one was a real lesson, wasn't it?"

The ranger imitated a sword in his hands. "It's all in the swing."

It felt good to laugh again and even better to see the elation mirrored in Avandriell, who flapped her wings and squawked with delight. Then she dashed off down the ramparts, forcing Asher and Gideon to follow her. The soldiers she passed were instantly dumbstruck by the mere sight of her and left gawping.

All but one.

Caught up himself, it took Asher an extra moment to notice the only Namdhorian guard who remained rooted to the spot. He was less animated than the others, who all pointed and gazed at Avandriell as she bounded down the nearest steps. Instead, *his* eyes shifted back and forth between the baby dragon and the ranger with a calculating expression.

Then the rest of the picture fell into place for Asher. The guard's uniform wasn't quite right for his size - too baggy. His helmet didn't sit properly on his head, sloping slightly to one side. The travelling boots were definitely his, but they weren't the standard issue worn by the others. Then there was the dark patch staining the black material on the end of his left sleeve. Blood.

Asher's heart thundered in his chest as the obvious answer struck him with dread: Arakesh.

The assassin's appearance was either a testament to his inexperience or the speed with which he had infiltrated the keep. The ranger was hoping for the former as he lunged for the killer.

The Arakesh knew his cover had been blown a second before Asher leapt at him, giving him just enough time to push one of the real guards into his path. The collision broke Avandriell's charm and riled the Namdhorians up, unaware of what was really going on around them. The ranger, however, had no time to explain, leaving him with no other choice but to push them aside and pursue his foe.

"Asher!" Gideon called.

"Stay with her!" he shouted, pointing down to Avandriell.

Leaving them behind, the ranger chased the Arakesh round onto the southern ramparts and over the platform that topped the main gates to the courtyard. Asher tried not to think about the fact that Avandriell was making her way down to the crowds that inhabited the large courtyard, confident that Gideon could take care of her.

Instead, he focused on tracking his enemy down. The Arakesh was younger than him, evidenced by his precise and swift movements. Youth, fortunately, was often trumped by experience. Asher looked ahead, calculating like an assassin. Thinking like the young man was all too easy and he saw the obvious path.

Past the walls, the nearest building was beyond any human's

ability to jump, but the scaffolding erected after the recent battle closed that gap just enough to make it possible. The climb down from the scaffolding, after the jump, would be slow and, in there, lay the opportunity.

Asher ceased his pursuit and descended the closest set of steps, leaping the bottom half into the bustling courtyard. With powerful strides he was outside the keep and on the main road in a few seconds, just in time to see the Arakesh leap from the ramparts as predicted. He managed to get a hold on the second platform down from the top, his chest impacting the wood with some force.

The Ranger raised his hand to draw the silvyr short-sword from his back. All he had to do now was wait for the fool to climb down, by which point he would be at the base of the scaffold, waiting. Asher's hand hovered over the hilt, failing to grasp it.

The assassin was climbing *up*.

Asher swore and broke into a sprint. By the time he was ascending the lowest rungs of the side ladder, the Arakesh was disappearing over the roof. He climbed up as fast as his limbs would take him, aware that any student of Nightfall possessed the training to vanish, once out of sight. It was in this regard that the young assassin displayed his inexperience further for, as Asher reached the top, he spotted him fleeing over the roof tops when he should have already climbed down, discarded his stolen uniform, and blended into the city.

Asher would teach him this lesson, though the dead had little need of such things.

A northerly wind blew out the ranger's green cloak as he navigated the broken roof and patches of slick ice. Without any great speed behind him, leaping to the next building required a lot of strength from his legs but leap he did. His arms stretched over the lip of the next roof and his hands scrabbled for purchase while his feet slipped against the wall.

The assassin was already jumping down to the next building, taking advantage of the city's sloping architecture. Asher heaved himself up and quickly put one foot in front of the other, renewing the chase. Approaching the other end of the roof, he caught a flash of steel hurtling up towards him. He twisted his shoulders, narrowly evading it, before he even processed the fact that it was a throwing dagger.

With a growl in his throat, Asher pushed off from the roof and landed on the next. The angled tiles were slippery, forcing him to edge around the sides to catch up with the agile Arakesh. Again, the assassin was already crossing the gap to a church tower and disappearing down the other side. It spurred the ranger on but, in his haste, it compromised his footing. First, his right leg went over the lip, swiftly followed by his left leg. In the blink of an eye he was hanging from the very edge by his fingers alone.

Whether the assassin had noticed or not, the younger man was now scaling down the side of the church, making for the street below. Once he hit the ground he could disappear down any number of alleys or inside a house or shop. Having not seen his face properly, there was every chance the assassin could walk past the ranger and he wouldn't recognise him.

He couldn't let that happen.

Falling into the mindset of a predator, Asher prepared himself to do whatever was necessary to catch his prey. That began with falling.

Keeping himself close to the wall, the ranger dropped down and gripped the windowsill on the next floor down. His fingerless gloves lent him extra grip, but he could already feel himself slipping. He had the briefest of moments to look at the ground where he discovered an abandoned cart. It wouldn't exactly cushion his fall, but it took some of the remaining distance out of the fall.

He kept any yelp to himself and crashed down onto the centre of the cart. The wood cracked beneath him, threatening to drop him further, but it held long enough for him to groan and roll off the side. As his feet touched down, so too did the assassin twenty feet away.

There was nothing to be said, only more running. The Arakesh darted down the alley immediately in front of him. Asher rounded the corner a moment later and ducked just in time to avoid the helmet being thrown back at him. By the time his focus returned, the young assassin was barging his way through someone's door. There was a scream from inside, followed by a clatter of debris, before the ranger darted in behind him.

A cleaver cut through the air and dug into the door's wooden frame, an inch from Asher's head. The ranger shouted a vague apology to the owners, both huddled in the far corner of the kitchen, and ran through and up their stairs in pursuit. The assassin kicked in another door, crossed the small room, and forced his way through a pair of shutters. A brief fall brought him crashing back onto the street.

Asher landed only seconds later. He tucked his legs up, absorbing some of the impact, and rolled away until he was able to jump up to his feet again. Ignoring the pain in his knees, the ranger propelled himself after the Arakesh. A young couple walked out in front of the assassin and he pushed his way through the pair, knocking the man to the ground. Having been slowed down, the killer charged through another door in the hope of putting enough obstacles between them that he might escape.

What he didn't know, however, was that Asher had been trained to track and capture his targets in the maze-like districts of Karath and Tregaran. Of course, that was seventy years ago or more.

Following the screams and yells of the new intrusion, he chased the Arakesh inside. There was a woman crouched over her husband, who was nursing a cut on his head, and a small boy cowering under the table. The child pointed at the next room but didn't dare come out from under the table. Asher nodded his appreciation and held his hands out to calm the parents, making it clear that he was only in their house to get the intruder.

The next room was dark, illuminated by a single gleam of light from the shutters. Where most might have been tempted to squint into the shadows, Asher observed the motes floating in the shaft of light. They were moving fast, their direction suggesting that something large had recently run to the right side of the room. Confident, the ranger planted a solid boot on the end of the dining table, shoving it into the shadows.

The sound of it impacting the assassin's head was satisfying.

Knocked back from his hiding position, the young Arakesh swiped at the sundries on the table. Asher raised his hands and protected his face from the projectiles, but the assassin used his moment of blindness to roll across the table top and swing a kick into the side of the ranger's head. The next thing Asher knew, he was collapsing through several shelves on the wall, bringing down plates and decorations.

It was the sound of steel sliding from leather that sharpened his focus. Aware of the assassin's general position, Asher launched his foot in that direction. He caught him in the gut, mid-swing, and threw him to the other side of the room. Emerging from the debris and splintered wood, Asher glimpsed the dagger in his enemy's hand, the blade catching the light.

"Where is Veda Malmagol?" the ranger growled.

The Arakesh responded with violence. His attacks were fluid and well-practised, every strike angled to deliver a killing blow. Asher deflected what he could with the leather of his bracers while inserting counterattacks to put his foe off balance. One such attack staggered the young assassin, giving his next attack a wide sweeping angle. The ranger easily snatched his arm from the air and shoved the tips of his finger up into the soft skin of the Arakesh's wrist, forcing his hand to snap open and release the dagger.

Without needing to look, Asher dipped and caught the falling weapon. One perfectly placed thrust drove the blade into the assassin's thigh, where it severed an artery. The ranger rammed his own head into the Arakesh's nose and forced him onto his back, careful to keep the dagger in place.

With one knee pressing down on his enemy's chest, Asher reached out and wrapped his fingers around the hilt of the precarious blade. "If I take this out, you'll be dead in minutes," he threatened. "There are Keepers in the city, mages who could save your life. Tell me what I want to know and I will bring them to you."

The Arakesh remained very still, sweating in the gloom. His

eyes, however, were wild. They scanned every inch of Asher's face before taking in the room.

"Don't listen to it," Asher warned. "Your training. Right now you're looking for solutions, opportunities, anything you can use to escape. Do you feel that cold steel in your leg?" The ranger applied a small amount of pressure, increasing the panic in the assassin's eyes. "Accept the reality of your situation. There's naught but magic that can save you now."

The assassin sneered. "You are a traitor!"

"Focus." Asher pressed the dagger just a little further. "Did Veda Malmagol send you? Or did he have you waiting here, watching?"

"They're going to kill you," the Arakesh spat. "My brothers and sisters... they're going to—"

Asher flicked the fool's eyeball, silencing him with a shot of pain. "Where is Veda Malmagol?" he demanded. "Where's the Father?"

"You won't see him coming!" the assassin boasted. "We might be few now, but we are still Arakesh. The order will live on." Without warning, he yanked at Asher's hand, tearing the dagger free from his leg.

"No!" the ranger protested, but it was too late.

Arterial blood gushed from the wound in his thigh. Asher moved to apply pressure and staunch the flow, but the logical conclusion was inescapable. Instead, he roughly grabbed the young assassin by the collar and lifted his head from the floor.

"Where are they?" he fumed. "Where are the others? Are they in Namdhor?"

The Arakesh boldly maintained his defiant expression, determined to meet his maker with some dignity.

"Fool!" Asher berated, letting him drop down.

"They're... coming for you," the assassin stuttered. "They're all... coming for you. Before this is over... you will know... real vengeance."

Asher imagined the full weight of the Arakesh coming down on him, now, when his focus was most needed elsewhere. And how would he defend Avandriell from some of the most efficient killers in the realm? It made his blood boil.

"When you get wherever you're going," the ranger uttered, "tell them *I* sent you. And tell them more are coming."

The Arakesh's look of defiance faltered. Perhaps he was beholding the doom of all his kind, there to see in Asher's eyes. Or perhaps he was seeing the great many that had fallen to the ranger's blade, there to take him to the beyond.

Asher stood up as blood pooled around his boots. On the one hand, he was glad to be looking down at another dead Arakesh but, on the other hand, he couldn't help but see the wasted life at his feet.

Turning away from the body, he reassured the family that the man who had broken into their home was dead. He also told them not to enter the other room until the body was dealt with. In the meantime, he needed some fresh air.

Outside, the winter chill was a refreshing balm. He felt the wind sting a handful of new cuts he had received in the fight and on the pursuit.

A shadow ran over the street and, before he could look up, Inara was landing on the stone in front of him. There was a touch of magic to her impact and it cast mud and snow in every direction. Rising from her crouch, the Guardian strode towards him with concern marring her expression.

"What happened? Are you hurt?" Inara clearly had a lot more questions than that, but she was content to hear those two answers first.

"I'm fine," Asher reassured, his chest still heaving. "There was an Arakesh inside the keep. Took a guard's uniform. He saw me, but Avandriell seemed to give him pause. Instead of attempting to kill me, he fled."

Inara peered through the broken door but there was nothing to see in the gloom. "Why would an Arakesh run instead of attack?"

The assassin's last words echoed in Asher's mind, answering Inara's question. "Because they're *all* coming for me," he relayed. "I think he was supposed to report back to Veda Malmagol. Then they could coordinate an attack."

By the look on Inara's face, the seriousness of that statement wasn't lost on her. "The last thing we need right now is the Arakesh threatening you."

"They're still in Alijah's pocket," Asher pointed out. "They were always going to be in the middle of all this."

"Did he speak to anyone?" the Guardian asked.

Asher shook his head. "He was too busy trying to evade me."

A sharp squawk bounced off the alley walls around the corner. The ranger would have known that voice anywhere. A moment later, Avandriell came bounding out of the alley with such speed that she ran part-way up the adjacent building and leapt towards Asher from some height. Her wings unfurled and the dragon glided into his arms. Her jaws snapped repeatedly before her emotions washed over him. His sudden departure had left her feeling frightened, but his own emotions had put the fight in her bones.

A few seconds later, a dishevelled Gideon Thorn skidded out of the alley with a handful of Namdhorian soldiers behind him. The old master visibly relaxed when he spotted Avandriell in Asher's arms. "She's *fast*," he panted.

Asher looked down at her. "You'd find me anywhere it seems." A low clicking sound resonated from Avandriell's throat and she nestled her head into his chest. The ranger was unfamiliar with dragon behaviour and sounds, but he could sense the hatchling's joy and comfort at being reunited with him.

"Since you're alive," Gideon remarked, "I'm assuming he *isn't*."

Asher simply nodded at the splintered doorway, where the soldiers were now entering to calm the family and see to the body.

"Arakesh," Inara informed gravely.

Gideon's mouth twisted in contemplation. "It seems your business with them is yet to conclude."

"It will," the ranger said gruffly.

"You have a plan?" Inara's raised eyebrow spoke of her doubt.

"I do," Asher replied, making for the alley that would take him back to the main road.

"And what would that be?" Inara asked with exasperation.

The ranger paused and looked back at them. "I'm going to help The Rebellion stop Alijah. Nothing else matters. When they come for me, I'll..."

"Kill them all?" Inara assumed critically. "That isn't a plan. We don't know how many are left."

"Don't worry," Asher smiled. "My plan was to stand behind you."

Inara sighed and looked to be on the verge of a verbal assault when Asher caught a glimpse of a figure behind her. They were further down the street, barely visible on the corner of an alleyway. Hooded and robed, there was something wrong about them, just as there had been with the young assassin on the ramparts.

The ranger strode forward, parting Gideon and Inara to get a better look. Between their movement and the onlookers who had steadily filled the street, Asher lost sight of the observing figure.

"What is it?" Gideon asked, following his gaze.

Asher didn't answer right away. Instead, he continued to investigate the crowd, assessing each of them for any sign that they were more than they appeared. Back in his day, it would have been impossible to distinguish an Arakesh in a crowd such as this. But this younger generation, trained outside of Nightfall's terrifying halls, were inexperienced and headstrong.

"Asher?" Inara probed.

"It won't be long," the ranger said ominously.

"And then what?" Gideon enquired.

Asher took a breath. "It'll either be them or me. It was never going to end any other way."

CHAPTER 15

FAREWELLS

P er winter's demand, the sun remained close to the horizon
as it passed over the world. Kassian tilted his head as he
scrutinised its position in the sky. They should have left
for the south by now. They had, at best, somewhere between four
and five hours before nightfall; then the darkness and drop in
temperature would force them to camp.

Perched on a ledge, beside one of the catapults, Kassian looked
down the main road of Namdhor, where he could see that they
were almost ready to depart the north. A good number had
amassed to take the fight to the enemy and an even larger number
was gathering to say farewell to their heroes.

He didn't like to think how many of them would never see
home again.

Then again, given the scant supplies they had scavenged from
every nook and cranny, there was a good chance they wouldn't
reach The Moonlit Plains before they ate each other. With that in
mind, he made sure to enjoy every bite of his small pie.

In quiet moments such as this, he liked to imagine Clara sitting
next to him. She would playfully accuse him of eating his pie with
all the manners of a pig and praise the incredible view before them.

She would also ask him what he planned on doing when they reached The Moonlit Plains.

The answer was clear to the widower, but he couldn't bring himself to say it, even to a person who wasn't really there. Kassian was immediately frustrated by that fact. Since that night, the night his world had been shattered, he had thought of nothing but killing Alijah Galfrey. Now, after so many days and nights of hate-fuelled violence, he wasn't sure he wanted to spill the blood.

Now he was thinking of legacy.

He had nothing left but to do something he knew Clara would have been proud of. Something real. Something important. For her.

As always, he battled the images of her final moments. Malliath engulfed her in flames without a care and Alijah showed no remorse for any he slaughtered in Valatos. If he saw his face or that of the dragon, Kassian couldn't rightly say how he would react. He only knew what Clara would want him to do.

His reverie was disturbed by Aphira, whom he saw approaching up the steps. In part, he was thankful for the disruption of his inner monologue, though, for the most part, he was just happy to see Aphira. He found her accent oddly soothing and he certainly appreciated her input. During their time as Keepers in Valatos, she had only been one level below him within their ranks and he had heard often of her great potential. Since then, of course, she had saved his life a handful of times.

"You've either come to tell me there's more pie or we're finally leaving," he called out. "Anything else will sour my cheerful mood."

"The dragons are flying south," she reported. "And there's definitely no more pie."

Kassian let his head hang as he sighed into his chest. "If they're leaving we must be soon to follow surely. Have they dealt with the assassin problem?" he queried, having seen Asher and Inara returning to the keep with the body.

"Well he's still dead if that's what you mean."

Kassian silently laughed to himself. "I suppose I only have myself to blame for that sharp wit of yours."

"My wit isn't the only thing that's sharp," she replied, resting a hand on the hilt of her mage blade.

Kassian rose from his perch. "Oh yes. I have sparred with you enough times to know that, Aphira." He nodded up at the keep. "I suppose we should say our farewells."

"*That* is why I came for you," the Keeper confirmed.

Kassian raised an eyebrow. "You came to get me just to ensure I said my farewells to Inara and Gideon?"

"Can't you see your own place in all this?" Aphira questioned bluntly. "It is important that you stay within the circle that governs the realm."

Kassian frowned and licked the pastry from his thumb. "What are you talking about?"

Exasperated, Aphira held her hands out and shrugged. "Are you still so blinded by hate that you cannot see a future for our kind? I had hoped our victory here would have given you some clarity."

"Nothing feels more real than the hate," he responded on reflex.

"Now you're just lying to yourself as well as me," Aphira retorted. "You have the ear of the king. Our efforts have ensured his victory in the north. That has to matter, Kassian."

"Matter for what?"

"For us!" Aphira clipped him round the head. "For mages everywhere! We have to assume we're going to win, Kassian. And when we do, we need to make sure there is a place for people like us."

"A place?" he repeated. "You mean a place like Valatos?"

"No," she said, shaking her head. "Something *better*."

Kassian absorbed the words though he knew he would need more time to truly understand them. In the meantime, there was only one response that felt right. "You've come to the wrong person for that."

"I know," Aphira replied drily. "But there is no one else. Like I said, you have found yourself uniquely positioned. And I will only tell you this once, Kassian. You are a fine Keeper and a damn good mage. You might even be the best of us. Whether or not you think you can be the man to see such a vision through is up to you. If you cannot, well, I would appreciate a proper introduction to King Vighon."

There was a witty reply on the edge of Kassian's lips, but some part of what Aphira had said had struck a chord in him, leaving the Keeper unusually silent. Instead of delivering his sarcastic response, he nodded his appreciation and understanding before making his way to the steps. Back on the main road, he instructed Aphira to join the others by the city limits and make sure they were ready to leave. He, on the other hand, began the trek uphill.

He was pleased to see the Namdhorians steadily returning to their homes after hiding in the keep. Here and there, stragglers were saying goodbye to their wives and children before jogging down the road to meet the company. There was one particular child, however, that caught the Keeper's eye. A young girl, no more than seven years, was standing by the corner of an alley, watching the father of another family say his farewells. The scene stopped Kassian in his tracks.

He observed for a moment, scrutinising her expressions. The child certainly wasn't part of the family she was watching, though she clearly yearned to be. Judging by her appearance, Kassian had to wonder where her own family were and why they weren't caring for the young girl. Compelled as he was, he crossed the road and approached her, sure to keep his movements slow and unthreatening.

The girl saw him and immediately retreated into the shadows of the alley.

"Wait!" he called, dashing in after her.

The girl quickly disappeared but her torn boots left distinctive prints in the snow, guiding Kassian to a strewn pile of empty barrels. Sure enough, the girl was hiding behind them, but she didn't remain there for long. With a face of fury, she hurled herself from the ground and pointed something at the Keeper.

"Stay back!" she hissed.

Kassian raised his hands but his eyes narrowed at the slender object in her hand. It wasn't steel or a blade of any kind, but the girl obviously thought she was wielding something he should be afraid of.

"I mean you no harm," he said firmly. "I saw you by the road. I thought I could—"

"Help?" the girl cut in, jabbing her weapon again. "You wouldn't be the first to try and *help* me!"

Kassian didn't like to think of the wretches who had tried to take advantage of the poor girl. "I'm not..." His attention returned to the object in her hand and he realised what he was looking at. "That's my wand!" he exclaimed.

The girl's demeanour changed in an instant. "You're one of them?" She looked out on the partial devastation that marred many of Namdhor's buildings. "You're a mage."

Kassian slowly lowered his hands and shifted his coat to reveal Fin's wand on his thigh. "I am a Keeper. And that," he said, pointing to the wand in her hand, "belongs to me."

"You lie!" she spat instinctively. "You have one right there!"

"This belonged to a good friend of mine." Kassian carefully withdrew the wand and displayed it handle-first. "He died fighting for this city." He crouched down to her height and nodded at the wand in her hand. "Where did you find mine?"

The girl seemed to be considering the threat he posed. Judging by her posture, she was relaxing somewhat. "It was poking out of the snow, two blocks up from here."

Kassian thought back to the moment he had lost the wand, when the cart he was hiding in exploded. "That seems about right." He sized the girl up for a moment, unsure how to proceed. "What's your name?"

"What's *your* name, Keeper?" the girl retorted.

Kassian smiled, despite the sigh he resisted. "I am Kassian Kantaris."

The girl twisted her mouth. "I am Clayda," she finally said.

"Clayda," Kassian repeated. "A strong name. How long have you been living on the streets of Namdhor, Clayda?"

The girl brandished the wand again. "Long enough to know that this will make me a queen in these parts."

"A queen?" the Keeper echoed with some amusement. Then, as he dwelled on the implications of her statement, his expression turned serious. "Have you used this, Clayda?"

"Maybe."

Kassian looked from the wand tip to Clayda's wild blue eyes. Knowledge of the ancient language was required to perform spells, but the Keeper knew well that children with a connection to the realm of magic possessed a raw power that, if aided by Demetrium, could conjure a spell or two given the right conditions.

"You look hungry, Clayda," he said, changing the subject. "Would you like to accompany me back to the keep? I can get you food there. New clothes perhaps. I'm sure there would be someone who could—"

"I'm doing just fine on my own," Clayda asserted. "With those smelly black knights gone I've finally got this place to myself again."

Kassian resisted the urge to simply pick the child up and take her to the keep. "Then I shall take my leave," he announced, rising to his full stature. "And I would take my wand with me."

Clayda took a step back and held the wand in both hands. "I found it. It's mine now."

The Keeper bit his lip, wondering how he had ended up in this alley. "I'll tell you what," he began. "I will give you this wand if you give me that one."

Clayda frowned. "Why would I want that one?"

"I can see that you know a lot about wands."

"I do!" she boasted.

"So you know that they are always far more powerful in the hands of the one who made them. You see, the Demetrium in their core attunes to the magic of their wielder over time."

"I knew that!" the girl clarified.

"Good. So then you also know that wand has spent too many years by my side to harmonise with the magic of any other. But this wand," he continued, holding Fin's in the air. "This wand has no master. If it were to be wielded by one as brave as my friend, however, it could make a fine mage out of them."

Clayda stared at Fin's wand, her imagination set alight. Without a word, she snatched it from Kassian's hand and thrust his own back at him. The Keeper relished in the feel of his own wand again. Its weight, grip, and size were perfect, made to his exact specifications.

He looked back down at Clayda. "Magic is a gift," he told her. "It should never be used to hurt people, only protect them; including yourself if you must. One day you're going to have questions about all this. When that day comes, go to the keep and tell them you wish to speak with Kassian Kantaris. Wherever I am in the realm, they will find me and I will return here to answer all your questions."

Clayda continued to look up at him for a moment, but her youthful features concealed her thoughts. Then, without warning, she turned on her heel and ran until she disappeared. Kassian's mind was faced by the guilt of withholding the wand from Fin's final resting place, but the young mage would never have wanted his wand to rot in the ground had he the choice. And he definitely would have liked Clayda and her fiery soul.

His wand returned to its rightful place on his thigh, Kassian backed out of the alley before turning to continue his journey up the slope.

Inara tied the last knot around one of Athis's spinal horns, securing their sack of supplies for the journey. Dropping back down to the snow, she watched her parents bid Gideon farewell. The three of them had so much history - it wasn't fair that they were reunited for a day before duty pulled them apart again. She would have continued to watch them, waiting for her mother to squeeze Gideon in one of her crushing hugs, but Vighon crossed her line of sight.

The king was about to approach when Nathaniel brought him into their conversation with Gideon. He flashed Inara an apologetic look before replying.

He makes you happy, Athis acknowledged.

Inara felt instantly awkward and she hated it. **You know it isn't him or you - I don't need to choose. There are just...**

Two halves to you now, Athis said. *I know this. The same is happening within me, though not so keenly. I know you continue to battle your emotions and there are limits to what I can help your human side with.*

So you're not... jealous?

The dragon chuckled in her mind but made no physical sign of amusement. *I am Athis the ironheart! I know who I am and I do not get jealous. But I will not lie to you; the thought of you sharing things with another instead of me does dampen my spirit. But it will never overcome the joy I feel for you. Love is an exceptional power in this world, one that can keep us standing when all else abandons us. I am glad you have found this in Vighon. He is a good man.*

Inara caressed the hard scales along Athis's jaw line. **I have love for you both, just as I feel love from you both.**

And it will never fade, wingless one.

Inara shared in the warmth that swelled in Athis's heart. She couldn't rightly say what path she would have taken had the dragon rejected Vighon as a suitable mate or expressed real hate at the idea of sharing her emotionally with another person.

A playful squawk turned Inara to her feet, where Avandriell skipped across the ground and bounded up the side of Athis. There was an immediate change in the red dragon as he took great pleasure in the hatchling. From his memories, Inara knew it had been decades since he had enjoyed the company of one so young.

As one always accompanied the other, Inara turned around to see Asher approaching her. Considering he had recently chased an Arakesh over the roof tops, pursued him through the streets, and fought hand-to-hand with the killer, the ranger looked strong, taller even. The same had been said about her, she knew, after bonding with Athis.

"She doesn't want you to go," the ranger said.

Inara smiled. "It's strange, isn't it, interpreting the emotions of another being?"

"It will take some getting used to," Asher admitted.

"It will be easier when you can communicate directly," the Guardian assured. "How do you feel?" she asked, glancing at the cuts on his knuckles.

The ranger clenched one of his fists. "Better than I should," he replied lightly. "A chase like that should have left me with sore knees and an angry back."

"Avandriell will make you stronger and faster, *but*," she added with a light-hearted laugh, "she will do nothing for your humility. Dragons are *proud*."

"I can live with that," Asher replied, his tone refreshingly contented.

"Have you disposed of the body?" Inara questioned.

"I've had the soldiers place it in the dungeons for now."

Inara took a second to cast her eyes over Vighon, who was still talking to her parents and Gideon. "Is it still customary to retrieve the bodies of any fallen Arakesh?"

"It was in my day," the ranger answered. "Lady Gracen and now Veda Malmagol are doing things their own way."

"And here I was," Kassian Kantaris announced from the road, "fearing that you had given up on killing assassins!" The Keeper patted Asher twice on the arm. "Good work! That's one less killer on the streets."

"Kassian," Inara greeted with a nod.

"Inara," he responded, bowing his head. "I would ask that you leave *some* Reavers for the rest of us."

"You cannot ask a dragon to hold back their wrath," she quipped.

"*Indeed*," the mage said with an amused grin.

Inara followed his gaze to Avandriell and Athis who, absent any hint of wrath, were clearly playing some kind of game on the larger dragon's head.

"I can't believe you have a dragon," Kassian said, directing his words to the ranger. "*I* want a dragon. Perhaps you should take me to Erador next time."

"I'm not sure you could stomach the rejection," Inara was quick to say, displaying her own grin of amusement.

"Safe journey," Asher interjected, ending their banter. "Make sure you both rest before entering the battle."

"We will," Inara said seriously, before embracing the ranger. "You just keep Avandriell safe. We'll see you in The Moonlit Plains."

Parting from Asher, Inara looked to the Keeper but he was already walking away. He disturbed the conversation between her parents and Gideon, giving Vighon a chance to step back and slip away. He offered a reassurance of some kind to Kassian in passing. Then he made directly for Inara, who led him around Athis for cover.

The king immediately pulled her in for a passionate kiss which, for a brief moment, Inara enjoyed. "Careful," she cautioned, pushing him back a few inches.

"I have waited too long to kiss you again," he expressed eagerly.

"You kissed me this very day," she instructed, struggling to hold back her smile.

"I have a lot of days to make up for," Vighon said enthusiastically. "And I'm getting tired of the world ending - it always seems to come between us."

"It certainly does," she agreed with a kiss. "But we need to be careful. You're the king of Illian, I'm the..." Inara wanted to say she was the Guardian of the Realm, but it was a title she had always felt was too burdening for just one person. It also sounded pretentious when said out loud.

"For years I was harassed to find a wife, a queen for Illian. There are none I would rule beside for there are none stronger or wiser than you, Inara Galfrey. Damn being careful." The northman leaned in again and they embraced with all their love for the other.

Inara allowed herself a few more seconds to take pleasure in it. Besides the fact that they were being split up again, there to face peril and possible death, she simply enjoyed the very human emotions that came with kissing the man she had loved for so long. She wondered how many other human things she had missed without realising it.

"Inara?" came her mother's voice.

They parted from their embrace but Reyna was already in view of them. Her mother made to speak, seeing them together as they were, but made not a sound. Instead, she corrected her expression of surprise and offered a quiet apology before wandering back towards the keep.

Both Vighon and Inara fell into each other, sharing a laugh that spoke of their amusement and awkwardness. "I'm going to have to deal with that," she reasoned.

"I would keep you to myself a moment longer," the king whispered.

Inara looked into his brown eyes, his concern evident. "We *will* see each other again," she promised. "We haven't come this far to be torn apart at the end."

Vighon gently placed his head against hers. "Fight hard. Come back to me."

"By the time you reach the battlefield," Inara replied, "I will be standing victoriously wondering what took you so long."

Vighon stared into her eyes for a long moment. "Let Gideon face Alijah."

Inara arched her back to better see the king. "What are you talking about?"

"I have no doubt that you could best him," Vighon explained, "but I do not want you to have to live with it."

The Guardian placed a hand against his cheek. "I will do what I must. Even if that means killing Alijah." Inara was momentarily surprised by her own tone; speaking so matter-of-factly. But she also knew it was the only way she could slay her brother.

Vighon could do naught but nod his understanding and kiss her again. "Then I will see you soon."

Inara squeezed him in her arms before making to move away. A hand each remained clasped until the last possible second.

Rounding Athis, Gideon was now talking to Asher while her mother clearly informed her father of what she had just seen. Inara took a breath and decided to get it over with.

"Have you said your farewells to the king?" Reyna enquired innocently.

Inara blinked slowly and flashed her teeth with a bemused smile. "Our exchange was long overdue," she said cryptically.

"I'll say," Nathaniel muttered before Reyna tapped his stomach.

"I always imagined this for you, when you were younger," her mother began. "My heart swells to see that such a future is still within your grasp. You deserve some happiness."

"I think happiness is a long way from here," Inara said dryly. "We all have quite the journey ahead of us."

Nathaniel broke away from Reyna and wrapped his arms around his daughter. "I hate having a hero for a daughter," he groaned. The old knight kissed her on the head. "Be as safe as you can. Don't do anything I wouldn't do."

"And don't do anything he *would* do," Reyna added with a smirk.

Inara was about to make her promises, empty as they would be, when her mother enveloped her in a firm hug. In truth, they were Inara's favourite and she took joy in the embrace.

"Inara," Gideon called. "We should be leaving."

"As should we," Kassian made known.

Tearing herself away from so many that she cared about, Inara ascended Athis's back as Gideon mounted Ilargo. They waited for Avandriell to find her way back to Asher before turning to face away from the keep. There was only just enough room for both dragons to safely manoeuvre without damaging anything.

Since Ilargo had already disposed of Karsak's ravaged corpse, the way was clear, offering them a view of the south. Their destination lay well beyond sight.

We will make it in time, Athis imparted confidently. *Magic will endure.*

The consequences, should they fail, made Inara feel sick to her stomach. ***Then fly swiftly, old friend.***

With a lasting look at Vighon, Inara braced herself against Athis's scales. Both dragons, one in front of the other, flapped their wings and battered the city with strong winds. Within seconds they were clearing Namdhor altogether and ascending into the heavens as The Rebellion's vanguard.

Now for the south. Now for war.

PART TWO

CHAPTER 16
A NIGHT ON THE PLAINS

Under a starry night sky, Galanör casually weaved through the camp, his movements appearing effortless, as he offered friendly nods and smiles to both dwarves and elves. For those among his kin who looked in need of courage, where the imminent battle was concerned, he took the time to speak with them. Most had lived in Ilythyra, under Lady Ellöria's leadership, and had shunned violence where they could.

Alijah had seen to the end of those days.

Where the elves were quiet, contemplating what tomorrow would bring, the dwarves were redefining the height of merriment for the ranger. Whatever their clan or history, the children of the mountain gathered around roaring fires and shared old mead and fresh hunts from the plains. They cheered and hollered, banging their shields and armour with abandon as they told stories from wars past.

Their laughter was infectious and tempted Galanör to join them. More than a few even invited him with an offer of food and drink. The elf always politely declined, more than happy to drift through and soak up the atmosphere. He had charged into several battles in his lifetime, but never had he seen such revelry before dancing with death. Elven as he was, Galanör preferred the quiet before the storm so that he might centre himself and focus.

It was his craving for such peace that cast his eyes out to the plains, searching for a quiet spot. Under a cold moon, the enchanted fields were luminescent and dotted with black silhouettes where the trees stood proud. There was one figure, easily seen as she moved towards the nearest trunk, that caught Galanör's eye. He knew Aenwyn even in the dark.

After receiving a pat on the arm from a fellow elf, the ranger broke away from the sprawling camp and made for Aenwyn. Sitting cross-legged, her face was illuminated by the glowing grass. Her quiver was on the ground beside her, the arrows spilling out. With barely a sound, Galanör took to the ground in front of her and enjoyed the feel of the supernaturally warm grass. Rather than speak, he watched her carve glyphs into every arrow head.

For a moment, he thought they were magical in nature, lending every projectile a deadly enhancement. He was about to offer caution, aware that using a degree of magic with every arrow was dangerous while simultaneously exerting physical energy on a battlefield. But then he glimpsed the individual characters.

They were names.

Galanör couldn't even count the number of arrows. "Have we lost so many?" he muttered.

"I don't have enough arrows for them all," Aenwyn lamented.

Galanör scrutinised her stoical expression and knew there was more she wasn't saying. "I know we—"

"Your name could have been on one of these," Aenwyn interjected, her eyes flashing in the green light.

Galanör held in his sigh, her anger more than justified. In fact, he had wondered when this particular conversation was going to happen. Aenwyn had clearly been showing a great deal of restraint while nursing him back to health.

"I'm sorry," he said, with as much sincerity as he could intone.

"For what?" Aenwyn countered. "For lying to me? Lying to everyone? Challenging Alijah by yourself? Getting caught in a spell that could have killed you?"

"Gideon has assured me the spell will have no harmful side effects," he quickly pointed out.

"You didn't know that!" Aenwyn argued. "You went into that tower to die, if that's what it took."

"Isn't that why we're *all* here?" the ranger questioned. "To die for The Rebellion? For the realm?"

"If that is what victory demands of us then we will see it through together. Those were your words the first day we set foot on Qamnaran. And then you left me."

Galanör deliberately slowed his breathing down in an effort to hold back any tears. "I'm so sorry," he repeated.

"That's all we have left now," Aenwyn continued, her shoulders sagging. "Dying together is the best we can hope for."

It broke Galanör's heart to think that that was their only future. "It cannot be," he pleaded. "I have only just found you." He closed the gap between them, a movement that Aenwyn acquiesced to. "I acted without thought," he admitted. "I told myself I would be saving you if I killed him."

"I have warned you, Ranger, about trying to save me," she replied, brandishing an arrow head in his face.

Galanör held his hands up. "I know. I allowed Alijah to get in my head. Tomorrow, you and I will be shoulder to shoulder when we meet his Reavers. But, I promise you, it will not be our end. There will be another sunrise for us."

"And after that?" Aenwyn enquired incredulously.

Galanör gave her his most confident smile. "An eternity of sunrises."

Aenwyn rolled her eyes. "Perhaps that spell does have some side effects after all," she remarked, touching the arrow to her head. "Was it an injury that saw you pledge yourself to Queen Reyna?" The question sounded innocent enough, but Galanör could hear deep curiosity in her voice. "Or was it guilt alone?" she added.

The elven ranger twisted his lips, aware that this too was a conversation he could not have avoided. "I went into that tower alone and unprepared. Had I not, Adilandra would still be alive."

Aenwyn put her arrow down. "You cannot know such things, Galanör. It was a battle and a fierce one at that."

Galanör raised his hand to halt any further protest. "Directly or indirectly, my actions led to her death and Reyna's ascension to queen - a position she must surely resent. Whatever I have to give in service to the realm, it will be at Queen Reyna's behest."

"That's quite the commitment for a ranger," Aenwyn commented, probingly. "The Galfreys will be expected to return to Ayda after the war. If you are to be in service to them, you will have to follow them across The Adean."

"*We* would have to follow them," Galanör corrected. "You are already in service."

Aenwyn leaned in to him. "You would make a new life for us? In Ayda?"

Galanör looked out at the land, at Illian. He had made it his home, however nomadic he had chosen to live. And he had come to love it, in his own way. He had even found a great fondness for the humans that inhabited it; a species he had once vowed to destroy. Then he turned back to look in Aenwyn's eyes, dark orbs that pulled him in.

"My home is wherever you are," he said softly. "If serving the king and queen offers us a roof over our heads... all the better."

Aenwyn gave him a contented smile and pressed the side of her head into his chest.

"I *am* sorry," he reiterated softly. "I should never have lied. And I should never have left you."

"And?" Aenwyn demanded, pulling away from him.

Galanör gave her last question a moment's thought before the answer dawned on him. "And I should have worn the cuirass."

Aenwyn was nodding along. "It took *some* magic to heal those wounds on your chest."

"If it were here I would wear it—"

"It's back at the tent," she inserted with half a smile.

Galanör let the rest of his sentence fall away. "Good," he said simply. "Then I will wear it tomorrow."

"Then you are soon to be forgiven," she replied, coyly.

"Soon?" Galanör raised an immaculate eyebrow.

"Don't worry, by sunrise you will have made it up to me."

A broad grin slowly spread across the ranger's face and he leaned in to kiss her. There was, indeed, a difference in her. It only added to his guilt for the grave concern he had put her through. Never again, he promised himself.

Resting back against the tree now, Galanör noticed Aenwyn's smile fade away as she regarded the arrow in her hand. Adilandra's name was engraved into the head.

"A great light has been extinguished from the world," she spoke softly, "now to light the heavens instead."

Galanör regarded the stars with dismay. "There is nothing up there so bright as Adilandra Sevari," he reasoned. "I would say she was welcomed by the sun itself."

Aenwyn added the arrow to the pile and picked up another. "Have you spoken to Faylen?"

The ranger scanned what he could see of the camp. He discovered Faylen's makeshift tent notably distant from the cluster. She was sitting outside, alone, staring into the flames of her fire.

"I have tried," he answered. "Outside of strategy, she does not wish to speak to anyone. Telling Reyna her mother had died must have been hard, *especially* when you're the High Guardian. But she also had to break it to her that she is our new queen."

"I cannot imagine the responsibility Reyna feels now," Aenwyn sympathised.

"Reyna can handle it," Galanör said with easy confidence. "I'm more concerned for how Faylen takes it all. She was close to Adilandra for centuries."

"Perhaps speaking to Reyna will make her feel better," Aenwyn posed.

The elven ranger sighed. "Reyna is days away from the plains. There's a lot to overcome before they meet again."

Movement crossed the edge of Galanör's vision and he turned to see Russell Maybury walking away from Doran's personal camp. The old wolf cloaked himself and disappeared into the night.

"I see conflict in you," Aenwyn commented, having turned to see what had drawn Galanör's attention.

"Conflict?"

"You fear the wolf that lurks behind his eyes." Aenwyn's words cut right to the heart of it.

"His condition worsens; that much is clear to see. But the full moon is upon us soon."

There was a pause from Aenwyn before she asked, "Do you know how to slay a Werewolf?"

Galanör didn't answer right away. He heard the question but to his mind it wasn't a Werewolf he would be slaying - it was a good friend. Still, he knew where her curiosity came from and it wasn't from a desire to kill Russell. She only wished to protect them all.

"The humans would have you believe you can only kill one with silver," he finally explained. "As usual, their legends are skewed. Werewolves are flesh and blood like any creature. You just need the courage and strength to bring one down. And preferably a big axe," he added.

His own words stayed with him for a time. He already knew someone with a big axe and no end of courage and strength. It was just too heartbreaking to consider.

Aenwyn was waiting for his eyes to find hers. "Go," she advised. "You know where to find me. But don't keep me waiting too long," she added. "My forgiveness has its limits, Ranger."

Galanör planted one final kiss on her lips before crossing to the tents once more. By the edge of the camp, there was nothing between him and Doran Heavybelly. The War Mason was accompanied by Thaligg and Thraal, his trusted generals. Galanör entered the light of their fire and looked directly at Doran, who carefully assessed the elf standing before him.

"Give us a minute, lads," he commanded, sending the brothers away.

Galanör nodded his appreciation and assumed the log they had been using. He picked up the wine skin at the end and sniffed the contents. That was enough to put him off ingesting a single drop.

Doran chuckled. "Thraal's home brew. It's not got the kick me own does but it'll get ye there."

"I can't believe you can drink that stuff and still walk," Galanör groaned.

"There's no ale out there that can stop me from walkin'... though there is a *quantity*," he added with a shrug.

Galanör found an easy laugh and he enjoyed it. "How are the clans holding up?" he finally asked, stalling the inevitable.

Doran held out his tankard towards the camp. "The answer lies before ye, good elf. Since I know ye're not blind, say what ye've really come to say an' unburden yerself."

The elf looked out at the camp, though he failed to see Russell anywhere.

"He's taken 'imself away," Doran interpreted. "He doesn' trust 'imself at night. He says the wolf never sleeps."

"And he is right," Galanör agreed. "The curse is consuming him. The wolf within is waiting for its moment to emerge. It's waiting for Russell to give in and—"

"Ye think I don' know that?" Doran spat. "For years I've watched as that monster eats me friend from the inside out. An' ye're daft if ye think he doesn' know it as well."

"He's a good man," Galanör asserted, hoping to calm the dwarf. "And he's a damn good fighter." The ranger let his words hang while he ordered his thoughts.

"Jus' say it, lad," Doran insisted.

"Tomorrow we fight," Galanör began. "The scouts have already reported a great number of Reavers guarding the dig site. There's a good chance we'll be fighting for days, Doran. *Days*," he repeated.

"Then it's a good thing we're all dwarves an' elves," the War Mason replied. "There's no human in the realm that could fight for so long."

"That wasn't what I was getting at," Galanör said.

Quite exasperated, Doran waved his words away. "I know exactly what ye're gettin' at."

"Then you know I am referring to the full moon two days from now," the elf continued. "You must know what will happen if he transforms during the battle. We'll be exhausted if we're still alive. And then what? A Werewolf to contend with? The monster won't choose sides; it'll just kill anything in sight."

Doran threw his tankard into the fire and sent sparks and rogue flames into the air. "He's fightin' with us, ye hear! I don' know how many more moons he's got in 'im, but if Russell Maybury is leavin' this world ye can bet he's doin' it with a bloody big pile o' monsters under his feet!"

Galanör spared a glance at the onlookers who'd witnessed the son of Dorain's outburst. "I know the two of you have a lot of history, but you're not thinking about Russell. If he transforms and kills even *one* of us he won't be able to live with himself."

Doran's frown creased all the more. "I won' let that happen," he declared earnestly, his tone lowered to that of a grave intensity.

"You can't take responsibility for him, Doran. You've seen more battlefields than I have. How many times has it gone sideways? How many times have you felt in control? The plains are sprawling, as will be the battle. You could be half a mile away from him when he turns."

The dwarf set Galanör in his gaze, his dark eye reflecting the flames. "In all the time ye've known me, elf, 'ave ye ever known me to say one thing an' do another?"

Galanör didn't need to mull it over. "No," he said, for there was no other answer.

"I won' let it happen," he repeated, only slower this time.

The elven ranger briefly closed his eyes and nodded solemnly. "I do not envy the task ahead of you. You have but to ask, Doran, and I would help."

The dwarf's chest puffed out as he took a long breath. "I would not ask another. The real burden has been Rus's. If... *when* the time comes, I will relieve 'im o' it."

Galanör had more to say on the matter, but he could see that he had pushed Doran as far as the dwarf could go. Instead, he promised himself that he too would keep an eye on Russell during the battle. If it came to it, he would end Russell's suffering himself.

"I wouldn' spend too much time worryin' about it, lad," Doran offered, his tone perking up. "The chances o' us still breathin' come the full moon are damned slim. We'll all be dinin' in Grarfath's Hall together before that monster rears its ugly head."

"Speak for yourself, dwarf," Galanör replied with a cocky grin. "I haven't faced Darkakin and orcs to be brought down by the wretched corpse of some Reaver."

Doran laughed deep in his chest. "O' course not! Ye're Galanör Reveeri, greatest sword dandy in all the realm!"

Now Galanör shared his laugh. "You know of my reputation then!"

As the evening stretched on, the elf finally picked up a drink, having chosen something less potent than Thraal's home brew, and poured Doran another cup. They put the horrible matter of Russell's curse behind them for now and enjoyed each other's company, just as they had before the war, and the war before this one. Neither had ever thought they would live to call a dwarf or an elf their friend, but that's what they were, *friends*.

Galanör would have loved to have taken some of the burden from Doran's shoulders and even counselled him on the dire situation surrounding his brother. But, in some ways, the dwarf was right - they might not live long enough to be troubled by such things. The battle they were heading into could easily be their last. Their numbers, after all, wouldn't begin to be bolstered for at least a day and a night of fighting.

With that in mind, Galanör let his focus wander for a time. He reminisced with Doran and the pair swapped stories of old contracts that involved the most terrible of fiends. It wasn't lost on either of them that many of their tales ended with a drink and a hot meal in The Pick-Axe.

"So Aenwyn's not murdered ye yet then?" Doran slurred.

Having only sipped his own drink, Galanör's response retained its clarity. "Her arrows could still find me from afar."

The son of Dorain chortled. "She swore all manner o' oaths to kill ye should ye ever wake."

Galanör gave a light shrug. "No more than I deserve."

"Ye came closer than the rest o' us to endin' this damned war,"

Doran praised. "Though ye went abou' it with all the finesse o' a bag o' hammers!"

"A fair assessment," Galanör agreed.

Doran took another swig of his drink, though most of it appeared to make its way down his beard. "An' now yer magic's yer own! Not bad! Better than bein' tied to some tree I suppose."

Galanör had spent some time trying to wrap his mind around Inara's revelation. The realm of magic had long been a highly regarded theory among his people, but actually knowing the source of all magic came from a mountainous tree, in a dimension that sat directly on top of Verda, left the elf bewildered.

"I feel no different. And it will make no difference. We will stop Alijah from destroying the tree and magic *will* continue to flow as it ever has."

"I like yer conviction, lad." Doran raised his cup to the notion.

Galanör was on the verge of responding when he noticed a buzz of activity along the edge of the camp. He shielded his eyes from the fire and sharpened his gaze to make sense of the hubbub. Dwarves and elves alike were rising from their places of rest and arming themselves, their attention turned to the east.

"Doran," the ranger warned, abandoning his drink.

"What are ye abou'?"

Galanör ignored the question when he saw Faylen striding past. Unlike many others, the High Guardian kept her scimitar in its scabbard, though her hand noticeably rested on the hilt.

"What is it?" Galanör called.

Faylen didn't halt as she replied, "We are not alone."

The elven ranger stepped out of Doran's personal camp, navigating his tent, and looked out into the dark. There, standing tall on a shallow rise, were a team of Centaurs. While the silhouettes of some blocked out the stars beyond, there were several standing in the light of torches held in their hands.

Galanör turned back to Doran. "Centaurs!"

The son of Dorain spat his current mouthful of ale, spraying the air with a wet fog. "Centaurs?" he echoed.

The dwarf heaved himself up from his log with a dazed expression as he searched the ground. When, at last, he found the bowl of water, he tipped the contents onto his face and shook his wild beard. He elicited a feral growl as he tried to take command of his dulled senses.

"I'm right behind ye," he promised, taking in hand the axe half of Andaljor.

Galanör left the inebriated dwarf behind and jogged to catch up with Faylen. As he arrived at her side, so too did Aenwyn, her bow slung over her back.

"What do you think they want?" Aenwyn pondered with just a hint of concern in her voice.

"I have no idea," Galanör admitted. "From what I know of them, they do not require fire to see in the dark."

"Then they are announcing themselves," Aenwyn concluded.

"Most likely," the ranger replied, "though I have no experience with their kind."

"I do," Faylen informed. The High Guardian half turned and gestured at the armed contingent to hold back. Only Doran continued, though his was not quite a straight line.

Approaching the Centaurs, Galanör began to realise there were a lot more than he had first believed. After counting two dozen, and rising up the hill to meet them, the ranger discovered scores more of them on the other side and decided to stop counting.

They came to a halt not far from the Centaurs. Galanör had used their last few steps to scrutinise the wild folk of the plains. Everything below the navel was that of a horse, well-muscled and strong. Everything above was the perfect combination of man and elf with, perhaps, a little bit of dwarf thrown in. They all possessed long matted hair that reached down the length of their human backs. The males looked down at them with braided beards and bushy eyebrows while the females of their species displayed their chiselled jaws and high cheek bones.

All appeared quite fierce. The armour they wore was clearly stolen for Galanör recognised pieces of iron and pads of leather from various groups, including the Reavers. It was worn sparingly, however, allowing the Centaurs to present their tribal tattoos; thick lines of varying colours.

In their hands, and slung over their backs, they wielded spears, bows, and axes, all of which were too big for any man or elf to master.

A dark male Centaur, situated in the very centre of their line, stepped forward and bowed his head. "El'shenae," he said respectfully in his native language. "I am Kelabor," he greeted in his deep voice in the common language.

Faylen bowed her head. "I am Faylen, High Guardian of Elandril. This is Galanör and Aenwyn," she added, drawing a bow from them both. "I am known to Xastus and his tribe."

Kelabor's face remained firm. "I am afraid Xastus fell to the orc invasion, sixteen cycles ago. Though it will please you to know that many of his tribe survived."

"I am sorry to hear that," Faylen replied thoughtfully. "Xastus was most welcoming to me and my companions."

Kelabor looked beyond the trio, clearly done with any talk of Xastus. "I did not think I would ever see El'shenae and stone dwellers together."

"I'm afraid allies are few and far between in these dark times," the High Guardian explained. "Thankfully, our people have a better history of fighting together than we have of fighting each other."

"Your enemy is worthy of such an alliance," Kelabor noted. "That black scourge has blanketed our lands. They attack us day and night without cause and without mercy."

"The Reavers," Faylen nodded. "They have a stronghold north of here."

"They guard it fiercely," Kelabor warned. "They forced out every tribe for miles in every direction."

"I apologise for our presence here," Faylen continued. "We would respect your lands in better times, but we are here to attack that stronghold and free The Moonlit Plains."

Kelabor scanned the distant camp. "There will be much blood on the ground." The Centaur puffed out the slab-like muscles in his chest. "We would spill our own blood for these lands. There are none among the tribes who would see others die for it. It would be our honour to accompany you into battle."

Galanör's broad smile was a reflex of the hope that sparked in his heart.

"The honour would be ours," Faylen replied. "You have our gratitude, Kelabor. Your numbers and strength will go a long way to helping us turn the tide."

Kelabor gestured to the Centaurs behind him. "These are but a few of my people. There are more across the plains waiting for my word. We will send messengers to the other tribes and they will join us."

Galanör's grin widened and then faltered as Doran finally caught them up. "What did I miss?" he panted.

The elven ranger half turned. "Kelabor, this is Doran son of Dorain, War Mason to Clan Heavybelly and a renowned ranger in these wilds."

Doran looked up at the Centaur and belched.

Kelabor looked less than impressed. "Stone dwellers," he muttered.

"Doran," Galanör continued, "the Centaurs have chosen to fight with us."

Surprise stretched the dwarf's dazed and haggard features. "Oh," he said pleasantly. "Would ye care for a drink?"

CHAPTER 17

A ROGUE MEMORY

All too vivid were the dreams that haunted Alijah Galfrey. He was pleased to finally open his eyes to that first glimmer of dawn. It was quiet in his chamber, the finest suite in Lirian's palace, and a stark contrast to the screams and clashing steel trapped inside his mind.

He wasn't even sure if they were his memories or Malliath's.

Soaked in sweat, the half-elf rose from the bed, curious as to why he had been asleep in it at all. The king had intended to meditate until first light, preparing himself to complete his task. His need for rest too great, he had clearly fallen asleep and in his scale mail at that.

Disappointed in himself, Alijah looked across the chamber and out of the oriel window. He couldn't see his companion out there, but he could sense his presence somewhere inside the palace grounds. The lightest of probes, across their bond, informed Alijah that Malliath was still sleeping. While he had fallen into The Hox, his companion had dived into it at some speed; it was no surprise they both needed rest.

Acknowledging the dragon's need to sleep, Alijah left him to it and tested the strength in his leg. There was still pain. He made for the window, dismayed to see that it still affected his walk a little. The pain in his back and shoulders was healing at a better rate, but it still made him doubt his ability to swing his sword with any accuracy or strength.

He cursed his grandmother.

Had they both faced the events on Qamnaran better, they could have torn right through Athis and Ilargo and taken Namdhor back in an afternoon. He could have faced Gideon and Inara and proven himself the better warrior, a fact that Gideon should know by now. And it would have been so satisfying to put Asher down for good. How many assassins had tried and failed over the decades? How many Darkakin and orcs? Perhaps he was the only one capable of killing the ranger. He would have the answer soon, he was sure.

Peering out of the window, he could see the palace servants going about their earliest jobs. Lord Starg was likely still panicking after Malliath had dropped unannounced into the courtyard last night.

Clipping his sword and scabbard to his belt, Alijah left his chamber and was immediately met by a dozen servants. For just a moment, he was taken back to his years in Erador where his reign had been more readily accepted. He took the offered food and water but consumed both while making his way to the grand balcony that looked out over Lirian. From there, he could now see Malliath, curled up below. In front of the dragon's maw was the remains of a horse, though it required some scrutiny to be identified as such.

Lirian itself was already a buzz of activity. Smoke rose from numerous chimneys, carts were driven up and down the streets, and even the market traders had already begun selling their wares. It never failed to surprise Alijah how the world kept turning when so much of it was on fire. For two years, Illian had been ravaged by The Rebellion's efforts to overthrow the peace yet here it was, going about its day as if it were any other. He commended them for that.

"Your Grace!" came Lord Starg's high born voice.

Alijah didn't turn to greet the man, content to observe his

people for a time. "This is why I am here," he proclaimed, confusing the lord. "Look out there, to the people. Their lives are all that matter. Their peace. This is why I will fight to my dying breath, Lord Starg."

The steward of Felgarn looked from the city to the king. "Indeed, your Grace!" he agreed with all the enthusiasm of a man who had no idea about what was really being spoken.

Deciding his thoughts were too involved for the lord to grasp, Alijah turned to a simpler subject. "Forgive my late arrival, Lord Starg," he began. "Our journey is long and rest was required. You have my thanks for the hospitality and the fine room."

"Lirian flies the banner of the dragon, your Grace," Starg blurted, bowing his head. "This will always be your city before it is mine or any of my successors."

"Successors..." Alijah muttered. "How have you found your appointment in Lady Gracen's stead?" he asked.

"I speak on behalf of all house Hamish when I say we are humbled by your confidence in us to steward the region, your Grace. I have lived in Lirian all my life. There is no better place," he added with a beaming smile.

"I too am very fond of the city," Alijah said earnestly. "That's why I was so disappointed to hear of rebel activity, right here in Lirian."

The smile fell from Lord Starg's face. "Rebel activity, your Grace? Oh yes, the *rebels*. There were multiple eyewitnesses who reported seeing..." The steward hesitated, licking his lips with uncertainty.

"I read the report," Alijah said, putting the man out of his misery. "I am aware that my father has been moving from city to city over the last two years in a bid to recruit more to their pathetic cause. It's just a pity you didn't capture him. Though I am interested in the subsequent arrests you made after his disappearance."

"Arrests, your Grace?"

Alijah looked round at the lord. "Those my father spoke to," he specified. "The men and women who are sympathetic to The Rebellion. I'm sure you arrested at least a few of them."

Lord Starg's body language shifted and not subtly. Alijah knew fear when he saw it.

"There were no arrests, your Grace," he confessed. "Many of the watch were replaced by the knights from Erador, none of which... take orders from me. I commanded the few I can to search the rebels out but they found no leads to pursue."

Alijah looked out at the city once more, his focus directed east of Lirian's heart, where one familiar building resided. His thoughts remained there for a while, distracting him.

"Your Grace?" Lord Starg enquired.

"My apologies for removing so many of my knights of late," Alijah managed, his mind elsewhere. "I have need of them on the plains - that is where my journey ends. You have my word they will return to keep the peace."

Without further instruction, the king walked away from the steward of Felgarn and made for the grand staircase that would take him down to the courtyard and the palace's main gates.

"I do hope that wasn't your horse, Lord Starg," Alijah remarked, gesturing to the carcass in front of Malliath.

Lord Starg hesitated, undoubtedly upset by the scene. "No, your Grace," he said, watching the king accept another horse from one of the stable hands. "It was my daughter's."

Alijah wasn't about to apologise for the dragon. "You're welcome to take it up with Malliath when he wakes," he replied with half a smile.

Lord Starg held up his hands. "There's no need, your Grace!" he fretted. "My daughter's a terrible rider. Better suited to carriages! Your Grace, perhaps you would like an escort into the city? I have good men who could accompany you."

Alijah gritted his teeth through the pain as he swung his leg over the saddle. "I require no such escort, Lord Starg. I do not fear my own people." With his last word, the king guided the horse through the main gates. From there, the road sloped down and round to the city below.

The king was acutely aware of the pain that plagued his ride. Thankfully, the streets of Lirian offered him some distraction. He could also feel the presence of his Reavers. They were few, having sent most of them to reinforce the dig site and protect the doorway. Alijah ordered them to keep to their patrols with their Seekers on their leashes. He wouldn't need them this day. Here and there, however, he did discover some of the city's watch and he was pleased to see them attired in his colours and sigil.

And, of course, they bowed. They *all* bowed; every man, woman, and child. Though, in truth, they likely had no idea who he was. His armour, cloak, and sword declared his status, but his exact title was probably a mystery to most. They knew Alijah Galfrey was their king, but how many had actually seen his face? Without Malliath behind him he was just another man of power and wealth. Still, they knew enough to bow in his presence.

When they had succeeded in destroying magic and brought peace and balance to the realm, Alijah told himself that they would visit every town and city. He wanted to meet his people and them to meet him. Then he would return to Erador and do the same. His work there had been all-consuming, barely giving him the chance to see the country outside of old battlefields and fortresses.

Alijah guided his horse into the centre of Lirian's eastern district. He unthinkingly jumped down from his horse and concealed his face behind the animal's neck. The pain in his leg contorted his expression and he didn't want any of Lirian's inhabitants to see him suffering. It didn't take long to subside, allowing him to turn and look upon the tired tavern that had drawn him from the palace.

The Pick-Axe.

This was where it had all begun for the half-elf. After exiling himself from the Galfrey home, destiny had guided him here, to the same decrepit green door that stood before him now. It had been over twenty years since then. He could still remember feeling like he didn't belong in there, among rangers and hardy patrons. Then an old mage had brought him a drink, a hot meal, and a welcoming smile.

Hadavad.

If only the mage could have seen him now, Alijah thought.

Even Hadavad, a mage of great vision and wisdom, could never have dreamt such a fate as this. It still saddened him to know that his old mentor had been destined to die so that he might break free of any and all who would lead him astray.

As he approached the steps up to the porch, Alijah asked himself what he was really doing there. There were pressing matters that warranted waking Malliath and continuing their journey but, instead, he was reaching out for the door handle. He just needed to see it again, to take in the tavern's musty aroma, and wander back through the halls of his memories to a different time. The king had believed he was above such trivialities as nostalgia but, here he was, aggravated by the lock that barred his way.

There were many ways he could remove the obstacle from his path, but he wanted to enter the Pick-Axe as he had so long ago. Alijah waved his hand over the lock and used a simple spell to pull it out of place. The door creaked on his way inside. He was immediately assaulted by the musty smell of the place, only it was far more pronounced than on his last visit. It reminded the king that Russell Maybury had sided with The Rebellion, leaving the tavern empty for nearly two years.

Still, the scent brought back numerous memories for the half-elf. He remembered the first time he returned with Vighon by his side. The northman had been sheepish, accustomed to the harsh ways of The Ironsworn, until Russell's dog, Nelly, had bounded up to him.

Walking up to the bar, from where Russell's pick-axe was clearly missing, he turned to the right, an area where the band had always set up when there wasn't a ranger telling a tale or two. He had enjoyed many of Doran's tales during his time with Hadavad. Those memories, however, felt spoiled now by the son of Dorain's actions against him.

With quiet contemplation, he slid his hands over the wood of the bar. How many times had he leaned over it and flirted with barmaids? It had all been so easy back then. He would cheat his way through a game of Gallant and use the coin for food, drink, and a warm bed.

Looking through the gloom, he picked out the booth where Galanör Reveeri had been sitting. The elven ranger had been watching him and Vighon on behalf of Hadavad and Gideon. From there, everything had changed, their courses altered forever. That led him to the door on the far left of the bar. Well and truly a victim of his own nostalgia now, he made for that door and descended the immediate steps.

The rangers' bar opened up around him with a small collection of tables and chairs and half a bar in the corner. He was drawn to the old armchairs, a little worse for wear, in front of the fireplace. He had spent many an evening sharing a drink with Vighon while staring into the flames. For all the venom he held for the northman, he couldn't help but recall those times fondly.

His hand ran along the top of the armchair as he left the common area. With what light there was, streaming through the high windows that revealed the street above, he navigated the only passage under the tavern. Ignoring the doors on his left and right, Alijah made for the door at the very end. Like the others, it creaked as he passed through to the next chamber. It was just as large as the common area, but it was devoid of furniture. The space had always been used for training and practising with new weapons.

Looking around, there were hardly any left on the walls anymore. Stepping onto the training mats, the king examined the long coat, belt, and sword that remained fixed to the far wall. It took him a moment to recall the ranger's name as Jonus Glaide, an old friend of Asher's and Doran's. Alijah had never met the man, but he had heard of his heroics during the Battle of Velia, in The War for the Realm.

Turning on his heel, the half-elf faced the small alcove built into the wall. A dusty curtain, poked with ragged holes, partially concealed the contents. With one hand, he drew the curtain back, his mind envisioning the row of identical swords and green cloaks. This had been Asher's personal locker. Now it was bare but for a single two-handed broadsword.

Alijah removed it from the rack and held it in both hands. The spiked pommel felt solid and heavy, but the blade evened the weight distribution to make it a finely balanced weapon. After so many years of disuse, however, it was in much need of care to make it battle worthy again. Not that its wielder would ever return to claim it, nor the tavern's owner for that matter.

The king sighed. "What am I doing here?" he asked himself.

The question evaporated from Alijah's mind when the tip of a stranger's sword came to rest on his shoulder. He chastised himself for being so wrapped up in his own thoughts that he had stopped listening to his senses. Now, a cursory glance to the side revealed four men had entered the chamber, one of whom had succeeded in getting so close that his blade now touched his very person.

"I wouldn't mind an answer to your question as well," came a gruff voice from behind.

Alijah held out Asher's sword with just his finger and thumb and slowly returned it to the rack before turning to face his attackers. They dressed like ordinary men, but the way they displayed their weapons and the formation they assumed to block his way, screamed their true identity: rebels. They were likely ex-soldiers from various places around Illian.

Though he now faced the man pointing a sword in his face, Alijah's attention was quickly drawn to the man on his right. Judging by the fear in his eyes, the rebel had recognised the person before them was the king of Verda, the most powerful and dangerous man in the world. And they were trapped down here with him.

"It's him," he said in a quiet voice.

"What are you talking about, Bervard?" the gruff voice demanded, his eyes never straying from Alijah.

Trembling now, the man uttered, "It's him... the *usurper*."

That word got stuck in Alijah's head, striking him like a physical blow. "Usurper?" he echoed acidly. "I am your *king*."

One of the four desperately shouted, "Kill him!" But it was too late.

Alijah had but to flick his wrist and the man pointing the sword in his face was hit by a wall of compressed air. The magic picked him off his feet and launched him into the back wall with enough force to spill some of the contents of his head across the stone. He didn't get back up.

The trembling fool who had recognised the king staggered backwards, his fear taking a hold of him. The remaining two rebels advanced from different angles, accustomed to fighting side by side. As they came at Alijah, he felt Malliath waking from his slumber with a start.

I'm coming! he growled across their bond.

The half-elf had no time to reply. He shifted his body one way to evade a thrusting sword before pivoting to avoid an incoming axe. A pained wince flashed across his face as his injured leg protested at the quick movement. The rebels turned around, ready to spring again. Alijah stood his ground, considering which destructive spell would be the most spectacular.

Then he thought about the battles to come. He would be the fool to believe that Inara and Gideon weren't on his tail. Clashing with them both was inevitable and, right now, he didn't know if he could even swing his sword without the pain getting in the way.

Using speed any human would find unattainable, the king freed his Vi'tari blade from its scabbard. His shoulder cried out but the pain only served to anger him which, in turn, led Alijah to lash out with his green scimitar. He batted his foe's sword aside and, in the same blow, sliced across his eyes, blinding him. The rebel fell away, wailing in agony.

The axeman hesitated, giving Alijah enough time to face him properly. When, at last, he attacked, the king snatched the haft of his weapon mid-strike and held it high. Again, the pain in his back was akin to a lashing whip, but he adopted some of Malliath's rage and pushed through, just as he slowly pushed his Vi'tari blade through the rebel's chest. Shock ripped through the axeman's expression. What pain there was didn't last long before Death claimed him and he slipped from Alijah's scimitar.

Keeping hold of the axe, the king twisted the weapon in his hand. He turned to face the trembling sop who was trying to disappear into the corner. Wherever he had seen Alijah before, he had obviously borne witness to his terrible might. He approached the man with deadly intent, a predator closing in on its prey. To silence the blind rebel's constant whimpering, he threw the axe into the side of his head, adding a third corpse to the training room. This made the survivor tremble all the more.

"Please!" he begged. "Please! Your Grace!" Pushing away from the corner, the man prostrated himself before the king. "I am your humble servant! I will do anything you ask! Please, your Grace!"

Alijah loomed over him. "What was your name?" he asked softly. "Bervard?"

"Yes, your Grace," he stuttered.

"Bervard, you have committed grievous crimes against the realm. Treason is punishable by death."

The man sobbed some more. "Please, your Grace! I'm begging you! I will do anything!"

Alijah sighed and sheathed his blade. "I am merciful," he said, giving the man hope. "Go," he instructed, nodding at the door.

Fearing a trick, Bervard hesitated. Then, he swallowed hard and rose to his feet, nervously looking from the king to the door.

"Do you wish to die down here?" Alijah questioned.

"No, your Grace!" Bervard blurted.

"Then why am I still looking at you?"

The fool bolted for the door and swiftly disappeared from Alijah's sight... but not Malliath's. The king heard the tavern's front door burst open as Bervard darted for the street. Then he heard the flames that engulfed the rebel and half the road.

All four of them were dead the moment they entered the chamber. Alijah had known that, just as he knew his own fate was sealed by his actions.

With a lasting look at the interior, the king made his way back to the street, ready to leave The Pick-Axe behind forever. It had served its purpose in his life.

Outside, the smell of charred flesh stung Alijah's nostrils, but he was sure not to display any discomfort. Instead, he took a moment to examine what remained of Bervard. That didn't take very long. Small flames licked at the street here and there but Malliath had kept the damage to a minimum, a stark difference to the devastation he unleashed upon the city during The Ash War.

With a force of their own, the dragon's purple eyes pulled Alijah in. *Why did you come here?* Malliath asked bluntly.

Alijah regarded the old tavern. ***I don't know,*** he confessed.

Malliath huffed, expelling a blast of hot air from his nostrils. *It has passed the time we were leaving. We have work to finish.*

Alijah could feel his companion's need to be in the sky again, to fill his wings with air, and soar with the kind of freedom that only a dragon could know.

"Your Grace!" Lord Starg called from astride his horse. Accompanied by a handful of his own men, the steward rode down the street but was sure to dismount before getting anywhere near Malliath's tail.

"Lord Starg!" the king called back. "Inside you will find the bodies of three dead rebels to add to this one," he said, pointing at Bervard's burning husk. "Upon my return, I expect you to have found the people aiding them and made arrests!"

The steward stumbled over his own words. "It will be done, your Grace!" he promised.

Alijah didn't much care for his promises. Instead, he ascended Malliath's back, his pained climb hidden by the dragon's wing, and readied himself for flight. It took only seconds to put all of Verda behind as they rocketed into the heavens.

With every beat of Malliath's wings, Alijah found his memories of The Pick-Axe fading away. It was, in fact, Malliath's words that echoed in his mind.

The past must die, so that the future may live.

CHAPTER 18
BATTLE OF THE MOONLIT PLAINS

A dwarven horn cut through the cold morning air just as it cut through Doran Heavybelly's head. He shot the blower a look so fierce it moved him on, deeper into their ranks and away from the War Mason's sensitive ears. It wasn't the first horn that had bombarded his sore head - the morning's march had been filled with them. Every time a new tribe of Centaurs joined their forces, both elven and dwarven horns would celebrate.

Doran hated them all just as much as he hated the one that had pierced his tent and roused him, hours earlier.

He had quickly come to regret joining in the evening's intemperance his people always enjoyed before a battle. He wasn't the young warrior he liked to think he was anymore. But now, astride Pig, as he looked out from the small rise in the plains, the most sobering of sights banished any and all ailments from Thraal's home brew.

Gone was the lush green of the everlasting Moonlit Plains. Instead, there was an ocean of black steel. Reavers, amassed from every corner of the realm, surrounded the enormous dig site. The inner-most ring, by the edge of the hole, was occupied by a camp of enslaved dwarves.

If only that was all the son of Dorain could see. He cursed under his breath upon sighting the lumbering Trolls. They easily stood out against the smaller Reavers, who controlled them with chains and spears. Indeed, Doran spotted two of the wretched beasts lying still in the western flanks, their jagged hides like hills on the flat land. They had clearly proven unruly and been slain by their undead masters.

Good, he thought. That was two less monsters to deal with. Of course, the remaining dozen or so, dragged from their dark dwellings, would create quite the problem when the real fighting began. That's *if* the real fighting ever began, for the Reavers and the Trolls were not their only foe. Scattered throughout were numerous ballistas and catapults, some of which were still in the process of being constructed.

They were dwarven in design.

That fact broke Doran's heart. Was there any greater humiliation for a dwarf than to be forced to build your enemy's weapons, weapons that would be used against your kin? He could only hope that some had been sabotaged.

Glancing back over his shoulder, he was pleased to see that his army - a collection of clans - had remained in formation. They would be relying heavily on their ancient battle strategies if they were to beat a superior foe. That all began with rigid formation. Of course, the elves made the whole affair seem effortless in their shining armour and with their stoical expressions. Even the Centaurs, who stood above them all, had found some kind of organisation that worked for them.

"I don't see him," Faylen stated from atop her horse.

Doran looked up at her and followed the elf's sight to the sky. "Well there's nowhere else for a big black dragon to hide out 'ere," he remarked, turning left and right. "Grarfath must be hurlin' a strong wind in his direction."

"If you are correct," Faylen went on, "then the same thing delaying Alijah and Malliath is also delaying Inara and Gideon."

That didn't sound right to the dwarf. "Perhaps it's jus' as Gideon said: Malliath's injured."

Galanör jumped down from his horse and walked a few steps ahead. "Dragons or not, this battle possesses challenges all of its own. Catapults, ballistas, Trolls. Add them to the Reavers and who knows what else awaits us out there."

Watching the Reavers rally on the southern side of the dig site, spreading their line out to meet the rebels, was more than enough to give Doran doubts about any victory. "We ain' 'ere to win, remember. We jus' need to keep 'em busy until we 'ave the numbers to defeat Alijah. Bring 'im down an' they all follow."

"Sounds gruelling," Aenwyn commented.

"Aye," Doran agreed. "An' that's before we face the damned Trolls."

"Leave them to us," Kelabor asserted, trotting over to their small group ahead of the army. "My people have experience with their kind."

Doran cast his only eye over the Centaur and decided, rather quickly, that he wouldn't disagree. Like many who had emerged from the plains to join them, Kelabor wore an armoured coat over his horse body, similar to the battle-wear of iron plates and chain-mail the dwarves clad their Warhogs in. It all lent to the already menacing appearance of his kind, given their significant tattoos and large weapons.

"If ye can bring 'em down then ye're welcome to 'em."

"We need to rethink our strategy here," Faylen suggested. "Charging at them, flat out, will see many of us perish by those catapults. And if they unleash the Trolls before we reach their front line, our formation will be compromised."

"Is there time for that now?" Aenwyn posed, her sharp eyes fixed on the Reavers.

"They're not advancing," Faylen replied. "And since surprise was never an option, I suggest we take the moment to decide our best course of action."

"Ye're not wrong," Doran added, before turning to look up at Kelabor. "It's great that ye've got experience bringin' down Trolls, but how do we get close enough before their catapults an' ballistas…" The dwarf tailed off, his mind falling back to his days in Dhenaheim.

"Doran?" Galanör cajoled. "What are you thinking?"

He was thinking war strategies, schemes designed to ensure death on a grand scale. He hated that his mind could so easily fall back on that way of thinking, though he had to wonder if it had served him during his years slaying the realm's worst beasts.

"I'm tryin' to do what no other has done before," he began, sounding somewhat harassed. "We've got elves, dwarves, an' Centaurs at our disposal. How do we best use our different skills to the advantage against an enemy with superior reach?"

Galanör looked to be really considering that question. "We could—"

"I wasn't really askin', lad," the War Mason interjected. "Kelabor. Can yer kin gallop faster than the average horse?"

The Centaur audibly expelled a breath of air from his nostrils, indicating his offence at such a question.

"I'll take that as a yes," Doran concluded. He turned back to the open fields and the vast enemy that awaited them. A fiendish grin spread across his face. "I 'ave an idea."

It took some time to organise the three different races, informing them all of what was about to happen next and what their part would be in it. For most of that time, Kelabor and his Centaurs were flooding the front lines, and blocking out the distant Reavers, as they positioned themselves into Doran's suggested formation.

Since he could no longer see his enemy, the son of Dorain kept a weather eye on the sky. If Alijah and Malliath arrived they would have no choice but to attack immediately. They would end up throwing away many lives, but stalling him from entering that pit and destroying magic was all that mattered. It made Doran shudder to think of Alijah being the only person in the realm with both magic and a dragon.

Astride his Warhog, Doran trotted up and down his line,

assessing his warriors. Most looked ready for battle, eager to settle old scores with the enemy that had destroyed their homes and robbed them of loved ones. They would have that opportunity soon enough.

Though he could see that some were not happy with the definition of soon, given their part in the battle, Doran cared little. They were warriors, *his* warriors. They would follow the orders he had given and stick to the plan that would keep most of them alive.

Eventually, to the sound of more horns, the Centaurs began to advance as one, closing the gap between them and the Reavers. They moved up slowly, taking the time to spread out. When their advance was sufficient, the elves steadily followed behind, their numbers spread out to match the Reavers in front and the dwarves behind.

With the rhythm of so many hooves growing distant, Doran took the moment to address his army. A nod to Thaligg instructed him to blow a particular horn, one which directed every dwarf's attention to their War Mason.

"*For five thousand years the clans have stood apart!*" he bellowed in his native tongue. "*For five thousand years we have stained Dhenaheim with each other's blood. Look to the dwarf beside you now! Battleborns, Brightbeards, Heavybellys, Goldhorns, Hammerkegs. Today they are just words! I do not care about words! I do not care about lines on a map! And I do not care about crowns! There is only one thing that means anything today!*" Doran shifted his broad shoulders in his saddle and gestured to the dig site. "*Dwarves! My blood is just as red as any of yours and I will spill every drop of it for the dwarves in that hole! Today we fight as one people! If there are any of you who can't stomach that notion, now is the time to walk away.*"

The son of Dorain paused, waiting to see if there were, indeed, any among them who couldn't stand to fight alongside different clan members. Not a single dwarf moved.

Doran nodded approvingly. "*Then prepare for battle, brothers, for I expect Grarfath to tremble at your roar!*" he shouted, eliciting a thunderous growl from the army. "*I expect Death itself to dread your fury!*" The dwarves began beating their shields and armour. "*I*

213

expect Verda to never forget the day the children of the mountain unleashed their wrath!" The cacophonous response was deafening, leaving Doran to simply raise Andaljor into the air.

The War Mason guided Pig around to follow the advancing elves and Centaurs. Russell was there, absent his horse now, with his new battle hammer in his hands.

"I didn't catch a word of that!" he shouted over the dwarven war cries.

"It was very inspirin'!" Doran informed. "Ye should feel inspired!"

Russell nodded once. "Inspired," he agreed, turning to the enemy.

Thaligg and Thraal blew their horns and every captain along the line did the same. The fiercest dwarven army in history broke into a charge, led by Doran himself. Russell sprinted alongside him, having no need of a mount over a short distance.

Now, the War Mason just had to hope the timing of his plan was perfect.

Further north, the Centaurs were ensuring just such a thing. Galloping towards the enemy, their numbers scattered across the plains, they were inviting the aim of the merciless catapults. Their projectiles were easily seen as they set sail across the sky like burning comets. Just one had the power to kill scores of Centaurs.

"Now," Doran muttered under his breath.

Far from the sound of his voice, Kelabor blew into his horn, signalling his people. Now, they were really running. They left the gallop of a horse behind and revealed their true speed. This was the undoing of the catapults, their first salvo destined to overshoot and strike naught but grassland. Indeed, the open plains between the Centaurs and the staggered elves were bombarded by flaming projectiles that exploded on impact. Not a single drop of blood was shed.

Now, galloping like demons, the Centaurs moved into Doran's suggested formation. He had described it as a spear to them, for they charged their enemy only four abreast but hundreds deep. Like a battering ram, they approached the

Reavers in the centre of their mass, hollering war cries of their own.

But the spear did not penetrate.

At the last possible second, the Centaurs split their force down the middle, veering off to the east and west. With great speed, they charged along the outer edge of the Reavers and lashed out with all manner of weaponry. There was nothing the Reavers could do against such thunderous might. Here and there, they succeeded in spearing a Centaur, but *their* numbers were taking the larger toll. It also pushed the dark army together in a bid to back away from the encompassing attack.

Now for the elves.

Faylen, Galanör, and Aenwyn led the immortals through fire and smoke, crossing into the catapults' threshold. From atop their horses, the elves released salvo after salvo of both arrows and spells. No aim was required to hit the Reavers, and those that were struck in the head dropped to the ground, out of the fight for evermore.

Leading by example, Faylen erected the first shield of magic over her head. The rest of her force quickly followed suit and did the same, just in time for the first wave of ballista bolts and the second wave from the catapults. Had the dwarves gone ahead of them, their dead would litter The Moonlit Plains. Doran's plan, however, played to their strengths and the elves remained safe beneath their magic.

Still charging from the rear of their attack, the son of Dorain could see their shields flaring and flashing as they took the punishment from the aerial assault. It wasn't a perfect strategy though and several elves were caught in the blast waves from burning projectiles. Others were flung from their mount when the animal was speared by a ballista bolt.

Time was against the dwarves now. The elves had taken the brunt of the siege weapons, but the Reavers would reload them all and fire again soon. They had to cross the field and get stuck in before that happened. Of course, before that, the elves had to breach their front line.

As the Centaurs disappeared around the edges of the Reavers, Faylen, Galanör, and Aenwyn were the first to have their mounts leap into the fray. Galanör's blades swung out, Faylen expelled destructive magic, and Aenwyn let fly her arrows. Then came the rest, their force aimed at a single point in the Reavers' line. Much like one of Aenwyn's arrows, the elves shot through their enemy, almost penetrating to the heart.

Now there was nothing between the children of the mountain and their already occupied foe. With a few hundred feet left to charge, the catapults hurled their load into the heavens. They would make no difference now - the dwarves were too close and too spread out to give anything to the catapults' range. Doran cheered with righteous glee before the inevitable and violent clash.

And violent it was.

Armoured Warhogs collided with armoured fiends from east to west in an ear-splitting crash. Russell alone performed an almighty leap that cast him deeper into the Reavers' ranks, a place where his battle hammer could come down with abandon.

Doran was oblivious to all but those directly in his path. He let Pig deal out as much damage as it could, the Warhog's momentum more than enough to crush a dozen Reavers before the dwarf dismounted and added his swing to the clamour. By then, he had separated Andaljor into axe and hammer, making him just about the most dangerous thing on two legs.

The hammer swung out to the left and the axe chopped down on the right, every blow spelling the end of another Reaver. And behind him, dwarf after dwarf added their mettle to the melee, pouring into the battle with a war cry on their lips and steel in their hearts.

Somewhere in the heavens, Grarfath was laughing.

Doran felt his ancestor's hammer crush helmets and skulls while the axe hacked through limbs and severed heads. It wasn't long before he was forced to step over the undead creatures to reach his next foe. As he moved to slay the Reaver in his sights, a Warhog barrelled into it and rammed the fiend into those behind. He was about to cheer the rider when he realised the dwarven warrior was dead, his body savagely impaled by five swords. Doran liked to imagine that he had fought until that fifth and final sword.

With a growl rising from deep inside his chest, the son of Dorain charged in behind the rogue Warhog and dropped his hammer down on the Reavers before they could recover. One of them, unfazed by their shattered legs, pushed up on one hand and thrust a spear towards the War Mason. The dwarf dodged left but the edge of the spear tip cut a neat line up the side of his cheek. Doran was barely aware of the pain. He batted the spear aside with his hammer and sank his axe deep into the Reaver's head.

Like sharks catching a scent of blood, a group of Reavers cut through a pair of dwarves and elves to reach Doran. Their swords were slick with the blood of his kin, while his own weapons were crusted with the rotten debris of theirs.

"Come on then!" he goaded, banging axe and hammer together. "I've got more than enough steel for all o' ye!"

The dead had no response but to advance on the dwarf, their hideous faces concealed behind their helmets. Gritting his teeth, Doran determined to break them all until their insides were squeezed through the eye slits. At least he would have done were it not for Galanör and his wicked blades. The elven ranger emerged from the battle like a dancer on a grand stage. Stormweaver slashed high and Guardian swept low, so that, after a handful of seconds, Galanör was standing amidst their headless bodies with a victorious grin on his face.

"Show off!" Doran yelled, before swinging both his hammer and axe into an oncoming Reaver. Galanör's blades flashed again and he was gone, absorbed by the battle.

A staccato of lightning nearly blinded the War Mason when an elven warrior unleashed his magic. He succeeded in repelling four Reavers and burning an entire ballista, but he missed the spearman off to the side. The Reaver launched the weapon with an accuracy it had brought from its previous life, eons past, and impaled the elf through the chest. Before he fell to the ground, there to join his brothers and sisters on the eternal shores, Aenwyn let loose an arrow that brought the Reaver down.

Then she fired five more in quick succession, each arrow well placed to kill a Reaver before they could deliver a killing blow to an ally. Her last arrow spent, Aenwyn dashed from corpse to corpse and retrieved them one at a time before firing them again. When one particular fiend jumped at her, the elf twisted her body and evaded its swing. A swift boot to its back sent the Reaver careering towards Doran's waiting axe.

Like Galanör, Aenwyn was quickly concealed by the chaos of battle. Doran hoped to see both of them again, but he didn't give it any more thought than that. They had a long way to go and a lot of Reavers to slay. It was going to be a long day.

At some point, the sun had given in to the progression of stars and a shining moon. Under this new reign, the fields of The Moonlit Plains came to life with their enchanted glow. For centuries, beings of intelligence had marvelled at its beauty and sheer majesty, but not this night. Even if those fighting for their lives weren't distracted by the heated battle, the enchantment couldn't be seen through the blood that stained the earth.

That blood belonged to countless elves, dwarves, and Centaurs, all of whom had fought side by side for untold hours and were now dying side by side. The inescapable truth came down on Doran Heavybelly again and again: they didn't have the numbers. Everywhere he looked, his kin and allies were falling to the many blades of their enemy. He wasn't convinced they weren't crawling out of the hole like demons escaping the pits of hell.

He thanked the Mother and Father he had been born a dwarf, lest his fatigue claim him like some human. With what strength remained in his hands and arms, he brought Andaljor to bear and blocked an incoming longsword. Locked between his weapons, the sword was braced as its wielder tried to sink it into the dwarf. Doran looked up at the Reaver with a feral glint in his eye. Then he pulled the axe and hammer towards him, yanking the sword from his enemy's hands. A strong boot to the knee put the Reaver on its back and a strong downwards swing significantly diminished the dimensions of its head.

It felt good. But it wasn't enough.

That thought was never so overwhelming as when he heard the deep rumbling growl of a Troll. The ground shook beneath its lumbering stride. Reavers, elves, and dwarves alike were flung into the air by arms as thick as trees. The monster's chains rattled and whip-cracked as they swung left and right.

The son of Dorain back-handed his hammer across a Reaver's ankles, taking its legs out from under it, before finishing the fiend off with a heavy strike from his axe. Now he could see the Troll and its rock-like hide. It was heading right for him, though the beast was most certainly oblivious to Doran's significance.

A tired sigh escaped Doran's lips. For all his hours of fighting, he had only glimpsed a Centaur here and there. It seemed the bulk of Kelabor's force were still battling in the north and along the flanks.

"I suppose I'll be killin' a Troll then," he muttered to himself.

The Troll in question, however, swept in with a back-hand that launched four elves and a dwarf into Doran's path. The War Mason was clipped by an elven boot and knocked to the ground. There were too many dead faces waiting for him.

With a bubbling wrath, he picked himself up and faced the Troll once more. "Now ye're goin' to get it!" he promised.

The Troll took no heed of the dwarf and continued to stomp ahead. Doran jumped to the side and avoided being stepped on, but he paused long enough to drive his axe down onto one of the monster's toes. The beast grunted and staggered right, only Doran's axe was still buried in the toe and his hand was still gripped to the haft. A sharp yell was raised from the dwarf's mouth as he himself was yanked from the ground.

Thrown loose from his grip, the son of Dorain tumbled across the battlefield with only his hammer in hand. Protected by his armour, the War Mason jumped back to his feet and came face to knee with a very angry Troll. It roared, blowing out his blond hair, and expelled an ungodly amount of spit upon the dwarf.

Unfazed by the display, Doran wiped the spit from his face and looked at all four of the Troll's bloodshot eyes. "Ye've got somethin' o' mine," he said, gesturing at the axe lodged in its toe.

The Troll growled and raised both of its arms, fists clenched. Doran leapt forward and dived into a roll that took him between the monster's legs. He felt the ground shudder under the double impact behind him, a blow that would have ground him down to a mangled mess. Rising from his manoeuvre, the son of Dorain rounded the monstrous foot and grabbed his axe, levering it by the top of the haft to pull it free.

Emerging on the other side of the Troll, he was forced to again dive out of the way as it turned to find him with swinging arms. One of the long chains threatened to take off his head, but the War Mason ducked as it swept through the wisps of his hair instead. Another hammering fist came down, followed by another, both of which he managed to evade by throwing himself around the battlefield. The third blow looked to be unavoidable, and so the dwarf went on the attack and hurled his hammer directly at the Troll's head. The block of steel caught the beast in the mouth and shattered several teeth but, more importantly, it knocked the monster backwards, saving Doran's life.

The Troll shook its head, regaining its senses, and focused on the small creature that had hurt it. The beast ignored the arrows that imbedded themselves between the rocky patches of its hide and the swords that chipped at its legs, and came for Doran with a vengeance. The son of Dorain backed up, desperately trying to think of an attack that would bring it down for good.

All he had left in his arsenal was the axe of Thorgen.

Assured of his own accuracy, Doran threw the weapon end over end having aimed for the Troll's ugly face. If it didn't kill the stupid creature it would, at least, blind it. From there, he could use what time he had to find another way to slay the monster. The axe, however, got no further than the Troll's forearm, which whipped up to protect its face.

Doran swore.

Weaponless, he now faced an angry Troll that had the power to crush him with a single hand. The dwarf braced himself, entirely unsure what he was going to do.

The answer was nothing.

He felt the pressure of a large boot pressing down between his shoulders before he saw Russell leaping over his head. The old wolf gained enough height to face the Troll at eye level, his battle hammer held above him in both hands. Using the flat of the hammer, Russell buried the weapon right between the monster's inner eyes. The force behind his blow was strong enough to crack the rocky hide and direct all four of its eyes inwards.

As Russell landed back on his feet, the Troll staggered backwards, one enormous foot after the other. Its balance came into question as it wavered one way then the other. At last, it grunted, shook its head, and locked its eyes on Russell with renewed fury. It took two confident strides when Kelabor and a trail of Centaurs burst from the fray, galloping straight past the Troll. Without faltering a step, Kelabor casually swung his sword and slit the monster's throat, taking advantage of both his height and the soft patch of skin under the creature's jaw.

Blood ran freely down the Troll's jagged chest before it fell to its knees and then flat onto its face. The Centaurs hollered victoriously into the night and circled around, forming a temporary defensive line around the War Mason.

"Where in the hells 'ave *ye* been?" Doran shouted over the melee.

Kelabor only shot the dwarf a look. Then he was gone and his Centaurs with him as they pushed deeper into the battle. With them gone, the Reavers closed in again.

"Doran!" Russell removed the dwarf's axe from the Troll's arm and tossed it to him. The War Mason regained his grip just in time to cleave the first Reaver's head from its shoulders. He shoved the next aside and buried his weapon in the knee of the third, dropping it with the other. Then he hacked repeatedly until he was confident neither would ever rise again.

With laboured breath, he made his way back to Russell's side. The old wolf had already found Andaljor's hammer and he held it out for Doran to take. His weapons back in his hands, the dwarf glanced up at the moon. It was so close to being full now. One more night and the curse would have its time.

"Are ye with me?" Doran croaked.

Russell's jaw was set, his yellow eyes cast over the dwarf. "Until the end."

Together, they turned and faced the next wave of enemies. With so few allies around them, the pair were soon forced to ascend the Troll's back. The climb slowed the Reavers down just enough to give them the edge, but their elevated position informed every fiend in the area of where to find them. Doran would never have admitted it aloud, but he could really have done with Galanör and his blades showing up right about then.

"Doran..."

The War Mason retrieved his axe from his enemy's head and kicked it off the Troll before following Russell's gaze. There above them, three fireballs were lighting up the night's sky as they arced towards the south. Doran tracked them to the distant plains. Upon impact, their flames illuminated the greatest thing Doran had ever seen.

Reinforcements.

Captain Nemir, Faylen's husband, led his fellow elves across the plains with scimitars raised. He had behind him every elf who had survived Malliath's attack on The Shining Coast and they all looked hungry for battle.

A flicker of hope dared to bring new life into Doran's aching bones. "Keep swingin'!" he growled to himself.

And so he did.

CHAPTER 19
A LARGER TAPESTRY

Viewing the world from the heavens, Gideon looked down and ahead of Ilargo to discover the southern edge of The Evermoore. The great forest dominated the landscape below, running from east to west with seemingly no end in sight. The Moonlit Plains, however, tinted orange in the setting sun, rolled across the realm like a blanket, taking Gideon's vision to the furthest horizon.

Were they to continue their journey through the night, they would arrive at the battle having completed two days of constant flying. Though Ilargo, nor Athis, would ever admit to it, neither could face the likes of Malliath and two Reaver dragons after such an exertion. They had already battled strong winds that had blown off The Vrost Mountains, determined to force the dragons ever westward.

We should rest here tonight, Gideon suggested, aware that Ilargo was connected to Athis. *There is a cliff just east of here, above the trees. It looks big enough for both of you.*

We can't afford to stay long, Inara cautioned through their shared bond. *Alijah has a head start.*

We will leave before the night is over and finish our journey under the stars, Gideon reassured.

Both dragons banked towards the clearing without a verbal response, a testament to their fatigue after days of flying across the world from Erador to Illian with barely a stop in the middle. Gideon harboured a real fear for his companion's life but, as strange as it still felt, he kept the thought to himself. A lot of his worries stemmed from the fact that, after years of imprisonment, he had only just got his eternal companion back and he didn't want to lose him again.

Adding to the waning shadows of the trees, Athis and Ilargo flew low over The Evermoore before gliding on the currents to bring them up to the rocky bluff that stood a little taller than the surrounding forest. It was slightly pitted in the centre, offering the riders some shelter from the wind, but the dragons still curled around the area offering a wall of muscle and scales.

Gideon patted Ilargo on the neck before making his way down the angled rocks and boulders. Meeting Inara there, they quickly set up a small camp with blankets and a fire to cook their food. They did all this in silence, their actions born of muscle memory more than anything. They had both camped in the wilds of the world and with far less than they had now.

They ate and drank, watching the stars creep over the sky. As the temperature dropped, Inara carved some small runes into the ground around them and the fire. Gideon recognised the spell and even remembered teaching the younger warrior how to enact it. When she was finished, an invisible bubble surrounded them, trapping the heat inside. Trivial as the spell was, it still made the old master proud.

"Did you ever think about me?" Inara asked, cutting through the sound of the crackling flames.

Gideon looked at her, across the fire, well aware of what she was talking about. "Every day," he assured. "And twice as much after Alijah captured me."

"What did you think?" Inara continued. "When your thoughts dwelled on me," she specified.

Gideon could see how awkward Inara felt asking the question. "For my years in Dragons' Reach, I longed for your opinion on *everything*. You've always seen things so clearly. But, most of all, I think I missed your laugh. Something I haven't heard since our reunion."

Inara's mouth twisted. "There hasn't been much to laugh about of late."

Gideon looked down at his food. "I suppose not." The old master took a breath before meeting her eyes again. "I worried about you," he confessed. "I knew you could take care of yourself - you were the most dangerous thing in all of Illian. But I worried you were lonely. I knew the order was a part of your identity. I feared that you were living in hope that every day would be the day we returned."

"I did," Inara replied quietly.

"I'm sorry," he muttered before finding his courage. "I am sorry," he repeated boldly. "I convinced myself that... Well, I don't know what I told myself. I've made one bad choice after another and leaving you behind to guard Illian on your own is right up there with the worst of them. You should never have had to shoulder that responsibility. If I could change things I would."

Inara stared at her old master and Gideon felt the weight of her gaze through the licking flames. "I forgive you. Just like I forgive you for keeping the Dragorn bond a secret," she added sincerely.

Gideon swallowed, unable to say anything in light of the absolution of his failures. Inara's strength and humility were boundless - as he well knew - but to experience it was like having his chains removed all over again.

"I also forgive you for taking the extra piece of bacon," Inara added, her tone bringing some levity to the conversation.

Gideon managed an amused smile and flicked his finger over the bacon on his plate. The telekinetic spell launched the strip of meat across the fire and into Inara's waiting hand. Her grin broadened as she consumed it in three quick bites.

"I do not deserve your forgiveness," Gideon uttered.

"And yet you still have it," Inara replied.

Gideon nodded his appreciation but failed to look at her as he busied himself with his water. He had nothing to offer in return for her kindness even though he knew Inara expected nothing.

"I'm surprised you haven't asked me yet," Inara announced.

The old master was taken aback by the confusing statement and, for the life of him, couldn't understand what she was referring to.

"It must have crossed your mind," Inara continued as if he was in on it. "We discovered an entire cavern full of dragon eggs. The bond you now have with Ilargo aligns with the ancient ways. You *must* have thought about the Dragon Riders. I'm just surprised you haven't asked me to join you yet," she finally clarified.

Gideon opened and closed his mouth, unsure how to respond. "I would be lying," he began, "if I said I hadn't considered it."

"Why would you only *consider* it?" Inara questioned with a frown.

Gideon was tempted to laugh at his own miserable history where leadership was concerned. "I haven't exactly succeeded in that particular area. You might recall your recent trip to Dragons' Reach."

Inara was shaking her head. "You're a leader, Gideon. It's in your bones."

Now *he* was shaking his head. "The qualities of leadership are not enough to build an order of dragons and Riders from the ground up. I brought too many potential Riders too soon to The Lifeless Isles. Our numbers swelled beyond my ability to teach with any significant instruction. There were too many young Riders and too many young dragons." Gideon paused and took a moment to think about all those that had perished in the orc invasion. "Elandril started the Dragorn and kept the order alive and relevant for thousands of years. I lost it all in a few decades."

"You said it yourself; you tried to rebuild an order designed by elves *for* elves. The Dragorn was never meant for humans. And when Elandril started the order, he was closing in on five hundred years. You don't even have a century to your name yet. You're too hard on yourself. What really matters is the cause of all the strife you put yourself through - you just want to protect people. I can see that hasn't changed in you, nor in Ilargo. And like Asher said: you always get back up. He believes that's what makes you dangerous but he's wrong. That's what makes you *wiser*. This isn't some fairy tale, Gideon. This is real life. When we fall, we pick ourselves back up and try again. There are none in the realm with your experience or better prepared to find Riders for those eggs."

Gideon couldn't help but get carried away in Inara's speech. "It would certainly take longer. Those eggs will only respond to a particular kind of warrior and they aren't in abundance." He shook his head in a bid to rid himself of the fantasy. "No. I had my chance at it all. Now there's blood on my hands. I don't deserve a second opportunity."

Inara held her tongue for the moment and stoked the fire. "The world is going to need some hope to cling to, something to assure it that evil will never return. Dragon Riders have ever been that promise, whatever form they took." She leaned forward. "It's because of your past, because of your failures that you are the leader Drakanan needs. You could build something new that bridges both orders."

Gideon smiled weakly. "I think the world is going to have all the hope it needs in you... and Vighon." Inara's eyes flicked up from the flames and fixed on the old master. "So there is something there," he concluded. "I thought so but I wasn't sure."

"I don't want to talk about it," Inara said, in a clipped tone.

Gideon held up his hands. "I'm happy for you both. I'm glad you're coming to terms with your bond; you're doing better than I am and I have a few years on you. My emotions were pretty focused while I was imprisoned but, since you rescued me, I've struggled to understand my own mind. I feel like I'm back in my first year at Korkanath."

"You're struggling too?" Inara asked in disbelief.

"Of course! I've always known I was Gideon Thorn, Master Dragorn. Now I'm just a man with greying hair and the emotional control of a young teenager. Did you know your mother is very attractive?"

Inara put a hand up. "There is a line, and you just crossed it."

Gideon laughed. "I apologise. I've known Reyna for decades and never once considered her appearance. And that's just some of it. I get angry over small things and upset over nothing. I have thoughts that I *want* to keep to myself and not share with Ilargo. I know he is the same."

Inara looked confused. "I haven't seen any of this since we left The Tower of Jain."

Gideon shrugged. "I still have my decorum to fall back on. We've also been dealing with the end of the world as we know it."

Inara gave a soft laugh that never made it over the sound of the flames. "Well, it's nice to know I'm not alone."

Gideon smiled. "I don't think you'll ever be alone, Inara Galfrey."

The Guardian bit her lip and frowned. "We both have to survive first, Vighon and I."

The old master could see that it was hard for her to talk so openly about it. "You've both forged futures through the darkest of times. You will again."

A look of deep sorrow shadowed Inara's features. "It's hard to see that future when it lies on the other side of killing my brother. If that's even possible."

Inara's words set off a chain reaction in Gideon's mind, taking him down a path he had tried to take before, in the halls of Drakanan. "Do you recall, before we discovered the bonding chamber, I was telling you about—"

"Your last conversation with Alijah," Inara cut in, eagerly. "You said it was your worst argument. Something about The Crow."

"Yes. As I said in Drakanan, I had a lot of time to think. The one thing that kept coming back to me was The Crow's part in all this. One day, I decided to voice my opinion to Alijah. He took it badly and he made Ilargo suffer for it. The next time I saw him was two days ago."

Inara tilted her head. "What burdened you so much that you felt the need to discuss it with Alijah?"

"I think a part of me wanted to anger him," Gideon confided, "to make him feel small and used."

Inara narrowed her eyes. "Tell me, Gideon."

The old master adjusted his position on the ground, allowing him to better see her across the flames. "I think The Crow lied to us."

"About what?"

"Well, maybe *lied* is too strong a word. I believe he was hiding the truth behind the truth."

Inara raised an eyebrow. "Now you're making about as much sense as The Crow himself."

"What was the last thing he ever said?" Gideon asked, already aware of the answer.

"Monsters only beget monsters," Inara replied flatly. "I spent years pondering over what he meant," she admitted. "Then Alijah invaded and I saw the monster for myself."

Gideon disagreed. "But that doesn't make sense," he argued. "Sarkas claimed to have seen a future where peace existed across all of Verda. He went to great lengths to ensure Alijah became the king he is right now, including the orchestration of events that brought him and Malliath together. Yet, in his final moments - after declaring *himself* a monster - he told you that monsters only beget monsters. Why would he allude to Alijah being a monster if he was supposed to be the one to bring about peace and unity?"

"The Crow was a very twisted man," Inara opined with a shrug.

"His methods were twisted, yes, but I can't believe his vision was *this*. Consider everything we know about The Crow - *Sarkas*. He grew up under King Atilan's reign, a notoriously selfish and greedy man - a *tyrant*. And Sarkas himself lived in The Citadel, his life dominated by the mage priests of The Echoes order. He knew real oppression. Why would he bring about a future that ensures the realm is ruled by another of their ilk? He had to know that Malliath would be a corrupting influence on Alijah besides his own tormenting in The Bastion."

Appearing agitated, Inara asked, "What are you getting at, Gideon?"

"It's not just what he said," the old master pointed out, "but *who* he chose to say it to."

"How so?" Inara questioned.

Gideon paused, wondering how to put it. "I don't think Sarkas orchestrated millennia of history just to ensure Alijah's birth. I think he also did it to ensure *yours*."

Inara's face dropped. "What are you talking about?"

"Alijah wasn't the only person born that day," Gideon explained. "If Sarkas saw the future, he saw your birth too. I think he always meant for Alijah to become the man he is. Look around; he *has* brought the realm together. There's never been this kind of unity before, not between all the races. *That's* the truth he told. The real truth, behind that, is Alijah's role in all this."

Inara looked away, her mind pulling on the thread. "You think Alijah was meant to be the monster that united the realm with a common enemy. And that I'm the one who..."

Gideon leaned towards her. "You're the one who slays the monster and brings real *lasting* peace to the realm. The truth behind the truth." He gave her a moment to absorb his theory.

"And you shared this with Alijah?" Inara asked incredulously.

"I wanted to hurt him, but I was also hoping he could see the logic in it. He didn't. And, like I said: there was pain." Gideon looked at his old student. "What do you make of it all?"

"I think we won't know until the end," she answered simply, her feelings her own. "Everything The Crow ever said came to pass, but he never told us how this really ends. He even damaged his second prophecy to make sure we only knew just enough to move events forward and keep us in the dark."

"He said there will be peace," Gideon reasoned, "knowing that could only come about with Alijah's demise."

"If my brother destroys the realm of magic," Inara countered, "the world will never face another threat he can't handle on his own. One way or another, Gideon, there will be peace."

"At what cost though?" the old master posed, fearful for those who would have to die to see Alijah's peace come about.

Inara gave him a hard look through the flames. "That's what we're fighting for."

CHAPTER 20
CROSSHAIRS

Death had come to The Moonlit Plains. It plucked souls from the battlefield by the score and reclaimed those that had been forced back into their rotting bodies. Yet the Reavers still possessed the superior numbers and not one of them showed an ounce of fatigue.

Galanör couldn't say the same.

The elven ranger had been fighting day and night and now, rising in the east, a red dawn graced the sky. All his long life, Galanör had never endured a battle for so long. Like everyone else, he was testing his limits and pushing himself beyond them.

He had lost count of how many Reavers had tasted his steel and been sent back to the grave. Devoid of blood, their detritus smeared the elf's scimitars, staining them black. His blue cloak was similarly ruined and heavier now as it flowed around him, slapping mud against his legs.

Then there was Aenwyn, a beacon of light in the darkest hours of the battle. Her movements were still light, ethereal almost, as she flitted from one enemy to the other. She balanced her attacks between blade and bow, picking up arrows wherever she might find them.

Galanör cut his way through two Reavers to fight by her side, intensifying their prowess. They quickly assimilated the other's style and began to complement each other in their attacks. Galanör ducked under a sweeping sword and Aenwyn used his position to roll over his bent back and fire an arrow into a Reaver's head. The ranger popped back up with a snap and a swirling attack with both Stormweaver and Guardian, protecting Aenwyn's blind side.

Of course, there was more than just Reavers to protect each other from. If Centaurs weren't charging through and Warhogs weren't rampaging in every direction, the dwarves of Dhenaheim were there to add their own flavour of chaos to the fighting.

Galanör dashed to the left in order to avoid a trio of dwarves barrelling into a Reaver, their combined weight more than enough to bury the fiend in mud: there to use their axes. Aenwyn too was forced to spin away from a dwarf swinging his hammer with wild abandon. Neither of them, however, could argue with their results. The children of the mountain could take some serious damage and every one fought with hardened experience.

Looking out at the sea of heads and elevated Centaurs, the ranger only hoped that Doran, Russell, and Faylen were out there somewhere. He wondered if Faylen had found her way to Captain Nemir, as his forces continued to dominate the south-eastern corner of the battle. Whatever happened to them, he hoped they were together.

Galanör shook his head. The fatigue was making his mind wander when he should be focused on his surroundings. That was how he missed the incoming Reaver and its thrusting sword. Aenwyn, ever his saviour, planted a firm boot in Galanör's chest and shoved him back into a pack of dwarves. The Reaver missed its target and, instead, found Aenwyn's scimitar lodged in its head.

The dwarves growled at Galanör's interference and, collectively, pushed him back onto his feet before Aenwyn. "That's six!" she shouted over the melee.

Galanör deflected a killing blow with Guardian and decapitated his foe with Stormweaver. "Six?" he doubted, sure that Aenwyn had only saved his life four times since the fighting began.

Aenwyn dodged a Reaver's sweeping sword and, in the same movement, yanked free a wild arrow protruding from its hip. "Six!" she confirmed confidently, before firing that same arrow point blank into her enemy's face.

Any witty retort he might have responded with was stolen by the ear-splitting roar that cracked the sky in half. Galanör cast his eyes to the dawn's red canvas above and searched for the greatest killing machine in the world. It was hard to feel relief upon spotting one of the undead Dragon Riders, but at least it wasn't Malliath the voiceless. Narrowing his vision, the ranger tried to identify the specific Rider, be it Vilyra astride her dragon, Godrad, or Gondrith astride his dragon, Yillir. They were the only remaining two of Alijah's fearsome generals but, from this distance, even his elven eyes couldn't determine which of the two had entered the battle.

"Incoming!" a fellow elf bellowed from within the chaos.

Galanör didn't need the warning - he could see the dragon flying down towards him. He turned around, barged his way to Aenwyn and grappled her to the ground only a moment before the monster snatched at any body it could. Looking up from the mud and blood, the ranger watched as the dragon ascended back into the sky, where it released elves, dwarves, and Reavers from all four of its claws. Their screams lay beyond Galanör's hearing, but their fall was well within his sight. He would have watched them to their end but he was quickly set upon by more Reavers.

"Get up!" Aenwyn yelled.

The elven ranger came up following the tip of his swords, both of which skewered a Reaver each and pushed them back. Aenwyn guarded him while he dispatched them for good. Now he could see the Reaver dragon and the Rider on its back. Yillir glided low over the battle with Gondrith and his mighty hammer seated in the saddle. Careful not to diminish the Reavers' numbers, Yillir chose victims on the outer edges of the fighting, where Captain Nemir's forces were still penetrating.

Galanör watched in horror as Yillir's tail curled down and

dragged through the ranks of his kin. "We need to bring that dragon down!" he growled.

"How?" Aenwyn demanded, slicing through the legs of two Reavers. "I'm a good shot but one arrow isn't going to bring it down!"

Galanör bashed the pommel of a hilt into an enemy's helmet, knocking it clean from the horrific face beneath. Stormweaver flashed upwards and the Reaver lost most of its head. As it dropped to the ground, the ranger glimpsed something between the maddening fray.

"Maybe one arrow *is* all we need!" he called back. "We just need a bigger bolt!" Answering Aenwyn's questioning expression, Galanör pointed one of his scimitars at the distant ballista.

"After you!" Aenwyn insisted.

It was a clear morning over The Moonlit Plains. The sky was still transforming as the dawn bid farewell to the night. It was a good day to change the world.

Alijah looked down on the sprawling battle that spread around the entire circumference of the dig site. Thanks to his bond with every Reaver, he already knew that Centaurs had joined The Rebellion. It was a pity, he thought. They were such a fascinating species with a long history in Illian and, indeed Erador. Now, however, the tribes of The Moonlit Plains would have to be purged for good.

Much closer to the battle, he spotted Yillir creating havoc among the elven contingent. He sent a mental command to Gondrith, instructing the Rider to add his hammer to the melee.

As Malliath flew directly over the dig site, Alijah considered his path to its lowest depths. There was nowhere to land around the edge of the site, a battleground in itself thanks to the dwarven prisoners in the throes of rebellion.

Get me as close as you can, he instructed, eager to see Malliath devastate the rebel forces.

If I land in the middle of that I will be surrounded by enemies, the dragon was quick to respond. *I am immortal, not invincible.*

The king hadn't expected such reluctance from his companion but, as always, he was right. And Alijah knew he would struggle to focus on his task if he thought Malliath was being harmed. Alijah considered diving down, plummeting to the very bottom, and using magic to safeguard his landing, but he didn't know what awaited him down there, nor in the realm of magic. He needed to be conservative.

Land in the east, he suggested, noting the edge of the battle was closer to the dig site. *I will forge my own path to the doorway.*

Malliath banked to the east and began his descent to the plains. Given the pain in his wings, it wasn't the fastest descent he had ever made. The dragon glided round in a broad arc until his claws touched down on the grass. The rebels fighting on the fringes turned to behold the greatest threat they had ever faced. That threat looked back at them with purple eyes.

Try not to destroy too many knights, Alijah advised. **We will still need an army when this is all over.**

Malliath replied with his fiery breath, a jet of flames so excruciatingly hot that it melted the elven, dwarven, and Reaver armour alike. Entire Centaurs were engulfed, disappearing inside the blinding torrent, their screams drowned out by the raw power of the oldest dragon in the world.

Alijah climbed down his companion's side and drew his Vi'tari scimitar, enjoying how the green steel caught the rising light. Now it was time to show them *his* power. He walked over the scorched ground and charred bodies, ready for the battle to swallow him up. One last push, he thought. Then he could rest, knowing he had saved the world.

Galanör put the last Reaver down that stood between him and the ballista. Aenwyn was close behind, her scimitar slashing to defend herself.

"It's not loaded!" Galanör complained, turning to see Aenwyn slice her foe into pieces.

"Here!" Aenwyn handled one of the spear-like bolts from the ground and passed it to the ranger.

"Watch my back!" Galanör shouted as he began to align the bolt onto the central shaft of the ballista. Of course, Aenwyn was already moving to defend him, dancing around the weapon to keep any Reavers at bay.

Satisfied with the placement of the bolt, the ranger attempted to winch the drawstring back behind it. His arms trembled with the exertion, an effort he would not have needed prior to the battle.

"Aenwyn!" he shouted desperately, seeing Yillir's flight path begin to line up.

Aenwyn ordered two elves to guard them as best they could while she jumped to Galanör's aid. They both groaned under the effort as they drew the string into place. Working together, it wasn't long before it gave a resounding and satisfying click.

"Take the shot!" Galanör urged, reaching for his blades again.

"Me?"

"You're a better shot than me!" the ranger encouraged. He pivoted just in time to block the downward stroke of a Reaver's blade. A boot to the chest shoved it back into the timely swing of a dwarven axe.

Then he saw it. Death.

It was as if the ethereal and ancient entity walked side by side with Alijah Galfrey. The half-elf, visible between a dozen fighting combatants, flashed his green blade in sweeping arcs. Every elf, dwarf, and Centaur he faced was collected by Death, their souls added to the extensive tally that already belonged to his cursed blade.

"Come on!" Aenwyn berated herself.

With what strength she had, the elf manoeuvred the ballista to keep the bolt head in line with Yillir's erratic flight. Galanör dashed to her side and added his blades to her defence. "He's here!" the ranger informed. "Alijah and Malliath are here!"

Aenwyn never took her eyes off her target. "One dragon at a time!" she replied, firing the bolt at last.

The missile sailed over the top of the battle, whistling as it cut through the air. Galanör watched it intently, willing it to find its mark. Yillir's flight path, however, was momentarily altered at the last second as it moved to avoid the wild swipe of a rogue Troll. The bolt careered off one of the spikes on the dragon's tail. Aenwyn cursed and slammed her fist onto the ballista.

"Load another bolt," Galanör muttered. "Load another bolt!" he bellowed. "Quickly!"

Time against them and enemies at their back, the elves worked to place another bolt onto the main shaft and draw the string back. Both elves and dwarves clashed with Reavers to protect the pair, but there was nothing any of them could do against a dragon.

"Pull!" Aenwyn grunted, her strength added to Galanör's.

Yillir ripped the Troll's head from its body and spat the mangled skull from its mouth. Rid of the temporary hindrance, the dragon roared and flapped its ragged wings, taking it back into the sky.

"Pull!" they both groaned.

Flying right for them, Yillir opened its maw, preparing to consume them in flames.

Click. It was the most satisfying sound in the world.

Aenwyn shoved Galanör away and assumed full control of the ballista's aim and trigger. Only seconds existed between them and death by fire. The elven ranger caught just a glimpse of the smile that flashed across Aenwyn's face before she let fly the lengthy bolt. It launched with a loud and powerful thunk, though its flight was short-lived when Yillir took the bolt directly in the mouth. The dragon was instantly brought down by the force of it.

The ground shuddered under the impact, which killed any unfortunate enough to be in its path, but its speed continued until Yillir skidded across the battlefield and its head slammed into the front of the ballista, knocking Aenwyn back a step.

Galanör wanted to celebrate the victory with her but there was no time. Another shadow was upon them. The ranger gave no warning before he wrapped his arms around Aenwyn's waist and brought her down with him. As they hit the blood-soaked ground, the meaty fist of a Troll crashed into the ballista and reduced it to splinters.

The roar that followed was deafening. Determined that such a savage noise would not be the last thing he ever heard, Galanör rolled to the side with Aenwyn still in his arms. They avoided the second fist, which dented the ground, and quickly split up to confuse the beast.

Four wretched eyes looked down on Galanör as he ran around the remains of the ballista, missing Aenwyn who weaved between a group of dwarves to flank the Troll. Using one of the dwarves' pauldrons, she deftly leapt up and found purchase on a spear jammed in the monster's ribs. From there, she scaled its rocky back until its stubby head was within her grasp. Galanör was preparing to evade the incoming hammer fist when Aenwyn took the dagger from her belt and rammed it into one of the Troll's eyes.

The next attack never came for Galanör, the Troll's wrath now directed elsewhere. One hand after the other snatched at the air around its hideous head, searching for the one who tormented it.

"Get away from it!" Galanör warned.

Before Aenwyn could jump down, however, the Troll found its attacker and yanked her from its shoulders. Aenwyn fought to free herself but the monster's grip was unyielding. The Troll growled in her face and brought her towards its open jaws. One bite would snap anyone in half, armour or not.

"NO!" Galanör raged, seeing Aenwyn's life coming to a gruesome end.

The ranger reacted without thought, his muscles falling back on centuries of practice. He rolled his wrist, twisting Guardian in a swift circle, until he was holding the scimitar like a spear. Despite the awkward angle, standing in the shadow of the Troll, he succeeded in launching the weapon up into the roof of its mouth.

It immediately flinched backwards and dropped Aenwyn to the ground. Its pain-filled roar was dampened by the steel lodged in its palate, the hilt poking over its bottom lip. It tried to pull the blade free but discovered more pain in the process. This made it mad, mad enough to ignore the fear of pain and simply clamp its jaw shut, shattering Guardian between its teeth. The hilt and half the blade fell to the ground while the top half remained stuck inside its mouth.

Galanör was elated to see Aenwyn alive on the other side of the broken ballista and simultaneously heartbroken by the loss of one of his swords. In the path of the Troll's burning ire, however, there was nothing he could do about either. Instead, he dived to the side, narrowly missing another fist. One after the other came down around the elf, each possessing the force of a falling tree. Galanör rolled left and right between crawling and jumping out of the way. With saliva and blood drooling from its mouth, the monster pursued him, swiping at anything and anyone that got in its way.

The ranger's ultimate undoing came in the form of a crazed Warhog. The dwarven mount burst forth from the melee and knocked Galanör to the ground, giving the Troll time to bear over him. He tried to get up but there was nowhere to go but a wall of dwarves and Reavers locked in battle. If he pushed into them, they would all suffer the beast's hammering blows.

With Stormweaver in hand, he rolled onto his back and faced the looming Troll. Its three remaining eyes narrowed on the elf and it sneered, revealing a sliver of the broken steel in its mouth. It raised its left fist, cracking knuckles the size of a man's head. If that fist was coming down on him, Galanör was determined that it would feel the cutting bite of Stormweaver first.

Like a meteor, the fist was dropped, blocking out the sky above. But it never found Galanör of house Reveeri.

From his grounded position, the ranger could only marvel at Ilargo's timely manner. The green dragon had snatched the Troll from the battlefield in his front claws and now carried the monster off into the heavens, there to be dropped from a dizzying height.

As Ilargo flew away, a new figure came to stand over Galanör. "What are you doing down there?" Gideon Thorn asked with a cocky grin and an outstretched arm.

The elf couldn't help but break out a broad smile of relief as he took the offered hand. "Oh you know, just catching my breath," he replied. "I'm glad to see you," he said seriously. "The cavalry is just what we need about now."

"*I'm* not the cavalry," Gideon told him. "*She* is."

Galanör followed his friend's gaze to the sky, where a small figure was leaping from the back of Athis the ironheart. Inara Galfrey hurtled towards the battlefield like a star thrown by the gods. The Guardian of the Realm was enveloped in a multitude of flaring colours as she not only protected her fall with magic, but also surrounded herself with a destructive force.

There wasn't a soul on The Moonlit Plains that didn't feel her impact.

Inara came down directly on top of a Troll and obliterated it. The shockwave of magic then expanded outwards into an area densely populated by Reavers. They too were reduced to smaller pieces of themselves, never to rise in their master's name again.

Perhaps, Galanör dared to hope, they could turn the tide after all.

CHAPTER 21
OFF THE BEATEN PATH

Having finally put the north behind them, it seemed that those who had left Namdhor were the heralds of winter itself. The thick powder of The White Vale no longer buried the hooves of their horses, but thick clouds swarmed overhead, depositing fresh snow with every mile they covered.

In the lead, Asher had guided the company away from The Selk Road before they reached Kelp Town and, instead, cut across the wilds. To have continued on the road would have taken them far west, further into The Ice Vales. Using his superior knowledge of the land - and his affinity with the dark - the ranger led them through most of their first night, allowing them to cover as much ground as possible. There had, of course, been more than a few protests but Vighon had kept everyone focused, reminding them of their need for haste.

By the first ray of dawn, he had them back on their mounts until they reached the western edge of The Evermoore. From there, the company followed the forest south for another day and camped not far from where The Selk Road cut in from the west and weaved through the trees to the city of Lirian.

Now, under the light of yet another new day, Asher had them cross the road rather than take it. In his opinion, which had been voiced to the king, Lirian was an unknown quantity.

"Better we keep to the tree line," he had said to Vighon. "If we follow it south we will eventually find The Moonlit Plains."

"And it should be quicker," Reyna had pointed out, easing the decision for Vighon.

With rolling hills to their right and The Evermoore's towering pines to their left, Asher tried to relax for the first time since setting off on their relentless journey. Snow continued to sprinkle the land, adding an extra layer of beauty to it all.

With only one route to follow, and an easy one at that, he decided to ease off on the reins and allow others to pass him by and take the lead for a while. The ranger offered Avandriell an arm so that she might climb out of the satchel and onto his lap. The hatchling scurried up his forearm and paused to flex her wings. She needed no encouragement to bound away and take to the snow.

"Easy now," Asher cautioned, helpless to do anything but watch her leap.

Avandriell quickly buried her head in the snow before emerging with a mouthful. From there, she explored every small rock and turned over every stone. Now and then she would pounce at something Asher hadn't seen. He could feel her happiness, infectious as it was.

Nathaniel sidled up beside the ranger. "I haven't seen you smile like that since... Well *never*, actually."

Asher instinctively made to return his expression to that of a stoical monk, but he found it much harder than usual. "I can't explain all the things I'm feeling," he said gruffly, "and I'm not inclined to try."

"I might not have seen that smile on *you* before," Nathaniel continued, "but I *know* that smile. I grinned like that every day watching Alijah and Inara growing up. It's pride," he explained. "Mixed in with a heap of love I suppose."

Unaccustomed to describing his intimate emotions, even to Nathaniel, Asher kept his eyes on Avandriell. He wondered if that's what it was. Pride. Love. It had taken a lot for him to figure out that his feelings towards Reyna and Nathaniel were love, Faylen too. That particular emotion had been twisted all his life. But he knew it now and could see that he did, indeed, love Avandriell, though its intensity was magnitudes beyond anything he felt for a person.

Pride was new. It was often reserved for parents and mentors, the former of which he had no experience of. During his time in Nightfall, he had mentored several students but being satisfied with them wasn't the same as being proud.

"Maybe she *is* like a child to me," he mused, watching her climb the trunk of a tree to pester the squirrels.

Nathaniel gave a short laugh. "Only you could be a father to a dragon."

Asher shared in the amusement. "Who do you pity more?"

"Oh, definitely Avandriell," the old knight quipped.

The two trotted side by side for a while, exchanging jokes about what hilarity might ensue while Avandriell grew ever larger and harder to handle. They kept the conversation light and off what the real future might bring their way. Asher did his best to keep one eye on the hatchling, concerned that she might dash between the horses and be trampled.

At some point along their journey, a pair of soldiers peeled away from the company and tried to find rest at the base of a small hill. Nathaniel sighed and begged his pardon as he broke away to confront the men with a firm reminder of the stakes.

Asher easily returned his attention to Avandriell, who had, apparently, declared war on all squirrels and birds. A melodic voice caught his ear, drawing him back to the riders beside him. Reyna's emerald eyes were waiting for him, and she displayed just the slightest curve of a smile on her lips. Her leathers, scimitar, and bow lent her the look of a fearsome warrior, the very thing Asher knew her to be.

"I have enjoyed seeing you two side by side again," she

remarked, glancing at her husband in the distance. "It reminds me of old times."

The ranger tried not to laugh. "By old times you mean when we were fighting Valanis and the Darkakin? Or perhaps you're referring to the orcs and The Black Hand?"

"I enjoyed the moments in between," the elf confessed. "We could probably do with making some new memories," she added. "Preferably ones without swords."

"Where's the fun in that?" Asher replied amusedly.

Reyna laughed. "Your decision to remain a ranger makes a lot more sense now. I applaud your decision by the way," the elf complimented.

"Thank you," the ranger said quietly, his eyes tracking Avandriell from one branch to another.

"I mean it," Reyna insisted. "You know who you are. After everything that's happened to you, *happening* to you, your lack of conflict reflects your true character. I know I speak for the whole realm when I say thank you for that."

Asher didn't know what to do with such kind words. He muttered a thank you of his own, reluctant to look the elf in the eyes.

"In some ways," he began self-deprecatingly, "it's the easiest decision I've ever made. Being a ranger is far simpler than being a Dragon Rider."

"That's not why you have chosen that path," Reyna reminded him.

"No," Asher agreed. "I *am* a ranger. There are just some things you can't fight, no matter how hard you try or how far down you bury them." The ranger finally turned again to look upon Reyna. "We are who we are," he declared.

"Indeed," she uttered, averting her own gaze this time.

"You *are* a queen, Reyna," Asher told her. "You've always been a queen, just like I've always been a ranger."

"And if I don't want to be a queen?" the elf pondered.

"Then be Reyna Galfrey," Asher suggested casually. "Forge a different life."

Reyna turned on him with confusion. "You just gave a whole speech about being *who we are*! You can't fight it you said."

"I know what I said and I stand by it," he argued. "But you still have to choose it. To do otherwise would take you down a path of resentment. Ayda doesn't deserve a bitter queen. Your people deserve a ruler who *wants* to serve them. I know I speak for the whole realm," the ranger echoed, "when I say they would be lucky to have you as their queen."

Reyna met his eyes. "Thank you," she said with great sincerity.

"Having Nathaniel for a king is another matter," Asher cracked, bringing out a joyful laugh from Reyna. He had missed the sound of it.

"Perhaps I should look for a better suitor," the elf jested.

With a cocky shrug, the ranger replied, "I do come with a dragon now, you know."

"Do you?" Reyna queried, searching the trees past Asher.

Whipping his head around, panic swiftly set in as he failed to locate Avandriell. His fears took his mind to the worst places, forcing him to imagine the Arakesh stealing her away.

"I saw her," Adan'Karth called from behind. The Drake climbed down from his horse and strode towards the tree line. "Avandriell went this way."

"Go," Reyna urged, taking Asher's reins from him.

The ranger dismounted and wasted no time following Adan into The Evermoore. The Drake took to the forest with a grace and fluidity Asher could never attain. It was as if the trees pulled him in, guiding his every step. It brought back memories for the ranger of his time in Ikirith, a heaven on earth. His mind was stunted, however, gripped with fear for Avandriell.

"This way," Adan directed, taking them deeper still.

Asher wasn't sure how his bond with Avandriell worked exactly. Should he be able to find her without sight? Could he call to her with his mind alone? He certainly couldn't feel her emotions right now, unless the hatchling was fearing for his life as he was for hers.

Then he heard her, the familiar hiss of a baby dragon. They

arrived at a small clearing dotted with jagged boulders and a fallen tree. It didn't take long to find Avandriell, nor the monster she had picked a fight with.

Adan'Karth held an arm out to stop Asher from entering the clearing. "Wait," he warned firmly. "That is an Arkilisk - very poisonous."

"I know what it is!" the ranger barked, aware that a single bite from such a creature could bring down the largest of men.

The monster and the dragon squared off, each gripping the same boulder at an awkward angle. The Arkilisk was twice Avandriell's size and its bark-like hide was covered in sloping spikes. Its six claws outnumbered Avandriell's and its much larger head possessed a mouth of razor-sharp teeth. Asher knew well that it could tear through leather, and even armour depending on the Arkilisk's age, but could it puncture dragon scales? That question led him to another question: how strong were a hatchling's scales?

The ranger cursed himself for not asking Gideon more questions when the opportunity had presented itself. "I'm dealing with this," he growled, reaching for his broadsword.

"Wait," Adan repeated, but it was actually his tone that stopped Asher in his tracks.

"What is it?" he demanded urgently, wondering if there was something worse than an Arkilisk lurking in the forest.

"Can you not feel it?" the Drake asked, searching the air around him.

Avandriell pounced at the Arkilisk and the two wrestled briefly across the rock before tumbling to the ground. Asher finally pulled free his two-handed blade having already visualised the way he would slay the creature. The monster scurried forward and attempted to take a bite out of Avandriell, but the bronze dragon proved the more agile of the two and evaded the attack with apparent ease.

Asher took a step forward when Adan'Karth gripped him by the shoulder and pulled him back. Surprising the ranger all the more, Adan raised his free hand and erected a shimmering shield between them and the clearing.

Only then did Asher feel something of what Adan had been warning him about. He knew it emanated from Avandriell. He could feel her heart racing within her chest. But there was another sensation against his skin that he hadn't felt since his days with Paldora's gem on his finger. He could *feel* magic in the air.

Then something terrifying happened.

Avandriell exploded in a myriad of colours, blinding anyone or anything foolish enough to have been looking at her. The air cracked in that same instance, assaulting their ears with an incessant ringing. Then came the heat. Asher almost choked on it as he wafted the air with his hand. Slightly in front of him, Adan'Karth was coughing and spluttering, staggering around in a daze. The pair blinked repeatedly and hard in an attempt to regain something of their sight.

"Avandriell!" Asher rasped. He squinted into the clearing but it was hard to see anything through all the smoke.

Adan'Karth tried to caution the ranger's advance but he had to know what had happened to her. Something crunched under his left boot and he paused to investigate. The ranger lowered his head and discovered he had stepped right through the charred remains of the Arkilisk. Everything from its hide to its blood had been scorched black.

"Avandriell?" he called softly.

Adan'Karth entered the clearing and waved one hand through the air. Again, Asher felt the use of magic roll over his skin before he saw the smoke being swept away by the Drake's spell. Ignoring the sensation, the ranger cast his eyes over the area. What he found opened a pit inside of him. It sucked in all his hope and left him in the company of fear alone.

There was no sign of Avandriell, only ruin. The rocks scattered around the area where she had stood her ground were blasted in the shape of a perfect circle. The edges of what remained were glowing orange from the heat. Two trees were on fire, threatening to torch The Evermoore were it not for Adan'Karth's swift intervention. Any grass, moss or bark on the ground was simply gone, leaving small patches of flames here and there.

As despair began to creep in, Asher tried again to call out her name. "Avan—"

The ranger was immediately startled and jumped back as the dragon leapt from cover onto the surviving boulders. She looked down at him with her golden eyes. There was so much intelligence behind them. Caught up as he was, Asher required an extra moment to realise this was not the same Avandriell who had just squared off with an Arkilisk.

She was bigger.

Asher stepped back to take her new size in. The best comparison he could conjure was to that of a dog, a *big* dog. Her tail, of course, made her longer than any dog he had ever come across. Larger as she was, he noted features he hadn't seen before, though he had to wonder if they were entirely new given her transformation. Her tail had more ridges, perhaps an extra spike or two, and the end - shaped like a flat leaf - was more defined, its edges sharper.

Her front claws curled over the lip of the damaged rock, drawing Asher's scrutiny. They were darker, much like her scales which had taken on a deeper shade of bronze. As they had deepened, however, her specks of gold and silver had increased, especially along her neck.

Asher...

The ranger's face dropped. Had he really heard that? The voice had been female and not a voice he had heard before. But it was familiar.

Avandriell? he replied mentally.

The dragon reared back, lifting her claws and head to the sky. Her wings fanned out, making her size all the more impressive.

"Asher?" Adan still had some caution in his voice but the ranger kept him back with an outstretched arm.

He knew what was about to happen.

Avandriell pushed up from the rock and beat her wings. She cleared the boulder and beat her wings again. Within seconds, the dragon was climbing into the sky, there to soar and experience her first taste of real freedom.

It was no time at all before she disappeared from sight but, somehow, Asher knew exactly which direction she had flown in. He turned in a slow circle, following the mental pull that kept him connected to her.

"What happened here?" Adan'Karth whispered.

"Energy," Asher grunted. "It had to go somewhere," he added with a shrug.

Backtracking, they eventually returned to The Evermoore's western edge. Most of the company had continued ahead, leaving Reyna and Nathaniel behind with the extra horses.

Reyna looked past them as they emerged, concern marring her expression. "Where is Avandriell?"

Asher looked up, guiding their attention to the sky. There, against the pale clouds of snow, Avandriell glided through the air. He enjoyed the awe that illuminated their faces, filling him with pride. She was beautiful, graceful, and exquisitely fierce.

Nathaniel glanced briefly at the ranger. "Is she..."

"She's bigger," Reyna confirmed, her eyes the superior of the two.

"How can she be bigger?" the old knight queried in disbelief.

"It's a dragon thing," Asher told him casually, unwilling to get into it.

"Is that what the noise was?" Reyna asked.

"Most definitely," the ranger replied, his ears still ringing slightly. "Adan, you felt it just before it happened."

"Yes," the Drake said, his eyes fixed on Avandriell. "She was drawing on an enormous amount of magic."

"Perhaps it's a good thing you stay with her then," Asher said. "The next time Avandriell... *grows*, the effects could be worse. The last thing we need is the king losing a leg."

Nathaniel whipped his head around. "Lose a *leg*? What happened in there?"

Asher mounted his horse and looked up at Avandriell with the same question on his mind. Had she really spoken to him? He could feel her looking down at him, watching him. If she could speak to him, the ranger knew she would do it again. And, though he would never admit it to anyone, he looked forward to the long conversations that would take them from dawn till dusk.

One day...

CHAPTER 22
WHERE WORLDS COLLIDE

As thick clouds rolled over The Moonlit Plains, it became harder to track the sun and grasp the passage of time. There was only death. Dwarves, elves, Centaurs. They all swarmed around Alijah and they all fell at his feet, there to add to the gruesome foundations of the battlefield.

So many dead. So many misguided fools.

It angered the king all the more. He was being forced to kill his kin because they had fallen under the spell of Vighon Draqaro. Even Inara and his parents had a hand in this. Alijah promised himself that these deaths would be placed on their shoulders when it came time to punish them.

The king welcomed the snowfall, sweating as he was. He decided that it must have been hours since he entered the battle. He blamed the chaos of it all for losing his sense of direction. Multiple times, he tried to use his bond with the Reavers to discern the right path to the doorway, but every attempt left him vulnerable to attack.

Malliath had tried to help him, guiding him from the sky, but Athis and Ilargo hounded him in and out of the clouds. In the briefest of reprieves, Alijah would look up and see the dragons exchanging blows and illuminating the clouds with their fiery breath. He reached out to get a sense of his companion's injuries and found them similar to his own, though his had been inflicted by a group of dwarves who had managed to push through his defence of Reavers.

Keep going, my friend, he urged.

Destroy the tree! Malliath fired back.

Alijah could feel him fighting through the pain, just as he was on the ground. *It will be done!* he promised.

I am flying over it now! Malliath growled, before Athis collided into his side and Ilargo snapped at his front leg.

Alijah dropped his scimitar as he too was wounded across his left arm. The king turned to see a dwarf raising his axe in the air, ready to bury it in the Reaver under his boot. Alijah quickly retrieved his Vi'tari blade and rammed it up into the dwarf's ribcage, slipping the steel between his armour just as the dwarf had sliced him between his dragon scales. He cursed the clumsy dwarf and shoved him from the end of the scimitar.

Ignoring the pain in his ribs, likely caused from overextending his previous injuries, Alijah felt for that pull in his mind and followed it to Malliath's location in the sky. The dig site was to his right. Then, using the most basic form of his bond to the Reavers, he commanded all those around him to close in on his position.

"Advance!" he bellowed, having them fight their way towards the pit.

After several minutes of pushing through the melee, a wild Centaur used its superior height to gain an advantage. Alijah glimpsed the incoming attack only a second before the spear was launched at him, skimming the tops of the Reavers. Evasion was out of the question with so many knights surrounding him. It was with instinct that the king turned to magic to save himself. The shield flared as the spear struck true, angled perfectly to have plunged through his head, before it snapped in half and careered away.

The knights of Erador closest to him broke away from their

master and swarmed the Centaur. All the while, Alijah became aware of new wounds he couldn't explain. He didn't recall being hit by any of those he had faced since entering the fray, but such was the turmoil of battle. His previous injuries had slowed him down and likely given his enemies more than one opportunity to land a blow that couldn't quite pierce his armour.

A shockwave of magic rippled through the battlefield, turning Alijah away from his wounds. He watched half a dozen knights fly skywards in a flash of blue light. Focusing on the source of the magic, the king tried to see between his protective circle. It could have been any of the elves, but they all appeared too exhausted to have used such a powerful spell. That left Inara and Gideon, though Alijah couldn't imagine the old master using what magic he still possessed.

Inara then.

As the knights guarded him against incoming attacks, he finally glimpsed his sister amongst the chaos. Her red cloak flowing around her, Inara was a maelstrom of devastating power and fury. Her Vi'tari scimitar, Firefly, was in constant motion, twisting and turning in her grip to deflect and attack almost simultaneously. When she wasn't using a double-handed attack, her free hand was expelling destructive magic.

Behind her, The Rebellion rallied. Alijah could see them all, an alliance of species, sweeping up behind her. She was the tip of the spear leading them all to the dig site.

Focus! Malliath chastised.

The king looked up to see his companion weaving between Athis and Ilargo's attacks, forcing them to change their flight path at awkward angles and chase him up into the clouds. Malliath was right. They were so close now. Falling back on his lessons, he heard The Crow's words in his head.

"Fear is not real, it is simply a product of the mind. Danger is real."

He had nothing to fear from his sister. He could overpower her, injured or not. But she posed a real danger to his work in the pit. Taking the lead in front of his knights, Alijah put his sword to use again and forged a path to the dig site. He had to get there first and see his task completed.

~

Inara saw him, fleeing like a coward. She had been directed to him, guided by his use of magic. And now, surrounded by his undead fiends, the would-be king of the world turned from her rather than face the consequences. It turned her blood to fire.

"I have him!" she called, drawing Galanör's attention.

"Where?" the ranger demanded, swiping Stormweaver across a Reaver's torso.

"He must be making for the site!" she reasoned, throwing her hand out to engulf a group of Reavers in flames.

"We have to stop him!" Galanör urged.

Inara set her sights on the path she intended to take. "We will," she said determinedly to herself. "On me!" she cried, rallying those behind her.

Elf, dwarf, and Centaur heard the Guardian and none hesitated to follow in her wake. She had more energy than all of them and her command of both magic and sword was vastly superior. Relying on the strength of her elven half, Inara flipped in the air and landed in the midst of the Reavers. Swifter than they could respond, she ducked down and swept her blade round in an arc, taking out their legs. On the ground, they were prey to the rushing dwarves of Dhenaheim as hammer, axe, and spear came down on them with a vengeance.

Before they were crushed into the dirt, Inara was already moving, gaining ground on her brother. Flashes of his jade scimitar pushed her on until she was stepping over the corpse of a Reaver and entering the campsite where the dwarves had been imprisoned.

A pair of Centaurs galloped in behind her, clearing one of the tents in a single leap. Against Inara's warning, they rushed the group of Reavers covering Alijah's back. One of them succeeded in cutting down a pair of the fiends, but the other received a sword to the chest, thrown by one of the Reavers. It was Alijah himself who turned and killed the surviving Centaur with a clean swipe of his Vi'tari blade.

He found Inara across the campsite and their eyes locked.

They each held a promise in their gaze. Alijah warned his sister that he wouldn't hesitate to kill her should she interfere. Inara assured her brother that there was nothing he could throw at her that would prevent her wrath from coming down on him. One of them was going to die today.

The Reavers closed ranks again and Alijah disappeared behind a wall of black knights. From her vantage, Inara could see that they were now on the lip of the dig site, meaning her brother was likely on his way down already.

They were out of time. "Are you with me?" she asked, glancing at Galanör.

The elven ranger assessed the Reavers blocking their way. "We can take them," he declared, turning to Aenwyn beside him. She flicked up her scimitar and nodded once with conviction.

Inara tried again to reach out to Gideon through their dragons' bond, but Athis and Ilargo were too occupied to bridge a connection between the four of them. She knew her old master was out there somewhere after having been separated by hours of battle. But she couldn't wait for him now. If Alijah had, indeed, found a way to open a doorway down there, he was, perhaps, only minutes away from destroying the source of magic.

Leading the way, Inara charged across the dwarven camp with Galanör and Aenwyn. Behind them, those of The Rebellion who had fought through to the heart of the battle spread out to join the chaos once more. Most of them had no real idea what was at the bottom of the dig site, believing that they were fighting simply to defeat their enemy. Only the few knew of the importance and only the few could do anything about it.

Faster than the weary elves, Inara collided with the Reavers first. Firefly blocked and batted away one sword after another before lashing out on the offensive. Her steel cut through limbs, necks, and heads until her path was clear. Those that survived her onslaught were faced with Galanör and Aenwyn who, between them, made short work of Alijah's protectors.

Stepping onto the wooden boards, Inara looked out on the largest excavation she had ever seen. With extraordinary tenacity and unparalleled skill, the dwarves had dug down, forging an abyss in The Moonlit Plains. The interior of the shaft was a mass of walkways, bridges, and pulley systems. The design was dizzying to Inara's eyes, but the dwarves weren't new to the art of digging large holes in the ground. She could see how, if one knew the structure, the miners could get to anywhere inside the shaft, but she was looking for the quickest way to the bottom.

Alijah crossed her vision, on the other side of the shaft. He was hurrying down the sloping walkway that lined the interior wall.

"Come on," she bade.

The trio dashed to the left and began their descent around the curve of the shaft.

"What are these?" Aenwyn questioned, referring to one of the stone tablets they passed every twenty feet.

Inara glanced at one as she ran past, having noted them pressed into the muddy walls. She instantly recognised the ancient glyphs carved across their surface. "They're warding stones!" she called back. "They were used on The Lifeless Isles to prevent the use of portals!"

"Good!" Galanör grunted. "Then he only has one way out of here."

Inara laid eyes on her brother across the way. "He won't be leaving here!" she proclaimed, in a bid to free herself of the emotions that tied her to Alijah. Then, without warning her companions, Inara jumped, kicked off the interior wall, and leapt into the shaft.

"Inara!" Galanör's voice disappeared above her.

As planned, Inara reached out and caught the rope of a pulley system. She slid down thirty feet until a bridge intersected the shaft and allowed her to spring the gap. Sprinting along the bridge, Inara made for the centre before hopping over the side and falling again. This time, she landed on the flat surface of a lift designed to haul tools up and down. The whole thing buckled under her weight and she heard chains rattling far above. Of course, she had never intended to be on it for more than a second. Springing away, before it fell into shadow, the half-elf gripped a stray rope hanging from another pulley and swung to the other side of the shaft.

Timed perfectly, Inara crashed through the railing and into Alijah. The siblings bounced off the wall together and tumbled down the walkway in a collision of limbs and stray punches. Falling over the edge of the boards was inevitable. They plummeted ten feet before careering off a lift platform and landing on the next walkway below.

Inara added her groan to Alijah's as she tried to get up, but his dragon armour had protected him better than any of her leathers. Rising first, he lashed out with a firm kick. Inara caught his foot an inch from her ribs and twisted, bringing him down on top of her. They grappled across the narrow walkway before, again, falling over the side.

By chance, they fell towards an intersecting bridge. Alijah hit the main bridge, landing flat on the boards, while Inara looked as if she would miss it. At the last second, utilising her elven heritage, she twisted and managed to grab hold of the railing, slamming her body into the side of the bridge. Every muscle cried out with new injuries, as well as a couple of ribs, but she refused to let go of the railing.

Again, Alijah was the first to recover. He crawled over to his sister, her fate in his hands. Or so he believed. As he hammered a fist down on her fingers, Inara let go with that same hand and reached up to snatch at his hair. One strong tug pulled his face down onto the railing, knocking him back in pain. Using the time she had, Inara swung her legs up and climbed onto the bridge.

Alijah was only a few steps away now, tending to his sore nose. Inara took the moment to look up and check on Galanör and Aenwyn. Both were still navigating the sloping walkway, too tired from battle to follow her dangerous route down.

"That hurt," Alijah commented casually, wiping blood from the fresh cut across his nose.

"You don't know pain yet," Inara retorted, her words as barbed as her tone.

"You can't stop this, Inara. It's already been seen and written in blood for thousands of years."

Inara looked at the man she knew to be her brother and numbed herself to the emotions that took note of his voice. He was just her enemy, another threat to the realm that needed dealing with.

"There are no words that will stop me from killing you," she stated flatly.

Alijah looked to be considering that. "How about these words?" He turned his palms down to the bridge and barked a spell of destruction that tore through the wooden boards.

Inara was accustomed to falling, an exercise she had practised many times with Athis, and instinctively jumped to the side as the bridge shattered into pieces under her feet. As the debris fell into the depths, she cleared the bridge altogether and grasped the edge of a lift platform. Alijah had made no such attempt to prevent his fall. He simply allowed himself to plummet and snatch at a loose rope. Determined not to let him get any closer to the bottom, Inara swung her legs and let go, her forward momentum bringing the Guardian in line with Alijah's rope.

"Inara!" Galanör and Aenwyn called from above.

Alijah began swinging his legs towards the lowest bridge in the shaft. A few seconds of back and forth and he was flying through the air, crossing the gap to the bridge. Inara ignored the calls of her companions and swung her own legs. From a greater height, she dropped down onto the bridge, testing the dwarven ingenuity. The boards, however, were saved from most of her impact by Alijah, who most definitely felt his sister's arrival.

They both rose back to their feet in an exchange of fists, elbows, and swift kicks. Inara relied on her knowledge of the Mag'dereth to inform her movements and fighting style. Alijah displayed a combination of martial arts that should have contradicted each other, yet he made his every blow move seamlessly from one to the next. His more barbaric inclinations surprised

Inara and she received a painful headbutt for the misinterpretation.

The Guardian of the Realm shook off the biting pain and came back at her brother with precise and calculated attacks. She had to be careful not to strike at his torso and cut her knuckles against the dragon scales. Alijah, on the other hand, had no such concerns and planted a strong uppercut into her solar plexus, folding her over. He tried to follow up with a knee to her chest but Inara blocked it twice before whipping her head up and catching him across the nose again.

Inara then extended her body into the fifth form of the Mag'dereth and flipped backwards. One foot after the other slammed into Alijah's chin and launched him off his feet. As he landed back on the bridge, Inara completed her flip and assumed her full height, her red cloak falling back into place behind her.

Alijah sat up and used the railing to stand again. A quick observation told Inara that her brother was favouring his right leg. She had also noticed a flicker of pain across his face whenever he used his arms to block her attacks.

"You haven't got it in you to kill me," he panted. "Your only hope is that Galanör reaches us before I enter the doorway."

Inara opened her mouth to deliver a sharp retort when she noticed something on Alijah's neck. Her head tilted to better observe the phenomenon. As she watched, small cuts were appearing along the side of his neck, forming a familiar pattern. Reaching out to Athis, Inara instantly became aware of their aerial battle and knew that Ilargo was currently entwined with Malliath, his jaws clamped across the black dragon's throat.

Her confusion slowed her down and Alijah took advantage. He jumped forward and landed a heavy side kick into Inara's midriff. She crumpled in the middle and flew backwards, along the bridge. After hitting her head, she skidded a few feet and lost a few seconds of consciousness. After that, rising back to her feet was a struggle and she depended on the railing to steady herself. After blinking her vision into alignment again, she set her gaze on an empty bridge.

Alijah was gone.

Bracing against the rail, Inara looked over the edge and found him on the walkway again. He paused and looked back at her. There was no arrogance or superiority in his expression, just resolution. Taking four more steps, Alijah disappeared entirely, as if he had never been standing there at all. Inara blinked, wondering if her head injury was more significant than she thought.

"Where is he?" Galanör questioned, his chest heaving beneath his armour, as he came up on her side.

Inara didn't know how to explain it. Instead of detailing the event to Galanör and Aenwyn, she made for the end of the bridge and began to make her way down in Alijah's footsteps.

"Inara, what is it?" Galanör asked. "Where did he go?"

"It's different down there," Aenwyn observed, looking over the edge. "The dwarves have lined the walls with stone."

Inara drew Firefly and took her first step off the wooden walkway and onto the stone steps. "He went down here."

With their own scimitars already in hand, Galanör and Aenwyn followed Inara down into the lowest depths of the dig site. Torches had been fastened to the walls, their flames showing the way. Inara removed one from its fixing and held it out in front to better see the steps. That wasn't all she discovered in the dark. They soon came across a pungent odour, followed by whispers in the shadows.

Aenwyn tried to pierce the gloom. "What is that?"

It was Inara who finally shone some light on the situation, turning her torch to the wall. Iron bars. Row after row of iron bars lined the shaft descending to its very bottom. The smell was certainly coming from the other side of the bars, but the whispering had stopped now.

"What is this place?" Aenwyn ran her hand up one of the bars.

"A prison," Galanör uttered with disgust.

"A prison?"

"Kassian got his hands on a Fenrig a few months back," the elven ranger explained. "He swore that's what the dwarves had been instructed to build down here."

Inara held the torch high and peered between the bars. "A prison for what?"

The answer emerged from the darkness, pushing the trio back a step. For the briefest moment, it would have been easy to believe that a monster was coming to attack them, but the horns and reptilian eyes were not those of a terrible beast. It was a Drake.

Then more stepped out of the shadows. Soon, every opening was filling with Drakes, their fingers curling around the bars. Turning slowly on her heel, Inara took in the entire prison around them. There must have been hundreds of Drakes, maybe more. An overwhelming surge of frustration and pity knotted inside the Guardian's heart. They were more than capable of melting the bars and reducing every Reaver to ash. They simply chose not to, avoiding any act of violence.

"You are not like the other," one of the Drakes announced, her voice just more than a rasp.

"She is," another remarked, his eyes scanning Inara from head to toe.

"You have come to free us?" the female asked.

"Yes," Inara whispered. "Yes, we're here to free you all," she said louder.

"How long have you all been down here?" Galanör probed, inspecting their dank living quarters beyond.

The female glanced at her kin. "Years," she stated, appearing somewhat broken by the answer.

"Years?" Galanör echoed in disbelief. "That's not possible. This entire shaft isn't even years old."

The Drake turned her gaze up to the light at the top of the shaft. "Down here, the sun does not hold sway over the passage of time. Only the currents can speak the truth of what we know." She set her sharp eyes on Galanör once more. "*Many* years," she reiterated.

Inara might not be able to read the currents of magic like a Drake, but the truth didn't escape her, horrifying as it was. She stepped back to the edge of the stone walkway and looked up. The flames of the torch revealed her worst fears and with it a memory.

The Guardian had seen this magic before, nearly twenty years ago inside The Bastion.

"*She* believes," the Drake asserted.

Galanör turned to Inara. "What is it? What's happening here?"

Inara directed them to the runes carved into the stone above the bars. They ran in perfect lines all the way around, starting where the prison began. There were even some etched into the walkway and along the steps.

Aenwyn reached up and ran her finger over one of the glyphs. "What spell is this?"

It was easier to show them. Inara removed a small dagger from her belt and tossed it high into the air. As soon it ascended beyond stone, the dagger slowed down to a crawl, its spin barely visible anymore.

"We're inside a time spell," Inara explained. "Hours and days up there are months and years down here." She looked at the Drakes again. "I'm so sorry." With one hand, she reached out and grasped that of the female Drake.

Galanör moved to the edge of the walkway and looked down at the very bottom. "That's how he did it. The doorway. He's kept their magic trapped down here for years."

"It also means he's been down here for some time," Aenwyn concluded.

"He sat there for many hours," the Drake told them, gesturing to the muddy ground.

"He just sat there?" Galanör doubted.

"Meditating," the Drake explained. "He entered here with injuries, but when he rose he was strong again."

"Alijah has had time on his side for too long," Galanör cursed.

"Well," Inara declared, removing the Moonblade from the scabbard on the back of her belt, "his time's up."

Bringing more light to the gloom, she raised the Moonblade to the ancient script above the bars. The opal blade glimmered with every colour over a base white, highlighting the dirt and blood on her face. With elven strength, she carved a line down and through the glyphs of the time spell. The magic within the

Moonblade broke the script, ending Alijah's hold over the lives of the Drakes.

A moment later, Inara's dagger - thrown high into the air - dropped back down and dug into the dirt at the bottom of the pit. "Get them out," she instructed, handing her torch to Aenwyn.

"Inara." Galanör's tone was full of warning.

The Guardian looked back at him. "Get them out. I'll handle Alijah."

Reluctantly, the ranger nodded once and turned to the cells with Aenwyn. Inara steeled herself and stepped off the walkway, jumping the remaining distance to the bottom. She slowly rose from her crouch, her eyes scanning the shadows between the sparse torches. With Firefly held high, and just a touch of magic, the crystal in the pommel brightened to dispel some of the darkness. Having seen many doorways in Drakanan, she knew exactly what to look for, but here there was nothing but dirt.

Alijah, however, must have gone somewhere.

Following the wall around, Inara soon came to realise her error. From their angle above, and where she had landed, the doorway was on its edge, making it thinner than a piece of parchment. Now, facing it front on, she could see right through to the realm of magic. Like some found in Drakanan, it didn't move of its own will, but was tethered to the ground by unseen forces. It was also smaller, coming up to Inara's neck and only just wide enough for her shoulders to fit through.

Rather than dwell on the fact that Alijah had actually achieved what she believed to be impossible, Inara focused on the bigger problem: he was already on the other side.

Once again, she took steps that would see her leave one world and enter another. The beauty of it hit her as if it was the first time all over again. Her eyes naturally lifted to the sky, a canvas of stalactites that glittered like stars. It was hard to say where the light came from, but nothing was in shadow. Mountains lined the horizon, their distance hard to gauge in a world so alien to her own.

Inara walked away from the doorway, her ankles submerged

beneath an endless ocean filled with shining crystals. Cutting through it all were thick roots that twisted, curved, and arched in and out of the ground. Following the roots back to their source, the Guardian of the Realm craned her neck to take in the tree. The white bark of its trunk stretched so far it was hard to see where it curved around. Much of the view above it was hidden by a mountainous canopy of red crystalline leaves.

Captivating as it was, Inara's gaze inevitably turned to the rising smoke. The black clouds were just visible over the tops of the distant roots on her left. Fear gripped the Guardian's bones and set her to a speed few could attain. She skipped over roots, slid under their arches, and leapt from one to another in a bid to reach the source of the smoke.

Sprinting between two wall-like roots, the water splashed round her before she finally bounced off one root to ascend over the adjacent one. She came down to land in more water, a patch of open space where the roots had parted long ago.

There was Alijah, his hands outstretched to the tree. Visibly sweating, he was a hum of magic as he expelled a jet of fire worthy of Malliath. The flames extended up the white wall of the trunk and turned the bark to black. From there, the fire climbed ever higher as if it had an insidious will of its own. Soon, branches were engulfed, setting the crystalline leaves alight until they shattered.

The sight of it enraged Inara. She buried Firefly tip down in the ground and flicked her palms out towards the tree. Responding to her magic, the water between the roots rushed forward in a crashing tsunami. Alijah was knocked forward, taken off his feet, and launched into the base of the trunk. Wasting no time, Inara then extended her arms to the burning tree and cast an outburst of water and sleet. It flowed from her hands in the same manner that the fire had been hurled from Alijah's. Unlike fire, however, water didn't have a life of its own.

As the drain began to pinch her hands, Inara stopped. There was only so far she could project her magic and Alijah's flames were always on the move, seeking out new branches and stretching across the trunk. In relation to its hulking size, Alijah's fire was no bigger than a single flame, but if she couldn't stop it from growing...

Just the thought of it boiled her blood. Inara clenched her fists, preparing another spell. If she had to give it every ounce of magic in her bones then she would. Anything else would be giving up. Anything else would mean the end for Athis.

A blinding flash erupted from the base of the tree and caught Inara across the midriff. There was no fighting the power that threw her backwards and dropped her into the shallow water. Groaning, the Guardian quickly recovered and patted the smoking leathers over her ribs and chest. Then she set her predatory gaze on Alijah.

He was on his feet now, a black sentinel between her and the tree. "There's nothing you can do!" he called confidently. "It's over, Inara!"

Rising back to her full height, Inara looked from Alijah to Firefly. The Vi'tari blade was between them, standing proud in the ground.

"Don't," Alijah warned.

The command only served to infuriate Inara all the more. She broke into a mad dash towards the scimitar. Alijah threw up one hand then the other, each casting a spell of fire at his sister. Inara raised her hand and caught the first with a quick shielding spell, but Alijah's magic was strong enough to shatter the shield in an explosion of light. Temporarily blinded, and determined to maintain her speed, the Guardian dived into a roll, tucking under the second ball of flames.

Emerging from her manoeuvre on one knee, Inara's hand grasped firmly around Firefly.

Keeping her head down below the hilt, she threw her will into the crystal set into the pommel. The magic discharged by the crystal spread out like a disk and impacted Alijah's hip, almost folding him in half before pushing him back into the tree with some force.

Inara rose triumphant, dwelling on the fact that the crystal in

Firefly's pommel had been a gift from Adilandra. Alijah, however, still found the strength to get back up, his jaw set.

"It wasn't enough that you killed our grandmother?" Inara barked, hurling a blast of destructive magic at her brother's waiting shield. "You had to kill magic too?" she pressed, casting another bolt. "Is there no one you won't murder?" The Guardian advanced on him, her every question punctuated by another offensive spell. "Would you take Athis from me? Would you execute our parents too?" Now she was so close that Inara switched to slamming his shield with her Vi'tari blade. "How could you be so weak? You should have been stronger than The Crow!"

Alijah took it all and he never let his eyes stray from hers. His shield flared with every blow, but he concealed the effort of maintaining it. For a fraction of a second, Inara thought she saw something of her brother behind his flat expression, a crack in his armour. With two hands around Firefly, she ignored the glimmer of hope and continued to swing her sword. Her emotions were beginning to get the better of her, and they would only get in the way of what needed to be done.

"Look at you," he said from behind his shield, his tone brimming with pity. "All that rage. All that power. You have no idea what to do with either of them. You should have joined me, Sister. I could have taught you things Gideon Thorn has nightmares about. Instead, you can only witness true power, never to be the one to harness it. Watch."

With one hand, he kept Inara's attacks at bay while, with the other, he unleashed a staccato of lightning upon the tree. Every blinding bolt tore into the bark and started more fires. The Guardian screamed with rage, threw her scimitar down, and thrust both hands at Alijah's shield. The magic she channelled was undefinable in its physical manifestation, pulsing from her palms like the sun itself. Soon, Alijah's shield arm began to tremble.

"That's it!" he patronised. "Dig deep, Sister! It's in there!"

"I am not your sister!" she yelled in his face. "I am... the line in the ground! I... am the shield in the dark! And you are nothing...

but-my-enemy!" The magic surging from her palms flickered as her bones began to ache.

"Poetic!" Alijah shouted back. "But you're going to need more than that to beat me!"

Inara gritted her teeth. "How about this?" she seethed.

Using every ounce of speed available to her, Inara ceased her magical assault, rolled backwards, and retrieved the Moonblade from her belt. Relying on skill and years of experience, she threw it clear across the gap without taking any time to line up her aim. It cut through the air until it collided with Alijah's shield. The power of the blade instantly shattered the protective magic and continued past the half-elf, slicing the side of his face in the process.

Shock and pain turned Alijah away, his attack on the tree brought to a swift end. By the time he had recovered and whipped his hair aside, Inara was upon him. Her last step became a leap, bringing her down on Alijah with a closed fist.

The blow turned him around with a mouthful of blood spraying across the air. Displaying a great deal of resilience to the pain, he turned his momentum into a full spin that saw his leg fly up and connect with the side of Inara's head.

On the ground, her vision fractured, a boot flung up into her ribs and forced her to roll in agony across the ground. Alijah gave no quarter, yanking her back to her feet with an iron-grip around her throat.

"You were supposed to be on my side!" he growled, followed by a punch to her gut. "We were supposed to do this together!" He laid another fist into her ribs. "You don't just betray me, but the realm itself!" Alijah lifted his fist and thrust it towards Inara's face.

But he wasn't the only one with an iron-like grip.

Inara caught his fist mid-air and held it steady. Her free hand wrapped around Alijah's thumb, currently digging into her neck, and prised it away.

"I'm going to kill you," she croaked.

A student of the Mag'dereth, Inara called upon her knowledge of form five to untangle herself from Alijah. It also came with a flat-handed attack to the side of his neck, a hammer-fist to his jaw, and strong elbow to the eyebrow. Each successive blow staggered the would-be king until there was enough distance between them for Inara to deliver a push kick to his chest.

His back impacted the ground, splashing water into the air. He was slow to rise, her attack designed to discombobulate. Inara used what precious time she had to focus her magic, drawing on it from her core, and harnessing it in her hands. As her power reached its apex, stymied by her fatigue, Alijah was back on his feet with a face full of rage.

Something close to a war cry burst forth from Inara's lips as she unleashed her magic, a combination of spells capable of reducing a man to ash. Alijah met her attack with outstretched arms and a new shield.

The light between them was blinding and the heat being generated sent ripples through the air. Theirs wasn't simply a battle of wills, however, but a battle of power. Alijah's power was built upon knowledge, a knowledge of which Inara could not boast.

"Gideon taught you a lot!" he yelled over the maelstrom of magic. "But he couldn't teach you what he didn't know!"

Alijah slowly pulled his arms back before pushing his hands into the back of the shield. It quickly expanded, forcing Inara's spell back on her.

For a second, the world went black. The next thing Inara knew, she was lying on her back, the water covering her ears. She could see Alijah casting more spells over the tree, the sound of his magic dulled by the water, but her mind struggled to comprehend anything.

A low branch, the size of a city street, gave in to the fire and impacted the ground with a violent earthquake. There was a part of Inara's mind that knew she needed to get up, to fight, to do anything. But everything hurt. Her muscles weren't responding and her bones felt so heavy she feared they had been bolted to the ground. More than that, though, her mind had been fractured by the blast.

After what felt like a lifetime, Alijah came to tower over her. His eyes, mirrors of her own, looked down at Inara. After a few seconds, he crouched down and used a small leather pouch, taken from his belt, to scoop up a handful of water and a crystal with it. Then, without a word, he stood up again and continued to observe his sister. His fingers twitched, though whether that was due to the volume of magic he had expelled or his temptation to draw his blade remained a mystery. He didn't say anything. Killing her would be easy now and Inara knew it.

As the realm of magic came down around them, brother and sister held a silent moment. Then he was gone. Inara remained on her back, her eyes fixed on the starry stalactites above. She could see the flames rising higher and higher up the tree. Every inch it lost was a portion of magic taken from the world.

Lost felt like the right word to Inara. That's exactly what they had done. Lost. All because she didn't have the power or the will to kill a single man. That thought brought some of her anger back and with it the power to move her hands and feet. Eventually, she was able to lift her head out of the water and even begin to sit up.

"Inara!" The familiar voice drew her to Galanör, who was dropping down from a tall root. "Inara!" he called again as he came to her aid.

By her side, he quickly checked the half-elf over before looking back at the burning tree. Most of the tree was untouched by the flames, but the fire's reach was high and beyond either of them now. Not far away, another branch lost its grip and fell to the ground. Everything shuddered beneath them.

"There's nothing we can do now," Galanör told her, his eyes roaming over the devastation rising up the tree. "We must consult Ilargo and Athis. Their wisdom will guide us."

"Did you see him?" Inara rasped. "Did you see Alijah?"

Galanör looked around. "We must have passed each other," he lamented. "The roots are tall here; it's like a maze."

Inara found her feet again, but Galanör was needed to steady her. "I failed," she whispered, her eyes reflecting the flames. "I tried..." She couldn't bring herself to relive the event, her energy on the verge of abandoning her altogether.

A light rain of red dust showered the pair, the remnants of the crystal leaves. "Come," Galanör bade, helping her up. "We need to go."

As he guided her away, back towards the doorway, the fire continued to spread and smoke billowed around them. Inara couldn't even think of a way to save it now.

The tree was dying.

All was lost.

Alijah stepped through the doorway and into the gloom of the pit. His bond with Malliath returned instantly and with perfect clarity. The king welcomed his companion's thoughts and feelings, both of which seemed to clear his head. It had felt unnatural to be so disconnected, leaving some of his own thoughts to fray at the edges.

He looked up to the circle of light, where snow flurries drifted down into the pit. He saw hundreds of Drakes running along the spiralling walkway, ascending to freedom. Of course, Inara had freed them all, and broken his time spell too. Despite his instinct to stop them escaping, he let his sister have her small victory. After all, the Drakes had served their role in his plan, a plan he had now completed. He would have preferred to have spent longer and torched a lot more of the tree, but the deed was done.

Now he just had to wait.

I'm coming to you, he said.

There were no words from Malliath. The dragon was all action as he battled two of his own kin, both fierce opponents, even for one so ancient and powerful as Malliath. Alijah could feel his companion's rage building with every claw and tooth that sank into his muscles. So intense was it, that the king believed he could actually feel some of the pain that accompanied those attacks. Alijah was tempted to withdraw slightly from their bond, so as to distance himself from the pain, but he *wanted* to feel it, to share as much of the battle with his dragon as possible.

Taking one more step away from the doorway, the king was struck by an arrow fired with greater accuracy and speed than any human could have achieved. The force of it sent him back a step, causing a portion of his cloak to interact with the edges of the doorway and disintegrate. The pain of it brought forth a roar from the half-elf and he instinctively reached for the missile. Looking down, the arrow had found the smallest of spaces between his scale mail, just below his shoulder. His fingers hesitated to touch it.

Whipping his head up, he saw an elf on the stone platform - she looked somewhere between determined and shocked. Using her own surprise against her, Alijah threw his hand out and caught her in his telekinetic spell. Her yell was cut short when she collided with the adjacent wall of the pit and fell to the ground.

"You must be... *Aenwyn*," he groaned, struggling to stand up straight. Bracing his open hand beneath the shaft of the arrow, the king flicked his fingers and drew it out with a touch of magic. It was agonising, but he had endured much worse.

A little dazed, Aenwyn rose to her feet, nocking a new arrow as she did.

"If you're here," Alijah reasoned, "so too is Galanör." He looked around the shaft but found no trace of the ranger. "A pity. I would have liked to have finished what he started on Qamnaran."

The muscles in Aenwyn's face subtly twitched as she took umbrage at his comment. The muscles in her face weren't the only ones to shift beneath the skin. Her arm pulled back the bow string half an inch and the knuckles in her hand paled. To Alijah, it was a glaring sign informing him of her imminent intentions.

"I wouldn't do that," he advised, his hand braced against the bleeding wound on his chest.

Aenwyn took no heed of his warning and raised her bow with enviable speed. In the same moment the arrow left the string, Alijah waved his free hand from left to right. The spell caught the arrow, Aenwyn, and most of the dirt beneath her feet, launching all of them into the air and back into the wall.

The fresh wound sent a spike of pain through his body and the king winced, his hands balling. Somewhere far above, he was sure he heard Malliath's almighty roar.

Without giving Aenwyn another look, Alijah made for the stone steps. Approaching the first pulley system he came across, Alijah wrapped his good arm around the rope and kicked out the mechanism holding the counter weight. In seconds, dwarven ingenuity had him rising up through the shaft, past the fleeing Drakes. After reaching the top, he swung across to the wooden boards and simply walked round the top level until he was standing on The Moonlit Plains again, his whole body sagging to one side in submission to the hole in his chest.

The sun was setting now, and not just on the world. Soon, magic would have its last day, then there would be no more battles for he could end them all, unchallenged. But that was not this day. As night approached, The Rebellion continued its stubborn attack on his Reavers, the battlefield as relentless as ever.

Time to leave, he said into his bond with Malliath, wary of losing too many more of his forces.

The black dragon dived down with Athis close on his tail. The two flexed their wings and glided low over the plains, just east of the battle. Athis proved faster, however, and caught up just enough to drive both dragons down in a tumble that tore up the ground for a hundred yards. Malliath was the first to recover, rising to club Athis across the face, but Ilargo was dropping fast with all four of his claws outstretched.

Alijah felt Vilyra and her dragon, Godrad, before he saw them. The pair intercepted Ilargo only seconds before he could rake at Malliath's back and head. The undead dragon pinned Ilargo to the ground, using its surprise to its advantage. Ilargo, however, was larger and would inevitably free himself, giving Alijah little time to make his own departure astride Malliath.

Where are you? Malliath pursued, his mighty chest heaving.

In the heart of the battle, Alijah might as well have been as far away from Malliath as The Narrows. But it had been The Crow who had taught him to always have an exit strategy. From his belt, he took the leather pouch, filled with water and a single crystal. He knew, having picked one up only seconds after entering the realm of magic, that the crystals lost their power when removed from the water.

The pouch was dripping in his hand as he prepared to throw it and open a portal. He paused, his attention momentarily stolen by a figure not far from the inner edge of the battle. Gideon Thorn, coated in mud and blood, stood watching him.

"What have you done?" the old master demanded.

"I've ended it," Alijah replied definitively, annoyed that the Dragorn had seen him looking so beaten after taking the arrow.

Without another word, he threw the pouch and commanded the magic therein to explode into the form of a portal. He stepped through and dropped down onto Malliath's waiting back, beyond the edges of the battlefield. He gritted his teeth against the pain that shot through almost every limb.

Not far away, Athis was shaking his horned head in a bid to regain his senses. When he did, and he inevitably would, the red dragon had only to unleash his fiery breath upon Malliath and the flames would consume Alijah. Such an attack could only be met with magic, the very thing the king knew he would struggle to conjure after opening a portal.

We've already won, Alijah insisted, watching Athis recover. *Their slow death will rob The Rebellion of what little resolve it has left.*

Though Alijah's consciousness was beginning to slip, succumbing to fatigue, he could still feel his companion's insatiable fury. Malliath wouldn't be satisfied until he felt their bones crack between his jaws.

Go! Alijah urged, unsure whether he would be able to keep his eyes open for much longer.

Malliath grunted, forcing a plume of smoke from his nostrils as Athis finally turned on them. His wings rose high and beat down, clearing them both from The Moonlit Plains and into a twilight sky. Vilyra and Godrad freed themselves from battle with Ilargo and quickly made to follow their master.

When the battlefield was so distant that it could be seen in its entirety, Alijah slumped in his saddle. His bones demanded rest for the magic he had let loose and he knew, given the time, he would fall into a deep sleep. Right now, however, he didn't care. Right now, he was content.

Rest now, Malliath whispered into his mind. *The war is over.*

No, Alijah uttered, a tired smile pulling at his mouth. ***Not just the war, but* war *itself.***

CHAPTER 23
CURSED

In the waning vestiges of light, Doran Heavybelly swung Andaljor with all his might, refusing to give up the fight. He had fought for two days without rest, stealing seconds here and there to down a mouthful of water, often taken from the corpses of his kin. The muscles in his arms stung with fatigue, his hands pulsed in pain, and his feet were on the verge of abandoning him altogether.

What remained of his senses had taken note of the dragons, their fight their own. A part of him acknowledged the fact that Alijah Galfrey must have entered the battlefield if not descended into the pit already, but he couldn't bring himself to care about the details surrounding that dilemma. There was only the fight.

Hours ago, he had glimpsed the power of Inara - her magic hard to ignore - and had even caught sight of a man he believed to be Gideon Thorn, though he hadn't seen the man in the flesh for over a decade and the dwarf had certainly been plagued by sweat in his eyes at the time. Alijah was *their* fight. As much as Doran would love to bury his axe and hammer into the half-elf's scrawny body, he knew the would-be king possessed magnitudes of skill above his own.

He settled, instead, for slaying Reavers. He was good at that. His axe cleaved and his hammer pummelled. Anything that survived that deserved to live in the dwarf's opinion.

From what Doran could tell of the battlefield, only two Trolls remained on their feet and one of them was currently being swarmed by Centaurs. If they all survived this, the son of Dorain promised himself he would reward Kelabor, and every tribe of the plains, with anything that the lands of Dhenaheim could offer.

That still seemed like a very big *if* to the War Mason.

For every Reaver they put down, two more seemed to spring up, as if the dead were waiting to replace the dead. Even now, as he drove one of the fiends to the ground, his axe lodged in the centre of its head, three more Reavers emerged from the melee. The dwarf retrieved his axe and backed off as the trio stepped over their dead and made to attack.

As they advanced, the sun's final rays of light faded and the grass came to life wherever it could between the bodies and snow. Cast in the green light, the Reavers appeared as menacing wraiths in their lunging attack. He would have spat some witty remark, words to goad, but he didn't have the energy to conjure words, let alone voice them. Instead, he let Andaljor do all the talking.

The nearest fiend went down quickly, its right leg hacked through. Tempting as it was to drop the hammer on its head and finish the job, Doran needed both weapons to deflect and block the remaining two Reavers. He shoulder-barged one, giving himself some space, before swinging his axe in a wide arc. The blade found its new home in the hip of the Reaver and declined to come out. Since the creature was knocked to the ground by the force of the blow, Doran had to abandon it and face the last standing Reaver with his hammer alone.

Seeing the incoming downward strike, the son of Dorain side-stepped and let the mindless knight decapitate the one-legged Reaver. With a grin on his face, he smashed his hammer down onto the back of the mindless knight's head, adding its corpse to the rest.

Turning to retrieve his axe and destroy the Reaver harbouring it, Doran was met by a new obstacle. With what energy he could conjure, the dwarf swore under his breath at the sight of Gondrith the Just and Hammer of the North. At least that had been his title many millennia ago, when Erador heralded him as a hero. Now, he was an undead Dragon Rider with a long hammer plastered with gore and dripping with blood.

Having already come across his dead dragon, Yillir, Doran knew that Gondrith fought without the aid of his companion, but that didn't mean the Rider wasn't a force to be reckoned with. With the son of Dorain in his sights, Gondrith shoved any and all aside to reach him. His hammer even knocked down Reavers if they got in his way.

"Ye've come for a piece o' Heavybelly 'ave ye?" he provoked, hunching his shoulders into a fighting stance. "Many 'ave tried. Yet 'ere I stand!" he bellowed, beating his chestplate.

Gondrith dashed forward, his hammer lifted high, while Doran charged forward in a frenzy of rage. The two collided in a clash of steel and a battle of wills. The War Mason swiped with his axe, just as he had for the last two days, but the Dragon Rider displayed a set of skills the other Reavers didn't possess. He evaded with swift ease and wielded his hammer as if it were no heavier than an ordinary sword. Doran had to work twice as hard to avoid its blow.

Concerned as he was with the slab of steel at one end, he forgot to block the end of the haft, which Gondrith slammed into the side of Doran's head. The dwarf reeled away, trying to move in the direction of the blow, but the force was still enough to knock him off his feet. Hitting the dirt was painful, but the incoming hammer triggered all of Doran's survival instincts. He ignored the aches and rolled one way then the other, narrowly avoiding the heavy strikes.

Stubborn as he was, the son of Dorain had no intention of giving up the fight. From the ground, he back-handed his hammer into the side of Gondrith's leg, bringing the Reaver down to one knee. Doran used the opportunity to get back on his feet and catch his breath. Gondrith required no such reprieve. The Dragon Rider rose to his full height, his hammer still firmly in his grip.

"Come on then," Doran muttered. "I'll knock that ugly head right off yer shoulders."

Gondrith twisted on the spot, bringing his hammer round in a sweeping arc. The War Mason wasn't foolish enough to believe he could block such an attack and so he didn't even try. Instead, he dropped and rolled under the swing. Popping up at Gondrith's side, Doran swiped and hammered at his enemy, but the Rider took it all before turning to continue the fight. The son of Dorain, however, wasn't finished. Using the curved blade of his axe, he hooked it over the haft of Gondrith's weapon and pulled it down, exposing his head. Without pause, he thrust the top of Andaljor's hammer into the Reaver's face and repeated the action three times.

A final shoulder barge forced the Rider back a few steps and gave Doran a good look at the damage he had inflicted. Gondrith's helmet was a crumpled mess, the iron digging into sections of his putrid face. So misshapen was it that one of his eyes had been crushed in by the hammer, giving him a blind spot.

It brought a smile to Doran's face. "Welcome to the club," he jeered.

Gondrith gave no hint of suffering or even offence. Using one hand, he dragged the helmet from his head without a care for the chunks of his face that came with it.

"Damn," the dwarf cursed. "An' I thought ye were ugly *with* the helmet."

There was no witty retort from Gondrith, only action. The Dragon Rider kicked the head of his hammer up and took hold of the weapon in both hands. He then proceeded to roll the hammer over itself left and right as he approached the War Mason. Doran stepped back in an effort to anticipate his foe's attack. When it finally came, his exhaustion slowed him down enough to have his axe batted aside and his hammer knocked from his grip. Gondrith brought his weapon to bear and shoved the haft of his weapon, horizontally, into the dwarf's face. The next thing Doran knew, something strong impacted his chest and he was on his back again, only now he was absent Andaljor.

Gondrith the Just came to tower over the son of Dorain.

Looking up at his foe, Doran spat a mouthful of blood at him. It was all the defiance he had left in him. He had no words, in this his final moment. The dwarf let his eye wander up to the emerging stars where, beyond their light, Grarfath's Hall awaited him. He almost giggled at the thought of Yamnomora's warm and comforting embrace, for the Mother was always the first to greet the children of the mountain.

Gondrith's hammer went high into the air, though Doran was hardly aware of it anymore. In fact, he would welcome the sweet release of it all. Release from the pain. Release from the burden of responsibility.

Down came the stroke, the killing blow that would take the light of Doran Heavybelly. Only it never got past the meaty fist and vice-like grip of Russell Maybury. The old wolf caught the hammer in one hand and quickly reversed its momentum into Gondrith's face. He followed it up with a swing from his own battle hammer and sent the Dragon Rider into a group of Reavers, knocking them all down.

Doran rolled over, supporting himself on his elbows, as he watched his friend do what he did best. "Give 'em hell, lad," he rasped.

Russell pursued his foe with determination, though both of his hands were trembling. His stance was no longer that of a man but more a beast, hunched and feral. He beat down the Reavers that recovered faster than Gondrith and none of them got back up again. His every blow was wild and brimming with untameable rage.

He was also much stronger than any of them, including the Rider. Gondrith discovered this when he got up and took his first swipe at Russell. The old wolf caught the end of the hammer in his hand and stopped it mid-swing. The impact would have shattered the bones in a normal man.

Baring large fangs, he roared at the Dragon Rider and snatched the hammer from his grasp before tossing it aside.

"No," Doran hissed, glimpsing the wolf. He looked up at the

night's sky, searching for the gleam of the moon in the lightly falling snow. "Don' give in to it, Rus!" he yelled. "Fight it!"

But Russell was a slave to the moon now; he heard only its call.

Gondrith lashed out at the old wolf with fists alone but he might as well have offered his head on a plate. Holding on to what he could of his humanity, Russell delivered an uppercut with his battle hammer and snapped the Rider's head back. As Gondrith landed on his back, Russell was already looming over him. The veins beneath his skin pulsed and his muscles began to expand, tearing the seams of his clothes.

"No, lad!" Doran cried. "Fight it!"

Before his bones broke and altered his appearance, Russell drove the haft of his battle hammer down onto Gondrith's mouth. With one hand flat to the hammer's head, he forced it down until the weapon sank into the ground, pinning the Rider in place. His hands shaking, the old wolf retrieved Gondrith's legendary hammer and gave one last swing with the arms of a man... of a ranger.

What there was of the Reaver's head came together between the two hammers in a spray of ancient remains. Gondrith the Just was returned to Gondrith the dead.

Russell staggered backwards and fell to his hands and knees. He was heaving, his chest panting at an unhealthy speed. Whatever he had managed to keep in his stomach was released across the battlefield. His fingers dug into the dirt as the bones in the back of his hand snapped and realigned into something worse.

Doran struggled to his feet and approached his old friend. Russell shot up a hand to halt him, displaying extended fingers and razor-sharp nails. The skin began to discolour, losing its pale complexion as it turned into a dark brown. It was his eyes, however, that truly stopped Doran from getting any closer. Though yellow, they were still Russell's. They showed something of the man trapped inside as well as his fear for Doran.

It quickly became too much after that and his head bowed. His clothes tore and his leathers ripped as his frame expanded. It looked like agony. Eventually, he was pushed off his knees when his feet changed shape and his arms lengthened. Doran was now slowly backing away, his eye scanning the ground for his axe and hammer.

The wolf's head snapped up at last. There was nothing left of the man Doran had come to call a friend. Sharp yellow eyes looked down a large snout at him. Thick saliva slopped from the Werewolf's mouth, between a jaw of deadly fangs. A low growl rumbled out of its throat.

Doran had no idea how he was going to fight the wolf - he could barely lift his arms anymore. Stepping on something hard and flat, Doran glanced down to discover the axe of Andaljor under his boot. He didn't dare reach for it or make any sudden movements.

His attention darted to the left when two elves emerged from the chaos to attack the wolf. Their scimitars sliced its arms, enraging the beast. As it lashed out with tooth and claw, Doran retrieved his axe and then his hammer, not far from where he was standing.

When next he looked back, the elves were dead, a mangled heap of bloody limbs at the wolf's feet. Its yellow eyes soon returned to the son of Dorain and the beast crouched, ready to pounce. For the first time, Doran was saved by Reavers after a small group of the mindless fiends were forced into the wolf's path by a Centaur and an elf. The cursed creature ripped their undead heads from their bodies like they were made of parchment.

"Stay back!" Doran warned the Centaur and elf.

The War Mason rocked from foot to foot, no clue as to how he was going to survive the next few seconds. The wolf closed the gap between them in a heartbeat and knocked Doran over with a hard shove to the chest. It took the air out of the dwarf's lungs, leaving him gasping on his back. The Werewolf then came to hunch over him, all four of its limbs boxing Doran in while its frame eclipsed the sky above.

This was not the way Doran wanted to leave the world, but at least it was Russell and not some meat puppet of Alijah's. The wolf opened its maw and the dwarf turned away from the foul breath that greeted him.

"Make it quick, lad," he instructed.

The wolf was happy to oblige. Its head dropped down, ready to snap its jaw around his entire head, when the unstoppable arm of a Troll slammed into its side. Doran heard the wolf's whine, like an injured dog, as it flew into the air and disappeared somewhere inside the fray.

The Troll continued its sweeping attacks, launching every combatant into the air with a roar on its dark lips. Doran managed to stagger out of the way, avoiding one of its lumbering feet, before its leg caught him across his right side and sent him careering into another dwarf.

Slow to recover, it took Doran an extra moment to realise the Troll had stopped its attack. The simple beast looked across the battlefield, its steaming breath spilling into the air. Without explanation, it turned to the west and fled with abandon.

"What now?" the son of Dorain grumbled.

As the Troll fled west, every Reaver on the battlefield was running to the east, breaking away from the battlefield. Exhausted, The Rebellion forces guarded themselves and simply watched as their foe retreated with no apparent cause.

"*What's going on?*" the dwarf beside him asked in their native tongue.

Doran couldn't say and he didn't dare hope that they had won. If Alijah had been slain the Reavers should have dropped to the ground. To his right, he could see Ilargo and Athis now, both looking weary by their hanging heads. There was no sign of Malliath but the black dragon had always been hard to spot at night.

As the battlefield began to clear of Reavers, the son of Dorain could see further and he was looking for something in particular. To the south, he found it - the Werewolf. The beast was limping away into the night and quickly fading from view.

Doran sighed, too tired to even muster a tear for his broken heart. He let the wolf go with a promise made to himself.

Plodding through the sludge and debris, the War Mason began to make his way towards the dig site. He barely recognised a soul on his way, their faces covered in mud and blood. He didn't have it in him to even pat the arms of his kin or offer a word to his allies. He just kept seeing Russell's eyes, warning him.

As he reached the edge of the pit, Galanör and Aenwyn emerged with Inara propped up between them. Not far, and striding towards them all, was Gideon. They converged on each other by one of the few tents to have survived the fighting. Galanör and Aenwyn carefully laid Inara down on the remains of a cot by the side of the tent.

"What happened?" Doran demanded, his throat horribly dry. "Did ye stop 'im?"

Inara could hardly keep her eyes open as she looked from him to Gideon. The old master crouched down and grasped her hand, their eyes locked.

"Well?" Doran pressed, glancing at Galanör and Aenwyn.

"He succeeded," Gideon announced on Inara's behalf. "The tree burns."

CHAPTER 24

AFTERMATH

Soon after the first rays of light, having had no sleep at all, Gideon stepped out of the doorway through which reality had been torn asunder.

Re-emerging onto Verdan soil, he inhaled Illian's air. Despite being deep beneath the surface, the air was much clearer and easier to breathe than that of the magical realm. Ash and smoke had assaulted his lungs from the moment he had stepped through.

He immediately reconnected with Ilargo, where the two shared equal dismay. They had already absorbed Inara's memories, thanks to Athis, but Gideon had simply needed to see it for himself. The tree was, indeed, burning and what magic he commanded had done little to help. The flames were too high and the damage too extensive.

Return to me, Ilargo bade.

Gideon happily ascended the shaft, pausing only to inspect the cells where Alijah had been holding the Drakes. He had given it much thought over the years - wondering how the half-elf might coalesce enough magic to open a doorway - but this was beyond his nightmares. It filled the old master with such sorrow to think of so many being trapped in the dark, for years and years.

Rising back to The Moonlit Plains, he closed his eyes and soaked up the morning sun. **This should have been a victorious dawn,** he lamented.

Every dawn we see in these dark times is a victory, Ilargo commented, drawing Gideon to the south, where the green dragon lay beside a sleeping Athis.

I fear your dawns are numbered, old friend, Gideon replied with glassy eyes.

We have had more than most. Though distant, Ilargo was still able to direct Gideon's attention to the battlefield that sat between them. It was littered with the bodies of heroes and villains alike, all scattered between the giant carcasses of Trolls and abandoned catapults.

Gideon began to make his way through it, weaving between the dead. Having taken the night to rest, elves, Centaurs, and dwarves had already started to clear through the fallen. They piled the Reavers and set the bodies alight while lining up their kin to prepare for funerals.

Is Inara awake? he asked of Ilargo.

She stirs, though I would say she needs...

Gideon frowned and shook his head. **She needs what?** he pressed.

Nothing.

There was nothing but his own thoughts inside his mind. Gideon reached out, as he had done countless times over the decades, in search of Ilargo's feelings. Nothing. The silence was deafening.

Ilargo? He repeated his companion's name over and over, his speed picking up as he crossed the battlefield.

Between the piles of bodies, he glimpsed Ilargo's head rising up to find him, similarly concerned. *Gideon?* Without warning, the dragon's voice suddenly cried out inside his mind, causing him to stop and wince.

I can hear you, he told him.

And I you, Ilargo replied.

Gideon continued his journey, a quick stride on him now.

What was that? The old master already had the answer to his own question but he didn't want to voice it.

Our bond is that of magic, Ilargo expressed for them both. *As the tree burns, the conduits of this world will lose their hold on magic.*

Gideon paused on his journey and looked back at the pit. **The realms are separating.**

Returning to the dragon, Ilargo dipped his head and the two stood together, skin to scales. As they parted, he got a good look at his companion, wounds and all. Malliath and Godrad had dealt out a good deal of punishment. Large claw marks cut red lines through Ilargo's majestic scales and Gideon could sense, if not feel, deep bruises beneath those that remained intact. Spikes were missing up and down the length of his body and the knot of bone at the end of his tail had been worn down and chipped.

Malliath evaded us for most of the battle, Ilargo explained, looking down at Gideon with bloodshot eyes.

Evaded? Gideon repeated,

Yes. He only revealed his aggression after Alijah descended into the pit.

Gideon met Ilargo's gaze as the companions put more pieces of the puzzle together. **Try to rest,** he said, rather than attempt to unravel the growing mystery surrounding their enemy. **I'm going to check on Inara.**

Leaving Ilargo to rest, the old master made his way around Athis, on the other side, until he could see the makeshift tent that had been moved over Inara. Faylen herself had seen to watching over the Guardian, no thought given to her own injuries and fatigue. She was seated on a small barrel, her elbows resting on her knees, and her head hanging over her chest.

"Faylen," Gideon greeted softly. The High Guardian of Elandril tried to stand in his presence but Gideon kept her down with a hand on the shoulder. "You need not stand for me," he told her. "You need rest."

Faylen looked into the tent at Inara, who appeared restless on her cot. "She is many things to many people, but she is the princess of Elandril to me. I will protect her to my end."

"The Galfreys have ever counted themselves fortunate to have you as their friend," Gideon offered. "Just as Ayda is fortunate to have you as its High Guardian."

Faylen managed a faint smile. "It is good to see you in the flesh again, Master Thorn."

There was too much dirt and blood on Gideon's face to reveal his flushing cheeks. "I'm afraid that title no longer applies to me. I'm just Gideon."

"There's no *just* about you, Gideon Thorn. Here you are again, putting yourself between the light and the dark. I see why Adilandra liked you so much."

Though he didn't think it was possible, Gideon felt new depths of sorrow upon hearing the late queen's name. "I will miss her all my days," he promised.

"As will we all," Galanör chimed in, approaching from behind.

His blue cloak flowed out, picked up by the winter breeze, and flecks of dried mud took off into the wind. His bronze-coloured chestplate was dented in parts and marred by scratches, the causes of which would have spelled his doom were he not wearing it. Since the battle had ended, the elf had tied his long chestnut hair into a knot, but his face was just as filthy as everyone else's. The most notable aspect of the elven ranger was the single scimitar sheathed on his hip. There would be no recovering its twin.

"How fairs Inara?" Galanör continued, peering into the tent.

"Better than others," Faylen answered, cocking her head towards the pain-filled cries of the wounded.

Galanör acknowledged the gesture. "Aenwyn is helping to organise the injured so that we might heal those most in need first. There are many."

"The dwarves will prove more difficult," Faylen commented. "Their natural resistance to magic won't help them."

"Where is Doran?" Gideon asked.

Galanör stepped to the side and set his gaze to a specific spot, searching between the foot traffic. "He's still out there," he said gravely.

Gideon moved to find the dwarf himself, following Galanör's

direction. Doran was just standing there with his back to them, removed from the camp. He was facing south, away from the battlefield, as if held by some trance.

"The dead weigh on him," Gideon assumed.

Galanör folded his arms. "The earliest reports actually suggest that the number of dwarves saved has increased their numbers. Doran has been told as much."

"Then why does he stand apart?" Gideon enquired.

Galanör glanced at Faylen, who appeared to understand whatever wasn't being said. "It's Russell."

The old master turned from Doran to look at the elf. "Russell Maybury? The owner of The Pick-Axe?"

"The *ranger*," Galanör added. "Russell has been fighting with us since Alijah invaded."

"What happened?"

"You know of Russell's affliction?" the elf questioned.

"I only met him a handful of times," Gideon recalled, "but I believe he was a Werewolf."

"An old one at that," Galanör said. "His curse finally ran its course. He had been struggling for weeks, months even. On the battlefield, he turned for the last time."

Faylen nodded her head in the War Mason's direction. "Doran said the beast ran south."

Gideon watched the dwarf for a time, wondering what was going through his head. "They were close?"

"Very," Galanör confirmed.

"Are you concerned?" the old master asked pointedly.

"His grief is a burden only his shoulders can bear," Galanör replied. "But bear it they will. I am more concerned that he will go after the wolf alone, to end Russell's torment."

"Whatever Doran decides," Gideon replied, "he needs rest first. You all do. You've been fighting for days without sleep or food. Go," he bade. "I will see to Inara."

Faylen nodded, if somewhat reluctantly. "I will find my husband first. I left him counting our fallen." The High Guardian made to move, pausing only to pat Galanör on the shoulder. "You fought well," she complimented.

The ranger found an amused smile. "Did you even see me out there?"

"No," Faylen admitted, as she walked away from the tent. "But you're still here, so you must have fought well."

Gideon couldn't argue with her logic and by the look on Galanör's face, neither could he. "Rest," the old master urged the ranger in Faylen's absence. "You and I have some catching up to do and I wouldn't have you falling asleep on me."

Galanör sighed and nodded along with heavy eyes and dark lids. "Gideon," he said, on the verge of leaving. "What do we do now?" he asked, glancing back at the dig site.

Gideon gave the only answer he had. "I don't know." He planted a hand on the elf's shoulder. "Get some rest, old friend."

After Galanör turned and walked away, Gideon ducked his head and entered Inara's shelter. She was rubbing her eyes, creating a deep frown between the two. Her leathers were a testament to not only the battle, but also the duel with her brother.

"Gideon?" Inara's voice was hoarse, like so many who had survived the fighting.

"I'm here," he assured, taking a seat beside her.

"I feel so weak," Inara complained, wincing at the light.

"You used a lot of your magic. You will recover." Even as he said those words he couldn't get the image of the burning tree out of his mind.

"You saw it?" Inara was looking up at him from her cot.

"Yes. I tried to put out some of the fire but there's too much."

Tears streaked down the side of Inara's face, cutting through the dirt. "I failed," she sobbed. "I failed us all."

Gideon's eyes welled with tears now and he reached out to comfort her. "You didn't fail."

"Of course I did," Inara protested. "We came to stop him, yet he still succeeded. I'm not the one you thought I was. My birth wasn't fated to happen. I wasn't meant to save the world. Everything The

Crow did was to make sure Alijah destroyed the world of magic. Now we have to watch them die."

Gideon didn't need to ask her to know that Inara was referring to their dragons. "I don't believe that," he stated firmly. "We are still alive, which means there is still a fight to be had. We will not let this be the end."

Inara squeezed his hand. "I can't beat him," she said defeatedly. "I tried. He's too powerful now. He..." Her words trailed off as her eyes glazed over.

"What is it?" Gideon demanded.

Inara made to answer but her thoughts and words collided with naught but silence for their efforts.

"Inara?"

"In the pit," she said at last, "when we were fighting..." Her hand reached up to touch her neck. "I was sure I saw wounds appear from nowhere. It looked like a bite mark." Inara shook her head. "It's all so fuzzy. I must have been seeing things - I hit my head more than once."

Gideon, Ilargo commanded. *I bit Malliath's neck after Alijah and Inara descended into the pit.*

Indeed, a flash of memory informed Gideon of the details, including the taste of Malliath's blood in Ilargo's mouth. It also offered new and crucial pieces to the puzzle that had plagued them since Namdhor.

This could change everything, Gideon concluded.

For some, yes, Ilargo agreed. *For others, it will not.*

Gideon could think of a few who wouldn't care at all. Then he wondered if he was one of those people.

"What's wrong?" Inara asked. "You're talking to Ilargo."

Gideon took a breath and leaned forward on his elbows. "I think you saw what you saw."

Inara groaned as she attempted to sit herself up but ultimately rested on her elbows. "How can that be? He told you their bond had never been like a Dragorn's to begin with."

Gideon nodded in agreement. "But what he told me and what we've both seen doesn't match up."

Inara frowned. "*Both* seen? What are you talking about, Gideon?"

The old master glanced out of the tent, in Ilargo's direction. "When we confronted Alijah and Malliath, in Namdhor, they both bore injuries from Qamnaran."

"Yes," Inara replied. "Adilandra threw him into The Hox and Malliath dived in after him; I saw those wounds myself."

"Did you notice Alijah's limp?" Gideon questioned. "Malliath's back left leg was barely touching the ground."

"That isn't proof," Inara said, shaking her head.

"And the cut above Alijah's eye?" Gideon continued.

"I saw it," Inara confirmed.

"Malliath had the exact same cut in the exact same place. It was harder to see because of his dark scales but Ilargo didn't miss it. Now you witness shared injuries as they actually *happen*. Inara, I don't think you hit your head and imagined it. I think—"

"They're still bonded like Dragorn," Inara interjected, the revelation washing over her at last. "They share pain."

"They share more than that," Gideon determined. "If they share pain, they are *one life*. That also explains why Malliath kept Ilargo and Athis chasing him for so long rather than turning to fight them."

"He couldn't risk Alijah suffering *his* injuries while he needed to get to the doorway," Inara continued, picking up the thread.

"It means Malliath has been, and is still, influencing Alijah's thoughts and feelings," Gideon elaborated.

Inara's mouth fell open. "How can this be?" she questioned absently.

"It's the only explanation for what we have both seen."

"No, I mean *how* can this be? Alijah believes his bond is that of a Dragon Rider. He would know that to be a lie if they shared wounds."

Dismayed, Gideon shrugged. "It is likely a testament to Malliath's control over Alijah. He has been blinded to it all, tricked into believing they are his injuries alone. Or perhaps Malliath makes him oblivious to the wounds altogether."

"How can Malliath's influence be so consuming as to fool Alijah?" Inara queried. "Athis may have guided my emotions now and then to ensure I didn't take the violent path, but he has promised me that was the *extent* of his abilities."

"Ilargo was the same," Gideon reassured. "He has never been able to directly control my thoughts and, from his mother's memories, no dragon ever has in Elandril's order."

"Then what? My brother is a puppet?"

"There are extraordinary circumstances involved where Alijah is concerned. He was tormented in every way by The Crow. His mind was already being broken down before his bond with Malliath matured."

"He was always strong of mind," Inara said, shaking her head. "There's a part of me that's still angry with him for giving in to the pain, for taking on The Crow's teachings."

Gideon looked down, his thoughts running away with him. "What if he did resist?" he posed. "What if The Crow didn't really get into his mind like we think? What if The Crow only sought to break Alijah down so Malliath could assume more control. He would seep into the cracks and bury Alijah under millennia of suffering and hate."

"This hate of magic that drives him so fiercely does speak more of Malliath's mind than his own," Inara opined. "I suppose Malliath's age could mean he is simply powerful enough to control Alijah."

"Possibly," Gideon reasoned. "He's older than history."

Inara leaned in. "If we're right, that means there might be something of our Alijah still in there somewhere."

"*Somewhere* would be accurate," Gideon told her. "If he is still in there, he will be buried beneath The Crow's brutal torment and Malliath's over-bearing mind. Asher has spent years just trying to rid himself of Malliath's *echo*. I can only imagine the oppression of being bonded to him."

The revelation brought some new life to Inara, who managed to sit up on the edge of her cot. "So what do we do now?"

Gideon opened his mouth but nothing came out. He could feel

Ilargo searching for an answer to that same question but even the dragon failed to grasp any option that could help them.

Finally, his response was identical to the last time he had been asked that question. "I don't know."

Inara sighed, the fight in her ebbing away. "Even if there was something we could do, we could also be wrong," she theorised. "There might be nothing left of him in there. And if there was, how many people do you know who would be willing to try and save him? Everyone has lost someone and they all put the death toll at Alijah's feet."

"What if it's the only way to beat him?" Gideon suggested. "He's powerful. He has Jainus magic at his disposal and Malliath's strength flowing through his veins. And that's without taking Malliath himself into account. What if separating them is the only way to beat them?"

Inara tilted her head. "You're talking about turning Alijah to our cause, pitting him *against* Malliath?"

Gideon locked his jaw while considering his next words. "Alijah might be the only one who can beat Malliath. We have to accept the fact that Ilargo and Athis cannot kill him." The old master could feel an argument rising in his companion, leading him to quieten his bond temporarily.

"I think you might be overestimating Alijah," Inara cautioned. "If we did find some way to pull them apart, the Alijah that we knew might not appear for some time, if at all. After all their time together, he could truly agree with Malliath and then we've just made it harder to kill them."

There was a hard edge to her voice that jarred with Gideon. "So you think we should use this knowledge to focus our efforts on killing one so that we might kill them both?"

"Alijah couldn't fight off all of us with Ilargo and Athis coming down on him," Inara reasoned. "We now know that if we kill Alijah, we kill Malliath. Surely that is our only advantage from this."

Gideon thought of the young man he had known, a man who only wanted to help the world, regardless of the cost to himself. It made his bones shiver to think of that same man being trapped inside his own mind, within a web of lies and deceit constructed by the one being who should love him the most.

"Do you *want* to save him?" he asked bluntly.

Inara held his gaze for a moment. "If we're right about all of this - if *you're* right about all of this - he was born to be the destroyer. He is here to be the evil that unifies the realm against him. Shouldn't we seek to kill him? To end his threat?"

"Ending the threat he poses and killing him are two very different things, Inara. I'm talking about a way to free Alijah and offer him a real chance at redemption."

"By having him kill Malliath?" Inara countered. "And that's *if* he can. You could bring forth a broken shell of a man who doesn't even know what world he's living in. And that's the good scenario. You could separate them and discover Alijah is just as twisted as we've thought all along. Then there's two of them to fight."

Gideon prepared his side of the argument as he shuffled forward, but Inara beat him to it with a blunt question and a clipped tone. "Do you know how to separate a dragon from their Rider?"

The old master swallowed, his confidence faltering. "No."

"What about the Jainus?" Inara pressed. "If anyone in history was going to try and find a way to do that it would be the Dragon Riders' sworn enemies."

"If they did I found no mention of it in their library," Gideon replied. "Given that the Dragon Riders won the war, though, I imagine they destroyed anything that might harm them."

Inara continued to look at him, her victory clear to see. "There you have it, from your own mouth. There is no way to separate them, which means there is no saving him, no redemption, and absolutely no chance of him killing Malliath for us. The advantage is simple - we focus *all* our efforts on killing Alijah alone."

Gideon didn't agree and he could feel Ilargo backing him up. "Our efforts should not be directed towards Alijah or Malliath right now. Both of our companions will die if we don't try and find a way to save the tree."

Their argument shifted, Inara paused to take a breath but it quickly led to her head dropping into her chest. Gideon could see the energy draining from his old student, her skin paling. He grasped her arms before she fainted and flopped onto the ground.

"Easy," he cautioned. "You need more rest."

Inara tried to argue the opposite as he guided her back down onto her cot. "We need..." Her chest heaved with the effort. "We need to..."

Gideon hushed her and draped a blanket up to her shoulders. "Sleep," he whispered, though she already was.

As he exited the tent, Ilargo's blue eyes were looking down at him. *Defeating Alijah and Malliath will not undo the destruction they have wrought upon the realm of magic. And I'm afraid we no longer have the luxury of dealing with one problem at a time.*

I agree, but I have no idea how to fix either problem.

Ilargo's head perked up and his reptilian eyes cast across the plains. *Captain Dardaris and his forces have arrived.*

Better late than never I suppose. Gideon turned and walked away to get a better view across the camp. ***I will greet them,*** he said, watching the few thousand men as they marched north. ***Faylen and Galanör need to rest. As do you,*** he added, looking up at the dragon.

You will hear no arguments from me, Ilargo replied, lowering his wounded head to the ground.

Gideon made to leave, but he allowed himself an extra moment to look upon his companion with adoration. Theirs was a love he could not live without.

CHAPTER 25
SURVIVORS

The far-reaching hand of winter travelled with Vighon and his company. However far south they journeyed now, its bitter cold was waiting for them, with the first falls of snow. It was these icy winds that kept most inside their homes. Absent any walls or a roof, the northman adjusted the furs around his collar, sure to keep his dark cloak over his knees.

More than once he had climbed down from his saddle and walked beside his horse to get some warmth into his muscles. He was expecting a fight at the end of their journey and he didn't want to be stiff entering a battlefield.

He hated to think of the carnage taking place only a few miles south of them. After an agonisingly long three days, they had entered The Moonlit Plains and even passed the ruins of West Fellion, but the ancient land just seemed to roll on, expanding into more open plains. He had hoped to arrive at the dig site that very morning, but that looked to be out of the question.

For most of their trek, the king had comforted himself with the knowledge that every mile they covered was a mile closer to Inara. Now, however, he couldn't get rid of that itch to simply be there, adding his flaming sword to the fray.

Avandriell had proven to be something of a welcome distraction along the way. Vighon looked up at the dragon now and marvelled at her flight. Her recent growth spurt had been explained to him during their last camp. Since then, he couldn't recall seeing her anywhere but in the sky. He hoped to live long enough to see her fully grown and Asher mounted on her back. *Now that would be a sight,* he thought.

Quite the opposite of *her* majesty, Sir Borin the Dread entered his vision astride the largest horse they could find for him. Thankfully, there had still been an armourer working in Namdhor. Now, the Golem's gruesome body and face were covered by plate and a flat-topped helmet.

The sound of hooves, moving faster than the others, turned Vighon away from his bodyguard. Kassian Kantaris came up alongside him, his face partially concealed by a scarf and the collar of his long coat. The mage didn't say anything for a while, content, it appeared, to ride beside the king. He wanted to say something, however - that much the northman could discern.

"Out with it, Keeper," Vighon urged. "You've more than earned the right to speak your mind."

Kassian licked his lips, his brow furrowed in contemplation. "We're going to win this," he said, without context.

Vighon glanced at him, assuming he could only be talking about the war. "Of course we are," he replied, with as much confidence as he could muster. "Has that only just dawned on you?"

"Until recently, I didn't really care." Kassian's tone spoke of honesty, a refreshing change to his usual sarcasm. "As far as I was concerned, I had already lost and there was nothing to win. There was just pain... and vengeance."

Vighon was reminded of the vengeance that once drove him. It had been maddening, like an ache in his bones. The pain had demanded that he find and kill his father, the man responsible for his mother's death. At least he had one or two people to blame and focus his wrath upon. Kassian lived with a burning hatred for the most powerful necromancer and dragon in the realm. Everywhere he went, Alijah's mark stained the land, reminding him of what he had lost.

"Take it from me," Vighon said, "there's no clarity to be found in vengeance. That sweet release it offers is all too brief. In the end, you're still left with the pain."

"You've walked this path yourself?" Kassian enquired.

"During The Ash War," the king answered.

"Did you have your vengeance?"

Vighon thought back, recalling with ease the moment he killed Godfrey Cross, the man his father had tasked with murdering his mother. Then, with perfect recall, he saw his father, Arlon Draqaro, walking down the main road of Namdhor, his wrists chained in manacles. The Peoples' Justice had seen to his end with brutal efficiency. Had he made it to the bottom of the slope, Vighon was still unsure to this day whether he would really have set him free.

"I suppose I did," he finally replied. "But it changed nothing. Vengeance never does."

Kassian kept his thoughts to himself for a moment. "So how did you... move on?"

Vighon considered the question. "It's hard to lose what you love. Your world shrinks. There is no tomorrow, only today." The king turned to look at the Keeper. "It's even harder to find a reason to keep going. Something to live for. But once you do, it soothes the soul. Then, like anything, time sweeps in and the pain begins to fade."

Kassian's head rolled back onto his shoulders and he sighed, exhaling a cloud of vapour into the air.

When he didn't reply, Vighon pressed. "You said until *recently* you didn't care." The king left it there, opening the space for Kassian to talk about it if he wished. He had come to value the Keeper and not just for his skill with magic. The northman could see something of a great man under all the mage's grief.

Kassian glanced over his shoulder at Aphira, his fellow Keeper. "We're going to win this," he repeated, as if starting again. "When we do, we need to be ready to rebuild the realm."

Vighon tried to contain his smile. "We?"

The Keeper took a long breath, his eyes struggling to meet the king's. "All I have left of Clara is the pain. Her memory deserves more than that. And the conduits of this world deserve more than being hunted by Alijah's beasts. I believe there is a way to serve both."

Now Vighon was very intrigued. "By conduits you mean…"

"People touched by magic," Kassian clarified. "The survivors of Valatos alone must number in the hundreds and they're all out there, lost and afraid. And they're just the ones with training. There could be thousands more out there who have no idea why they're different. Without the proper guidance, they can be a danger to themselves and everyone around them."

Vighon drew an easy conclusion. "You're talking about a new Valatos? A new Korkanath?"

Kassian looked pained by the comparison. "Yes and no. They both possessed a good foundation but their vision was executed poorly. I'm talking about something that is better than both."

"Which is?"

"I don't know yet," the Keeper confessed. "But I would like your help in building it. And I'm not talking about your coin," he added quickly. "I want you to help me find a way that benefits the realm as well as these people. Coexisting is the only way we can forge a lasting future. I see that now."

Vighon nodded in agreement. "I wish Alijah saw it your way," he remarked.

"He sees people like me as a threat to the realm," Kassian said.

"He's not wrong about that," Vighon replied, bringing out a frown in the Keeper. "His response to that fact is disproportionate," the northman continued with a calming hand in the air. "I had similar fears when Valatos was built. We were still rebuilding in the wake of the destruction caused by The Crow. He showed all of us what magic is capable of when wielded by the wrong person."

"The Crow and Alijah are the reason why we need to do this together," Kassian elaborated. "With your approval, and Inara's wisdom, the people will trust what we're doing."

"Inara?" Vighon questioned.

Kassian shrugged. "Well, besides you being the king and queen of the realm, Inara carries the wisdom of the dragons. Not to mention the people's love and respect for her. They probably like her more than you already," he quipped with an amused grin.

Vighon, however, appeared dumbfounded. "King and queen?" he managed, having never thought of the titles side by side.

The Keeper raised an eyebrow. "Is that supposed to be a secret?" He glanced back at the company. "It might be a little late for that, your Grace."

The king wasn't sure what to say. "Does everyone know about us?"

"I'd say so. Though why you'd both keep it a secret is beyond me. The fact that the two of you have managed to find each other in this mess of a world is nothing short of a miracle. If you ask me, you should hold on to each other and never let go."

Vighon would have loved to do just that, but Inara was still miles away, her fate unknown. "It's been a long time coming," he commented quietly. "And you're right," he continued, "Inara's wisdom would be crucial to your plans."

"So you agree then?" Kassian probed eagerly. "There should be a place for magic?"

"If Alijah's schemes have shown me anything," Vighon said, "it's how important the world of magic is to Verda. And whether a person can wield magic or not, they are a subject of my kingdom and I will serve them as such. The real question is: are *you* ready to serve them?"

Kassian didn't reply with a bold declaration but, instead, a humble nod of the head. "I would like to. But, I suppose I'm bringing this to you now because, well... let's face it, there's still a chance I won't survive this war. I need to know that you will still do something in my absence."

"For what it's worth," Vighon offered, "I don't think you will be added to the fallen. You're too stubborn. But, if it gives you peace of mind, know that I will do all that is in my power to help people like you. You have my word."

Kassian gave an appreciative nod and half a smile. "It wasn't that long ago I considered you to be just as ordinary as any other northman. Now, I know the value of your word."

Vighon smiled. "I hope, in time, you come to value the word of every northman. We are an honest breed."

"Well if it's honesty you appreciate, I should tell you and every northman: you need to find somewhere else to live. Namdhor is bloody freezing!"

The king laughed. "You're not wrong," he said. "But the cold is good for us - it keeps the fire in our veins at bay!"

The two men shared a laugh before falling into deeper conversation, sharing ideas and possibilities for the future. It felt good to talk about the world in such a manner, pretending, for the moment, that the realm wasn't hanging in the balance.

As the waning sun showed its face, between the thick clouds and the distant horizon, their discussion came to an end. They were approaching the last rise in the plains where smoke could be seen rising into the sky. Naturally, Vighon scanned the sky in search of Athis or Ilargo.

"Prepare for battle!" he bellowed over his shoulder.

With his horse spurred into a gallop, the king rode towards that final rise. He did his best to ignore the anticipation that dug deep into his gut and focus on the fight to come. There was only him and his sword.

Trailed by his company of warriors, Vighon drew his sword and pointed it to the south. His confidence, however, was instantly knocked when he realised his enchanted weapon remained dormant. The silvyr, as always, appeared exquisite, but there were no flames.

The northman stared at the blade, his attention stolen by the phenomenon. How could there be no flames? The enchantment had never failed, not once. As the answer struck him, his horse reached the apex of the rise and began the gentle descent towards the dig site. There was no battle, at least not anymore. There were plenty of dead though - proof that one had been fought there.

In the distance, just south of the battlefield, a makeshift camp sprawled across the snowy plains. That appeared to be the source of the smoke, where numerous fires had been lit. The dig site itself was a black void in the middle of the land, a portal that transported one down into the depths of the realm.

Then, without any warning, the sword of the north came alive with blinding flames. Vighon held it away from his cloak before again holding it high into the air, signalling their arrival to the others. He couldn't acknowledge, even to himself, the obvious conclusion.

Skirting around the edge of the battlefield, the king noticed the largest corpse amongst the debris. He couldn't identify the dragon, but he knew it to be one of Alijah's Reavers. By his calculations, the wretched necromancer only possessed one more. It was a small victory if nothing else.

Soon after, they were greeted by a throng of elves, dwarves, and Centaurs, the latter surprising Vighon. Seeing some of the flames dampen on his sword, he returned it to the scabbard on his hip. He offered nods to any and all who met his eyes, but the king was searching for a few among them.

Athis and Ilargo were easily spotted, lying to the east of the camp. Even from this distance, Vighon could see the damage both had taken. Before he could make his way to them, Faylen Haldör emerged weary and exhausted.

"Your Grace," she greeted with a bow of the head.

"High Guardian." Vighon offered the same gesture. Faylen, however, was quickly distracted by those behind the king, directing him to Reyna and Nathaniel.

Reyna brought her horse to the front of the company and removed her hood, revealing golden hair and emerald eyes. Faylen shouted something in elvish over her shoulder and every able elf and Centaur stood up before genuflecting with bowed heads. Reyna responded with a gentle word in her native language and Faylen rose from the mud with the others.

"Where is my daughter?" she asked in the common tongue.

Faylen's expression subtly dropped and her head turned to the east. "She rests, your Grace."

Vighon felt a distinct lurch inside his gut. "She is injured?"

"Inara is already recovering," Faylen assured. "Gideon is with her."

Nathaniel turned his horse to the east and set off at a quick trot. There was no stopping the father, nor Reyna who followed after him.

Vighon was torn between his love and his duty. Were he to take off behind them, he would be revealing priorities unbefitting of a king, especially since he had missed the battle. "What happened here, Faylen?" he asked urgently.

"We lost." The words sapped Vighon and his company of energy and hope, but the words had not come from Faylen. The king turned with everyone else to see Adan'Karth. The Drake remained astride his horse while his reptilian eyes searched their surroundings. "The two realms have already begun to separate."

Vighon turned back to Faylen as Galanör arrived by her side. "He's right," the elven ranger confirmed. "I have seen the tree with my own eyes. Alijah has taken fire to it."

The king gripped his hilt, his worst fears laid bare. "And our enemy?" he uttered.

"As soon as his task was completed," Galanör replied, "Alijah fled with Malliath. The Reavers followed thereafter."

Faylen opened her mouth to add something when a distant squawk drew her gaze to the sky. There she set eyes on a young Avandriell and was lost to the dragon's majesty.

Galanör craned his neck and narrowed his vision. "Is that..."

Vighon had waited as long as he could. "I would see Inara," he insisted. "Then I want a full report." He didn't wait for their response, his horse set to a swift trot down the line with a large Golem on his tail. Athis and Ilargo were the perfect markers, directing him to Inara's position within the encampment.

He was dismounting before the horse came to a complete stop, his attention directed to the tent where Reyna and Nathaniel were crowding. He barked a command at Sir Borin, ordering him to remain where he was. The Galfreys parted as he arrived, giving the king a good view of Gideon Thorn. The man was filthy and marred by a plethora of minor injuries.

"Your Grace," Gideon greeted with a dip of the head.

Vighon looked through the gap and found Inara lying on a cot. He tried to push past but Gideon placed a firm hand in the centre of his chest, barring the way. The king fought the instinct to slap it away and remind Gideon who he was.

"Forgive me," the old master began. "Inara used a considerable amount of magic against Alijah. Added to her injuries, it's imperative that she rests..." Gideon trailed off as he looked up, beyond the northman.

Vighon turned to see Athis's head looming over them all, his magnificent blue eyes fixed on the king. Vighon had no idea what the dragon was thinking nor his intentions, but he knew they were holding a moment. Athis gave a slow blink and glanced at Gideon before returning to his place of rest beside the tent.

Without explanation, Gideon stepped aside and gestured for the northman to enter the tent. Vighon nodded what little understanding he gleaned and ducked to walk inside the torn canvas. He crouched down by Inara's side and grasped her hand under the blanket. She was cold. The king didn't hesitate to remove the furs from his shoulders and place them over her.

Outside, he heard Gideon recounting events for Reyna and Nathaniel but he hardly listened. His thoughts were so consumed by his fears for Inara that he couldn't focus on much else.

Rather than perch beside her and do naught but watch her sleep, Vighon used the rag and a small bowl of water beside her cot to begin cleaning the muck from her face. She didn't so much as stir, despite how cold the water was.

"We should have waited," he whispered. "We should have attacked together." The king squeezed her hand and planted a soft kiss on her forehead. "I love you," he professed with glassy eyes.

The northman held her hand for a few minutes more. He wanted to stay with her until she woke again, but even without a crown on his head he could still feel the weight of it. Given the significance of their defeat, Vighon made to leave and fulfil his other duties.

A light touch of snow sprinkled across his face as he met Gideon and the Galfreys again. "She's strong," he said reassuringly to Reyna, who looked at him with great concern. "But Gideon is right: Inara needs to rest now."

"I'm not leaving her," Nathaniel stated.

"Nor will I," Vighon echoed. "The circumstances and location aren't ideal, but I want to convene the council immediately. Right here," he added, pointing at the space beside Athis. Gideon and Nathaniel nodded in agreement but Reyna's gaze had drifted back to her daughter. "Reyna," the northman said, taking her hand. Only when her eyes met his own did he speak directly to her. "I have valued your counsel for years. I need it now."

"And you have it." Her response was bold but her voice lacked the tone of dependability he had come to expect from her.

Vighon, instead, glanced at Nathaniel, who gave him a reassuring nod that his wife would be up to the task.

"I will summon the others," Gideon offered.

As the old master walked away, Vighon advised the Galfreys to sit with their daughter until the council was ready. He hoped some time with her would ease their concerns but, like the northman, they wouldn't be content until she opened her eyes.

Rounding the tent, the king looked out on the camp. He could see Kassian and many of his Keepers were already spreading out to put their magic to good use where the wounded were concerned. There were so many of them. Like the sun, Vighon's hope was waning. A familiar face, though, brought a much-needed smile to his face.

The captain of the king's guard, Sir Ruban Dardaris, approached with a number of soldiers at his back. Beyond them, Vighon could see a growing camp of soldiers, men gathered from around the realm, though predominantly from the south. They all bore the sigil of the flaming sword and they all bent the knee in his long shadow.

Ruban didn't bow.

The captain gave Vighon a hard look, though the pause in his approach allowed the king a cursory inspection of the man and his forces. That was all he required to see that none had been in the recent battle. A closer scrutiny of Sir Ruban's face, however, informed the king that his old friend wasn't entirely glad to see him. The captain raised his arm, putting Vighon on edge - he had promised to put him on his back, after all. But then, in the blink of an eye, his demeanour changed with a broad and delighted grin breaking out across his face. Happy to be surprised, Vighon clasped his friend's forearm and crushed him in a tight embrace.

"Forgive me," Vighon whispered in his ear, his tone pleading.

"You do not need forgiveness for being flesh and blood like the rest of us," Ruban replied. "I have seen the kind of king you are time and time again. I saw that in you before you were king, in fact. But the realm is not yours alone to hold up. You should have confided in me. Your fears are mine."

"I know," Vighon said, shutting his eyes tight.

Ruban increased the strength of his embrace. "The next time you feel the weight of it all, you come to me. If you don't - should you falter again - I will hunt you down myself."

Vighon smiled through the cutting guilt that stabbed at his heart. "Never again, old friend," he promised, stepping back from the captain. "I know who I am."

Ruban mirrored his grin. "It is *good* to see you," he said earnestly. "Though the company you keep is questionable," he added, looking over the king's shoulder.

Vighon glanced back at Sir Borin. "It's a long story."

"I would hear it over a drink and a hot meal," Ruban replied.

The northman patted his captain on the shoulder with an agreeable smile and moved past him. "Rise, all of you!" he commanded to the force beyond. "For two years you have kept the flaming sword alive with your courage! For the rest of your days I will not see you kneel to me! I would always know who you are! And there will always be a place for you at my table!" The men took the honour in their stride and cheered the name Draqaro.

Vighon turned back to his captain and placed a hand on his

pauldron. "The council is convening - I want you there. Fetch Kassian too."

Ruban's face lit up with the contented smile of a man who was happy to have his king back. "As you command, your Grace."

The northman stepped away and let his gaze drift over the survivors. It dawned on him then. If Alijah had truly won and the realm was, indeed, his now, they would face naught but dark days and forever be known as *survivors*, nothing more.

"No," he muttered to himself, his fists clenching by his side. He would make heroes of them all, even if it killed him.

CHAPTER 26
FAMILIAR FACES

As a bitter wind picked up his green cloak, Asher climbed down from his horse with both eyes on the sky. He found Avandriell with ease, his mind drawn to her. But his gaze travelled further still, to the thick clouds that threatened more snow. The ranger thought of Malliath piercing those winter clouds and descending upon his young companion with merciless wrath.

It brought back memories from his time under the thrall of The Crow. Even now, years later, Asher could still hear the screams of Dragorn and the cracking bones of their dragons within Malliath's jaws.

The memory stirred his emotions which, in turn, affected Avandriell. The bronze dragon tucked in her wings and dived towards him in search of comfort.

Too fast! he called out across their bond. *Too fast!*

The ranger quickly assumed a wide gait, preparing to catch Avandriell and cushion the impact - if his knees were up to it. At the last second, her wings fanned out and she crashed into his chest with all four claws, some of which tore his leathers. He staggered back, thankful for her last-second attempt at slowing down.

"Easy!" he reassured, moving his head to avoid her new horns, each the length of his hand now. "Easy," he repeated in a softer tone.

Avandriell looked up at him with her golden eyes. Whispers echoed in the back of his mind but the speech was too chaotic to discern. Amidst the chaos, however, one word pushed its way forward with clarity.

Asher.

Her voice struck his mind like a bell, but the moment was broken when her meaty tongue ran up the bristles on his cheek. The size of a large dog, there was no stopping her from pouncing away. Happy to have her on the ground again, Asher took a few seconds to scan his surroundings. Vighon had left soon after Reyna and Nathaniel, all disturbed by the news of Inara. The ranger himself felt a pang of unease where her health was concerned, but Adan's words had cut right through him.

"What do you see?" he asked the Drake.

Adan climbed down from his mount, his eyes still surveying the land around them. "The world is losing its colour," he uttered. "The light of the elves is already beginning to fade. Soon they will be shells, a shadow of what was." Adan crouched down and ran his fingers through the snowy grass. "It's all dying," he lamented.

Asher turned back to Avandriell, who was examining a Centaur with curious eyes. His concern for her quickly rose to the surface. "What about..." He couldn't bring himself to ask the question since he wasn't entirely sure he could handle the answer.

Adan stood up and pulled his hood back to look at the dragon. "Avandriell's magic will outlast us all, even that of Ilargo and Athis. Her connection to the realm of magic is still so raw and, after thousands of years in her egg beside her brothers and sisters, she is a powerful conduit."

Asher took his first breath since the Drake had started talking. But then his world came crashing down on him. All Avandriell had was more time than the rest of her kin; her fate was still sealed. Before the ranger could sink into that depression, a hand landed on his shoulder, turning him around. For all the misery dragging him down, seeing Faylen brought a smile to his face.

"Hello, stranger," she said with a coy grin.

Asher spread his arms and pulled her in. There was a time when all he had wanted was the feel of her skin, the smell of her perfume, and the sound of her sweet voice. And, though he could not deny any lingering feelings towards her, he had found a place in his heart to be happy for her.

There was also a part of him that still wanted to punch Nemir, her husband, right in the face. He felt that all too keenly upon spotting the elf emerging from the camp to greet them.

Asher stepped back from Faylen and gave the elven captain a nod. "Nemir," he said politely enough.

"Asher," the elf replied with a slight bow of the head.

Awkward as it was, Faylen ploughed through and gestured to Avandriell. "Is this..."

Asher couldn't help but smile - he loved the way people marvelled at his companion. "This is Avandriell," he declared with pride.

"Avandriell!" Faylen repeated, clearly enjoying the way it sounded in her mouth.

"She is magnificent," Nemir commented, his stiffness easing.

A contented smile ruled Faylen's expression. "You are bonded to a female dragon. Somehow that seems perfect."

Perfect was a word that kept coming to the ranger when he considered any aspect of Avandriell. "She still has a lot to learn," he said gruffly, which led his thoughts back to a dark place.

"Does your life ever get dull?" The lighter tone was familiar, leading Asher to the angular face of Galanör Reveeri.

The ranger flashed a smile and clasped hands with the elf. Like all the others, Galanör was grubby from head to toe, his elven demeanour - a regal stature - diminished by exhaustion. Still, Asher could feel the strength in his grip.

"*You walk with Fate, old friend,*" Galanör said in his native tongue.

Asher cast a cursory eye over the elf. "And you walk with only one blade. What happened?"

Galanör placed his hand over the empty scabbard. "Trolls.

Though I would gladly have given both swords if it would have saved more lives."

"I'm sure many more would be out on that field if it weren't for you," Asher encouraged.

Galanör thanked him with a nod before joining Faylen and Nemir, who had both crouched down to greet Avandriell. "She is exquisite," the elf complimented.

"She gets that a lot," Asher quipped, his sight lost to the sea of dwarves and elves.

"*Captain Nemir?*" came a call from the thick of the camp.

The captain ceased his interest in Avandriell and stood up to meet the approaching elf. They exchanged a brief conversation in their melodic language. The captain nodded, signalling the end of their discussion, before turning to Faylen. "I must see to something." Husband and wife shared a gentle kiss before separating.

The ranger was pleased to see that such affection didn't sting him half as much as he had expected it to. Instead, he waited for Nemir to disappear back into the camp before asking, "Where's Doran?" There was something about the way Faylen looked up at him that made Asher steel himself for the worst of answers.

The High Guardian rose to reply, leaving Galanör to stroke the scales under Avandriell's jaw. "He's just south of here," she said, easing some of the tension in the ranger's muscles. "Asher..." Her tone pulled his eyes from the south and back to her. "It's Russell. He transformed during the battle. The wolf fled but Doran seems to think that Russell will never return."

Asher sighed and dropped his head into his chest. "I had hoped to be there for his last moon," he said with a heavy heart.

"So it's true then?" Faylen continued. "Russell will never return?"

"His curse has been bearing down on him for some time. Being consumed by it is an inevitable conclusion for any Werewolf. I had hoped there was more time." The ranger had really hoped he would be given the chance to say goodbye.

Galanör returned to them, his arms folded. "The weight of it has robbed Doran of reason. He has barely said a word since the battle ended yesterday. I don't think he's slept either."

"He just stands there," Faylen explained, "staring at the south."

Asher was about to speak when he sensed something from Avandriell. It was a craving, he knew, and not for food or water. He was naturally drawn to the sky, an ocean of freedom that the dragon had recently discovered. It was addictive. That much of her experience he shared. She let out a low squawk and flapped her wings. Many stopped what they were doing and simply watched her take flight, most completely unaware of who her companion was.

"I told you she would get big!" Gideon called on his approach. "Though I have to say, I wasn't expecting her to fly so soon."

Happy to busy his mind from the news of Russell, Asher turned to the old master. "You failed to mention the circumstances of her growth," he replied.

Gideon finally reached the trio and frowned at the response. "Ah, yes," he recalled after some thought. "It can be somewhat dangerous in the wrong environment."

"There's an Arkilisk out there who learnt that the hard way," the ranger said dryly. "Had I not been with Adan I would likely be a pile of ash in The Evermoore."

Gideon looked past the ranger to set eyes on the Drake. "Of course... He can read the magic." The old master's eyes glazed over for a second, his thoughts consuming him. "My apologies, Asher," he eventually said. "I should have mentioned the danger. Sadly, time eludes us again. The king calls for a council."

By the time a fire pit had been constructed and The Rebellion's council had gathered around it - absent Doran Heavybelly - the sun had dropped below the western horizon and the thick clouds had thankfully rolled away with it. Now, under a canopy of stars, Asher listened to reports from Faylen, Galanör, and Gideon about the end of the world. At least it sounded like the end of the world to him.

The battle sounded bloody, claustrophobic, and unbalanced where numbers were concerned. Adding to the enemy's might, they had guarded the dig site with Trolls, catapults, and ballistas. As tempting as it was to believe that he could have made a difference in the fight, the ranger knew losing odds when he heard them.

He just liked to think that he could have saved the tree.

Saved Avandriell.

Her head was currently resting over his leg, her scales bright in the light of the flames. Asher stroked the top of her head, between her two horns, and watched her eyes get heavier and heavier. Could Fate be so cruel as to take her away from him? Why not? he mused. It had spent a thousand years learning new ways to torment him.

The flat of his hand came to rest on her head and he simply enjoyed the rhythm of her breathing.

"You can't grasp the size of the tree," Gideon was saying to Reyna. "It's as big as any mountain and the fire has spread to the canopy. It would take a *lot* of magic to put out the flames and every second that goes by, we lose more of our connection to it."

Vighon leaned forward on his log. "What are the realistic repercussions of this?"

Gideon glanced at Asher before answering the king. "Our ability to wield magic will diminish day by day until the tree is gone. We've already heard from Captain Nemir," he said, gesturing to the elf seated beside Faylen, "that the healers among us are failing to aid common wounds. Even The Moonlit Plains," he added, pointing at the luminescent grass beneath their feet, "will lose its enchantment. And we have no idea what will become of the Drakes, but they are half dragon and..." The old master took a long breath in an effort to conjure the words. "And the dragons of this world will die without magic."

Nathaniel turned to Galanör. "But not you," he stated. "Your magic is no longer tied to the tree?"

"Time will tell," the elven ranger replied. "It seems likely given what Gideon told us of Alijah's plan on Qamnaran."

"Sadly," Gideon chipped in, "Galanör's ability to retain his magic cannot help us. No one person can save the tree, however powerful they might be."

"No!" Kassian said forcefully, shaking his head. "We're talking like all hope is lost, like we've lost the war. This isn't over yet. The tree isn't gone and our enemy is still out there."

"He's right," Nathaniel added supportively. "We can't let magic *die*. There must be a way."

"What about the dragons?" Sir Ruban queried. "I have seen them put out the worst of fires."

Gideon was shaking his head before the captain had finished. "The doorway is barely large enough for a human to fit through." The old master cast his eyes over Asher's sleeping companion. "And Avandriell is too young and too inexperienced to fight a fire this big."

"So what *are* our options?" Kassian pressed.

"Perhaps," Sir Ruban suggested, "we should take the fight to Alijah while there is still enough magic in the world to aid us."

"Our options are few," Gideon admitted. "But I don't think we should even consider challenging Alijah and Malliath until we have a better understanding of the damage done to the tree."

"If we wait," Sir Ruban countered, "do we not risk having no magic at all?"

Vighon shook his head. "Regardless of the magic at our disposal, The Rebellion is in no shape to face Alijah and his Reavers right now. As much as I would like to make our enemy pay for what they've done, our priority is seeing to the wounded, gathering our strength, and investigating the damage to the tree. We aren't going to beat Malliath without Ilargo and Athis and we're not going to beat Alijah without magic on our side."

"What if you only need to beat one of them?" The question came from the shadows, beyond the firelight. There were none on the council, however, who didn't recognise the voice of Inara Galfrey, no matter how weak it sounded.

Gideon's head whipped around. "Inara?"

The Guardian of the Realm entered the light, her fatigue there for all to see. Inara waved away the concern of many and declined the offered seat from Vighon, choosing to stand instead.

"What are you talking about?" Kassian asked her.

Inara looked at Gideon. "Have you told them?"

The old master appeared reluctant to answer her. "No," he confessed.

"Told us what?" Kassian blurted impatiently.

"Malliath and Alijah are still bonded by one life," Inara declared. "We have only to kill one and they will both perish."

Asher's attention sharpened to a point, the old assassin in him demanding action. It was like a sweet voice in the back of his mind. Avandriell stirred and opened her jaw to yawn. The voice in the back of his mind then quietened and he reminded himself that he was a ranger, not an Arakesh. He was part of something here, something more important and bigger than himself. Besides, he had tried to kill Alijah once before using the methods of the Arakesh and it ended badly.

He returned to stroking Avandriell's head, discarding the urge to sink into the shadows and track his prey across the realm.

Nathaniel adjusted his position on the small barrel. "What do you mean, Inara?"

Asher listened intently as the Guardian went on to explain what she had discussed with Gideon the previous day. She detailed their findings and laid it out for those who might not be accustomed to the way of dragons and their companions. Ultimately, it came back to the ranger's initial conclusion: focusing their efforts on killing Alijah alone would end the war.

Throughout Inara's speech, Gideon remained seated with his arms folded and his hand covering his mouth. The look in his eyes told Asher that he didn't fully agree with his old student.

"So we only have to kill one or the other?" Vighon questioned out loud and mostly to himself. "Focusing our attack on Alijah alone would improve our odds."

"It would if we knew where he was," Asher announced, speaking for the first time.

"I thought you could track anything," Kassian quipped.

"Not through the sky," Asher replied dryly. "I agree this changes the way we view our enemy, but they're in the wind and beyond our reach. There's a reason Alijah and Malliath have fled rather than secure this site. They have only to wait now. When magic is gone," he said, glancing at Athis and Ilargo, "so too are their greatest threats. Right now we have a foothold. We should take advantage of our enemy's absence."

"Asher is right," Gideon spoke up, though his words were directed at Inara. "We have access to the tree here."

"Until the doorway closes," Inara countered. "The Drakes fled before we even set up the camp. Without their magic down there, the doorway will close."

"All the more reason to do what we can now," Gideon argued. "I do not wish to return to Drakanan while Alijah and Malliath could follow us. I will not put the eggs at risk needlessly."

A tension filled the gathering until Queen Reyna shattered it. "I think we can all agree on our priority here. Nobody wants to live in a world without dragons, therefore we cannot allow magic to fade away."

"*Are* we all in agreement?" Vighon asked, looking from Inara to Gideon. "Magic *is* our priority? And only *then*, we take the fight to Alijah?"

"Aye," Inara voiced first. "As long as we are in agreement on our *strategy*," she added, looking pointedly at Gideon.

One member after another gave their aye in agreement, but it was Gideon's response that drew Asher's gaze. He watched the old master's jaw clench as he agreed with the council and Inara's stipulation.

"Aye," Asher finally said, the last to do so. He continued to watch the old master, vowing to speak to him later rather than in front of the council.

"We cannot speak for the dwarves," Faylen said.

"I will speak with Doran," Asher volunteered. "I don't think he will be ready to leave the plains yet, but I wouldn't rely on them staying too long - this land is too exposed for any dwarf's liking."

Vighon gave Asher a look of appreciation before addressing the council again. "I would like to see this tree for myself. Though, I must admit, I have no idea how I might be of any aid."

"Perhaps," Gideon began, looking across the fire to Adan'Karth, "we could try *talking* to the tree?"

The king raised an eyebrow. "Perhaps you need rest, Gideon."

"I agree," Inara said pointedly, taking a seat beside Vighon. "But he isn't wrong," she added in a softer tone and without meeting her old master's gaze.

Vighon found the Drake across the fire. "You can speak to trees?" he asked incredulously.

"The trees of this world are just as alive as you or I, good king," Adan'Karth explained. "Though I fear their voices will fade soon."

"Why?" Inara questioned.

"Magic has long been a part of Verda's nature, just like the wind and the tides. Without it, much of this world will pale to shadows in the twilight."

Again, Adan's words cut through the group and lowered morale, though he only lived to speak the truth and it could not be held against him. Asher was, in fact, rather proud of the Drake. He was the only one among his kin who was doing something to save the realm. And he had stayed by the ranger's side day and night, enduring Asher's every habit and bad attitude.

"If there is any hope," the Drake continued, "it may lie in the tree itself. I will gladly reach out to it, but I must pass through this doorway; my people can glean a lot from touch."

"I can testify to that," Asher muttered, recalling his first visit to Ikirith, before the war.

"I will take you," Gideon volunteered.

"I will come as well," Kassian interjected.

Gideon appeared reluctant. "We don't know what's over there. It might be safer to keep our numbers down."

Vighon raised a hand. "I want Kassian to go," he said, raising a few eyebrows - the Keeper's included. Since he wasn't going to give his reasons for the edict - nor did he have to - Gideon simply bowed his head. Kassian did the same, though his was more of a thanks than a sign of respect.

"Urgent as this may be," Reyna spoke up, "might I suggest a night of rest for all."

"I'm not going to argue with that," Gideon replied, obviously exhausted.

"I would see to some of the wounded," Adan declared, rising from his seat.

"I will assist you," Galanör offered. "My magic should be put to good use."

Reyna reached out and touched the elven ranger's arm. "Make sure you rest."

Asher patted Avandriell's neck, rousing her before he stood up. He didn't want to sit around. Being still felt wrong, even if he wasn't in a position to do anything.

"I will speak with Doran," he repeated. Turning to leave, the ranger hesitated, aware that he was in the presence of the king. Vighon flicked his head, encouraging him to depart the group with a silent dismissal.

Asher cast his eyes over Inara and Gideon. The old master was watching her, though it seemed the Guardian was determined not to look at him. The ranger wasn't one for getting in the middle of things when it came to the emotions of others but, of all those around the fire, Inara and Gideon were The Rebellion's - if not the realm's - greatest hope. And though they might not need to be in harmony, they at least needed to agree on the same strategy.

This was not the time or place, however, to call out either of them. He had other business to attend to.

With Avandriell close by his side, the pair made their way across the camp. They weaved between dwarves huddled around fires and elves sharing out food. Every Centaur that crossed their path bowed to Avandriell. Though the night was getting on, the camp was far from quiet; the still air disturbed by the cries of so many wounded. Asher could see frustrated Keepers and elves alike

as they struggled to enact their healing spells; a notoriously difficult magic to perform.

The ranger hardened himself to it all, well accustomed to the
consequences of war. Avandriell, however, was not so versed in the
reality of battle for there was only so much she could take on from
her mother's memories. Asher had expected her to absorb his
emotions on the matter but her individualism, it seemed, was a
new development in her growth. More than once, the young
dragon paused to look at an elf or a dwarf in pain.

Her heartache and desire to help made him stop and crouch
down. "They're in good hands," he assured her, though he didn't
know how much she truly understood. "There is one, however,
who does need our help."

Avandriell looked at him, her golden eyes wider than normal.
Even if she didn't know what he was saying, she could interpret his
feelings and she trusted no one more than Asher. Together, they
finished their journey across the camp and broke away, to the
south.

Doran was easy to find, sitting on a lone boulder with a cloud
of smoke rising from his mouth. He was still wearing all of his
armour, though Asher and Avandriell could have discerned that by
smell alone. Andaljor rested upright against the boulder, its steel
stained with detritus. Also resting beside the weary dwarf was his
trusted mount, Pig. The animal snored into the night, weary itself
judging by the injuries crossing its hide.

"That Warhog is as stubborn as you," Asher remarked. "I'm
starting to wonder if it will outlive us all."

The dwarf glanced to his left, taking in the pair. "I'm happy for
ye, lad," he said, oblivious to the ranger's comments. "Ye deserve a
companion as fierce as yerself," he muttered.

Asher remained beside the boulder as Avandriell pounced on
some insect in front of the dwarf. Doran got a better view of her
now and allowed his eye to wander over her rather than scout the
southern plains. He didn't display the look of wonder and amazement as everyone else did when seeing the young dragon, but
dwarves weren't known for their appreciation of the natural world.

"Her name is Avandriell," Asher told him.

"A fine name," Doran complimented. "A fine dragon too. Me kin could work steel an' silvyr for centuries an' never make anythin' so exquisite as her scales. Ye're a lucky Rider," he added, before exhaling another cloud of smoke.

Asher puffed out his chest and hooked his thumbs into his belt. "I'm still a ranger," he replied adamantly.

The son of Dorain gripped his pipe between his teeth. "A ranger with a dragon? Ye'll be puttin' the rest o' us out o' business then."

Asher couldn't see many more days ahead of Doran as a ranger, but he kept that opinion to himself. "The battle was unforgiving," he said, instead.

"The battle was *hell*," Doran corrected. "But aren' they all?" he muttered with a heavy heart.

Asher took a breath, his eyes still roaming the darkness. "He's out there somewhere."

The dwarf removed the pipe from his mouth and sighed. "Aye," he drawled.

Asher finally looked down at his old friend. The weight of the world was upon him. The ranger placed a hand on his shoulder, drawing Doran's eye towards him. "Russell should not be left to torment. Inside the beast he is a prisoner."

"He charged me with killin' 'im should it come to this," Doran blurted, averting his sight. "I know I should already be out there, huntin' the wolf down. But when I swing me axe that's it. Russell will be gone... forever."

"He will *rest* forever," Asher said softly. "But only after we have slain the wolf."

Doran looked at him again. "Ye don' 'ave to do this, lad. Rus charged me, not ye."

"I brought him into this world of monsters," Asher maintained, recalling the moment he had introduced Russell to the life of a ranger. "I will make sure he does not remain as one."

Doran nodded once. "Ye'd 'ave made a good dwarf, ye know."

"And had naught but *rocks* between my ears?" the ranger quipped.

The son of Dorain chuckled half-heartedly. "I can' argue with that."

"Come," Asher bade, turning back to the camp. "Eat, drink, and find some rest. We hunt in the morning."

Doran frowned. "We should leave now!"

"Trust me," Asher said. "Hunting Werewolves at night is a mistake; especially when the wolf in question knows our scent. It will likely be sleeping in the day - that's when we hunt." The ranger gestured to the camp. "Now rest or you will be useless to me."

Doran huffed. "Are ye sure ye're not half dwarf?" he asked, rising begrudgingly from the boulder.

With Avandriell bounding beside them and Pig sniffing every inch of ground behind them, they returned to the camp and found somewhere to rest. Asher was unaccustomed to seeing Doran attended to by others, but his station as War Mason made him important now. They were brought what food could be spared and settled for water instead of ale.

His mind allowed to stray from Russell's fate for a while, the son of Dorain asked many questions concerning Avandriell and what events had led to their pairing. Asher was more than happy to talk about her, though he struggled to contemplate the future right now. It wasn't long, however, before the dwarf gave in to his exhaustion and fell asleep. Asher draped a cloak over him and sat back against the wheel of a cart. He raised his arm to let Avandriell nestle in beside him.

The ranger let his thoughts drift rather than dwell on the pain the morrow would bring.

CHAPTER 27
FIRST CONTACT

A new dawn greeted the world from the east, though it failed to bring with it a clarity to match its light. Kassian looked out on the camp feeling just as lost as he had the previous day. They had arrived to a field of bodies and defeat, both of which had stolen the hope from many a heart. Every one of his Keepers had come to him at some point with their fears. None could imagine a realm without magic in it.

Nor could Kassian.

After taking Aphira's advice and speaking to Vighon about the future, Kassian had finally begun to envision his place in a world without Clara. In fact, the world he now dreamt of was so perfect *because* of Clara.

And now it was in jeopardy, hanging on a knife's edge. The Keeper was eager to enter the realm of magic and see the damage for himself. With that in mind, he strode across the camp to join Gideon, Vighon, and Adan'Karth by the northern edge. They were easy to find since Sir Borin the Dread was standing beside the king and the Golem could be seen from almost anywhere.

Not far away, nearer to the large dragons, Reyna and Nathaniel were sharing some food and water with Inara. The Guardian of the

Realm appeared in better health today, which was more than could be said for everyone else in the camp.

Rounding a pair of Centaurs, Kassian discovered Asher talking to Vighon, the ranger previously hidden by Sir Borin's frame. Once the Keeper was within a few feet of them, their conversation could be heard over the general hubbub.

"How long will you be gone?" the king was asking, some concern in his voice.

"I cannot say," Asher replied honestly. "This land is unknown to the wolf. It has likely found refuge nearby and is seeking to carve out territory."

"I understand what lies ahead of you," Vighon said, sympathy lacing his tone. "Russell's fate pains us all. He was a good man. I hope you bring him rest and soon."

Asher bowed his head. "Your Grace." The ranger gave Kassian a passing nod as he walked away but the king's call gave him pause.

"Do not linger in the wilds any longer than you need to," Vighon pleaded. "The Rebellion needs you in the fight and the dwarves need Doran now more than ever."

"You have my word," Asher replied.

Kassian watched the ranger disappear into the camp before returning his attention to the group. "Shall we?" he asked, looking to the dig site beyond. "Time is ever against us."

They crossed the battlefield on foot, navigating around the heaps of burnt bodies and discarded weapons. The dead Trolls and dragon carcass required the most forethought, their girth considerable. Most of the fallen dwarves, elves, and Centaurs had already been collected from the field and lined up beyond the camp, ready to be identified before any funeral.

Arriving at the edge of the enormous pit, the companions peered over the edge. Kassian examined the wooden walkways and bridges before looking back at Sir Borin.

"Is it going to take his weight?" he questioned.

Gideon stepped onto the first boards that curved round the outer wall. "It's dwarven engineering," he remarked, as if that was answer enough.

"Let's not take the chance," Vighon replied, before turning to his bodyguard. "Sir Borin, you will remain up here."

The Golem groaned from within its iron helmet.

"The battle is over," Vighon told him. "I will be safe down there. You *will* remain here."

The king didn't wait. He stepped onto the wooden boards and strode down the ramp until his head disappeared below the lip of the pit.

As was his humour, Kassian had a sharp quip for the Golem but, upon meeting his unnatural eyes - seen through narrow slits - the Keeper held on to his words and trailed after his companions.

Down into the pit they descended. After the fight between Inara and Alijah, there were few lifts still in service and those that had remained intact looked too precarious. Following the walkway around the wall, they continued until the dirt became stone.

Adan'Karth slowly wrapped his fingers around one of the bars to a cell and opened it wide. The Drake scrutinised the disgusting dungeon Alijah had forced his kin to endure. If the numbers Galanör and Aenwyn had reported were accurate, these cells were far too cramped.

The king stopped beside the Drake. "I understand that your people abhor violence, Adan, but there must be a limit. Any one of them could have broken free."

"My people remember little to none of our existence as orcs, your Grace. But what we do remember is their hunger for violence and death. It's naught but a leaf carried in the wind for us now, a thought whispered in the back of our minds. But it lingers. And so we walk a different path, one that will never breed violence."

"And a noble path it is," Gideon encouraged. "Orcs believe that everything can be solved with violence, and if violence isn't solving the problem, you're not using enough of it."

"Quite," Adan'Karth agreed.

"Well," Vighon said, "I am thankful we can count you as our friend, Adan.

As the Drake tilted his head in thanks, Kassian's gaze wandered up to the glyphs etched into the stone around the pit.

"I know pieces of this spell," he announced, a little dumbfounded by the intricacy of the extensive glyphs. "I can slow a person down, for a short while at least. But this... *This* magic would have been beyond even the masters of Valatos."

"As is that." Gideon looked down at the pit floor, directing the Keeper to the doorway.

Kassian pressed himself up to the railing, his eyes wide in fascination. Without waiting for the others, he rushed down the remaining steps to better see it. The mage in him wanted to investigate every facet of the gateway, but the sands of time were pouring inside the hourglass and, with every grain, they lost more magic.

"Will it hurt?" Vighon asked, eyeing the ragged edges of the doorway.

"No," Gideon reassured. "Just be sure to duck your head. I can't say for certain what would happen if you touched the edges."

"Let's go," Kassian said, eagerly.

He was the first to pass from one realm to the other. His eyes naturally tracked up the mountainous tree, its branches extending to a sky of glimmering stalactites. It would all have been so much more beautiful if it wasn't for the black smoke and ash billowing into the air. There was still a considerable amount of the tree's white bark left, and thousands of red leaves, but the flames that fought for domination were enough to engulf several towns if not a city.

"I would get closer," Adan told them, breaking the daze that held Kassian.

"We will have to climb the roots," Gideon said. "This way."

Kassian was happy to be led, allowing him more opportunity to take in the foreign land. Climbing over one of the snake-like roots, the Keeper noted its warmth and smoothness. It was almost comforting, as if he had known its touch all his life.

They journeyed to the base of the trunk in silent awe, though a glimpse at Adan showed the Drake to be in pain. Kassian was often envious of his connection to magic, but, right now, he was thankful to be no more than an ordinary mage.

"Can you hear it?" the king enquired of the Drake.

Adan'Karth pulled back his hood to fully reveal his pained expression and shaven horns. "It is deafening," he informed them, his voice a little louder than necessary. "But it cannot hear me," he added.

The Drake moved to the trunk, its bark a glorious white that even snow could not boast. Dropping to his knees, Adan placed the flat of one hand to the tree and bowed his head. A moment later, his muscles stiffened and he gasped.

"Adan?" Gideon stepped forward.

The Drake could not answer and, it seemed, he could not remove his hand from the trunk. His free hand, resting by his side, began to tremble uncontrollably.

"Adan!" Gideon's alarm was shared by them all.

"Help him!" Vighon shouted.

Kassian dashed, as they all did, and gripped some part of the Drake's body. The Keeper paused, astonished and utterly perplexed by the phenomenon taking place before his eyes.

"What is that?" he uttered.

Gideon and Vighon hesitated. They watched as Adan's hand began to blend into the tree, his skin transforming into bark. Without words, they all agreed the Drake needed to be ripped from the tree. It took the combined weight of three men, but they managed to yank Adan away, his hand included. He screamed in agony as flakes of bark broke away from the trunk and his individual fingers.

"Adan?" Kassian tried to get through to him, but he had clenched his fist and curled up into a ball at their feet.

A distant sound, similar to that of a tree being felled, reached them all, turning three pairs of eyes to the stalactite sky. A burning branch was snapping and tumbling through the canopy.

"We need to go!" Gideon warned.

"Agreed!" Vighon replied, bending down to pick up Adan.

"Leave him to me." Kassian retrieved his wand from its holster and pointed it at the Drake. A simple levitation spell raised Adan from the ground and gave the Keeper complete control over his direction. Navigating the large roots was trickier on their return journey, but it wasn't long before they were passing through to a familiar reality.

In the gloom of the pit, Gideon crouched down beside the injured Drake. "Adan?" At some point on their journey, he had passed out. As he lay limp in the dirt, the old master gripped the wrist of his wounded hand and held it up for them to see.

The king narrowed his eyes. "What do you make of it?"

Kassian took in the detail with grave concern. Every inch of Adan's hand resembled the bark of the white tree.

"I don't know," Gideon voiced. "But it's not good."

CHAPTER 28
ON THE HUNT

In the wake of mid-afternoon, after winter's snowfall had further graced the plains, Doran and Asher had put enough distance between them and The Rebellion that the sprawling camp was long lost to sight. Journeying south, astride horse and Warhog, they were the only ones to have made tracks in the snow. Thick clouds had rolled in and fresh powder had wiped away any trace of the wolf.

The rangers had only their instincts where the monsters of the world were concerned.

Agreeing that the Werewolf would feel vulnerable in unknown land, and wish to get as far away from the ruckus of The Rebellion as possible, Asher and Doran had cut a straight line south of the battlefield. Added to a sense of vulnerability, the beast's injuries would only spur it on to seek shelter in the wooded land south of The Moonlit Plains.

This land was blemished with rocky outcroppings and forests that had taken root centuries past. Weaving between them all was The Selk Road, a path that would take any traveller to the major cities and towns of Illian. Finding it in the plains, between the dotted forests, was unlikely in winter and following it was even harder as the snows took hold. Such had been the tale of one unlucky merchant who had brought his cart to a halt on the road and tried to make camp.

Doran took it all in from left to right, his imagination putting the scene together in all its violent detail. The cart was beyond repair, the crusted wood splintered from one end to the other where something large had assaulted it. Just off from the road, the merchant himself lay strewn across the ground, half buried in snow. At least part of him was. There were other parts of him further away.

"Well, it wasn't the cold that killed him," Doran remarked.

"Nor his horse," Asher said gruffly.

The son of Dorain followed his companion's gaze to the south-west. There he saw a larger lump on the ground, though he could only assume it had been the merchant's horse given the state it was left in.

"It ain' fresh," Doran stated. "Two days I reckon. Probably the first thing the wolf came across."

Asher didn't disagree which, in Doran's experience, meant he agreed.

"Speak yer mind, old man."

Asher drew a line with his hand from the cart to the dead horse. "The wolf dragged it away, likely until it got tired." The ranger pointed to the tree line of a dense forest south-west of their position. "From here, that's the closest source of shelter, and the wolf would have had no problem seeing it in the dark."

It was a reasonable assessment of the situation. "Let's go then." Doran pulled on his reins and guided Pig towards the wall of trees. They left the remains behind and crossed the land until they were confronted by the towering pines.

Doran scrutinised the trees, catching sight of a rocky peak somewhere in the heart of the forest. "What are ye thinkin'?" he asked of his companion.

Asher adjusted himself in his saddle and looked up. It wasn't the darkening clouds, however, that drew his focus. Avandriell was gliding around in a large circle, her wings fanned out beside her.

The young dragon let out a single squawk before tucking her wings in and diving down towards the trees.

"What is it?" Doran enquired.

"Blood."

Asher's response pushed Doran's eyebrow into his forehead. "She told ye that? I thought ye weren', ye know, speakin'."

"Trust me. She's found blood." Without further explanation, Asher guided his horse between the trees and into the forest.

"I never thought I'd see the day ye got *more* mysterious," Doran chuntered to himself.

Trailing Asher, Doran soon heard Avandriell as her claws danced across the forest floor. It was only after the ranger directed his horse round to the left that the dwarf got a good look at the scene. It was certainly gruesome and Doran could see why the dragon had been attracted to it.

"Is that a bear?" As he asked the question, his eye wandered up a nearby tree, following the blood and gore that splattered half the trunk.

Asher climbed down from his horse. "It *was*."

The son of Dorain dismounted and joined the investigation. "Eviscerated," he quickly surmised after inspecting the ghastly state of the bear's midriff. He pulled a dagger from his belt and raised one of the rib bones to better see it in the gloom of the forest. "Large teeth marks on the bone," he reported. Moving on to a furry patch, just below the bear's savaged head, the dwarf examined a raking wound that had cut through to the muscle. "There's not much round these parts that could do this to a bear. An' these definitely look like the claws o' a Lycan to me."

Asher had already moved on from the frozen carcass. He was further into the forest and crouched with one hand supporting himself against a small rock.

Doran shook his head and looked across at Avandriell, who was studying him intently. "He always did prefer to work alone. Perhaps ye'll 'ave better luck." The young dragon made a series of clicking noises in her throat and leapt over the bear, towards her companion. "Or maybe it's jus' me," the dwarf pondered aloud.

Making his way around the dead bear, the War Mason came up on Asher's side. The old ranger was running his fingers over an impression that had barely dug into the snowy ground. Most would have missed it, but never Asher.

"This is a big print," the ranger commented.

"Aye," Doran agreed. "When was the last time ye saw the wolf?"

Asher resumed his full height, his eyes narrowed in recall. "Before The War for the Realm," he said.

"I'd say it's grown since then," the dwarf voiced. "I saw it on the battlefield. It tore through elves, dwarves, an' Reavers like butter."

Asher glanced back at the unfortunate bear. "At least we know we're in the right place."

Doran looked from the bear to Avandriell before finally settling on the ranger. "Are ye sure this is the right place for her? I know they're tough but we're talkin' about a fully-grown Werewolf. Even ye an' I will be lucky to get out o' this place alive."

Asher gave his companion a long hard look. "Avandriell stays with me. I can't protect her from everything and she needs to learn."

Doran nodded his understanding. "As ye say." He returned his attention to the print at their feet. "Shall we get to trackin' it then?"

Asher crouched down again and gave the paw impression another look. "These won't be easy to follow. Werewolves are light on their feet and very fast."

The son of Dorain twisted his mouth as he considered their options. As he did, his eye took note of the broken twigs and branches further along the trail. The bear's impressions were much easier to see.

"Maybe we should think like the wolf," the dwarf suggested, drawing a curious expression out of Asher. "It's feelin' vulnerable. It's lookin' for territory." He looked back at the carcass. "An' we know it's fed. I'd say it's likely our prey has followed the bear prints back to its dwellin'."

"A cave perhaps," Asher interpreted.

"Aye. To the victor go the spoils an' all."

Before going any further, they trekked back to the edge of the forest and tied their mounts to the trees. Tracking a Werewolf was hard enough without the noise and smell that accompanied a horse and Warhog. Doran only prayed that his mount would still be there upon his return.

With Avandriell stalking beside them, the three companions cautiously journeyed deeper into the trees. Over the next couple of hours, Doran came to realise how rusty his ranger skills had become. He sighed and chastised himself every time his boot snapped a twig or crushed fallen leaves. His armour brushed against the environment, the clatter disturbing the birds. Asher shot the dwarf a look over his shoulder more than once.

As the shadows grew long, it became apparent to the rangers that the bear hadn't come directly from its lair. Its recent travels even took them as far as the western edge of the forest before the tracks curled back into the thick of the trees.

Only when dusk settled on the land did Asher come to a halt on the trail. "We can't track it in the dark. We should make camp while we still have *some* light."

Doran agreed, though he wasn't entirely convinced. "If we stop now there's a good chance the hunters will become the hunted. The wolf will surely see our fire."

"We would need fire to follow the tracks," Asher countered. "We have little choice in the matter."

Doran grumbled but made no further protest. They found a small clearing and went about starting a decent fire that would stop winter from claiming their lives while they slept. The son of Dorain chopped up some extra logs for the pair to sit on and share some rations. By then they were steeped in the darkness of night.

The wood fell silent. Doran didn't like it. The fire was the brightest and loudest thing for miles around - the wolf had to know they were there. Still, the War Mason could not deny the fatigue that bit into his muscles and bones. He was still recovering from two days of non-stop fighting and a severe lack of sleep.

Whether this was obvious or not, Asher offered to take first watch while he got his head down.

Despite the unnerving surroundings, it was only seconds after shutting his eyes that sleep robbed the dwarf of conscious thought.

~

A noise beyond the crackling fire awoke Doran with a start. Years of experience, however, prevented him from jumping up. Instead, his eye snapped open and he remained perfectly still, lying on the forest floor. He had no idea how long he had been sleeping for and, right now, he didn't care. He couldn't say what the noise had been and, worse still, he couldn't discern the direction from which it had originated.

Carefully, he adjusted his position to try and see Asher on the other side of the fire. An alarm sounded in his mind when he failed to spot the man. It shouldn't have been that hard since there were only three of them around the fire and one was a dragon no bigger than a dog. Yet, the ranger was missing. Doran slowly pushed up from the ground and cursed when he noticed Avandriell was gone too.

"Typical Outlander..." the dwarf mumbled, rising to his feet. "Don' ye 'ave any new tricks up yer sleeve?" he asked the shadows in frustration.

Another noise pierced the sound of the crackling fire, turning Doran to his right. There was nothing but trees and darkness. He didn't want to take his eyes away from the gaps between the trees, but he needed to get his hands around Andaljor. The cold steel felt reassuring in his grip and even better after separating it into axe and hammer.

A rustling followed by rapid steps turned the dwarf on his heel. Nothing. Doran widened his gait and braced himself, his knuckles cracking around the hafts of his weapons.

"I know ye're out there, beastie," he called.

Claws raking down a tree spun the dwarf around but he caught only a glimpse of something darting through the shadows.

"Me friend sent me for ye!" Doran yelled, working himself up. "Ye might know 'im! He went by the name Russell Maybury!" A low growl rumbled from the darkness, turning the War Mason in another direction. A wicked smile broke across Doran's face. "I thought ye might know 'im. He sends his regards!"

A pair of eyes shone in the pitch black beyond the firelight and slowly rose up until the Werewolf was standing on its back legs. The son of Dorain spat on the ground and bashed his hammer and axe together.

"Come an' get it!" he provoked.

The Werewolf exploded from between the trees and crossed most of their camp in a single bound. Its claws were outstretched and its jaws of razor-sharp fangs ready to clamp around Doran's neck. It was damn fast, faster than the dwarf remembered. He swung his axe and hammer simultaneously but, even as he raised his arms, he knew he had mistimed it.

That was the moment when a two-handed broadsword plunged down through the monster's back. It also had Asher's weight behind it. The ranger had dropped down from the surrounding trees with, thankfully, perfect timing. The wolf was brought down by the piercing steel and most of Asher, bringing it to a stop at Doran's feet.

A sword through its ribs, however, was not enough to finish the Werewolf. It roared with rage and thrashed about, knocking Asher clear with a backhand across his face. With the sword still impaled, the beast tried to rise, only to discover an ancient hammer slamming onto its head. Some of the roar was taken out of the wolf as its jaws were driven into the ground. Doran meant to follow up his attack with a swing of the axe, but the monster found a burst of energy and barrelled into the dwarf, hurling him into a tree trunk.

Falling onto his hands and knees, it took every bit of Doran's iron will to keep his weapons in his hands. As it had been for Thorgen, his great ancestor, Andaljor was an extension of his arms and he refused to give it up. Instead, he offered the wolf a roar of his own and threw himself into the beast. The axe took a chunk out of its right leg and the hammer impacted the side of its head as it crouched down to bite him. Neither attack was strong enough to deliver a final blow, but they were enough to turn the wolf away and into the waiting claws of a dragon.

Avandriell swooped down from the canopy, her movements far more gracious than that of her companion. All four of her claws sank into the Werewolf's back while she snapped at its neck and face. The monster staggered back and howled in pain, but even that wasn't enough to quash the wolf's rage. The young dragon was gripped by the neck and thrown to the ground.

A primal roar tore through the still air as Asher leapt over the fire, his silvyr short-sword raised over his head. The ranger collided with the wolf, his blade flashing high and low as he scored red lines up and down the beast. It swiped at him with enough strength to break his neck, but Asher ducked under the claws and spun on his heel. Returning to his full height in one smooth motion, he pulled free his broadsword and swung it at his enemy's head.

The wolf caught the blade in its meaty hand.

Blood trickled down its dark hide, running the length of its arm. As it lowered its head towards the ranger, its teeth already stained red, Doran brought his axe to bear. The steel was embedded in the creature's leg, drawing a pain-filled howl from its lips. Asher didn't hesitate to drive his short-sword into the wolf's hip, their combined attacks dropping it to one knee.

The intelligence of Werewolves had been debated by many a ranger over the centuries but, judging by the look in its eyes right now, Doran could see this beast knew its time was up. And, like all animals, the instinct to survive kicked in. The wolf forced Asher's broadsword aside and directly into Doran's face. The dwarf stumbled backwards and took his axe with him. Using its free hand, the beast shoved Asher away, launching him clear from the ground.

With hands not dissimilar to a human's, the wolf gripped the hilt of the silvyr blade and removed it from its hip. By the time the short-sword could be heard clattering on the ground, the beast was gone, vanishing into the night.

Doran shook his head and blinked hard. The broadsword had left a dark line across his forehead. Asher was already picking himself up, coaxed by Avandriell beside him. The dragon appeared to have gained a limp but, like the rangers, she had emerged from the fight intact. Asher ran a hand over her head and under her jaw before returning his broadsword to its scabbard.

"What are ye doin'?" Doran demanded. "We didn' kill it."

Asher bent down and retrieved his silvyr short-sword. "The wolf won't be coming back tonight," he replied boldly. "We might not have killed it, but we definitely wounded it. If it has claimed that bear's lair for its own, we'll follow the blood until we find it."

"Well let's be gettin' on with it then!" Doran huffed, making for the gap in the trees.

"At first light," Asher stated.

Doran gave the ranger a double look. "At first... Are ye mad? It's injured an' badly so. We should hunt it down an' finish the job before it heals."

Asher rubbed his chest where the wolf had struck him. "These are not hunting conditions."

"Oh, but they were good enough for settin' a trap!" Doran countered. "An' with me as the bait no less!"

The ranger shrugged. "You make good bait." He took a seat by the fire and drove the end of his silvyr blade into the ground beside him.

His heart still pounding like a hammer on an anvil, Doran fumed. "Rus didn' ask *ye* to do this. So ye stay 'ere an' get cosy if that's what ye fancy, lad! But every second that goes by, that beast's existence makes a mockery o' his life!" His voice broke towards the end and he had to pause to collect himself. "I'm goin' out there to hunt that wolf with or without ye!"

"Doran," Asher called before he could set foot beyond the trees. "Russell wanted you to slay the wolf. He didn't want you to die trying."

"Ye doubt the strength o' me swing?" Doran spat, itching for a fight.

"I doubt the strength of your eye," Asher said bluntly, stoking the fire. "Even bleeding, the wolf won't be easy to track at night."

"Bah!" Doran waved the ranger's comment away and turned back to the darkness.

"Doran." Asher said his name sternly this time, adding the hint of a growl to his voice. "You cannot be this foolish."

"Don' lecture me abou' such things!" Doran barked. "Ye throw yerself into every hair brain situation without so much as a thought!"

Asher stood up. "You are to be king," he declared as a matter of fact.

Doran was stumped, his mind and mouth disconnected.

"And not just any king," Asher continued. "All of Dhenaheim will fall under your rule."

"I don' need ye to babysit me! An' don' talk abou' things ye don' understand," Doran warned.

"I understand well enough," the ranger argued. "I fear it is Doran, son of Dorain, who is burying his head."

The dwarf threw his axe into the ground and pointed a stubby finger at Asher. "Ye'd do well to shut yer mouth before I shut it for ye!"

"You can't ignore what's right in front of you. I know Kraiden's blade is lost to The Hox. It isn't the end any of us would want for Dakmund, but his fate is just as sealed as yours, Doran."

Hearing his brother's name took some of the fire out of his veins. "Stop," he pleaded.

"Would Russell have stopped?" Asher questioned. "He was practically the voice of your conscience."

"Ye're not him," Doran pointed out.

"No," the ranger agreed. "And he didn't charge me with killing the wolf either. But, many years ago, he did give me another task; one far more difficult than slaying any beast."

Doran raised a bushy eyebrow at the ranger, though he suspected he knew what Russell would have asked of him. Still, he remained quiet and allowed Asher to finish.

"He told me to watch out for you when he couldn't. *He* wouldn't let you ignore your destiny."

The son of Dorain wasn't ashamed of the tear that escaped his eye, nor the heartbreak he wore on his sleeve. "An' what is that?" he asked.

"You're not a ranger anymore," Asher answered simply. "Your kin are depending on you now - every one of them. If you go out there, you put them all at risk."

Doran's shoulders sagged and his hammer slowly slipped down his grip. "I feel like I'm losin' everythin'," he grieved. "To put me friend to rest means drivin' me axe through his chest. To rise up an' lead me people means standin' on the bones o' me brother. Hells, to even win this war we've got to kill the son o' dear friends. I'm tired, Asher. Me bones are weary, me muscles ache, an' me mind can' make sense o' the world we're tryin' to save."

Asher closed the gap between them and placed a hand on Doran's shoulder. "Everything that's happened to you. Everything you've done. Everything you're *going* to do. It hasn't just been for a crown on your head. It's all for what you will do with that crown. Be the king Dhenaheim deserves. Be the dwarf Russell knew you to be."

Doran blinked hard and squeezed Asher's hand. "Ye're a good friend, lad. Even if there's naught but hammers bangin' around in that skull o' yers." He gave a short laugh, shared by the ranger. "Come then. Let's lick our wounds. Tomorrow, we finish this."

CHAPTER 29

INSIDE THE CAGE

Alijah's eyes opened to the familiar black stone above his bed. He remained still for a while, staring at the dark blocks. The longer and harder he gazed at them, the easier it became to imagine there was nothing but that peaceful abyss. It always pulled him in and emptied him out, freeing the half-elf of his burdens. But he was to enjoy no such peace this night.

He had awoken in pain. Again.

A groan pushed through his lips as he forced himself to sit on the edge of his bed. Everything hurt, especially the wound beneath his shoulder. Rising to his feet, he could feel that every previous injury had been replaced by another.

"Why do I suffer?" he growled. His words may have pierced the air, but his thoughts conveyed that very same question to his eternal companion.

Malliath moved through the shadows of his mind, as if the dragon possessed a physical presence inside. *We are at war - pain is to be expected.* Malliath's voice expressed irritation and impatience.

I recall every blow, Alijah said, his pain adding venom to his reply. *Yet my skin burns, my muscles ache, and my bones feel hollow. Inara did not inflict such wounds.*

You were struck by an elven arrow, the dragon pointed out. *Had it been an inch lower you would have bled into your lungs and died.*

It is not just the sting of the arrow that ails me, he complained, sure that he had been burnt somewhere across his back.

An overwhelming weight pressed down upon the king's mind and he collapsed onto the end of his bed. His thoughts fractured. Words failed him, their meaning entirely lost on him. An acute sting bit into his neck, forcing his hand to the skin. His fingers came away with blood. Where he had disturbed the wound, more blood trickled down his bare chest.

Alijah thought the pattern of those wounds familiar - a bite mark. But he had not been bitten. The thought evaporated in his mind. He tried to grasp at it but he would have had better luck catching smoke in his hands. With what focus he was able to maintain, the half-elf waved his hand through the air and conjured a mirror image of himself.

He looked dreadful. His face was bruised and swollen, his eyes bloodshot. Raking wounds marred his skin, the flesh torn. He even possessed what looked like a burn on his right hip.

"I don't understand," he muttered.

The oppression on his mind increased. Alijah leaned forward and rested his elbows on his knees, his head bowed. Malliath oozed soothing emotions across their bond.

You were injured in the battle, the dragon purred. *You were injured by Inara Galfrey. She challenged you. They all challenged you. Yet you endured. You wear your wounds with pride and honour, for you have done what no other could. You have changed the world.*

Alijah straightened and examined his mirror image. The blood streaking down his chest faded from view, as if it had never been there. Indeed, he could not recall whatever had drawn his attention to his neck, for there was only a dark bruise there now. Only the burn on his hip remained, but he suddenly remembered Inara casting the spell that had scorched him. The swelling across his face even eased, returning some of his chiselled features.

You see, Malliath whispered in his mind.

Yes, Alijah replied absently. ***I suffer from the battle.***

You suffer because of your sister! Malliath fumed, snapping the king from his haze. *I have seen your memories. You faltered in the realm of magic,* the dragon scolded. *Inara Galfrey should be dead!*

Alijah waved a hand through his own image and it faded to mist. **Burning the tree was the priority. Verda's future is finally assured.**

Malliath filled more of his mind, shrinking the half-elf's surroundings. *You let our enemy live! The first time our bond is compromised and you reveal your weaknesses.*

"I have no weaknesses!" Alijah yelled.

You are a man! Malliath provoked. *You are riddled with weakness!*

Alijah lashed out with magic and blew the windows out of his chamber. "I am a dragon!" he roared.

Yes! Malliath roared, expressing his pleasure. *We are to be the only dragons in the realm. As such, we have no sisters or parents. There are no ties, blood or otherwise, that bind us. When next you meet another Galfrey, you will destroy them.*

His chest heaving and heart thundering, Alijah nodded along to his companion's edict. "We are dragons," he breathed.

Malliath's presence relaxed in his mind. *What now, king?*

Alijah draped himself in a heavy fur cloak and left his chamber as it filled with snow. **Now we wait,** he replied. **The tree is burning as we speak. With each passing moment, magic retreats from the world. Bereft of this gift, Vighon and his rebellion will lose all hope as they watch their most powerful allies fall into shadow. The elves will likely lose any sense of self and seek shelter in their homeland.**

The king gritted his teeth, bearing the pain that begged him to rest. **Then, when the world is at its darkest, we shall emerge from these mountains and remind the realm who wears the crown. After we purge The Rebellion's remnants, including my sister and Vighon, we can finally get to the business of peace.**

I fear you have taken refuge in the future, Malliath said. *The land and its people - our people - do not stand united. The capital flies the banner of the flaming sword, The Arid Lands is restless without a clear leader, and The Rebellion's forces are amassed in the heart of the realm.*

Alijah paused in the hallway and turned his mind inward. He reached out to his Reavers, detecting the bulk of them on the east road, having just passed Darkwell. They would enter the valley of The Vrost Mountains soon and stand guard at the base of The Bastion. Beyond them, he could feel hundreds more scattered throughout the realm, patrolling cities and towns.

He left them all to their tasks and focused on The Moonlit Plains. There were but three of his knights with enough life in them to grant him their eyes. They were severely mutilated, missing most of their limbs and all three were pinned down by the scores of bodies that had been piled on top of them. Of the trio, only one could see the snowy fields and even the camp of rebels.

Look, Malliath, the king bade, drawing the dragon in. **They are in disarray. They have been beaten and broken and they feel it. When the truth sinks in, when they accept their fate, they might even lay down their swords and beg for our forgiveness.**

And would you have us grant it? Malliath enquired.

Alijah displayed a wicked grin. **Dragons do not forgive. They devour.**

Indeed. But do not underestimate our enemy. Until magic has fled the world and our dominance over the sky and land is assured, they remain a threat.

We will keep a watch over them, Alijah reassured. **And we will do so from the safety of The Bastion. Let the realm breathe for a moment. Uncertainty breeds unrest and unrest breeds violence. The Rebellion has shattered this country and soon every man, woman, and child will see that. I want them to reject Vighon in their hearts. I want them to despise him and everything he stands for. Then, when the fires rise, we will return to restore peace. There will be no dragons to challenge us and no magic to threaten us with. We will be invincible.**

Very good, Malliath expressed. *Very good.*

CHAPTER 30
OLD FRIENDS

The morning returned to the forest accompanied by a white mist, a concealing vapour that spread across every inch of the land. Asher cursed their luck as he kicked dirt onto the fire. Doran was already by the edge of their camp, crouched low to better inspect the wolf's departing tracks. Whatever his mood, the dwarf had certainly found some sleep that night if his snoring was anything to go by. Asher was just pleased to see his old friend in better spirits and rested for the hunt.

The ranger himself had only found sleep after Avandriell had relaxed and closed her eyes beside him. He watched her closely now, looking for any sign of lasting damage to her injured leg. Judging by the way she stalked a mouse through the foliage, the young dragon had fully recovered. While she devoured the mouse, he moved to Doran's side and cast his experienced eyes over the ground.

"This damned fog'll slow us down," the War Mason complained.

Asher stepped ahead and to the side as Avandriell bounded through the gap. "Forget the tracks," he told the dwarf. "The blood

343

will lead us to its lair." Even as he spoke, the dragon was sniffing the ground and following the trail of blood.

"I could get used to huntin' with a dragon," Doran quipped.

As beneficial as Avandriell's natural talents were, Asher wasn't comfortable with her leading the way. Every now and then she would get excited by a different scent, or simply the prospect of hunting their prey, and dash ahead. The ranger could always find her, but that didn't mean he enjoyed losing sight of her. Still, he had been impressed with her assault on the Werewolf and the dragon knew it, his pride filling her with happiness.

As the morning dragged on, the mist refused to fade away. They relied on Avandriell alone to guide them across the landscape. Without her, it could have easily felt like being stuck in a labyrinth with the trees and fog closing in on them.

It was hard to measure the amount of time that had passed since setting off from the camp, but Asher guessed it to be nearing midday when they came across their first real obstacle. The ranger looked up at the rock wall, unable to see the top or any ledge beyond the mist. What he could see, however, was blood and claw marks running up the stone.

Doran tapped the steel of his axe against the wall. "Sheer," he observed. "We won' be followin' it this way."

Avandriell rested her front claws against the wall as if meaning to mimic the wolf's ascent. "No," Asher warned her with an outstretched hand. The dragon dropped her claws back onto the ground and exhaled sharply.

"No bear could make that climb," Doran said, craning his neck. "There must be another way up there."

"Agreed. Let's keep the wall on our left and follow it round."

Filled with confidence from a morning of leading the hunt, Avandriell moved to the front again and pounced between the trees.

Asher focused on their bond, an almost tangible part of his mind. *Avandriell,* he called, giving the dragon pause. *Stay by my side. A cornered wolf is a dangerous wolf.*

Avandriell raised her head and assumed a regal pose. There

were no words in response but Asher could feel the confidence of a creature that knew it was an apex predator.

Soon, he reassured. *For now, stay with me.*

The young dragon waited for the ranger to catch her up before falling into line beside him. He enjoyed the level of understanding that currently existed between them, though he longed to talk to her, to know her thoughts and opinions on the world.

"There," Doran said, breaking the ranger's reverie.

Asher looked over his shoulder and followed the dwarf's finger to a muddy slope. The path had been forged in a break in the rocky wall and gently rose up and round the stone. Avandriell moved towards it and ducked her head. Asher came up on her side and crouched down to waft away some of the fog.

"Bear prints," he announced.

Doran took a long breath as he examined the slope. "Let's finish this."

Together, they took to the slope and navigated the cliff side. In most places, the path was only wide enough for single file, certainly a width where even a bear would have been forced to tread carefully.

"I don' like the look o' that," Doran voiced, staring at a cut in the rock. It was a straight path that led into the heart of the cliff but, if they were attacked while passing through, they would struggle to swing their weapons.

Asher checked the prints at their feet. "This is the way - we have no choice."

"I'll lead," Doran volunteered, his courage never to be questioned.

Following him in, Asher was sure to keep Avandriell between the two of them. At least, of the three of them, she could fly away, her wingspan just within the walls. Of course, the ranger knew that would be the last thing she would ever do. The dragon would rather die fighting by his side than abandon him and survive. Asher both loved and hated that fact.

Sacrificing stealth for speed, they crossed the narrow path while constantly scanning the fog above and behind them. Asher's head twitched to the side, sure that he had heard something scrape across the stone. A few moments later and a small collection of loose pebbles trickled down the wall on his right. Looking up, there was nothing but fog and more wall.

Thankfully, it wasn't too long before they emerged on the other side, where the path was wider. Even the mist seemed clearer here, giving them a better view of the surroundings. Continuing to follow the rock face round to the left, they soon came across a smear of blood where the wolf had climbed over the edge.

Doran frowned with disgust. "Ye smell that?"

Avandriell certainly did, her nose pointed to the sky. "We're close," Asher concluded.

The dwarf adjusted his grip around the haft of his axe. "If we can smell the wolf... the wolf can smell us."

Asher drew his broadsword. "Surprise won't be on our side this time."

Using the blood, they trailed it round the path until it brought them to a wide cave opening and a shelf with a sheer edge that dropped down into the misty wood. There were signs everywhere that a bear had taken residence here, perhaps even generations of bears. But it was the blood that weaved between the debris and bones that held the rangers' attention.

Doran beat the flat of his hammer against his armoured breastplate. "Are ye in there, beastie?" he yelled.

Asher sighed inwardly, suddenly reminded of their different styles when it came to facing monsters. He caught the dwarf's eye and nodded for him to take the left-hand wall into the cave while he followed on the right. It took them both a moment to adjust to the gloom of the cave, though Avandriell, it seemed, had no such issue. The dragon stopped halfway into the cave, her golden eyes piercing the shadows. For just a second, Asher assumed Avandriell had seen the wolf, but her emotions didn't correspond to that. She was calm, perhaps even a little confused.

The wolf wasn't in the cave.

"It's not here," he stated confidently.

"Ye're sure?"

Asher looked down at Avandriell. "It's not here," he repeated, relaxing his sword arm.

Doran huffed. "Then where in all the hells is it?"

Avandriell heard the wolf first, a fraction of a second before her alarm rang like a bell inside Asher's mind. The dragon whipped her tail around to aid in her spin while Asher gripped his sword in both hands and swung blindly behind him. That fraction of a second saved the ranger's life as his blade clashed with the wolf's claws. The force of it, however, knocked him back a step. There was no opportunity to fall into a defensive stance as the monster came at him again and again. Asher parried those raking claws and batted the creature's hands away, buying Avandriell time to line up her lunging attack.

The wolf howled when its ankle was caught in the vice-like grip of the dragon's jaws. The beast staggered, giving Asher time to adjust his style and put an aggressive foot forward. His broadsword arced through a chunk of the Werewolf's arm before coming back around to swipe across its chest.

Pained and enraged, the wolf dropped down and slammed a heavy hand onto Avandriell's head. The dragon released its foe and cried out, a sound that boiled Asher's blood. The ranger gave in to that anger and hacked at the monster with two-handed hammer strokes. With strong arms, almost twice the length of an ordinary man's, the wolf only had to swipe at Asher's legs to take him off his feet. The impact hurt, but it wasn't nearly as painful as the bite he was about to receive.

The wolf came down on him with an open maw and a breath that spoke of death. It was then that Asher was reminded why it was a good thing that his style differed from Doran's. The dwarf charged into the side of the wolf, barrelling them both into the cave wall. Amidst the chaos of their wild limbs, the son of Dorain managed to yank the monster's mane of matted hair and slam his hammer into its snout and face.

"Don' worry, old friend!" Doran grunted, lifting his hammer high again. "I'll set ye free!"

Unfortunately, the wolf retained enough of its senses and

strength to snatch the head of the hammer before the next stroke fell. It growled from somewhere deep in its throat and looked Doran in the eye. The dwarf swore, though the word was barely given time to escape his lips before the beast hurled him across the cave, towards the shelf.

Asher picked himself up, sparing Avandriell a glance, and renewed his assault on the wolf. He cut a line across its face, ripping a gash through its black nose and bloody snout. In a display of supernatural strength, the wolf scaled the cave wall in a heartbeat and pounced from above. The ranger turned his broadsword horizontally and gripped the flat of the blade, barring the Werewolf's attack across the neck. The weight of the monster, however, was still enough to flatten him beneath it.

Pressed against the wet floor again, Asher writhed on his back and put all of his strength into keeping his foe at bay. With open jaws, thick saliva drooled between its fangs and coated the ranger's leathers and face. The flat of the blade quickly began to bite into his hand, threatening his only defence.

Out of sight, Avandriell let loose her fiery breath, the flames illuminating the cave. The wolf roared and then howled as the pain set in, relenting its attack on Asher. The beast leapt to the side and rolled across the cave floor, a portion of its mane set alight. Avandriell bared her fangs and growled at her enemy, her stance low and ready to attack.

The flames extinguished, the wolf rose with a smoking back and a look of wrath in its black eyes. Dragon and Werewolf collided in a clash of claws and gnashing teeth. In the air, Avandriell's wings flapped furiously, disorientating her foe as she tore through its chest. The sound of the wolf's claws scraping across her scales made Asher wince. He desperately wanted to enter the fray but he risked striking his companion in the process.

As Avandriell opened her jaws, preparing to breath fire upon the wolf, the wretched monster thrust its head forward and clamped its fangs around her neck. The young dragon couldn't so much as squawk, her breath taken away.

"NO!" Asher charged with all his fury and plunged his broadsword into the wolf's gut.

Everything happened so fast after that. Avandriell was released and dropped to the cave floor, the wolf's attention turned to the ranger. It backhanded him into the wall and removed the blade from its gut. Before Asher could even think to retrieve his silvyr short-sword, the beast took his head in its hand and shoved him into the rock face. The knock to his skull robbed the ranger of his immediate senses and he crumpled to his hands and knees, blood dripping from the side of his head.

"Beastie!" Doran yelled from the mouth of the cave. "I'm not done with ye yet!" he goaded.

Asher looked on, his sight fractured. The wolf walked towards the dwarf on its two powerful legs, its hands and claws reaching out in anticipation. Asher tried to stand and offer aid but he dropped back to his hands and knees and slumped against the wall. Not far away, Avandriell lay coughing and spluttering. They were out of this fight.

Doran slowly backed out onto the shelf, his eye locked on the approaching wolf. He dared to spare a glance at Asher and Avandriell - they were alive but certainly injured. Getting a good look at the wolf in the light, the dwarf could see the damage both had inflicted on it. A particularly nasty wound continued to bleed out from its gut and down its leg. It had, however, already healed the majority of wounds suffered the previous night.

"Ye've got the advantages o' age," Doran remarked, falling into a circling pattern with the wolf. "So 'ave I," he quipped with a wicked grin.

Words had no place in the monster's life and so it reacted with violent action. Doran braced himself, his feet firmly planted. At the last second, in the face of a charging Werewolf, he threw all of his weight to the side and rolled away. The beast came down and skidded across the rock shelf, its claws digging up loose stone to cascade over the edge.

Back on his feet, Doran pressed his attack. He came at the wolf with hammer and axe swinging, determined to slay the monster that had ruined his friend's life. Though its actions were erratic, the dwarf felt both of his weapons impact its body multiple times, splashing blood across the ground. Thankfully, he could barely feel the wolf's claws tearing at his skin when they found the gaps in his armour.

Inevitably, the son of Dorain was thrown to the ground - and more than once - but his hammer always slammed into the wolf, giving him the opportunity to find his feet again. His heart was pounding in his chest now and his lungs burned from the exhaustion. He still hadn't fully recovered from the battle and his muscles informed him as much. How long could he keep this up?

Such thoughts and questions were banished from his mind when the wolf chomped down on one of his pauldrons and swung him around. Dragged by the shoulder, he could only retaliate with his hammer, but the wolf seemed oblivious to the beating he delivered. At last, the beast cast him free, tossing the dwarf towards the edge. The War Mason skidded on his knees and managed to assume his full height before the wolf could take another swipe at him.

"Come on," he growled.

The Werewolf roared and charged at him with no hesitation. Doran had naught but his instincts to call upon, aware that these would either be his last moments or the wolf's. He threw his axe at the ground, directly in the path of the wolf. The creature altered its assault, adapting quickly, and leapt over the weapon. As it leapt, however, the dwarf stepped forward, placing himself closer to the wolf than it had anticipated when it avoided the axe. Now, when it came down, Doran was perfectly placed to drive the top of his hammer into the beast's throat, using its own weight against it.

The son of Dorain was already rolling across the ground, towards his axe, before the wolf could catch its breath. As it choked and gripped at its throat, Doran reclaimed his axe and launched it at his foe in one smooth movement. The steel made a satisfying sound when it dug deep into the creature's chest. Its eyes bulged in surprise and the monster staggered closer to the lip, barely concerned with its collapsed windpipe anymore.

With a single glassy eye, Doran adjusted the grip around the haft of his hammer. "Rest, old friend."

The dwarf lobbed his hammer underarm, his aim unerring. It crossed the gap like a bolt from a ballista and slammed into the wolf's face with all the might of his ancestors behind it. Andaljor took the cursed beast from the rocky shelf and cast it into the white mist. Doran moved to the edge and peered over, making certain that the creature had succumbed to the fall.

There was nothing but fog.

Asher's spine cracked in several places as he straightened up, finally back on his feet. His head still didn't feel right, as if it wasn't quite connected to the rest of his body. Still, he counted being on his feet as a victory where head injuries were concerned.

Avandriell weaved between his legs having overcome the assault on her throat. Her claws and horns were stained with the wolf's blood, but her scales had protected her from serious harm. Asher bent down to stroke her head but stopped himself when a dizzying wave washed over him. Instead, he made for Doran and welcomed the cold breeze that picked up his hair.

"It is finished?" the ranger asked.

"Let's find out," Doran replied sombrely.

Retracing their steps, the companions made their way back down to the forest floor and journeyed around the rock face. Asher wasn't sure exactly what they would find when they came across the wolf; an uncertainty that kept one of his hands resting on the hilt of his broadsword. What they discovered, however, stumped even the experienced ranger.

The Werewolf that lay sprawled across the hard ground, with an axe in its chest, was completing the slow transformation before their eyes. Its long and broken limbs retracted as the leathery brown hide faded to Russell's pale complexion. Razor-sharp claws sank back into the fingers that had birthed them while its furry strip of a mane decayed and fell away. Within seconds, Russell Maybury's naked and battered form lay before them.

His yellow eyes fluttered open.

Doran quickly dropped to one knee by his side. "Rus!" he exclaimed, clasping his friend's hand.

Asher moved to the other side and crouched down as Russell looked from one to the other. The ranger had encountered the dying often enough to know that his old friend was nearing the end. Asher placed a gentle hand on his bare shoulder, making no attempt to prevent the tears that welled in his eyes.

"We're 'ere, Rus," Doran told him. "It's goin' to be alright."

Russell struggled to turn his head to look at the dwarf. His lips quivered. "Thank... you," he breathed.

Doran couldn't hold back his tears any longer. "Rus," he blurted.

Asher waited for the son of Dorain to find his gaze before shaking his head, discouraging him from holding on to hope. This was the end of Russell Maybury and there was nothing they could do to stop it. Nor should they, Asher thought. The man deserved some rest.

Russell relaxed and his eyes turned to the mist above. A faint smile curled his lips before his grasp loosened around Doran's hand. With the final beat of his heart, the dwarf carefully placed Russell's hand over his still chest and left it there.

"Grarfath keep ye, old friend," he whispered, his tears disappearing into his beard.

Asher ran his hand over Russell's eyes, closing the lids. He looked to Doran. "A pyre," he said.

The dwarf sniffed. "A bloody big pyre," he specified.

Asher nodded in agreement. "A bloody big pyre," he echoed.

After Doran removed his axe and recovered his hammer, they took it in turns to carry Russell's body to the edge of the forest, where their mounts awaited them. They spent the rest of the afternoon building their friend the pyre he deserved. The companions did so in silence, their grief realised.

In the end, the pyre was humble in size, their time limited before nightfall. They carefully placed Russell's body on top, his arms positioned at his side. A soft sprinkling of snow fell from the dark heavens as Avandriell breathed fire into the pyre. The flames spread steadily across the wood until it was engulfed and Russell with it.

Asher raised his hood and bowed his head. He knew of no god to offer his prayers to, but he cast quiet words into the ether, hoping his friend had found a peaceful rest. The ranger remembered nothing of death from his own experience, but he knew there had been no pain. What more could men such as them ask for?

Beside him, his hands resting on the axe planted in the ground, Doran Heavybelly sobbed.

Eventually, after taking a deep breath and composing himself, he declared, "Never has a ranger - nay a man - possessed the courage, strength, an' heart that Russell Maybury displayed every day o' his life. He saved lives, damn it!" the dwarf growled. "An' he deserved a better end than the one we gave 'im. But, with Grarfath as his witness, he didn' give up without a fight on that battlefield. He fought to the end." Doran sighed and blinked a fresh tear from his eye. "Ye will be missed, lad. Every day."

With Avandriell curled around his leg, Asher reached out and placed a comforting hand on Doran's shoulder. After paying their respect for a while longer, they retired to a smaller campfire, not far from the pyre. There they drank to their friend and told stories of his life, recounting his heroic deeds and amusing encounters.

There, they said their final farewells to Russell Maybury.

PART THREE

CHAPTER 31
BENDING THE KNEE

Night and day, The Moonlit Plains were freezing, drawing many to compare them to The White Vale in the north. The winds that howled through The Rebellion's camp brought misery, robbing the inhabitants of any fight that might have lingered in their bones. And, accompanying the wind, the wounded and dying cried out for mercy from dawn till dusk.

Despite the icy blasts and calls for help, Galanör Reveeri was sweating through his clothes, his brow furrowed in deep concentration. His hands were overlapped and pressing down on the ribs of a young dwarf. Beneath his hands, a mortal wound threatened to claim the dwarf's life.

The wound had begun to smell, a rotten and vile odour, the ragged edges darkened with infection. The elven healer who had asked for Galanör's aid had informed him that the infection would soon spoil his blood. Death would swiftly follow.

Galanör drew on his magic and poured his will into the dwarf's body. A faint light glowed between his fingers and under the skin surrounding the wound. He envisioned the blood running clean, the muscles knitting back together, and new skin to cover the injury. As he did so, the dwarf's eyes fluttered rapidly and a groan rumbled in his throat.

A firm hand gripped Galanör's shoulder - Aenwyn. He had almost forgotten that she had entered the tent with him. Her voice, a tone of caution, sounded in his ear, though he couldn't hear the shape of the words themselves. Ultimately, he ignored her and renewed his focus. He wasn't going to let the young dwarf perish.

Seconds, minutes or perhaps, even hours went by before Galanör finally opened his eyes. He had spent most of his magic on the infection spilling out across the dwarf's body, coursing through his veins. After ridding him of that, bringing the wound together had felt relatively easy.

"Thank ye," the dwarf uttered, shocked by the power of his own breath. "Ye saved me life!" he exclaimed, emboldened by the return of his strength. "I am forever indebted to ye," he promised.

Galanör could barely lift his hand to wave the notion away. "There is... no debt. Just help the others," he managed, gesturing to the row of wounded dwarves and elves outside.

The dwarf stood up from his cot and marvelled at the healed skin over his ribs. "I will never forget nor sully the power o' elves. Thank ye." He patted Galanör on the back as he left, though he might as well have hit the ranger with a shovel.

"Easy," Aenwyn said, catching him before he fell into the cot. "You're done for the day," she stated.

Galanör shook his head, though he did accept her help to leave the tent. "There are more," he croaked.

"You've been healing all morning," Aenwyn argued. "You need to rest."

"Just one more," Galanör told her.

Aenwyn sighed. "At least see to one of our kin, a Centaur even. That was the third dwarf this morning - their natural resistance to magic is crippling you."

Galanör was more than aware of their stubbornness. "I have a responsibility," he said, regaining his breath. "My magic remains intact. I need to use it."

"It's use to no one if you can't even keep your eyes open,"

Aenwyn countered. "You have saved lives today, Galanör. Let that ease your burden while you rest."

Galanör knew a losing argument when he heard one, and he did feel hollow from head to toe. "Perhaps something warm?"

Aenwyn smiled, though it was out of relief more than victory. "Rumour has it there is an excellent broth coming out of Sir Ruban's camp."

"The northmen?" Galanör said incredulously.

Aenwyn guided him away from the wounded and offered a playful shrug. "I was just as surprised as you are."

After a few hours of sleep and a steaming hot broth - likely revered for the large quantity of salt the northmen added to it - Galanör was able to meet the rest of the day without feeling as if he was being turned inside out. The cold, however, still crept into his bones, reminding him that he was experiencing the drain that came with healing magic. He wished, now more than ever, that he had devoted more time to study and picked up his scimitars less.

His blue cloak billowed in the breeze, but his furs kept it weighted down around his shoulders as he slowly walked through the camp. He paused when the wounded came back into view, in the distance. It was tempting to return and give them all he had. Aenwyn, as usual, was right to caution over-use of his magic lest he end up lying amongst the wounded, adding to their number.

Walking among them was Vighon, easily seen thanks to his entourage and a lumbering Golem. The king was taking time to visit the wounded, offering them words of encouragement no doubt. Galanör held a moment of pride, recalling all too well the young rogue Vighon Draqaro had once been. He really was the king Illian deserved.

Turning to his right, Galanör discovered another worthy of her title. Reyna was four rows over, directing various captains in the elven army as well as taking in reports from others. Nathaniel was beside her, his elvish tested to its limits in the middle of it all. The old knight was certainly the most unusual king Ayda would ever have. Galanör only hoped his kin accepted the man.

A shadow swept over the camp, turning the ranger's eyes to the sky. It was the first break in the clouds he had seen and the light from the waning sun cast strips of orange across the heavens. Passing over that light, in the west, were Athis and Inara. The red dragon glided with all the ease of a blade cutting through air. It was the first time he had seen them take flight since arriving at the battle. It pleased the elf to see them both recovered enough to soar again.

"Galanör!" The call returned his gaze to Reyna and Nathaniel; the old knight beckoning him to join them. As he approached, Nathaniel asked, "Would you share some food with us?"

Galanör beamed at the offer. "How could I refuse my king and queen?" His comment gave Reyna pause before she took her seat around the fire.

Like almost everything else in the camp, their makeshift stools were made from the catapults and ballistas that had been torn down for parts. The larger tent that had been erected for the council certainly had beams and other supporting structures from the catapults.

Nathaniel glanced at the elves who had taken up positions around them, just beyond their cosy camp. "Reyna," he said, almost pleading.

Reyna acknowledged her husband's discomfort and issued an order in elvish. The servants faded away to give the king and queen some distance while still being attentive. It was enough for Nathaniel.

"They will obey you too," Reyna told him quietly. "And your elvish is just as good as mine."

Nathaniel shrugged off her suggestion. "I don't think I'll ever get used to it."

Galanör was tempted to make a joke about taking the knight's place, referring to the betrothment that had once existed between Reyna and himself. Deciding it was too awkward a subject, he accepted the food and drink and filled his stomach with both.

"Aenwyn asked that we keep an eye on you," Reyna said, changing the subject. "She was worried you might return to the wounded." Galanör looked up from his food, his eyes naturally scanning the environment for any sign of his love. "She has joined some of the hunters," the queen went on to explain. "I dare say her skill with a bow surpasses my own."

"That's very kind of you, your Grace," Galanör replied. "I fear I have aided all I can today," he added. "My skill with healing magic is lacking."

Nathaniel leaned forward to rest his elbows on his knees. "You don't need to use such formal titles with us - we're old friends."

"Yes he does," Reyna said, her tone clipped and her gaze averted from them both.

"What?" Nathaniel questioned.

Reyna took a breath and looked at Galanör with an apology in her eyes. Then she turned to her husband. "He does have to use our titles." Her gaze flickered to the distant servants and back, drawing a sigh from Nathaniel.

Galanör waited until the old knight was looking at him. "It is the way of things... your Grace."

Nathaniel's expression soured with a hint of amusement behind it. "*You* were supposed to be on *my* side."

The elven ranger raised his hands in mock surrender. "Any elf with half a head of sense knows to always side with their queen."

Reyna wore a smug smile before turning serious again. "You speak of lacking skill but I hear there are dwarves and elves walking about the camp who should be walking hand in hand with Death."

"I did what I could, your Grace," Galanör replied, humbly. "The effects aren't wide spread yet, but every healer is complaining of a... *disruption* in their magic."

The queen made an expression of agreement. "It is among the hardest of spells to weave."

Galanör looked to his left, though he couldn't see the Drake. "How fairs Adan'Karth?" he asked. "Has he spoken yet?"

Reyna shook her head. "Not yet, I'm afraid. Gideon and Kassian are with him."

The elven ranger nodded, disturbed by the lack of news. "And Asher? Has he returned with Doran yet?"

"No," Nathaniel answered this time. "Though I am keen to see both again."

"There is little in the wilds that could trouble a pair like that," Galanör reasoned. "Though I do not envy their task. I will count Russell Maybury as one of humanity's best for all my long days on this earth."

"The casualties in this war will live in our hearts for eternity," Reyna uttered, before sipping her water.

Galanör shared the shadow that overcame the queen's face, for he too thought of Adilandra Sevari in that moment and his heart sank all the further. "Your Grace," he began, his voice on the verge of trembling. "Before you now, I would like to reiterate my condolences and beg not only for your forgiveness, but for the opportunity to serve you and, perhaps, elevate myself in your eyes once more."

Reyna couldn't hide the pain that stirred in her. "Galanör..."

"I was reckless," he continued. "Queen Adilandra would never have entered the tower with so few if she hadn't been trying to save me. I put her in that position." Galanör slid off his stool and took a knee beside the fire. "I am so sorry, your Grace."

Reyna reached out and lifted his head with a gentle finger under his jaw. "Faylen has recounted events for me. My mother commanded them to leave her. She knew exactly what she was doing. Like you, she chose her own path. Facing Alijah was inevitable." Galanör made to speak but the queen hushed him. "I would not have you carry this guilt for eternity. My mother counted you as a good friend and an honourable elf. She was always proud to have fought by your side.

"So," Reyna said, her tone firming up, "in regard to this debt you speak of: there is none. My court - the entire elven nation - would be a better place with Galanör Reveeri in service to it, but I would not have you assume such a position out of guilt or some presumed debt. If you wish to really serve us and our people, you must desire it in your heart."

With tears glistening in the corners of his eyes, Galanör removed Stormweaver, his one and only scimitar, and planted it tip first in the ground. His grip firm and head lowered, he vowed in elvish, "*I, Galanör of house Reveeri, pledge myself and my sword to the house of Galfrey, the bloodline of Sevari, and the kingdom of Ayda.*"

Reyna gave the elf a broad grin and instructed him to rise. Then she told him to take his seat again and finish his food and drink. "I have no official position for you yet," she went on to explain. "Though I do have one in mind. For now, however, I would like you to work alongside Faylen as you have been doing. She remains your superior; her word to be counted as my own."

Galanör bowed his head again. "I understand, your Grace. And thank you for accepting me into your kingdom."

"It is good to have you back in the fold," the queen affirmed. "I promise you, no matter what is to come, I will never command you with the ill will of my father. He took advantage of your skills with a blade - perhaps it is us who should be asking for your forgiveness," she posed.

"Never, your Grace," Galanör assured.

"I am more interested in your mind, your perspective," Reyna specified.

"You've certainly seen and done a lot," Nathaniel pointed out.

Truly humbled, Galanör nodded in appreciation. "Thank you for the promise, your Grace." The elf swallowed a mouthful of bread and cleared his throat, unsure whether this was the right environment to make his enquiry. "Has there ever been any word of your father, your Grace? Of King Elym?"

Reyna glanced at Nathaniel, though the meanings behind their expressions were known only to husband and wife. "Not long before The Ash War," Reyna disclosed, "before King Vighon tasked us with investigating Valatos, we had some time to ourselves. I had been curious for some years as to what had become of him. It took time and a lot of leg work up and down the east coast, but we finally found him."

"His journey out of Velia was simple," Nathaniel began. "After Adilandra exiled him, he took to The Selk Road and headed north. It seems he didn't stop until he passed through Longdale and into The Lonely Wastes, as far north as Illian goes."

"It was the tales coming out of Longdale that ultimately led us to him," Reyna continued. "They spoke of a man from the north - not something you hear people in Longdale talk of. They said he came every few months to trade fish for materials and supplies. This might not seem extraordinary, but they said he had been coming for thirty years and never aged a day."

Galanör was enraptured by the tale. "Did you go to him?" he asked, forgetting any formality.

Again, husband and wife shared a look. "We made the journey," Reyna answered. "Those frozen wilds are no easy place to survive so we could not stay long. I laid eyes on him, though he did not see me. His dwelling is a simple hut, not far from the shore. His existence is equally simple... and lonely. It cannot be an easy life to bear for an immortal," she concluded.

"Such is his punishment," Nathaniel reminded them. "He nearly steered the realm into war and genocide. He was lucky Adilandra only banished him."

Galanör didn't disagree, though he couldn't help but notice some heartache where Reyna was concerned. Her relationship had never been good with Elym, but he was still her father and now her only living parent. He felt for her.

Eventually, the queen waved the topic away. "These days are dark enough without dwelling on the misdeeds of my father. Let us pretend, if only for a moment, that all is right in the world. Lighten the mood, Galanör, and tell us of Aenwyn. I want to know everything," she added with an eager smile.

More than happy to, Galanör took them back to his arrival in Ilythyra, when Ellöria was the lady of the wood. For a time, the three of them were able to fall into conversation and talk like the old friends they were.

CHAPTER 32

A HEART OF THREE

Illian boasted every kind of terrain Verda had to offer and every inch of it was magnificent in its own way. It had been appreciated by numerous races and their countless generations for millennia. For Inara Galfrey, however, there was no better place than the sky. It might be devoid of rolling hills, snow-capped mountains, and glorious forests but, in comparison, it was an oasis for those who could navigate it.

Athis bore his pain willingly for the opportunity to soar through the heavens. His wings hurt to be so extended and his joints ached with every flap, but it did not stop him from gaining height nor gliding on the currents. The effects of Malliath's fangs and claws still lingered up and down the red dragon's body, their sting keenly felt. Yet they did not get in the way of his delight - flying with Inara.

His head broke the wind, allowing her to take in their surroundings. Inara would have preferred to keep her sights on the sky and the clouds or even the distant horizon, but there was no avoiding the eyesore that marred The Moonlit Plains. The battlefield remained littered with the dead, their bodies either piled or ordered into rows.

Inara was taken back to the battle, back to her failure.

The entire realm had been put in jeopardy because she had failed to defeat her brother. Thinking of Alijah brought back their last moment together. He had stood over her, the victor. In the last two years of war he had never had such an opportunity to kill her as he did then. But he faltered. Or did he? she questioned. Perhaps he merely wanted her to see his victory in all its terrible glory.

We both know that is not the truth. Athis's voice focused her immediately.

It isn't? she responded innocently enough.

When you entered the realm of magic, Athis continued, *we lost contact with each other. We should assume the same of Alijah and Malliath.*

That proves nothing, Inara countered without thought.

Perhaps not, Athis admitted, *though it certainly adds to Gideon's theory. There might be something of your brother left in there, Inara. A part of him that, without Malliath, recognises you for who you are.*

Inara hardened her heart and mind to the possibility. ***No,*** she simply rejected. ***He is the enemy; nothing more, nothing less. As the Guardian of the Realm, it is my duty to—***

Kill him? Athis questioned incredulously.

Again, Inara hardened and pushed her emotions down. ***If I must,*** she declared.

I share the title of Guardian, Athis said delicately, *yet I do not consider it my duty to kill anything. We are to hold back the darkness. We are to be the hope that carries the light. We are to stand for those who cannot. If Alijah needs our help, should we not try?*

Inara looked down at The Rebellion's camp, her sharp eyes running along the many wounded and dying. ***No,*** she replied firmly.

Athis turned his head to briefly lay a single blue eye on his companion. *Your thoughts and feelings may be your own now, but I still know what lies in your heart. I know that you—*

Inara blinked in confusion. The dragon's voice had simply disappeared. She looked at her companion and tilted to one side to try and see his face. She couldn't feel him in her mind.

Athis?

There was no reply. There was nothing at all. Though their bond had changed, she could always reach out and feel the edges of his consciousness. Not anymore. Her confusion was quickly replaced by panic.

Athis?

The dragon looked back at her, concern in his eyes, as he was clearly experiencing the same thing.

"I can't hear you!" she shouted over the wind.

Athis growled in frustration and banked to the north, his head angling down to return them to the ground. All four of his claws beat down in the snow, his wings fanning the powder into the air around them. Inara climbed down and dashed to face her companion.

"What's happening?" she questioned out loud.

Athis moved his head as if he was replying, but no words sounded in her mind. Inara reached out and touched his hard snout, desperate to connect with the dragon in some way.

Inara? his voice finally rang clear in her mind.

Yes! she exclaimed. **I can hear you again!**

That was unpleasant, Athis understated. *I couldn't sense you at all.*

Inara could feel her heart pounding in her chest as she turned to look at the distant pit. **It's the tree.**

Athis's head bowed, his dismay clear to see. *I do not wish to spend my final days in this world alone.* His bleak statement turned Inara back to him. *If I am to find my way to the eternal shores,* he continued, *I would very much like to do so in the company of your voice.*

Inara's eyes immediately welled with tears and she reached out again to stroke the scales under his jaw. **You are going nowhere,** she vowed. **We will find a way to undo this. We have an eternity together, remember?**

The red dragon exhaled a hot breath and drew Inara in to his rich blue eyes. *Eternity is a long time for one whose heart is held by a mortal,* he said, shifting the topic.

Inara looked away. She knew she had ignored the reality of Vighon's mortality.

I will enjoy what time I have with him, she said earnestly. *To do anything else would give me an eternity of regret.*

Athis leaned forward, bringing him even closer to her. *Not if you were mortal,* he uttered.

Inara frowned and stepped back. "No," she replied with her voice, emphasising her response. *I will not even entertain that,* she continued across their bond. *We both know there's only one way that can happen and I will not hear you speak of it. You will* **not** *perish,* she added with some force.

The life of a mortal is not so bad, Athis began gently. *On the contrary, I would argue it is all the more beautiful because of their mortality. Every moment is precious. They experience life like a flash of light; every colour, sound, and taste is more vibrant because of it. And, at the end, you would return to me on the eternal shores.*

Inara waved the conversation away. *It doesn't matter. You're not going anywhere.*

Athis lowered his head so that she could rest her own against his warm scales. *I only want for you to be happy.*

You make me happy, she stated.

Life is more complex than that, the dragon told her, his innate wisdom showing through. *You are part dragon, human, and elf, wingless one. Your heart has many desires, all of which you feel so keenly now. And I am glad. This is who you are. I was wrong to deny you your whole self. The realm could never be threatened by one who loves it so much.*

Inara pulled her head back to meet his eyes. *You know I—*

Have forgiven me, Athis finished. *I know; that much I can feel in you. And with the forgiveness I feel your love for me. I also feel your love for Vighon. I think everyone can see his for you. There is great happiness to be found in his embrace; happiness I cannot give you, a life I cannot give you. Both your human and elven self naturally seek those relationships; they should not be denied.*

The dragon glanced at the camp before returning his attention to his companion. *Should we survive what is to come or not, be with him, Inara. Together, we will cherish the memories of him forever.*

Inara wiped a solitary tear from her cheek and placed a hand on the dragon. ***I love you,*** she declared.

And I you, wingless one.

~

As night closed in on The Moonlit Plains, Inara found herself waiting for Sir Ruban and a handful of captains to leave Vighon's tent. She stood patiently beside Sir Borin the Dread, one of very few people who could, in fact, stand beside the Golem without trembling.

Through a gap between the tents, she caught sight of Gideon in the distance, just beyond the camp. He was with Ilargo, as he had been all day. The pair had been in deep discussion since before the dawn, their conversation their own. Athis had noted more than once that Ilargo had prevented him from making contact.

Inara let it go when, finally, the occupants filed out of the tent. She gave them all a friendly nod before entering. The king was leaning over a table, constructed using the base of a ballista by the look of it, and scrutinising several maps of Illian.

Catching sight of Inara, his mood immediately brightened. "It's good to see your feet on the ground. I've missed you."

Inara couldn't help but smile. "Athis and I have been testing the limits of our injuries," she explained. "It seems nothing can keep us from the sky."

"I wish there was something that could keep me from these maps," Vighon complained, his mood diminishing again. "We're just guessing at everything," he continued, fingering a pile of papers. "All the reports are old. Alijah's moved his Reavers round since they were delivered." The king shrugged in despair and took his seat. "It all seems so pointless. The tree burns and Adan'Karth has said nothing. None of this means anything if we lose magic."

Inara moved to his side, squeezed his shoulder, and leant down to plant a soft kiss on his lips. "You will never lose this."

After she pulled away, Vighon remained still, his head back, and eyes closed. He sighed and, with it, exhaled some of the tension that had been knotted inside him. "I needed that," he said.

"As did I," she replied, taking a seat beside him. The king continued to look at her expectantly. "What is it?" she asked amusedly.

"You haven't come to tell me something grave?" Vighon pondered. "You're not here to strategise? Share a burden or two?"

Inara gave a gentle giggle and poured herself some water. "Am I usually such a bearer of bad news?"

"No," the northman was quick to respond. "I suppose it's just the times we live in."

"I am sick of the times we live in," Inara groaned. "I want to eat, drink, and talk of... Well, perhaps not too much talking." For just a second, she saw her coy grin mirrored in Vighon's expression.

"No," he said with half a laugh. "I have not waited all this time to lie with you in a grubby tent, surrounded by every man, elf, and dwarf in the realm."

Inara's coy smile turned into a warm one as she leaned towards him. "I didn't realise you were such a romantic, your Grace."

"Not every northman possesses a block of ice for a brain," he insisted. "Though I would flatten The Vengoran Mountains for another kiss."

Inara happily obliged. "There's no need to reshape the world," she whispered.

And so the night stretched on, the couple undisturbed. They shared drink and food, their portions no bigger than those which the rest of the camp enjoyed. They talked for hours and nothing of the war or Alijah. Any memories recounted only involved the two of them and often ended in laughter. Vighon was very interested in chatting about their future, one he held great faith in. It seemed he had been dreaming of their life together for many years. Every detail he fantasised about brought a smile to Inara's face, even the part where they had several children.

And, all the while, he never once dwelled on their most distant future, when most would accept their old age. He only spoke of the fantastic things they would do together and for the realm. In his imaginings, they were young forever.

Inara didn't correct him; it was all too wonderful to spoil.

Instead, she listened and even contributed, adding fantasies of her own; dreams she had let go of decades ago. They all resurfaced now, her human side coming alive with it all. More than once, Vighon referred to her as queen, a title that took her aback. Like her mother, that was the last title she had ever expected to receive.

It led her down the path of proposals and weddings, events she had witnessed with no intention of experiencing. Now, however, the idea of marrying Vighon Draqaro made her stomach flutter and her heart race. Just the thought of it conjured a picture of happiness she had never imagined.

A hand brushed her cheek, drawing her from the reverie. Vighon's dark eyes were boring into her, searching for the woman he loved.

"Where did you go?" he asked.

"The future," she replied quietly.

Vighon tilted his head, curiously. "And how does it look?"

Inara looked past any sadness until her mouth shaped into a beaming smile. "It looks good."

Day had passed into night without notice from Gideon. He had spent most of the day sitting beneath one of the few pines that dared to have taken root on the plains. Lying beside the tree, his head curled under the canopy, Ilargo exhaled warm air across his human companion. The dilemma that had beset them was of intentions, decisions, and actions, all of which plagued their high-minded sense of morality.

Rider and dragon had used much of the day to debate the worst of any life, good or bad. There was no mistaking that Alijah had been corrupted to his core, but that was not to say that he couldn't yet be saved.

Gideon groaned and let his head rest back against the trunk of the tree. *He wouldn't be the first to be put to death for crimes against the realm,* he argued.

But he might be the first redeemable person to commit such crimes, Ilargo countered.

And so their conversation had gone on for many hours. Gideon would question the weight of so many demanding Alijah's death and whether such a large number was a valid reason for execution, given that most people knew nothing of Alijah Galfrey. Then Ilargo would bring up the matter of duties, especially those of Inara, Vighon, and Reyna, all of whom were expected to uphold the laws of their countries, laws that demanded Alijah's death.

For every point one would raise, the other had a reasoned conflicting point. It was infuriating.

We are no longer governed by the codes and laws of others, Gideon said, the thought having been lingering on the periphery of his mind all day. *We could act on our own will. Accomplish our own goals.*

Ilargo's blue eyes took in the vast camp before settling on Gideon. *Acting in such a way brings about an entirely different ethical dilemma. Rogue dragons, and especially rogue Riders, have always been treated with great suspicion and rightly so. We are too powerful to simply roam the world without any allegiance to the rulers of the land.*

Then perhaps now is the best time to behave in such a manner; while the realm is in turmoil. We could set out to do what we know is right without fear of reprisals.

I agree that the timing is right, Ilargo replied, *but what exactly would we accomplish? We are both aligned when it comes to Alijah - we believe he should be saved over death. But how would we save him? Malliath's hooks go deep. What could we do to part their minds? And where would we go to accomplish such a deed?*

Only an hour earlier, Gideon had found a spark of hope when recalling the ancient runes that had lined his cell in The Tower of Jain. He brought it to the discussion, wondering whether they could replicate them using Ilargo's perfect memory, but the dragon had quashed any hope.

Where would we place such runes? the dragon had asked. *Alijah is waiting us out. There will be no time to use the magic of those runes before magic itself no longer exists. Besides, I believe there was more to those spells than the scrawls that decorated our cells.*

Gideon sighed and rubbed his eyes. **I can think of no path that leads to sparing Alijah's life.** The old master balled his fist and fought the urge to lash out at the ground. **This is all my fault. I should never have tasked Hadavad with recruiting Alijah in the first place. My own actions were all part of The Crow's plans for him. I just want him back, Ilargo. I want to save that young man who only wished to fight for good.**

Ilargo's eyes sharpened on his companion. *The decisions we made came from a good place. The Crow had nothing to do with it; he simply used our actions against us. Something he could have done without dark magic. And I would remind you that it was those same decisions that ultimately led Vighon Draqaro to the throne of Illian.*

Gideon slowly nodded along, unable to fight the dragon's wisdom. **Perhaps Alijah's fate is beyond us. He has wronged so many, some powerful enough that we could not stop them from killing him if we tried. I suppose our place is here, guarding the doorway. We need to save the tree or there's no point in...** His words trailed away as he watched Ilargo's head rise from the ground, his gaze distant. So complex and layered was the mind of a dragon that Gideon had to accept the fact that his companion could think through multiple scenarios at once, while *his* capacity could only cope with one of them at a time. **What is it?** he asked.

Ilargo looked down at him. *There is another way to separate the minds of Rider and dragon,* he explained ominously. *We have experienced it first-hand.*

Gideon saw the green image in the dragon's mind. **Crissalith?** he queried, recalling the crystals well.

It is the only thing I have ever known that could sever our bond, Ilargo went on. *If we could use it against Alijah, Malliath's influence would be wiped away.*

I agree, Gideon said, his tone matching his disheartened demeanour, **but you're forgetting the most important fact about Crissalith: it's all gone.**

The dragon's eyes narrowed. *I forget nothing.*

Gideon saw his companion's thoughts as if they were his own and, with them, came a new spark of hope.

CHAPTER 33
WHY WE'RE HERE

O n the dawn of the third day, Asher and Doran crossed the snowy plains in sight of the sprawling camp. Cutting through the air overhead, Avandriell soared and dived, still too young and fearful to venture into the heavens above. The ranger could feel her elation upon spotting Athis and Ilargo in the distance.

As their approach advanced, every able dwarf either rose to their feet or stopped what they were doing to face their War Mason. It was a great sign of respect for Doran, one Asher had feared his friend would never gain from his kin, a people notorious for having heads as thick as stone, long memories, and grudges that bore roots.

Asher turned to look down at Doran. He didn't envy what lay ahead of him, but he *was* happy for him. He deserved a second chance and the children of the mountain sorely needed a king such as him.

After receiving a grand return from the dwarves, the pair were stopped in their tracks by Galanör. The elf cut a lithe figure, his navy cloak flowing out beside him.

"It is done?" His words were carried in a grave tone to match his expression.

Asher glanced at Doran before responding. "It is."

Galanör nodded slowly. "The world has lost a fine man and The Rebellion a fine warrior. Russell Maybury will remain in my thoughts always."

"An' ours, lad," Doran agreed.

Galanör took a breath. "I will leave you here. I am to spend some more time amongst the wounded."

Asher squeezed the elf's shoulder and moved aside to let him go. Only a moment later they were met by Sir Ruban, who relayed King Vighon's request to join them in the council's tent. Avandriell glided down to pad alongside her companion and hear the captain's brief report concerning Adan'Karth's unusual injury. The news perturbed ranger and dragon alike.

Entering the council's tent, Asher acknowledged the familiar faces but, after discovering the Drake resting by the far wall, he moved past them to crouch by Adan's side. He lay curled up on a cot, his body draped in blankets and furs. Words, barely a whisper, escaped his lips in a steady stream while his eyelids fluttered incessantly.

The ranger tried to make sense of it but Doran's recounting dominated the tent. A few kind words were said as those who knew Russell offered something close to a prayer. A moment of silence was held for him, a moment Asher used to inspect the injury to Adan's hand. Sir Ruban's description hadn't done it justice. Turning it over to examine the palm as well, he could see the extraordinary bark had taken over his whole hand. It was also just as soft as his skin, making it all the more unnatural.

Avandriell came up by his side and gave Adan's hand a sniff. "What do *you* make of it?" he asked in a hushed tone. The dragon tilted her head inquisitively before giving it a lick. Outside of her curiosity, he sensed nothing more from her. "Stay with him," he said, stroking the scales on top of her head.

Returning to the central table, Asher was immediately greeted by Reyna. Whether he wanted her to or not, she gave the ranger a hug, embracing him with her strong arms.

Looking up at him with her emerald eyes, she said, "I am sorry you have lost Russell. I know you were good friends with a rich history. Perhaps you could honour him one day and tell me of his life."

Asher managed a smile. "I would like that."

Nathaniel patted him on the arm before squeezing his muscle. "You are a good friend. Both of you," he added, taking Doran in.

The son of Dorain nodded with a sober expression. "An' what has happened in our absence?" he asked, looking to Adan'Karth.

Vighon rested both of his hands on the table and glanced over the rough map that had been laid out using various materials. "We have made little to no progress," he reported gravely. "We entered the realm of magic and..." The king gave half a shrug as if he could go no further.

"Adan touched the tree," Gideon continued in his stead. "I believe he was trying to talk to it. None of us can explain exactly what happened next but, it seems, the tree tried to... *absorb* him."

"Absorb 'im?" Doran echoed. "Ye mean to say it tried to eat 'im like some Mud Slug?"

"We can't say," Kassian spoke up, his expression never more serious. "Adan is yet to say a word we understand."

Inara stepped in beside Vighon, their proximity notably closer than any other pair in the tent. "I touched the tree," she announced. "It did not harm me in any way."

"Has anyone returned to the tree?" Asher queried.

"A couple of times," Gideon answered. "The fire continues to spread. The entire realm looks to be crumbling around the tree."

Asher could feel his heart quickening as his concern for Avandriell bubbled over. "How do we stop it?" he demanded, driven by fear.

Gideon, who had just as much to lose as the ranger, could only shake his head. "So little is known about it. We would need to observe it for decades, perhaps centuries, to know more."

"We don't have that kind of time," Asher pressed, his fist

thumping down onto the table. "You were supposed to find a way," he growled.

"This isn't one of your typical problems," Kassian retorted on Gideon's behalf. "You can't just swing a sword at it and make things better."

Asher eyed the Keeper with some ferocity. "There aren't nearly enough winters behind you to lecture me, boy."

Kassian's face dropped and he started for the ranger. Inara's hand quickly found its place in the centre of the Keeper's chest, an immovable object he could not overcome.

"That would be a mistake," she warned.

Doran let out a little chuckle. "I wouldn' o' minded watchin'," he remarked.

"Emotions are high," Reyna said diplomatically, watching Kassian relax. "That is to be expected. We all have something to lose and we are wading through uncharted territory. We must be reasonable and work together if we are to undo this calamity."

"My mother is right," Inara said. "Time is our enemy. Without the combined magic of the Drakes in that pit, the doorway will soon close. At the rate we are losing magic in this world, we might not be able to rely on Athis or Ilargo to fly us back to Drakanan."

"We would need magic to enter the bonding chamber anyway," Gideon added, folding his arms. "This doorway is our only option."

"What about Alijah?" Asher posed with little explanation.

"What about him?" Vighon questioned.

"He has Jainus magic at his disposal," the ranger stated. "Is it possible he possesses the knowledge to stop the situation from getting any worse?"

"He has used time spells," Nathaniel chipped in.

Asher briefly pointed at his friend. "Time spells. Perhaps he knows of a way to reverse what's happened. Or maybe we could even go back and..." He could feel himself grasping at straws.

Gideon was shaking his head. "Time is a fragile thing, Asher. It can be fractured and manipulated to extreme lengths, but it cannot go back on itself."

"I am no master in these matters," the ranger admitted, "but there must be something he has that can stop this."

"So you want us to abandon the site and attack Alijah and Malliath?" Kassian jibed. "Wherever they might be," he added, throwing his hands in the air. "And all for what? Something he might not even have?"

"It's better than staying here and doing nothing!" Asher argued, his fists clenching into knots.

"This is typical!" Kassian spat. "You can't fix it so you just want to hit it!"

"Shut ye gob!" Doran barked. "The man's got a point. The answer might lie with our enemy. He did this, after all!"

Vighon waved his hand. "We are in no position to take this fight to Alijah. And Kassian is right. We have no idea where he's gone."

It was then that Inara gave her opinion, in Asher's favour, but was quickly opposed by Gideon. With Vighon stuck between them, the three bickered venomously. Reyna and Nathaniel stepped in to meet Kassian's next bout of abuse towards the ranger, though Reyna quickly peeled off to interfere with Inara and Gideon. Doran also took umbrage with the Keeper's choice of words and placed himself directly in front of the man, a threatening look in his eye. Faylen tried to diffuse things between them by putting a hand on each, but Kassian appeared to be getting fed up with people physically holding him back. All the while, Asher was poking his finger into the table with every point he made, each one an argument for finding and attacking Alijah while there was still time.

A nudge to the side of his leg turned Asher away from the heated arguments. Looking down, Avandriell was pressing her head into his calf. At the same time, he could feel her reaching out to him across their bond, filling his head with unintelligible whispers. Her golden eyes directed the ranger back to Adan'Karth, but the Drake was no longer curled up on his cot.

Asher's eyes narrowed as he assessed his young friend. "Adan..."

"Quiet," Vighon commanded from the other side of the table.

The king's gaze turned the tent's occupants to Adan, who was slowly approaching them draped in furs.

Asher offered to steady him, but the Drake managed to reach the table unaided. His skin was paler than usual, making him almost white and his patches of paper-thin scales nearly undetectable. His reptilian eyes were sunken and surrounded by dark rings.

"Avandriell's presence is most soothing," Adan complimented, directing a smile at her. "Forgive my absence, as it were, I have not been myself. I needed time to piece my thoughts back together."

Kassian moved away from the others to better see the Drake. "You haven't said anything since we left the tree."

"Was that some time ago?" Adan asked.

Gideon put himself on the other side of Vighon, away from Inara. "It's been days, Adan. We haven't been able to get through to you."

Asher caught the Drake's eyes. "What happened down there?"

Adan held his gaze for a moment, his thoughts his own. When he was ready, the Drake revealed his hand from within his furs. He turned it over so that all could see.

"I spoke to the tree," he breathed. "It is dying and it knows it."

Nathaniel cocked an eyebrow. "The tree is... *alive* then?"

"It is more alive than any of us," Adan'Karth replied with an edge of awe in his voice. "It has been around since Verda was naught but dust swirling in the ether."

Had Asher been a scholar, he was sure such information would have invigorated him. Since he hunted monsters by trade and his companion's life hung in the balance, he didn't care at all. "Did it tell you how to save it?"

"No," Adan reported, robbing the tent of hope. "Though I believe there is a way."

All eyes returned to the Drake, hungry for more. "You would keep it a secret?" Asher contested.

"I have been considering that," Adan revealed, taking everyone by surprise.

Asher glanced at Avandriell before focusing on Adan. "Why would you keep it a secret? You know what's at risk."

"Because if I am right, saving the realm of magic will come at a great cost." Tears welled in his exquisite eyes. "And I do not know if I can bear it," he added.

"Whatever the cost," Inara said, "it must be paid, Adan. Without magic on our side, this war is as good as lost. Whatever the future may be, it will rest under the shadow of Malliath."

Adan's head bowed and he clenched his bark-like hand. "The tree meant me no ill will; it was barely aware of my consciousness. It could only sense the magic that dwelled within me. When I touched it..." The Drake rubbed his thumb over his finger, feeling the grooves in the bark. "It naturally tried to take my magic," he finally said.

"Take your magic?" Reyna's concern was well-founded given her past.

Adan furrowed his brow. "Perhaps *take* is the wrong word. Take *back* would be more appropriate. The tree emits so much magic that it cares little for that which bleeds across the realms. Nor does it care that conduits in our world harness that excess magic. Touching the tree, however, allowed it to bond with my magic and, I have to say, it felt as if my magic *wanted* to return. That's why it hurt so much; because I was resisting."

"I did not experience this," Inara told him.

"I do not mean to offend," Adan said, "but your magic is... *quieter* than mine."

Inara didn't hide her look of surprise. "Quieter? There is no offence, Adan, but I am bonded to a dragon; surely there is nothing quiet about my magic."

"And yet the tree could not sense you," the Drake pointed out. "To the tree's perspective, you are of no consequence. As would be any elf or human mage."

Asher took a breath and fell back on his years of mental discipline to remain calm. "What are you saying?" he probed.

"The tree has lost magic," Adan declared simply. "Being the source, it has nowhere else to draw upon. We need to replenish it."

The revelation dawned on Asher, striking him a blow he had not expected. "It needs you," he uttered, looking again at Adan's hand.

"No," the Drake answered, shaking his head. "Were it so simple, I would gladly become one with the tree so that it might live on." Adan'Karth steadied himself and raised his chin. "It will need every Drake in the land."

Asher stepped back and turned away from the group, so as to hide his dismay. There would be no saving the tree now. Avandriell's death was assured.

"You are certain of this?" Vighon asked, the first to find words in light of the news.

Adan looked away for a moment, consulting his own thoughts. "I cannot assure the tree's survival, but there is no greater source of magic in all of Verda than that which resides in my people. And, besides our magic, I believe a degree of conscious thought will be required to direct our magic to extinguishing the flames. Being part elf and dragon, your Grace, I feel my people possess a sharp enough mind to do so."

Kassian's head dropped to his chest. "This is folly."

"Perhaps we should consider findin' Alijah," Doran suggested carefully. "If we are to fight 'im, we should do it now, while we 'ave the firepower," he added, thumbing at Inara and Gideon.

"We could track the Reavers," Nathaniel mused, his tone suggesting he had little fight in him. "Their numbers should leave quite the trail - we just have to hope they return to Alijah."

When Asher finally turned back, he could see the heartache experienced by both Inara and Gideon. They would lose companions they had been bonded with for decades, a pain magnitudes beyond his own.

"Keep the hope alive," Adan'Karth asserted, glancing at Inara. "All is not lost."

"Not yet," Kassian reminded him, his arms folded tightly across his chest.

"I will speak to my people," Adan continued. "I believe their choices to be simple: give up this life and save magic or do nothing and die with it."

"We don't know that for sure," Kassian told him. "You could very well survive it."

"Even if we survive," Adan countered gently, "half of what makes us who we are is certain to die. I would not know *how* to live without magic."

Asher consciously relaxed the tension in his jaw. "There must be some other way," he appealed. "The price is too high."

Adan gave the ranger a warm smile. "There is no death in the realm of magic. Only an outpouring of life."

"Tell that to yer hand, laddy," Doran remarked.

"It would not be the life you know," Adan went on. "We would be in the very currents of magic that we see around us."

"That's not life," Asher countered. "*This* is life. I will not let you give it up - magic or no magic."

Adan reached out and put one hand to Asher's chest. "Perhaps *this* is why we are here."

~

Heated debates, long discussions, and deep conversations dominated the rest of the day. The council had gone round in circles, off on tangents, and struck dead ends that threatened to raise tempers again.

The council had finally parted ways after nightfall, each seeking refuge from the end of the world. Asher was exhausted, a state brought on by frustration and hopelessness. With Avandriell by his side, the ranger had taken himself off and started his own fire to the north.

In the light of the flames, Avandriell asleep beside him, Asher removed his broadsword. He was dismayed by the blood that stained the steel. Russell's blood. With some water and a rag, he went about cleaning the blade from guard to tip.

His mind wandered, restless.

For every memory he recalled of the old wolf, he was brought back to Adan'Karth and his inescapable revelation. As hard as he had tried, the ranger had become attached to the Drake after so much time together. He owed his life to him more than once.

"I would ask what troubles you," Nathaniel said, walking into view, "but that would seem in poor taste."

Asher suppressed the sigh that so desperately wanted to be released. He had left the camp for a reason. "Unless you brought ale, this isn't the fire for you."

Nathaniel's mouth broadened into a smug grin as he held up a pair of dwarven horns. "Thaligg assures me he *didn't* brew it himself."

"That just means it won't kill us," Asher quipped, accepting the horn. He gave it a brief sniff, recognising the scent of an established dwarven cider - Thundergrog perhaps.

"I know you wanted to be alone," Nathaniel commented, taking his seat opposite the ranger, "but you should know those days are behind you now. Even friendships come at a cost," he added with some amusement.

"It seems everything comes at a cost these days," Asher muttered, tasting his drink which was sickeningly sweet, just the way dwarves liked their cider.

Nathaniel took a mouthful of his own but his focus remained fixed on the ranger. "You dwell on what was said in the tent."

"A *lot* was said in the tent," Asher pointed out, avoiding the real topic.

"Adan'Karth's words cut through you," Nathaniel said, cutting through the ranger in his own way. "Do you reckon there is any weight to his suggestion."

"If Adan says his people can heal the tree then I believe they can heal the tree," Asher responded, his tone clipped.

Though the ranger's mood didn't deserve it, Nathaniel was patient with him. "That's not what I'm talking about and you know it."

Asher brought the rim of his horn to his lips but failed to drink even a drop. He averted his gaze from across the fire and finally exhaled a sigh.

"When I retrieved that relic from Haren Bain," he began, "I thought it was a weapon. I thought I was going to kill every orc under the sun - genocide. Monsters or not, I knew it would haunt me for the rest of my days. When it... *created* the Drakes, for the first time in decades of killing, I had been instrumental in the spark of life. It felt *good*.

"I know everything I did had been manipulated by The Crow; the memories of Haren Bain taken from my bond with Malliath. But I couldn't hate him for that."

"And now?" Nathaniel pressed.

"Now I think of everything we have learnt about The Crow," Asher replied gravely. "We foolishly believed that Alijah was his endgame, but I don't think we're there yet. He knew the future, Nathaniel - *all* of it. He needed the orcs to be decimated and the Drakes to be brought into being, and he used me to accomplish both in one fell swoop. He had me create a whole race just so they could all die."

Nathaniel absorbed his every word. "Gideon holds a similar theory, one he told in your absence. If The Crow did intend for the Drakes to be created, that means he knew they would save the tree. It means he saw it."

The quiet rage building in the ranger awakened Avandriell before he threw his horn of cider at the fire. "At what point do we consider the cost and tell The Crow to stick his prophecies?"

"Well," Nathaniel said with a shrug and a quick sip of his drink, "The Crow is very dead, so there's no telling him anything. And the cost..." The old knight trailed off as he took a breath and lowered his tone. "The cost is not ours to pay. Only the Drakes can decide their fate; we will not force them."

"It may not be ours to pay," Asher countered, "but it will be ours to live with."

Nathaniel lowered his drink, his expression as serious as Asher's words. "Aye," he agreed. "That and so much more."

CHAPTER 34
KING TO KING

Braced against a bitter wind, Doran Heavybelly stood as a sentinel on The Moonlit Plains, his gaze set to the northeast. Out there, beyond land and sight, was The Black Wood. Never had a forest called to the dwarf, yet here he was, drawn to it like some *elf*. He could feel the sands of time slipping through his fingers, only it wasn't really *his* time. With magic fading, how long did Dakmund have before the elven spells' efficacy dispersed? Without their magic, his wound would surely have claimed his life by now.

A cold wind battered his face and forced a tear from his eye, streaking it back towards his hair. He refused to look away. His heart still grieved for Russell and the numerous dead and dying, yet there was more to come and he could not escape it.

It was all so hopeless and he didn't dare think about the consequences of his brother's death; a selfish fear given Dakmund's fate. He also couldn't bring himself to turn around, aware that thousands of dwarven eyes were upon him as they went about their day. They were waiting for his command.

"It's not easy, is it?" came the last voice Doran expected to hear.

"Yer Grace?" he questioned, turning to see Vighon Draqaro walking towards him, draped in a dark cloak and furs.

"Forgive my intrusion," Vighon continued. "The council is gathering and I thought I would stretch my legs first. I saw you..." The king trailed off, gesturing to the north-east as he came to stand beside the dwarf. "It's not easy, is it?" he said again. "They all look to you. Your every word carries weight. They get etched into history and judged long after we're gone."

Doran nodded along, noting the small group of king's guard that held back, closer to the main camp. "Ye've worn yer crown well, yer Grace," he replied, his tone as low as his spirits.

"Crowns don't make kings," Vighon said reflectively, his own gaze set to the horizon now. "Nor do words, no matter how heroic they sound. We're all forged by our actions, regardless of whether we succeed or not."

Doran glanced up at the king, wondering if the latter was specifically directed at him. "How did ye do it?" he asked quietly, his words barely reaching Vighon. "How did ye come back an'... *face* it all?"

Vighon took a breath, a hint of shame and guilt still lingering in his demeanour. "Leaders, whatever their role, don't set an example by being perfect. They set an example by getting back up. My judgment faltered and I made a mistake. In the end, I had to accept that and rise above it, whatever the punishment. And, like you, it helps that I have loyal supporters who believe in me."

Doran half chuckled to himself when considering his own *loyal supporters*. "Ye're well loved an' yer past deeds well remembered. I wouldn' put me in yer camp, yer Grace."

"You sell yourself short," Vighon argued, before noticing the dwarf's raised eyebrow. "I meant no offence," he quickly added with some amusement.

"Hmm. I'd say ye've spent too much time around Asher," Doran remarked, his skin far too thick to take any real offence.

Vighon stifled his laugh. "What I meant to say is: you have plenty of supporters here, and back in The Black Wood. You haven't just been fighting for The Rebellion all this time, Doran;

you've been liberating your people. In just a couple of years you've broken down clan lines that have separated dwarves for thousands of years."

The son of Dorain looked down at his boots, his mouth contorted to match the turmoil within. "When I left for Qamnaran, I made a promise to return with that wretch's blade. Without it, I've done nothin' to change Dakmund's fate. An' what o' me Ma? How will I look her in the eye after he's gone? I've failed to save the last king o' Dhenaheim. How am I to return? Ye say I 'ave supporters, but who could support me when I can' even protect me own brother?"

"I spent a year with questions like those," the northman began. "They preyed on me every time I strayed too far from a bottle. They kept me prisoner, trapped in a cycle of fear. They held me back and stopped me from doing the one thing I should have been doing."

Doran furrowed his brow and looked up at the king. "An' what was that?"

Vighon smiled to himself and turned his head to look back down at the dwarf. "Fighting for what's in my heart instead of what's on my shoulders. But the questions that haunted me are not those that haunt you. Only you know what you must face to put them to rest. There can be no peace for you until you do."

Doran absorbed every word; no easy task for a stubborn dwarf. And, right at that moment, he knew what he needed to face if he was ever to move forward, along with his kin.

A light chortle escaped his lips. "Ye're nothin' like the young pup I remember," he shared. "I used to see ye in The Pick-Axe, when ye weren' out runnin' around with Alijah that is. The two o' ye would come in, young, dumb, an' full o' yerselves. Nothin' could bring ye down; ye were *invincible*." The son of Dorain laughed again before growing serious. "Now look at ye. Ye've got the wisdom o' an elf, the strength o' a dwarf, an' the heart o' a *good* man."

Vighon bowed his head by way of thanks. "I hope you remember me that way five hundred years from now."

"I'll be lucky if I remember me own name five hundred years from now," Doran quipped.

"Your Grace!" one of the knights called, after dismissing a messenger. "The council is ready."

Vighon stepped aside and gestured at the camp. "There can be no council without Doran Heavybelly."

The dwarf grinned. "Too right."

Unlike the rest of his kin, Doran was more attuned to humans and elves after so much time living amongst them. He picked up on their subtle cues, be it in their facial expressions or body language. Elves, naturally still and poised creatures, were often more animated when irritated. And, it seemed, they could say a lot more with their eyes than their mouth. Humans, on the other hand, went rigid and cold, usually a precursor to an explosion of energy. Looking around the tent now, Doran's experience informed him that calmer heads had prevailed after a night's sleep.

Naturally, all eyes fell on Vighon as he invariably led these kinds of meetings. The king, however, directed them to Adan'Karth at the other end of the table. "It was Adan who requested we meet again," he explained.

The Drake bowed his head in thanks before addressing the council. "Thank you for gathering again; I know there are many out there who look to you all for guidance now. We discussed many things yesterday. We *disagreed* on many things yesterday," he added, clearly uncomfortable with any kind of conflict. "You are all within your rights to remain here and continue discussing your next steps, but I have already decided on mine."

"Adan..." Asher's tone had just an edge of pleading to it.

"I have accompanied you across the sea and back," Adan replied, meeting the ranger's blue eyes. "I made your path my own." The Drake glanced down at Avandriell. "But I cannot follow you - you belong in the sky now. It is time I walked my own path. I will journey to The Evermoore and seek out my people. If I can, I will convince them to join me in bonding with the tree."

Silence filled the tent like a thick mist.

"You are sure, Adan?" Inara questioned, her soft tone breaking the tension.

"You have all given or lost something for the realm," the Drake replied. "My people and I could never fight for this land as you do but, perhaps, we can still serve it in a way that matters. My mind is settled."

Inara nodded once. "Then Athis and I will hasten your journey," she offered. "You will reach The Evermoore by air."

"I would like to accompany you," Kassian told them, with a quick look at his king.

Inara made no protest, though she did turn to Vighon.

"Adan carries a precious message," the king said. "The more to protect him the better."

"While we're there," Inara added, "I will seek an audience with the governor of Vangarth. It's the closest town. Perhaps I can convince him to send supplies to aid us."

"Do what you can," Vighon replied.

There were no further objections, the decision Adan's alone. Doran could see, however, the way it tore through Asher. He felt for the ranger, trapped between a rock and hard place.

"We should leave immediately," Inara suggested. "Athis cannot fly every Drake back to the plains; they will have to make the journey on foot."

"I'm ready," Kassian agreed, in time with Adan bowing his head.

Doran cleared his throat, giving them pause while simultaneously drawing everyone's attention. "Ye're not the only ones to be leavin' this day," he announced. "An' before ye start worryin', I'm not talkin' abou' marchin' every dwarf off the plains." The War Mason stopped and sighed. "I 'ave to return to The Black Wood," he said, catching Vighon's eyes.

"There's unrest brewin' between me kin. I'm hearin' talk o' new kings an' challenges risin' up amongst 'em every day. With the clans leaderless an' broken, chaos an' violence will break out an' consume 'em. Right now, while they're all lookin' to me, there's an opportunity to unite 'em all that I cannot ignore. But, to do that, I 'ave to be there for me brother before he meets the Mother an' Father. I would not 'ave 'im slink into death, his passin' unnoticed. Dakmund is the last an' rightful king o' Dhenaheim - he deserves to be recognised as such."

Reyna reached out and rested a hand on his shoulder. "I am so sorry, Doran."

"Will you travel alone?" Nathaniel asked, concern in his voice.

Doran harrumphed. "Those days are behind me whether I like it or not. As War Mason - the *only* War Mason - I won' be allowed to travel across country without at least a hundred dwarves at me back. Don' worry though, I won' be takin' me best. We will help ye defend the plains."

Reyna lowered her head and planted a kiss on the dwarf's cheek. "You are the best of your kin, Doran, son of Dorain. Return to your brother and do what you must, for his sake as well as for your people." The elven queen paused to hold a brief, yet silent, conversation with Vighon. "We will return your forces to you in The Black Wood when our victory here is secured."

Doran was still trying not to blush at the kiss while he nodded his head in agreement. "I'll make sure Thraal introduces ye to me replacement before we depart. An' I have no doubt ye will succeed here," he declared with confidence. "Some in this tent are already heralded as *heroes*, others *legends*. Mark me words, the deeds o' ye all will be recounted in the history o' every race from east to west for all time. An'... I am proud to call ye all me friends."

All but Gideon Thorn had some form of farewell to offer the dwarf. The old master looked lost to his thoughts and Doran left him, eager to be getting on his way. A handful of words, and stern ones at that, were all Thaligg and Thraal required to begin preparing for his journey. They had argued, initially, that he should be accompanied by their best warriors, but Doran had put them to the task with naught but a look in the end.

He also made certain that enough of his kin learned the reason for his departure to ensure that word travelled across the camp. The last thing he wanted now was for them to believe he was abandoning them, especially with the number of would-be kings amongst them. If there were any who did seek to challenge his claim to rule, he would meet them in The Black Wood, *after* he had seen Dakmund into the waiting arms of Yamnomora.

He soon came across Pig, the Warhog's frame hard to miss. He patted the beast on the head before inspecting its damaged tusks. "Ye gave 'em Reavers what for," he commented mostly to himself. "Good Pig."

Working his way around the Warhog, he came to the broken pick-axe strapped to the saddle. He had kept it since Qamnaran, hoping to repair it and give it back to Russell. He ran his fingers over the notches carved into the haft, each a monster Russell had sent to the next life. The son of Dorain had no idea what to do with it now. He only knew that he didn't want to discard it. Leaving it where it was, he moved round to see Lord Kraiden's head, his crown of spikes still bolted to his skull. The wretch's head could remain tethered to Pig a while longer, he decided.

His inspection completed, the son of Dorain mounted his Warhog and guided it by the reins. Thinking like a ranger rather than a War Mason, he envisioned a journey that would cut across the land until they came to Barden Bridge, outside of Whistle Town. From there, they could take The Selk Road north. He was done hiding. If any Reaver or bandit fancied their luck challenging a company of dwarves, a hundred strong, then let them.

Waddling under the weight of his armour, Thaligg approached the War Mason with a hint of apprehension about him. "If ye've words for me then spill 'em," Doran commanded.

Thaligg waited until he was right beside Pig to speak his mind. "Are ye sure to be puttin' Commander Rolgoth in charge in our absence, me Lord?"

Doran looked down on him, already aware of the dwarf's concern. "Ye've a problem with Rolgoth?"

Thaligg glanced over his shoulder, checking for those who might be eavesdropping. "He's a *Battleborn*, me Lord."

"Oh," Doran replied sarcastically, "was it the sigil tattooed across his entire *face* that gave 'im away?"

The younger dwarf ignored the jibe. "Our clan is in a place o' strength right now. Shouldn' we put a Heavybelly in charge while we're gone?"

"It's *because* he's a Battleborn that I'm puttin' 'im in charge," the son of Dorain countered. "Battleborns 'ave been at the top o' Dhenaheim's hierarchy for centuries. That's hundreds o' years forbidden from attackin' the clans beneath 'em an' hundreds o' years spent diggin' in an' defendin'." He paused to point at the distant pit. "That's exactly what we're doin' 'ere."

Thaligg's mouth twisted this way and that as he considered Doran's choices. "Aye, I suppose that makes sense," he finally muttered.

Doran's eye went wide. "Oh, well if ye *suppose*..." The War Mason thumbed over his shoulder. "Get saddled an' get this lot movin'!"

With Thaligg's departure, he turned Pig to better see those of his company. He was glad to see a great number of volunteers step forward to join him. He only hoped they chose to do so out of loyalty rather than a desire to depart The Moonlit Plains. He had cause to look twice at one particular dwarf joining his company. The tattoo on his arm identified him as a Hammerkeg, a clan that had resided beneath the Heavybellys for centuries.

"*You, lad!*" he called in dwarvish. "*What's your name?*"

The younger dwarf hesitated before approaching the War Mason. "*Finrig, son of Fearn, my Lord.*"

"*You would cross Illian with me, Finrig? To The Black Wood?*"

"*Aye, my Lord,*" the dwarf answered without his previous hesitation.

Doran licked his lips. "*It's mostly Heavybellys up there,*" he warned.

Finrig appeared tempted to avert his gaze but he possessed enough military discipline to look his superior in the eye. "*You saved my life on the battlefield,*" he explained as a matter of fact, though Doran could not recall anything of the such. "*And my friend, Kalagad, would have perished on Qamnaran were it not for your axe and hammer, my Lord. There are more like me and Kalagad. Thousands more, all saved by those of another clan who march on your orders. We would follow you into The Dread Wood if you so commanded it."*

Doran was quite taken aback by the response. *"There's no place for great names and hard lines on a map anymore. We need to look after each other. Oh, and should the day come that I issue a command to enter The Dread Wood, Finrig, you have my permission to strike me on the head with Andaljor!"*

CHAPTER 35
AN INTIMATION OF HOPE

Deep inside his sanctuary, a physical realm that bridged his mind to Ilargo's, Gideon turned away from the perpetual night sky and ocean of stars. Instead, he looked to his companion, who rested on the lush plains of their quiet haven. The dragon's rich blue eyes bore into the dark orbs of the old master's.

You're sure? the old master asked him for possibly the tenth time, aware that Ilargo could think twice as fast as any human or elf.

No more than I was the last time you asked. Our options are limited and time is against us. If this is truly the path we wish to commit ourselves to, we must simply act.

Gideon slowly nodded in agreement, though he would have liked their odds of success to be a little higher. Still, it felt like the right thing to do, so what else could he do?

I will take this to Inara, he said.

I would not, Ilargo cautioned. *We have disagreed with them on this matter. I do not believe their minds have been changed since last we spoke.*

Gideon quietly sighed. *I have to try. She has buried her feelings. I know there is still a part of her that wants to save him.*

Ilargo's head shifted and his gaze with it. *They are preparing to leave. If you must speak with her, now is the time.*

Gideon took a breath, closed his eyes, and re-emerged in the real world. He was standing beside Reyna and Nathaniel, who had both offered farewells to their daughter. Asher and Avandriell were a little further away, closer to Ilargo who was watching Gideon with sharp eyes. Kassian and Adan'Karth were already astride Athis, though the Keeper looked as if he was ready to get down before they took off into the sky.

Only Inara remained on the ground, pulling away from Vighon after a tight embrace and a handful of private words. It was the most open either had been about their relationship and Gideon could see the joy it brought to Reyna, beside him.

"Inara!" the old master called, breaking away from the Galfreys. He passed the king and continued until he was face to face with his previous student. "I know time is short," he began before Inara could make any protest. "Just listen to me," he pleaded. "Ilargo and I have been thinking about Alijah."

Inara gave him a patronising look and half turned as if to walk away from him. "We've been over this, Gideon. Malliath or not, Alijah has made himself the enemy." After delivering her response, the Guardian turned her back on him.

"We think there's a way to save him." Gideon put it as simply as he could, but kept his voice low enough so that only Inara could hear him.

Inara stopped on her way to Athis and reluctantly turned back to her old master. "I don't even know what you're thinking, but I know you must be clutching at straws, which we don't have time for."

"If you can't stand the idea of saving him," Gideon replied with his last ditch effort, "then consider it another tactic to defeat Malliath."

Inara looked on him with pity. "Not everyone can be saved, Gideon."

"I know you, of all people, do not really believe that."

His words may have cut through her, but Inara was quick to harden herself against any truth he might spout. "Stay here," she said firmly, though careful not to sound aggressive. "Guard the doorway." Giving him no opportunity to say more, she made for Athis and climbed up his scales.

Gideon stepped back as Athis's red wings gave them rise into the sky, a plume of snow and debris lifting with them. He quickly turned north and continued to ascend, heading for The Evermoore.

You tried, Ilargo said into his mind. *She requires more time. I sensed a much greater curiosity in Athis.*

In their absence, Gideon replied, **we will turn to those who can aid us.**

Ilargo arched his neck, raising his head to the west. *He is among the wounded.*

While those of the council who remained began to naturally gather, Gideon strode back into the thick of the camp. He weaved between the individual sites, avoiding the areas where food was being prepared and served to larger groups. The elves he passed knew exactly who he was and always bowed their heads out of respect. Most of the dwarves, however, didn't know his face, but the children of the mountain had a better eye for steel than they did faces. The red and gold hilt of Mournblade turned more than a few heads among their number.

On the far side of the camp, where the wounded had been triaged into a system from injured to dying, Gideon began his search in earnest. A nudge from Ilargo, whose height gave him a view of the entire camp, pushed the old master in the right direction.

"You must be Aenwyn," he said with a genuine smile.

The elf bowed her head. "It is an honour, Master Thorn."

Moving past the lump in his throat, he waved the title away. "Please. It's just Gideon."

Aenwyn bowed her head one more time. "As you say."

Gideon looked at the entrance to the tent beside her. "Is Galanör..."

"He is healing," Aenwyn answered pleasantly.

Gideon battled the sense of urgency that demanded action. "Very good," he said instead. "Actually, I'm most pleased to have met you. Galanör was telling me everything... Well," he reconsidered, "Galanör's never been one to tell everything."

Aenwyn smiled knowingly. "He certainly makes you work for it," she agreed.

"He spoke of his fondness for you though," Gideon quickly added. "Indeed, I don't believe he's spoken of anyone the way he speaks of you. I have long worried that he was fated to wander the wilds with naught but his swords for company. I'm so happy for..." He trailed off as Galanör himself emerged from the tent, coated in a fine sweat.

"Gideon?" The ranger looked a little pained to straighten his back.

"Are you well?" The old master couldn't hide his concern.

Galanör took Aenwyn's offered arm to steady himself. "I'll be fine by midday," he reassured. "Healing magic is—"

"Hard," Gideon finished. "That's because you give a portion of yourself to every person you heal. You are not nearly schooled enough in this art to continue as you are."

"There are no healers amongst my people who can teach me," Galanör told him. "All are affected by the tree."

Gideon nodded gravely. "You are a hero in more ways than one, Galanör Reveeri."

The ranger shook his head. "The real heroes are dying all around us."

Gideon didn't want to disagree with him. "You're doing good work here. How many are you able to save?"

The elven ranger looked like the weight of the world was on his shoulders. "Two or three a day."

"Any more and he risks his own life," Aenwyn pointed out.

The old master looked out on the numerous makeshift tents, all filled with wounded warriors. "When we take the fight to Alijah, there will be fields of tents like these."

Galanör narrowed his eyes questioningly at his old friend.

Gideon caught his look. "What I mean to say is: we need to stop this war before there's no one left to rebuild whatever remains."

Now Galanör looked suspicious. "Is there a reason you have sought me out, Gideon? Faylen has filled me in on the meetings."

"I'm afraid there is no more to be gained from meetings," Gideon stated boldly. "Now is the time to act."

Galanör found the strength to stand on his own, regaining some of the posture that identified him as a warrior. "What are you hatching, Gideon?"

The old master responded with a coy smile. "One last adventure."

A few hours after midday, when the winter sun was beginning its decline into an early rest, Gideon found his path blocked by six foot of human ranger. In all the time he had known Asher, Gideon could confidently say that he had never been truly intimidated by the man, but he still wouldn't try and forcibly remove him.

"Asher." The old master looked from the ranger to Avandriell, whose head rose just above his knee.

"Schemes do not become you," Asher said, his eyes flitting over Gideon's shoulder.

A quick glance informed Gideon that the ranger could see Galanör and Aenwyn collecting supplies from various sources. Further still, Ilargo had taken himself away from the bulk of the camp and was in the process of flexing his wings, preparing for a long flight.

"You don't miss much, do you?"

"Apparently I've missed *something*," Asher quipped.

Gideon held up his hands. "We weren't going to leave without explaining."

"You shouldn't be leaving at all," Asher told him. "With Athis gone, Ilargo is our best chance of holding this position." The ranger's eyes flashed over Avandriell. "I don't have to tell you how important this is."

"There's a way to save Alijah," Gideon blurted, halting Asher's train of thought.

"Save him?" he questioned sceptically.

"You know more than anyone what it's like to be trapped in a cage with Malliath. Inara and I have both seen the truth - he *is* being influenced. The fact that Alijah thinks their bond has been altered, blinding him to his own injuries, tells me that he is barely aware of his own actions." Gideon put a finger to his head. "He's stuck in there, Asher. The Alijah we all knew. The Alijah that loved his friends and family. The Alijah who wanted to save the world. He deserves to be saved like everyone else."

The ranger's hard features softened somewhat. "I agree," he said, taking Gideon aback. "But our efforts should be focused on defeating Malliath, not saving Alijah."

Gideon couldn't hide his frustration. "I'm aware that most of the people in this field, perhaps the entire realm, would prefer to just kill them both and be done with it. They might even be right," the old master considered. "But there is another way to look at this."

"Would that other way be the scenario you suggested to Inara?" Asher replied. "I saw her reaction after you spoke to her."

"She has hardened herself to all matters concerning her brother," Gideon lamented.

Asher nodded his understanding, reminding Gideon that the ranger had spent a lot of time with Inara while searching for him in Erador.

"As to your perspective," Asher pointed out, "you suggest that saving Alijah rids us of a powerful foe *and* unbalances Malliath at the same time. It's a good twist on saving him, but everyone will see it for what it is and, like you said, they want Alijah dead, not redeemed."

"*They* don't get to decide that," Gideon argued. "I cannot be commanded by king, queen or *ranger*. And I know this is the right thing to do. I thought you would too."

Asher looked away, his thoughts always his own. "We all deserve a second chance," he said reflectively. "Some of us are on our third or fourth. And no one should have to endure the mind of that monster." The ranger turned back to Gideon. "I'm only asking you to consider the timing of this. We need you here, *now*."

"The timing is *why* we must leave now," Gideon countered. "Even Adan couldn't say for certain that his people would be able to save the tree, if they agree to try at all. We need to do something while we still can and, for that, I need Ilargo."

It was clear to see that, no matter how pragmatic the ranger was, Asher found it hard to accept that they could lose magic and all the dragons with it. "And how *exactly* are you going to save Alijah?"

"Yes," came a voice that startled them both. "How will you save him?" Reyna echoed, rounding the council tent to meet them.

Gideon made to speak but he retracted the words before they could leave his mouth. This was a sensitive topic to discuss with anyone, but Alijah's mother made it so much harder to articulate.

"Are you asking as the queen of elves?" Asher posed. "Or Alijah's mother?"

Reyna held the ranger's gaze for a moment before looking at Gideon. "Perhaps we should take this inside," she suggested, her eyes directing them to a pair of curious dwarves within earshot.

With some reluctance, Gideon followed Reyna and Asher into the council tent. The absence of Sir Borin immediately informed the old master that the king was elsewhere. In fact, with Reyna's guard commanded to stay outside, they were the only occupants.

"Where are Vighon and Nathaniel?" Gideon enquired, wondering if he could ever get used to calling them kings.

"They are both dispatching scouts to widen our perimeter," Reyna replied. "Alijah knows where we are and that we have suffered heavy casualties. He could still have Reavers as close as Galosha, Whistle Town, *and* Tregaran."

Gideon nodded along while casting his eyes over the maps on the table. When he finally looked up, Asher and Reyna were watching him closely.

"Can you really save him?" Reyna pressed, her emotions bubbling just under the surface. "Can you save him from Malliath?"

"There might be a way," he said with some reticence. "And when Ilargo tells me that - I listen. But I would caution against hope. Though I'm confident this will separate Alijah from Malliath, I cannot guarantee it will bring back the man we all knew. The best case scenario is that it unbalances Malliath and disrupts their command over the Reavers."

Asher gave a quiet sigh and leaned over the table, his blue eyes piercing the old master.

Gideon bit his lip, buying just an extra second of time to collect his thoughts. His attention ran over the maps and landed on the coastal city of Velia, a place of memories for them all. "Do you recall the events immediately after the battle of Velia, at the end of The War for the Realm?"

"This is already sounding too long-winded," Asher complained, folding his arms.

Gideon held up a hand, requesting patience, but it was Reyna who answered his question. "Which event are you referring to? We took the fight to Valanis after the battle."

The old master shook his head. "Before that, when we were all together for the first time. I had come from Mount Garganafan, having claimed The Veil."

Asher gestured at him. "You had killed someone..." The ranger's eyes shifted to a distant gaze, though the ranger possessed more memories than just his own these days.

"Lord Krayt," Gideon informed. "He was Atilan's Minister of War."

"He fancied himself a god," Reyna said. "Like his master."

"Next to most, he was," Gideon stated. "Like Atilan, he always kept Crissalith on his person. It lined his staff."

"Crissalith?" Asher repeated. "Let's pretend I'm not an elf; you're talking about something that happened nearly fifty years ago."

402

"That's your plan?" Reyna interrupted, doubt and curiosity fighting for her tone. "I thought it was all gone."

The old master shook his head. "The *mine* was destroyed," he specified. "The Crissalith and Atilan's private lab should still be down there."

"For those of us who died after you explained this the first time," Asher cut in, "what is *Crissalith*?"

Gideon apologised with his expression. "Crissalith is a form of crystal, green in colour. I first came across it in the south of Ayda. The Darkakin were using it against the dragons."

By the look on Asher's face, his memories had just caught up with him. "It kills magic."

"That's something of a *ranger's* description, but you're close. Crissalith was designed by Atilan to deflect the currents of magic. He was looking for a way to bring dragons down but, from what records there are, he mostly enjoyed the power it gave him over his subjects. Like Krayt, his staff was lined with the crystals. Any room he entered rendered the occupants blind and deaf to the realm of magic. It made him powerful among the powerful."

"But he couldn't use magic either," Asher reasoned from Gideon's description.

Revelation illuminated Reyna's face. "The blue crystal..." Her words trailed off, much like her sight, as she tried to follow her understanding through to a logical conclusion.

"There's a *blue* crystal?" Asher's frustration formed his every word.

"The one you brought back from Mount Garganafan," Reyna continued. "You said you had taken it from Lord Krayt."

"Yes," Gideon confirmed. "It was the only way I could beat him." He recalled yanking the ring from Lord Krayt's bony finger, reducing him to naught but an old man, feeble when compared to Gideon's youth.

Asher shook his head. "Besides the fact that I didn't have any eyes at the time, I've taken a few blows to the head since then - some quite recently. I don't remember any blue crystal after the battle of Velia."

"They're called Hastion gems," Gideon explained.

One of Reyna's eyebrows lifted in curiosity. "I thought they had no name."

"At the time we didn't know of one," Gideon explained. "Atilan's grimoire - the one Galanör and your mother found in the mine - made no mention of it by name, but I found a single reference to it in the Dragorn library, on The Lifeless Isles. Elandril himself investigated a few ancient sites, during The First Age. He collated what he could—"

"I'm appreciating the history lesson," Asher interjected, "but what does a Hastion gem do?"

Gideon tried to think of the simplest way he could put it. "Like Crissalith, Atilan designed it with a single purpose. Whoever wields a Hastion gem retains their connection to the realm of magic - Crissalith cannot affect them. Atilan wore such a gem on his finger. He also gifted them to his most trusted and loyal servants, like Krayt."

Reyna leaned forward on the table, her gaze almost predatory. "Do you still have it?"

Gideon nodded. "Locked away in the Dragorn library."

Asher released something close to a groan from his throat. "Why do I feel like I've missed a step?"

Reyna turned to the ranger. "With a Hastion gem in his possession, Gideon can retrieve a piece of Crissalith from the mine and safely bring it back to Illian without Ilargo falling ill to its effects."

Gideon added, "It also means we could get close enough to use it against Alijah without losing what's left of our own magic. At least one individual could," he added.

Asher didn't look convinced. "For the last two years, Alijah has proven to be one step ahead of us at every turn. If you've considered this, won't he have?"

"He won't even know it exists," Gideon replied with the hint of a smile. "I locked the Hastion gem away in the library years before he was born. And Malliath was there for the mine's destruction. As far as he will be concerned, Crissalith is no longer a threat."

Asher looked away as he came to his own conclusion. "They would be blind to it."

"Yes," Gideon said with some satisfaction. "This could be our best chance at really stopping them. The Crissalith will cut right through their bond. Alijah will be able to think for himself for the first time in years. Malliath will be put off balance, perhaps enough to subdue him until Alijah can alter their bond. After that we can slay Malliath and spare Alijah."

The ranger shook his head again. "This Hastion gem you possess - it's a ring?"

Gideon looked from Asher to Reyna and back. "Yes," he answered hesitantly.

"So you could retrieve a piece of Crissalith without it blocking your magic," Asher went on, "but how will Ilargo fly back to Illian if it only protects the one wearing it?"

"Ilargo has already considered that," Gideon reassured. "We have a plan."

"And does this same plan also help you to enter a mine destroyed by a dragon?" the ranger hounded.

"No." The answer turned every head to the tent's entrance, where Galanör was standing with Aenwyn. "I believe that's where I come in."

Gideon pointed his finger at the elven ranger. "Galanör has been inside Atilan's lab. He's *seen* it."

Again, Reyna put it all together before Asher. "You could open a portal *inside* the mine," she voiced.

Galanör nodded. "It's been several years since I opened any portal, but I recall the method. And I recall Atilan's lab with enough clarity."

"You don't look like you have the strength to open a door," Asher said bluntly, "never mind a portal."

"He will have time to recover," Gideon assured. "We must fly to The Lifeless Isles to recover the Hastion gem first."

"What about crystals to open a portal?" Reyna questioned. "I doubt there are any among us who can create one now."

"Before departing Illian at the end of The Ash War," Gideon told them, "I concealed three crystals in my private chamber."

"One to get in," Galanör said with a finger in the air. "And one to get out," he added with a second finger.

"And one for luck," Gideon commented.

Asher gave a false laugh. "You're going to need it. Hell, we all are."

Reyna acknowledged his comment without a direct response. "The magic in those crystals will be degrading along with the tree," she said instead.

"All the more reason for haste," Gideon reminded them.

Asher, clearly the one burdened by the most doubt, leaned over the table and hung his head. Reyna mimicked him to better see his face between the strands of hair. "Is this the part where you say we're all going to die?"

The ranger waited a moment. His eyes crossed them all before resting on Reyna. "Not this time," he replied resolutely. He returned to his normal height and took a breath. "Well. What are you still doing here? Go. We can defend the doorway if needed."

Gideon looked at Galanör and Aenwyn with a question in his eyes. They both nodded, informing him that they were ready to take flight.

"What will you tell the others?" Gideon enquired of Reyna and Asher.

"The truth," Reyna answered. "You have gone to retrieve a great weapon that will end the war."

Gideon could see the hope that now lived in her, no matter how much she tried to hide it behind a narrative. Judging by the way Asher looked at her, he too could see the fire ignited within her soul.

He hoped he didn't break her heart.

Soon after, Gideon was ascending Ilargo, taking his place in front of Galanör and Aenwyn. Many eyes were turned to their departure, most of which looked concerned. The old master trusted the reason for their absence to spread quickly.

He looked down at Reyna and Asher while Avandriell jumped about beneath Ilargo's head. "Protect that doorway," he said.

"Save my son," Reyna replied quietly.

Gideon maintained eye contact with the queen, his old friend.

Asher glanced at her with concerns of his own pinching the muscles on his brow. "Go," he urged, looking back up at Gideon.

The old master turned back to his companion, catching one of his blue eyes. *Take us home, Ilargo.*

The green dragon walked away from Avandriell and the others before bursting into a run. Once he was away from everyone, Ilargo beat his wings and soared high, leaving the world behind. Avandriell flew after them but the younger dragon soon banked in a bid to return to her companion, her bronze scales disappearing into the mass of the camp below.

Gideon looked down at the pit as one opened inside his stomach. Now it was he who dared to hope. Hope that Adan succeeded and saved the tree. Hope that their journey to Ayda bore fruit. Hope that they would return to a world of magic where he could watch Avandriell mature.

He feared he too was destined for heartbreak.

Not if I have anything to say about it, Ilargo declared with determination.

It brought a warm smile to the old master's face and not just because his companion was so fierce. He enjoyed the fact that, while their bond had been irrevocably altered, they could still dwell in each other's thoughts with ease.

In his despair, it would have been easy to shut Ilargo out and keep his thoughts to himself. In all his years, however, Gideon had found no better place to be.

CHAPTER 36

MESSENGER

Every second in the sky was a gut-wrenching moment for Kassian Kantaris. His body was tensed from head to toe, braced between Athis's spinal horns. The muscles in his thighs, back, and arms ached, begging him to relax. He dared not, just as he dared not look at anything other than Adan's back. He caught glimpses of Inara's red cloak, flapping in the wind, but he never shifted his focus from a particular stain on the Drake's robes.

Thankfully, it was a straight flight north from the camp to Vangarth. Had Athis needed to bank left or right or ascend over mountains, Kassian would have ruined the dragon's exquisite red scales with the contents of his stomach.

Up ahead, Inara turned her head over her shoulder to face them. "We're nearly there!" she called over the wind.

Kassian didn't even bother to nod his head. Instead, he hunkered down and adjusted his grip on the spike in front of him, preparing for the change in altitude. Adan, on the other hand, felt very differently about their flight, his arms outstretched as he embraced the thrill of it.

It wasn't long before Athis angled his head down and his body followed after it. The tall pines of The Evermoore, coated in snow, were there to greet them, stretching far into every corner of the land. As the ground rushed up towards them, Kassian instinctively turned his head away and settled his sight on the western horizon. Only then did he realise the sun's final light was upon the realm, tinting everything a glorious orange.

The beauty of it all was immediately lost on him when his stomach lurched, threatening to jump up into his throat. Kassian closed his eyes, shutting them so tight it hurt. He felt all four of the dragon's claws impact the ground and he heard the trees and snow react to his mighty wings. Still, he didn't open his eyes until he heard Inara's voice as she climbed down from her companion.

"The town is just north of here," she told them.

Kassian peeled himself off Athis and happily followed Adan'Karth down to the ground. The snow made a satisfying crunch when his feet touched down. He had never been so grateful to have the earth beneath him.

Inara strapped one bag of supplies over her shoulder before giving them each their own. "I will go into Vangarth," she continued. "If I can, I will persuade the governor to send any supplies they can spare to the camp. We're going to need everything we can if we're to make the journey to The Black Wood when the time comes."

"We will accompany you," Adan began. "Vangarth is too vast to go around and my people will have sought refuge deeper into the woods."

"Can't you just speak to the trees here?" Inara queried, clearly hesitant to have them accompany her.

"Yes," the Drake agreed. "But the closer I am to them, the less they have to travel. They will be more likely to seek me out this way."

Inara nodded along but she harboured reservations. "Fine. But I will enter Vangarth separately. Two strangers walking into town after sunset is less likely to draw unwanted attention than three strangers."

"Are you expecting trouble?" Kassian questioned, his hand coming to rest on the hilt of his sword.

Inara ran her hands around her belt, checking the Moonblade amongst her other items and small knives. "Always," she replied. "It's highly likely that Alijah still has Reavers patrolling the town."

Kassian shifted the holster on his thigh so his wand was better concealed within his coat. "The last time I was in Vangarth there were quite a few of them," he remarked. "Seekers too," he added gravely, aware that all three of them reeked of magic.

"That doesn't surprise me," Inara replied. "Vangarth is the biggest town in all of Felgarn. Only Lirian would have more of the wretches."

Adan, who had been standing as still as the trees, announced, "We should go. The currents continue to fade."

Inara gave a nod to Athis, their personal farewells private. Kassian was only too glad to stretch his legs and leave the dragon behind for a while.

Thanks to Adan's uncanny ability to navigate the maze-like forest, they eventually found themselves on the southern border of Vangarth.

It was quiet on the edge as families settled down for the night, smoke rising from their chimneys. Warm light poured out of windows here and there. Kassian knew from his last visit that Vangarth was a sprawling town, the majority of buildings single storey. Even from the ground, the guard towers could be seen on the periphery, looming over the people. At its heart lay the Great Lodge, the largest building in the town, where countless governors had dwelled during their reign.

"That is my destination," Inara informed them, looking to the Great Lodge at the end of the main road. "I suggest you take the western streets and enter the forest again in the north."

Kassian agreed. "Be careful," he warned.

"I will meet you in the forest when I'm done," she said, stepping out from between the trees.

"You can track us?" the Keeper asked in disbelief.

Inara looked from Adan to Kassian. "I can track *you*."

Kassian wanted to argue but she was probably right. Instead, he watched her disappear down the main road, her red hood draped over her head. For just a moment, the Keeper felt real concern for her going off into the town alone, but then he remembered who he was concerned for. Inara was called the Guardian of the Realm for a reason, and she didn't need a dragon by her side to claim it.

With Adan by his side, the pair cautiously entered Vangarth. Kassian kept his scarf wrapped around his neck and half of his face while the Drake concealed his shaven horns inside a dark hood. Unfortunately, the first people they came across were not people at all.

A pair of Reavers, clad in their usual black suits of armour, were patrolling the street around the corner. Kassian whipped his arm out and kept Adan pressed against the wall before either could walk into view. Without speaking, he directed the Drake to an alley that would take them the back way to the western streets.

From the next corner, they could see more Reavers standing guard at the top of the nearest tower. Exiting the base of the tower was a lone Reaver, accompanied by a pale Seeker on a lead. Kassian took Adan by the arm and dashed out of the alley and further up the street. A quick glance over his shoulder informed the Keeper that the Reaver and its pet were taking the same route. Kassian cursed and guided the Drake further west, putting a row of buildings between them and the enemy.

They passed a tavern, the windows brimming with firelight. It wasn't the liveliest place Kassian had ever seen but it was full enough that they could disappear inside and blend in with the patrons. But the presence of the Seeker kept his feet moving and his heart pounding. If their trail was followed into the tavern, they would have no way out but through the Reaver, creating a ruckus that would surely bring more down on them.

No, he decided. They kept walking through the gloomy streets, though the Keeper began to worry that they would never end. One street led to another which led to another. He had them heading north as soon as the path became clear but, more often than not, the Reavers emerged from the shadows as if birthed by the darkness, forcing them to take the long way around.

By the time they reached the northern edge of the town, Kassian should have been very aware of the freezing temperature, but he remained oblivious. Every ounce of his focus was on the dark corners and high towers. So close to the forest again, they opted to run, making a mad dash for the cover of the trees. They kept up their speed until Kassian's human lungs demanded rest.

"I would suggest a little further," Adan remarked, his reptilian eyes surveying the hidden wilds.

"Fine," Kassian agreed, his chest heaving. "But we might have to walk."

Grateful for a slower pace, the Keeper followed Adan's lead as they pierced The Evermoore and left Vangarth behind. He couldn't say how long they walked for, but the evening's clouds had moved on, replaced now by a shining moon and sea of stars. They finally came to a stop in a small clearing, illuminated by the hanging moon above.

"Here," Adan'Karth announced.

"What now?" Kassian asked.

The Drake approached the nearest tree and placed his hand to the bark. The Keeper noted it was not the hand affected by his interaction with the mountainous tree in the realm of magic. As he had done then, Adan closed his eyes and communed with the tree, a conversation that remained entirely undetectable to Kassian. He simply waited, calling on what patience he still possessed.

It was in times like this, quiet moments where he had nothing to do, that he would dwell on Clara, often reliving her death. He was pleased, however, to find his memories cast back to their playful games, when he would try to find her from the rooftop of the central hall in Valatos. He envisioned her smile and then recalled the sound of her laughter. Kassian vowed to make something beautiful in the world, something that would reflect her.

Adan stepped back from the tree, bringing the Keeper back to reality. "Is that it?"

The Drake answered with action rather than words. With both hands raised, Adan conjured a spell that brought forth a wave of cold air. It blew through the tree, rustling the needles, and continued to the next tree and so on. Moving his hands around, he cast his magic in an arc until every tree around them was rustling with the artificial breeze.

As he turned on the spot and came face to face with Kassian, Adan stopped and his eyes went wide. The Keeper knew that look. He had seen it in the faces of his mages time and time again. Acting protectively as well as instinctively, he pushed Adan'Karth back while, at the same time, throwing himself to the ground. As he rolled over his shoulder, he heard the sound of steel cutting through the air where he had just been standing.

Reavers!

There was no opportunity to rise before another swing came at him, this time high to low. Kassian launched himself backwards, narrowly avoiding the tip of the blade.

Landing on his back, he scrambled away from the Reaver as best he could but the undead wretch advanced with confident strides. As a third blow came down on him, the Keeper parted his legs and avoided amputation.

As the Reaver heaved its sword back with both hands, Kassian retrieved the wand from his thigh - he wasn't going to let it deliver a fourth blow. Thrusting the wand, he poured his will into the spell, his focus harnessed by the Demetrium core. He squinted his eyes, preparing for the blinding light that would explode from the end and destroy his foe.

There was no explosion, however. Instead, his wand spat a shower of sparks at the Reaver, a spell no more potent than throwing a bucket of water over the fiend. Inevitably, that fourth blow arrived; this time aimed to slice through his head and torso.

The Keeper swore and rolled to the side at the last second. He tried to jump up but a boot pressed into his side and kept him down with a fierce push kick. Kassian used this forceful momentum to continue his roll, thereby avoiding a fifth strike from the Reaver's sword. With what precious moments he had, the Keeper aimed his wand again and flicked his wrist this way and that to expel the destructive magic. Nothing. Sometimes there weren't even sparks.

As the sixth hammering blow came down on him, Kassian rolled to the side one last time before shoving his boot into the Reaver's knee. The creature felt no pain, but the damage to its limb caused it to stagger away, giving the Keeper the time he needed to finally get off the ground. It was only then that he noticed the Seeker advancing on Adan'Karth.

Giving up on his wand, he exchanged it for the sword on his hip. Muscle memory demanded that he draw the blade over his left vambrace, an act that would ignite the spell laid in the steel. He had done it hundreds of times and never once had it failed to come alive with that blinding white heat.

Except now.

The blade remained dull, its only shine from the moon's reflection. With the Reaver limping towards him, he had only his skill with a sword to fall back on. He deflected three successive strikes while deliberately positioning himself to have a clear line to the Seeker. It growled and hissed as it stalked closer and closer to Adan, its jaws dripping with thick saliva. With few options, Kassian did the only thing he could to save the Drake's life. He launched his only weapon.

The sword flew through the air, spinning end over end, until it slammed into the centre mass of the Seeker. The creature yelped as it was thrown into the side of a tree, there to die. Now, of course, the Keeper was left to face the Reaver with naught but his hands and his wit.

"The currents!" Adan shouted from across the clearing. "The currents are aligned with you again!"

The Reaver managed another three strikes - all of which Kassian managed to evade - before Adan's words sank in. He gripped his wand again and whipped it up into the Reaver's chest. Now there was an explosion of light. And the force that accompanied it was enough to take the fiend from its feet and hurl it into the forest.

As the dust settled, Kassian stepped out of the clearing and approached the Reaver. It was easy to find, impaled on a branch, its feet hanging above the ground. It writhed and struggled to free itself, but Kassian's spell had severely damaged its arms and legs, leaving the resurrected knight to remain pinned to the tree. He aimed his wand at its head, intending to destroy the creature once and for all. This time, a harmless jet of water shot out of the tip and did nothing more than soak the Reaver's armour.

The Keeper groaned and tapped the wand against the palm of his hand. It still refused to obey him, this time emitting a low humming noise.

"It's your lucky day," he remarked, before returning to Adan. "Are you alright?" he asked.

"I am unharmed," the Drake replied evenly.

"Good." Kassian planted one boot on the Seeker's ribs and yanked his sword free. In his hand, the blade now came alive with a searing hot glow that took him by surprise. "This is getting tiresome," he complained before looking to Adan. "What you said back there... You can see when the currents are flowing through me?"

"Yes," Adan confirmed. "They are not flowing through you now." With his last word, Kassian's sword lost its enchantment and returned to ordinary steel.

Just to be sure, the Keeper ran it over his vambrace anyway before sliding it back into his scabbard. "They must have tracked us from town," he concluded, gesturing to the Reaver that was still trying to escape.

"Could there be more?" the Drake asked with curiosity more than fear.

"There's always more," Kassian replied dryly. "How long will this take?"

Adan'Karth looked around, as if the answer lay before him. "I cannot say. My people will hear my message, but whether or not they choose to come remains to be seen."

The Keeper took a breath to continue his recovery and let his head fall back. "Were you telling the truth back at camp?" he asked, though the question didn't look to surprise Adan.

"I have never lied," the Drake told him.

"So it wouldn't be death," Kassian probed, "if you... *gave* your-selves to the tree?"

"Does this worry you?"

"Death?" he echoed, wielding the word as if it carried no weight. But then it began to sink in, the finality of it, an absolution from all things. He then grew more serious in both expression and tone. "Of course," he said honestly, if quietly. "You are an entire people. As much as I fear you all losing this life, I fear what Verda will lose without Drakes in it."

"I did not lie," Adan reiterated. "The tree is a source of life. It is not the life we know, but our presence will forever be felt. Those currents that flow through you and those like you will have a touch of us in all of them." The Drake's expression finally cracked, displaying a hint of apprehension. "That is not to say I look forward to such a thing. Change is difficult and... frightening. As much as I know it is not death that awaits us, I know it is not the life I have come to enjoy. But what choice do we have? I am half dragon and wholly magic. I cannot fathom life without it."

Kassian had to look away, lest Adan see the tears welling in his eyes. "When this is all over," he began, finding the courage to look Adan in the eyes, "I am going to build a new world for the conduits of this realm. The king will help me. It will be safe and purposeful. It will be a place where people and magic can come together in harmony. A place where your sacrifice will live on in all of us."

Adan'Karth offered the Keeper a warm smile. "This place you speak of, it reminds me of Ikirith, our home." The Drake turned to the north. "Its remains are not that far from here. For me at least."

Kassian's hand twitched by his side, hesitant to perform an act of compassion he had long forsaken. Finally, he managed to rest that hand on Adan's shoulder and squeeze.

"I wish there was another way," he whispered.

Adan placed his hand over Kassian's and smiled before looking to the sky. "What is it Asher says about wishes? Ah, yes. Wish in one hand and spit in the other and see which one fills up first."

Kassian maintained his serious expression before it cracked in amusement. "Of course he does," he laughed.

CHAPTER 37
HARD TRUTHS

U nder a still and cold night, beneath an ocean of watching stars, Inara strode up the middle of the road towards the Great Lodge, her red cloak floating out silently behind her. A handful of people passed her by, hurrying to their homes. Like most towns and cities under Alijah's reign, there were curfews in place that only granted so long outside after dark - an attempt to track down rebels no doubt.

An example of such a thing could be seen down an adjacent street, where a pair of Reavers were watching every patron as they filed out of a closing tavern. Inara returned her sight to the gates ahead, using her hood to conceal much of her face.

Two human guards, those allowed to remain in the governor's service, saw her approaching and stepped forward to bar her way with a halberd each.

"I pray you stop, lady," the older of the pair commanded.

Inara did not wish to create a scene and so she obeyed. "I request an audience with Governor Harlan," she announced with clarity.

The same guard who had spoken to her raised an eyebrow in

doubt. "The hour is late - the governor's appointments are finished for the day."

"Curfew is almost upon us," the younger man chipped in. "Best you return to wherever you came from and be quick about it."

Inara only briefly regarded the younger man before returning her full attention to the first guard. "Tell the governor," she said, moving her cloak aside to reveal Firefly's crystal pommel, "that Inara Galfrey is at his door."

Her name struck both guards like a hammer to the head. They quickly turned to each other sharing the same perplexed expression before giving each other a knowing nod.

"Go and inform the master," the older man instructed. "We'll enter via the kitchens. I'll bring her to his study." The other guard gave Inara one last look before rushing off into the Great Lodge. "Quickly now," the older guard said to her. "We need to get you off the streets. The governor will want to meet you."

Inara allowed the man to usher her through the gates, though his attention was mostly cast over the streets, checking for Reavers if she had to guess. As was explained to the younger guard, they entered the Great Lodge via the kitchens and quietly made their way through the decorated halls until they reached the ornate door of the governor's study.

"Wait inside," the guard insisted. "The master will be with you shortly."

Inara entered the study and drew back her hood as the door was closed behind her. It was a large room, larger than any one person required of a chamber to read and sign documents. The walls were lined with books, the shelves separated by the stuffed heads of bears and stags. It was sparsely lit by a handful of candles and a single torch on the far wall.

The Guardian wandered by the desk, its proportions designed to intimidate any who sat opposite the governor. She ran her fingers over a piece of parchment and examined the seal of Governor Harlan. Inara considered what she knew of the man. It had been some years since they had met at some royal function or other. She recalled his honest nature as a good sign where his loyalty to Vighon was concerned. And, judging by the way his men had sneaked her into his study, Inara assumed his loyalty was still standing.

A few minutes later, the door opened again and a shadowed figure entered the study. Instinct drove Inara to grip Firefly before she successfully identified the figure as Governor Harlan. He was smaller than her, older too, but the man appeared almost haggard. Most with his title, and the wealth that came with it, were somewhat plumper.

"Guardian," he said with a bow of the head. His almost pleading tone concerned Inara.

"Are you well, Governor Harlan?"

He swallowed and licked his lips, his eyes searching the shadows around them. "The transition of power has been taxing to say the least. The king's... *knights* have no mercy in their hearts. And the king himself... Well, let's just say he is not *my* king. Unfortunately, I get the sense he knows this. He gave Lirian and all of Felgarn to Lord Starg, a loyal supporter of any who can grant him power. Sadly, he now wields that power over me."

Inara felt for the man, one of many throughout Illian who were powerless to challenge her brother. "I speak for King Vighon when I say your loyalty to him and your people is admirable *and* appreciated."

Governor Harlan tried to smile but it faltered and became no more than a twitch. "Please," he said, gesturing to the chairs, "you are a guest in my home, however secret your presence might be. Can I have you some food and drink prepared?"

Inara declined the food and drink as well as the chair. "I am here on urgent business, Governor. I am sorry to add to the weight you are already under, but The Rebellion is in need."

Governor Harlan took a deep breath and glanced at one of the three large windows set into the south wall. "Does this have anything to do with what's going on in The Moonlit Plains? I am aware of vast forces amassing down there."

Inara nodded, trying not to recall too much of recent events. "There was a battle. Alijah has ordered his army to retreat but The

Rebellion has been left in dire need of supplies. We cannot hope to renew the fight if we cannot leave the plains."

The governor cupped his jaw and turned his back on her, but she could still feel the waves of fear coming off him. "I cannot move anything from this town without word getting back to Lord Starg. His wrath aside, I cannot say how the king's knights would react."

"I know there is peril in my request," Inara continued, "but good people are dying on those plains. Strong warriors are wasting away. We need to get them moving again and start preparing for the next fight."

The Governor's head hung low onto his chest, the weight of his responsibilities pressing down on him. "I... I cannot help you, Guardian. It would bring ruin upon my people and it would most certainly be a death sentence for me."

A loud and violent clatter erupted on the other side of the study door. One of the guards called out in warning before steel clashed in the narrow hall. The guard never spoke again before his body hit the floor. A moment later, the door was opened from the outside and a Reaver stepped inside, followed by five more.

"I wouldn't worry, Governor," the lead Reaver announced, its voice broken and distorted, "your death sentence has already been passed." The Reaver's head turned to regard Inara. "Hello, Sister." It was in those two words that she finally heard some semblance of Alijah's voice.

Athis! Inara called out across their bond. There came no reply from the dragon, however, only silence. *Athis?* The Guardian quickly concealed her dismay and held out her arm to guide the governor. "Get behind me."

Of all the Reavers, the fiend with Alijah's voice was the only who held itself like a person. The rest stood as sentinels, perfectly motionless like puppets awaiting their master's controlling hand. With its sword pointed to the floor, and both hands resting on the pommel, the Reaver tilted its head as Alijah would, were he really present.

"You should know by now that standing behind you or with

you is to dance with Death." The Reaver held out its hands. "And as you can see, Death and I are partners now."

Inara eyed the creature with disgust. "You've been so corrupted by dark magic that you can't even see your true reflection anymore. You are a necromancer, Alijah! There is nothing more abhorrent in this world than that which you have become."

"Such hate, Sister. You wear it like armour now."

"I don't hate you," Inara retorted, getting her tone under control. "How could I when I feel nothing for you. You're just another twisted fool who thinks that breaking the world is the same as saving it."

"Saving the world?" Alijah replied, turning the Reaver's visor to the window. "Is that what the Drake and the Keeper are doing in the forest?" Inara couldn't keep the surprise from her face. "Yes," Alijah continued smugly, "I know what they're doing. Even now I can hear them, waiting, *hoping* for more Drakes to arrive. It won't work. My victory was seen thousands of years before either of us were born."

Inara's surprise was swept away by her resolve. "We *will* save the tree."

The Reaver let loose a short sharp laugh from within its helmet. "I commend you for trying. *Keep the hope alive.* I have heard rebels muttering those words right up to their death. Hold on to hope if you must, but it will only make the defeat that much more crushing. You should be spending your last days with Athis, not pleading for supplies."

"We are coming for you," Inara promised threateningly, though her biting response was more reflex than anything. "There's nowhere you can hide, be it sky, earth, or sea."

The Reaver continued to stare at the Guardian through the narrow slit in its helmet. "Who is *we* exactly? Are you referring to the poor souls freezing to death on The Moonlit Plains? Perhaps you speak of the dwarves and their broken clans, bereft of kings and leadership. Or the elves? Without their magic they will fall to dragon fire by the hundreds!" The Reaver laughed again. "What will you do, dearest Sister? March thousands of men through winter with naught but the dying flames of Vighon's sword to keep them warm?"

Inara could feel her heart pounding in her chest as her grip tightened around Firefly , the blade itching to be freed from its scabbard. "Before the last vestiges of magic ebb away, Athis and I will descend upon you with wrath and ruin. This I promise you, Brother."

"You are welcome to try," Alijah goaded. "I'm not hiding. I'm *waiting*. Unlike The Rebellion, I don't rush into everything with a war cry. I'm a dragon," he boasted. "I observe my prey and wait for the opportune moment to strike. Though I would urge you to find me soon, before Athis loses his place in the sky."

Inara felt the sting of his words but she used the time to reach out to her companion again. Nothing. She cursed the sound of her own voice as she longed to hear that of her dragon's.

"How can you do this to your own kind?" Inara demanded. "Are you that broken and twisted?"

The Reaver's head tilted, suggesting a degree of curiosity on Alijah's behalf. "What are you talking about? I'm not doing—"

"I wasn't talking to you," Inara snapped. "I'm talking to your master, the one holding your strings."

The Reaver's head whipped back into an upright position. "You sound ridiculous, Inara. *I* am the one who told *you* about the true bond between dragon and Rider. You just can't accept me for who I am because you've always underestimated me," he fumed.

"I saw the truth with my own eyes," Inara told him, relishing every word. "I saw your wounds, wounds inflicted upon Malliath by Athis and Ilargo. I *know* who I'm talking to. So hear me, Malliath the voiceless. I know your weakness now. And I *will* kill him to destroy you."

The Reaver housing Alijah's consciousness twitched. Her brother's voice came out but his words were fractured. Then the Reaver staggered backwards as one of its hands reached up to touch its helmet in distress. The warrior in Inara had enough sense to know a fight before it broke out. Firefly was freed of its scabbard with a satisfying sound and a flash of steel, just in time to parry the first attack from one of the other Reavers.

The Guardian spun on her heel, bringing her into the heart of them. For most warriors, such a move would assure their doom but, to a master of the Mag'dereth, the Reavers were right where she wanted them. Firefly's steel edge lashed out in a sweeping arc, pushing four of her enemies back before she brought a two-handed strike into the neck of the fifth, relieving it of its head.

At the same time, Governor Harlan dashed for cover behind his desk. Inara tried to keep herself between him and the knights of Erador but the remaining four pressed towards her. Between their approaching helmets, she glimpsed Alijah's Reaver standing to the side as if struck by a daze. There was no time to ponder on its condition for she needed to move every limb to deflect and counter all at once.

These undead fiends, however, were no match for one who had spent the better part of two years cutting them down. One by one they fell at her feet absent the body parts that identified them as humans. When there were four more heads added to the floor, rolling around her feet, a familiar voice resounded inside her mind.

Inara! Athis called with alarm.

With no time for words, Inara transferred her recent memory across their bond, informing the dragon of her situation in less than a second.

I'm coming! he replied with a growl in his tone.

Alijah's Reaver snapped back to life with a wild swing of its sword. Inara easily avoided it with footwork alone and responded with a flick of Firefly's sharp edge across its leg. The force of it dropped the Reaver to one knee before the Guardian. Its eyes flashed from within its shadowy helmet and, for just a moment, Inara was sure they had been the purple reptilian eyes of Malliath looking back at her.

It was incapable of looking at anything after she thrust the tip of her scimitar through its visor and head.

No sooner did she pull her blade free than yet more Reavers poured into the room. Given the limited space of the study and the swelling number of enemies, Inara concluded that the odds were quickly stacking against her. Out of the corner of her eye, Inara could see Governor Harlan sinking further under his desk and disappearing into the shadows. Since he was as safe as he could be, the Guardian of the Realm decided to take control of the environment.

"Come and get me." Her words were the only warning they were going to get before she turned on her heel and dived through the nearest window.

Alijah pushed off from the ancient throne of Atilan and stumbled across The Bastion's main hall. Beads of sweat ran down his face and dripped onto the cold floor as he fought back the urge to be sick. Inara's voice reverberated through the passages of his mind, her every syllable creating destruction and chaos.

"Malliath," Alijah called out, falling to his hands and knees. Pain shot through his chest and shoulder, spreading around the arrow wound.

"I saw the truth with my own eyes," Inara had said. *"I saw your wounds, wounds inflicted upon Malliath by Athis and Ilargo."*

Her claims splintered his memories, taking the king back to their fight on the way down the pit. His mind clawed at his recollections, desperate for the truth. It was right there, right in front of him; he knew it. But every time he pieced the images together they misaligned, robbing him of clarity.

"Malliath!" he yelled this time.

He could feel the dragon trying to get through to him, his vast mind navigating the mess Inara had made. Alijah managed to rise to his feet and turn to face the oldest of thrones. He focused on it, using its details as a harbour in the storm. It was a slab of black stone, with flat angular features and a high back that had severely cracked at some point over the millennia. It wasn't beautiful and it wasn't meant to be. It was there to display Atilan's strength.

With little thought, he was rubbing the indentation where his shoulder met his chest. There was an itch beneath his scaled armour that irritated him. Memory struck him, though it was not his. He saw, and even felt, the jaws of Ilargo grip around Malliath's neck and shoulder, piercing the muscle beneath. The memory brought pain, staggering the king.

"What's happening..." His words trailed off, along with his attention. Alijah tried to sharpen his focus but an inferno swept through his mind, all to the sound of beating wings.

Follow my voice.

Alijah hesitated, though he couldn't say why. Malliath's voice had always possessed a soothing allure that comforted him in his darkest hour. His thoughts stopped there when a searing hot jolt plunged through his mind. The king was cast back through his own memories, taking him to moments over the last fifteen years he didn't recognise. He saw himself experiencing the same confusion and agony in the halls of his palace in Valgala and then again in The Red Fields of Dunmar.

This wasn't the first time his mind had split open.

Gathering what strength he could, Alijah balled his fists and roared, "MALLIATH!"

The doors at the far end of the hall blew open, turning Alijah on the spot. Cold mountain winds filled the chamber and snow spilled across the floor. The stone beneath his feet shuddered when the largest dragon in the realm landed in front of The Bastion's main entrance. Alijah felt Malliath's purple eyes upon him, as if they were only feet apart.

It was within that gaze that Alijah lost himself. His past melted away, consigned to the darkest depths of his mind where he could never hope to grasp it.

He closed his eyes and then snapped them open. The doors to the hall were closed, though he could not recall the last time they had opened. He was still sitting on the ancient throne with no memory of having left it. There was an itch in his mind that questioned it all, sure that he had forgotten something crucial. The king shook his head and decided it was the disorientation that accompanied the inhabitation of a Reaver.

His thoughts quickly turned to his sister. Inara had levelled her usual threats but it had been satisfying to witness her fear after revealing his knowledge of their plan. It would be even more satisfying when he finally saw the light fade from her eyes and that of his parents'. Then he would be rid of his mortal trappings, free to exist solely as the king of Verda and nothing else.

There was, however, a small fear of his own. Its voice grew louder in his mind, bringing him to his feet. *Could they do it?* he asked Malliath, sensing the dragon's presence somewhere above him. *Could the Drakes be just as instrumental in the undoing of our work as they were in the making?*

There came no response.

Frustrated, Alijah stormed across the hall, his face angled to the ceiling. *Malliath?* he demanded.

I am thinking, came the dragon's reply, his tone one of impatience.

I don't see how they could, Alijah continued, pacing now. *Their magic will be fading like all other creatures. Hells, even the doorway will be closing soon.* The king stopped to cast a quizzical eye over the snow dispersed across his floor. He could see with a glance that the doors were closed, a Reaver posted either side. As he tried to recall the last time they had been open, Malliath spoke into his mind, turning his sight back to the ceiling.

All things are possible, the dragon said.

Yes, Alijah agreed. *But some things are certain. The Crow has seen our future. He warned us that we would be challenged, and by those who claim to love us. If there was a chance our great work could be undone, he would have orchestrated events to prevent it. The Rebellion plans to use the Drakes no less, a race brought into being by the guiding hand of The Crow.* The king shook his head, his own reasoning filling him with confidence. *No,* he muttered. *They have no hope.*

Malliath's presence settled around Alijah's mind, adding weight to his words. *All things are possible. We would be foolish to underestimate our enemy now, when we are so close to victory.*

Alijah ran his hand over his jaw and nodded in agreement.

You're right, he said absently. *This could be one last challenge we need to meet. But our forces have just arrived in the valley,* he added, sensing the thousands of Reavers entering The Vrost Mountains.

Time is against our foe, Malliath counselled. *Empty the towns and cities of Reavers and have them make for the doorway. They have but to create chaos, preventing any Drakes from entering the realm of magic, until the door closes.*

Alijah was already relaying such commands to every knight in the surrounding areas. He didn't, however, empty Vangarth of every Reaver. The king was sure to keep some behind to pursue Inara to her end.

When this is all over, Alijah remarked, *we will have to review the size of our forces. The Rebellion has reduced our numbers beyond expectations.*

We will require no such review, Malliath countered. *The realm is inhabited by mortals. We have only to pass a new law, conscripting every man and woman who dies into our army.*

Alijah considered the dragon's suggestion. *Elegant,* he complimented. *And no waste. Even in death, every man and woman will have purpose.*

The king liked it. He walked back to the throne and sighed as he took his place upon it. All they had to do was crush The Rebellion and that world would be in his grasp. With that in mind, he wondered how his sister was doing.

Inara dashed across the rooftop, just as she had across every other, to escape the incoming arrows. The archers, firing at her from the surrounding towers, forced the Guardian to remain in the heart of Vangarth, where the majority of Reavers hunted her from the streets.

Skidding the last few feet, Inara dropped down onto a lower roof and narrowly avoided an arrow. Refusing to give up her momentum, the Guardian dropped into a roll before leaping up the adjacent wall and renewing her climb. Returned to her previous height, she was in the sight of multiple archers. It was instinct to fall back on her magic and keep the arrows at bay with a shield, but she dared not rely on it. Instead, Inara put her faith in her physical abilities.

Again, she jumped from one building to the next and just missed the arrows seeking her heart. Though the strength of her jump was more than any man could have dreamt, her timing was off. Instead of landing perfectly on the next rooftop, her chest slammed into the side of the building as her hands gripped the ledge above. Besides taking the wind out of her, it gave the Reavers below a chance to catch up.

Keep moving! Athis urged.

Where are you? she asked, heaving herself up.

You will know when I am there, the dragon promised.

By the time she was firmly on the roof, a pair of Reavers were ascending from the other end. Adding to their number, three more were climbing up behind her.

"Damn..." she panted.

What is it? Athis questioned.

Dead men can climb, she complained.

Left or right, the adjacent buildings were too far even for her. An arrow whistled past her face, reminding her that standing still wasn't an option, and leaving her with one path. With no time to conjure a plan, Inara burst into a sprint. By her second step, Firefly was in her hand, its cold steel hungry for action. With little more than six feet between her and the two Reavers, the Guardian covered the remaining distance in the air. Her red cloak twisted, following her body round, until she came down on the nearest Reaver. Firefly cut through the top corner of its head before her feet touched down.

The second lunged at her without hesitation and the two fell into the rhythm of battle. Inara gained the advantage when an arrow, meant for her, caught the Reaver in the back, behind its shoulder. It wasn't a killing blow for the fiend, but it was enough to push it forward and into Inara's sweeping scimitar. As the body crumpled to the rooftop, absent its head, three more Reavers appeared at the other end. The Guardian only gave them a glance, however, her real concern lying with the archers on the nearby tower. Their aim was getting better.

Even now, she could see four of the undead fiends aiming their bows down in her direction. She knew a dozen spells that would either protect her or reduce the top of the tower to kindling, but her open palm failed to conjure little more than sparks.

Athis was not so hindered.

The dragon shot over the town like a spear hurled by a vengeful god. His breath was that of fury and flames and it brought a light more blinding than the sun to Vangarth. The top half of the nearest tower exploded and the Reavers with it. Before the shower of debris found the earth, Athis had already moved on and destroyed the next with his front claws. His tail swept in and tore the rest of it to splinters. Flying around the edge of the town, immune to petty arrows, he continued to light up the night and bring fire to their enemies.

One by one, the towers fell to his might and ringed the town with sentinels of fire.

Inara smiled. There was no missing a dragon's entrance. **We need to rid Vangarth of every Reaver,** she said, bracing Firefly in both hands. **We need supplies and we need to create a safe passage for the Drakes.**

Athis held his reply while she weaved and ducked between the three attacking Reavers. *There are dozens leaving the town as we speak,* he informed.

Inara deflected two blades at once and kicked the third away. **Leaving the town?**

They're marching south, Athis reported gravely.

The Guardian shoved one Reaver from the roof, removing it from the fight altogether, and drove her sword up through the jaw of a second. **He's marching them back to the pit,** she concluded, before manipulating the lifeless Reaver to shield herself against the third.

Inara, Athis intoned, *if Alijah knows what Adan'Karth and Kassian are doing, there must be Reavers close by.*

Discarding the second body from the end of her scimitar, Inara pivoted and sliced one way then the other across the last Reaver. The second attack decapitated it, leaving her alone on the rooftop. Absorbing the dragon's words, she turned to regard the forest north of the town. A sense of dread swelled in her chest.

Go, Athis urged.

Inara turned around to see her companion igniting the main road to the south. Through their bond, she knew that dozens of Reavers just went up in flames, never to hear their master's commands again.

Go! he repeated.

Inara didn't waste another second. She climbed down and returned to street level having already planned her route to the northern edge. Passing numerous houses, she saw fearful onlookers daring to peer out of their windows to catch a glimpse of the violence. The Guardian, however, didn't plan on stopping to explain, even if it would put them at ease. She continued through the streets until the pines of The Evermoore stood in her way. Leaving Athis to his work, she entered the forest.

Her progress would have been slow, given the lack of light with which to locate their tracks, but the Guardian was shown the way in the most unexpected manner. At first, she feared it was a trick or perhaps fatigue on her part, for she had never seen trees move as they did now. The needles of particular trees blew in the breeze, revealing a distinct direction that led deeper into the forest. Whenever she displayed caution and considered another route, the trees in front of her would blow in that same direction.

Adan...

It had to be the work of the Drake. Inara knew of no other who could manipulate trees this way. It gave her hope.

And so she followed the breeze that blew through the forest, watching for the movement of the needles and the rustle of the trees. When the sound of destruction was too distant even for Inara's ears, she came across a disturbing sight. Pinned to a tree by a piercing branch, one of Alijah's Reavers writhed and struggled to free itself.

"You found us," came Kassian's voice from behind, his tone hinting at some relief. Adan'Karth soon appeared beside the Keeper, his hands clasped inside his voluminous sleeves.

"I'm not the only one apparently," Inara replied, eyeing the Reaver.

"It followed us with a Seeker," Kassian explained, "but I took care of it."

"You should have *killed* it," Inara chastised as she removed Firefly for a third time that night. Using her free hand, she cast a simple spell that tugged the Reaver away from the tree. Before all of its weight came down on its feet, the edge of her scimitar cleaved the fiend into two parts, separating head from body. "Alijah knows you are here now," she told them, returning Firefly to her hip. "And worse: he knows what you're doing here."

Kassian frowned and opened his mouth to argue until his eyes tracked down to the headless corpse. He swore.

"I have had the displeasure of speaking with my brother," Inara continued. "He has heard you speaking of our plans and, as we speak, is commanding Reavers to attack the dig site. We need to move, *now*."

The Keeper stepped aside, revealing a handful of Drakes huddled in the light of the moon. "I think we're going to need more than six if we're going to save the tree."

Inara took in the sight of them, noting the caution that each carried in their demeanour. "Do they know why you have called on them?" she asked Adan.

The Drake shook his head. "This is a decision that must be made by my people as a whole. They will arrive at their answer with haste if they are altogether and convening as one."

Inara couldn't hide her impatience but, from his place of dominion over Vangarth, Athis reminded her, *Theirs is a great sacrifice, wingless one. They cannot be pushed. We must wait.*

The Guardian took a breath. "As you say," she reluctantly replied to both Adan'Karth and Athis. Considering the options that now lay before her - one of which was sitting on her hands - Inara turned back to the south and made to leave.

"Where are you going?" Kassian questioned.

"You're safe here," she answered, gesturing to the dead knight. "I'm going back to the town."

"What for?"

Inara's hand tightened around Firefly's hilt. "To kill some more Reavers."

CHAPTER 38

THE FUTURE LIES IN THE PAST

t was a privilege to accompany a dragon in flight, something most would kill to experience. For Galanör Reveeri, this was his ninth time soaring through the heavens and he hoped he was never going to have to stop counting. He wondered if he had enjoyed such an honour more than any other in the realm who was not bonded with a dragon.

Of course, they had not all been as exhilarating as sitting astride Ilargo. His first flight, on the back of Malliath, had been terrifying at times. And he could still recall, with horrifying clarity, the time Rainael the emerald star had scooped him up in her claws and taken him to Dragons' Reach. Given that he had also had the pleasure of flying with Athis, during The Ash War, and one of the elder dragons, during The War for the Realm, he was sure he held some kind of record for non-Riders.

For Aenwyn, however, this was her first time and it showed. Galanör was certain her cheeks must be sore from so much smiling. Even after the sun had gone down and they flew through the night, she had beamed with glee to observe the stars from so high up. And now, as the glorious sun bounced off the waves of The Adean, she grinned with pure happiness.

Her joy was infectious and Galanör lapped it up. The days they were leaving behind had been of misery and exhaustion and the days ahead of them only threatened to be worse. The elven ranger was glad to have his mind taken elsewhere and his mood uplifted, even if it was only briefly.

His wings flexed and held steady, Ilargo glided away from The Shining Coast, Illian's eastern shore, and set his sights on the archipelago on the horizon. Galanör narrowed his vision to try and see it in better detail. How long had it been since he had laid eyes on The Lifeless Isles? It had been longer still since he had last set foot on them.

The closer they got, the lower Ilargo flew, bringing them within a few feet of the sea. It was a magnificent display of the dragon's speed, though he was flying no quicker than when he had been among the clouds. Aenwyn tensed in front of Galanör and lowered her head, but it was not fear that moved her. She was loving it.

Eventually, Ilargo crossed the gap and entered between the cliffs of The Lifeless Isles. He banked left and right, high and low, to navigate the labyrinth of islands big and small. Here and there were signs of an ancient settlement where the Dragorn of Elandril's time had carved their homes out of the stone. For a time, even Gideon had called this home.

Galanör tilted his body to see the old master further along Ilargo's body. He was looking out at the platforms and balconies that extended from the cliffs, an air of melancholy about him. It wasn't the happy return the elven ranger had once hoped for his friend.

Rising above the cliffs, Ilargo angled his body towards the largest of the islands, further south, before diving back into the channels below. Galanör knew exactly where the dragon was taking them and he recognised that particular cliff face when they came upon it. Halfway up, a wide cave had been carved out of the stone, large enough to accommodate most dragons. Ilargo came to a halt inside that cave, his claws scraping across the ground.

Gideon was the first to dismount, accustomed as he was to the contours of his companion's body. He paused in front of Ilargo and took in the familiar sight. Galanör and Aenwyn climbed down and joined him, pausing themselves to run a hand along Ilargo's jaw and thank him for bringing them so far.

"Is this what I think it is?" Aenwyn pondered, scrutinising the four pillars that held up the jagged ceiling. Beyond them lay a single chamber that housed a long table and a collection of high-back chairs, though it was all cast in gloom.

Gideon walked over to the nearest pillar and grasped one of the torches from its mount. He waved his hand over the head but nothing happened. He tried again and again, his third attempt producing a flicker of light but no flames. Aenwyn offered her help but found her own magic wanting when it came to the simple spell. Only Galanör possessed the power to bring light to the cave, his magic setting the end of the torch on fire. Turning to the rest of the cave and the chamber beyond, the elven ranger raised both of his hands and flipped them palm up. Half a dozen braziers and twice as many torches came to life with flickering flames, illuminating the ancient dwelling.

"For seven thousand years," Gideon began, "since the time of The First Age, this was the council chamber of the Dragorn." The old master crossed the cave and approached the head of the table, his dark eyes fixed on the chair at the other end. "Elandril, Valtyr, Aerilaya... The best of the Dragorn. They all sat in that chair. They all held back the darkness of their time."

Galanör could see the guilt and shame Gideon was putting upon himself. "As did you," he pointed out. "*Twice.* The Darkakin, the orcs; they all faced you in their pursuit of conquest. Now Reavers and necromancers threaten the realm and here you are again. You have placed yourself on the line between good and evil every time."

Gideon was shaking his head. "If history has shown us anything, it is that standing up for the light isn't enough. Every leader of the Dragorn gave their *life* to keep back the darkness, and to keep the order alive."

"Then I would say it is a good thing you are *not* Dragorn,"

Galanör replied softly, having no wish to see his friend die for the cause.

The old master eventually nodded, though whether he was agreeing or simply avoiding further discussion remained to be seen. On the other side of the table, Aenwyn's attention had been captured by the stone murals that lined all three of the chamber's walls, just as they had once enraptured Galanör.

"Amazing," she commented, running her fingers over the carvings.

Her choice of words brought back an old memory for Galanör, bringing a smile to his face. "Adilandra said the same thing when she saw it for the first time. That is Valtyr," he explained, looking at the depiction of an elf astride a dragon. "He fought—"

"Against the Darkakin in The Second Age," Aenwyn finished. "Assisted by Lady Syla," she added with a bashful smile. "I know my history, Galanör."

"Then you know more than me," the ranger replied with amusement. "I'm just repeating what Queen Adilandra told me."

"If you think this is something," Gideon said, making his way to the door on the right of the table, "wait until you see this." His hand clasped the door handle, his touch enough to deactivate the wards he had placed over it before he left for Ayda.

Galanör watched Aenwyn closely, eager to see her expression when she laid eyes on the library of the Dragorn. Unlike the chamber outside, the library was instantly illuminated by a series of torches and an enormous hearth. Gideon led the way, taking to the steps first and descending to the lowest level. Galanör remained beside Aenwyn as she pressed up against the railing and absorbed her new surroundings. He enjoyed the awe and wonder that lived in her eyes as she looked up at the tiers of books and relics. Beneath them, in the open-plan ground floor, there were even more relics of the past, all encased in displays and cabinets.

"As a child," Aenwyn revealed, "I dreamt many times what this library would look like. My mother described it as the heartbeat of history itself, though she was never as fortunate as me to actually see it. I want to explore every corner of it!"

Galanör laughed and his voice carried up to the highest tier. "I could have guessed." Looking down at Gideon, who was currently rummaging through the lower half of a tall cupboard, the ranger's tone took on a more serious edge. "Perhaps another time though," he said, planting an affectionate kiss on the side of Aenwyn's head.

They joined him on the ground floor, though Aenwyn was quickly lost after drifting towards one of the glass cabinets. Galanör rounded the long table to meet Gideon, only to pause at the sight of a familiar sword mounted horizontally on the wall. The ranger rapped his knuckle against the dragon bone. "I remember this," he remarked. "What did he call it again?"

Gideon stopped for as long as it took him to see what Galanör was talking about. "Dragonslayer," he said with a hint of disgust.

"What a foul name," Aenwyn opined. "Who did it belong to?"

"Karakulak, the orc king." Galanör's tone was that of Gideon's.

Aenwyn's eyes lit up in understanding. "I only glimpsed him during that last battle - he was *big*."

"He was a head shorter by the time Gideon was finished swinging Mournblade," Galanör quipped.

"Good riddance," Aenwyn commented, returning to her exploration.

Galanör left the horrid sword where it was and turned to Gideon, who was frantically shifting the contents of another tall cupboard, his eyes scanning its every nook and cranny.

"Where is it?" he muttered to himself. "I know I left it around here somewhere."

"What are you searching for?" Galanör enquired with some concern. "The Hastion gem?"

"No," Gideon answered, moving to the next set of shelves. "The gem is locked away over there," he said absently, gesturing in the direction of the hearth.

Galanör left Gideon to his task and approached the area beside the hearth, though he discovered naught but books either stacked on top of each other or lined along the numerous shelves. "I don't see it," he called over his shoulder.

"Don't touch that!" Gideon warned.

437

Galanör spun on his heel and quickly followed Gideon's outstretched hand to Aenwyn. She froze, her finger under the golden latch that secured a vertical glass display. Slowly, the elf retracted her finger and removed her hand before turning back to Gideon.

"My apologies," the old master said, calming down. "I should have told you: certain items in here are warded, especially that one. Best not touch any of them."

Galanör looked past Aenwyn to examine the particular item in question. Inside the glass case, hanging on a simple hook, was a long chain with a large ruby on the end. He would know that ruby anywhere, having seen it around Hadavad's neck for many years.

"The Viridian ruby," Galanör uttered.

"*A* Viridian ruby," Gideon specified. "There are supposedly five of them…" His words trailed off as he stood back from the cupboard to look at every shelf in frustration.

"This is the ruby used by the mage Hadavad?" Aenwyn checked.

Galanör was glad to know that she had been listening to his tales after all. "Yes. It's how he moved from one host to another." The ranger turned back to Gideon. "I didn't know you possessed it."

"I couldn't leave it for just anyone to find," the old master replied without looking back at him. "And it was no easy task. Before leaving for Dragons' Reach, I returned to the site where we faced The Crow. There was a lot of debris to clear, but Ilargo saw to most of that. I was just thankful the Leviathan wasn't covering it."

Galanör let his sight linger on the ruby for a moment. There were still times when he missed the old mage and their days hunting down The Black Hand. Taking his mind from such memories, the ranger returned his attention to the Hastion gem. "There's nothing but books over here, Gideon," he reminded him.

The old master tore himself away from his task and joined Galanör in combing the books. He scanned along one of the shelves, his finger running across numerous spines before stopping on one nestled in the middle. "Here it is," he announced, handing the book to the ranger.

Galanör read the cover. "Merdians of the Blue," he said curiously.

"Merdians are among the deepest dwellers of The Adean," Gideon explained to a quizzical elf. He flashed an amused grin before opening the hardback cover to reveal a hollow cut into the pages. Sitting inside was an ornate ring, the finest craftsmanship to house the Hastion sapphire.

Galanör shared some of his friend's humour. "Merdians of the *Blue*. Very imaginative. Shame about the book though," he added, removing the Hastion gem.

Gideon lifted a finger to the air. "There's another copy on the third floor - fascinating read."

The elven ranger was sure to secure the gem on his belt before responding. "I'm sure it is," he agreed, though he had made a personal vow, decades earlier, to steer well clear of all Mer-folk for the rest of his immortal days.

"What are you looking for?" Aenwyn asked Gideon, who had already returned to his personal hunt.

"This!" he declared, retrieving a leather satchel from the last cupboard on the ground floor. It was a disgusting looking thing that appeared to have seen more years than all of them combined. "Don't you recognise it?" Gideon held it up for Galanör to see.

The ranger shook his head. "Should I? It looks like the inside of an orc."

The old master stifled a laugh and turned the satchel upside down. From within, half a cupboard's worth of books were emptied onto the floor at his feet. Seeing the pocket dimension in action, Galanör's memory was cajoled into recalling the ancient satchel.

The elf pointed at it. "Adilandra brought that back from Davosai. She found it in Atilan's lab." His eyes looked down to the pile of books, searching for a specific tome.

"It's not there," Gideon told him, deciphering his thoughts. "Atilan's grimoire - the one Adilandra placed inside - is locked away and warded." He looked down at the other books. "I just needed somewhere to put all of those."

Galanör raised an eyebrow. "So you used the ancient satchel of a self-proclaimed god."

Gideon shrugged. "It did the job."

"How will this aid us?" Aenwyn enquired, bringing them back on track.

"The satchel is enchanted with a pocket dimension," Gideon said rather redundantly. "If we place the Crissalith inside, we can transport it anywhere without it affecting us. Of course, as soon as we retrieve it from within, we will require the Hastion gem to maintain our advantage when facing Alijah or Malliath."

"Won't the Crissalith prevent the enchantment from working?" Aenwyn pointed out.

Gideon shook his head. "No. My first up-close encounter with Crissalith severed my bond with Ilargo, but it didn't affect the enchantment on Mournblade - a fact that saved my life once upon a time."

"It doesn't affect objects," Aenwyn said with revelation.

"Exactly," Gideon replied with a broad smile.

"Well, what are we waiting for?" Galanör took the satchel from Gideon and draped it over his shoulder and hip. "Let's go and dig up the past."

As hard as it was for Aenwyn to leave the library behind, they returned to the council chamber. The trio paused briefly so Gideon could retrieve the three crystals he had hidden in his room, two of which were vital for their errand. Despite having everything Gideon had outlined in his plan, Galanör held loosely to any hope that they could actually free Alijah from Malliath's influence. After all, they still had a long way to go and no end of perils in their path.

Ascending Ilargo's green scales once more, they braced themselves as the dragon dived from the cliff and spread his wings to carry them into the vast blue of the heavens above. He turned south-east, to a murky horizon of waves, and put civilisation behind them.

CHAPTER 39
AN ALLIANCE OF TWO SHORES

F eet firmly planted in the land, *his* land, Vighon Draqaro ignored the icy blast of wind that sent his dark cloak billowing and kept his eyes fixed on the misty plains to the north. Nothing. It had been two days since Inara had left with the others and he believed another whole day would come and go without any sign of them. He knew it wasn't nearly enough time to complete their errand but his attention continued to divert to the north.

He sighed, his eyes narrowing in the rising sun.

The king had enjoyed every minute of his time with Inara since her return to Illian, but it had been all too brief. Fate continued to intervene and find some new way of separating them. There was a growing part of him that feared the war would rob one of the other before the end.

"You are watching for her too," came Reyna's distinct voice. It was melodic and soft and drew the northman's attention to his side, where she had quietly joined him.

"I have been watching for her all my life," he replied dryly. "Why should I stop now?"

Reyna glanced up at him before returning her emerald eyes to the plains. "I am sorry to have seen Gideon and the others set off without you. Time is against us."

Vighon considered looking down at the elf, who had been like a mother to him, but he couldn't deny the sting of being left out of such a pivotal discussion, especially when it resulted in The Rebellion losing a dragon. Instead, he kept his gaze distant and said, "I have spoken with Asher." His response turned the queen's head. "I know this *weapon* they have gone to retrieve offers Alijah some kind of redemption. Or, at least, that's what you're hoping for." As Reyna made to speak, the king continued. "I would have sanctioned such a mission," he clarified. "Though I realise neither you nor I command the likes of Gideon Thorn and certainly not Ilargo. But I would not have objected."

Reyna took a moment of contemplation. "Inara would have," she remarked.

"You're not wrong," he replied, well aware of her feelings, or lack thereof, where her brother was concerned.

"I thought," the queen pursued, her sight moving away, "given everything he's done to you - *taken* from you - that you would want to see Alijah dead."

Vighon swallowed. "I would be lying to you if I said I hadn't dreamt of killing him. Many times. I would settle for *Malliath's* head," he continued. "But I could live with Alijah in chains." His last comment had the queen's head whipping around to look up at him again.

"In chains?" she echoed, her tone incapable of disguising her dismay.

Vighon met her gaze. "What else?" he asked. "His crimes against the realm demand punishment. Chains and a locked cell are the best I can do. And I will face opposition from those who want a more... *permanent* punishment." Reyna looked away but the wind could not steal the stray tear from her cheek before the northman noticed. "What had you desired?" he enquired softly.

"The fancies of a hopeless mother I suppose," she muttered. "I had dared to dream, should he be made to see sense, that I could take him back to Ayda. Without Malliath..." Her voice faltered before she found her courage. "Without Malliath he will be mortal again. I know it is more than he deserves, but I would have liked for my son to spend his final years among the trees of The Amara. A simpler life."

Vighon recalled, with painful clarity, the young man Alijah Galfrey had once been. "I'm not sure even he would allow that. If he truly saw himself for the monster he has become, I think he would want to be locked away. Perhaps worse."

Reyna's shoulders sagged and her head dipped down to her chest. Vighon didn't hesitate to reach out and pull her into his embrace before more tears streaked down her face. He was sure to keep his back to the camp, concealing their moment.

The king's shoulders bobbed with a silent chuckle. "What are we doing talking about the future? Has there ever been a more uncertain thing? The realm of magic is crumbling to ash and our enemy has but to wait it out. If we lose the dragons our fight is over. Then it will be us in chains... or worse."

Reyna pulled back from his chest, her beautiful eyes marred with redness. "There *will* be a future for us all. Illian has never known a better king than you. I am so proud of the man you have become. I weep because I *know* you will find victory and it will come at the cost of my..." Unable to finish her words, the queen patted his chest. "You have overcome more than any king could bear. And with Inara by your side, there is nothing the two of you will not accomplish together. Your fates have been entwined since you were children: that much I have always known."

Vighon squeezed her hand. "So much of who I am is because of you and Nathaniel. I owe you both everything."

Reyna finally managed a smile. "You owe us nothing," she insisted. "You are the man you were always meant to be."

The northman took her kind words as best he could, sparing a glance at the distant plains. "How is Nathaniel settling into his new title?" he asked, naturally thinking of the man he had long measured himself against.

"He hates it," Reyna replied with a degree of amusement.

Vighon enjoyed her lighter tone. "Wearing a crown is never

what you expect. You think the whole world is yours and you can do what you like with it, but it's quite the opposite. Your world is small. Your every step is watched. Your every word written down. It will take some adjustment on Nathaniel's part. I suppose he never considered the possibility of being a king." The northman noted his companion's pensive expression. "You miss her," he surmised, without saying Adilandra's name.

Reyna slowly nodded. "Growing up, my mother often told me the qualities required of a queen, more so than those required of a princess, as I was. I would always tell her how little it mattered when she would be queen for all time. I can see her face now, as if I was back there with her. She knew. Somewhere deep down, she always knew. My mother was a better student of history than me - she knew there had never been a queen *for all time*. I should have listened to her lessons," Reyna lamented. "I just never thought she wouldn't be here."

"You are already a good queen," Vighon reassured. "You have had the respect of your people *and* mine for many years. Nathaniel too. My own deeds as king pale in comparison to what you have already accomplished for both Illian and Ayda."

"In this future you doubt is to come," Reyna suggested, "we will have to be more than good kings and queens. Ours is an alliance of two shores. The realm is going to need piecing back together, on both sides of The Adean."

"If only it were just Illian and Ayda," Vighon contemplated. "Erador will fall into war without Alijah and his Reavers to keep order. We cannot ignore our neighbour."

The queen made to speak on the matter when her gaze shifted away from the northman and down the eastern line of the camp. Vighon turned to see Faylen and Captain Nemir astride a pair of galloping horses. They broke away from the camp and crossed the plain to join them.

"Why do I have a bad feeling?" the king pondered.

"I share it," Reyna replied, stepping away from him to greet her High Guardian. "You have news, Faylen."

Their horses came within feet of the king and queen, though

Faylen was already leaving her saddle behind before the mounts came to a complete halt. "Your Graces," she began with a quick bow of the head. "Word from our scouts in the east: Reavers are departing Whistle Town and Galosha."

"Departing?" Reyna queried.

Faylen clarified, "They have been sighted on mounts of their own ilk, all heading west, towards *us*."

Vighon felt his jaw tense. "Galosha is a large city - there must be hundreds of Reavers stationed there. Any word from the scouts in the south?" he asked, concerned they would be attacked on more than one front.

"We didn't have the numbers to set up a relay line of scouts to the south," Captain Nemir told him. "We have heard nothing from those dispatched."

"We were wrong to assume Alijah intended to wait this calamity out," Faylen continued. "He means to press the attack while we care for so many wounded."

"That makes no sense," Reyna reasoned. "If he meant to destroy us he would have stayed and done so."

Vighon turned away, his gaze fixing on the north once more. He couldn't hide his concern from the woman who had all but raised him.

"You think Alijah knows of our plan?" the queen concluded from his expression alone.

"If he does," Vighon replied, "he could only have learned of it from Inara and the others."

"I'm sure they remain unharmed," Faylen offered. "They have Athis with them."

"Unlike us," Nemir countered. "We have enemy forces advancing on our position and now we have no dragons to assist us."

Vighon cast his eyes over the sprawling camp, all the while his grip tightened around the sword of the north. Only the dead would dare to face an army - even half an army - comprised of elves, dwarves, humans, and Centaurs. But it was the dead they faced, and the dead feared nothing.

"Who among them isn't hungry?" Captain Nemir continued, having followed the king's sight. "These freezing winds are enough to take the fight out of anyone, never mind empty stomachs and aching wounds. Between the cold and our dwindling rations, this rebellion is a pale shadow of what it was only days ago."

Vighon knew the elven warrior was voicing their collective fears, but he didn't need to hear it now. "Fight or die," he told the captain, his tone full of foreboding. "That has never changed and I see no reason why it should now. We will rouse any and all among us who can hold the line, and we *will* hold the line. My men have not seen battle and nor have I; we will defend from the front." The king raised his hand and beckoned one of the guards keeping watching over him from afar. The Namdhorian only looked too happy to get away from Sir Borin, who stood sentinel beside him.

Reyna glanced at the pit, on the other side of the battlefield. "We should focus our defence around the doorway. We have to secure passage for the Drakes."

Vighon faced the Namdhorian soldier who quickly approached. "Find Captain Dardaris and have him inform Commander Rolgoth of the Battleborns that I must speak with him immediately." The soldier bowed his head before running back to the camp with his orders.

The queen issued commands to Faylen and Nemir, sending them out to spread the word. "Even if Alijah has emptied Whistle Town and Galosha," she said, watching them ride away, "the number of Reavers will be in the hundreds, not thousands. We can face that."

"We have to," Vighon said boldly. "The future of the realm depends on us saving that tree." He lifted the sword of the north halfway out of its scabbard, dismayed by the absence of the flames that had always licked at the silvyr. "We cannot count on magic in this fight."

"Inara and the Drakes may yet return before the Reavers arrive," Reyna pointed out. "Then we will have magic *and* a dragon."

There was a voice in the back of the northman's mind and it

was not so quiet in speaking its fears. He considered the strong possibility that the Drakes wouldn't help them. And, if they did, there was no guarantee that they would heal the tree with their sacrifice, their deaths only adding to the great loss.

The king sighed. "Then pray that they return with all haste."

Reyna turned to him, her own fears laid bare. "Pray to what?" she wondered.

Vighon looked up at the sky and narrowed his eyes. "To whatever keeps testing us."

CHAPTER 40
OUT OF TIME

Three days after arriving in The Evermoore, Kassian Kantaris could feel what precious time they had slipping through his fingers as the realm of magic collapsed on itself. After the sun had set and the moon held sway over the night, the Keeper had begun to weather a sense of panic, fearing they would be too late.

As the hours and days had pushed on, more and more Drakes had arrived, filling the clearing and spilling out between the trees. As their silent presence grew, so too did their calming aura swell. They stood motionless, like the trees around them. Every one of them was touching another, their outstretched hands creating a web that spread beyond sight.

As Kassian walked among them, ducking under their arms and weaving between the trees, his fascination was beginning to get the better of him. It was clear to see that the Drakes possessed a form of communication that required no more than physical contact. The inquisitive mage that had always dwelled within him was curious to experience it for himself, and see if it worked on other races.

Presented with a tall male Drake, his horns thick and dark

against his pale skin, Kassian removed one of his gloves and held up a hesitant hand towards his bare shoulder. At the last second, his fingers curled in and he retracted his hand until he was sure the Drake's eyes were closed, like all the others. Confident he remained unobserved by any of them, the Keeper held out his hand again.

This time, he gripped the Drake's shoulder.

The shadowy Evermoore dropped away as he was sucked from reality and consumed by streaking stars. He was moving faster than anything he had ever seen yet he couldn't feel an ounce of resistance against his skin. His final destination was an indefinable place of colour and sound. Only his consciousness inhabited this new plane of existence. That was until the voices filled the space. So many voices. They all spoke at once, yet Kassian was able to understand them all.

"The realm of magic is dying." Adan's familiar voice was the strongest among them, his words looped on endless repeat. "The tree is burning," he continued. "If that realm falls, so too will this one."

Kassian was bombarded with sights and sounds from Adan'Karth's memory as he showed every Drake what he had witnessed in the realm of magic.

"It is not our place to save or protect the realm," another Drake replied. The smallest amount of focus from Kassian revealed the Drake's name to be Laga'Thak. The Keeper knew that if he delved a little deeper he would see all of her memories too.

He withdrew, however, when he heard the voices of five others say, "You have been corrupted by their ways."

"Ours is not a path of violence," another added.

"Listen to him," Laga'Thak's voice insisted, opposing her own previous comment.

"What do you propose?" another female voice asked.

"It would be a peaceful existence," a gentle male voice opined, as if they already had the answer.

Kassian listened a while longer, lost to it all, until he finally understood why their collective discussion made no sense to him.

They were all speaking out of time.

For those who were just joining the extraordinary forum, the conversation was in its infancy, even though others had been talking for days. Some, it seemed, were nearing the end, having heard and seen what happened to Adan's hand when he touched the tree. While Kassian knew it was Adan'Karth's plan to become one with the tree, adding his magic to it, he could sense that many of the Drakes were coming to that same conclusion before he explained it. He took that as a good sign.

The whole experience was maddening to the Keeper, whose human mind was struggling to inhabit an environment that didn't adhere to a linear construct.

"There is life in the tree," Adan was saying, his words overlapping his older ones. "But what life could we expect if we do nothing? The tree would surely perish and with it our magic. Without magic, would we not be forced to live as humans? To defend ourselves like humans? We would descend into madness and violence. If we *save* the tree, we do not just save ourselves, but everything else too."

"We will die if we do nothing," a deeper male voice added to the collective. "The essence of dragon flows through us like water courses through a valley. Without magic, I believe we would simply die and become one with the forest."

"We don't know that," another Drake countered.

"We could live," Laga'Thak said, her opposing comment nearly two days old.

"We could survive," a softer voice put forward.

"We do not live to merely survive," Laga'Thak replied, though her response was very recent now, contradicting her earlier opinions. "We live to be in harmony with magic."

Adan'Karth's voice pushed through the ether. "Could we really live with ourselves knowing we could have done something, but chose to do nothing?"

Laga'Thak made to respond when her consciousness turned on Kassian. The Drake poured her mind into his and saw all that he was and all that he had been. "You do not belong here," she said simply.

Before the Keeper could respond, his presence was ejected. His mind felt like it was slammed back into his body and with it a wave of nausea assaulted him. He staggered away from the tall Drake he had been touching and leaned against the nearest tree. After succeeding to keep his stomach in check, he straightened up and became aware of the freezing cold again. How long had he been standing still for, his muscles idle?

Working his way back to the clearing, the centre of the Drake-web, Kassian discovered that Adan'Karth was still at the heart of it all. He had been standing on that spot for two days, never once pausing to eat or drink the supplies Inara had brought back from Vangarth. A quick count informed the Keeper that seven other Drakes were currently touching Adan and each of them was being touched by three more and so on.

Just the sight of them made Kassian feel weary. He returned to the small fire of his makeshift camp, nestled between the Drakes. It took more time than he would have liked to warm up again, though he was hesitant to define it as warm. He decided he was simply less cold than before. At least, he thought, his appetite was coming back.

While consuming his flat bread and cold sausage, the Keeper heard a pair of feet crunching through the snow. This wasn't unusual and didn't give him pause, as Drakes had been appearing at all times of day. When the footsteps grew closer, however, he had cause to look over his shoulder.

Inara Galfrey.

Her red cloak was dark in the firelight of her torch. Kassian only needed a quick look at her face to know that she hadn't found restful sleep in days, if any sleep at all. He was thankful to see her though. Besides the calm emanating from the Drakes, there was an eerie silence that permeated the forest from dawn till dusk that made him feel isolated. He also liked the food she brought him.

"Please tell me you stopped by a bakery on your way here," he pleaded in a hushed tone.

Inara came to sit beside him with a knowing smile. From within her satchel, she provided a small cube wrapped in cloth and tied with a piece of string. Kassian stopped himself from snatching it and thanked her before even removing the cloth. The smell of the lemon cake was more intoxicating than any ale or cider that had crossed his path.

"How are things here?" Inara asked, casting a cursory glance over the Drakes.

"More turn up all the time," Kassian replied with half a mouthful of cake. "They're so far back now, you can't see them all."

"Have any of them moved? Said anything?"

The Keeper shook his head. "No. At least not in the way we understand. They're as unmoving as the trees, but inside," he added, tapping the side of his head, "they're all talking at once, their emotions bleeding into each other. They share memories right down to the smell and taste of a thing. It's incredible."

Inara turned so that her blue eyes could bore into the Keeper. "Did you touch one of them?"

Kassian kept his gaze on the last few crumbs of cake inside the cloth. "I might have... *brushed* past one of them, yes."

"Kassian!" she admonished. "I told you not to interfere."

"So did they," he muttered. "And besides, I've been stuck out here with them for days! It's freezing and my magic is barely working. Pretty soon I'm going to have to keep this fire going the old-fashioned way." Kassian stared at the flickering flames for a moment before realising he had no idea how ordinary people started fires. "I can't stay out here forever," he concluded. "Maybe you should stay here and I'll go back to Vangarth."

"We don't have forever," Inara agonised, ignoring his last comment.

The Guardian didn't need scrutinising to see that the weight of the world was sitting on her shoulders. "How are things in Vangarth?" he asked, changing the subject.

"Athis and I have cleared it of Reavers," she reported.

"That sounds like fun," Kassian lamented.

"It had its moments," Inara replied, a touch of levity added to their conversation. "Governor Harlan is very much on the side of

The Rebellion thankfully. He's already sent several carts of supplies to The Moonlit Plains."

Kassian nodded along, glad to hear it all. He couldn't help but notice, however, the look of concern that crept across Inara's face. "What is it?"

"What's *what*?" she countered, perhaps brusquely.

"What's the cause of your concern?" he asked specifically.

"Besides the end of magic," Inara quipped, "and the realm falling under the rule of a mad dragon and his pet?"

"Those are usually my words. You even got the tone right. All of which tells me you're compensating for something. What is it?"

Inara rubbed her eyes and sighed. "Athis is getting worse," she told him. "He's already slower and I can tell he's cautious of flying now. Our bond is sporadic. I can feel his life ebbing away. It's like a part of me is rotting from the inside."

Kassian almost winced at the description. Though he couldn't understand her exact feeling, he knew what it was like to have a part of himself rot away, spoiled forever. He knew it could never be fully healed, but the rest of him would find a way to grow and to live with it. Of course, he could never say such a thing to Inara.

"This is going to work," he said instead, his tone determined. "It has to."

A flicker of a smile strained Inara's face. "You are not the man who has plagued countless council meetings for the last two years."

"Plagued?" he echoed with amusement. "I always thought my contributions were vital to The Rebellion's morale."

The two shared a quiet laugh before assigning shifts in which to sleep during the rest of the night. Kassian insisted on taking first watch to ensure that Inara did, indeed, get some much-needed sleep. And, not for the first time, the Keeper was pleasantly surprised to have enjoyed the company of another Galfrey.

~

Unfortunately, the next morning wasn't so far away and, before he knew it, Kassian was being woken by a rough hand pressing into his chest. The Keeper opened his eyes to see Inara standing over him. He squinted his eyes in the light, dazed and confused as to why the sun was directly overhead.

"What's wrong with the sun?" he asked, sitting himself up.

Inara raised an eyebrow. "It's midday - the sun is right where it's supposed to be."

"Mid... Midday?" Kassian rubbed his eyes, his confusion no better off. "Why is it midday?"

"Why is water wet?" Inara asked with more wit than Kassian could conjure right then. "Why is the sky blue? Why is your breath so bad?" The Guardian shrugged. "It's just the way of things."

"You shouldn't have let me sleep so long," the Keeper said, choosing to ignore her remarks.

"Kassian." Inara's impatient tone stopped him from reaching for his waterskin.

Instead, he followed her gaze beyond their little camp and realised the Drakes were no longer standing like statues. "What's happening?" Kassian rose to his feet as the Drakes broke their web.

"I think they're finished," Inara reasoned.

Kassian looked around in search of answers but it was chaos with so many Drakes now wandering between the trees. With Inara, he began to weave his way through to the heart of the clearing. Before they reached the centre, Adan'Karth emerged with a handful of Drakes at his back.

"What's happening?" Kassian asked with urgency, painfully aware that they had now been away from The Moonlit Plains for four days. "You've been talking for an age," he added with some exaggeration.

"There were many facets to be discussed," Adan replied coolly. "Unfortunately," he continued in a graver tone, "a general consensus could not be found." The Drake turned to direct their attention to a dozen or so of his kind. They were walking away from the clearing and steadily vanishing into the forest.

"What do you mean?" the Keeper pressed.

"There are some among us," Adan explained, "who do not wish to get involved in the wars of the realm. There are others who wish to take their chances in a world without magic."

Inara looked back at those who were leaving. "They're not coming with us?"

"They cannot be forced," Adan'Karth stated. "This was always a choice."

Kassian quickly scanned the Drakes who remained, though he couldn't see them all to count their number. "Are there enough? Can you save the tree?"

"Even if we were twice what we are," Adan said, "I still could not answer that question. I only know seven-hundred and thirteen of us wish to try."

Kassian wanted to voice his concern that seven-hundred and thirteen would not be enough, but he reminded himself what sacrifice those Drakes were making. With that in mind, the Keeper bowed his head out of respect for them.

"History will not forget you," Inara declared. "Any of you. I won't allow it."

"Nor shall I," Kassian promised.

"The *future* is our concern," Adan replied, "not history. We will do all that we can to ensure there is one."

Inara bowed her head as Kassian had. "We should make for The Moonlit Plains immediately," she urged. "It's a four day journey on foot and time is against us."

Adan'Karth surveyed his kin before meeting the Guardian's eyes again. "We are ready."

By the time they reached the streets of Vangarth, the last rays of light were gracing The Evermoore. Naturally, Kassian looked up to spot Athis in the sky, but there was no sign of the dragon. Inara's words came back to him and made all the more sense when he finally laid eyes on the dragon. Kassian would never have described Athis as small, yet he did not hold himself to the size the Keeper recalled from only days previously.

Standing in the road, by the town's southern edge, his horned head was bowed, his wings tucked in, and his tail curled to line up with his body. Even the red of his scales appeared dull compared to Kassian's memory of him.

Leading the procession of Drakes, Kassian came face to face with Athis first. Of all the dragon's features, his blue eyes - sapphires cut with a slit of black - had always stood out, imprinting on the memories of any who looked upon him. Now they were darker, absent their usual intensity.

Inara reached out to run her hand along the edge of his mouth. "We're going to make it," she said. The dragon's only response was to turn around and start down the southern road.

Governor Harlan appeared with a small entourage of high borns and guards. "Guardian?" he enquired with a curious look down the line of Drakes.

"Our business in The Evermoore is concluded," Inara told him without explaining the Drakes' presence. "We will return to the plains at once."

"Very good," the governor replied. "I am glad to have been of service to The Rebellion. I'm sure King Vighon will see to our protection in light of our allegiance."

Inara flashed the man a confident smile before glancing at the Drakes trailing Athis. "If we succeed in the coming days, Vangarth will have no reprisals to fear from the likes of Alijah Galfrey and his *knights*."

"Then I pray the gods bless you," Governor Harlan offered.

Kassian watched Inara stumble over her response before finally saying, "And you, Governor. And thank you for sending so many supplies - your generosity will not be forgotten."

The Keeper joined Inara as the pair fell in beside Adan'Karth and the hundreds of Drakes. Seeing them all together, heading to their deaths as far as any human was concerned, Kassian felt sick, just as he had when Laga'Thak had cast him out of their extraordinary network. As far as he was concerned, the future came at a cost: seven-hundred and thirteen lives.

CHAPTER 41
CAST OUT OF THE HEAVENS

It had been nearly a decade since Gideon or Ilargo had seen Ayda, the dawning country. Having crossed over its shores in the dead of night, they were now presented with a vista of colour in the sunrise. After two days of naught but ocean waves in every direction, it was pleasing to take in the land and its variety. That variety, however, gradually faded the further inland they journeyed. It soon became an inhospitable realm of sand and rocks: a harsh place to live.

As the morning went on, Gideon periodically checked on Galanör and Aenwyn over his shoulder. Both had slept most of their journey away, finding little stimulation in the new environment. For Galanör, an elf of five hundred years, his time in Ayda's southern lands might have been brief but, for Gideon, it was a significant turning point in his life.

I still remember it like it was yesterday, he said to Ilargo. *I remember crossing over The Opal Coast while hanging on to Malliath for dear life.*

Ilargo briefly turned his head to lay an eye on his companion. *For all his evil deeds, I am thankful for Malliath. He did bring us together, after all.*

Gideon rubbed Ilargo's scales but held his next words back, his attention snatched away. The old master narrowed his eyes and looked to the distance. Despite the hazy line of the horizon, there was no missing the enormous blotch of green against the surrounding desert.

The Great Maw, he uttered.

Aptly named, Ilargo remarked. *That jungle is filled with all the predators who could not survive outside of it.*

There was only one predator in there that concerned me, Gideon replied, his memories threatening to recall all he had seen of the dreaded and savage Darkakin.

Ilargo made for the jungle, his mighty wings keeping them clear of the violent habitat beneath. It wasn't long before the ruins of Malaysai came into view, though many of its buildings and temples had been consumed by the encroaching jungle.

"Is that what I think it is?" Galanör called from behind.

Gideon turned to see the elven ranger. "Welcome back to Malaysai!"

Keeping to a south-easterly heading, Ilargo continued to fly over the dilapidated city. It wouldn't be many more years before there was nothing left visible to the eye but the pyramid in its centre. The Great Maw was never satiated.

Without the usual warning, Gideon felt his stomach rise as Ilargo descended. *Ilargo?* **What are you doing? We need to be higher if we're to clear the city.**

There came no reply from the dragon.

Again, the old master felt the sudden drop in altitude and Malaysai came ever closer. Galanör questioned their flight path but Gideon ignored him as he adjusted his position to better see Ilargo's face. His companion appeared dazed, drowsy almost. At first, Gideon feared he had flown for too long and needed rest, but he would have sensed such a thing long before now.

All the while, Malaysai was rising up to meet them, and fast.

Ilargo? he called again. *Ilargo!*

"Gideon!" Galanör shouted, his voice panicked. "What's happening?"

"Brace yourselves!" Gideon yelled back. *Come on, Ilargo,* he called across their bond. *Hear my voice. Come back to me!*

There was a faint presence in Gideon's mind, just a hint of his companion. Though brief, he could feel the weakness spreading throughout Ilargo's body and even his mind. His magic was fading.

With the wind pummelling them, the trio held on to Ilargo wherever they could and prepared for the roughest of landings. His wings continued to glide over the city, but he had dropped so low now that Gideon heard the tip of a wing scrape against one of the tallest spires. Yet the ground was still so far. At their current speed, Ilargo would slam into the remnants of a building or skid across one of the ruined streets and kill them all, himself included.

His mind racing, Gideon desperately searched the surrounding area for anything that might help them, regardless of how futile it might be. Besides the pyramid, there was only one other structure in all of Malaysai that drew the eye: the barbaric arena. It stood above the city on three rocky columns and was large enough to accommodate several dragons. It was the arena's height, however, that gave Gideon a glimpse of hope.

"I have an idea!" he shouted back to the elves. "Hold on!"

Without delay, he scrambled further up Ilargo's neck, thankful the dragon was only gliding. Well-accustomed to his companion's body, Gideon positioned himself to the left of Ilargo's head and slowly rose until he was upright and braced. He had no time to lose - his window of opportunity was quickly disappearing.

"Gideon!" Galanör bellowed. "What are you doing?"

The old master clenched his fists just once, flexing the fingers in preparation. Then he jumped. His leap was true, bringing him alongside Ilargo's face. Before his momentum could take him any further, Gideon reached out and gripped one of the dragon's largest horns, just above his eye. Using what was left of his momentum, he yanked outwards and slammed his feet into his companion's jaw.

Fortunately, Ilargo's dazed state had rendered him relatively limp, at least enough for Gideon to pull his head out to the east. The dragon's body naturally followed the direction of the head and steadily glided towards the arena. When they were lined up, Gideon eased off and pushed himself back the other way to straighten Ilargo's flight. There was no climbing back onto his neck now - he was going to see the landing through from the front.

As the wall of the arena approached at speed, Gideon saw Ilargo's pupil sharpen. A number of subtle movements rippled across the dragon's features, indicating his alertness. His bulk and speed made it impossible to miss the arena now, but Ilargo managed to raise his wings just enough to give them some extra lift and avoid the worst of impacts.

Instead, they skimmed the lip of the wall before all four of his claws tore through the seating and he inevitably tripped over himself. His armoured underbelly took the brunt of the skidding impact, and his jaw struck the arena floor with enough force to reduce his regained alertness and knock Gideon free.

The old master rolled over himself half a dozen times, barely aware of his companion's wing as it momentarily blocked out the sun. Ilargo came to a halt after his entire body was on the arena floor and a trail of rubble was behind him. Red dust clouded the air, concealing the fate of Galanör and Aenwyn. Gideon could only say that Ilargo was still alive - that much he could still feel through their bond.

"Gideon!" came Galanör's voice from somewhere in the haze.

"Over here!" he shouted back, relief in his voice.

Two silhouettes pushed through the debris until the true forms of Galanör and Aenwyn were revealed. Like Gideon, they had suffered minor injuries though they had, perhaps, fared better on Ilargo's back.

"Is Ilargo still alive?" Aenwyn blurted.

"He lives," Gideon answered, his eyes guiding them back to the rising dragon.

Ilargo shook his head, freeing more dust into the air. Some of the sharp ridges and spikes under his jaw and along his neck were either chipped or worn down completely. Blood was visible between some of the scales on his face and legs.

Can you hear me? Gideon asked via their bond.

Ilargo turned his head and looked down at him. *Yes,* he replied, his voice uncertain.

Is anything broken? Gideon's eyes surveyed Ilargo from head to tail. It wasn't that long ago he wouldn't have needed to ask.

Only my pride, the dragon said, though Gideon could sense a fair amount of pain on his companion's part.

Galanör looked from Rider to dragon. "What happened?"

Gideon held Ilargo's gaze a moment longer. "Magic is dying," he stated before breathing a sigh.

The currents fluctuate, Ilargo told him. *They fade here and there, but this is the first time the loss of magic has taken my senses with it.*

"It's only going to get worse," Aenwyn surmised, unaware of Ilargo's response.

"What do we do now?" Galanör questioned, dusting off one of his arms.

Gideon looked back at Ilargo. "Can you fly?" he asked aloud.

Yes. But I will not fly now, the dragon added.

Why not? Gideon pressed, falling naturally back into their bond.

Because I do not trust myself, Ilargo said simply.

Aenwyn is right: it's only going to get worse. We need to reach Davosai.

I know what we must do! Ilargo snapped, his head rushing down to Gideon. Both Galanör and Aenwyn flinched as they took a step back. *I said I will not fly,* the dragon repeated. *Not today.*

Gideon could sense so much more going on under the dragon's surface. Besides an injured pride and grave concern for those he was responsible for, he was also experiencing some of the same emotional outbursts that had plagued Gideon and Inara from time to time.

Aware that his companion's emotional state was close to turning from irritated to angry, Gideon left it there. *Rest, old friend,* he said instead. *I have faith in your wings yet.*

Ilargo huffed, expelling a jet of warm air from his nostrils, and moved away. He flexed his wings once, revealing new injuries across the thin membranes. His right wing shuddered as he pulled it in to his body. Gideon remembered the specific pain of a wounded wing and felt for his companion.

"Is everything alright?" Galanör enquired tentatively.

Gideon glanced at Ilargo, who was now lying down in the arena. "We won't be going anywhere for the rest of the day," he informed them.

"We can rest easy enough here," Aenwyn replied diplomatically. "We are above ground. Galanör's magic can start a fire - I imagine it gets cold here at night."

"*Very*," Gideon emphasised.

"I can look at your wounds too," Galanör offered, looking at a particular nasty cut that Gideon could feel above his left eye.

"I will be fine," the old master insisted. "Save your magic."

It wasn't too long before the sun was setting on Ayda, casting the ruins of Malaysai in an orange tint. Aenwyn and Galanör had set up a small place to rest beside Ilargo and already started a fire. Thanks to their supplies, they had blankets, food, and water to keep them going.

Gideon stood apart from them, atop the highest tier of the arena. He had stood on this very spot nearly fifty years ago and looked out on Malaysai and the jungle beyond. Even now, he felt as if he could see Adriel and Adilandra out of the corner of his eye, standing where they had so long ago. His heart sank to think that both of them were gone.

Can you see her? Ilargo asked, speaking for the first time since he snapped.

Gideon knew who he was talking about. He turned his sight to the north, where an enormous mound of flowers and plant life appeared to have sprung up from the ground and taken over everything around it. ***Angala the wise,*** he said with reverence. Thanks to the clarity of Ilargo's memory, he could still see the mighty dragon being brought down by the Darkakin.

It feels like recalling the life of another, Ilargo began. *We were different back then. The future seemed so bright and full of hope. I felt so strong.*

You are stronger now than you ever were, Gideon encouraged.

I do not feel it. As magic flees this world, I can feel it taking me with it.

Gideon wasn't sure how much he believed his own words but he said them anyway. **Have faith in our friends. They will save it. And when they do, we will be there to make sure this war comes to an end, one way or another.**

Will you make me a promise, Gideon?

I don't need to make that promise, he replied, well aware of what his companion was going to ask of him.

I need to hear you say it, Ilargo pressed. *Promise me you will find a way to go on, to find a new life without me.*

You think after fifty years that's even possible. Could you? he fired back.

Yes.

Gideon rolled his eyes and glanced back at the resting dragon. **Liar.**

A quiet moment existed between them for a time, each settling in to the thoughts and emotions of the other. *I am sorry for the way I spoke to you earlier,* Ilargo said softly.

You don't need to apologise, Gideon replied. **Were I in your position I would be angry too. What's happening to you isn't fair. It isn't right.**

I believe the true source of my anger lies in our bond, Ilargo admitted.

How so? Gideon asked, unable to sense the truth behind the words.

As much as I hated to see you share my wounds, everything was easier when we bore it together. This new existence, though practical and fair, is somewhat... lonelier.

Gideon couldn't argue with that. **Life did seem less complicated. But we will find a way to make this work. Dragons and Riders lived this way for eons. We'll find a way,** he promised.

Ilargo shifted his front right leg and twitched with the pain that ran through it. **Rest, old friend,** Gideon bade, hoping the dragon would regain some of his confidence to fly again soon.

"Gideon." The call came from Galanör, who had wandered a little further ahead of Ilargo.

Since there was no tone of alarm in his voice, Gideon made his way down the arena in his own time and met up with Aenwyn, who had also come to see what had attracted the ranger. Galanör's back was facing them, his blue cloak perfectly still in the cool evening air. He pulled back his hood as they approached and stepped to one side so that they might see what lay on the arena floor.

Gideon frowned in his attempt to understand what he was looking at. Human as he was, his eyes quickly detected the familiar shape of a person's skull. It was filthy and severely cracked across the top. He crouched down and moved some of the debris away to discover the rest of the skeleton, though the limbs were notably far away from the main body. Most of the bones were damaged in some way and decades old by their colour.

Standing up, he stepped back to take in the whole scene while his memory caught up with him. Looking around at the arena, Gideon quickly placed Rainael the emerald star and Queen Adilandra, both of whom had once stood where they were now. At the time, the Goddess of the Darkakin had been stuck between them.

"The Goddess," he announced.

"She liked to think she was," Galanör replied.

Gideon examined the gaps between the limbs and the main body again. "I remember Adilandra breaking a lot of her bones. I don't remember her tearing them *off*."

Galanör kicked one of the leg bones with the tip of his boot. "That's because she didn't. If I had to guess, I would say her subjects found her up here and—"

"Perhaps you don't need to guess," Aenwyn interjected. "This is picture enough I feel."

"You know," Gideon said, "for all her wickedness, I never gave her another thought after leaving here."

"Nor would she have been deserving of it," Galanör stated. "This is what she deserved," he added, gesturing to her broken remains.

"Then let us not disturb her," Aenwyn suggested, half turning back to their camp. "I would hear of Queen Adilandra though. The two of you spent much time with her."

Gideon and Galanör shared a brief exchange of looks. "The Darkakin tried to break her, but she left these shores a stronger person," the ranger declared. "You should have seen her when we rested in The Hook of the World, surrounded by dragons of every size and age," he went on, returning to the fire beside Aenwyn. "She met Rainael face to face and convinced the queen of dragons to fly immediately to Velia. Had she not, that battle, nay the entire War for the Realm, might have ended very differently."

Gideon gave the Goddess one last look before trailing them. "She was a demon on the battlefield too," the old master recalled. "She required no aid that day."

The trio took a seat around the fire, shared food and drink, and swapped stories well into the night. For a brief moment, Gideon forgot all about the troubles of the world and enjoyed the company of his friends and the rhythmic breathing of his companion behind him.

CHAPTER 42

PREPARATIONS

A heavy slumber had settled upon Asher, taking the ranger back through the eons to a time of dragons. He sensed his young companion's consciousness entwined with his own as Avandriell's inherited memories gripped them both. It was an extraordinary experience to be awake yet trapped in his sleep, helpless to do anything but be carried along in the currents.

Though he saw naught but mist and shadow, the sound of beating wings and rushing air filled his ears. A familiar female voice called out to him through the ether, tethering him until the memory sharpened into light and colour. Asher wanted to hear Avandriell's voice again but he was presented with a scene from millennia past, stealing his attention.

The sun shone brightly from its place in an ocean of pure blue, its light intensified by the desert sands. Seeing through the eyes of a dragon, nothing escaped Asher's gaze. He looked out on a line of Riders as they awaited the arrival of another group, approaching from the south.

Thanks to Thessaleia's memories bleeding through their bond, the ranger knew he was looking out on The Glimmer Lands,

Erador's most southern territory. He was instantly enthralled, curious as to what he was witnessing.

Thessaleia glanced to the side, giving Asher a good look at three other dragons. They were all watching their Riders as they met the southern strangers. The ranger's curiosity peaked when that group came to stand at three times the height and width of the Riders. They possessed the features of humans, for the most part, and were well-muscled; easily noted by their scant clothing. Their size could only identify them as Giants, though Asher had never seen Giants like them, accustomed as he was to the lumbering behemoths that behaved in the manner of beasts and monsters.

The Giants that stood *conversing* with the Riders looked to have all the mannerisms of an ordinary person. The words that passed between the two groups were indistinct, but Asher knew Thessaleia was tense and ready to spring should the untrustworthy Giants prove violent.

As interesting as this had probably been, it felt wrong to Asher. This wasn't their land and it wasn't their time. They were taking on memories and experiences that would do little to aid them in the present.

Avandriell, he said, searching for his companion in the void. **This is not our world.**

It is all our world, Avandriell countered, her words and the strength of her voice taking the ranger by surprise.

Her words also brought an end to the memory. A flash of lightning tore through the desert, replacing the vast landscape and heat with the confines of West Fellion and a hammering rain. Asher was back in his own body, caught between the gates of the Graycoats' fortress, as countless Arakesh poured in to take their pound of flesh.

Blindfolded, he raided the world for all it had, detecting every scent, hearing every breath, and feeling every raindrop against his skin. Blood spoiled the air and he tasted the hot liquid as it ran down the steel of his blade. While his every sense was more alive in the thrall of the Nightseye elixir, assassins were mounting at his feet, dead.

You have been stuck in the dirt all your life, soaking in blood. Avandriell's voice expelled the memory, transporting Asher to the top of Syla's Gate, where he had faced the wild Darkakin. *You have been surrounded by enemies with no way forward but through the tip of your sword.* Syla's Gate crumbled beneath his feet and he landed on the high walls of Velia as Giants and Trolls assaulted the walls. *You have suffered for those around you, forced to always sacrifice yourself for them.* Asher saw himself plunge his broadsword into the eye of a Giant and follow it down to the ground, where a sea of Darkakin vied for his blood.

As the Giant slammed into the ground, however, he was suddenly sinking beneath the enchanted waters in one of the pools of Naius as Kaliban fell into ruin around him. *We will soar over the realm,* Avandriell promised. *We will soar together. Erador, Illian, Ayda... all of Verda. You do not face the world alone anymore, nor your enemies. Now you have me.*

Asher could feel the passion, love, and wrath, that formed the core of every dragon - a three-stranded cord that could not be broken. Avandriell was a warrior from an ancient time, her confidence gifted to her by a powerful mother and father. It was similar to his own, though his confidence was born of decades being honed in the shadows of Nightfall.

As he dwelled on that terrible place, a nightmare from his past, Avandriell broke through and brought light to the darkness. His tortuous lessons fell away and the sting of those memories faded, just as Malliath's had. Piece by piece, she was renewing him, making him whole again.

Whether the ranger wanted to or not, his eyes opened to the real world and discovered a young dragon perched on his midriff. She was careful not to press down with her claws but there was nothing to be done about her weight, which was becoming considerable.

A slit of dawning light shone through his makeshift tent but he couldn't take his sight from Avandriell's golden orbs. "Morning," he said aloud, intrigued by her intensity.

When there came no reply of any kind he tried the same greeting again using their bond, eager to hear her voice. Nothing. Somewhat frustrated by their lack of communication, the ranger rolled over, ushering her onto the ground beside him.

"So you can speak to me in my dreams," he surmised, his voice gruff from disuse. Avandriell tilted her head at the words, displaying some understanding in her eyes, though she failed to give any kind of verbal response. "Do you know what I'm saying?" he asked, aware that the dragon had heeded his words previously. Avandriell pounced without warning and landed on his cot, her nose rooting around in the folds of the blanket. Asher sighed. "I'll take that as a no," he said.

Gathering his swords and equipment, the ranger departed his tent and greeted the cold morning. His breath clouded the air in front of his face while his back audibly cracked with only the most minor of stretches. Avandriell soon bounded through the flap of the tent and raced around the available area. A passing dwarf was forced to move his leg and hop to the side in a bid to evade the excitable dragon. A pair of elves, eating their breakfast, paused with spoons to their lips to marvel at her.

Asher took the opportunity to fasten his belt and broadsword to his hip before strapping the silvyr blade and quiver over his back. The folded bow required some adjustment to keep it latched to the quiver and his fingers naturally ran over the small knives and hunting daggers on their way, checking that everything was where he liked it.

Raising his head, the ranger inhaled a deep breath and orientated himself to reality - no easy task after hours of living in the past. Just having his feet on the ground was a peculiar sensation having soared across the Eradoran skies as a dragon.

"Avandriell," he called, heading away from his tent.

Navigating the various species and campfires was second nature to Asher. Blending in and flowing through crowds was considered just as important as the art of assassination in the halls of Nightfall. Avandriell appeared to share some of those same skills, though she didn't exactly blend in. She was nimble and quick enough, however, to weave between broad dwarves, numerous elves, and even under the occasional Centaur. Of course, her keen sense of smell often got in the way of any progress, leading her to every source of food.

Asher sighted one of the carts from Vangarth, the origin of the new food. They had arrived nearly two days ago and been met with cheers from all, including the elves. Vighon had instructed his men to ration it all and share the food and supplies amongst the camp. It had increased their spirits, something which was much needed since news of advancing Reavers had spread three days past.

Making his way towards the council tent, the ranger happily accepted a red apple from one of the Namdhorians and proceeded to eat it as he approached the entrance. The absence of Sir Borin outside the tent immediately informed Asher that Vighon was not inside. A brief glance at the surroundings also informed him that neither Reyna nor Nathaniel were inside the tent, their guards missing from their usual stations.

Wandering a little further down the northern line, Avandriell in tow, he soon discovered Reyna in deep conversation with Faylen. The pair were looking out at the battlefield and the enormous pit, their hands outstretched as they pointed at various places. Following their focus, Asher laid eyes on several ranks of elves taking up positions at specific locations closer to the pit. Further to the east, Captain Dardaris was trotting up and down Namdhorian lines, ordering soldiers into formation. Among them was Vighon, only visible at this distance thanks to Sir Borin's inescapable size.

Standing just beyond the camp's northern line now, Asher caught sight of Nathaniel not far away. The knight, as he would always be to the ranger, was overseeing the distribution of food from one of the carts. Still eating his apple, Asher crossed the gap to meet his old friend. Nathaniel's personal guard of elves noted his approach and responded in kind to the ranger's nod.

"See that the wounded are tended to first," the immortal

knight commanded. "But make sure some is left for those out on the field... they will need their strength." His words were met with obedience by humans and elves alike.

"I see preparations are well under way," Asher remarked, his eyes leading Nathaniel to the battlefield.

"Aye," he agreed. "We can only hope it's enough. I don't need to ask if you'll be out there with us."

Asher turned to regard the distant Namdhorians. "I'll stand beside the northmen," he declared, confident in his abilities to meet the attacking wave of Reavers. "And you?" he queried.

Nathaniel looked wistfully at the king and his soldiers. "I would fight where I always do; beside you." His eyes flitted from the guarding elves to his wife before returning to Asher. "Alas, I am expected to fight with... *my people*, defending the perimeter of the pit should the enemy break through the Namdhorian line. Perhaps you could let just a few through," he added with a coy smile.

Asher looked down at Nathaniel's hip. "How long has it been," he joked, "since his Grace had need of a sword?"

The old knight gripped his hilt. "This sword took Namdhor back," he said determinedly.

The ranger finished his apple and threw the core away. "I'm sure it *helped*," he quipped with a mischievous grin.

Nathaniel's mouth twisted in amusement. "Avandriell might have made you immortal, old man, but she hasn't made you any quicker."

Asher pulled his broadsword a few inches from its scabbard. "Care to test that theory?"

Though he heard four blades of steel leaving their fine elven scabbards, the ranger barely had the time to blink before they were all pointed at him, one even resting on his shoulder. He glanced back to see the elf in a battle stance, prepared to defend his king with bloodshed. The elf, however, did show some unease upon hearing Avandriell's aggressive hiss beside his leg.

"Stand down!" Nathaniel barked. The elves didn't hesitate, moving as one to draw back their scimitars and return to a guarding stance. "This man is never to be treated as our enemy."

"I'm afraid such a man does not exist." The response led them to Captain Nemir and his small entourage of warriors. "At least, the royal guard cannot afford to believe as such. Your Grace is our king now. You will be defended as such for the rest of your days." Nemir looked to Asher. "Should you require a sparring partner, I would offer myself in place of the king."

The ranger opened his mouth to reply with a resounding yes when his gaze found Faylen. Both she and the queen had stopped their conversation to watch the event, though whether they could actually hear what was transpiring from so far away remained to be seen.

He couldn't say what Faylen was thinking but he had a good idea of how she would feel watching him clash swords with her husband. With that in mind, he lowered his broadsword until the cross-guard met the scabbard.

Nathaniel stepped between them. "As much as I would like to see such a spectacle, there is still much that needs to be done in defence of the doorway. Besides, I don't think it will be long before all of our swords are needed." He gave the captain a nod, dismissing him with a look.

Asher glanced back at Faylen and Reyna again, though both had quickly returned to their plans.

"I thought there was no bad blood between you two," Nathaniel said quietly in Nemir's absence.

"There isn't," Asher confirmed. "Doesn't mean I wouldn't like to break his nose."

Nathaniel laughed and patted the ranger on the arm. "Come. You can help me with the supplies from the next cart."

Asher nodded along before looking down at Avandriell. "Next time, don't announce yourself - just take the leg."

CHAPTER 43
END OF THE ROAD

The midday sun struggled to rise much higher than the horizon, and struggled all the more to pierce the thick clouds rolling over The Moonlit Plains. Snow reigned silently over the land, blanketing everything as it removed the finer edges from the world. Looking back over her shoulder, Inara could no longer see the great pines of The Evermoore, the forest nearly two days behind them now.

Instead, she looked upon the many Drakes that walked without complaint through the icy weather. It would have been enough to break the spirits of any, even more so given their final destination, yet Adan'Karth and his kin continued diligently. Inara was both inspired and heartbroken by their march.

Turning back to the south, she could just make out Kassian Kantaris through the snowfall, leading the procession beside Adan. Had she not been astride Athis, there would have been no view but the backs of numerous Drakes. Of course, it helped that Athis was bowed under the weight of his own horns, as he had been since they left The Evermoore.

With every passing hour, Inara could feel the heat leaving his body. When they had set out from Vangarth, the dragon had been near the front, well within range of calling Kassian or Adan. Now, sluggish as he was, Athis had slipped further and further down the line of Drakes. His every step was clearly an effort, his tail simply dragging along the ground behind him.

Inara patted his scales. *Keep going,* she encouraged. **The doorway isn't far now. We might even reach it by tomorrow's dawn.**

I fear that the next dawn is beyond me, wingless one. Athis's voice was just as weak as his limbs.

It filled Inara with a cold dread. **Do not say that,** she rebuffed. **You are Athis the ironheart! If you could fly you could be over the pit in a few hours.**

But I do not have my wings, Athis pointed out. *Soon I will not even be able to rely on my legs.*

The sorrow weighing on Inara's heart kept her mouth closed and her words locked in her mind, beyond even Athis's reach. She feared the worst was upon them, but how could she voice such a concern? Not when Athis needed her strength - now more than ever. How many times had he pulled her through the darkest of days? How many times had he lent her his strength and seen them both to victory?

But what could she really do? That question echoed in her mind, extinguishing any light of hope. Words alone would not bolster Athis, for magic was dying and it cared little for sentiment.

With so little to offer the dragon, she simply pressed her body to his and stroked his scales.

~

Time and land slipped by under the relentless snow. Having taken to the road herself now, Inara's thoughts had been torn between memories of Vighon and Athis. She recalled Kassian joining her at some point, the Keeper in need of sleep himself. He was walking only a few feet in front of Athis, though they were a few hundred feet behind the Drakes.

Inara was instantly struck by the danger posed to the Drakes by her companion's reduced speed. Looking at Athis, it didn't take someone well versed in the culture of dragons to see that he was ailing. His blue eyes, absent their vividness, were closed more than open. Where he had recently been able to hold his head up, the hard ridge of his jaw was currently dragging through the snow and mud. Even his claws had lost their smooth motion and now twitched with the strength required of them.

I cannot... I cannot go any further. The dragon's slow plod had come to an end before his words. His jaw took the full weight of his head until the rest of his body slid to the ground, flat.

Athis! Inara rushed to the side of his head and placed both of her hands over his scales. He was so cold.

I am... not strong enough. You must—

Whatever he said next was hidden from Inara. She reached out across their bond and even plunged into the sanctuary they shared, but Athis's presence couldn't even find the strength to inhabit it.

"What's happening to him?" Kassian asked.

Inara tried to fight back the tears that welled in her eyes. "He's dying," she uttered, falling to her knees beside him.

"His aura is beginning to dim," Adan announced, turning Inara and Kassian back to the south. Behind Adan, every Drake had stopped in their tracks to look upon Athis, as if paying their respects.

It maddened Inara. "He will not die!" she fumed.

Adan'Karth simply bowed his head, his hands folded within his voluminous sleeves.

Inara ignored the Drake and returned her attention to Athis, finding one of his large eyes. "Fight it," she urged, relying on his hearing instead of their bond. "You have to fight it. For me."

"Inara." Kassian's voice was as soft as the falling snow.

With an outstretched hand she kept him and his words at bay, refusing to take her gaze from Athis. "This isn't how Athis the iron-heart dies," she declared, though her voice lacked the conviction. "You are a hero," she continued. "A warrior without compare. With tooth and claw you have saved the realm. You've bled for it. The realm still needs you. I need you. *Fight it.*"

There was a flicker of life in the dragon's eyes as he focused on Inara.

"The currents return," Adan stated. "But they are weak."

A blast of cool air escaped the dragon's nostrils. *You must fight... for us both now, wingless one.*

Inara's heart quickened at the sound of his voice. *I can't. Not without you. Stay with me.*

There has never been a day... when you needed me, Inara. There is no greater strength in this world... than that which lies in your heart. I have seen it.

A defiant tear ran down Inara's cheek as she pressed her hands deeper into his scales. *I won't leave you.*

You must, Athis insisted. *Save the tree. Save the world. You must go now.*

"He still has time," Adan'Karth told her, his hand placed against the dragon's chest. "Though his will fades, his heart is still strong. If we can save the tree, there is still hope for Athis."

Inara wanted to tell him where to stick his hope. The rage bubbling under the surface had begun to erode the anguish that had settled over her. Now the Guardian of the Realm was imagining the idea of cleaving her brother's head from his shoulders.

Focus, wingless one. Athis's voice brought her back to him. *Leave me here. Do your duty.*

After a moment of contemplation, Inara rose from her knees, her chest heaving. She was torn between action and inaction. The latter, however, would spell Athis's doom for certain.

"Let's go," she said, battling her own voice to remain even. Looking at her companion, their bond still connected by slivers of magic, she promised, *We will see each other again.*

A few extra seconds were required before Inara was able to turn around and force her feet to march behind Kassian and Adan. She couldn't look back at her companion. To do so would root her in place, never to leave his side.

After a hundred yards, Athis's voice whispered in her mind as the last vestiges of their bond lost their hold. He only said three words, but they were enough to both break and bolster Inara's heart.

CHAPTER 44
THOSE BELOW

With the sun camped in the west, the shadows of the nearby mountains reached across the dry ground in a bid to touch the edges of Davosai. Seen from the sky, the Darkakin city was naught but a ruin of broken stone smashed against the landscape, its original shape barely recognisable.

Such was the wrath of dragons.

Galanör had seen as much with his own eyes nearly fifty years ago. Looking out from Ilargo, the elf even caught sight of the cliff from which he and Adilandra had witnessed Davosai's fall. The desert heat had been mild compared to the inferno the dragons wrought upon the city that day.

The ranger recalled it all with horrifying clarity, for who could forget such a spectacle? There were few throughout history who could claim to have watched and survived a dragon attack, especially in those numbers.

Of course, there had been one particular dragon who delivered destruction upon the savages with gleeful and terrible abandon. Galanör leaned out and looked down at an area of destruction that led out of the city's main gates and across the sun-baked land. It had been there that he had seen Malliath the voiceless pursue

478

hundreds of fleeing Darkakin only to bathe them in fire. None had survived.

Ilargo dipped his head, angling them down towards the inner city. It gave them all a good view of the circular pit that sat in the centre of Davosai. It was twice as large as the shaft dug into The Moonlit Plains, though its purpose had been just as singular in nature. Down there, in the dark, Atilan had forged his greatest weapon against the Dragon Riders.

"Hold on!" Gideon shouted over his shoulder.

Not again, Galanör thought, bracing himself.

Ilargo dived for the ground, pressing Aenwyn's back into the ranger's chest. They held on together, fearing that the green dragon would never level out. Fortunately, Ilargo possessed enough strength to flex his wings and catch the currents. His tail and claws skimmed along the ground as he sailed between the ruins of the city, bringing them closer and closer to the pit.

When the debris closed in on them, Galanör could feel the dragon's leg muscles already moving as he matched his speed, closed his wings, and continued the remaining distance on the ground. That, however, did not last long. Ilargo slowed and eventually collapsed to his hardened stomach, his jaw flat.

Gideon took a breath and patted his companion's scales. "That was close," he remarked.

"He did well to remain aloft for so long," Aenwyn offered.

"Had he flown any longer we would all be stains on the ground," Gideon replied, climbing down.

Galanör tried not to think about that alternative as he navigated his way down the curves of Ilargo's body. Having worried about the dragon's health since leaving Malaysai, the ranger felt good to have his feet on the ground again.

He walked by Ilargo's head and stroked the scales around the back of his right eye. "Your strength knows no bounds, old friend. Thank you." The dragon could only blink in return.

"He says he wishes that were so," Gideon relayed. "Though I am in agreement with you," he added, looking at his companion. "It *is* your strength that has brought us this far." Ilargo had just enough energy to lift his nose, gesturing towards the pit. Gideon nodded. "We will," he said. "You stay here and rest."

Galanör felt the latter was redundant given Ilargo's condition, but he knew Gideon was speaking aloud for their benefit. Bidding the dragon farewell for now, the three companions made their way through the remaining debris until they were standing by the edge of the mine. It was too dark to see the bottom.

"The Crissalith was down there?" Aenwyn asked sceptically.

Galanör pointed to the inner wall of the mine shaft. "There was once a network of walkways and pulleys, much like the ones in The Moonlit Plains. The Darkakin were mining the Crissalith for generations."

Aenwyn surveyed the inner walls. "What happened here?"

Galanör looked up at the sky before returning his vision to the darkness below. "Dolvosari," he said simply.

"The storm maker," Gideon verified.

"Dolvosari is a dragon?" Aenwyn questioned.

"An old one," Gideon answered.

"A *big* one," Galanör added.

"Like Malliath," the old master elaborated, "he had spells etched into his hide that could conjure storms after reaching a particular height. His choice apparently. He had the ancient Riders do it when they were at war with Atilan."

"I had never seen a storm like it," Galanör told them. "With rain he flooded the mine and with lightning he destroyed the Darkakins' work. Nearly killed me and Adilandra in the process."

Aenwyn crouched down and peered into the abyss, her apprehension clear to see. "We're sure this is the best option?"

"It's the only option," Gideon said, removing the three crystals from his belt. "Can you open a portal into Atilan's lab?" he asked Galanör.

The ranger accepted the crystals but his mind pondered something else, causing him to glance back at the way they had come. "I can open a portal," he affirmed. "But I can't get us back to Illian."

Gideon looked from Galanör to Ilargo and back. "He just needs to rest," the old master assured.

"He's been getting worse since Malaysai," the elf reminded him. "How many stops did we have to make between there and here?"

"He's fine," Gideon said firmly.

"And if he's not?" Galanör countered. "If Ilargo can't fly us home we're going to have to brave Drowners' Run - a name those islands have well-earned. Not to mention the time it will take on foot."

Gideon looked away. "I said he's fine, Galanör. He'll have time to rest while we look for the Crissalith."

"Time is the one thing he doesn't—" Galanör's words were stopped by Aenwyn's hand pressing against his chest.

She gave him a subtle shake of the head before saying, "We have come this far. We have no choice but to continue onwards, whatever our way back to Illian. If Crissalith is The Rebellion's path to victory and Alijah's path to redemption, I say we go and get it."

Galanör nodded once in agreement, fingering one of the crystals in his hand. "Give me a moment."

Stepping away from the others, the ranger closed his eyes and cast his mind back to The War for the Realm. The decades between melted away and he visualised Atilan's ancient lab with the clarity only an elf could conjure. He placed the desk and chair in the chamber, focusing on the largest open space in the middle of the room. He had it.

Drawing on his own well of magic, Galanör began to pour his will and power into the crystal, enhancing its brightness. His fingers were hot and the hairs on the back of his neck stood on end. It had been a long time since he had used this kind of magic and he had forgotten the extent of its requirements. He continued to give it all he had, balling it up in his fist now. As the first beads of sweat began to make their way down the side of his head, the elf flicked his wrist and tossed the crystal into the air.

A blinding flash erupted before their eyes, eclipsing the crystal and all else for a brief second. What remained could only be described as a void in reality, a place where nothing had shape or texture. Sparks and bolts of lightning flickered around its edges, scorching patches of ground.

"Quickly," Galanör uttered.

One after the other, they dashed through the portal before it collapsed on itself, leaving Ilargo alone on the surface.

Crossing from one place to another, the cold air was immediately noticeable, as was the even colder water that filled the chamber to their knees. It was also pitch black, an unnerving and disorientating condition. Warriors all, the companions naturally reached for their swords, though Galanör was more aware of Stormweaver's weight after opening a portal.

"We need light," Gideon stated, his words aimed at the ranger.

Galanör felt nauseous just thinking about using more magic, but what choice did he have? Without light they would never find the Crissalith. The muscles in his arm pinched and his fingers ached as he cast an orb of white light. It floated up, revealing the flooded chamber in stark shadows, lending the ancient site a menacing appearance.

Unsure of his ability to keep the orb alight - and aware that he needed to recover his strength to open a portal back to the surface - Galanör examined the chamber's details and scanned the walls, searching for torches resting in the fixings. He found two and quickly set them aflame, not wishing to dwell on the use of more spells.

"Take them," he urged.

With a torch each, Aenwyn and Gideon moved to different parts of the room to expel the lingering darkness. The far left corner of the chamber had suffered the worst under Dolvosari's assault, the space now occupied by rock after a cave-in. The collapsing rock had torn through one side of Atilan's desk, reducing it to splinters and leaving the rest of it at an awkward angle.

Exhausted as he felt, Galanör could still remember his time with Adilandra in this room. The memory turned him around to set his sights on the door that led out into the base of the mine.

"We need to go that way," he directed, breaking Gideon's

reverie. The old master was obviously fascinated by their surroundings, his free hand having already glided over a dozen relics along the walls.

Aenwyn reached the door first. "It won't budge," she reported, her shoulder leaning into it.

"There's going to be tons of debris on the other side," Galanör replied. "Can you pull it from its hinges?"

Aenwyn handed her torch to the ranger and retrieved a dagger from her belt. With both hands, she dug the blade in and prised the hinges away from the rotten wood. She removed the lowest hinge blind, her hands working beneath the water.

Her work completed, the elf found her grip on each side of the door and yanked it backwards. The top half split almost entirely before a few strands of the wood took the lower half with it. Discarding the door, they looked out on a wall of dirt and rubble that rose to shoulder height.

"We can fit," Aenwyn reassured. Using her dagger as a lever, the elf cleared some of the larger rocks, thus increasing the size of the gap. Her torch returned, she was the first to climb up. Flat on her stomach, she crawled through the narrow gap until it opened up to the base of the mineshaft.

"It's clear!" she called back to them.

Following her example, Galanör and Gideon scaled the rubble and squeezed through to join her in the main shaft. The torch's fire and Galanör's dimming orb cast light on the uneven floor and revealed the half-buried debris from the old mining equipment and walkways. Looking up, the visible sky was beginning to turn orange as the sun brought an end to the day.

"Is the Crissalith beneath us?" Aenwyn's tone matched the look of concern on her face.

"There will be some yes," Galanör said, crouching down to grab a handful of dirt. "But we should think of it as lost and look elsewhere - we won't be getting through this."

"Agreed," Gideon said, moving across the shaft. He rounded a large mound of rubble and lowered his torch in search of other passages that might still be accessible.

Galanör turned on the spot to get his bearings. He recalled the six entrances that had lined the inner wall, one of which they had just crawled out of. Having never entered any of the others, however, he couldn't suggest the best one to investigate.

"Over here," Gideon called. Using his torch, he illuminated another gap between the rubble and the top of a passage.

Aenwyn crouched down to examine it better, her eyes squinting into the darkness. "We could crawl through it," she surmised.

"Good," the old master said, "because it's the only one I've discovered that isn't completely blocked."

"I will go first," Galanör volunteered, but Aenwyn was crawling through before he had finished his sentence.

With no choice but to follow her, all three were soon on their stomachs again, crawling through the dirt. It was longer than the tunnel that connected Atilan's lab to the main shaft. Galanör had to steel himself in the enclosed environment, the ranger being more accustomed to open spaces. It was a relief to hear Aenwyn finally drop down to the passage floor.

Back on their feet - and up to their knees in water again - with their torches held up to the dark, Aenwyn tilted her head. "How far do you think it goes?"

Galanör couldn't fathom the answer, though he imagined the passage leading into a labyrinth from which there was no return. "Who can say?" he replied. "Keep your wits about you and stay close."

Gideon moved to run his torch along the right-hand wall while Aenwyn took to the left. Galanör guided his orb towards the ground in front of him and walked down the middle of the path, his eyes scanning for even a hint of green crystal.

Though it was hard to define, the passage appeared to curve around to the right. It wasn't long either before they came across another passage, offering them a new direction. Galanör had to wonder if it was just another way to get lost.

"Which way?" he asked aloud, his voice carried away down the passage.

"I see no reason to deviate from our current path," Gideon opined. "Let us see where this leads first. At least we know there are other tunnels to search."

Galanör agreed with a nod of the head, though he kept his concerns to himself for now. There was no need to share his growing worry that this entire endeavour was futile.

A few hundred yards further ahead, they were presented with two more tunnel entrances, each as mysterious as the other. None of them felt the temptation to investigate the new passages. As they moved on, however, a single sound reverberated through the passage to their right. The three companions stopped in their tracks, waiting to hear another noise. Galanör's best guess was a rock falling to the ground. It was also his hope.

"Let's keep going," Gideon bade.

The elven ranger inhaled a breath having held the last one for the moment. He turned away from the passage entrance to follow Gideon when he paused, sure that something significant had just caught his eye. While Gideon and Aenwyn walked a little further, Galanör approached the nearest wall and narrowed his eyes. What was it? What had he seen against the jagged wall that jumped out at his senses and told him to stop?

By the time he realised what he was looking at it was too late. A pair of pale eyes were looking back at him.

A creature with the form of a man leapt from the wall and barrelled into the elf, taking them both down into the water.

"Galanör!" Aenwyn yelled.

Submerged and under the weight of his attacker, the ranger shoved his foe and quickly pushed himself up above the water. The creature rose to its feet a moment later and screamed with rage before renewing its assault. Galanör hadn't seen it before, but his enemy was wielding a crude dagger, or perhaps it was a sharpened rock: he couldn't say in the gloom and the figure was coming at him with some speed. Never one to be flustered in a fight, the ranger's sharp instincts took over and he side-stepped the incoming attack. At the same time, his left hand darted up like a knife's edge and caught the creature across the throat. A swift kick to the chest launched it back, right in line with an arrow from Aenwyn's bow.

Falling like a stone, it collapsed into the water, dead.

Galanör looked to his right, locking his gaze with Aenwyn's. She saw the thanks behind his eyes and nodded once, a second arrow already nocked on her bow. Unfortunately, she had been forced to drop her torch in favour of her weapon, leaving them with a single source of light in Gideon's hands. The ranger looked about, half aware that his orb had vanished when his focus had been broken by the attack.

Aenwyn stopped him from producing another one. "You need to save all your magic for the portal out of here. I will do it." Deftly holding her bow and arrow with one hand, she used her other to birth an orb of light. It flickered to life, threatening to collapse on itself, as her remaining magic strained with the effort. At last, a new orb lifted into the air above them and the black water that filled the tunnel.

"What was that?" Gideon asked, nodding his chin at the water.

Galanör crouched down and searched for the edges of the body. "I think *it* was a *he*." With a hand behind his attacker's neck, the elf raised the body from the dark water and revealed the creature's identity.

"A human?" Aenwyn queried with disbelief.

"A *Darkakin*," Galanör corrected grimly.

Gideon and Aenwyn immediately turned their sights to the rest of the tunnel, her bow string pulled taut and his Vi'tari blade free of its scabbard. Galanör used his free hand to wipe away the crusted black substance that coated the savage's chest. Beneath was a skin so pale as to be compared to an orc.

Gideon was running his torch along the wall, checking for any more of them. "How can there be Darkakin down here?"

"There must have been some down here when the mine was destroyed," Galanör reasoned.

"That was nearly fifty years ago," Gideon pointed out as he turned back to the ranger. "That man is no more than twenty years."

Galanör used one thumb to lift the lid over the man's right eye. "Though I hate to consider it, the survivors must have bred down here." He beckoned Gideon with a hand. "Bring your torch," he instructed. Under the firelight of Gideon's torch, they could better see the savage's eye, a pale and unused thing. "I think he was blind. Or mostly blind."

"He was born in the dark," Aenwyn said. "What use are eyes in this hell?"

Gideon stepped back and adjusted the position of his torch. "We should assume there's more of..." His words trailed off as his sight was drawn to the water beyond Galanör.

The elven ranger turned around to discover the source of Gideon's distraction. Ripples glided across the surface of the still water, lapping with barely a sound against Galanör and the body in his hands. Searching for the source of those ripples, he found only darkness. Very carefully, he lowered the body back into the water and remained in his crouching position. Turning his head over one shoulder, he silently gestured for Aenwyn to direct her orb further down the tunnel.

Lowering her bow, the elf focused on her control of the orb and guided it along the ceiling, into the abyss. It moved without protest, its white light battling every inch of the darkness.

At around fifty yards, it revealed a group of Darkakin cautiously advancing on their position like wraiths sent for their souls. Their every step was so silent they could hardly be heard to disturb the water.

Galanör's heart quickened in his chest to that of a thundering drum. So loud was it in his ears that he was sure they would be able to hear it.

Narrowing his eyes at the approaching Darkakin, Galanör held up a hand to warn his companion's against moving. Blind as they were, there was a chance this group would simply pass them by - the better option considering a battle could bring more of them.

It wasn't long before the blind Darkakin were upon them. They wielded the same type of crude dagger as the one who had attacked him, but Galanör knew that crude was still capable of taking life. Having assessed their approaching pattern, the ranger was satisfied that the savages would miss them as they passed through, though only just. The elf made the slightest of adjustments, shifting his shoulders to avoid one of the silent hunters.

Looking back, Aenwyn was perfectly still, her muscles tensed in place as only an elf could accomplish. By comparison, Gideon was practically swaying on the spot, though he was incredibly sentinel-like in his stance.

Soon, four of the eight Darkakin were completely past them and into the tunnel beyond. Turning quietly back, however, Galanör was alarmed to see the remaining four had stopped moving. What were they doing? Casting his eyes over his shoulder again, he now saw that the leading four had come to a stop and even turned to face them.

It was only then that the truth of the matter occurred to Galanör: they could hear the flickering flames of Gideon's torch.

"It's an ambush!" the ranger yelled as Stormweaver rang clear from its scabbard.

The eight Darkakin closed in as one, drawn to the distinct noises of all three of their prey. Aenwyn's bow sounded as she drew back the string, Mournblade cut through the air, and Galanör's explosive charge was impossible to miss. Bloody chaos erupted and the black waters grew darker still.

The ranger's wrist flicked one way then the other, his scimitar slicing through all that got in its way. He felt the resistance of human bodies but the naked savages could do nothing in the face of such fine steel and skill. The first two were buried beneath the water in two beats of the elf's heart. They simply hadn't realised the prey they had ensnared was, in fact, a much more powerful predator.

The remaining two homed in on the sound of the ranger's movements, bringing their stone daggers to bear. Galanör evaded the swing of one with a dash to his left before quickly ducking under the swipe of the second. Experienced at finding their targets in the pitch black, the Darkakin knew exactly where the elf was standing and turned on him with deadly precision.

The ranger's free hand shot out to block the incoming dagger of the closest attacker, a prelude to his counterattack that had the elf slamming the end of his hilt into the savage's nose. A simple, but swift, downward stroke of Stormweaver then split the man down the middle. He was dead before he hit the water.

The last of the four Darkakin leapt the gap between them and grappled Galanör's back. With only a moment to spare, the elf raised his hand and snatched the wrist that was about to plunge a jagged dagger into his shoulder. Wild, like an animal, the Darkakin revealed more of his ferocious nature when he tried to bite the ranger's grasping hand. Superior strength won the day, however, when Galanör flung his foe forward, over the top of him. Thrashing in the water, the blind savage could do nothing to stop the cold steel of Stormweaver from driving down through his chest.

Prepared to now aid his companions against the other half of the ambush, the elf could see he was not required. Gideon was already removing Mournblade from one of the two dead bodies slowly submerging at his feet, while Aenwyn brought her scimitar round in a sweeping arc to lay low the last of the Darkakin.

"Is anyone hurt?" Galanör asked to a pair of shaking heads.

"Are you?" Aenwyn echoed.

"No. Though I do miss having two blades," he added, his chest heaving.

"Quiet," Gideon commanded, his head tilted to direct his right ear down the tunnel.

Both Galanör and Aenwyn heard it too now - a tapping sound against the tunnel wall. The ranger imagined one of the Darkakin knocking their crude weapon against the stone. They were either using the sound to locate their prey or it was their idea of an alarm, alerting others to the presence of intruders.

"We need to move," Gideon urged, turning back to face the adjacent tunnel entrance. "That way. Quickly."

With every direction as much of a mystery as the next, the elves made no objection and fell in behind the old master, who led with the torchlight. Looking up, it was becoming clear that Aenwyn's orb was faltering, soon to fade altogether.

"Look," Galanör hissed, directing them to the ripples pushing against their own. "More are coming towards us," he warned.

Gideon turned left and right, moving his torch to investigate their surroundings. There was only one other tunnel, though its entrance was no larger than an ordinary door. Without discussion they passed through, avoiding the oncoming savages for now. The narrow passage curved round to the left before the ground gradually began to descend, leading the companions to a large rectangular chamber.

Aenwyn moved her hand through the air, directing the last light of her orb further into the chamber. Before it died completely, they glimpsed another doorway on the other side, where the ground rose back up. Before they could consider alternatives, the sound of water breaking against the walls behind them spurred the group on. They descended into the larger chamber, submerging them up to the waist in water, and made for the doorway on the other side.

At the back of the group, Galanör was sure to keep checking over his shoulder for any sign of their pursuers. By the time they reached the new doorway, the side they had come from was steeped in darkness, concealing any trailing Darkakin.

Following the new tunnel, the water now returned to below their knees, they paused at a junction offering four alternative paths. "This place is a maze," Aenwyn groaned.

Galanör turned back to the way they had come and raised his sword to point into the shadows. "Just pick a tunnel. It doesn't matter which."

"This one," Gideon declared, making a decision for them all.

Taking little care for the sound they made, the three companions hurried down one of the four paths, passing other tunnels as they did. It was the fourth passage though, that caught Aenwyn's eye and she brought them to a stop.

"What is it?" Galanör asked.

"I thought I saw..." Aenwyn tilted her head and narrowed her eyes down that fourth passage. "Bring the light," she instructed, shifting her stance to let Gideon by. His torch lifted high and forward, they all saw a flicker of something green in the firelight.

"Crissalith," Gideon muttered, his tone verging on disbelief.

Approaching the green hue, they entered a rounded chamber of jagged walls and abandoned mining equipment poking above the water's surface. Holding the torch up, Gideon revealed for them all a small cave brimming with green crystals protruding from the walls.

Galanör extended his hand and attempted to conjure a simple fire spell. "Nothing," he reported, his hand absent any flames. "I cannot use magic," he added with a hint of relief he never thought he would entertain with such a bleak statement.

Gideon returned Mournblade to its scabbard and ran a finger along a crystal's edge. "Try again," he requested, turning back to look at Galanör's belt.

The elven ranger understood and quickly took the Hastion ring from the pouch on his belt. Worn on his index finger, Galanör held up his hand to marvel at the blue gem. "If this doesn't work—"

"It will," Gideon interjected boldly.

"Some light perhaps?" Aenwyn suggested.

Galanör clenched his fist and voiced the right spell in his mind. Opening his hand again, a glowing orb of light took flight above and between them. All three companions smiled in relief - they finally had a weapon that would give them the advantage over their enemy.

"We need to prise it from the rock," Aenwyn said, reaching for her dagger again.

Her words took a moment to sink in as Galanör was still holding a moment of triumph with Gideon. "We need a piece large enough to be used as a weapon," he finally suggested.

Aenwyn inspected various collections and clumps of the crystal before settling on a particularly pointed gem, its shape close to that of her own dagger. "This one will do." She hacked with the steel and hammered with the hilt, her mining abilities far from those of a dwarf. "I thought you said Atilan *made* the

Crissalith," she observed during her efforts. "This looks to be a natural formation."

"The *crystal* is natural," Gideon explained, "and found only in this location apparently. Atilan's grimoire detailed little regarding his discovery of it, but it did tell of his experiments with the crystal. He used spores from a strange type of plant he found in The Silver Trees of Akmar, in Erador. Combined with magic of his own engineering, the crystals turned green and developed their unique property of severing one from magic." The old master pointed around the cave. "Atilan spread the spores everywhere he could find the crystal."

Galanör listened to it all, fascinated, but he never took his eyes from the passage they had passed through. They were making enough noise to be easily located, even without the sensitive ears of the Darkakin. Another confrontation was inevitable.

Hearing the crystal break, the ranger dared to glance back and watch Aenwyn place the Crissalith inside Gideon's satchel. Swallowed by the pocket-dimension, the crystal might as well have ceased to exist.

"We have the Crissalith," Gideon summarised. "And we have the Hastion gem. Time to get out of this nightmare," he finished, looking to Galanör.

Galanör exchanged a silent conversation with Aenwyn and they swapped places so that she could cover them with her bow while he drew on his magic to create another portal.

"Have you had enough time?" Gideon enquired with concern.

Galanör could still feel the strain from opening the first portal, a fatigue that manifested in a slight tremble present in both of his hands. "Why?" he replied sarcastically. "Do we have time for me to rest down here?" The ranger took a breath to compose himself. "Just be ready to catch me on the other side."

His fingers reached into the pouch on his belt and investigated every inch of the leather. A cold dread rushed through his veins as he found the hole in the bottom. Removing the pouch completely, he opened it with both hands and looked in dismay at the lack of crystals therein.

"What's wrong?" Gideon demanded, likely aware of the calamity.

"The crystals are gone," Galanör stated, his tone hollow.

"Gone?" Aenwyn repeated, tearing her eyes from the passage.

"They must have fallen out when the Darkakin attacked me," he concluded, meeting Gideon's eyes to share in his trepidation.

"Without them we will be—"

"Stuck," Galanör cut in, finishing the old master's obvious statement. "We will just have to retrieve them."

"That is easier said than done," Gideon retorted.

"It's either that or accept this place as our tomb," the ranger spat, angry with himself more than anything.

"He's right," Aenwyn said, agreeing with Galanör. "This is just another problem. We will face it and overcome it or die trying."

Gideon nodded in agreement. "Then let us face it. I would not linger in this foul place any longer than we need to."

With no time to further chastise himself, Galanör took up the lead and guided them back the way they had come. Eventually, the light of his orb pushed forward into the rectangular chamber and reflected off the black surface of the water. Unlike the first time they had passed through this chamber, the ranger had a bad feeling about it now.

Slowly, with Stormweaver in hand, he descended back into the deeper waters. By the time he was crossing the middle of the chamber, Gideon and Aenwyn were up to their waist in water behind him. He could see the slope and the adjacent doorway up ahead.

Something brushed past his leg.

The ranger looked down, though he could see naught but the orb shining brightly on the water. Then he heard Aenwyn yelp behind him. He only glimpsed her before she was dragged down into the black.

"Aenwyn!" both Galanör and Gideon cried.

The water exploded all around them. Darkakin filled the chamber, lashing out at their prey. Gideon abandoned his torch and met the attack with Mournblade in both hands. Galanör skewered the first savage to come at him, forcing Stormweaver up to the hilt in the man's scrawny gut. He yanked it back and flowed into a sweeping arc that cleaved the next Darkakin's head from his shoulders.

"Aenwyn!" he yelled, as yet more came for his blood.

Gideon had been quickly piled upon and was under threat of being weighed down under the water. He slashed Mournblade high and low, relieving savages of limb and life alike but his sword arm was nearly submerged. Galanör fought his way across the chamber, cutting down Darkakin with every flash of his steel. One of them, however, succeeded in landing a blow to the side of the elf's face, knocking him off course from Gideon's plight. He was then faced by another pair of Darkakin who intended to stab him in the chest.

That was when Aenwyn burst from the water, her bow coming up as she retrieved an arrow from her quiver. In the blink of an eye she let loose her missile and took down one of Galanör's opponents. He dispatched the other with a swift horizontal strike of his scimitar, only to be relieved of the third savage - who had previously struck him in the face - by another arrow from Aenwyn.

Thankful as he was to see Aenwyn unharmed, Galanör immediately turned to renew his aid to Gideon. The old master, however, proved that the word *old* only referred to the number of years he had lived, not his state of health. With one mighty shrug, he freed himself of the surrounding Darkakin. What followed were the movements of a wraith, not a man. Flowing through the smooth forms of the ancient Mag'dereth, Gideon sliced, hacked, and slashed through every one of his foes until he was ringed by floating bodies.

Gideon's shoulders sagged while he caught his breath. "You're injured," he pointed out, looking at Aenwyn.

The elf shrugged off the concern. "Nothing serious," she replied, though Galanör would have preferred they took a moment to properly examine the multitude of cuts she had acquired under the water. "Gideon!" she said with some alarm, directing them to the stone dagger protruding from under his ribs.

Galanör waded through the water at speed to join his friend. "Don't touch—" His advice was moot when Gideon pulled the dagger free and tossed it away.

"I'll be fine," he groaned, placing a hand over the wound.

"That would kill any man," Galanör warned, fearful for his friend's life.

"Then it is a good thing I am not *any* man," Gideon quipped. "Ilargo's strength will see me heal quickly."

Galanör wanted to ask him what strength he spoke of, but now wasn't the time. "Let's get out of here," he said determinedly.

Keeping Gideon between them, the companions back-tracked through the tunnels, ever wary of ripples in the water. Only once did Galanör question their direction, but Gideon confidently directed them, proving his mind remained sharp despite his blood loss. For how long that would last was a bridge to be crossed when they got to it.

Any lingering doubt on Galanör's part was eased when his glowing orb cast light over eight dead bodies floating in the water. The ranger navigated the corpses until he found the young savage who had leapt out from the wall at him. He moved the Darkakin, pushing the body further up the tunnel, before getting on his hands and knees. The tunnel floor was rough and layered in loose stones and debris - he could have touched the crystals and never known it.

Groaning in frustration, the elf rose to his feet. "I could search this one patch of ground for a hundred years and never find even one of the crystals." He held his hands out, keeping them close together.

"What are you doing?" Aenwyn asked, though her judgmental tone suggested she already had a good idea about what he planned to do.

"I need to use magic."

"You will need all of your magic to get us out of here," she corrected.

"I can do it," he reassured. "Besides," he added, glancing at Gideon leaning against the wall, "we don't have time."

Galanör parted his hands and with them went the water around his feet. The waterspout gradually expanded, revealing the hard ground. The crystals were easy to spot, their glistening exterior exaggerated against the black stone. The elf reached down and snatched them both up before the water rushed in once more. He secured one of them in a pouch he knew wasn't torn or compromised.

"Galanör..." Aenwyn's dark eyes were set over his shoulder, but he knew what she was looking at.

"We'll keep them off," Gideon told him, sighting the Darkakin himself. "Open a portal back to the surface."

As Aenwyn took up her position in front of Galanör, the old master stood his ground behind him, Mournblade braced low by his hip. The ranger clenched his fist around the crystal and tried not to think about the peril that closed in on them. He needed to focus. While the orb had done little to deplete his reserves of magic, the waterspout had taken a part of what he had recovered after the first portal. Now, at such a crucial moment, he could feel that hollowness that always accompanied taxing magic.

As Gideon took his first swing and Aenwyn unleashed her first arrow, Galanör shut his eyes. He sharpened his power to a single point, directed through his body and into his hand. So much of him began to go numb, including his attention. He was barely aware of the body that dropped at his feet. Aenwyn cried out in pain, chipping away at his discipline. He could hear the effort in Gideon's breathing every time he raised Mournblade.

The elf scrunched his eyes and gritted his teeth. The heat building in his hand was like a naked flame. His heart thundered in his chest. It wasn't long before the muscles in his arm began to seize and he feared he would be unable to release the crystal from his iron grip.

Aenwyn called out his name, though the words that followed were lost on the ranger. Everything he had was pouring into the crystal, preparing to tear through the fabric of reality.

"Now," he uttered, his voice just more than a whisper, but he couldn't be heard over the violence around him. "Now," he repeated, sure that the crystal would explode in his hand if he didn't release it soon.

Finally, Galanör's eyes snapped open and he called on the last ounces of his strength. "NOW!" he growled.

Unable to lift his arm and launch the crystal, the ranger used what control he had to simply drop it at his feet. Magic tore through the world and ripped open a portal from one place to another, taking Galanör with it. He fell through the hole with gallons of water and landed hard on the ruined ground of Davosai's surface. He tried to keep his eyes open under the deluge and crawl away from the portal fixed in the air above him.

Seconds later, Aenwyn and Gideon dropped through the portal, though only Aenwyn managed to stay on her feet. The old master rolled aside, narrowly missing the Darkakin that followed him through. An arrow from Aenwyn's bow caught the savage in the side of the head and ended the threat.

Galanör could only watch as the portal snapped closed, to be replaced by Ayda's night sky. Not far away, he saw Gideon rest his head against the ground and close his eyes, his midriff red with blood. He desperately wanted to reach his friend but his limbs refused to move.

Aenwyn rushed to the ranger's side, her face framed by stars. The ranger tried to speak, to encourage her to tend to Gideon. Instead, the words died on his lips and his vision fell prey to an enclosing darkness.

CHAPTER 45
'TIS LIFE

Vighon's eyes snapped open only moments before Sir Ruban entered his tent. The captain's expression was enough to inform the king that calamity was upon them. Already dressed, it took no time at all before he was mounting his horse alongside the captain and Sir Borin, his enormous guardian.

A pale and cold dawn had risen to meet them in the east and, with it, a light mist had blown in over the snowy fields. It was in that mist where Vighon discovered his enemy.

Reavers on horseback were steadily approaching like demons come to herald the end of the world.

Riding across the plain, Vighon spared a glance to the north and caught sight of Reyna and Nathaniel taking up positions amongst the elven ranks. Faylen could be seen shouting orders in her native tongue and her kin responding by nocking arrows.

The king set his steed to a gallop and joined his men as fast as he could. His gaze never strayed from the advancing Reavers as he dismounted and unclipped his cloak. He barely registered the soldier who took it from him or the one who handed him his shield. Feeling its familiar weight on his arm was enough to drag his eyes from the enemy. He squeezed the leather handle in his glove, bracing the shield close to his body.

Hadavad's enchantments still lingered, the ancient runes a part of the shield for evermore. It was a pity, the northman thought, that those enchantments would only protect him against magic. He faced steel this day. Steel and madness.

Pacing along the front line, he cast a critical eye over every man, checking for loose or ill-fitted plates. They were fine soldiers all and better prepared for battle since the supplies from Vangarth had arrived. There was, of course, a handful among them who couldn't hide their fear and he wasn't about to command them to do so. Fear was to be overcome with action, never quashed with words.

Trailing behind him, Captain Dardaris was barking orders across the ranks, ensuring the archers were the first to make themselves known. When the enemy was too close, they would fall back and be replaced by spearmen, who would be immediately backed up by row upon row of swordsmen.

Reaching the end of the line, Vighon had a clear view of the empty plain that lay between them and the elves guarding the pit's eastern perimeter. Commander Rolgoth of the Battleborns was in the process of marching his dwarves, accompanied by the Centaurs, across that empty plain, ready to fill out the smaller elven force. Still battle-weary, Vighon hoped that none of them, elf, dwarf or Centaur, would need to see violence.

"Your Grace." Ruban's tone quickly turned the king further north.

Vighon took what felt like his first breath in a week. Drakes, hundreds of them, were crossing The Moonlit Plains and making for the pit. The northman moved away from his soldiers and narrowed his eyes. They were too distant to make out individuals, though he was confident he could see Inara's red cloak as she led from the front. Sure that it was her, he looked to the sky in search of Athis. A single dragon would decimate the incoming Reavers.

There was no sign of him.

Clouds continued to roll ever westward, undisturbed by a

flying dragon. His absence weighed on Vighon. He couldn't fathom anything between here and Vangarth capable of slaying the iron-heart. It had to be the tree. Was he dead already? That and so many more questions demanded answers in the king's mind but, more than anything, he wanted to reach Inara.

The northman's attention shifted back to Reyna and the elves. A portion of their force was moving around the pit to meet the approaching Drakes, hopefully to escort them down to the doorway.

"Your Grace." Sir Ruban drew his focus back to the advancing enemy, all of whom were riding undead horses.

Vighon was already calling on his warrior's discipline to rid himself of the distraction of Inara's return, but seeing the Reavers' numbers up close did it for him. There were, indeed, hundreds of them, as he had feared when hearing that the city of Galosha was being emptied.

"They're still the smaller force," Captain Dardaris said so that only the king could hear him.

Vighon sighed. "I'm not sure numbers entirely count when one side fights without all the mortality of the living." Looking at his men, he could see that most of them were thinking something similar as their own thoughts and fears preyed on them. "PREPARE FOR BATTLE!" he bellowed.

Every soldier loyal to the banner of the flaming sword took steel in hand or nocked an arrow. Striding back down the front line, Vighon glimpsed a shadow in the pale sky, turning him to Avandriell in flight. Returning his sight to the ranks, he quickly found Asher staking his ground between a pair of Namdhorians. The ranger removed his two-handed broadsword from its scabbard and plunged it into the ground. Without pause, he snapped his bow to life and nocked an arrow like the others before offering the king a nod.

"From all four corners of the realm you have gathered!" Vighon shouted. "Our fate, scribed long before we were born, brought each and every one of us to this place! It brought us here for one reason and one reason only! We are here to protect that which is most precious: the future! Today, you don't just fight for family and you certainly don't just fight for king and country! Today, you fight for all the unborn sons and daughters of Illian! The blood you give will fill these sweet lands with generations for the next millennia! What say you?"

There wasn't a man present who didn't beat their shield, stamp their spear, or roar into the dawn. Vighon freed his sword and held it high, rallying their cry all the more. Flames or not, it was still the sword of the north and it was in the hand of the one true king.

Placing himself dead centre of the front line, Ruban beside him, the northman gripped his sword and shield and slowed his breathing down. To his left, Sir Borin the Dread stood with all the movement of a rooted tree. To be so calm, the king mused.

"Archers!" he yelled. Two hundred bows were aimed high, awaiting the command to unleash hell on the enemy. Vighon watched the undead riders begin to gallop towards them, armoured in black, unwavering in the face of true death. A little closer, he thought. A little closer. "Loose!" he shouted. A cloud of arrows feigned their reach for the heavens before raining down amongst the Reavers. "Fire at will!"

Three more salvos bit into the enemy's numbers before the spearmen slipped between the archers and stood their ground. Vighon tried not to be disheartened by the lack of Reavers brought down under the hail of arrows, for most had taken them to the chest or limbs, their charge unhindered. Even the undead mounts rode through it all with only a handful dropping to the ground.

The king quickly turned his head to Ruban. "Get behind the spears!"

The captain scowled. "What about you?"

"I have the strongest spear of them all," Vighon quipped, nodding his head in Sir Borin's direction.

Reluctantly - a display of bravery in itself - Sir Ruban Dardaris backed up and took his position beside Asher, who now had his broadsword in hand.

With a few seconds left, Vighon braced himself, crouched in a battle stance with his silvyr blade resting tip-first over the rim of his shield. There wasn't time for anything else after that. Sir Borin leapt forward and met the charging horse with his plated shoulder and supernatural strength. Both horse and rider were upended and shoved back into those behind. It created chaos on the front line and dented the enemy's attack, sparing Vighon a gruesome death.

A passing Reaver swung out wide with its sword and clipped the side of Sir Borin's helmet, turning the Golem back towards the Namdhorians. In that same movement, the hulking creature snatched one of the horse's back legs and brought it to a spine-shattering halt. The rider was flung forward, into the human ranks, while the undead horse succumbed to Sir Borin's thundering boot, a blow so powerful it caved in the animal's skull.

There was no stopping the Golem now.

Vighon was satisfied to leave Sir Borin to his horrifying work and get stuck in himself. The spearmen had done their job admirably and prevented most of the horses from breaking through the ranks. Absent their mounts, the Reavers were now on foot among the warriors of Illian and following their cruel master's wishes.

Considering the space available to them on The Moonlit Plains, the battle appeared to be confined to a small area. Vighon was made aware of this with every shoulder and back that barged into him, both friend and foe. More than once he turned on an ally with the point of his sword ready to end them, only to push them away and swing his blade into the enemy.

Hacking his way through the mess of it all, the only space he came across surrounded the ranger. The intensity and sheer mayhem of the battle around him appeared to have no effect on Asher's style of fighting, which was brutal and efficient, yet displayed all the grace of a dancer. He dropped Reavers on all sides, his green cloak flowing out beside him. The mounting bodies never tripped him up or got in his way. If anything, he often used them to his advantage, gaining some height over his opponents.

Vighon decided to lend his sword and fell in beside Asher. He utilised the extra space the ranger had forged and swung the sword of the north with all his might. He parried high and low before slamming his boot into a Reaver's chest, launching it into Asher's timely strike. Another came for the king's head but met his shield, raised just in time. A swift thrust drove his blade through the fiend's head and dropped it to the ground.

More closed in on the northman, perhaps sensing the threat he posed, and attempted to overwhelm him. Shedding their number, Asher spun around and flashed his steel from left to right, decapitating one of the Reavers with a single blow. Vighon shielded himself against another while parrying a second with his sword. No further action was required after that. Sir Borin barrelled his way through and ripped the head off one with his bare hands. Captain Dardaris, never far from his king, lunged in and cut down the other.

The king nodded his thanks and turned to face the next Reaver. There was always a next Reaver.

He pushed one of the fiends away with his shield, giving his swinging arm the perfect distance to come down and chop through its helmet and head. Nothing stopped the fine edge of a silvyr blade.

"Your Grace!" Ruban yelled, turning the king around. The captain was elevated above most, having mounted atop the pile of bodies Asher had created. "There's a second wave!" he warned.

Vighon parried and slashed his way to Ruban's side and cast his gaze over the furious melee. The captain was right; a second wave of mounted Reavers had held back from the initial attack, waiting, it seemed, for the northmen to be distracted in battle. Now, with no front-line defence to stop them, the Reavers were navigating around the chaos and heading towards the pit.

The king pointed his sword in their direction. "We can't let them reach the Drakes!"

Of course, there was no disengaging from the pitched battle that had already consumed him and his men. Once he descended the pile of bodies, it became increasingly hard to discern north from south amidst the blood and incessant attacks.

He did, however, glimpse Asher's green cloak disappearing

with haste.

~

The ranger burst out of the northern edge of the battle, his broadsword cleaving through a Reaver as he did. He staggered across the plain for a few steps, pausing briefly to place his sword in the ground and lean on it in a bid to catch his breath. His blue eyes scanned the landscape, tracking the second wave of Reavers riding towards the pit and approaching Drakes.

Asher cursed and hefted his blade before breaking into a run. He wasn't in the habit of leaving good men to die, but there was so much more at stake than the lives of Vighon and his warriors.

Halfway across the plain, he watched the Reavers collide with Commander Rolgoth and his burly dwarves. The Centaurs reinforced them, leaping over the first line of dwarves to meet the enemy head on. The elves added a volley of their arrows into those bringing up the rear, but the fight was certainly upon them now.

Glancing skyward, the ranger quickly located Avandriell, her wings keeping the dragon far from peril. Asher could sense her irritation, desperate to join the fight but struggling to find her place in it all. Though he hadn't told her to stay out of it, the ranger hadn't kept his feelings to himself, expressing his apprehension through their bond.

In truth, he was just glad to see the tree's slow death had yet to affect her. It hadn't escaped him that Athis had not returned with Inara. He kept going over Adan'Karth's words like a mantra, willing Avandriell to retain as much of her raw magic as possible until they could save the tree. Asher had always put a lot of stock in age and experience, but Avandriell's youth would be the single factor that saved her life.

Closing the gap between him and the secondary battle, the ranger was almost brought to a halt by what he saw. The Reavers hardly cared about engaging their fierce enemy, using their undead horses as nothing more than battering rams to get closer to the pit. They immediately freed themselves of their mounts, turned away from the rebels, and deliberately avoiding as much conflict as possible on their way to the edge of the pit.

Then they jumped.

In droves, the Reavers leapt with abandon into the shaft as the Drakes descended the walkway around the outer wall.

Sprinting the last fifty yards, Asher took up pursuit behind the last of the Reavers. Spotting him from above, Avandriell sent waves of concern across their bond. The ranger could only ignore them and do what any other would consider madness.

He leapt in after them.

The billowing green of his cloak was added to the black of the Reavers as he left the security of Illian's earth and plunged into darkness. The undead fiends slammed into everything from beams and walkways to bridges and pulley systems, their falling weight more than enough to splinter the wood. A handful of Drakes were caught in the downpour of bodies and taken to their deaths.

Mid-fall, Asher reached out with one hand and grasped a stray rope that flew across his path. In order to prevent any serious injury to his shoulder, the ranger immediately turned his momentum into a swing and aimed his body at the nearest bridge. He hit it hard and his knees objected to the impact, causing him to roll and, ultimately, slip between the gap in the railing supports. At the last second he succeeded in grabbing the ledge with both hands, though he was forced to let go of his broadsword in the process.

Heaving himself up, Asher quickly dived to one side, narrowly evading a Reaver who was making the leap from one of the pulley platforms onto the bridge. Since the dead required no time to recover, the Reaver advanced on Asher with a downward stroke of its sword. He heard the steel dig into the wood only a couple of inches away from his head, but the ranger already had his feet coming under him, ready to spring him back into the action.

The Reaver's next swing was blocked when Asher snatched at its wrist, halting the blow mid-strike. A firm hand to the side of its helmet, his footing perfectly braced, the ranger launched the fiend through the railing and over the side.

Further along the bridge, two more Reavers were picking themselves up after their fall, no mind given to their broken limbs. They sighted Asher but quickly turned to meet the Drakes rushing down the spiralling walkway.

"No!" Asher growled, too far to stop them from cutting down a pair of Drakes.

He exploded into a charge only to be knocked off his feet after the second step. The Reaver that had collided with him took them both through the railing and on to a swaying platform. A good deal of pain shot up one side of the ranger's body, but he didn't let it stop him from raising a boot and kicking the Reaver off the edge of the platform.

Rising to his feet, he looked up to see that the two Reavers who had attempted to stem the flow of Drakes were meeting their end. Had they ever possessed any real sense, they would have known not to challenge Inara Galfrey. Firefly was a blur in her hands, its deadly edge reducing her foes to pieces in seconds. Behind her, Kassian Kantaris broke away and stood his ground on the bridge, holding back another group of Reavers.

Arriving with a style all of their own, Reyna, Nathaniel, and Faylen descended the other side of the shaft at some speed. The rope taking their platform's weight, however, was clearly fraying, promising to release its hold on the lift altogether and drop them to their deaths. Seasoned warriors, they jumped from the platform only a moment before that eventuality and landed on another bridge just beneath Asher.

Having followed their descent, the ranger could see that all their problems were only just beginning. Reavers were picking themselves up in various places around the shaft and preparing to slaughter the passive Drakes. Asher grimaced, envisioning a lot more Drake deaths before they could reach the doorway at the bottom.

"We need to clear a path!" Inara shouted across to him.

Looking down, Reyna, Nathaniel, and Faylen had already taken up that task. The three warriors laid into the Reaver force, fighting with their backs together. Free of pain and fear, the undead fiends threw themselves relentlessly at the trio, some leaping from deadly heights to assault them.

Turning his head back to Inara, the ranger yelled, "Keep them going!"

Before pivoting away, he caught Adan'Karth's dragon-like eyes. The Drake's gaze held the ranger in place for a second, almost slowing the entire moment down. This was not how he wanted to say goodbye to his friend, a friend who had saved his life more than once and stuck with him through dark times regardless of the peril it had put him in. He hadn't wanted to say goodbye at all. But he also wanted to thank Adan for gathering so many of his people, theirs a sacrifice that would echo through the eons.

The moment was broken when Kassian returned from his skirmish on the bridge and ushered the Drake along with the others. Asher found his focus again and quickly planned his route back into the thick of it all. With no room to run, he was forced to jump from standing still, a leap that only just saw him grab hold of the broken beam in front of him.

His legs hanging, the ranger shimmied across until he could grasp the rope that was long enough to take him down to the next bridge. Applying his weight to the rope increased the strain on the broken beam. Inevitably, the wood snapped at one end and swung to the side of the shaft, taking Asher with it. Whether it was luck or fate - neither of which the ranger particularly cared for - he swung down perfectly in line with the surrounding walkway and half a dozen Reavers.

Raising both of his feet, he rammed into one of the fiends and slammed it against the wall of the pit. A strong shove pushed another Reaver back and gave the ranger the time he needed to retrieve the silvyr short-sword from over his shoulder. He met the first blade swung at his head with a two-handed parry. The silvyr bit into the Reaver's steel, weakening the whole sword. Asher's counterattack was more than enough to shatter the blade and continue through the side of the fiend's head.

The remaining five rushed towards the ranger, but the width of the walkway restricted them to two at a time. Asher dispatched the first pair with experienced efficiency, his shorter blade easily finding the gaps in his enemies' attacks. The three bringing up the rear posed no threat at all thanks to Inara and Kassian who, between them, created a frenzy of slashing steel. The Keeper was unlucky enough to be caught across the arm by one of the Reavers, though he still managed to lift his blade without issue.

"Keep moving!" Asher urged them all.

Following the walkway down and round, the ranger stole a glance up the shaft. The handful of Reavers who hadn't crashed down to the lower depths were being slain by the elves and dwarves, preventing them from attacking the Drakes from the rear.

With Inara and Kassian behind him, the ranger led the advance into the darkness below. He darted out across a connecting bridge and met the cluster of undead fiends homing in on their procession. Ducking under the first blade, Asher shoved the Reaver back, into Inara's waiting swing. The tip of his silvyr short-sword plunged through the narrow visor of the next and sliced neatly through the creature's head. Displaying her heritage, Inara moved past him to challenge the remaining Reavers, a touch of fury to her fighting style.

Firefly spun, slashed, and hacked the fiends to pieces in seconds, freeing Asher to leap over the rail and catch the edge of a platform with his hands. The ranger swung his legs forward and dropped down onto another bridge, bringing him side by side with Nathaniel. Mimicking old times, the two warriors fell into a battle routine that complemented the other.

The last Reaver to face them succeeded in batting Nathaniel's blade aside before landing a solid fist into his face, a blow that nearly saw him topple over the rail. Asher lunged to his friend's aid and reached out to pull him back from the rail.

"Watch your back!" Faylen's warning preceded her scimitar. The fine blade swept through the incoming Reaver's chest, staggering the fiend enough to keep it at bay.

Asher turned on his heel and added his attack to the High Guardian's, ending the threat altogether.

A little further down the bridge, Reyna was proving herself the best archer in the realm. Her enchanted bow, though a long-range weapon, did not hinder the elf when it came to close quarter combat. Between her powerful kicks and martial prowess, often intertwined with the use of her bow's deadly limbs, Reyna would launch her arrows with pinpoint accuracy. Never once did the chaos or threat of death stop her from taking the shot and bringing down a Reaver.

At the end of the bridge, Kassian was driving his sword through an enemy in a bid to keep it away from Adan and the others. He tilted his head at the last moment and evaded the swing of another blade by less than an inch. It seemed that even without magic the Keeper was a more than proficient fighter, a fact that elevated the man in Asher's eyes.

Inara dropped down between Kassian and her mother and hurried to the Keeper's side. Asher gave Faylen a nod of thanks and joined the others in aiding the Drakes. Continuing down, the companions were regularly forced to split up, taking to the adjoining walkways, bridges, and platforms that the Reavers attacked from. It pained Asher every time one of the fiends made it past their defence and killed a Drake, but they were dealing with a large force and reinforcements were stuck behind the hundreds of Drakes.

"Look!" Reyna shouted, directing them to the very bottom of the pit.

Asher rammed his short-sword up and through his opponent's head before pausing to look over the rail. The Reavers who had hit the hard ground at the base of the pit were filing through the rip in reality, crossing the threshold into the realm of magic, there to wait for the Drakes.

"We need to clear them out!" Nathaniel yelled from beside the ranger, his sword flashing high and low.

"We need to clear a path first!" Kassian pointed out, not far from the stonework now.

On the lowest bridge in the pit, Asher turned to the Galfreys and Faylen, all three having followed him to stem the largest flow of Reavers yet. With the last of the creatures lying at their feet, the four companions held a brief, but silent, conversation with their eyes alone.

Asher whipped his head around to Kassian and Inara. "Keep pushing forward! We'll secure the doorway!"

As they once did, decades earlier, the four companions leapt over the railing and dropped down to face their enemy together. Nathaniel and Asher had no choice but to hit the ground and drop into a roll lest they damage their feet and legs. Reyna and Faylen required no such measures, their landing secured with a simple crouch.

The Reavers guarding the stone steps broke away from the cells that had imprisoned the Drakes and challenged the most experienced warriors in the pit - a choice only the fearless could make.

The Galfreys especially worked well together, their fighting style unique to the pair and only achievable after decades of fighting side by side. Faylen was the demon Asher remembered, her focused fury not to be taken lightly. The ranger's back pivoted in time with the High Guardian's, allowing them to dispatch a Reaver each without fear of being flanked. One went high while the other went low, their strikes always timed perfectly to aid the other.

"Drop this?" Nathaniel called as he retrieved Asher's broadsword, the tip plunged into the ground.

Asher side-stepped a Reaver's blade and caught the two-handed sword. On reflex, he incorporated the weapon into his spinning attack. That same Reaver soon found an edge of steel biting through its neck, releasing the fiend from its master's strings. Its head rolling across the ground signalled the last of Alijah's puppets on this side of the doorway, though Kassian and Inara were still beating back the few who attacked from elsewhere.

"Keep going!" Inara shouted down at them. "We can take care of this!"

Reyna gave her daughter a nod and nocked another arrow on her bow. "Shall we?" The elven queen was the first to pass through the doorway and enter the realm of magic.

Asher paused for the briefest of moments and looked up to

catch Adan's eye. There was so much he wanted to say to the Drake and no time for a word of it. He poured as much as he could into his expression, hoping Adan could see everything he wished to convey, be it his hope for their success or his agony that his friend would soon sacrifice himself for the greater good.

Setting foot into the realm of magic, it would have been easy to have given in to the sheer majesty of it all and simply stood in awe of such an alien world.

To Asher, there was only the enemy in front of him.

Having sheathed his silvyr blade on his back, the ranger added his broadsword to the battle. They were fighting between two enormous roots, their ankles submerged in warm water, while smoke and ash from the fire swept over them all, lending the Reavers a wraith-like quality.

Catching one of the smaller roots, beneath the water, Asher lost his footing and took a swift backhand across the face. Staggering away, he was then clipped across the shoulder by a stray blade from one of the fiends fighting Nathaniel. Tightening his grip around the hilt of his broadsword, the ranger returned with a vengeance. His shoulder cried out in pain, protesting the might behind his swing, but it didn't stop him from adding another body to the tally.

Soon after, the first of the Drakes poured in through the doorway, guided by Kassian and Adan'Karth around the small battle. Inara was quick to join the skirmish, her Vi'tari blade never one to be left out of a good fight. In the presence of the Drakes, however, the Reavers became twice as hard to pin down and slay as they repeatedly attempted to slip through the gaps and target them. Asher even resorted to grabbing one by the cloak and yanking it back to face him.

Continuing in this vein, the ranger moved through his stances and put steel to steel. The Drakes flowed through one after the other, scaling the roots between the doorway and the trunk of the tree.

Asher had no idea how much time had passed before he realised there were no more Drakes coming through the doorway.

Looking back at it now, he could see elven soldiers daring to enter while the dwarves remained firmly on Illian soil.

Confident that the few remaining Reavers could be dealt with, Asher bashed the nearest Reaver around the head with his spiked pommel, kicked it back, and made for the shorter of the two surrounding roots. His broadsword slotted back into its scabbard a second before his hands found purchase on top of the root. Exhaustion threatened to claim the last of his strength but the ranger pushed on, his training having more than equipped him to do such a thing.

Elevated now, he could see the hundreds of Drakes not far away, gathering at the base of the tree which, in itself, almost floored Asher with its scale. Now he really had seen everything. He could also see enormous stalactites falling from the star-like ceiling. A few seconds after they impacted the ground, a shudder rippled across the extraordinary realm. Careful to keep his footing, Asher broke into the fastest run he could manage and made for the Drakes.

He didn't cross the distance with nearly as much grace as the Drakes had, but the ranger finally made it to the base. Looking left and right, he could see that they were spreading out so that all of them could touch the bark. Seeing them now, next to the mountain-like tree, he couldn't help but fear this was a lost cause.

That fear led him to Avandriell, who would surely die with the tree. It was then that Asher realised he could no longer feel his companion. Her most basic thoughts and feelings were entirely absent, leaving the ranger with a cold and hollow sensation in the pit of his stomach.

Catching sight of a hornless Drake, Asher shrugged off his ill-feelings and focused on the present again. He was desperate to reach Adan'Karth before he touched the tree.

Approaching the trunk, he watched as dozens of Drakes placed their hands to the snow-white bark and drop to their knees. Slowly but surely, they began to glow, as if the sun itself was in their veins. The skin became hardened and crusted to mirror the bark of the tree until they stood as wooden statues.

"Adan!" the ranger bellowed, halting the Drake from pressing his hand to the tree.

"Asher?" Adan stepped away from his kin and met his friend with confusion. "Why are you here?" he asked, glancing back at the tree. "Time is against us - it will take all of us to focus on the fires."

Asher stood before him, unsure now of what he had wanted to say exactly. "I... I just... It's not fair!" he shouted over the increasing wind. "You shouldn't have to do this!"

"There is no other way," Adan told him. "We have to try!"

Asher was shaking his head. "This should never have fallen on you - any of you! You had a second chance at life!" The ranger's shoulders sagged. "You spent so much of it saving me, over and over again. I'm so sorry, Adan. I'm so sorry. I failed you."

Adan gave him a warm smile and gripped his arms. "You have not failed, good ranger! Fate comes for us all! If my people were destined to do naught but save the world, I can live with that!"

Asher could feel tears in his eyes. "If you touch that tree, you won't be living with anything!"

The Drake offered him a knowing smile this time. "Every time you use magic, you will feel us in the currents that flow through you. Do not fear for us, Asher. It is not death we face this day. 'Tis *life*."

With that, Adan's hands slipped from Asher's arms and he turned back to the tree. The ranger gave in to his impulses and grabbed the Drake, pulling him into a tight embrace. "You will not be forgotten," he vowed.

Adan'Karth squeezed Asher once before extracting himself and moving deftly towards the tree. He slotted in between his kin and pressed his hand to the tree, accepting his fate. He fell to one knee before his pale skin took on a hue that could scarcely be viewed by the naked eye. As the brightness intensified, Adan looked back at Asher with one last smile, an image that the ranger would carry with him for the rest of his long days.

Then, the brightness died away, leaving a wooden extension of the tree where Adan'Karth had been kneeling. Up and down the base, the last of the Drakes were succumbing to the incomparable power of the tree. Craning his neck, Asher watched the fire intently, willing it to die out.

Nothing happened.

"Come on," the ranger muttered under his breath. "Come on!" he growled. He had no god to pray to, only faith in his friend. "You can do it," he insisted, wondering if he was already seeing a reduction in the size of the fire.

"Asher!" Nathaniel's voice turned the ranger around. "The doorway is closing!" he warned. "It's unstable! We need to leave, *now*!"

Asher didn't want to leave - he wanted to watch, he *needed* to watch.

"Asher!" Nathaniel yelled again. "Get moving! Before it's too late!"

Afraid that his friends would get stuck on this side of the doorway waiting for him, the ranger finally moved away from the wooden Drakes and joined Nathaniel on top of the root. They made all haste to return to the site of the doorway, regularly glancing back to scrutinise the flames. There seemed more smoke than fire now, a sight that sparked some hope in Asher.

Arriving at the small battle site, the doorway was, indeed, closing up, having already lost much of its height while its edges fluctuated and contracted. Reyna, Inara, Faylen, and even Kassian were still on this side of the doorway, all waiting for their friends. They would leave together or not at all.

"What happened?" Kassian asked, upon their arrival.

Asher met the Keeper's glistening eyes before turning back to the tree. "I think they saved us," he panted. "They saved us all."

The companions watched for a few seconds longer, noting the lack of flickering flames that had burdened the top of the tree. They were doing it, the Drakes were bringing magic back to the world.

The cost of it would haunt the ranger for evermore.

A hand gripped his shoulder and he ducked to follow Nathaniel and the others through the shrinking gap. Returned to a reality he recognised, Asher watched the doorway collapse on itself.

Avandriell filled his mind almost instantly and he felt her great elation upon reconnecting. It was a bittersweet moment for the ranger.

~

Under an empty and bitterly cold sky, Vighon Draqaro slipped in the mud as he came down, sword-first, on his foe. The steel slid down through the fiend's visor and face before slicing through the other side. There was little that could stand up to silvyr. When the king rose from his kill, bringing the blade with him, he marvelled as searing flames licked at the exquisite metal.

Vighon hardly had time to notice as he raised it high and parried an incoming blow. He could, however, feel the heat of those enchanted flames on his face. With renewed vigour, he spun his enemy's blade away and cleaved its head from its shoulders in one smooth motion. Stepping on its lifeless body, the king thrust the sword of the north towards the sky and roared with all the passion he could muster.

It rallied what strength remained in his men and they fought on with increased determination. Sure now that they would overcome, Vighon threw himself back into the battle and tore through his enemies with righteous anger. They had tried to tear down his kingdom and plunge the world into darkness and death. They would be made to pay, just as their master would.

It felt like an exhausting lifetime before the last of the Reavers was returned to the true death, their black husks cast into the mud with the rest. Vighon desperately wanted to sit down, if not lie down, and consume his bodyweight in water. His every muscle ached and he was steadily becoming aware of fresh wounds up and down his body. But then he saw her. Inara. Backed by familiar faces and a large group of elves, dwarves, and Centaurs, the Guardian of the Realm was walking towards him. Just the sight of her kept him on his feet, his head held high.

Like those behind her, Inara wore a forlorn expression. Had the flames not returned to his sword, the king would have assumed the Drakes had failed and that magic was lost to them forever.

Instead, it was their sacrifice that weighed on them all and rightly so.

Fighting his battle fatigue, Vighon sheathed the sword of the north and moved to meet his love. They drew together in a tight embrace, oblivious to each other's odour and filthy appearance.

"They did it," she uttered, her own fatigue coming through in her voice. "Adan, his kin, all of them. They gave themselves to the tree. They're gone."

"They will be remembered as heroes," Vighon promised.

Inara's eyes looked past the king. "Where are Gideon and Ilargo?"

"Look!" someone shouted in the distance, shattering their moment. "They're coming from the south!"

Vighon swore under his breath and moved with Inara to get a better look. Beyond the battleground, a dark stain was riding over the snowy plains, heading towards them. "They must have come from Tregaran," the northman reckoned, thankful that their longer journey had kept them from the previous battle.

Turning to his men, he knew he needed to call on them, but how could he? Every one of them had given their all to prevent reinforcements from overwhelming those in the pit.

But what choice did he have?

"Men of the flaming sword!" he cried, freeing his fiery blade once more.

The king was proud to see so many rally to him, ready to fight for The Rebellion. Behind him, Asher was drawing his broadsword, the last to do so among the Galfreys and their elven warriors. Kassian spun his wand around between his fingers before stopping to admire the small glare of light that ignited at its tip. Only Inara stood without her trusted Firefly in hand, the Vi'tari blade still resting on her hip. It was the hint of a smile, however, that brought a question to Vighon's expression.

"Wait for it," she said, her eyes fixed on the advancing Reavers.

The king's curiosity took form in his mouth but the words never left his lips. The answer cast a shadow over them all.

He saw now that the sword of the north was nothing compared

to a dragon, for Athis the ironheart rallied every man, dwarf, elf, and Centaur: a mighty roar exploding from deep in their chests. They cheered him on as he soared across the sky, cutting through the air like a scaled spear. In no time at all, the red dragon had flown well beyond The Rebellion's camp and was now angling down towards the Reavers from the south.

Athis scorched the earth.

His first jet of fire cut them down the middle, sending at least a hundred back to the afterlife. Banking to the west, he quickly came back around and unleashed his fiery breath upon the fiends. An inferno consumed the southern horizon as a column of black smoke wafted up to the heavens. After several minutes, his final pass finished those lucky enough to have escaped his previous attacks, ridding The Moonlit Plains of the last Reavers.

The Rebellion gave a resounding cheer, celebrating their victory as a whole. Only those who truly understood why hundreds of Drakes had gone down into that pit and never returned maintained their sombre expressions.

Athis landed on the snow, directly in front of them. Inara didn't hesitate to meet her companion and share a quiet moment, their heads bowed together. Vighon could only imagine the anguish of their recent separation and was filled with joy to see them together.

"It is done," Reyna announced, though her words carried no further than those on the council. "Alijah and Malliath have been proven fallible."

"And with them The Crow," Nathaniel added smugly.

"The latter remains to be seen," Inara replied, her eyes scanning the area.

Vighon looked to Reyna and Nathaniel. "We will take the day and night; give our forces the rest they deserve. Tomorrow, at first light, we make for The Black Wood and join Doran."

"And then?" Kassian queried.

Vighon took in the sight of those around him, all as tired as he was and sick of war. "Then we end it," he declared.

CHAPTER 46
ETERNAL COMPANIONS

T he midday sun beat down over Ayda's southern lands, its intense light pressing upon Gideon Thorn. Even with his eyes closed, the brightness urged him to awaken from the depths of his great slumber. Slowly, his eyes began to flutter as they adjusted to the oppressive light.

"He's waking," someone said.

A moment later, his mind caught up with his surroundings and he realised it had been Aenwyn who had spoken. He was also aware of the desert heat now, reminding him where he was. With that thought, he remembered where he had been.

The Darkakin!

Willing his eyes to open, the old master took in his environment, eager to be free of his disorientation. He was lying on his back amidst the ruins of one of Davosai's shattered buildings. Above, the sun had found a crack in the debris and shone over his face. To his right, Aenwyn was approaching from another corner of the ruins. Gideon was pleased to see that she was unharmed except for a few cuts and bruises - a testament to her skill given where they had escaped from.

There was movement behind her, guiding the old master to

Galanör who, like him, was lying in the rubble under his blue cloak. He possessed no injuries that Gideon could see, but the elf possessed a haggard look about him.

Aenwyn crouched by Gideon's side. "How do you fair?" she asked softly, her hands probing the area around his ribs. "You've been unconscious since we portalled back to the surface." A broad grin spread across her face. "You've spent the time well it seems - this is healing nicely."

That surprised Gideon, for he recalled the weapon that had pierced his side and the subsequent blood loss. He adjusted his shirt to better inspect the skin, though it was hard to see clearly due to all the dried blood around the area. He felt the momentary sting as his finger brushed the wound.

Then it occurred to him, the truth of the matter.

There was only one reason he could heal so quickly and the source of it stemmed from his closest companion. But Ilargo's light had been fading, his life entwined with the tree of magic...

The green dragon cast a quick shadow over the ruins as his awesome form landed on the ground before the trio, his wings fanned out to increase his majesty. Regal in his stance, Ilargo looked down at Gideon with his sparkling blue eyes. There was so much life behind them.

"They did it," Gideon uttered in disbelief.

Beside him, Aenwyn held up her hand and cast a frost spell that sent cold vapour into the air around her fingers. "They did it," she beamed.

I am whole again! Ilargo exclaimed before bowing his head to focus his sharp eyes on Gideon's wound. *And so are you it seems.*

With tears in his eyes, Gideon rushed forward and pressed himself against Ilargo's head. His green scales were warm again and his golden speckles had returned with their exceptional gleam. **I thought I was going to lose you,** he confessed.

You almost did, Ilargo replied. *Though I dread to dwell on the cost of our victory,* he added dourly. *Lives have been spent. We can only hope there are Drakes left to grace this world.*

Gideon nodded gravely and patted the dragon's scales. **I fear** *those added to the dead will only fuel the fires for Alijah's execution. He moves ever further from redemption.*

Redemption or not, Ilargo said, *we now have the means to bring this wretched war to an end.*

The dragon's words turned Gideon back to Galanör. His pale skin was all the more obvious when contrasted with his dark sunken eyes. Despite his drained appearance, the elven ranger looked back at the old master with a smile. The Hastion gem flashed a brilliant blue on his finger as he reached out and gripped the old satchel, propped up against a broken wall.

"We did it," he croaked.

Gideon mirrored his friend's smile and moved to crouch by the elf's side. "*You* did it," he praised. "Opening two portals so close together isn't just hard it's dangerous. We would never have got down there and back without you, never mind escaping the Darkakin."

"What do we do now?" Galanör questioned. "I only ask because I have big plans to sleep for the next week - perhaps we could put off saving the world until then."

Gideon was thankful the elf still had some humour in him. "As soon as you're able to sit on Ilargo without falling off, we should begin our journey back to Illian. I'm not sure the world can wait."

"That is not today," Aenwyn pointed out, a hint of firmness in her voice.

"I agree," Gideon said. "In the meantime, we should look for better shelter and fresh water. We could..." He trailed off seeing a look of amusement on Galanör's face. "What is it?"

"We both know there's only one thing you want to do right now," the elf told him. "There's time. Just go."

Gideon held his expression before it broke and he glanced back at Ilargo. "We might better spot what we need from the air..."

"Go!" Galanör insisted, his smile broadening.

Gideon and Ilargo didn't need any more than that. The old master found his familiar place at the base of the dragon's neck and braced himself for the most exhilarating feeling there was.

After breaking into a sprint, Ilargo's wings unfurled and beat hard towards the ground. In seconds the world was falling away, the pair beckoned by the heavens.

It was glorious.

PART FOUR

CHAPTER 47
A MASTER'S WRATH

Through the eyes of the dead, the world was laid bare for the most powerful necromancer to have ever walked the earth. Alijah Galfrey looked out on the snowy Moonlit Plains, his time limited. The Reaver he commanded had been added to a burning pile and soon the flames would rob him of one more soldier.

Besides the cheering and general celebration taking place among the rebels, there was one thing that captured his attention, one thing that set a fire in his veins. There in the sky, flying with exuberance, was Athis the ironheart.

Soon after, Alijah's sight was engulfed by flames as the Reaver succumbed to its burning fate. The king withdrew from his undead servant and opened his real eyes to the throne room of The Bastion.

"HOW?" he raged, erupting from Atilan's throne.

His wrath manifested itself in the form of a spell and exploded outwards from his entire being. The stone floor rippled and broke apart around his feet. The throne behind him, a relic that had survived the eons, was reduced to pieces and launched towards the back of the hall.

He opened his mouth to bellow the same question but froze as a savage roar could be heard from beyond The Bastion's black stone. A burning fury had ignited in Malliath's heart, a feeling that soon took physical form when the dragon unleashed a torrent of fire into the air, the flames seen through the narrow slits in the far wall.

Alijah's seething anger was white hot, demanding he use his voice. "How could they do this?" he growled, storming towards the main doors.

A flick of the wrist and a touch of magic would have been sufficient to open the doors, but the half-elf threw his hand at them and cast a far more powerful spell. The doors were instantly ripped from their hinges and launched onto the frozen steps that had been carved into the plateau. A blasting wind slammed into the king, dragging his cloak out and up as high as his neck.

Alijah's hair whipped about his face as he turned to look upon his companion, whose black scales blended in with The Bastion.

The dragon dropped down from his perch with a ground-shaking quake and turned his horned head on Alijah, his purple eyes boring into him. *You were to do what I could not!* Malliath fumed.

Alijah's mind split open and the ancient dragon poured his rage inside, dropping the king to his knees in agony. Millennia of images, sounds, and experiences bombarded his smaller mind. Malliath made him relive the worst parts of his existence, ensuring that Alijah felt every spell and shard of steel that had pierced his scales and hide. Through it all, the king screamed, his pain spreading across The Vrost Mountains.

Your hands were to open the pages I could not, Malliath continued, his voice cutting through it all. *Magic has ever been at the fingertips of you mud-walkers and your precious books! It's not fair! I am magic incarnate! I am as old as the mountains, my mind as deep as the oceans. Yet your kind has lorded over the realm with absolute power. You were a gift. You were to be my hands, to delve into the magic hidden from me.* Malliath stalked across the plateau and loomed over Alijah. *You have failed me.*

Alijah wanted to look away from those terrible eyes, from the judgment, but he couldn't move. His body was trapped in the thrall of Malliath's memories. They continued to fill him up, taking him back to countless wars throughout history.

Alijah relived a moment from thousands of years past, when a Jainus mage had struck the dragon with a spell so wicked it flayed one of his back legs. From there, he was transported to a brawl between Malliath and a rogue dragon, the two fighting for territory in a time before the great Riders. The rogue dragon clubbed him around the face with a tail of spikes. The damage done was agonising and it took most of the next year to recover his left eye.

Taking the half-elf back even further, Malliath recalled his part in the fight against the last of the Leviathans as the dragons chased it into The Hox. Malliath, a young dragon at the time, had made the mistake of landing on the behemoth's black hide, a surface that bubbled and oozed with a toxic acid. There had been no cure, only pain for weeks and weeks. Alijah lived every day of it in seconds.

Then there were the mage knights of Atilan, who brought the dragon down with Crissalith and harvested more than half of his scales before Garganafan intervened, saving his life. Malliath made sure Alijah felt every scale that was torn from his body.

And on and on it went. There was no end to the torment that had befallen Malliath the voiceless. It fuelled his rage, bolstered his wrath, and plagued him with a mind of fury for all time.

When next Alijah opened his eyes, he was standing in the broken doorway of the main hall, his breath even and hair immaculate. He looked at the twisted doors, half-covered in snow. His memory stitched the scenes together, making him aware that he had just struck the doors with a spell. Any curiosity surrounding the amount of snow that buried the doors was erased and, with it, he lost his grasp on the passage of time. A strong wind was sucked into the hall, throwing his cloak out, before he strode outside to find Malliath for what felt like the first instance.

He found the dragon, sitting like a gargoyle, in front of The Bastion's outer wall. He was perfectly still, his purple eyes lost to the mountains around them. Alijah could feel the cold calculating fury that quietly resided in his companion. In some ways, it was more terrifying than a feral outburst such as his own.

Alijah moved towards him, his fist clenching with the anger that swelled in him. He quickly unfurled his fingers, however, when they protested with a painful ache. The half-elf simply explained the pain away as fatigue from his recent over-use of magic in general.

"How could they do this?" he asked again. Malliath continued to stare at the distance, his mind closed to Alijah. Using their bond, the king tried again. *I said, how could they do—*

I heard what you said, Malliath interjected, his eyes never straying. *You saw all that I did,* he continued, referring to the Drakes that flooded the realm of magic.

They used the Drakes against us, Alijah complained as he paced in the blistering cold, protected by his scale mail. **How could this have happened? The Crow orchestrated their creation for our purposes. He would have seen this. He** must **have! We are to rule - he foresaw it! Have we been betrayed? Have we...** The king trailed off as his mind succumbed to the controlling influences of Malliath.

Calm yourself, the dragon bade, preventing Alijah's thoughts from spiralling. *Everything that challenges us is part of a greater design, The Crow's design. We will only grow stronger, and tales of our victories will only spread further when we have faced the mightiest of foes. Magic or not, we will crush this rebellion. Then, we will destroy the elves - abominations in the eyes of nature - and the threat of their magic will be destroyed with them. We will...* Malliath winced and exhaled a slight groan, exposing some of the injuries along his neck. *If we cannot erase magic, we will simply wipe out any and all who know how to wield it.*

Alijah stopped rubbing his neck as the last of the dragon's words sank in. **Yes,** he agreed. **With fire and steel we will bring the world to heel... for its own good.**

The dragon cast his eyes over Vilyra, who was patrolling the mountain pass astride her dragon, Godrad. *This victory will make them bold,* Malliath remarked. *And we shall let them be bold. Let them gather their meagre forces. The Rebellion will wash over The Vrost Mountains like water on rock: they will make no difference. The Bastion has stood for thousands of years and it is our territory. We control it.* He finally looked down at the king. *Let us prepare.*

CHAPTER 48
THORGEN'S BLOOD

After a long and tiring nine days on the road, Doran Heavybelly finally looked upon the trees of The Black Wood. The journey had been arduous and longer in places where a degree of stealth had been required - no easy task for a dwarf and even harder for Warhogs. But, at last, there he was, standing before the forest that concealed so many of his people, families mostly.

His family.

Despite the chill that surrounded him, the dwarf could feel the palms of his hands becoming clammy. He wasn't sure what he would find in there and a part of him didn't want to discover the truth. But he hadn't come this far to sit idly in his saddle. In fact, he had a feeling his days of sitting idle were long past him now.

A tap of his heels set Pig to a trot, closing the gap between them and the wood. Behind him, a modest escort of a hundred and twelve dwarves trailed diligently. There had been a few among them who had complained about their journey, but Doran had heard the whispers that silenced them, whispers of what they would witness in The Black Wood. It seemed the entire company wished to be present to see history unfold before their eyes. All but Doran.

Finishing the last leg of their great trek, the dwarven company finally emerged from the trees and entered one of the vast clearings where the heart of the rebellion had long camped - a hub of advanced civilisation compared to what they had left on The Moonlit Plains. Dwarves, humans, and even a few elves ceased their roaming to pay homage to the battle-weary dwarves. Doran lowered his hood and bowed his head at those they passed, appreciating the respect he thought he would never again receive from his kin.

As they progressed through the camp, people of every race approached the riders and offered them fresh food and water. Unlike those behind him, Doran declined them all, his appetite having dwindled from the moment they passed into the northern realm. Instead, his eye was on the largest tent in the middle of the sprawling camp. There, either side of the entrance, he could see the banners of his clan flapping in the wind.

Before reaching it, the War Mason was impressed to see that several forges and sturdy workstations had been erected, the heat from which washed over the side of his face. Wherever they were in the world, the children of the mountain could not be stopped from reshaping the natural gifts of Grarfath and Yamnomora. It almost brought a smile to Doran's face. Almost.

The son of Dorain was soon dismounting Pig and standing before the royal tent, his journey at an end. He dismissed Thraal and Thaligg with a look and the pair dispersed his unspoken orders to seek shelter and rest while they could. Doran had to face this next part on his own.

The guarding Heavybellys bowed their heads as he passed them by and entered the deep blue tent. There was little light inside, the flaps closed to keep in the heat. Torches and a hearth in the centre brought firelight to the environment, though Doran almost missed the sight of his mother altogether, her black dress absorbing the light.

His lips moved to call her name but the word got stuck in his mouth when he looked beyond her, to the single bed that occupied the tent. Dakmund lay upon it, his skin still a sickly pale colour and exaggerated all the more by the dark veins. Worse still, there was no sign of the encapsulating spell that had been keeping him suspended. He was so still that Doran feared the worst had already happened in his absence. The War Mason took his first breath, however, when he witnessed his younger brother utter something, drawing their mother's ear to his face. Whatever Dakmund said, it turned the queen mother to her oldest son.

"*Doran*," she croaked, moving to greet him. Before taking him into her embrace, Drelda paused to look her son up and down. The spark of hope she had expressed slowly died away, leaving a lump in her throat. "*You do not have it,*" she observed in their native tongue. "*You do not have the blade. We cannot discover the truth of the spells that spur on the poison...*" The lump got the better of her, stealing her words.

Doran reached out and pulled his mother in as she began to sob. He muttered his apology over and over again but nothing he said was enough to make the queen mother embrace him back; she simply rested her head on his shoulder and quietly wept.

"*When did the spell fade?*" he asked, breaking his mother's grief.

"*Yesterday morning,*" she replied, stepping away from him. "*The elves in the camp know nothing of the magic that kept him alive - they left with Queen Adilandra.*"

That magic wasn't keeping him alive, Doran thought. It was just prolonging the inevitable. "*Queen Adilandra perished on Qamnaran,*" he told his mother. "*She and many more have died since last we saw each other,*" he added, unable to say Russell's name. "*I came back to... to...*" The dwarf couldn't find the words now that he stood before his family.

"*You came back,*" Dakmund breathed, "*to say... goodbye... brother.*"

Doran glanced at his mother, who ushered him on with a short nod. Moving to his brother's side, he perched on the edge of the bed and cast his eye over him. Dakmund had always been broad in the shoulders, his build larger than Doran's. The War Mason had always thought it ironic given his preference for the arts over war, but he had always loved his brother for being the dwarf he was. Now, sadly, he appeared frail, his size diminished by the poison that had spread throughout his once strong body.

Tentatively, he took Dakmund's hand in his own. Doran's brow twitched as he failed to conceal his surprise at how cold his brother's fingers were. He couldn't help but think of Russell's hand, at the end.

Dakmund slowly turned his eyes on Doran. "*Grarfath has... walked with you... I see.*" His every word was a labour, draining him of what precious life he had left.

A lone tear instantly broke free of Doran's eye. "*I don't know how you can say that. I have failed you, brother. I could not retrieve the blade.*"

Dakmund gave the subtlest shake of his head. "*You... are here,*" he managed. "*How else... could you have... crossed all the hells... if the Father was... not walking with you?*"

The oldest son of Dorain nodded along, unable to argue. "*I can't decide if I am blessed or cursed,*" he confessed. "*I do not want to live only to say farewell to those around me.*"

With his free hand, Dakmund called on all his strength and pointed at a small chest beside his bed. "*Open it,*" he whispered.

Doran let go of his brother's hand and retrieved the small chest, easily carried in two hands. Returning to his perch beside Dakmund, the War Mason rested the chest on his lap and unlocked the latches on the lid. It creaked as he opened it and an old musty smell found his nose.

"*Take it,*" Dakmund insisted.

Doran put the chest aside. When his hands returned, they brought with them the crown of Grimwhal. He was very familiar with it having seen it atop his father's head all his life. He realised then that this was the first time he had ever held the crown. Thinking back, it was easy to believe that it had been a part of his father's skull, permanently attached.

He turned it over and over in his hands, feeling the cool silvyr between his fingers. It was jewelled in places though not overly so - the sapphires and rubies small enough to almost blend in with the crown's intersecting pattern of lines. The silvyr rose up at four different points around the circlet, their harsh lines removing any possibility that it could ever be described as delicate.

"*Do they live?*" Dakmund croaked. "*The other kings... do they live?*"

Doran turned back to his brother. He opened his mouth to explain the circumstances of King Gaerhard's death, but Dakmund's time was limited and didn't require filling up with needless details. "*No,*" he said instead. "*You are the last king of Dhenaheim, Dak.*"

There was no change to Dakmund's expression. "*Our clan?*" he asked.

"*We are strong,*" Doran explained. "*Unfortunately, there is no other clan who can boast of our numbers anymore. We saved all that we could though, and at the price of Heavybelly lives.*"

"*Then... you have made... heroes of our people.*" Dakmund slowly reached out and attempted to squeeze Doran's hand. "*They will... look to you... now, brother. You must undo... the failures... of our ancestors. Unite Dhenaheim. Make us... whole again. You must... do this... while we are... strong.*"

Doran wanted to offer his brother hope and tell him he might still recover, that he might still live to be king of all Dhenaheim. But even now, Dakmund looked to have lost some life since they began their conversation. It wouldn't be long.

With the crown in one hand and his brother's in the other, Doran looked Dakmund in the eyes. It saddened him to see so little of the creative dwarf he had always known. "*I don't know if I can,*" he admitted. "*I don't know if I have the courage, let alone the supporters, to be king. Not without you by my side.*"

Dakmund blinked once, and slowly, his eyelids almost sticking together. "*You have walked... the lonely road... of a ranger... for over... a century. You know... how to survive the wilds... of the world. You were meant... for this... from birth.*"

At the bottom of the bed, a small moan escaped their mother's lips before she buried her face in a handkerchief. Like Doran, Drelda could see the end was fast approaching.

"*I do not deserve this,*" Doran continued, holding up the crown. "*I cannot be king because I failed to save you.*"

"*You will be king... because Thorgen's blood... runs through your veins. And you will be... king... because Grarfath himself... has brought you... to this place in time.*" A flicker of the old Dakmund flashed behind his eyes as he added, "*Also... you have father's head.*" His subsequent laugh descended into a rough coughing fit that ended with blood running from his mouth.

Doran managed a smile at his brother's humour, if only for his benefit. "*Do you suffer?*" he questioned. "*We can get you some relief.*" He turned to his mother who directed the War Mason to the empty vials on the other side of the bed.

"*My pain... is almost over.*" Dakmund's gaze gradually wandered from Doran, to their mother, before finally settling on the tent above. "*Unite them... Doran. Be better... than those who... came... before...*"

His last word was taken to the great Hall of Grarfath with him.

Tears streamed down one side of Doran's cheek as he carefully closed his brother's eyes. Drelda fell to her knees at the base of the bed and wept into the blankets, the light of her youngest son finally extinguished. Doran squeezed Dakmund's hand before placing it by his side. His fingers hesitated, insistent on maintaining a hold on him. But he was gone, and into better company at that.

"*The open arms of Yamnomora await you now, brother. Save me a seat in the Hall.*"

Doran picked up his mother and swaddled her in his arms. He held her close and let her weep into his shoulder while they shared in their grief. They remained that way for some time, until the queen mother needed to sit down. Doran offered to call someone and have her taken care of elsewhere, but she insisted on staying by Dakmund's side for now. Who was he to tell a mother otherwise?

With heavy feet and his father's crown held in one hand, the only living son of Dorain walked out of the tent to a waiting audience. It seemed every dwarf in the camp had gathered round after he had entered to find his brother. In the middle of them all, Thraal and Thaligg stood side by side with ashen faces. They all knew the truth of the matter.

Doran declared, *"King Dakmund, son of Dorain, ruler of Grimwhal... my brother... has ascended to the Hall of Grarfath with all honour. Let it be known that he fell defending our city, our home, and our lives. His last act as king was a heroic one. He will be remembered in our history, his name never forgotten."* The dwarf sighed and dropped his head to his chest. *"The king is dead,"* he muttered despairingly.

Thaligg and Thraal stepped forward, the first to bend the knee and lower their gaze to the ground. Their response rippled across the gathering with dwarves following their lead by the dozen. Doran cast his eye from right to left, watching them all drop to one knee before him, until he came across a familiar young dwarf. It was Finrig, son of Fearn, the Hammerkeg who had volunteered to join his company. Finrig bowed his head once before taking the knee with the others. He wasn't the only dwarf of another clan who showed their respect and allegiance, for Doran noted three Goldhorns, a pair of Brightbeards, and even a Battleborn drop down.

The son of Dorain tightened his grip around his father's crown - *his* crown - and looked down at it. Everything was going to change now.

CHAPTER 49
PALIOS

The days following the victory on The Moonlit Plains had been bitterly cold, the realm truly within winter's hold, but those of The Rebellion had found warmth in their daily camps, the fires sustained by *magic*. Under the shadow of Athis, they had also journeyed across the land with their heads held high, for none dared to challenge them.

On the sixth day, having crossed The Unmar at Barden Bridge and broken away from the road to travel north across the land, Vighon looked upon the high walls of Palios, the city of knowledge. It was the second largest city in the region of Alborn, after Velia and, more significantly, home to the All-Tower.

After getting back onto The Selk Road to approach Palios, the All-Tower grew ever larger as it loomed over the heart of the sandy-coloured city. All four of its walls, which narrowed from bottom to top, were lined in text telling one thousand years of human history in Illian.

Unlike Velia, whose walls were lined with gargantuan statues of the region's most famous kings, the road to Palios was lined with twenty-foot statues of ancient scholars, the first men to compile the records from across the realm and build a home for the most powerful thing in all of Verda: knowledge.

Like Velia, however, Palios was protected by a forbidding pair of enormous doors. And they were sealed shut. In all his time, not only as king but as a rogue, Vighon had never known the gates of Palios to be locked. A quick word to Sir Ruban had a couple of scouts ride on ahead to inform the city's guards that they had soon to be open. The northman didn't want to be seated in his saddle for a moment longer than he needed to.

He looked to his right to ask Inara her opinion on the matter, thankful that she had decided to ride beside him; if only for the day. Seeing her pensive expression though, the king asked her a different question.

"Are you still mad?" He was careful to use an even tone, lest he sound as if he was suggesting she had descended into sulking after six days.

"Perhaps," she replied, her voice leaving no doubt that she was.

Vighon took a breath while composing a slightly different speech to the one he had heard Reyna give her. "Gideon is only doing what he thinks is right."

"Gideon's problem is always thinking he *is* right," Inara countered. "I just can't believe my mother agreed with him. It was a crucial time; The Rebellion was vulnerable. Even if Ilargo hadn't been able to help, Gideon and Galanör are among the best swordsmen in the realm. And Aenwyn can rival my mother with a bow."

Vighon glanced over his shoulder to make certain their words could not be overheard. "We still found victory without them," he pointed out. "The tree was saved. Magic is no longer under threat. And besides, their mission has its own role to play. Alijah and Malliath won't even have considered Crissalith; that makes it a powerful weapon."

"You're assuming they find any," Inara responded. "They could be looking for a needle in a haystack."

"If anyone can, it's them," Vighon replied optimistically.

"To what end?" Inara muttered.

Vighon frowned at the Guardian. He couldn't hide his frustration; especially after six days. "To *the* end," he told her. "You heard what your mother said. The Crissalith will separate Alijah from Malliath. Divided, they will be more easily defeated."

"We both know that is not the reason Gideon has flown all the way to Ayda," Inara countered. "And it's the same reason why my mother was happy for them to go."

Vighon nodded to himself, sure that they were getting to the truth of her ire now. "You do not want redemption for your brother," he stated.

"Do you?" Inara put back to him.

Vighon didn't answer right away, his gaze taking a moment to drift across the land. "I want my kingdom back," he finally said. "I want my people to live without fear. I wouldn't mind mounting Malliath's head in the throne room. Do I want you to lose your brother? Your parents to lose their son? Do I want to lose my oldest friend?" That last one brought back so many memories for the northman: experiences by Alijah's side that clouded his judgment.

"Sometimes I wonder if his would be a death too many," he continued. "Selfishly, I wonder that because I know his death would affect those closest to me. The realm is filled with people - many of whom are right behind us - who have already suffered the loss of those closest to them. As their king, I know I should avenge those deaths and kill the one responsible. There have certainly been many times when I can think of nothing but running him through with my sword." Vighon paused to look at Inara. Her features had softened but she maintained an air of resolution where the subject was concerned. "In the moment though," he added, "I imagine Alijah won't give us a choice. We will be forced to kill him or be killed ourselves, Crissalith or not."

"In the moment?" Inara repeated incredulously. "The moment has passed. We are already without a choice."

Vighon sighed inwardly and nodded in agreement. "Perhaps you are right," he lamented. "Either way; I believe Gideon's decision to be the right one. Had I been present, I would have encouraged them to go."

Inara continued to ride beside him in silence, though her thoughts might as well have been on the outside.

"Just say it," Vighon urged. "I can see it's killing you."

"You would have been wrong," Inara was quick to say, her tone low enough to reach Vighon alone.

Vighon couldn't help but smile. "I'm allowed to be wrong. Such are the privileges of being king."

Inara rolled her eyes. "You're insufferable."

"You know, if you were... *queen*, we would have to make all of our decisions together. We could be *wrong* together," he said, hoping to bring some levity to their conversation.

Inara turned to lay her blue eyes on him. "That, Vighon Draqaro, is *not* a proposal. Though you would be wrong far less of the time," she added with a hint of a smile.

Vighon realised it was the first he had seen on her face since Athis had returned with all his considerable strength. Whatever their future, the northman knew there and then that making Inara smile was his reason for living.

"When the time comes," he said, adopting a serious tone once more, "we will face Alijah and Malliath together. And whatever happens, we will live with the consequences together."

Inara reached out and squeezed his hand, a genuine look of appreciation on her face. "Together," she echoed.

"Your Grace!" The call drew their attention to the road ahead, where both scouts were quickly returning on horseback.

Captain Dardaris intercepted them first. "Report!" he commanded.

"They do not answer to our calls, Captain," one of the Namdhorians replied. "There sounds to be a battle taking place."

"A battle?" Vighon scowled as he narrowed his vision at the gates. There did, indeed, appear to be people moving frantically atop the walls but the details were still hazy from this distance.

Without a word to Ruban or his men, the king set his mount to a gallop and rushed ahead of The Rebellion. He was quickly followed by Inara and the captain before the bulk of the force caught on and hastened after the northman. Closing the gap, he witnessed a man fall to his death from the top of the wall, shortly followed by a pair of Reavers, one of which had a spear impaled through its chest. The fiends crashed into the ground and struggled to rise with so many broken bones, but rise they did - just in time to glimpse the flaming sword of the north.

From atop his horse, Vighon cut down the closest Reaver with a single strike across the head, before kicking the second back. An arrow whistled past him and took the Reaver in the face. The fact that the Reaver's head exploded and the arrow continued until it drove into the stone of Palios identified the archer as Reyna. Looking over his shoulder, he saw the elven queen was hanging over the side of her saddle, another arrow already nocked.

Bringing his horse to a halt, he could hear the fighting taking place above - the clash of swords, the screams of men, and the wretched howls of Alijah's twisted Seekers. "We need to get up there!" Vighon yelled to his arriving forces.

"I can do up," Inara remarked, jumping down from her horse before it even came to a stop.

Beside the road, Athis thundered to the ground with such might that he rattled Palios's towering doors. Inara had been running towards the dragon before he landed and was quick to ascend to his back. Not one to miss a good fight, Asher was close on the Guardian's heels before he too climbed onto Athis's back. One beat of his wings cleared them from the ground and one more brought them in line with the top of the wall, ideal for Inara and Asher to leap from the dragon's head to the battlements. Even Avandriell followed them into the action, her bronze scales glimmering in the sunlight.

That was the last Vighon saw of the pair and the young dragon. Athis continued higher into the sky before vanishing somewhere over the city. Behind the king, Reyna shouted something in elvish - reminding the northman that he really must get round to learning the language. The meaning of her foreign words became clear when a contingent of elven archers let loose a salvo of arrows towards the top of the wall. A handful of Reavers subsequently fell from the wall, never to rise.

Feeling rather redundant and wholly useless, Vighon remained astride his horse and simply listened to the violence unfold beyond Palios's walls. More than once he shared an impatient look with Sir Ruban and he couldn't help but notice Nathaniel's proud expression as he watched his daughter dart about the battlements like a Fury of the gods given life.

As time went on, the king finally dismounted, along with many others. He held a few conversations here and there, mostly checking in on the wounded they had transported across the land. The more seriously injured that had been among them were now being taken care of in Vangarth, but there were still men, dwarves, and elves in their great company who suffered.

Of course, there were no longer any Centaurs among them, having declined to leave the plains, their home. With nothing to offer them, Vighon and the others had given their thanks and promised to find some way to repay them in the future. Kelabor had spoken on behalf of his kin and refused any such payment. They had been fighting for their land and freedom, both of which had now been returned to them.

Vighon was left with only the utmost respect for them.

It felt like the Fourth Age had come and gone when, at last, the city's hulking doors began to open. Vighon hurried back to the front with Sir Borin trailing him like an overly large shadow. Asher was standing in the middle of the entrance, his chest heaving and sword filthy with Reaver debris. Behind him, Inara had her boot resting on the chest of another Reaver as she pulled Firefly cleanly from its head.

Vighon passed through the doors and patted the ranger on the shoulder.

"The people of Palios saw the banner of house Draqaro coming," Asher explained, gesturing to a mob of armed men and women. "They wanted to welcome their king." Never one to say more than he needed to, the ranger sheathed his broadsword and walked away.

The northman faced the crowd, though their attention had been turned to more Reavers approaching from the side street. "Sir

Borin," Vighon said. "Assist those people." The Golem strode away with a sword more befitting of a Troll in hand.

Turning to Inara, he saw that the Guardian of the Realm was reaching out towards a lone Reaver emerging from the nearest alley. Her hand snatched at the air as she grasped the fiend within her magic. Its arms and legs bent at awkward angles, its feet taken from the ground, before she swiped her arm and launched the Reaver head first into a stone wall.

Vighon raised an eyebrow. "Has anyone ever told you you're something of a brute?"

"It's the dragon in me," Inara replied with a wry smile.

Moments later, the entrance to the city was flooded with rebellion forces of all three dominant races. Vighon, Reyna, and Commander Rolgoth issued orders to sweep the streets and buildings and destroy any Reavers and Seekers. It wasn't long before Sir Borin the Dread was returned to the king's side, his wide sword coated in bits of Reaver.

Halfway towards the All-Tower, a small crowd approached the king and his much larger entourage. Leading them was the familiar face of Governor Tarlan, a man in his late sixties with a slender build and thinning white hair. Vighon had entertained the governor in The Dragon Keep numerous times during his reign as king and knew the man to be a good supporter of his - at least he hadn't heard otherwise in the time since.

"Your Grace!" Governor Tarlan gave a deep bow before the crowd behind mirrored his action. "Palios is truly blessed to have you here! I have had men, *good* men, waiting for the right time to strike. There isn't a Palosian within these walls that could suffer the rule of any but you. When we saw your banner and, of course..." the governor said, looking from Inara to Athis flying overhead, "we knew the hour was upon us."

"Your loyalty will never be forgotten, Governor Tarlan," Vighon assured. "You know our Guardian of the Realm, Inara Galfrey," he said, gesturing to his side. "And this is *Queen* Reyna, the Lady of Ayda," he quickly added, before the governor could greet the elf by her old title of ambassador. "And, of course, her husband, *King*

Nathaniel." Behind Vighon and slightly to the side, a stout dwarf cleared his throat. "And you also have the honour of Commander Rolgoth, son of Bolgayne, of clan Battleborn."

Again, Governor Tarlan paid his respect with a deep bow, though not as deep as the one he gave to Vighon. "It is the honour of my life that such esteemed guests should grace this fair city. You are most welcome."

Vighon looked up at one of Alijah's banners - a black dragon on a red background - as it blew in the wind. "Has the enemy's rule here been hard on the people?"

"Yes, your Grace, though indirectly. The usurper's laws come to us via Lord Gydon, of house Bairn." The governor's tone spoke volumes about the lord's treatment of Palios, a city within the steward's region.

Vighon absorbed the information with a quick glance at Sir Ruban, who said, "Lord Carrington's replacement, your Grace."

The king nodded along. "One wretch replaced by another; and not by me," he defended, aware that Alijah had publicly executed Carrington before bestowing the title of steward on Lord Gydon. "It's been a long time since Velia had a respectable lord and Alborn a steward worthy of its land. I must see to that in time." Vighon paused to cast an eye over some of his weary men filling the street. "Governor Tarlan, our forces are tired and in need of shelter, rest, and hot food."

"Palios will treat every one of you like the heroes you are," Tarlan reassured. "And you shall all have chambers made up in my estate," he added, taking in the royal gathering.

"We won't be staying long," the king informed him. "A day, perhaps two, while we gather our strength. From here we are taking the fight to the enemy. I won't issue a command, but I would have you spread the word: any who wish to volunteer to join our force will be rewarded and carry a great honour for the rest of their days."

"I will of course spread the word of the king," Governor Tarlan promised. "And you will all have a place at my table this evening."

A distant scream turned Vighon to the western district. "I look forward to it, Governor." The king drew the sword of the north, its flames enough to make Tarlan step back. "Until then, there are still Reavers to put down."

~

It was a satisfying evening as the sun, heading to its rest, had cast the city of knowledge in a burnt orange. A strong wind had blown in from the east and evicted the thick snow clouds that had threatened to unleash fresh powder. In their place, a crystal-clear night looked down on the Palosians, offering the people a heavenly vista of stars. It was still bitterly cold, but the stillness of it all had beckoned Vighon to the veranda between his chamber and the dining hall.

Standing sentinel in the passage, Sir Borin watched over his master. Vighon was happy enough not to have the Golem's overbearing shadow for a time, however brief it might be. How often he pondered on Queen Yelifer's witchcraft, undecided on whether it was a gift or a curse.

Hearing the door to the veranda open, the king casually looked over his shoulder to see Nathaniel Galfrey, the closest thing he had to a father. The old knight was hardly recognisable having had a bath and retired his mud-covered coat for clean clothes. His hair, short as always, appeared washed and free of the debris it had picked up on their journey north. Having bathed himself and welcomed the clean clothes from Governor Tarlan, Vighon wondered if he too looked a different man.

"You're easy to find," Nathaniel quipped, thumbing at the giant in the doorway.

Vighon chuckled lightly. "He is lacking a certain... *stealth* element." The northman gave another look over his shoulder. "Where's your better half?"

"She said something about a *second* bath. Elves," he added with a shrug. "Where is Inara?" he queried.

Vighon felt an instance of awkwardness. It would still be some time, he reasoned, before everyone's knowledge of their relationship was a comfortable affair. There were times, even now, when he could hardly believe he was in a relationship with the woman he had longed for all his life. It was all new and happening at the worst time, a time of turmoil and chaos.

"She went for one last flight with Athis before dinner," the king answered.

Nathaniel laughed to himself. "Another? Her feet barely touched the ground on the journey here."

"They nearly lost each other," Vighon explained. "I think they're going to be more inseparable than usual for a while."

"I can imagine," the old knight replied, searching the starry night for any trace of his daughter. "So what has left the king of Illian brooding in the cold?" he eventually asked, turning his attention back to the northman.

Vighon continued to lean against the railing, his arms folded over the banner. "I'm not brooding," he insisted.

Nathaniel gave him a once over. "You're definitely brooding. Trust me; I know brooding."

An amused smile pushed at Vighon's cheek. "From your time with Asher?"

"Of course," the old knight said. "You might be the king of Illian, but Asher is the king of brooding. He'll die on *that* hill."

Vighon's gaze drifted over the city and turned skyward. "Kassian said they set off from Vangarth with seven-hundred and thirteen Drakes. *Seven-hundred and thirteen*, Nathaniel. That's how many people had to willingly sacrifice themselves to keep this world in the light. Kassian tells me they aren't dead as we know it but... Now I can't help but wonder how many of them are left."

Nathaniel, ever the pragmatist, replied, "The Drakes' sacrifice has given us another chance to win this fight, but it's no different to all the men and women who have died in battle against Alijah and his Reavers. The Drakes fought back in the only way they could, in a way that fits with their beliefs. And like all those who died before them, the Drakes will be honoured in all our deeds. Moving forward is all the living can do. It's our duty."

Vighon sighed. "You're right, of course. Don't you ever get tired of duty?" he asked wearily.

"All the time," Nathaniel said honestly. "That's why we have strong women like Reyna and Inara in our lives. Duty is in their blood."

The northman couldn't disagree. "How long *have* you and Reyna been married for now?"

Nathaniel slowly turned his head to look at Vighon, though his expression was one of suspicion and calculation. "I believe this year marks our forty-sixth anniversary," he said evenly.

Vighon turned a display of disbelief on the immortal man. "You don't even look forty-six."

"I have Asher to thank for that," Nathaniel said as he leaned against the rail.

The king gave the veranda a cursory glance. "Where is our fearsome ranger? I haven't seen him since we entered the city."

Nathaniel half turned to take in the governor's grand estate. "This isn't really Asher's scene. He said something about finding a tavern." The old knight's gaze came to rest on Vighon, where he deliberately held it for a long moment. "Are you going to ask her?"

The sudden question took the king aback and he feigned ignorance for a second. There was no getting around Nathaniel's intense scrutiny, however. Instead, Vighon lowered his rising defences and exhaled a cloud of vapour into the cold air.

"I was thinking about it," he admitted.

"Just *thinking* about it?" Nathaniel echoed. "Is there something wrong with my daughter?"

Vighon heard the jest in his voice. "The timing seems a little... inappropriate."

"You've been in love with each other since you were teenagers," Nathaniel pointed out. "I would say it's overdue."

The northman was shaking his head. "I was referring to the war we're still in the middle of. I don't think my people will be too happy to know that their king has priorities besides fighting the enemy."

"I'm not suggesting you end your campaign to organise a

wedding," Nathaniel explained. "I just think it's time you two stopped waiting. It was hard enough watching you mope around the halls of The Dragon Keep all those years."

Vighon scowled. "I never moped!"

"You moped a little," Nathaniel said with a shrug.

The king laughed it off. "I know I want to spend the rest of my life with Inara. I'm just not sure how much life that is. We still have a long way to go..." Vighon let his words fade into hot vapour before he talked of killing Alijah in front of Nathaniel.

"All the more reason not to wait," Nathaniel uttered quietly, his own thoughts likely drifting to Vighon's unsaid words and the war's inevitable conclusion.

The king slapped a hand on the old knight's shoulder. "Come," he bade with some enthusiasm. "Let us enjoy a drink before the meal. Kassian has come to me with an idea about the future and I would know your thoughts on the matter."

CHAPTER 50

ENDINGS AND BEGINNINGS

There wasn't a tavern in all of Palios that wasn't caught in the thralls of celebration. The Palosians drank to a city freed of Reavers and the return of their king, while those who had fought on The Moonlit Plains toasted to soft beds, hot food, and a significant victory under their belt.

The general ruckus was amplified by the bands that brought their music to every watering hole in Palios. In The Giant's Eye, several patrons had taken to dancing on the tables while others stamped their feet and sang along. Ale was going everywhere, sloshed into the air with every beat in the rhythm.

It reminded Asher of The Pick-Axe.

Sitting alone, the ranger brought his tankard to his lips and paused. He dwelled on memories of both Russell and Adan'Karth before taking a drink.

Asher spared a moment to wonder about Gideon and the elves. If they had succeeded in their task, there was, perhaps, a path to ultimate victory. And from there... The ranger could not comprehend the true meaning of immortality yet. Endless sunrises and sunsets. The fatigue of old age never to grip his frail body. The idea of it was too much for him to fathom.

A Namdhorian soldier gave him a rough pat on the shoulder as he passed the ranger's table. He shouted something unintelligible, known only to the inebriated, and the entire tavern chanted Asher's name - a brief interlude before the singing continued. The ranger threw out some friendly nods and half a smile while lifting his tankard in appreciation.

To be known was an unfamiliar and wholly unsettling feeling. It felt wrong to be recognised. Learning to move unnoticed had taken years of training in Nightfall, an art he had practised until it became second nature to pass through the world like a ghost. Now complete strangers were chanting his name in a tavern in Palios.

Unable to reconcile his mixed feelings on the matter, Asher shook his head, put down his tankard, and left The Giant's Eye. He had rented a room in the tavern but he had no intention of sleeping there - another lesson from his past. Instead, he had always planned to slip away and sleep in the large stables on Governor Tarlan's estate, north of the All-Tower. It was there that he had left a young sleeping dragon, nestled in a pile of hay.

Without thinking about it, Asher ducked into the first dark alley he came across and began a circuitous route to the grand estate. He meandered the winding streets, sometimes doubling back on himself, while his thoughts wandered the halls of his mind. He could still see and even smell Thessaleia's memories. It was an extraordinary feeling, but the ranger was quite sure Avandriell was dreaming of those same memories as he walked the streets.

Eager to see his companion, Asher found a more direct route and began a swifter journey to the stables. He passed one lively tavern as Kassian and a large group of his Keepers were coming out. They were laughing amongst themselves having enjoyed an evening of revels, though Kassian himself wore the expression of a man carrying a good deal of weight. He noted Asher's passing and offered the ranger a friendly nod before following his fellow mages to another tavern down the street.

Having met the soldiers guarding the governor's estate on his way out, Asher was welcomed back with a short bow of their heads. He nodded his thanks as they opened the gates for him, revealing the gardens that stretched to the small fortress. Smaller buildings dotted the grounds: places for servants to rest and guards to take breaks.

Taking the path to his left, between the rows of neatly-trimmed hedges, the ranger made for the large stable-block that had been abandoned by the governor in favour of the newly erected one on the other side of the estate, closer to the main gates. Having heard of these details earlier in the day, Asher knew he had found his bed for the night.

Taking care with the creaky door, the ranger entered as quietly as he could, sensing Avandriell's sleeping form nearby. She was exactly where he had left her, in the back right stall, curled up on the hay that had been left behind. Her tail was curved around the shape of her body and resting against the side of her jaw.

Lying down beside her, Asher reached out and ran a gentle finger along her snout, feeling the ridges of her scales. It was only a flash but, for just a moment, he saw through Avandriell's eyes as she dreamed of flying over mountains. The ranger absorbed some of her peace and rested his head in the hay. Perhaps they would dream together.

Before the dawn, when the world was in a deep slumber and the night still held sway, Asher's eyes snapped open. He remained still, on his back, while his senses did their best to inform him of the environment. What remained of the moon cast the stables in a pale gloom; enough light to prevent the Nightseye elixir in his veins from activating.

The air was still and noticeably cold since Avandriell was no longer beside him. The latter set alarms ringing in Asher's mind. When had she moved? Where had she gone? Focusing on their bond, he knew she was nearby but... The ranger quickly shifted his focus away from the dragon, his attention captured by that sixth sense he had spent his entire life honing.

He wasn't alone.

Asher cautiously rose into a sitting position and scanned his immediate surroundings. His quiver, folded bow, and short-sword were still propped up against the wall, his broadsword lying on the ground in front of them. Fully attired in his leathers and green cloak, he only had to take his weapons in hand to be ready for anything.

Somewhere above him, further along the building, one of the wooden beams creaked. It was subtle and easily explained away with half a dozen reasons, but something told the ranger to arm himself sooner rather than later. Instead of picking up his broadsword and quiver, Asher simply grasped the hilt of his deadly short-sword and pulled it free from its hourglass scabbard.

Leaving the stall and his other weapons behind, the ranger crept into the main area of the stables. His eyes roamed from left to right, surveying the web of beams overhead, where he discovered naught but impenetrable shadows. Though he was careful not to cross a shaft of moonlight and potentially expose himself, his silvyr blade passed through and glistened as if it was inlaid with hundreds of diamonds.

"Exquisite," came a low voice, turning Asher on the spot.

Facing the back of the stables, where there was no door, the ranger watched as the shadows gave birth to a lone figure clad in black hardened leathers. Asher would have recognised the outline anywhere, an outline made all the more distinct by the short-swords poking over each shoulder.

"I can hear it," the voice continued as the figure moved towards the ranger. "The silvyr," he elaborated. "It's excited by the moonlight." Entering some of that light himself, his bald head and dark skin were contrasted by the red blindfold that concealed his eyes.

Asher's grip tightened around the hilt of his blade. "Veda Malmagol," he said casually, as if the man in front of him wasn't among the best killers in the realm.

"I love its duality," Veda continued, his head tilted to suggest his gaze was lowered. "Its beauty is paired with a deadly edge. How many people have you killed with it, I wonder."

The ranger twisted the blade in his hand. "I'm about to revise the number," he threatened with half a smile.

Veda met it with a broader smile. "You have more than earned your confidence, Asher. Today, however, I fear it is arrogance." The Father of Nightfall remained perfectly still as multiple Arakesh emerged from the darkness all across the stable. They were high and low, positioned to come at the ranger from a variety of angles.

"After all this time," Veda drawled, "tracking you down was so easy. To think I had eyes looking out for you everywhere." The Father laughed. "There was no missing a force of thousands trudging across the realm. I never thought you would be so careless," he taunted.

Asher took a breath, his expression one of boredom. "Your mistake was thinking I cared to begin with."

Veda's mouth twisted with amusement. "Your words may sound as hard as that blade in your hand, but we both know that you have spent a lifetime running from the past. Well," he said, raising his hands, "*we* are your past. And we have cornered you like the animal you are."

"Don't flatter yourself," Asher retorted. "You're not my past. You're *barely* Arakesh. You're just survivors, a faded echo of an order long dead."

Veda's expression shifted, losing any and all amusement with it. "*We* are the future," he insisted with an edge of fury in his voice.

"Was that before or after I whittled your numbers down?" Asher prodded.

The Father's chest puffed out with his breath. "I have rallied every living Arakesh to this one spot so that, together, we can eliminate the last remnant of an old order."

Asher made a cursory inspection of the men and women surrounding him. "This is all of them?" he enquired eagerly. "Do you promise?"

His hungry smile enraged the Father all the more, causing him to step forward and draw both of his short-swords. Mirroring their leader, every Arakesh pulled free their weapons and braced themselves in an attacking stance. Asher didn't move a muscle. Instead, he waited and watched.

"Which one of you is the bravest I wonder. I suppose it's whoever doesn't want to watch the others die."

"We are Arakesh," Veda stated. "We do not know fear."

To Asher, that was just another reason why none of them were real Arakesh. He tilted his head to better see the scar that ran down from Veda's left eye to his jawline. "You were afraid when I gave you that," he pointed out. "Or was running away part of your strategy?"

Veda flashed his teeth with a quick snarl. "You will not get the honour of a quick death."

The ranger was hardly aware of the man's last words, his attention having shifted to his faithful companion. It brought a fresh smile to his lips.

"What are you smiling at?" Veda spat, clearly distressed with what had likely been a rehearsed conversation gone awry.

"She listened to me," Asher said, confusing the Father.

Any misunderstanding was immediately cleared up when Avandriell darted through the open window, situated high on the far wall, and collided with the Arakesh at Asher's back. Even with their heightened senses, their human bodies were incapable of responding to her speed and ferocity. The dragon's claws, combined with her speed and force, took the man by his leg, snapping it out of shape and, ultimately, taking him off his feet. With ferocious haste, Avandriell dragged the assassin into the adjacent stall, out of sight. His screams were quickly silenced by razor-sharp fangs.

Before either dragon or man had even impacted the ground, however, Asher had leapt forward and brought a downward swing onto Veda Malmagol. The Father managed to parry the silvyr a few inches from his face before countering with his twin short-swords. The ranger jumped back and evaded that second blade only to be assaulted by two more Arakesh. He twisted his body to avoid one before ducking under the second. Rising to his full height, Asher planted a solid kick in one of the assassin's gut, throwing the woman into Veda.

Free of them both, he met the challenge of the third with a style of parrying known to the elves. It saw him release his grip on the hilt of the weapon as he swapped hands again and again, deflecting the incoming attacks from a multitude of angles while simultaneously confusing the opponent. After a few seconds, the ranger had found his enemy's opening and he sprang, slashing across the Arakesh's midriff once and then again after spinning on the ball of his foot. The second strike cut through his leathers and chest to deliver a mortal blow to the man's heart.

The assassin's body had barely hit the floor before another of his ilk was upon Asher. Gripping the ranger's cloak in both hands, the Arakesh yanked him back with enough force to put Asher on the ground. The impact was almost enough to take the wind out of his lungs, but he retained enough sense to know he was being dragged across the stables. Asher tucked in his legs and twisted his hips to narrowly miss the blades of those surrounding him.

A feral anger erupted from somewhere deep in his mind, only it wasn't *his* anger. A bronze blur flew across the stables and slammed into the assassin dragging the ranger. Like the other, he was swept from his feet in a splash of blood and gnawing fangs before his body shattered the wood of the closest stall.

Asher used what was left of his momentum and rolled backwards in order to jump up to his feet. Seeing three Arakesh dashing towards him, the ranger quickly unclipped his cloak and let it fall to his feet in a heap.

Throwing himself into the next fight, Asher deflected and parried, but their combined number and angles of attack left the ranger with stinging cuts across various limbs. Growling with the pain, he twisted his body around and brought a sharp elbow into the face of the closest. The Arakesh's head was whipped back, making him unaware of the silvyr blade plunging towards his gut. After securing the man's death, Asher lashed out with a foot and kicked back one of the other two, giving him time and space to pull free his bloody short-sword.

That was all he had time for.

Veda had recovered from his fall and was coming down on Asher from a leaping start. The two combatants fell into the rhythm of their lethal dance, their blades clashing between them. The ranger often had to work twice as fast to meet and counter both of Veda's blades, the Father proving himself the most capable among them with Nightfall's fighting styles.

Asher grunted and growled as a few swipes and slashes got through his defences and tore at his skin. One particular slice opened a healing wound on his leg and caused him to stagger back, offering Veda the perfect opportunity to jump and kick the ranger across the face. The pain spread through his jaw before a greater pain struck him in the head after colliding with a supporting post. Knowing his enemy, Asher pushed away from the post and evaded the Father's incoming swing.

Where most men would have succumbed to their pain, the ranger welcomed it as an old friend. Pain always brought back his earliest of lessons in Nightfall, reminding him of the strength he had needed to overcome every obstacle, and it had been a life of obstacles. Using his pain to focus his thoughts, Asher planned his next three moves.

The first: relieve Veda of one of his blades and even the fight. He did this with ease, since the Father's last swing had buried his short-sword in the post. Asher had but to chop down with his silvyr blade and the Arakesh's weapon was knocked to the ground and taken by the shadows.

The second: drive the pommel of his short-sword into the Father's eye. It was an agonising blow for any creature and Veda was no exception. He threw his head back and howled as he clutched the strip of fabric over his bleeding eye. His throat exposed, Asher rammed his open palm into his foe's neck, stealing his breath.

The third and final move: the ranger snatched at the red blindfold, removing it from Veda's head altogether. When, and only when, the Father met his eyes did Asher drive his silvyr blade into his gut. It wouldn't be a quick death.

Veda's eyes bulged with pain and shock. He released his remaining short-sword, letting it clatter to the ground, and gripped Asher's arm. With what he had left of his strength, he held the ranger's arm in place, preventing him from removing the silvyr.

"I'll live long enough to watch you die," he hissed.

Asher made to pull his blade free but Veda refused to let go. It was all the time the assassin hiding in the rafters needed to drop down and wrestle the ranger away from the Father and his precious blade. While Veda fell to the ground and began to crawl towards the stable doors, Asher was launching himself into the wall of the nearest stall.

His bid to remove the Arakesh on his back succeeded, but the younger man was quicker to recover. From a prone position, the assassin heaved his body up and caught Asher in the face with his knee, stopping the ranger from rising. The next thing he knew, rough hands were grabbing him by the collar and the waist and throwing him out of the stall.

A low grunt escaped Asher's lips as he pushed himself up onto all fours. Various parts of his body were crying out in pain, demanding his attention, as blood oozed from every limb and half a dozen smaller cuts on his face. Wounded as he was, he could still see and hear the chaos Avandriell was causing further down the stable. The dragon raked with her claws and opened arteries with her fangs when she wasn't picking assassins up and dropping them from the ceiling. If it wasn't for her, he would have been swarmed by Arakesh and probably be dead already.

The assassin who had thrown him out of the stall was storming towards him, his quick strides visible in the corner of the ranger's eye. His instinct was to reach for his weapon, but the silvyr short-sword was halfway across the stables, impaled in Veda's gut. Asher swore and took a breath, preparing himself for the brutality he was about to unleash on the younger man.

Those familiar rough hands grabbed at him again, but they failed to lift the ranger. In fact, they failed to do anything after Asher reversed his kneecap. The Arakesh fell back, raging with pain, and tried to crawl away, just like his master. Asher took a hold of the man by the waist of his trousers and dragged him back. Snapping his neck was muscle memory.

A light that felt as bright as the sun suddenly expelled every shadow in the stable, turning the ranger to Avandriell. Hovering in the air, the young dragon had set two of the assassins on fire. They ran into each other, their arms flapping around uselessly, before finally dropping to the ground, dead. Asher would have smiled at his companion's efforts but a boot to his chest launched him from his knees and onto his back.

The woman that came down on him had a single short-sword, but both of her hands were driving it down towards Asher's throat. At the last second, he managed to grip her wrists, halting the tip of the blade as it touched his skin. They both groaned under the effort, one driving down, the other braced. Again, Avandriell came to his aid. He saw her wings flap either side of the Arakesh before her claws sank deep into the woman's back. Her attack on Asher was immediately over, giving him the time to twist the short-sword from her grip and run it across her throat.

Avandriell, the ultimate predator, wasted no time bounding over the ground and barrelling into another assassin. Asher spared a glance at Veda, who was still desperately trying to crawl away. The ranger gripped his enemy's blade and started towards him, intending to finish what he had started. His first step, however, was the closest he got to the Father.

He heard the whistle of flying steel, but his senses had failed to locate its location before the blade was sinking into his arm. Asher roared and dropped the weapon he had taken. As he moved to take the dagger out, two more came hurtling in his direction, the blades thrown from the darkness. A last second shift of his shoulders allowed him to evade the first dagger which went on to find the post behind him. The second was lower and more central, catching him in the left hip.

The new pain in his hip forced Asher down to one knee, where he watched two Arakesh take shape from the shadows. Veda, it seemed, had staggered the attack on him, ordering a pair to hold back and ensure a fatigued ranger was met by fresh assassins.

Regardless of the doubt it clearly showed on the Father's part, it was a new tactic that must have come out of Asher's time hunting them down. The ranger swore again.

The pair of killers ran at him, their short-swords coming into play now. Asher gritted his teeth against the inevitable pain and yanked the dagger from his arm. He launched it with years of experience behind him, but the blindfolded assassins felt the steel in the air and dodged it with little effort. By the time he got round to removing the blade from his hip, the duo were upon him. Asher could do naught but throw his arm out and hope to stop at least one of them from swinging their sword.

There was barely any time to perceive it but, in that fraction of a second, Asher felt the hairs on his outstretched arm stand on end. There was a rush of heat, pulsing from the bones in his arm down to the smaller bones in his open hand. The air in front of his hand fractured and rippled outwards at great speed, picking up the loose hay and dirt from the ground before slamming into the Arakesh. Their direction was instantly reversed and with violent consequences. Both men hit the side of the stables with enough force to push their bodies through the hard wood to the outside. They didn't get back up.

Still in significant pain and down on one knee, Asher brought his hand back and examined the palm. There was a dull ache in his fingers but they were perfectly normal in appearance. He hadn't used magic like that since his days with Paldora's gem on his finger. The thought led his gaze back to Avandriell. The dragon was walking out of a stall with blood around her mouth and up her legs.

The ranger tried to get up and walk towards her but the pain in his hip brought him down again. Avandriell hurried to his side and nuzzled her head into his chest, where he was apparently very bruised. He patted her scales and eased her away before attempting to rise again. On his feet, if a little hunched, Asher surveyed the bodies scattered across the stable, two of which were on fire. There was one, though, who continued to move, if very slowly.

Sensing his disdain, Avandriell bounded and pounced until she was blocking Veda's way to the doors. The dragon lowered her head to the Father's and growled at him, baring her gore-coated fangs. Avandriell knew everything that had happened to Asher in Nightfall. She knew that it was men like Veda that had tormented her companion and twisted who he was to fit their needs. It brought out her wrathful side.

"Wait," Asher croaked, limping across the stable.

Asher reached down and unceremoniously retrieved his silvyr blade from Veda's gut. The Father cried out in agony and curled up in a ball, though there was nothing he could do to stop the blood loss now.

Looking down at the pathetic man, the ranger's vision blurred, creating two images of the Father. Asher touched his fingers to his head and discovered a decent amount of blood on his hairline. He had no idea when that particular blow had struck him, but he knew a blackout was coming his way and soon.

"Just do it," Veda moaned. "Or get your... *pet* to do it. Whatever helps... your conscience, traitor. Just know... you will always be... one of us. Killing me... killing all of us... just proves that... you were the best of us..."

His blade gripped in hand and pointed at Veda, Asher prepared himself to finish the Arakesh, ending the ancient order once and for all. But it wasn't the first time he had heard words like those. Words that had stuck with him since the last assassin of Nightfall had been at his mercy. Like Veda did now, that Arakesh had looked up at him and seen themselves reflected back. But what else could be done? The Arakesh were a scourge, a plague that had brought its rot to every corner of Illian for a thousand years. They needed eradicating. If Veda was allowed to escape or if he found some way to survive, the order would continue.

Pressing the silvyr tip to Veda's chest, Asher offered the man a final grimace to take to hell with him. "I can live with that," he replied.

As his arm tensed, ready to drive his blade down, an unusual and overwhelming feeling swept over the ranger. In that same moment, he was taken back to the first time Avandriell had swelled with magic and grown in size. Like then, Asher felt the cautionary arm of Adan'Karth hold him back.

Looking beyond Veda, Avandriell's golden eyes were waiting for her companion. Though she gave no outward suggestion of what was to come, Asher could feel it in her. Around the dragon, small pieces of debris and dirt began to lift from the ground and float in the air. Ignoring Veda altogether, the ranger turned on his heel and dived in the opposite direction.

The gloom and even the firelight from the bodies were eclipsed by the bright star that was birthed inside the stables. It expanded for six feet in every direction, propelled by the rawest magic there was. Everything inside that sphere was disintegrated, including all but a single foot of Veda Malmagol.

Succumbing to his injuries now, Asher slowly rolled onto his back and searched through the smoke for any sign of his companion. The intense burst of magic had spread to one of the supporting posts, removing a chunk of the wood while setting the rest of it alight. The fire and smoke made it hard to see anything, though Asher wasn't sure his head injury didn't have something to do with his poor vision.

A silhouette began to take shape near the doors, beyond the scorch mark that Veda's body had left on the ground. The silhouette rose and continued to rise and expand, taking on a hulking shape.

"Avandriell?" he uttered.

The smoke curled as that silhouette pushed through to reach him. A single head, a little larger than a horse's, emerged to rest over the ranger. Avandriell's reptilian eyes blinked once as she looked down on her wounded companion. They were the same shade of gold, if a few sizes bigger. The two horns, one above each eye, were thicker and much taller now.

Asher desperately wanted to see all of her, to marvel at the way she had grown, to admire her increased beauty. But the world was fading away and the smoke was making it harder to breathe.

Asher... Avandriell's voice was a soothing balm that gave him just enough life to keep his eyes open a moment longer.

In that time, the wall behind Avandriell was ripped away in a violent explosion of splintered wood. There, with the stars and moon at his back, Athis the ironheart stood tall on his back legs, his mighty fangs bared in a snarl.

Asher, Avandriell said again, her golden eyes drawing the ranger in. *Hold on...* Her voice was the last thing he heard before the black took him.

"I think he's waking up," came a voice from the ether.

It was familiar, but the ranger struggled to place it.

"Quickly," the same voice said, "alert my mother."

"Inara," Asher croaked, his throat horribly dry.

"I'm here," the Guardian replied.

The ranger's eyes fluttered open and protested against the light streaming in through a large window to his left. Inara's elfish face slowly grew in detail until all the blurry lines were gone, leaving naught but her smile.

"You're in Governor Tarlan's guest house," she informed him before he could begin his stream of questions. "It's a few hours past midday. You've been out since the pre-dawn, but we've taken good care of you. And you certainly needed it," she added, leaning away to cast her eyes over his body. "You can take a beating, I'll give you that."

Asher's hand instinctively moved to the pinch he felt on his left hip. He could feel a rough scab but nothing else.

"You had a dagger in there," Inara told him. "And besides the plethora of gashes and bruises, you also had a nasty cut on your head."

"Why am I not dead?" he asked.

"The power of the elves," Inara beamed. "My mother and a handful of her kin have worked through the morning to heal you as best they can." Her expression was serious. "I saw the bodies in the stable. They were Arakesh."

Asher nodded along. "They had been tracking me since Namdhor."

"There were a lot of them," Inara remarked.

"*All* of them, to be precise," he corrected. "Veda is dead, and the last of the Arakesh with him. Nightfall is no more."

"They're all gone?" Inara enquired with disbelief.

Asher thought about that question. "All but one," he said quietly.

Inara gripped his hand and squeezed. "You walked away from that path long ago, before I was even born. Yours is the way of the *ranger* now," she declared with encouragement. "And I have to say, what you two can do together is... a little *scary*." There was something in her eyes that reflected the horror the pair had left in that stable.

Asher hardly acknowledged her final words as something intangible tugged at his mind, drawing his gaze to the window. It looked to be a cold, yet cloudless, day outside. But it wasn't the weather that had demanded his attention. He could feel Avandriell out there, waiting for him.

Turning back to Inara, the half-elf was displaying a knowing smile. "Would you like to see her?"

As always, Asher answered the question with action and immediately tried to get out of bed. There was no particular thing that stopped him but, by the time he reached the edge of the bed, everything hurt in some way.

"Easy!" Inara bade. "They stopped you from bleeding but they didn't give you a new body."

Asher groaned with frustration. "I thought Riders were supposed to heal fast."

"We do," the Guardian said. "But you've still got a way to go before then."

Inara assisted the ranger in finding his clothes and, with a heavy fur added to his shoulders, Asher limped to the door. Inara showed him through to the foyer and the guest house's main doors. Not one to have doors opened for him, the ranger went to the extra, and painful, effort of opening it himself.

The sunlight was blinding, though its heat did nothing to counter the bitter wind that picked up his green cloak. With all the haste his injuries could afford him, Asher hurried away from the building and into the gardens. His blue eyes scanned the heavens in search of his companion. He could feel her, up there in the sky, but she was moving faster than before, making it harder to track her movements.

Something cut through the sky behind him, but his wounds prevented him from turning around quickly enough to spot it. Despite the glare from the sun, concealing her approach, the ranger knew the dragon was finally flying towards him.

When Avandriell was close enough, her wings fanned out and eclipsed the sun. All four of her claws came up before digging into the ground in front of him. Asher's mouth failed to close - he was in awe of her.

Avandriell maintained her regal stance, allowing the ranger to get a better look at her. The dragon now stood a head taller than a horse and at least twice that length. Her scales gleamed in the sunlight, a shade of bronze that no dwarven smith could ever achieve in his forge. Her claws were thick and her legs even thicker. She looked strong enough now to lift an ox clean off the ground. A long ridged tail swayed gently behind her, ending with an oval-shaped chunk of dark bone.

Perhaps the most noticeable difference, besides her increased size, were the spikes along her spine. Asher tilted his head to take in their new shape, noting how flat the majority of them were. Athis and Ilargo possessed similar protrusions along their spines, but both displayed sharp spikes rather than flat ridges.

"It's a female trait," Inara told him, watching his gaze. "They have flatter spinal horns, but they're twice as strong as the spikes found on a male."

Asher appreciated the information, though he was unable to tear his eyes away from the dragon. Following the flat ridges up to her head, he discovered a pair of small tusks either side of her jaw.

They were small changes, but every one of them made her all the more fearsome and beautiful at the same time.

Quick footsteps came up behind them. Asher didn't need to turn around to discover their owners' identity, for Avandriell could see them with ease. The dragon's knowledge was instantly his and the ranger knew that Reyna and Nathaniel had arrived with Faylen and a handful of elves. It was the most peculiar thing to know something with absolute surety without actually seeing it.

Inara held up a hand to hold them back. "We will give you both some time." After offering Avandriell a polite bow of the head, the Guardian of the Realm walked away and took the others with her.

Once they were alone, Avandriell dipped her head a little lower and tilted it to one side. *It must be so frustrating to only have two legs and no wings,* she observed with a touch of humour to her voice.

Asher couldn't help but grin like a fool. "So I didn't imagine it. You did talk to me, in the stables."

You need not use your voice, Avandriell reminded him. *The bridge between our minds is* strong.

The ranger opened his mouth to speak again but quickly sealed his lips. **Can you hear me?** he asked through their bond.

Of course, the dragon replied. *I have heard quite a lot while you have been sleeping the day away.*

Asher was still too stunned at hearing her voice to defend himself. Instead, he remained quiet and hoped to hear more of it.

Our enemy has been found, she stated, revealing some of the fierce warrior that her mother, Thessaleia, had imparted to her. *I heard a report given to Inara,* she continued. *Ravens from both Dunwich and Darkwell have arrived with news of Reaver tracks entering The Vrost Mountains. Inara and Athis believe Alijah and Malliath are holed up in The Bastion, biding their time.*

Asher had to shake his head to catch up with the details, so enthralled was he with his companion's level of intelligence and personality. Already, the ranger could tell that Avandriell was from a fighting stock of dragons that had long served the order of the Riders in Drakanan. She thought like a predator and dreamed of the hunt. Her significant bond to Asher was what tied her to current events, making Alijah and Malliath her prey.

Again, Asher had to shake his head and blink to focus his thoughts. He felt as if he could fall into Avandriell's mind and way of thinking for days. There were parts of her that just came to him without question or reason.

We have today, she informed him, *but The Rebellion is moving on from Palios at dawn. We will meet up with Doran before taking the fight to the enemy.* Avandriell looked away for a moment, her mind flitting through Asher's countless memories of the infamous Heavybelly. *I think I will like the dwarf,* she remarked offhandedly. *He would make for a good Rider.*

Asher couldn't help his scoff. **Doran would disagree. As would his dragon...** he added with amusement.

A rapid guttural sound resonated from Avandriell's throat as she shared in the joke. *You are not wrong,* she agreed.

Asher laughed all the more. **I can't believe we're actually talking to each other. It doesn't seem real.**

Avandriell lowered her head until the flat of her snout was within the ranger's reach. *Does this feel real?*

With his free hand, Asher pressed his palm to her scales and felt the warmth within them. They weren't as smooth as he recalled, when she was no bigger than a dog. Now, her bronze scales had a weathered texture to them and felt harder.

You are not alone anymore, good ranger. I live in you. And you live in me. There is nothing of the sky or earth that can come between us. We are free.

Those last three words struck a chord in Asher and he retrieved his hand so that Avandriell could raise her head to see him. **We are free,** he repeated.

The dragon tilted her head again. *What was it you said? I am ranger. Yes. I like that. My mother and father have memories of dragons who lived free of the order. They were known as rogues; dangerous and territorial creatures who could not be trusted. But rangers live by a code. I have seen that in you. It would be a life no other dragon has ever* known. *Quite an adventure,* she concluded with delight. *Yes. I am ranger.*

We *are rangers,* Asher emphasised.

Though nothing changed on her face, Asher could sense the pleasure that resided within his companion. *Perhaps,* Avandriell suggested, *if you're done bleeding everywhere, we could find somewhere quiet to rest together. Somewhere we can talk.*

Unlike the dragon, Asher displayed his pleasure with a contented smile. ***I would enjoy that,*** he replied, limping away from the gardens beside her. ***What would you like to talk about?***

Oh... everything.

Asher let out a short sharp laugh. ***Everything sounds good.***

CHAPTER 51
HOME IS WHERE THE HEART IS

Descending beneath the clouds, Gideon Thorn was met by the white cliffs of The Shining Coast. The jagged cliff stretched from north to south, beyond even that of Ilargo's vision. To millions of others, it would have been a welcoming sight, to see those white walls and know they were home.

It didn't feel like home to Gideon.

He had lived in many places during his life; enough to have good and bad memories of Illian, Ayda, and even Erador. They had all felt like home at one point or another, though some had also felt like prisons. These days, home was in the sky, free of the lines drawn over the land below.

Of course, it was never the land that drew him anywhere - it was the people. He cared for the everyday lives of the families that inhabited the realm, be they humans, elves, or dwarves. He had fought and suffered for them all during his long life and the old master knew it was a habit he could never break. It was a duty that surpassed the codes of any order, a sense of responsibility that came with the power he and Ilargo both harnessed.

Perhaps, Ilargo said, *we could find others who share that sense of responsibility.*

Gideon looked over the snow-covered fields of Alborn, his gaze drawn to the far west. Further than any could see was Erador and, further still, was Drakanan, the ancient home of his predecessors. It was there, hidden deep in the mountain rock, that any hope might be found for a future filled with Dragon Riders.

No, Ilargo corrected, turning Gideon back to him. *The hope you hold in your heart does not rest in Drakanan. It lies out there, in the vastness of Verda. Those eggs will not bond to just any. They demand a companion who embodies all the virtues of a true warrior. Nothing short of that will do.*

I'm not even sure it's the right thing to do, Gideon replied. **We've done this before. We've made this same decision before. Restarting the Dragorn came from a sense of duty, regardless of the outcome. Now, I have to wonder if my heart desires this because I don't want us to be alone.**

We will never be alone, Ilargo countered softly.

You know what I mean. Asher and Avandriell have their own path and it has nothing to do with the Riders or the Dragorn. And then there's Inara and Athis, Gideon said with a sigh. **I see their future being very tied up in royal duties. And you know I'm happy for them both,** he added. **I just can't make a decision like this without considering all the reasons why we should do it.**

Ilargo turned his head just enough to lay a single blue eye on his companion, though he said nothing.

What is it? Gideon asked, unable to read the dragon's thoughts. **Ilargo, what aren't you saying?**

Your human side has made you indecisive and unsure of yourself, the dragon chastised. *I can feel it in you. You have lost sight of who you are and what you are capable of. Our bond might have changed, but there is still a dragon in you.*

Gideon clenched his jaw. **I want to trust what's in my heart.**

A heart you still share with me, Ilargo pointed out.

And what is in your heart? Gideon asked. **What do you think we should do?**

The dragon continued his flight for a moment, his thoughts coalescing into poignant words. *Drakanan,* he began, *deserves a leader befitting of their legacy. As do the eggs and their potential Riders. They need a leader who has been knocked down and got back up again. A leader who knows their failures and has learnt from them. Did you ever consider that our life, our experiences have been forging that kind of leader out of you, out of us? Drakanan and the entire order of Riders fell eons past and without your hand in it. As did Elandril's Dragorn. Unlike those that came before us, we are still around.*

But is that enough? Gideon agonised, still haunted by all the young dragons and Riders Malliath had slaughtered in The Lifeless Isles.

Nothing is ever assured and nothing is ever truly safe, Ilargo asserted. *But our ability to try* is *assured. Our promise to always get back up* is *assured. And our oath has ever been to die keeping the realm safe.*

The old master rubbed his companion's green scales, his mind falling ever deeper into thought. There was so much to consider and yet the future still teetered on a knife's edge. The greatest challenge of their lives lay ahead and there was no certainty that they would even survive to see Drakanan again.

Gideon, you know what we must do. What we must commit ourselves to.

An exasperated sigh escaped Gideon's lips and got lost in the wind. **You know, sometimes your innate wisdom is tiresome.**

No it isn't, Ilargo said with an edge of smug superiority.

Gideon laughed in his agreement before realising those behind him would have no idea what was so funny. Instead of explaining it all, he simply told the elves that Ilargo would be following The Selk Road north in the hope of joining The Rebellion once more.

Galanör and Aenwyn readily agreed with the plan since the rebels had always planned to meet up with Doran in The Black Wood should they find victory in The Moonlit Plains. They briefly discussed the merits of checking the plains, but it was a long way to go only to find an empty hole in the ground when they knew where The Rebellion would be going.

And so Ilargo banked to the north and flew inland until the white cliffs fell away and The Selk Road snaked through the region of Alborn. The dragon continued his flight for several hours, his sharp eyes scouring the land below. The sun moved across the winter sky, chased westward by the approaching night. As it touched the distant horizon, Ilargo dipped his head and raced towards the ground, bringing a city into view.

What is it? Gideon asked, bracing himself.

Bodies, Ilargo stated gravely. *Lots of bodies.*

Gideon narrowed his eyes and saw a great pillar of smoke rising high into the sky. Beyond the smoke, the All-Tower of Palios stood tall in the heart of the city. As captivating as the scholars' tower was, Gideon was drawn back to the smoke. Following it down to its origin, he soon discovered the bodies Ilargo had mentioned.

Reavers, the dragon confirmed.

The Rebellion's forces have been here, Gideon deduced with some excitement. **Take us down,** he urged. **We will question the governor before moving on,** he added, glancing to the northern road their friends had surely taken.

Having met with Governor Tarlan, Gideon and his companions came to learn the truth of events in Palios. It was a relief to hear of so many in the company of the king, including their friends. It was disturbing, however, to learn of the attack on Asher and Avandriell, though the governor could give no further details on those who had ambushed them. Only that they had met a gruesome end for their efforts.

Considering the many days of travelling behind them and the distance The Rebellion's army could have travelled since they had left Palios, Gideon and the elves accepted Governor Tarlan's offer of hospitality.

And so the trio enjoyed the most comfortable night in a long time: soft beds, hot meals, and the protection of a city that had already been liberated. Eager as Gideon was to reach The Rebellion again, his eyes closed with ease and his mind fell into a deep slumber that one never enjoyed in the wilds.

Though he awoke the next day feeling refreshed and clear of mind, Gideon could feel Ilargo's fatigue lingering. The dragon had covered more miles than he could count since setting off from Drakanan and there were only more to put behind them. Given that Ilargo was capable of catching up with the army before they even reached Dunwich, Gideon suggested to Galanör and Aenwyn that they remain in Palios for the day and another night. Considering the battle that lay ahead of them, the elves offered no protest and happily took the rest of the day to recover from their journey.

And so it was the dawn of another day before they gave their thanks to the governor and the people of Palios and ascended to their place on the dragon's back.

The day seemed to stretch on ahead of them until it was night once again, extending their journey to agonising lengths. Ilargo continued through the night, his vision unimpaired by the dark. In the pre-dawn, they flew over Darkwell, the most southern city in the northern realm; a marker for all that they were passing from one region to another.

As the sun rose again, Gideon cast his eyes out on the world, hoping that he might discover a trace of The Rebellion. To his left, in the west, The Evermoore's tree line appeared as a faded darkness resting on the horizon. Following the great forest north, there was no missing The Vrost Mountains that curled around its northern boundary.

I see them! Ilargo exclaimed.

Gideon pushed up from the two small spikes his feet had always rested on. Looking over Ilargo's head, he narrowed his eyes and tried to make out The Rebellion's forces. Considerable as their numbers were, though, the dragon's eyes proved vastly superior as Gideon failed to discern them against the terrain.

With some impatience, he waited for Ilargo to close the gap. As he was informing Galanör and Aenwyn of their imminent arrival, another arrival met them in the sky. Gideon's words trailed off, leaving him speechless and wide-eyed.

Avandriell was flying beside them, her bronze scales catching the rising sun.

Galanör leaned forward, bringing his words closer to Gideon's ears. "Avandriell seems to be... *bigger.*"

Gideon laughed at the blunt assessment and nodded in agreement. "I would say so!" he called back.

Coming up on their other side, an even bigger dragon made his presence known. Athis glided in beside Ilargo, their wing tips almost touching, as he reached out to speak with Ilargo. Gone were the days when their thoughts were one. Now, Gideon had to request permission to join the bridge between Athis and Ilargo, though it was freely given.

It is good to see you, Gideon, Athis said after greeting Ilargo.

And you, Athis, the old master replied with a genuine smile lighting up his face.

Rather than waste time with words and endless questions, Athis gave Ilargo access to his recent memories. After they were absorbed at some speed by Ilargo, the green dragon filtered them through to Gideon at a pace his mind could comprehend. They witnessed events from Vangarth and The Evermoore, where the Drakes had taken days to decide on their action.

It was hard to experience Athis's weakening condition as the tree burned, though Gideon noticed anything to do with Inara, including her feelings, were guarded from him, protected as they were by her companion. The old master didn't push it, content for them to maintain their privacy. Instead, he accepted the memories that pieced together the events surrounding the tree itself.

A monumental weight pressed upon Gideon's heart as it all came together. Adan'Karth and hundreds of Drakes were all gone, their life force and magic offered up to the tree. It was an enormous sacrifice. Both he and Ilargo only wished they could have been there to pay their respects to the brave Drakes and say farewell to Adan'Karth.

Athis pushed on and Ilargo broke it all down for Gideon. While they had been flying across the world, eager to return to Illian's shores, The Rebellion had been moving across the land. In Palios, Gideon looked down through Athis's eyes and saw a ruined stable littered with bodies, all Arakesh. Asher lay unconscious among them, watched over by newly grown Avandriell. It felt a revelation to hear that those bodies were supposedly the last of Nightfall's wicked order. Fitting, Gideon thought, that they should finally be brought down by Asher of all people.

Since then, they had journeyed north intending to reach The Black Wood and meet Doran. As they had to pass the mouth of the valley that formed The Vrost Mountains, where it was believed Alijah and his forces were holed up, The Rebellion had made a substantial camp before going any further.

Gideon looked over at those mountains again. He didn't need to experience Athis's memories to know where their enemy was. The Bastion. A cold and dark place that had never known warmth or light, its black stone forever reigned over by the corrupted and evil beings of the realm.

Soon after meeting Athis and Avandriell in the sky, Ilargo was setting down on the snowy plains at the foot of the mountains. To the north of the camp, a large group of dwarves looked to be amassing while hundreds of elves and humans saw to fortifying the gap between the camp and the valley that cut through The Vrost Mountains. As before, a large tent was situated near the heart of it all, a place where The Rebellion's council could meet, and Gideon's current destination.

Many broke away to greet them, though most were elves. They were offered good food and hot drinks from the fires that dotted the camp. Gideon promised himself he would indulge in whatever they had soon enough, but not before he met with his friends. The elves who had approached them looked only too happy to move past and tend to Ilargo, as always.

Navigating the camp was no easy task. The Rebellion had clearly been restocked since leaving The Moonlit Plains and now possessed hundreds of carts with supplies, not to mention fresh horses from Palios. Of course, it was the Warhogs that proved the more difficult to negotiate, boisterous as they were.

As the pavilion began to loom large in Gideon's vision, he found his path blocked, though it wasn't by Asher this time. The old master stopped in his tracks and met the vivid blue eyes of Inara Galfrey. It quickly became clear that the Guardian of the Realm wasn't going to move out of his way. Instead of protesting, Gideon gestured for Galanör and Aenwyn to go on without him. Inara offered them both a friendly nod as they passed her by before returning her steely gaze to her former mentor.

Gideon hadn't missed, however, her brief glance at the satchel draped over Galanör's shoulder. Thanks to Ilargo's shared memories, Inara already knew what prize they had returned with.

"You saved the tree," he complimented with half a smile.

"That's an overstatement," Inara corrected flatly. "Though I lent my sword to the effort, which is more than you can say," she added sourly.

The old master took a breath to steady his rising temper - no easy feat since altering his bond with Ilargo. "You know as well as I that any war requires fighting on more than one front."

"Is that what you've been doing in Davosai?" Inara questioned incredulously. "Fighting on another front? Is this the part where you convince me that Crissalith is naught but a weapon to kill Alijah and Malliath?"

"With the Hastion gem," Gideon replied, "Crissalith *is* a weapon in our hands. It will sever Alijah's bond with Malliath but, more importantly, it will sever the strings Malliath has used to control Alijah all these years."

Inara raised a hand to stop him. "I've heard this argument from my mother. I am not so naive as to believe your intentions towards Alijah. You still believe he can be redeemed, that he *deserves* to be redeemed. A ludicrous notion when we can't even count the number of bones he stands upon."

"He's your brother, Inara. Have you forgotten that?"

"How could I forget that?" Inara spat. "Because of him, my very name has been tainted, my bloodline questioned. When this is all over and my *brother* is dead, do you really think the people of Illian are going to tolerate another Galfrey with a dragon?" She shook her head, exasperated. "No, Gideon, I have not forgotten that he is my kin. The difference between you and me, is that he's already dead in my eyes."

Gideon didn't hide his disappointment in her perspective. "We have a duty to save every life, Inara. *Every* life."

"Duty?" she queried with a frown. "We are neither Dragorn nor Dragon Rider. We have no such duty. I am the Guardian of the Realm, a title thrust upon me in *your* absence. I am honour-bound to protect the people of Illian from evil, whatever form it takes. Killing Alijah and Malliath will ensure their protection. There ends my duty."

Inara turned on her heel and made for the pavilion. "I need to save him, Inara!" Gideon growled, halting her mid-stride. "I need to save him," he repeated hopelessly. "I am the one who failed him. He could have been so much more. His destiny could have been as glorious as I'm sure yours is. But I failed him. And because of my failings, he ended up in the hands of The Crow. So you see," he said with a tired shrug, "I have to undo my mistake."

Inara held his gaze a moment longer. "No," she responded evenly. "You have to *live* with your mistake."

Gideon remained rooted to the ground, the wind taken out of him by her sharp words. "Keep the hope alive," he blurted, preventing Inara from completely turning away from him. "That is also your duty, is it not?"

The Guardian's hard expression faltered ever so briefly before returning tenfold. "You will have to be quick about your report," she said, changing the subject.

"Why?" Gideon asked with a hint of concern. "What's happened?"

"Word from The Black Wood: King Dakmund has passed away." Inara's tone was simply matter-of-fact, though Gideon suspected it was caused by talking to him rather than the subject matter. "As he was the last dwarven king of Dhenaheim," she continued impatiently, "a great deal of his kin wish to pay their respects before the next battle. There's also the matter of a new king. Given its significance and subsequent impact on the realm, the council has decided to accompany them further north. It's been decided that our forces will remain here and prepare to take The Vrost Mountains when we return."

Gideon remained where he stood for a few seconds longer, watching Inara disappear inside the tent. *She is carrying so much,* he said to Ilargo. *This is not the Inara Galfrey I know.*

A great deal has happened to her, the dragon replied. *We all change.*

The old master shook his head slightly. *Not like this. She has shut part of herself off to cope with it all.*

Perhaps, Ilargo posed, *that is what is required to kill her own brother.*

Gideon was tempted to turn around and spot the dragon across the camp, well aware that his companion didn't truly believe that. *Whatever Alijah's fate, we both know she will need all of herself if she is to defeat him. He is too powerful to be faced by anything less. I will speak to her again.*

And soon, Ilargo prompted. *When next they meet, I fear only one will survive.*

CHAPTER 52
FEELING IT

H aving taken on Gideon's and Ilargo's memories of their time in Ayda, Inara felt no need to be present for the report to Vighon and the others. Instead, she ascended to the heavens with Athis in the hope of finding fresh air to breathe, air that wasn't shared with her old master.

From the sky, they watched the world go by. As the day waned, the council eventually set out from the mountains, trailed closely by several hundred dwarves of varying clans. She could also see the four human scouts on horseback, riding off into the valley.

Taking in The Vrost Mountains as a whole, Inara liked to think her brother and his forces were trapped in there. They had retreated in the belief that all they had to do was wait: wait for the tree to burn, wait for their most powerful foes to die away, and wait for The Rebellion to be at its most vulnerable.

Inara held her head high in defiance. After so much fighting, The Rebellion had finally shown their might, undoing Alijah's schemes, and cornering the treacherous necromancer. It was all coming to an end; she could feel it.

Turning away from those ominous mountains, Athis began a slow glide towards The Black Wood in the north-east. The red dragon inevitably caught sight of Ilargo and Gideon, for there was only so much sky to share. Curiously, Athis closed a portion of his mind to Inara, keeping his immediate thoughts to himself.

As they had previously established, it was perfectly alright for them to close off and have more private thoughts and feelings, but the timing of it stood out to Inara. She spared a moment to look at Gideon and Ilargo, to her right and slightly lower.

Do you agree with them? she asked a little too bluntly.

Athis held on to his thoughts a while longer. *I share your passion for justice,* he began, *but I have been speaking with Ilargo.* That surprised Inara and she couldn't hide it. Athis acknowledged the feeling, noting the hint of a sting among her emotions, and continued. *What if Alijah is just another victim in Malliath's war on magic?*

You do agree with them, Inara concluded.

No, Athis countered with irritation. *But I am willing to listen and consider. Our duty requires more than our ability to swing a sword and breathe fire. Listening is a powerful tool. It can elevate you in the eyes of your allies and grant you knowledge where your enemies are concerned. And,* the dragon added, his tone growing more serious, *if we are to make judgement on another, should we not seek the counsel of others to ensure we are informed? Anything else would be an abuse of our power.*

Inara was on the precipice of replying, but there was something about the poignant words of wisdom, words only a dragon could spout, that stopped her in her tracks.

I don't want to talk about this, she finally said.

Athis made no comment. Instead, he maintained his course and flew through the onset of night and over Dunwich, the only town to border The Black Wood. He continued to circle the wood until the council and dwarves were among the others.

Inara hardly waited for his claws to touch down before she was preparing to jump. Walking past her companion's head, the dragon simply said, *We will speak later.*

Inara didn't correct him. She, instead, gave a short nod of the head and let her true emotions wash across their bond. Athis, however, already knew the truth of her emotions. He knew she wasn't really angry with him; she just wanted to run away from it all. It was an ugly task that the realm required of her and she would see it done. That's all there was. Athis wholeheartedly disagreed with her approach to it, but Inara severed their bond before he could voice as much.

All she had to offer her companion was a look of apology. She just couldn't face it right now.

~

A quiet and aching sorrow had beset the atmosphere of The Black Wood, a contrast to the mesmerising sky above, bejewelled with an ocean of stars. The council's exchange with Doran and his mother had been brief. Like the others, Inara had offered her condolences, though the queen mother looked to be in a permanent daze while Doran appeared to have the weight of the world on his shoulders.

For all the pressures and grief that plagued him, the dwarf still made time to enquire about recent events. Though short-lived, Doran's spirits looked to be lifted upon hearing news of their victory.

"I knew ye'd do it," he had said, sparing an extra second to comment on Avandriell's increased size. "She looks like a weapon with wings." His remark had even come with a genuine smile.

There had been no time for anything else after that - there was a king to bury.

Amassed in the largest area, the camp of dwarves, humans, and elves stood silent with either a candle or a torch in hand. For the humans and elves, it was a moment to pay their respect to the dead liege but, for the children of the mountain, it was a time to grieve.

Those of clan Heavybelly felt it the worst, their king of many years finally lost to them. But there was grief also among the dwarves of other clans for they had all lost someone like Dakmund, be it their king, brother, father or son. Here, with Doran and his clan, they shared it together.

Emerging from the royal tent, Doran and three of his kin

carried Dakmund's body on a simple bier. Drelda would have fallen to her knees and sobbed were it not for her maids catching her by the arms. Doran had no tears to speak of, though the red skin around his only eye suggested he had already wept for his brother. With a set jaw, white knuckles, and steady gaze that never wandered from his destination, the son of Dorain put one foot in front of the other.

Leading them was a bald dwarf whose beard nearly dragged on the ground. His voluminous robe and plethora of necklaces indicated he was some kind of priest or cleric of the dwarven faith.

After a short walk to parade the king, Doran and the others placed his body down and took the bier away, leaving Dakmund to rest on the cold ground. Only Doran remained by his brother.

"Here lies King Dakmund, son of Dorain!" he called out. "This is..." Doran faltered and swallowed before continuing. "This is no place to bury a king. Me kin, be it me father Dorain or me ancestor Thorgen, 'ave been given back to the mountain stone. This is not Vengora an' nor is it The Whisperin' Mountains. But, since it would be disrespectful to send a king on such a journey, we 'ave brought the mountain to 'im."

Inara followed Doran's gesture to the pile of large rocks resting on the back of a cart. Given the time since Dakmund's death, she assumed the rocks had been mined from Vengoran stone, just north of the woods.

Without another word, Doran took the first jagged stone from the cart and laid it beside his brother. He was shortly followed by a handful of dwarves who joined him in the silent work. While they piled stone upon stone, the cleric stepped in and began to offer up dwarven prayers in their native tongue.

It was a lengthy process to entomb the king and Doran was flushed and sweating by the end of it. Still, with bleeding fingers, he had laid one stone after the other until his brother was hidden from the world and returned to Grarfath and Yamnomora.

Inara had never met Dakmund, and so the tears welling in her eyes were for Doran and his kin. She could feel their collective grief and would have been lying if she denied the effect it was having on her.

There was something more to it, though, something that gripped Inara's heart. Looking at Doran, she saw someone who was burying their brother. It conjured up thoughts and memories of Alijah, feelings and events that she could never forget. For Doran, there was never going to be a second chance, another opportunity to speak to his brother. They had shared all the days they were ever going to.

That was her future. For two years she had sharpened her resolve to a deadly point, one she intended to unleash upon Alijah. And then, when it was done, he would be gone forever.

Inara shut her eyes tightly and took a steadying breath. No, she told herself; he was already gone. Her kind and caring brother, who had always found a way to make her laugh, had died years ago inside the very place he now resided. As hard as that was to believe, she knew it to be true. It had to be, for how else would she find the courage to kill him?

Doran took the place of the cleric, bringing Inara back to the present. The son of Dorain puffed out his chest and raised his chin. "Tonight, we grieve," he instructed. "Tonight, we mourn our loss an' not jus' that o' King Dakmund, but all who 'ave fallen to this scourge. Every king o' Dhenaheim. Every warrior who now dines with the Father. But tomorrow, we celebrate! We celebrate their lives! Their achievements in life! We will drink to their bones that they might enrich Grarfath's soil an' better His world! An' then, with *steel* an' *wrath*, we march on our enemy!"

Every dwarf gave a short sharp roar into the air. What followed was a quiet dispersal as the various elves, dwarves, and humans found fires to huddle around and swap stories and share food. Those of the council naturally came together in the royal tent. Doran was sure to keep his mother close and within the comfort of his arm.

"Tell me everythin'," Doran said, eager, perhaps, to think of something other than his brother.

Between them all, they recounted recent events for the War

582

Mason, filling in the details from their different perspectives and quests. Inara remained relatively quiet for the most part, only speaking of her time in Vangarth. When it finally came to Gideon, Galanör, and Aenwyn, who had travelled further than them all, Inara subtly removed herself from the tent. Vighon had squeezed her hand and shot her a questioning look, but she had calmed him with a look before leaving.

In the cold night air, Inara reached out to Athis and quickly discovered he was deep in conversation with Avandriell and Ilargo. Deciding to leave them to it, the Guardian settled for a stroll through the camp, pausing briefly to look upon Dakmund's tomb. She envisioned herself doing this years from now, only it was Alijah's tomb she visited.

What would she say in that instance? She knew of no real god to offer a prayer to and she didn't believe in the dwarven religion. Where was Alijah going after death? Would he ever know peace? Did he even deserve it? Inara had none of the answers, though she wondered if her future self would be plagued with regret.

After leaving Dakmund's tomb, it wasn't long before the fire light of the camp was behind her and she was standing in the gloom, surrounded by trees. Despite the tranquility of the environment, she just wanted to scream. Her human emotions collided with each other, leaving the Guardian unsure of how she felt about anything.

That wasn't true.

She was angry. Of all her emotions, anger fought its way to the forefront and dominated her. Inara was angry at Athis for ever dampening her human side. Then there was her mother, who was willing to forget everything Alijah had done if it meant saving him. And Gideon. He had been imprisoned by Alijah for years, tortured even, and yet he was trying to save him.

Of course, as much as her anger was aimed at others, it always came back on her. She was angry with herself for ever altering the bond with Athis and inflicting these human emotions on her life. And she hated herself for being cross with her mother, who only wanted to save her son from death. And then there was Gideon, who had been trying to save everyone since before she was born. Being angry with her old master, a man she had looked up to for most of her life, was hard.

A snapping twig turned Inara on her heel. She recognised Gideon by his silhouette, though he was easily identified when the golden dragon's claw that formed Mournblade's pommel caught the distant light.

"We need to talk," he said determinedly.

Gideon's words immediately got Inara's back up and her emotional defences rose into place. "What is there to talk about?" she asked, her heart hardening once more to the approaching task. "You've already made your move and it appears you have the backing of the council."

Gideon stepped forward. "Is that how you see it? We're all making different moves like pieces on a board?"

"Aren't we?" Inara questioned. "Even Doran has lost some of his fire. Now he just wants the war to be over, whatever Alijah's fate."

"You cannot deny the truth you have seen with your own eyes," Gideon argued. "Alijah has no idea he is still under the thrall of Malliath. He has told us both that he believes himself to be free. That makes him a..." The old master lost his patience for words and gave an exaggerated shrug. "You know all this."

"I know that Malliath's influence is powerful," Inara acknowledged, "more so than anything we ever experienced with Athis and Ilargo, or the entire Dragorn for that matter. But it's still *influence*. There's some of Alijah in his actions, Gideon. There's a part of him that wants the realm in an iron grip, a part of him that wants the only dragon in Verda."

Gideon didn't say anything. He was *listening*. After Athis's words, earlier that day, it stood out all the more to Inara. Unlike her, he wasn't blindly following a single thought or belief; he was considering everything. It took some of the sting out of her anger towards him and left her feeling disappointed in herself.

"You're right," he finally replied. "It would be naive to think that Alijah is nothing more than a puppet. Like all of us, he has his flaws and he always struggled with living in the shadow of you and your parents. It's not hard to believe that there's a part of him that wants ultimate power, whatever the cost." The old master sighed and his shoulders sagged. "And perhaps he should be killed with Malliath. It's not a justice I believe in, but it might be the one the realm needs to heal and move on.

"I spent years teaching you how to think for yourself," he continued, somewhat disheartened, "so I won't tell you how to think now. And I certainly wouldn't tell you what to do. And, in all likelihood, Alijah won't give either of us an option. That's why I've given the Crissalith to Doran. He's going to have his smiths work it into something that can be wielded as a weapon. If Alijah is truly lost to us, the Crissalith won't just sever his bond with Malliath, it can be used to pierce his heart."

Hearing those words said aloud, and by Gideon no less, struck Inara deeply. It now felt all the more real that she was heading towards a confrontation with her brother and that one of them had to die. As she attempted to add another layer of shielding to her heart, disconnecting her from the task, her old mentor spoke again.

"You need to feel it," he stated with conviction.

Inara frowned in confusion. "What do you mean?"

"You might not like it, but I *know* you. Since you found me in Erador I've seen you withdraw more and more when Alijah comes up. You've been burying your emotions, steeling yourself to face him. I did the same thing when I challenged him in Erador. I watched him for weeks until I was able to look at him and see only my enemy. And it wasn't enough. I didn't let myself feel any of it.

"When it comes to that final blow," he averred, "you must let yourself feel it. The anguish. The heartbreak. Every ounce of pain must tear at you. It's the only thing that will give you the strength to do what needs to be done."

It was a powerful thing to hear and, though she couldn't absorb it all immediately, Inara knew his words would sink in and leave a mark. "I thought you would be the last person to give me advice on killing him."

"If it comes down to you or him, I choose you. But, like I said, I know you. When it comes to that moment, I know you will do what you believe is right." Gideon took a breath. "I can live with that."

Inara made to reply but her thoughts slowed her down enough for Gideon to turn away and return to the camp. She wanted to go after him and continue their conversation, remembering now how much she had always enjoyed talking to him. Instead, Inara watched him fade into the camp and disappear.

She had much to think about.

CHAPTER 53
THE BEGINNING OF SOMETHING BEAUTIFUL

After a dark and sorrowful night, a bright dawn brought a new day to The Black Wood. The grief remained, as it would for some time, but a new atmosphere was becoming palpable within the camp. Preparations were beginning for an evening of celebrating the dead and drinking to the coming battle. Dwarven as the tradition was, every elf and human was happy to join them, Asher included.

Having dwelled in the mourning and grief of so many, the ranger couldn't help but feel guilty, an emotion he was mostly unaccustomed to. Though he had lost Russell, a good friend he had long counted among the few he trusted with his life, and Adan'Karth, a being who had often acted as his conscience, Asher had gained new life that nourished his own.

Crossing the camp now, he looked up and saw that new life cut a bronze line through the sky. Avandriell was following him from above, her curiosity and apprehension bidding for dominance. She knew where her companion was going.

"Gideon tells me it's only temporary," he said aloud, garnering an inquisitive look from a passing dwarf.

A wave of amusement washed over their bond. *You have to stop doing that,* Avandriell insisted.

Even after days of almost constant talking, Asher could still be captivated by his companion's voice. It was new to him, yet it felt like a voice that had always existed inside his mind.

I'm never going to get used to this, he replied mentally, offering the dwarf a polite nod. **And Gideon tells me the effects of the Crissalith are only temporary. There's no pain, just... silence.**

Hmm, the dragon mused. *Must you experience it first-hand?* she asked.

I have no desire to be parted from you either, Asher stated. **But if there's anything out there that can harm you or our bond, I want to know about it.**

The warrior that lived in Avandriell's core agreed with the logic, but there was certainly more to her than just a fighter. *I still don't like it,* she complained, having no desire to be separated from him.

Asher couldn't help a smile. He knew there were people who would say they loved him - and he would never tell them they didn't - but it was a very different experience to feel the love of another resonating in his heart.

The work stations of the dwarven smiths weren't too far away from the main camp, but their seclusion made for perfect conditions where Crissalith was concerned. Still, the elves and dragons were sure to keep their business on the other side of the camp.

Only the slightest chill graced Asher's skin as he passed between the heat of each station. Hammers beat with a steady rhythm and sparks were born and died in the blink of an eye. For most, the ranger included, it was a headache-inducing environment, but for the dwarves it was the sound of home.

The smiths barely glanced away from their work as they took note of Asher's observation. He admired the blades and shields they produced, especially given their limited resources in the wood. Nothing, it seemed, could prevent the children of the mountain from doing what they did best.

I can still feel you, Avandriell told him.

Asher didn't need to look up to know that the dragon had glided away to a safer distance. *And I you,* he replied.

Approaching the furthest work station, the ranger's eyes caught a flash of green on an anvil. The closer he got, the more detached and isolated he felt. Avandriell's thoughts and feelings faded, as if the distance between them actually applied.

Asher... Her voice was reduced to a whisper.

It was wholly unnatural and every fibre of Asher's being told him to get away from the Crissalith. But he needed to know. If it could be retrieved from the mine in Davosai once then it could be retrieved again. Now he knew how close the crystalline rock had to be before he began to experience the side effects. Two more steps and his mind was an island again, absent Avandriell's exquisite presence and Thessaleia's extraordinary memories and experiences.

He was just a man.

His fist clenched, the ranger studied the work of the dwarves closely. They were detailed in their approach to any weapon's crafting, but they were also incredibly fast. Even now, before his eyes, the rough piece of crystal was beginning to resemble the blade of a dagger. It was beautiful. And abhorrent.

Like so much from that time, Crissalith was just another nightmare from the mind of Atilan. The secret history of the world would forever remember the wicked king as nothing more than a genocidal tyrant who couldn't live with his own mortality. His only saving grace was the accidental creation of the elves, though it was something of a taboo subject among the woodland folk.

Satisfied with his new knowledge regarding the Crissalith, Asher wasted no time in bidding it farewell. He strode from the area without a glance back.

There you are! Avandriell exclaimed. *Come and meet me!*

Asher welcomed her presence as she filled up his mind. There was instant transmission of memories, informing the other of their brief time apart. Both were in agreement that Crissalith was to be avoided at all costs and, if possible, destroyed so that it could never be used against them.

I have been reviewing your memories of orcs, Avandriell said with excitement, and much to Asher's amusement. Her mind worked quickly, dashing from one subject to another with hardly a breath between. It reminded him how young she was.

And what do you make of them? the ranger asked, heading deeper into the main camp.

I would like to face them! the dragon declared eagerly. *They possess a ferocity worthy of challenge.* Before Asher could comment, Avandriell blurted, *And Giants! Illian is home to a gruesome breed my mother never encountered. And Sandstalkers! I wish to test my fangs against their outer shell.*

Asher chuckled to himself as he passed a pair of dwarves stirring a large vat of stew. **This world is full of monsters,** he assured. **You'll get your chance at them all before long.**

Navigating a tight cluster of tents, the ranger offered Captain Dardaris a greeting nod, though he didn't stop to talk to the man, still unsure as to how he spoke to someone while conversing with a dragon. Continuing towards the large field that parted the trees, a place he could meet up with Avandriell, Asher almost paused his step. He could feel his companion moving around inside his mind.

What are you doing? he asked curiously.

You're different, Avandriell told him.

Different? he echoed incredulously, though he only required a moment of thought to realise he was completely different to the man he had been before he stepped into that bonding chamber.

You are not entirely the man I met, Avandriell went on. *You have let go of so much since then, even more so since Palios. The end of Nightfall and the Arakesh has changed you. I feel relief in you, a weight lifted. Yet, you still believe yourself to be the last of them. I can feel the shame that lingers. I do not like it.*

Asher glanced at the sky, catching a glimpse of her. **In time, their mark on the world will fade and their name will become an old legend. But I'm... immortal.** The word didn't come to him with ease. **I will live on, and so Nightfall's teachings will remain in the world. There's no escaping that.**

Avandriell remained uncharacteristically quiet for a moment, though Asher was convinced he could feel an impression of Thessaleia in her thoughts. *Are you an Outlander?* the young dragon asked.

Her tone suggested it was a trap of sorts but the ranger took the bait. **No,** he answered confidently.

Are you sure? You bear the mark of an Outlander. And, however long ago, I can still see and hear all that your time amongst them imparted to you.

Unconsciously, Asher reached up and touched the patch of skin under his left eye. The faded black fang tattoo had been etched into his face as a young child, an event he could not recall.

I see where you're going with this, he said, aware now that Avandriell was calling on some of her mother's wisdom to help him through it.

You are not Arakesh, the dragon asserted, *just as you are not an Outlander. Everything that came before has given you the foundation on which you can build a new life, a life with me. And we are rangers! Alidyr Yalathanil, Nasta Nal-Aket, Lady Gracen, and now Veda Malmagol. They are all gone. There are no more Mothers or Fathers. No more Nightfall. It is done.*

The ranger hadn't heard a couple of those names in a long time, nor had he paid them much thought. He wondered how long it would be before Avandriell's grasp on his memories stopped being so strange.

Asher gave a resigned smile. **Perhaps you are right.**

I am right, Avandriell replied boldly.

The ranger was almost upon the field now, the camp once again falling behind him. **Who am I to argue with a dragon?**

Avandriell's focus sharpened and her tone grew serious. *Never forget, you have a dragon heart. Whatever else, now and for evermore, you are a dragon. That makes us equal.*

A warm and genuine smile lit up Asher's face, a smile he would always hold in reserve for Avandriell alone. He knew his responding feelings were passing through their bond and so he didn't need to speak.

Navigating the trees, Asher didn't have to enter the field to know that Ilargo was already in it. Piercing the trees, the morning sun struck the green dragon and highlighted his golden speckles.

Catching Ilargo's eyes, the ranger offered a bow of the head before making his way towards Gideon. The old master was standing with his hands on his hips and looking down at Doran, who was issuing orders to a handful of his kin as they arrived with a small cart.

"What's all this?" he enquired on approach.

Any answer was delayed when Avandriell dropped out of the sky at a run. She came to a stop beside her companion with a cheeky glint in her golden eyes. It occurred to Asher that only he could see that expression in her and he liked it, even if it did leave him feeling a little suspicious.

"Ah, there ye are, lad!" Doran beckoned him closer with a gesture. "I've not long - I'm needed in a dozen other places. While ye lot were still makin' yer journey this way, I had me boys make somethin' for the three o' ye. Though," the dwarf admitted, "we've had to make some quick adjustments for Avandriell. We didn' know how big she was goin' to be."

"Three of us?" Asher looked questioningly to Gideon and found a good deal of doubt in his demeanour.

"Aye, the three o' ye; Gideon, Inara, an' yerself." Doran turned back to his fellow dwarves. "Come on lads, get to it!"

Asher turned briefly to Avandriell. *Why do I get the feeling you know what's happening?*

The dragon glanced at Ilargo before returning her companion's look. *Because I do.*

"It was very good of you to think of us, Doran," Gideon voiced.

Doran shrugged at the compliment. "Ye don' 'ave to use 'em. I jus' thought it might even out the field a bit. After all, Alijah an' Malliath 'ave one."

The tarps pulled back, the team of dwarves revealed three saddles and a tremendously long set of straps. An abundance of excitement and anticipation rose up in Avandriell.

Gideon twisted his mouth as he examined them. "Dragons

aren't meant to be *ridden*," he muttered. "But I suppose we aren't Dragorn anymore," he added, looking up at Ilargo.

Following his gaze up to the towering dragon, Asher was amazed to see Ilargo's expression in a way he had never noticed it before. Until that moment, the changes in his reptilian face had only been noticeable when his mood changed drastically. Now, he could see the subtle movements in the finer muscles and the emotion in his eyes. Ilargo appeared content with Gideon's assessment.

Doran raised his hands in a display of innocence. "I would never compare a dragon to a horse or even a Warhog. I know they're not mounts to be guided. That's why there's no reins. Instead," he added, tapping the front of the long saddle with his foot, "they've been fitted with a pair o' handles. That should give ye somethin' to hold on to when things get hairy." The son of Dorain looked directly at Asher. "There's saddlebags too. I know a ranger needs space for their gear."

Asher gave an appreciative smile. "Thank you, old friend."

Doran nodded once. "A long time ago, there was an alliance between dwarves an' elves, between dwarves an' *dragons*. We made weapons for ye." He gestured to Mournblade on Gideon's hip. "We fought with ye. An' we died with ye. Followin' the victory o' our alliance, the world seemed to fall apart for us all. Me kin looked inwards an' we shunned all else. I don' know what the future holds for ye, either o' ye. But jus' know, ye, an' all like ye, will always 'ave friends in Dhenaheim. That I promise."

Gideon placed a hand on the dwarf's shoulder. "And Dhenaheim will always have friends in the sky."

Doran responded with a tight-lipped smile before a sigh escaped him. He looked back at the main camp, through the trees. "I need to get back to it," he said half-heartedly. "We only 'ave today. Who knows what tomorrow will bring? They will assist ye as ye require," he added before walking away.

As the dwarves went about fitting the new saddles and measuring the straps that would have to go all the way around the dragons' chests, Asher found his feet firmly rooted to the ground.

He met Avandriell's eyes and found a quiet resolve in them - she would not be budged on what had to happen next.

"I wasn't aware you possessed such nerves," Gideon remarked, tightening one of the straps around Ilargo.

Feeling vulnerable under the scrutiny, Asher forced himself to relax and move from the spot. "I don't," he lied, walking around Avandriell to inspect the saddle. "I just thought Avandriell was too young."

You and I are flying today, the dragon declared unequivocally.

Unaware of her words to Asher, Gideon replied, "Avandriell is twice the size of a horse; she'll hardly feel your weight. The trick is balance, for both of you." The old master walked up to the bronze dragon and paused with his hands held out. Only when Avandriell bowed her head did he actually touch her. "You need to feel her muscles shifting beneath you," he continued, pressing into the scales above her front legs. "Your bond will give you an intuitive understanding when it comes to day to day flying, but Avandriell will always detect threats before you do. When that happens, her body will respond more on instinct and you won't always get a warning via your bond. You'll need to learn to interpret her every movement if you're to battle in the sky with her."

"You sound like you've had experience," Asher quipped.

"That's because he has," Inara called, approaching from the tree line behind them. Athis glided down and came in alongside Ilargo, their combined bulk taking up most of the area. After finding her place between them, the Guardian gave her old mentor a meaningful look. "Gideon knows what he's talking about. You should take his advice," she said to Asher.

The ranger didn't miss the moment of harmony that appeared to exist between the two. He had no idea what had been said, but he was glad to see they had found some common ground.

"And they look great," Inara commented, referring to the saddles now properly strapped to the dragons. "Athis and I have been talking about using one for years."

Now I feel like my mother, Avandriell announced proudly.

"Dragon Riders used saddles," Asher said aloud, drawing on

Thessaleia's memories. "They definitely knew a lot about aerial combat; they practiced it like a religion."

Gideon beamed. "I envy the memories you carry. Perhaps Avandriell's ancient heritage will give you both an advantage up there."

Asher followed the flick of Gideon's eyes to the blue ocean above before coming all the way back down to Avandriell's hungry expression. *Let's go!* she cried, turning to present her side.

When he didn't move, Inara turned a questioning look on him. "Do I detect some hesitation in the stoical ranger?"

"No," Asher quickly replied through a tense jaw.

Inara did not look convinced. "You've flown before," she reminded him. "And not just on Athis. You even flew on—"

"I'm aware," the ranger cut in, with no doubt in his mind as to which dragon she was about to name.

Confused, Inara asked, "Then what is it?"

It's the memories, Avandriell revealed, only she also shared it with Ilargo and Athis, which is to say she shared it with Gideon and Inara.

"Memories?" Gideon queried.

Having shared just enough to coax the ranger, Avandriell offered them no further explanation. *Speak your burdens,* she urged him, *and they will lose their hold.*

Asher flashed his companion a brief scold. **I'm already growing tired of this dragon wisdom.**

"Asher?" Inara probed.

"I remember everything I ever did under The Crow's spell. I remember my time bonded to Malliath." He took a breath. Just saying that much made him feel more vulnerable than he could usually bear. "Avandriell has already started to take the sting out of those memories. Even now they continue to fade, as if they were someone else's life. But it's harder up there. There's nothing like being astride a dragon. Those memories are the sharpest." The ranger turned to Gideon. "I was with him when... when he attacked The Lifeless Isles. I saw the dragons and Riders fall from the sky. I felt his fury. And I felt their death." Asher shut his mouth and puffed out his chest as his chin dipped to meet it.

He heard Avandriell walking towards him, though there was some inexplicable part of him that sensed her approach regardless of his human senses. When her head hung just over his, he finally looked up to meet her beautiful yet fearsome eyes.

So much shame, she began, *So much guilt. How quickly you forget your great deeds, your heart and soul trapped under the weight of your past. Well here it ends,* she declared. *Today, this very moment, is where the line is drawn. No longer will you suffer from the dark corners of your life. You and I will leave the earth in our wake and embrace a new world of our own making.* Avandriell's face edged closer, her hot breath washing over him. *You have atoned. It's time to start living.*

Her determination became his, a fire they shared in their veins. Within seconds, Asher was seated comfortably in his new saddle and looking down on Gideon and Inara. Both were grinning up at him and, through the bond shared between all three dragons, he could tell that their hearts were swelling with happiness. The old Asher would have recoiled from it all and used his previous skills as an assassin to simply disappear but, instead, he responded in kind and accepted their love for him.

For the first time in his life, it didn't feel so strange to have friends.

Holding lightly to the handles, the ranger let his body move with Avandriell's as she walked away from the others. Following her instruction, he leaned forward and gripped the handles. He immediately felt her body tense beneath his, a slight crouch in her legs as her claws sank into the ground. Her wings swiftly unfurled, the tips pointing to the sky. With white knuckles and a racing heart, Asher held his breath.

Proving her strength and displaying the might of her heritage, Avandriell cleared the ground in one beat of her wings and launched into the air. The wind swept Asher's hair and green cloak out behind him and even tried to force him to close his eyes. But he refused. He wanted to witness every second of it.

Avandriell was awash with joy. She climbed and climbed until

The Black Wood was naught but a dark smudge on the earth. With her wings tucked in, she twisted her body so they skimmed the clouds blowing in from the east. Asher had braced himself for the moment and managed to stay in his saddle during the corkscrew manoeuvre. It was exhilarating. He hollered and cheered and urged his companion to reach for the heavens.

Not until you have a better grasp on magic, Avandriell cautioned.

Satisfied with the majestic view from below the clouds, Asher settled into the flight and focused on the dragon's micro movements. Every few minutes she would change her flight path while deliberately withholding the decision from him. Every time, he discovered something new about the way her body moved in the air and he committed it to memory. Only once did he lose his grip on one of the handles, causing his entire left side to flip over to the right. Avandriell had only to make a quick correction in the opposite direction to put the ranger back in his saddle.

And, just when Asher was beginning to feel like he belonged in the sky, two enormous dragons cut through the heavens, one after the other. Ilargo was first, shooting up in front of them and hurtling through the clouds. Avandriell was left with no choice but to bank sharply to the right and avoid the collision. That was when Athis appeared, his red scales dominating their view as he raced to catch up with Ilargo. In order to avoid the new collision, Avandriell pointed her head up and took the rest of her body with it until she was vertical.

It proved too much for Asher, who struck his head against one of Avandriell's blunt protrusions and lost his grip on both handles. Before he knew it, his companion's tail whistled past his ear as the distance between them continued to grow. It would have been easy at this point to believe he was falling to his death and cry out with great protest. And, perhaps he would have were it not for Avandriell speaking into his mind.

I'm coming!

He believed her.

The bronze dragon darted through the clouds, her wings flat to her sides. Avandriell homed in on him and closed the gap in seconds. Following her lead, Asher twisted his body until he was head down, mirroring his companion.

Now! she commanded.

Asher reached out and grasped the handles of his saddle as they came together. Lining himself up, his legs either side, the ranger prepared himself for the sudden change in direction and, indeed, it was sudden. Avandriell arched her body, flexing her spine back on itself, and launched them into the vastness of the sky once more.

Soon after, Athis and Ilargo came up on either side of them, Inara and Gideon seated in their new saddles. Both of them were clearly amused, much to Asher's chagrin.

It's good to fall off, Gideon said across their shared bond. *It reminds you who has the wings. Always follow Avandriell's lead. Listen to her body.*

Asher nodded his head in understanding, but he was somewhat distracted by the size of Ilargo and Athis. In the air, with their wings spread out, they seemed magnitudes larger than Avandriell. He had to wonder how big she would eventually grow to be. Thessaleia had been comparable to Ilargo or Athis, but Avandriell's father, Garganafan, dwarfed them all.

There isn't enough time to teach you everything you need to know, Inara pointed out from the other side. *When we enter those mountains, we face Malliath and Godrad. They're big dragons,* she added gravely. *Speed and quick manoeuvring will be your advantage. Athis and Ilargo can help you practise but, the truth is, you first need to be confident when flying. Otherwise, all the manoeuvring in the world isn't going to matter. And drill after drill isn't going to instil that.*

Asher raised his eyebrows. *Then what will?*

A gleeful smile took over Inara's face. *Let's have some fun!*

CHAPTER 54
CHOOSING JOY

L ong after the sun had set, Inara was still beaming from a day in the sky. She couldn't recall the last time she had flown with such abandon beside other dragons and their Riders. The three of them had soared through the heavens and raced only feet above the ground.

Towards the end, as twilight was upon the world, they had practised specific manoeuvres that showed Avandriell different ways to weave in and out of battle. While her smaller size put her at a disadvantage, it could also be used in her favour.

It was all so much harder for Asher who, for the first time to Inara's eyes, was a fish out of water. There was next to nothing the Arakesh, nor his time as a ranger, had taught him that could be used. Though, where he lacked the skills of aerial combat, he made up for it with bold determination and control of his fears.

Once they had returned to the ground, Inara privately suggested to Gideon that they leave Avandriell and Asher out of any aerial attack on The Bastion. Though Gideon agreed, the pair decided between them that they could never conjure an argument strong enough to dissuade the new companions.

And so, with nowhere to go but forward, they soon found

themselves returned to the large camp and a very different atmosphere to the previous night. A sense of anticipation had spread among the rebels, particularly the dwarves.

"Is this typical of dwarves before a battle?" Inara asked while talking to her parents, though it was Galanör who answered as he approached with Aenwyn.

"It's not just the coming battle," the elf said. "A new sense of unity has begun to spread among the children of the mountain. Since Qamnaran, there have been a few *louder* dwarves who believe they would replace their fallen king, but they have proven to be all talk and no action. None have stood up to lead."

"I would say one has," Aenwyn remarked knowingly.

"Indeed," Galanör agreed.

"If begrudgingly," Inara added, after catching on.

"Doran has had this thrust upon him," Reyna observed, her tone suggesting a deeper level of understanding where the dwarf was concerned. "Yet he has faced every challenge in the name of his kin, even when it was them who challenged him. Doran might not want to be the king of Dhenaheim, but he is certainly the one they deserve."

Inara reached out and squeezed her mother's hand. She was sure to put an apology in her eyes, there for Reyna to see. That was all it took to bring them back into harmony, their disagreement regarding Gideon and the Crissalith quickly forgotten. It wasn't enough for her mother, however, who pulled her in and planted a soft kiss on her head.

"Doran as king," Nathaniel said with a laugh. "He's going to hate it."

"Or perhaps," Reyna was quick to reply, "he will come to appreciate the new power he wields and use it to serve his people with love and respect."

The old knight held his wife's gaze a moment longer, her words not lost on him. "Perhaps he will," he said earnestly.

"I thought there would be a lot more celebrating," Aenwyn commented. "Before the battle on The Moonlit Plains, the dwarves were behaving as if they had already won."

"They're waiting," Gideon told her, arriving with a cup of ale in each hand. Before he could give one to Inara, her father swiped it from the old master's grip.

"You're flying tomorrow," he reminded her with a wink. Inara gave a light groan through her amused smile.

"Waiting for what?" Aenwyn enquired.

"Their king," Gideon said with a grin.

Before any discussion on the matter could begin, Vighon arrived with Sir Borin the Dread at his back. All but Reyna and Nathaniel responded to his presence with a courteous bow of the head.

"Good evening," he greeted, his breath visible in the air.

"Your Grace," Gideon replied, the hint of a question in his voice.

"I have been speaking with Doran," Vighon explained. "The war isn't even won yet and he's concerned about a lasting alliance between Dhenaheim and Illian."

"He *is* to be declared king then," Nathaniel surmised.

Vighon appeared hesitant to answer. "Soon, I believe," he said, his dark eyes glancing at Inara. "It is believed the dwarven force will fight with better morale if they are united under one banner and one king."

"Can he not be challenged, your Grace?" Aenwyn asked.

"Who would challenge him?" Nathaniel questioned before the northman could reply. "Doran has freed thousands of his kin and defeated every foe he's come up against. Not to mention the fact that he wields Andaljor. That weapon is legendary throughout *all* the clans."

"As you say," Gideon said. "And the prospect of ruling all of Dhenaheim would be enough to give anyone pause. There is unity now, but in the absence of foreign enemies, the cultural differences between the different clans will become apparent. Doran has a very long and difficult road ahead of him."

Vighon simply nodded his head in overall agreement. "And he will have Illian to call upon should we be required."

"Ayda too will come to his aid," Reyna stated.

"He knows all that," Asher said, emerging from the gathering crowds with a pipe between his teeth and Kassian behind him. "Tonight, he just needs his friends."

"Agreed," Nathaniel cheered heartily. "We should all have drinks for the occasion," he added, looking to some of the passing dwarves who hefted a keg of beer between them.

As Faylen and Nemir arrived, Vighon used their collective greeting to discreetly lean in to Inara's ear. He asked to steal her away for a moment, before the night's activities truly began. She quickly agreed and he instructed Sir Borin to remain where he was.

Taken by the hand, Inara was happily led away from the throng and deeper into the woods. When the camp became imperceptible background noise, Vighon finally stopped and turned to face her.

"I think everyone knows about us," Inara pointed out. "You could probably kiss me in front of them," she added with a wry smile.

Vighon had a smile of his own, one that Inara couldn't interpret the truth behind. As a question formed she felt Athis shrinking away in her mind.

Why are you going? she asked the dragon. They didn't often separate without a cause.

This is a moment for just the two of you, Athis replied, one step ahead of Inara.

Instead of saying anything at all, Vighon maintained his smile and subsequently dropped to one knee. Inara felt her heart quicken and her breath get away from her. Before she knew it, her hand was in his.

"Inara," he began confidently. "I have no token to offer you, and this is, perhaps, the last place a king would make a grand proposal. But I do have a promise." The northman took a breath. "I have loved you for so long I can no longer recall a time I didn't. With my word and my life I promise you that that will never fade. I will love you and honour you from now to my last breath." Vighon's hand tightened around hers. "Inara Galfrey, will you do me the honour of being my wife?"

There was an immediate answer behind her lips, desperate to

be set free. Rather than let her thoughts give her pause, a hesitation in Vighon's eyes, Inara withdrew into the sanctuary she shared with Athis, a place where time almost stood still. Sensing her disquiet, Athis re-formed the bridge of their bond and quickly joined her in the heavenly mountains of their own design.

Athis recovered her recent memories in an instant. *That was very sweet,* he opined. *You would imagine a king to make a spectacle of such a thing.*

He knows me, Inara explained. **But I fear I do not know myself.** She walked out onto a plateau of varying types of long grass, their colours more vibrant than anything possible in the real world. **I know what I want to say,** she continued.

Then say it, Athis advised, gliding down to join her in the grasses. *You need not fear yourself. You must learn to embrace who you are, who you really are.*

Inara sighed, torn between angst and excitement. **If I take this path, if I marry Vighon, I will be giving my heart to a mortal. I will have to watch him fade away until death finally claims him. And what of children? They would have some elven blood, but it might not grant them everlasting life. It didn't for Alijah. I would live on only to watch my entire line eventually die. I would have to say farewell to them all.**

Athis lowered his head, angling it at a slight tilt. *Inara, you have already given your heart to Vighon. Even now I can feel it beating for him. I sensed your love for him when we first met and it has never faltered. I simply prevented you from feeling it.*

None of that changes my future, Inara countered. **If I say yes, I will know only—**

Love, Athis interjected. *You will know the love of a family. The companionship of a husband. The joy of children. They are unique experiences that no Dragorn has ever known. Yes, there will be pain. But there will also be happiness. I know you, Inara. If you deny your feelings now, you will live with regret for the rest of your days. Even if your time with Vighon is a spark in your lifetime, let it be a spark so bright that it lives in you for all time.*

Inara reached up and ran a loving hand along her companion's jaw. ***What will it mean for us?***

We will find a way, Athis promised. *Though I see children on my back in the future,* he quipped.

Inara smiled, blinked once, and returned to the same moment she had inhabited standing before Vighon. "Yes," she replied to his question. As she witnessed a wave of joy overcome Vighon, she felt the same thing cross her bond from Athis.

The northman leapt to his feet and pulled her in to a tight embrace and a passionate kiss. "You have made me the happiest man alive," he exclaimed before kissing her again.

"We are such fools," Inara said through a giddy smile. "Tomorrow, we go into battle."

"Now I have something more to fight for," Vighon uttered, his expression locked in a moment of joy.

Hand in hand, they made their way back to the camp and returned to the gathered council. A drink was waiting for them both and more than a few questioning faces. The couple, however, offered tight smiles in response and kept their engagement to themselves. The night was about someone else.

CHAPTER 55
THE VALLEY OF DEATH

"*They're waiting for you,*" Drelda said, her voice hoarse from days of weeping.

Seated beside his brother's bed, his elbows resting on his knees, and his head hung low, Doran nodded absently. He had taken note of the quiet beyond the royal tent as the camp's anticipation reached its apex.

Doran looked up and cast his eye over the empty bed. Once upon a time, long before he exiled himself to Illian, the son of Dorain had imagined the day he would be crowned the king of Grimwhal. On that day, he had always envisioned his brother standing beside him.

"*Your father would never have stood for this,*" the queen mother continued in the absence of a response. "*A king should be crowned by the Iron Priest, not some lowly cleric. And it certainly wouldn't be done in a forest.*"

Doran let her vent it all, aware that she was only trying to busy her mind and keep the grief at bay. "*The Iron Priest was killed when the Reavers invaded Grimwhal, Mother. A lowly cleric will do the job just fine - all he has to do is place a damned crown on my head. And we have no mountain to call home right now, so The Black Wood will have to do. Soldiers always do better when they have someone to follow."*

As he stood up, his mother was right in front of him, a stern look on her face. *"That damned crown you're so loath to wear means something. From King Thorgen's head to yours it has brought power to our family."* Doran wanted to remind her that it was not the same crown worn by their ancestor - the original lost over two thousand years ago during a clan war - but he didn't dare interrupt her right now. *"Your father didn't know what to do with that power. He had no ambition for the Heavybellys nor our people as a whole. Your brother..."*

Drelda caught herself before new tears escaped. *"Your brother wanted to change everything. He wanted peace across all of Dhenaheim. He wanted prosperity for all dwarves. But for all his wants and desires, such a future was beyond him, beyond any dwarf, even King Uthrad Battleborn."* The queen mother gripped Doran's arms. *"But you, my son, have found yourself at a very precious point in history. What you do here and now will shape the children of the mountain for generations. Only Grarfath and Yamnomora have done more for our people."*

Doran considered the declaration he was minutes away from making. *"It's bold,"* he said. *"There will be those who oppose my taking of Grimwhal, let alone Dhenaheim."*

"They might oppose you, but none can oppose your deeds. Kings are always defined by their actions—"

"Exactly," Doran interrupted. *"You're talking to the dwarf who abandoned his post, his family, his home. My actions speak only of—"*

"A hero," Drelda stated, cutting him short. *"You have proven yourself to be worthy of Thorgen's blood. This was always to be your fate. You have just arrived at it from an unusual place. It only adds to your story and legend."* The queen mother pressed her hands to his chest. *"But, if it makes you feel better, you are not elevating yourself. Wearing that crown is a sacrifice, a burden you bear for all. Till the end of your days, you are a servant to our people. You will be judged not only by us but history itself."*

Doran gave a light chuckle. *"You know, that doesn't make me feel any better, but thank you, Mother."* He took a deep breath and looked to the tent's entrance. *"Let's be doing this."* He loudly cleared his throat, signalling Thaligg on the other side.

"Pray silence!" the cleric bellowed in man's tongue, bringing an end to the quiet conversations still taking place. "We may not be in the shadow o' the mountains, but we stand on ground as hard as Grarfath's skin, ground the Father laid 'imself at the dawn o' time! It is on that ground that we pay homage to Doran Heavybelly, son o' Dorain Heavybelly, an' descendant o' the mighty Thorgen Heavybelly!"

Taking his cue, Doran emerged from the tent and, with Thaligg and Thraal at his back, walked into the clearing behind the cleric. Just as they had when he announced his brother's passing, the gathered crowd dropped to one knee and bowed their heads, including the several hundred dwarves who had come with the council. Only Reyna, Nathaniel, and Vighon remained standing, their own stations demanding they bow to no one.

A subtle flick of his fingers signalled the cleric alone to rise, who motioned for another dwarf to approach from the side, a cushion held out in both hands. Doran watched the cleric remove the crown of his ancestors from the cushion and hold it high.

"In the eyes o' the Mother an' Father, I ask Doran Heavybelly to kneel before his people an' for his people to rise an' accept his pledge!"

On his knees, his head held high, Doran declared, "For as long as Grarfath gives me breath an' Yamnomora gives me favour, I give me life not only to the Heavybellys o' Grimwhal, but to every dwarf on this rocky earth! As we lived thousands o' years ago, in an age o' heroes, we will live again! As one people under one banner, the children o' the mountain will rise again! We will take back our homes, our land, an' our heritage! My every wakin' moment will be devoted to this cause, *our* cause! Only death itself will stop me!"

"I'd like to see it even try!" came a cry from one of the dwarves in the crowd.

"Pray silence!" the cleric admonished.

Doran looked down to conceal the brief smile curling at his mouth.

"It is with the blessin' o' Grarfath that I, a cleric o' the Mountain Order, bestow upon ye, Doran Heavybelly, the crown o' Grimwhal... an' the crown o' *Dhenaheim!*"

Doran felt the circlet of silvyr as it came to rest on his head. Light as the metal was, it felt oppressively heavy on his head. Now he knew why Vighon rarely wore his own.

With nothing to do now but stand up, he rose to his feet and was met with a blasting roar from the crowd. Due to his lack of peripheral vision, the dwarf had to turn his head left and right to take them all in. The applause continued until he raised his hands to quieten them.

"Tomorrow we go into battle!" he yelled. "Stand behind me an' Andaljor an' victory will be ours! It *must* be ours, for this is not to be our end! Only when the mountains themselves perish will we perish with them! So tonight, drink to our inevitable victory! Drink to those who 'ave fallen to get us this far! An' drink to me while ye at it, yer one-eyed king!" The crowd cheered with his laugh, a sound that surely rocked the earth.

What followed was a haze of congratulations from friends and strangers alike. Drinks and food flowed through the camp, some of which even graced Doran's lips. Unlike the last time, however, the new king was cautious where the ale was concerned - he wanted a clear head for battle. It was with the battle in mind that the council eventually came together, much later into the night when Doran had lost some of the attention he had garnered. Around a roaring fire, watched over by guards of varying races, they planned The Rebellion's final assault on the invaders.

"If he thinks that cold piece o' stone is goin' to keep 'im safe he's got another think comin'," Doran remarked of The Bastion.

"The mountain path is treacherous," Inara put forward. "You could not march an army up there."

"Alijah knows this," Vighon added. "He will have been forced to leave his Reavers in the valley. If they block the path, the only way to The Bastion is by air."

"Then it's a good thing we have dragons," Kassian commented.

"Three dragons cannot ferry an army up The Vrost Mountains," Gideon pointed out, holding his cup at his mouth.

"They don't need to," Asher said. "If Alijah doesn't have an army up there, we need only face him with a small team of skilled fighters."

"It would be foolish to believe he doesn't have *any* Reavers up there," Galanör replied.

"Then we had better put an emphasis on the *skilled* part," Asher responded with a wry smile.

"He could call on his army with a single thought," Reyna reminded them. "Treacherous as the mountain path is, Reavers move without fear and without need of rest. If he wanted to, Alijah could have Reavers reinforcing The Bastion before we have time to defeat him."

"And defeating Alijah is far from guaranteed," Nathaniel told them. "Especially since Malliath will be up there with him."

"Malliath is not all that stands between us and Alijah," Gideon addressed. "He still has one Dragon Rider under his thrall. Vilyra of Freygard and heir to Carstane was a fearsome Rider of her time. And Godrad, her dragon, was known for his appetite for Giants."

Doran looked to Gideon and Inara. "If ye can handle the dragons an' whatever else awaits ye in The Bastion, me kin will keep the Reavers in the valley from flankin' ye."

"As will the elves," Nathaniel proclaimed. "Though I must insist on accompanying you to The Bastion."

Inara sat forward. "Father," she pleaded.

"I believe we fall within the *skilled* category that Asher referred to," Reyna added to her husband's words. "Faylen is more than capable of leading our forces in battle," she assured, looking to her old friend across the fire.

Doran watched Inara, waiting for her to rebuke her parents' desire and deny them a place on the dragons but, rather surprisingly, the Guardian of the Realm took a breath while she scrutinised them. "We will face him together then," she said. "You may accompany me on Athis."

"Is there room for another king?" Vighon enquired. "And,

612

perhaps, a stubborn Golem?" he added, glancing at Sir Borin over his shoulder.

"You need to lead your forces against the Reavers," Inara was quick to tell him, an edge of protectiveness in her voice.

"Sir Ruban," Vighon began, gesturing to his captain, "has led my forces across the entire realm and faced all manner of opposition. He has more than proven himself capable. No, I must face Alijah. He took my kingdom. If I am to truly reclaim the throne, I must be seen to challenge my usurper."

"And if he kills you in the process?" Inara questioned.

"That's what you're there for," the northman replied with a confident smile.

Inara's next breath came through a clenched jaw. "Very well," she reluctantly agreed.

"Your challenge of him is understandable," Gideon commented to the king. "Though I must insist on taking Galanör," he stated, glancing at the elven ranger. "He retrieved the Crissalith and he has the Hastion gem. With his skillset, both can be used as a weapon, one our enemy knows nothing about." Aenwyn cleared her throat beside Galanör. "And Aenwyn, of course," the old master quickly added.

Since their number was growing, most eyes naturally turned to Kassian Kantaris. It hadn't escaped Doran's notice that the loudmouth mage had been unusually quiet.

"An' what o' ye, young Keeper?" the son of Dorain asked bluntly. "I would 'ave thought that burnin' hot vengeance o' yers would 'ave ye jumpin' at the bit to get up there."

Kassian tapped the wand holstered on his leg, his eyes lost to the flames.

"Kassian?" Vighon prompted.

The Keeper finally looked up. "I will fight in the valley," he made known. "We will give you as much time as we can."

Doran licked his lips. "Ye know Alijah an' Malliath will be in The Bastion, don' ye? For two years I've sat through countless meetin's an' listened to ye tell us how ye goin' to *kill the necro-*

mancer for what he's done. Are ye tellin' me now that you won' take yer wand to that fight?"

Kassian ran a hand over his beard, contemplating his words. "There have been many sacrifices to get us to this point. More deaths than I can count anymore. I see now that they didn't die just so we can defeat our enemy. They gave their lives for Illian's future, for *our* future. I have glimpsed what that may be. I would not throw my life away fighting a superior foe - I see that now. Instead, I would fight to live so that I might build something new out of the ashes, something worthy of my wife."

Doran offered the man an approving grin. "Good on ye, lad. Fightin' with hatred in yer heart is a path to destruction, take it from me."

"Good decision," Vighon expressed.

"Then it's settled!" Doran announced, rising to his feet with a horn of ale in one hand. "Tomorrow we fight! But, tonight, we make what we can o' the time we 'ave left!"

The dwarven king knocked the horn back and gulped the ale, his gaze cast to the stars above.

It felt to Doran as if the next time he was parting the horn from his lips, he was throwing it into the snow and facing The Vrost Mountains. Time had moved so swiftly that he could scarcely recall the latter half of the night nor the journey from The Black Wood to their waiting forces. He did, however, remember cursing the dawn as it pierced the trees and woke him from what had only been a short slumber.

Now, attired in his black and gold armour, Andaljor strapped to his saddle, and a crown on his head, Doran had nothing but an angry frown for the snow-covered valley. Behind him thousands of dwarves stood in their tight ranks, awaiting his command to advance. To their left, the elves looked to Faylen Haldör for their own orders while, to the right of the dwarves, the human soldiers stood ready for Captain Dardaris's word. It was among them that Kassian had dispersed his Keepers, having instructed them to add their magic to that of the elves.

Atop their horses, Faylen and Sir Ruban closed in on the king from each side. "The scouts we sent into the mountains have not returned," the captain reported. "I fear they never will."

"Hmm," Doran mused with a rough throat. "I believe this valley intends to swallow us whole."

"At least we know they're in there," Faylen replied.

"They're in there *waiting* for us," Ruban specified. "The advantage is already theirs."

"Trap or no trap," Doran said, looking up at the three dragons circling in the sky, "that's where we're goin'. We only 'ave to keep 'em occupied until they defeat Alijah an' Malliath. Without 'em, the puppets 'ave no strings." Turning his mouth over his shoulder, the king bellowed, "ADVANCE!" The order was echoed across the numerous ranks and repeated by elves and humans alike.

As one, The Rebellion entered The Vrost Mountains, prepared to make one final stand in defence of their realm.

Doran led them astride his loyal Warhog, his first battle as king. It could also be his last battle as king. That was a typical thought before any fight, especially on this scale, and he embraced it as his potential fate. To fear such a fatal outcome would weaken his resolve and, today and every day that followed, his resolve was an example that needed to inspire.

That in itself was a daunting thought that would see most run away, never to return. Fortunately, the old ranger in him knew exactly how to tackle such a fight: the knights of Erador were just monsters. He had fought and slain more monsters than he had eaten hot meals. That's all this was. Just another day killing monsters.

With that thought underlying his determination, he kept Pig on a straight heading and ploughed deeper into the mountains. Overhead, the dragons deliberately double-backed on themselves again and again to stay close to the army until they reached The Bastion. The valley, however, was mile upon mile of mounting snow, so thick in parts that the Warhogs struggled to move through it. Costing them vital energy and resolve, their journey went on and on, hour after hour, until the sun was hidden behind the western mountains.

"Camping in this is going to be hellish," Sir Ruban called out against the wind.

Doran was about to agree when he noticed the dragons fading away into an evening sky. They were angling into the north, to the dwarf's right, and heading for the top of the nearest mountain.

"I don' think we'll be campin'!" the king replied, returning his gaze to the open valley before them. He held up a balled fist and orders were immediately called out to halt their incessant march.

Faylen's horse approached to bring the High Guardian over. "The Bastion must be up there," she reasoned.

Kassian Kantaris came up from behind Doran, having left his horse with his Keepers. "If The Bastion is up there," he posed, "where are all the Reavers guarding the passage?" The young mage surveyed the valley as they all had. "It's just... more *snow*."

"And the sun is dropping fast," Sir Ruban added, as the wind whipped snow about them. "It will be dark soon."

The son of Dorain scowled at the setting. "I don' like it."

"Perhaps our assessment was wrong," the captain continued.

"Alijah must have ordered his forces up to The Bastion," Kassian said gravely. "If we don't find that path before nightfall we'll never get up there."

Doran shook his head, his eye never wandering from the valley. "We're dealin' with a necromancer," he reminded them. "He's not playin' by our tactics." The dwarf climbed down from his Warhog and was dismayed by the deep snow he discovered.

"What are you thinking?" Faylen enquired.

Doran squared his jaw and frowned. "What am I thinkin'?" he echoed. Unable to answer the question, he started forward, through the snow. Thaligg and Thraal naturally made to follow but the king stopped them with a gesture. Instead, he looked back at Kassian. "Bring yer wand, lad."

With the Keeper beside him, Doran broke away from The Rebellion forces. Together they walked further into the valley, though no further than their ability to call back. As light faded from the world, Kassian brought his wand to bear with a glowing light shining from the tip.

PHILIP C. QUAINTRELL

"What are we looking for, Doran?" he asked.

The dwarven king ran a hand through his blond beard, taking some of the snow out of it as he did. "Somethin' ain' right," he muttered, though the wind snatched it from the air before the words could reach the Keeper.

Standing still, his sight battling with the feeling in his gut, Doran let some of the tension go in his hand, allowing Andaljor's hammer end to dip into the snow beside him.

Doran froze and not from the plummeting temperature.

He looked down at where the end of his hammer would be, where he had just heard the familiar sound of steel knocking against steel. Kassian had heard it too and quickly turned on the dwarf, his wand pointed down at the pile of snow. Now that the light was directed at the ground, they could see the definition in place of the white out. The ground was covered in piles of snow similar to the one Doran was standing beside.

The king looked up to meet Kassian's eyes and found the same cold dread of realisation that lived in him. Without wasting another second, Doran turned back to The Rebellion and cried, "SHIELDS!"

At the same moment, thousands of Reavers sprouted from the valley floor, their numbers curling around the edges of the rebel forces, at the foot of the mountainside. The Reaver beneath Doran's hammer shot up from the snow only to receive a destructive blast to the face from Kassian's wand, the tip ignited with a devastating spell.

Enemies rising left and right, the son of Dorain had no choice but to heft Andaljor and swing with all his might. After hammering the closest Reaver in the chest, he took the opportunity to unclip the two halves of the ancient weapon. By the time he was wielding both axe and hammer, Kassian had unleashed a torrent of colourful spells and sent undead fiends back to the afterlife.

Not far away, Faylen and Sir Ruban gave the order to close ranks and organise a shield wall - they had only seconds before the Reavers were upon them. Doran glimpsed Thaligg and Thraal darting away from the formation and riding towards him on their Warhogs, and Pig close behind them. Inevitably, the Reavers swelled between them, cutting the brothers off from their king.

Now, with Kassian already disappearing behind a wall of Reavers, the son of Dorain faced the battle of his life, alone.

CHAPTER 56
WHERE IT ALL BEGAN

Alijah's maniacal laughter echoed through the halls of The Bastion. The Rebellion had entered The Vrost Mountains with all the finesse of a Troll and wandered into a fight they couldn't possibly win. Even now, he watched through the dead eyes of his knights as they fell upon Doran Heavybelly with sword and spear. The mettle of dwarves would be tested this night, their arrogance laid bare.

The elves, however, were already proving themselves a wicked foe. Their magic tore through the ranks of his Reavers, lighting up the darkness as they cast numerous bodies into the air. It only bolstered Alijah's resolve to extinguish their entire race. With the death of magic, they could have experienced full and rich lives, but they had taken that option away with their reckless action.

It was with reckless action in mind that Alijah turned to the eyes of his Dragon Rider, Vilyra. Through her, he saw a small band of rebels who believed they alone could defeat him in his own fortress. They were brought to his door on the backs of Athis, Ilargo, and a third dragon he couldn't name.

Is that Asher I see? he queried through his bond.

Malliath, who was also watching events unfold via their

connection with Vilyra, replied, *It is of no consequence. His dragon is a youngling - their scales will not stand up to my bite.*

A pity, Alijah mused. **In another life, Asher would have made an excellent Dragon Rider.**

Soon, Malliath purred, *he won't even have this life.*

As the dragons neared and Godrad acquired a better look at their passengers, Alijah rose to his feet, knocking the chair out from behind him. Inara was always going to challenge him, chained to her duty as she was, but she had brought their parents along to aid in killing him.

I told you, Malliath said. *They have chosen their side.*

Alijah's fists balled into tight knots until his knuckles cracked. This was it, the day The Crow had warned him about so many years ago, the day when those who claimed to love him would challenge him.

Sacrifice without hesitation.

Now he truly understood what that lesson meant. Tonight, he was going to spill his family's blood for the sake of the realm, sacrificing any hope of rekindling what they had lost. And he knew there were none who could ever love him as Inara and his parents had, but he would find a way to live without it - what other choice did a good king have?

The northman is among them, Malliath informed him, bringing Alijah back to the present. *I would taste his flesh.*

He is protected by that wretched Golem, Alijah remarked. **They are notoriously difficult to destroy.**

I have slaughtered my kin by the score, Malliath boasted. *I pay no mind to the likes of a Golem.*

Indeed, Alijah could feel his companion's appetite coming alive at the thought of it all. Rather than comment on the dragon's desires, the king returned his gaze to the mountain tops. Vilyra and Godrad were following closely from behind, using the encroaching clouds as cover. Sharpening Godrad's reptilian eyes, Alijah quickly spotted Galanör and Aenwyn astride Ilargo. Though he was to be attacked by the few, The Rebellion had brought together the realm's fiercest warriors.

Let us begin, Malliath declared with hungry glee.

Wait, Alijah cautioned. ***They are a menacing group to be sure, but their real strength is drawn from their belief that together, they can overcome anything. I would break them first, and let them see the end, before that final blow.***

Hmm. Malliath mulled it over with growing anticipation. *Fear does make the meat sweeter.*

Alijah couldn't attest to that but, in their fear, he hoped his enemies - those who had been so close to him - reflected on their misjudgement of him and the error of their ways before they died. **Let us divide and conquer,** he suggested.

Vighon narrowed his eyes at the black stone of The Bastion. As dark clouds rolled in, dimming any light from the moon, the ancient fortress almost disappeared entirely into the mountain. He had never seen the desolate place before but, seeing it now, he decided that none of the accounts had given its aura of malevolence enough credit. From Atilan, to The Crow, and now Alijah, The Bastion had provided shelter to naught but evil.

Before Athis touched down on the wide steps that led up to the main doors, the red dragon released its grip of Sir Borin. The Golem landed on his feet and required only the slightest bend in the knees to absorb the bone-breaking drop.

Along with Reyna and Nathaniel, the king climbed down and joined Sir Borin on the icy steps. Inara remained in her new saddle for the moment, surveying the walls that stretched high into the mountain rock.

The ground shuddered when Ilargo came down on the snowy slope beside the steps. Galanör and Aenwyn practically glided down the dragon's side. Like Vighon and the others, they quickly, without the dragon's radiating warmth, adjusted their hoods and cloaks to protect them against the vicious winds that battered the mountain side.

Being smaller, Avandriell was able to land on the hewn stone between the steps and main doors. With his green hood up, Asher cut a formidable figure astride the bronze dragon, his silvyr blade and quiver over his back and his broadsword on his hip.

"What's wrong?" Reyna shouted up to Inara.

"Malliath's scent is in the wind!" Inara yelled down.

No sooner had she said his name than the black behemoth thundered onto the steps behind them. His purple eyes appeared to almost flare as he lowered his head to reveal Alijah astride the base of his neck. Vighon braced both his stance and his courage as he stared the pair down. From his back, he retrieved the rounded enchanted shield and, from his belt, the flaming sword of the north, its flames a gift of elven magic.

"As king of these lands," Alijah boomed, "I sentence every man, elf, and dwarf in that valley to death!" A wicked grin spoiled his features. "Death by fire!"

With that decree, Malliath launched back into the air and curled his body round to take them into the mountains. Vilyra and Godrad swiftly dived out of the clouds, summoned by their masters to join in the fiery carnage.

Athis and Ilargo didn't hesitate to leap back into the air and give pursuit. Not to be left behind, Avandriell pounced towards the lip of the steps and beat her wings, taking Asher into the chase.

"Wait!" Vighon called after them.

"That's not our fight!" Galanör shouted over the wind.

"We can't stay out here!" Nathaniel warned them. "Get inside!"

Vighon followed them to the doorway but hesitated on the threshold. "All of our forces are down there," he agonised.

"The path down to the valley would doom us all before we got there," Reyna cautioned. "We have no choice now."

Vighon entered The Bastion and watched the outside world narrow until Galanör and Aenwyn sealed the doors shut. The northman turned around and pulled back his hood to take in the cold and empty void of the fortress's throne room, its ceiling oppressively low.

"You've been here before," he stated, talking to the Galfreys.

"Yes," Reyna answered. "And we had hoped to never return."

Another question parted Vighon's lips but the words never left his mouth. Instead, he held his breath and listened. It had been a distant sound that had caught his attention, but there was something to it that had given him pause - something insidious. The noise continued to grow, echoing through the passages and filling the throne room.

"What is that?" the king whispered.

Aenwyn slowly removed an arrow from her quiver. "It sounds like... *claws.*"

Nathaniel groaned. "Some things never change." The old knight removed his sword cleanly from the scabbard and brandished it in both hands.

"What is it?" Vighon asked again, preferring to visualise his enemy before actually seeing them.

Reyna nocked an arrow onto her enchanted bow and pulled the string taut. "Darklings," she uttered.

The wind howled as it rushed past Gideon's ears. Ilargo had the lead in their pursuit, his wings closing the gap to Godrad and Vilyra. Ahead of them, Alijah and Malliath buffeted the air like a hurricane, a force of nature that none could withstand.

We have to get ahead of them! Inara commanded across their bond of three. *Even one attack from Malliath will devastate our forces!*

Gideon failed to see how they would achieve such a feat - Ilargo was flying as fast as he could. Before they could begin to strategise, the mountains fell away and the valley floor was revealed below. Like a ravenous maw, the Reavers were slowly devouring The Rebellion, engulfing the bulk of the army while closing in from the sides. Brilliant colours flashed across the battlefield as elven spells pushed Alijah's fiends back.

Above it all, Godrad closed his ragged wings and plummeted towards the chaos. Gideon and Ilargo hesitated when Malliath not only continued his flight but began to climb even higher.

What's he doing? Inara questioned.

No time! Gideon's response came as Ilargo imitated Godrad and dived after the powerful Reavers.

They're dividing us! Asher growled.

Just keep him away from the battle! Gideon instructed them.

To preserve their focus, Ilargo closed off his mind to Athis and Avandriell. Gideon kept himself flat to his saddle, his hands fixed around the handles. The ground rushed up to meet them, bringing the battle into more detail. Godrad had positioned himself to approach from the east, allowing him to fly over the majority of The Rebellion's forces.

Hold on! Ilargo warned with fierce determination.

The green dragon twisted his body mid-dive and brought his claws into Godrad's back leg. The collision interfered with their dive as claws and gnashing fangs lashed out. The attack run completely ruined, Godrad fanned his wings, leaving Ilargo to continue downward until he corrected his fall and glided over the top of the battle. Gideon looked up to discover that Vilyra was already instructing her dragon to renew their attack on the rebels.

They're lining up for another attempt! Gideon warned.

As soon as Ilargo was free of the western tip of the battle, he beat his wings and ascended the valley. A quick banking roll brought him around to face Godrad, who was now only moments from bringing his fiery breath within range of the rebels. Ilargo dipped low and then hammered his wings to soar up into the ravaged beast. Again, the dragons slammed into each other with feral abandon, spinning and flipping out of their flight pattern.

Gideon held on through it all. He could feel the blows that Godrad's claws brought to Ilargo's body, but the pain was his alone. Enraged by the pain, Ilargo roared with defiance and dropped Godrad into the side of the nearest mountain, all the while their claws raking at each other.

In a daring move - the likes of which Gideon had never seen - Vilyra avoided being crushed between Godrad and the rocks by leaping and skipping through the chaos of the dragons' attacks. Her movements seemed effortless as she darted across their scales and found her way onto the bony frame of Ilargo's wing. From there, she dashed across his back and even took a swipe at Gideon with one of her twin blades. The old master parried the flash of steel with Mournblade and turned his head to watch Vilyra continue her journey and jump over the other side. It was all coordinated perfectly with Godrad, who detached himself from the vicious grapple with Ilargo and returned to flight as his companion came down on his neck once more.

Did you see that? Gideon asked, bewildered.

I was a little busy! Ilargo replied, pushing off from the rock in pursuit.

Gideon quickly came to the conclusion that he had wildly underestimated the prowess of Dragon Riders when it came to aerial combat. Vilyra had practically glided over Ilargo, having navigated the rough contours of both his and Godrad's body, and even found time to lash out at him.

Don't be impressed, Ilargo told him, his fangs gritting against the pain. *Be better.*

Gideon took on his companion's words as well as his grit and maintained Mournblade in one hand. Ilargo relayed an image across their bond, informing Gideon of his intentions. The old master shifted his body to one side, his muscles braced for the manoeuvre. The green dragon came down at Godrad from an angle and an orientation that gave Gideon a clean opening to attack Vilyra.

Cutting across the valley, Ilargo flew over Godrad's back. To Gideon, upside down, the enemy was above him and well within the reach of his sword arm. Vilyra, however, raised one of her swords and parried the swift strike in a clash of sparks. Shooting straight over the undead dragon, Ilargo quickly corrected his orientation and banked to the left, bringing them back in line with Godrad.

They're lining up for another attack run!

Ilargo agreed with Gideon's assessment and spat a ball of fire across Godrad's flight path. The undead dragon veered away to escape the flames and shot over the battle. Forced to race along the sloping banks of the southern mountain side, Godrad's left wing skidded through the snow before he launched back into the air.

Angling up behind them, Ilargo homed in on his prey. Gideon felt the drag try and pull him free from his saddle as he held on with one hand. In the other, his Vi'tari blade grew hungry.

Gideon, Ilargo began as he climbed higher, *those clouds are unnatural. They are forming too fast.*

The old master narrowed his eyes at the black sky beyond Godrad and Vilyra. His human sight wasn't comparable to his companions, but he could see the clouds moving in over the valley with great speed, swirling into themselves over and over again.

Gideon grimaced at the nightmarish spectacle. Flashes of lightning erupted within and thunder rippled through the mountains.

Malliath, he seethed.

~

High above The Vrost Mountains, Asher swore at the top of his voice. After being engulfed by a storm cloud, a staccato of lightning had erupted from within and blasted past his head.

Where did this come from? he demanded.

It's Malliath! Inara replied, frustration in her tone. *The spells etched into his body only come to life at a certain altitude!*

Before the half-elf finished her explanation, Asher lost sight of both her and Athis, taken by the storm. The conditions worsened after that, with the temperature plummeting and torrents of rain drenching them. The lightning increased, as if the clouds were at war, their bolts hurled across the heavens.

Avandriell banked towards Athis's last location but found no trace of them. *I can't see anything!* she fumed.

Asher shared her exasperation, but it wasn't Athis and Inara he was searching for. Somewhere in this gargantuan storm was its equally gargantuan maker.

Your spell is slipping, Avandriell warned him.

The ranger could feel the biting cold creeping in even as his companion told him as much. He recited the spell Gideon had taught him, going through the ancient words a couple of times before enforcing them with his will. A sensation of warmth swelled from within him and pushed the cold away. Now he just wished he knew a spell to keep the rain out of his eyes.

Avandriell's muscles suddenly tensed, giving Asher a fraction of a second to interpret her immediate action. He interpreted wrongly. Avandriell tucked in her left wing and her entire body followed. The ranger should have leaned with her, keeping them streamlined as one, but he shifted his bodyweight in the opposite direction. Having instantly lost his grip on one of the handles, Asher's legs took off into the sky and tried to take the rest of him with them. It was then, in that desperate moment, that he saw them.

Duelling gods.

Athis and Malliath thundered past, locked in a battle of claws, fangs, and beating wings. Lightning flashed all around them as their blood was added to the rain, their tails whipped around to club the other, and their Riders hurled spells of destruction through it all.

In the same moment Asher witnessed their collision of wills, he lost sight of them altogether. Avandriell dived down through the cloud and arched her back to ascend once more, giving the ranger a few seconds to find his place on the saddle again.

I sense doubt in you, she blurted on her way up.

Is that really a fight we can get in the middle of? Asher voiced his concern as plainly as he could.

It's the only fight worth *getting in the middle of,* Avandriell countered.

I've spent most of my life assessing opponents, Asher told her, his head close to the saddle. **I know fights I can't win.**

Avandriell flew through a pocket in the storm clouds, offering them a larger vista. *Is that fear I detect in your voice, Ranger?*

Asher groaned - she had too much of her mother's confidence in her, confidence earned after years of fighting for her order. **Don't** *confuse fear with weakness; it's kept me alive and my enemies dead for decades.*

I have seen your memories, Avandriell replied, banking to the west to continue her hunt. *I have seen you acknowledge certain death and still throw yourself into the fight.*

I've earned the right to go with my gut and trust my skills and experience to claim victory. You're up here with nothing but Thessaleia's memories of battle. There's a difference!

Avandriell spared a moment to lay a single golden eye on him. *Remember who has the wings,* she quipped. Her attention was quickly snatched by a glimpse of Athis and Malliath, one giving chase to the other. So quick was their passing, however, that Asher could only guess at who was winning.

Can you speak to Athis? he asked.

No, Avandriell answered, flying towards them. *They've closed off for battle.*

Asher was processing the inevitable fight between them all, visualising it as he did before most violent encounters. *How exactly are we going to get in the middle of this?* he questioned. *Their size alone increases our chances of being swatted out of the sky by either of them.*

Avandriell pierced the next cloud, missing an explosion of lightning by a mere second. *As I said; I've seen your memories. Combined with my mother's, I see only one way of striking at our enemy.*

That sounds like a violent combination of memories to call upon, Asher opined. Before he could enquire of her idea, he saw the scenario play out in her mind. Initially, he was dismayed to see that it had been his time as an assassin that Avandriell had recalled, but she reminded him to embrace all that he was and all that he had been - only then could he ever move forward.

His hands gripped to white knuckles, the ranger lowered his head and gritted his teeth. *Do it.*

Avandriell weaved between the lightning and pierced cloud after cloud until she heard the roars of larger dragons. *Get ready!* she advised.

Like a knife shooting out of the dark to take its victim in the back, the bronze dragon speared through the last cloud and slammed into Malliath's back. Her claws sank in, crunching through her enemy's scales and into the rough hide. With a roar of her own, Avandriell quickly raked her way towards Malliath's left wing and clamped her jaws around his scapula, a technique Thessaleia had used to disable enemy dragons from flying.

Avandriell soon discovered, however, that the strength of her bite was not that of her mother's. Rather than lose his ability to fly, Malliath became enraged and twisted his body into an erratic flight pattern. With no intention of giving up the fight, Avandriell beat her tail again and again, hammering the black dragon's side. Between the frantic beating of her wings, Asher caught sight of Alijah in his saddle. That was *his* target.

Leaping from the safety of his companion's back, Asher found himself navigating the various spikes that lined Malliath's back. His progress towards the half-elf was slow as every other step required him to brace against the spikes to avoid being thrown into the sky.

"You should have stayed on the ground!" Alijah called to him, having turned around while Asher was clinging to a spike.

Asher's brow furrowed into a hardened scowl. "And you should have stayed in Erador!"

The ranger reached for the silvyr short-sword poking over his shoulder and wondered how he was going to advance while Malliath was writhing. Alijah, accustomed to such aerial acrobatics, had no problem finding the required footholds and closing the gap between them.

Kill him and Malliath goes down too! Avandriell encouraged, her fangs scraping against the behemoth's bones.

Though he didn't need the reminder, Asher visualised his silvyr blade thrusting forward and sinking into Alijah's heart. It would be quick and efficient, just as he had been taught.

Asher hesitated, catching movement in the corner of his eye. Approaching from Malliath's right, at a slightly lower altitude, Athis intercepted the black dragon's flight. As one dragon flew under the other, Inara launched herself up from Athis's back and crashed into Alijah, taking them both over the side and into a cloud.

"Inara!" Asher shouted after her.

Predicting the inevitable, Avandriell released her grip on Malliath and let her wings catch enough air to lift her off. Burdened with a human mind, Asher came to her conclusion too late.

Malliath dived.

The ranger wrapped two hands around the nearest spike and held on with all his strength. It wasn't enough. His fingers lost their grip and he was swiftly left behind as Malliath continued to drop through the clouds in pursuit of his companion.

Avandriell! Asher bellowed her name across their bond.

I'm coming! she replied desperately.

Asher could do nothing but fall through the heavens, blind to what awaited beneath every cloud. *Avandriell!* he called again, concerned that any number of mountain tops were rushing up to greet him.

Hold on! she cried.

The ranger fell through a pocket in the storm, an area of empty sky waiting to be filled with lightning and rain. Only it wasn't empty. There was another occupant inhabiting the pocket and it was flying up, directly beneath him.

Avandriell! The ranger passed on the image of Malliath rising towards him, his mighty jaws extended to swallow him whole.

There was no response from Avandriell, leaving Asher to watch his fate grow ever closer. Within seconds, they were close enough that he could see Alijah safely returned to his companion's back.

I'm too far away! Avandriell's tone spoke of her agony. Like Asher, she knew this would be his end.

Deciding he wouldn't die feeling helpless, the ranger gripped the hilt of his broadsword.

What are you doing?

With seconds left of his life, Asher gave his last words. ***I'm going to ram it down his throat.***

Malliath's wet fangs glistened and his tongue curled at the air in anticipation. Perhaps that was why he forgot to mind his surroundings and missed the hulking red dragon flying into his side. With Inara astride, Athis barrelled into Malliath and sent them both careering to the north, their lashing tails missing Asher by just a few feet.

The ranger turned his head to watch the dragons continue their battle, but the storm soon took them in, leaving only a pair of silhouettes as more lightning erupted within the clouds.

There you are! Avandriell's voice preceded her by a couple of seconds. After falling through a rain cloud, the bronze dragon appeared by his side as the snow-covered mountain tops came back into view. Lining themselves up, now under the pouring rain, Asher reached out and found his place astride his companion.

Perhaps you were right, she remarked. *That particular battle is beyond* us.

Something about the way Avandriell emphasised her last word made Asher question her current flight path. **You're taking us back into the mountains,** he concluded. **Why?**

You're not ready for an aerial battle yet, the dragon quickly replied.

You're not going back up there alone!

Yes I... Avandriell trailed off, her head turning to the right. Asher followed her stolen attention and discovered Malliath dropping out of the storm, closely followed by Athis the ironheart.

They look like they're heading back to The Bastion, Asher said.

Avandriell banked in their direction and took after them. The lashing rain prevented the ranger from seeing anything more than a few feet in front of his companion's head. He felt her body shift one way then the next as she navigated the mountainous terrain, weaving her way back to that wretched fortress.

When, at last, it returned to Asher's view, there was no sign of Athis or Malliath, nor their Riders. The main doors were blowing wildly in the wind.

They must have gone inside, Avandriell considered, her bronze head searching the black sky as she came in to land. *You must go after them,* she insisted.

Asher climbed down to stand beside his companion. **You can't go back up there, Avandriell. With or without me, you're not powerful enough to face Malliath.**

Avandriell arched her neck and puffed out her hardened chest, adopting the most regal of stances. *Learn this lesson, Ranger, and learn it well,* she said, leaning down to bring her golden eyes to his face. *You can't stop me.*

Asher was taken aback having expected her to spout some nugget of wisdom passed down from Thessaleia. Taking advantage of his surprise, Avandriell bounded away and leapt back into the sky.

"Avandriell!" he cried aloud, his face turned up into the rain.

Go, Asher, she urged. *You have your fight and I have mine.*

The ranger growled as he pulled free his two-handed broadsword. ***If you survive, I might just kill you myself...***

～

Deep in the bowels of The Bastion, a place that had long been kept by the dead, Vighon Draqaro slammed into a wall as he tried to navigate the corner at speed. With his shield between him and the stone, the northman pushed himself off and renewed his mad dash to escape the horde of Darklings.

Not far in front, Reyna and Nathaniel led the way through the labyrinth, their swords lashing out left and right as Darklings burst from the side passages. Vighon held his shield out in front of him and rammed his way through a pair that emerged to separate him from Nathaniel. Their rotten skulls cracked and twisted out of shape but, even knocked to the floor, the Darklings didn't give up their savage attack.

Vighon gave a sharp yell as one gripped his ankle and brought him down. He instinctively kicked out and put a boot in what remained of one of their faces. It didn't free him of its grip but it stopped the fiend from biting his leg. The second Darkling scurried across the floor and leapt for the king, its bony fingers sharpened to points. The sword of the north flashed from up to down, its fiery blade of silvyr slicing the Darkling in two.

The other Darkling, the one intent on taking a chunk out of his leg, was clawing its way back to him. Vighon would have prepared himself to vanquish the creature but, unlike the Darkling, he could see what was coming. Sir Borin the Dread brought his large boot down on its head, and nothing remained between his foot and the stone floor.

"Vighon!" Nathaniel shouted from further down the passage, his eyes looking beyond Sir Borin.

The northman quickly picked himself up and saw the incoming Darklings scrambling over each other to reach them. "Pick up your feet, Sir Borin!" With the Golem thundering behind him, the king ran after the Galfreys.

Reyna was waiting for them at the next corner. The elf nodded for them to continue after Nathaniel as she brought her bow to bear, an arrow nocked on the string. The enchanted weapon launched the arrow with enough force to reach the far end of the passage, where Vighon had slammed into the corner. On its way, the missile burst open a dozen Darklings, reducing them to rotten debris. Yet still their numbers swelled from every passage until the undead were crawling along the walls and ceiling.

"Go!" Reyna shouted, nocking another arrow with great speed.

This time, she didn't aim for the Darklings. The arrow went high and struck the ceiling a few feet in front of the horde. Vighon felt the explosion rock the fortress while his ears were overwhelmed by the sound of the passage collapsing on itself under tons of stone. He came to a halt after reaching Nathaniel and the pair turned around to see Reyna emerge from the dust.

"That's only bought us some time," she said. "They'll find another way through to us."

"Any idea where Galanör and Aenwyn are?" Nathaniel asked, his chest heaving.

Vighon shook his head. "We got separated when the Darklings came through that wall," he told them.

A sudden noise echoed from further up the passage. Reyna was aiming her bow before Vighon had even taken his eyes from her.

"We can't stay here," Nathaniel stated gravely.

"We should ascend to The Bastion's upper levels," Reyna suggested.

Vighon wasn't going to protest. "You know your way around here better than I do - lead the way."

Nathaniel eyed the towering Golem. "Perhaps he should take the lead. Just in case."

The northman agreed. "Sir Borin," he began, gesturing down the passage. "You will lead us that way."

Behind the Golem's thundering steps, the trio began their journey up through The Bastion. Shrieks and howls reverberated through the fortress and, here and there, they even heard the clash of swords. They quickly surmised that, somewhere in the maze of black stone, Galanör and Aenwyn were fighting Reavers. Try as they might, however, they could never locate the source of these sounds.

"This is useless," Vighon fumed, turning down another empty hall. "We just have to survive up here while all of our forces are fighting for their lives in the valley. We should be down with them if we can't face Alijah. And who knows how *that* battle is going," he added with a quick nod at the ceiling.

"We have no choice in the matter," Reyna whispered. "Alijah has proven adept at anticipating our moves."

Leaving Sir Borin to continue walking, Vighon stopped in the passage and turned to face the elven queen. "Where are we even going? Nowhere in here is—"

The king's last word was stolen from him, drowned out by an almighty crack of stone as the wall ahead was blown in. Behind that force was Malliath the voiceless. His horned head forced its way into the The Bastion in a shower of debris and dust and, in the chaos, his jaws snapped around Sir Borin and yanked him from the passage.

Vighon ran to the jagged hole in the wall with Reyna and Nathaniel in tow. Outside, amidst a raging storm, Malliath whipped his head up and clamped his jaws, tearing the Golem in half at the waist. Before his legs could fall to the ground, the black dragon opened his wicked maw again. With the entirety of the Golem now in his mouth, Malliath chewed vigorously, turning Sir Borin into pulp before gulping him down.

Then, rain bouncing off his glistening scales, Malliath turned his purple eyes on the three sovereigns of Verda.

"Run," Vighon uttered. "Run!" he yelled.

Before he had even taken his first step, the northman knew this was the end - they weren't faster than a dragon, especially this dragon. In that briefest of moments, Reyna had come to the same conclusion as Vighon and didn't even try to escape. Instead, she aimed an arrow at the ancient beast, intent on doing as much damage as possible before death took her.

The fate of all three, however, was altered at the last possible second. To Vighon's eyes, Avandriell came from nowhere as she rammed into the side of Malliath's head, forcing him away from the hole in the wall. The smaller dragon grappled with the much larger horned head, her claws scraping and her jaws gnashing. Malliath roared and moved back from The Bastion so that he might swat her away but, by then, Avandriell had succeeded in dragging her claws down and over his left eye.

Vighon recoiled from Malliath's next roar, a sound so loud and fierce it could have cracked the sky. Avandriell pushed off from his face and beat her wings with all haste. Malliath did not require so much effort to take off in pursuit of her, his enormous wings buffeting the wind and rain towards the fortress.

Only seconds later, Athis cut through the sky behind him. Vighon leaned out of the hole to follow the red dragon, looking to see if Inara was with him, but the storm battering the mountain side concealed everything.

A strong hand gripped the king's arm, turning him back to the passage. Nathaniel let go of him to return both hands to his sword and face the six Reavers striding towards them. Reyna adjusted her aim, sighting the fiends down the length of her arrow. Vighon looked back at her when she failed to release the devastating missile. The elven queen's attention had been snatched away, her head tilted to one side and a look of concern growing on her face.

The northman stole a glance at the approaching Reavers, checking the time they had left. "What's wrong?" he asked her urgently.

Following her gaze to the hole in the wall, Vighon moved back to the threshold where the wind attempted to steal his cloak. Besides the raging storm, there was another sound carried in the wind, a terrible cacophony of shrieks and screams. Daring to poke his head through the gap, Vighon looked upon the black stone above the hole.

"Darklings!" he warned, stepping back and raising his fiery blade.

Nathaniel bent his knees, bracing himself into a defensive stance. "We sure could do with a Golem right about now," he remarked.

Vighon never thought he would miss Sir Borin and he certainly didn't have time to miss him now. A violent clash turned the northman to the head of the passage, from where the Reavers were still advancing. He had to look twice when he realised that it had been caused by a familiar ranger. Asher had charged out of a side passage swinging his broadsword.

Reyna didn't hesitate to burst into a charge of her own, lending her bow and scimitar to the fight. Vighon was close behind her, his flaming sword held high. By the time they reached the Reavers, Asher had cut down three of them and savagely maimed two others. Reyna challenged a one-armed Reaver, easily besting the disadvantaged fiend with a clean swipe across its neck. Vighon met the remaining two, one of which took searing silvyr through the visor, leaving the last to be kicked back and decapitated in a wide swing with the sword of the north.

Asher straightened up, his breath ragged. "Where's Galanör and Aenwyn?" he questioned, no doubt wondering where their secret weapon was.

"We lost them," Reyna told him, half-turning to face the hole Malliath had opened in the fortress wall. "Because of them," she said with disdain as thirty or more Darklings poured into the passage.

"Where's Inara and Gideon?" Vighon asked quickly.

"We got separated," Asher said, making for the side-passage from which he had emerged.

"Wait!" Reyna blurted, looking back at the Darklings. "Where's Nathaniel?" she asked with panic in her voice.

Asher and Vighon scanned the passage but only a glance was required to determine Nathaniel's absence. "He was with you?" Asher checked.

"Only a moment ago," Vighon confirmed.

"We need to find him!" Reyna was taking a step towards the Darklings when Asher grabbed her by the arm.

"We need to keep moving," he told her to the sound of terrible shrieks and growls. Reyna protested but allowed the ranger to drag her away. "This way!" he commanded. "Quickly!"

Vighon was right behind the ranger. "He was just with us!"

Asher paused at a junction before dashing to the left. "Nathaniel can take care of himself."

The northman's frustration wasn't going anywhere, just as Reyna's concern wasn't. "Where are the others?" he asked, hoping to piece together something good from this mess.

"Gideon went after Vilyra and Godrad, down into the valley." The ranger stopped in the new hallway to take in the various doors that lined the walls. "In here!" he instructed, opening the second door on the right. After everyone filed in, he gently closed the door, bade them to be silent, and braced himself with his sword pointed at the wood.

The Darklings were soon scurrying down the passage, their bony fingers and limbs clattering against the stone. They had slowed down, suggesting they were on the hunt again, their prey momentarily lost. It felt like a lifetime waiting for them all to move through and disappear elsewhere in the fortress, especially since Asher had failed to inform them about Inara's whereabouts.

They took a collective breath when silence reigned beyond the door.

"I think they're gone..." The ranger trailed off. "Where's the big one?" he asked, referring to Sir Borin.

"He was *eaten* by the bigger one," Vighon replied.

Asher accepted the loss of the Golem. "He was a monster, but at least he was a *useful* monster."

Vighon shook his head and all talk of Sir Borin away. "Where is *Inara*?" he asked specifically.

Asher gestured at the walls. "Somewhere in The Bastion." The ranger ran his thumb over a cut in his eyebrow and inspected the blood. "Alijah returned and Inara gave chase," he elaborated. "I haven't seen either of them since. They could be anywhere in here."

"Then we need to find them," Vighon asserted, making for the door. "Nathaniel too."

"We didn't *lose* Nathaniel," Reyna corrected, speaking for the first time since realising the old Graycoat was missing. "He's gone."

"Gone?" Vighon echoed.

"Yes, *gone*," Reyna repeated. "He's gone for Alijah, just as I once did."

"We need to find Galanör," Asher said, cutting through it all. "We need to help him get the Crissalith as close to Alijah as possible."

Vighon wanted to argue his point and even throw some of his kingly weight around, but it was Inara's voice in his head that reminded him of their duty. "Well we're not going to do that in here," he said, opening the door. "Let's get that Crissalith and end this."

Under sheets of rain and blasting winds, The Rebellion's forces met their enemy with grim determination. If this was to be their last stand, if victory was to elude them this day, then they would make it such a stand as to inspire countless rebellions to echo down through the generations and challenge the house of the dragon.

More to the west of the battle, well behind Reaver lines, Doran

Heavybelly was making his last stand worthy of history's note. With the axe and hammer of Andaljor, he swung with abandon, crushing and hacking at the fiends. Thaligg and Thraal had finally found him at the cost of their Warhogs' lives. Now, the trio fought back to back to back, parrying and countering while trying to avoid killing each other.

Of course, the stakes had been raised when the dragons entered the fight. Most of the time, they were dark wraiths that cut swift lines over the top of the battle, their presence never anything more than a threat. But, like now, the undead dragon, Godrad, would occasionally spit fire across the battlefield, lighting up the night. It never lasted long, thankfully, the dragon's attacks ever halted by Gideon and Ilargo.

Doran elevated himself on top of a dead Reaver, killing another with his axe as he did so, and witnessed Ilargo drop out of the sky and dig all of his claws into Godrad's back before dragging him away from the battle. After chasing Godrad away, Ilargo didn't waste the opportunity to turn his head and breathe fire across the ranks of Reavers closing in from the northern flank. The king cheered him on, though he would have liked the pair to be in the middle of slaying the one who controlled the enemy.

"*Watch out!*" Thaligg cried as he barrelled into the son of Dorain.

The Reaver's spearing attack went over them and met Thraal's shield before the stout dwarf buried his axe in its head. Doran and Thaligg staggered back to their feet, defending themselves with every movement. It wasn't enough. Doran could feel his bones aching from all the impacts and his focus was slipping. It didn't help that, with only one eye, he had to turn his head so much to take in the full range of enemies.

The king cried out when his axe was beaten down by a Reaver's sword, its curved edge only an inch from his boot. Bringing his hammer to bear, Doran tried to put all of his strength behind the mighty swing. Fortunately, there was no need. Pig came blasting though and slammed into the attacking Reaver, giving the dwarf some space.

Doran laughed. "Good boy!" he hollered, reaching to retrieve his axe.

That moment of triumph and luck was darkened by an agonised cry. The king turned around to discover Thaligg staggering away from his opponent, a spear through his chest.

"NO!" Doran raged.

Thraal, Thaligg's brother, beat him to it and chopped the Reaver down to one knee before sinking his axe down through its head. He then joined his dying brother and used whatever time Doran and Pig could grant them to say farewell. Their words were lost to the king, his ears filled with battle. Between blows, he glimpsed the brothers clasping arms. A last glimpse revealed Thaligg lying on the ground, his eyes lifeless.

Thraal let loose an angry roar and threw himself back into the fight. His grief brought new life to his muscles and kept the pain at bay. Such raw hatred would lend him strength, but Doran knew it would only be temporary. He moved in behind Thraal to keep the Reavers off his back, but the knights of Erador were only one of their problems.

The other was falling out of the sky.

Gideon braced himself flat to his saddle, a touch of magic added to his grip. He could see the battlefield expanding in his view, a writhing creature that rippled from one side of the valley to the other, as Ilargo rushed down to meet it.

Hold on! the green dragon cried.

Gideon could feel every ounce of Ilargo's strength directed to his grip on Godrad. Trapped under Ilargo's claws, the undead dragon was powerless to do anything but be rammed into the ground. Scores of Reavers were flattened beneath the weight of both dragons and a tidal wave of dirt and snow was thrown into the air.

Though his grip withstood the intensity of the impact, Gideon's breath was taken away. Worse still, he didn't have time to recover before Godrad fought back and Ilargo was forced to shift his weight.

Move! Ilargo warned him.

The old master leapt from his saddle as Godrad's tail hammered down across the green dragon's back, eliciting a pained roar from him. Still trying to catch his breath, Gideon landed and flowed into a roll to avoid the grappling dragons, their every movement crushing more Reavers.

Keep him this side of the valley! Gideon instructed, fearful of the rebel forces who could get caught beneath the winged titans.

Ilargo speared his head upwards and clamped his jaws around Godrad's neck. With the weight of his body behind him, the dragon shoved the undead beast further west, away from the clashing armies. In their absence, the Reavers quickly moved to swarm Gideon Thorn.

As they closed in, the old master held his hands close together. He called on the limited magic he had at his disposal and let it build in the gap between his palms. Then, when the fiends were within a few feet of him, he swept both hands out wide and unleashed his spell. The Reavers were tossed back and high in an arcing wave, their armour crumpled into their bodies and their bones shattered.

In the space it afforded him, Gideon took Mournblade in hand. He had seconds to prepare himself for battle. Quietening his mind, he heard his breath fall away, then the sound of the wind, and the rain hitting his leathers. All that remained was the rain striking the steel of his Vi'tari blade. The elven scimitar had been by his side for years - it was the only sword he had ever wielded. They were one.

The first group of Reavers to descend on him took the old master through forms one to three of the Mag'dereth. When they lay still on the ground and the next wave fell upon him, he was moving through form four to the most violent form five. This was a dance with Death. His scimitar flashed in every direction, cutting in at every angle, while his body moved like a snake, coiling in and out of encounters. His feet barely touched the ground as he weaved through the Reavers, dropping them with single strikes of precision.

To his left, a light as bright as the sun banished the night when Ilargo's fiery breath blew in the wind. Their positions had reversed now, with Godrad's jaws locked under Ilargo's neck and manipulating the direction he faced. Gideon could feel Ilargo's frustration and rage mixing together. His front claws came up and sank into Godrad's face, tearing and shredding what there was of the dragon's rotten features. When the tendons between his jaws were severed, Godrad lost some of the strength in his bite and Ilargo was able to free himself from the fangs.

Gideon knew what was coming. **Do it!** he urged, ducking under an incoming spear.

Ilargo needed no encouragement to destroy his undead kin. With Godrad's head still under his own, Ilargo used his front claws to prize open his enemy's mouth, stretching it beyond any dragon's natural capacity. Then, with unrelenting fury, he lowered his own head towards the open maw and exhaled a jet of fire. The hungry flames spread throughout Godrad's innards and escaped through the jagged holes that marred his body.

Only when Godrad's body grew limp did Ilargo release the flaming beast. The ground shook, the last impact Godrad would have on the realm.

Emerging victorious, if bloodied, Ilargo roared into the night and unleashed his fiery breath on the surrounding Reavers. It was the light of his flames that revealed Vilyra only a second before she brought her twin swords down on Gideon. Through his eyes, Mournblade felt the incoming attack and shot up horizontally to intercept them.

Vilyra's boot spear-headed her second attack and slammed into Gideon's chest, taking him clean from the ground. His spine protested against the impact, but the knock to the back of his head dulled its intensity.

He naturally rolled onto his front in an attempt to get up, but he saw Vilyra dashing towards him out of the corner of his eye. It was instinct that caused him to raise his hand towards her, the spell echoing from long ago into his mind. Only his level of power held him back, though the telekinetic blast still succeeded in pushing the Dragon Rider back several feet.

It was enough to give him time, a precious thing on a battle-field. On his feet again, Mournblade gripped tightly in his hand, Gideon had nothing but a grimace for Vilyra. She was the last on a short list of ancient heroes who needed putting back in the grave.

Her leaping attack appeared frenzied, her blades coming in at wild angles, but Gideon could see the fighting style emerging through it all. Maintaining the fifth form of the Mag'dereth, he kept up an aggressive response and pushed her back step after step. Soon, the area was beginning to flood with dwarves, humans, and elves as they took advantage of the hole Ilargo had punctured in the Reavers' line. Gideon welcomed them, thankful to have his back protected.

We must return to The Bastion! Ilargo insisted, his tail sweeping through hordes of Reavers.

Gideon cried out in pain when one of Vilyra's blades stabbed into his shoulder and the other sliced along his thigh. Spinning on his heel, the old master flourished his scimitar behind his back and deflected her next attack while positioning himself to face the Dragon Rider in form four, a style that balanced defence evenly with attack.

Would you like me to intervene? Ilargo enquired, snatching a Reaver from his shoulder and spitting it back onto the battlefield.

Gideon responded by countering Vilyra's low strike with a twist of his own, a flick positioned just right to send the weapon flying from her hand. He then advanced with a strike to her left and right, all the while pushing her back. He found gaps in her defence three times but his every slash had no effect on the Reaver.

Might I suggest aiming for the head, Ilargo chimed in, his voice strained as he unfurled his wings to banish the fiends crawling all over him. *This was not to be our fight,* he reminded his companion.

Gideon was too ensnared by his duel to reply or even contem-plate another fight. He was forced to step on a dead dwarf and use the height to bring a strong two-handed blow down on Vilyra. She blocked it, as he had expected her to, and then came at him with a counter strike he had predicted after scrutinising her style. That counter strike was delivered across his waist after she had ducked to one knee, but Gideon had already tucked his knees up to his chest and leapt over himself and the sweeping blade. Before he landed beside her, Mournblade was lashing out to take her arm.

The limb fell to the ground, added to a field of other limbs and bodies. It didn't seem to bother Vilyra, her sword still grasped in her remaining hand.

The head, Gideon! Ilargo reminded.

Like a banshee, she flung herself at the old master. He shifted his shoulders one way then the next, avoiding every stroke of her blade by an inch. Using her aggressive advance to his advantage, Gideon shifted his whole body to the side, pivoting on his heel, and brought Mournblade around in a cutting arc. He felt the brief resistance as the edge of the steel passed through her neck, though the pelting rain prevented him from hearing her head hit the ground.

At last, every Dragon Rider was returned to their rest.

"Good to see ye gettin' stuck in, lad!" The familiar voice turned Gideon to King Doran, who was yanking his axe out of a Reaver's skull. "Now, get back up there an' end this madness!"

CHAPTER 57
A CLASH OF FATES

A crack of lightning flashed through the narrow slits in the dark passage, bringing momentary life to the faces of a dozen Darklings. They had been waiting in silence, motionless in the shadows, while their prey moved ever closer. But Inara had seen them now and they knew it. As one, they burst forward, their nightmarish shrieks bouncing off the cold stone.

Inspired by the storm outside, Inara extended her hand towards the creatures and let loose a staccato of lightning bolts. The searing energy cut through them as if they were old parchment. For those that escaped the barrage, there was only fire. The jet of flames erupted from between her hands and engulfed the passage from wall to wall.

Nothing moved after that.

Inara looked down at the burning bodies, the flames reflected in her eyes. They were people once. Men and women who had likely committed petty crimes and been sent to The Bastion instead of the cells, there to be transformed into the tools of a wicked necromancer.

The ringing of duelling swords pulled Inara from her reverie and turned her to the northern passage, a hall that led deeper into the fortress. Firefly was freed of its scabbard, its steel flashing in the firelight, but Inara had to lean against the nearest wall before she could investigate.

Everything hurt. Between their physical battle and intense exchange of magic in the sky, Inara was aching from her bones through to the cuts and bruises that marred her skin. She knew there would be more fighting and more spells required before the end, for everything inside The Bastion was hostile.

Inara gritted her teeth and took a steadying breath. Nothing was more hostile than her. She poured that belief into her muscles and forced herself to push away from the wall and find her brother. One stroke of Firefly could end it all.

Taking to the northern passage, Inara spared a moment's thought for her companion. Even now, she could feel Athis locked in battle with Malliath, their claws and fangs ripping each other to pieces. She wanted to offer him encouragement, to bolster his strength, but the red dragon's mind was in a primal place.

Following the sound of ringing swords, Inara pushed through her injuries and quickened her pace. She soon arrived at an archway that opened up onto the gallery of a vast chamber that possessed two more levels above and one below. Thick chains hung from the ceiling and rusted manacles lay strewn across the ground floor, easily seen without any railing around the gallery. To the left of the chamber was a pair of enormous rattling doors that were continually blasted by the ferocious winds outside.

All manner of great beasts could have inhabited the chamber. And, by the look of the Giant and Troll bones littering the ground floor, Inara guessed that Atilan had once experimented on a number of them in the vile chamber. Having taken it all in with barely more than a glance, the half-elf was guided by sound to the battle below.

Galanör was leaping from atop the Giant's skull, Stormweaver gripped over his head in both hands. He tore through the Reaver from shoulder to groin, which was not a killing blow, but enough to knock it back into Aenwyn's sweeping scimitar. That was a killing blow. The head flew from its body and crashed amongst a pile of smaller bones.

Aenwyn didn't stop there. The elf launched her blade as if it were a spear and impaled an incoming Reaver in the head. Before it had dropped to the floor, she was already nocking an arrow in her bow and firing at the next fiend. Galanör didn't hesitate to retrieve Aenwyn's scimitar and wield it alongside Stormweaver. A flurry of steel was brought to bear on the remaining knights from Erador's ancient past.

Inara decided to lend Firefly to the assault on the last of them and stepped off the edge of the first storey. She would have landed with her usual elven grace, but recent injuries forced her to drop into a roll and almost collide with what looked to be a large femur bone. By the time she had corrected her stance, Galanör had cut down two of the three Reavers and kicked the last towards her. Inara had only to thrust out her sword arm and stab the knight in the back of the head.

"Inara!" Galanör sounded relieved. "Are you hurt?"

"Nothing that can keep me down," Inara replied firmly. "You two look to be on top of things," she added with a glance at the armour-clad bodies around them.

"We were separated from the others," Aenwyn informed her, ridding Inara of her next question. "There are Darklings everywhere."

Inara flicked her head over her shoulder. "I've already had the pleasure."

"Are Gideon and Asher with you?" Galanör asked, looking up to the floor she had come from.

Inara shook her head. "We too were separated."

Galanör looked despondent. "I fear this was his plan all along; lure us in to the mountains and then divide us."

"We wouldn't be the first to be devoured by The Bastion," Inara remarked darkly.

"So dramatic, Sister!" Alijah's voice came from every corner of the chamber, setting off the warrior instincts in the trio.

Backs together, they held up their blades and bow and frantically searched the shadows. There was no sign of Alijah, only the slight rattle of a chain from the upper levels.

"The Bastion is where *power* is forged!" Alijah continued from everywhere. "If you don't have what it takes to survive, then these walls will become your tomb!"

"Show yourself!" Galanör commanded.

"I'm right here." Alijah's whisper turned all three of them around, but then an amused bout of laughter turned them back to the upper levels. "Would showing myself make a difference, Galanör?" The question preceded his appearance on the highest floor.

Aenwyn released her arrow without any hesitation. It sailed through the air with such speed and accuracy that no man could rightly stand against it. But Alijah was no ordinary man, if he could be called a man at all. He casually waved his hand and disintegrated the arrow in a cloud of fiery ash.

"Clearly not," Alijah said, answering his own question. "Shall we move on to the part where you all die?" he asked smugly.

"You're acting as if you've already won!" Inara called up to him. "We saved the tree, Alijah! Magic thrives in us! You can't stand up to us all!"

Alijah tensed his jaw before pursing his lips. "Did that victory make you feel mighty, Sister? Destroying that tree was going to be a mercy!" he hissed. "In the absence of magic, every elf and Drake would have had eternity ahead of them! But now you and your rebellion have forced my hand! Now, I will have to eradicate them all! That blood will be on your hands!" the half-elf accused.

"The only blood on my hands will be yours, Brother," Inara assured.

Alijah took a breath, taking the measure of her, perhaps. "We shall see," he finally replied.

Athis's mind suddenly came alive inside Inara's and it was full of warning. *He's coming!* the dragon blurted desperately.

Inara's eyes flitted to the large doors on the other side of the chamber. "Shields!" she yelled, raising one hand.

Her warning was punctuated by a deafening crash. Both doors

were blown inwards, the force of which tore them clean from their hinges. Behind them came Malliath's gargantuan head and neck. With his jaws already ajar, the Dragon's fiery breath was quick to create an inferno. The first to be alerted, Inara was the fastest to enact her shield spell, its fringes just wide enough to protect Galanör and Aenwyn until they erected shields of their own.

The fire washed over their magic and tried to creep in at the sides, but the elves extended their shields and kept it at bay. Facing Malliath, Inara's efforts took the brunt of it. Ancient and massive as he was, the force of Malliath's fiery breath was considerable; more than enough to test Inara's magic, having used so much of it already. To her left, Galanör began to falter - the least schooled in the way of magic.

"Hold it!" she growled through gritted teeth.

As the heat inside their collective shield began to intensify, Malliath's jaws clamped shut, leaving a cloud of dark smoke in the air. Unfortunately, Inara realised, he was just taking a breath. Her hand tightened around Firefly's hilt as she started to draw on the magic stored in the crystal pommel.

But the next attack never came.

Claws as big as a man bit into Malliath's sides and dragged him from the chamber. The black dragon roared in pain and writhed about, his bulk smashing through the stone archway. Athis the ironheart had him now. The red dragon sank his fangs into the back of Malliath's neck and forced the behemoth away from The Bastion. Returning to the storm, their battle was renewed.

Inara lowered her hand and her shield with it. Through the smoke, she turned her head up to the highest tier of the chamber in search of Alijah. He appeared in a haze as he staggered away and disappeared through a door.

Galanör stepped forward, crossing the line from untouched stone to a charred and rough surface. The waves of heat rising from the floor were blown away in the mountain wind forcing its way into the chamber. "We have to go after him," the elven ranger declared, tossing Aenwyn's scimitar back to her.

Inara raised her hand to halt him. "We must tread carefully. He is likely baiting us into the next trap."

"Of course he is," Galanör replied. "But what choice do we have?" He placed a hand over the satchel clipped to his belt. "Our plan only works if we can get the—"

"Don't say it!" Inara snapped, before the word *Crissalith* left his lips. "Assume the walls have eyes and ears in this place."

Galanör gestured his understanding. "We still need to pursue him, regardless of the risk."

"We've come too far to do anything else," Aenwyn added.

Inara nodded her agreement before releasing a short sigh. "Do you still have the crystal Gideon gave you?" she asked.

A moment of confusion passed over Galanör's face. "I do. It's the only one of the three I have left."

"Good," Inara replied, her tone clipped. "Give it to me."

The elf hesitated as his hand moved to the pouch on his belt. "You have a plan for it?"

"I do," Inara said, noting the blue gemmed ring on his finger. "I've been here before, remember. I think I know where he's going. I can get us there first."

"A portal will drain you," Aenwyn pointed out with obvious concern.

Inara sheathed Firefly on her belt and tapped the crystal pommel. "I have reserves to call upon. Besides, it's like you said - we've come too far to do anything else. The best we can do now is get ahead of potential traps and lay one ourselves." The Guardian held out her hand to Galanör, waiting for the crystal.

Galanör removed the crystal from its pouch and moved to drop it into Inara's waiting palm.

Inara didn't catch it.

Instead, she flipped her hand and let the crystal continue its fall to the floor. The moment her hand was above Galanör's, she snatched at it with a vice-like grip, ensuring the pressure was intense enough to keep his fingers extended. Her free hand whipped up like a viper and called the Hastion gem to her grasp with a touch of magic.

Before the crystal had even hit the floor, Inara took advantage of Galanör's surprise and yanked him forward. At the same time, she put all of her weight behind the elbow she drove into the centre of his chest. The air from his lungs was instantly expelled in one sharp breath. She then released his wrist and threw a knotted fist into his jaw, taking him off his feet. Aware that she needed to continue her momentum, the Guardian dropped into a crouch, scooped up the crystal, and rolled across the floor to meet the elf as he landed.

Coughing and wheezing for breath, Galanör was helpless to stop Inara from removing the satchel on his belt and clipping it to her own. As she attached that last clip, an arrow tip came to rest beside her head.

"What are you doing?" Aenwyn demanded, her bow string pulled taut to her cheek.

Inara held out her hands, one still closed around the crystal, and slowly backed away from Galanör. "Saving your lives," she answered.

Confident that Aenwyn would never actually fire on her, Inara flicked her wrist and sent the crystal to the floor. It landed perfectly between the two elves and tore a circular portal through the stone. Taken by surprise, Aenwyn released her arrow high into the air as she fell through beside Galanör. Inara didn't allow the portal to linger, a drain on her energy, and closed it the second they were clear of the abyss. Though she could no longer see them, the Guardian knew they had just dropped into The Bastion's throne room.

The drain in energy was immediate and unforgiving. Inara felt her knees buckle and the charred floor rise up to greet her. The urge to vomit was overwhelming, though not so powerful as the urge to simply lie down and give in to sleep. Before oblivion claimed her, and it was coming for her, the Guardian gripped Firefly's crystal pommel and absorbed the magic therein. Strength returned to her bones and her stomach settled, as did her spinning mind.

Rising to her feet, Inara took a breath and clenched one of her fists. The crystal pommel hadn't restored all of her magic, that much she could feel. She could only hope it was enough.

Now to finish her hunt.

~

Tap. Tap. Tap.

The incessant noise turned Alijah's gaze to the floor. His brow furrowed in confusion. Blood was worming down his hand and dripping from the tips of his fingers. But where had it come from? The question began to evaporate before he could even finish the thought. He blinked and the blood was nowhere to be seen and the small puddle beside him was gone, concealed from his eyes.

He pushed off from the cold wall, barely able to wonder why he had been leaning against it in the first place. Before he could turn the next corner, however, a fissure was ripped open in his mind. He staggered to the other wall and reached to steady himself. He saw flashes of lightning and glimpses of Athis and a smaller dragon coming at him with fangs and claws.

Then there was pain. Lots of pain. Alijah cried out, sure that a dozen blades had pierced his skin. Then came the rage and the fury. It rose up in Alijah and manifested itself in the form of a savage roar that resounded through The Bastion.

When his outburst came to an end, he was in an entirely different part of the fortress with no memory of how he got there. But he knew *where* he was. In the pouring rain, under a wrathful sky, Alijah looked out on The Vrost Mountains from The Bastion's highest platform, a balcony that had seen its circular edge weathered and broken in parts.

How had he found himself here? Why did he always end up here?

His mind was unable to hold on to any question, let alone answer it. A thundering drum beat inside his head, drawing his hand up to nurse it. When it came away, the rain was washing blood from his palm.

"What is happening to me?" he whispered, staggering towards the jagged edge.

An ear-splitting roar defied the storm and turned Alijah to the sky. Malliath swooped out of a dark cloud and clubbed Athis around the face with his tail. The red dragon was taken from flight for a moment before his senses returned and his wings kept him from smashing into the mountainside.

Focus! Malliath's voice cleared through his mind like a purging forest fire. *Return to the fight. Kill them all!*

Alijah's pupils shrank to points. He could no longer see the blood on his hand nor feel the pain that had racked his body. His emerald Vi'tari blade was free of its scabbard and in his other hand, catching the rain. Playing over and over again in his mind, he saw himself killing his parents and Inara, their blood on his sword. Malliath desired Vighon and Asher and so he would deliver them to his companion.

The king of Verda turned around, set on his course, only to be confronted by an obstacle in the form of an old Graycoat. "Hello, Father."

Nathaniel Galfrey stepped out of the doorway and into the rain, his sword already in hand.

Alijah tilted his head, taking the man in. "Is this the part where you throw down your sword, tell me you won't fight me, and try to make me see *sense*?" he asked mockingly.

Nathaniel continued to approach his son. "No," he stated boldly. "I fear you are beyond all sense now."

Alijah straightened up. "Then you have come to kill me," he concluded with an edge of surprise in his voice.

Nathaniel came to a stop just short of his sword's reach. "I've come to make sure you don't suffer."

The half-elf raised an eyebrow and glanced at his father's blade. "And you're going to do that with your sword?"

The old Graycoat looked down at the weapon in his hand. "This is the best I can offer you, Son. There are those who want to save you, to give you a chance at redemption. I know it's all your mother thinks about. Hell, even Gideon wants a second chance for you. And there's a part of me that wants that for you more than anything. But if they save you, if you find some way out of this madness, you will be brought before the realm for your crimes. You will be made to suffer.

"Humans, elves, dwarves. They're past wanting you dead now. They want you to *hurt*. They want you to feel some of the pain you've unleashed on their lives. And they'd be right to," he added, tears mixing with the rain on his face. "But I love you too much to let that happen."

"A lovely, lovely speech, Father," Alijah responded patronisingly. "But *I am the realm*," he continued darkly. "The crimes committed against it are judged by *me*. And, right now, one of its greatest criminals stands before me with no more than the training of a simple Graycoat. There's a reason you're the last," he added with a look of wickedness.

"This isn't you," Nathaniel stated with a shaking head. "Those aren't my boy's words. Whatever you are, you killed my son."

"You tell yourself whatever you have to," Alijah goaded. "You won't have to live with your actions for much longer."

Nathaniel held up his sword in both hands. "If there's *anything* of you left in there, Son, know that I will always love you..."

Again, it was the clash of steel that drew Inara's attention in another direction. More distressing this time were the pained cries that came between blows. She hastened after them, searching desperately for the source of the fray. A voice in the Guardian's mind told her she knew who those pained cries belonged to.

Higher and higher she had risen through The Bastion's cold embrace. The sound of the storm increased with every new level as she ascended into an area of disrepair. Lightning frequently struck the fortress, knocking loose stones free while the relentless rain found its way into every nook and cranny.

"Liar!"

The stark cry stopped Inara in her tracks and turned her to the spiral staircase on her right. She raced up the steps, her hand running over the wet stone as she climbed ever higher.

"You never loved me!" Alijah's voice bellowed, before steel collided with steel.

Inara left the staircase behind and entered a shadowed tunnel. There were no other passages and no doors to choose from, just an archway that led outside. It was there that she saw her father's sword knocked from his grasp and a flash of green steel before his leg gave out, dropping him to one knee. Defenceless, his leg bleeding into the rain, Nathaniel looked up at his opponent, his *son*.

"It should never have been a choice for you!" Alijah screamed at him. "It should always have been me!"

Inara didn't even think. She saw Alijah's cursed Vi'tari blade come up, ready to thrust into her father's heart, and she reacted instinctively. Her hand retrieved the Moonblade from the back of her belt and let it fly with all her hope behind it. Be it the sound or the glow of the blade, Alijah became aware of the incoming dagger and adjusted his stance at the last second. Instead of catching him in the chest, it collided with his swinging sword and ricocheted off at an awkward angle.

His life extended, Nathaniel launched himself at Alijah and grappled him around the waist. The added weight put Alijah off balance and sent the pair to the floor in a tangled heap. While they rolled about, swapping sharp elbows and hammering fists, Inara sprinted through the tunnel and out into the rain.

Alijah, however, emerged the victor and jumped to his feet. An underarm sweep of his hand cast a blast of telekinetic energy across Nathaniel and sent him flying into Inara. She couldn't decide what hurt more: the impact of her father or the impact against the floor with his weight on top. Between them, they groaned and grunted onto their hands and knees, though Nathaniel was unable to rise beyond that feat. Inara gave him a quick look over, dismayed to see so many bleeding wounds and dark bruises.

It enraged her.

Inara spun around to face her brother. She was ready, there and then, to run him through and bring a bloody end to it all. Seeing him properly, however, only feet away, the fire in her veins cooled just enough to make her falter. He looked almost as ravaged as the knights he had twisted into Reavers. His angular features had hardened, lending him a gaunt and wasted appearance, as if he was slowly being hollowed out. When was the last time he had eaten or found restful sleep?

On top of his haggard look, a savage gash ran over his left eye, of which there was nothing but red to be seen. And a bruise, almost as dark as his armour, crawled up the side of his neck and across his jaw to a bleeding nose. It was hard to see which injuries could be attributed to his duel with their father and which had come from Athis and Avandriell's assault on Malliath. Even now, in front of her very eyes, new cuts were slicing through his skin, yet Alijah seemed oblivious to them all.

"I suppose it was always going to come to this," he announced. "This... *clash of fates* was foretold. The Crow saw this. He told me you would challenge my reign, that you wouldn't settle for any *peace*," he spat. "And here we are, destiny fulfilled."

Inara slowly shook her head in the rain. "He told you a version of the truth that he needed you to believe, Alijah. But it was a lie all the same."

"You still have no idea what you're talking about!" he retorted angrily.

"He promised you would be king of all Verda," Inara continued. "That your rule would reshape the realm and bring about a unity that has never existed before. True," she conceded. "At least, that's the version of the truth he wanted you to hold to. But the unity he spoke of was the one that rose up to challenge you. In this world, a world you *have* reshaped, the races have come together under one banner for the first time. And The Crow knew I would oppose you because he knew I would have no choice but to fight the evil he was unleashing on the world."

She thought of Gideon's words to her, before the battle on The Moonlit Plains. "I didn't want to believe it," she said earnestly, "but, standing here, now, *destiny fulfilled*... how can I not? Our birth *was* orchestrated, Alijah. *Our* birth. Because our fate was always to meet here. To end it all, one way or the other."

"Those sound like the narcissistic words of Gideon Thorn," Alijah rasped. "You always were his favourite puppet. He told me the same thing once. Since then, I've taken command of everything from the east to the west. I've brought peace to future generations. Thousands, *millions* more will be born into this world and know a full and happy life because of what I'm doing here! With no magic, there can be no threat! Who are you to challenge that?" His Vi'tari blade came up in his hands.

"And those sound like the bitter words of a frightened dragon," Inara countered. She had more to say, more words to twist her brother into knots, but there was no time - the would-be king lunged at her, proving himself to be as quick as ever.

Firefly came up just in time to block the green blade from taking her head. At the same time, the enchantment set into the Vi'tari blades caused an outburst of multi-coloured sparks. Alijah pressed into his sister, dragging his blade along hers until their faces were inches apart.

"Look at yourself!" Inara hissed. "You're being torn apart!"

Alijah growled and twisted his body into the next attack. Inara anticipated the move and adjusted her grip to meet the cursed sword. Again, their weapons collided in a spray of colourful sparks that died all too soon in the rain.

Rather than wait for his next attack, Inara fell upon her brother with a flurry of slashes and swipes. Her last strike, an upwards swing of Firefly, scraped along his scale mail and finally cut a line up his chin. As the blood rose into the air, Inara put a swift boot into his chest and sent him across the platform.

In a display of strength Inara hadn't believed he still possessed, Alijah flipped forward onto his feet from his back before his legs even hit the floor. His Vi'tari blade cut a fine line through the rain, demonstrating an edge of discipline to his form. They soon came together again in a battle of wills and ringing steel. Alijah's style reminded Inara of Asher's fighting form, his attacks precise and always deadly: intended to kill, not maim.

Misinterpreting one of his attacks, Inara received a dragon-scaled elbow to the face and a quick slash of steel across her hip. She screamed and fell face first against the stone, her tongue able to taste her own blood as it mixed with the collecting rain water.

Sensing a kick coming for her ribs, the Guardian rolled to the side. She avoided Alijah's boot but not the swing of his blade, which she was forced to meet with Firefly before rolling away again.

Instead of continuing their dance of steel, her hand shot up and released a blast of ice. Alijah stopped the freezing spell with a quick shield spell of his own. When he dropped the shield, a small sheet of curved ice fell to his feet and shattered into pieces. Inara used her precious time wisely and returned to her feet, despite the protests of her injured hip. Alijah, however, had no interest in crossing swords with her. Before their battle could begin again, he threw down his Vi'tari blade and raised his hands into the air.

"We've done this once before!" he yelled. "Do you remember how that ended?"

There was no time to conjure a destructive spell of her own - bolts of lightning were already sparking between his fingers. Inara dropped Firefly and held out both of her hands. Her shield flared to life with only a fraction of a second to spare before Alijah's display of lightning crashed into it. Between them, they lit up the night.

Alijah soon added waves of telekinetic energy to his lightning, putting more strain on Inara's shield. Inevitably, the drain began to take its toll on her physically. Within seconds of holding off the barrage, the Guardian was down to one knee. Leaving herself with one hand in the air to continue her defence, Inara's other hand dropped to her waist and found the satchel clipped to her belt.

Gaining ground, Alijah stepped towards her, his spells intensifying. Through the flashes and blinding bolts, Inara could see a grin of wicked glee on Alijah's face. It didn't look like her brother's face. Instead, she saw the insidious malevolence of his companion behind his expression, a beast who wanted nothing more than to break the surface world and its ties to magic.

Then, inexplicably to Alijah, his lightning spell began to shrink away from her shield, as if it was retracting into him. Within seconds, his hands held nothing but smoke.

"What is this?" he fumed.

Inara, gritting her teeth against the pain in her hip, and just about everywhere else, rose to her feet. In her right hand, she presented the Crissalith dagger, a sturdy weapon now, thanks to the dwarves.

Alijah's eyes narrowed. "Is that..."

With the Hastion gem sitting comfortably on her finger, Inara flicked her wrist and struck her brother with a fiery spell that launched him from his feet. "Crissalith," she declared, walking towards him.

The force of the spell certainly inflicted a fair amount of pain upon Alijah, though his smoking scale mail held up to the flames. Before he could get up, Inara unleashed a short burst of lightning and shocked him with enough energy to make him howl in agony.

Enjoying her superiority, the Guardian waved her hand left and right, flipping him one way then the next into the hard stone. Her last outburst shoved him across the platform, to the very edge.

Inara displayed the back of her hand and the blue gem that adorned her finger. "It's not so easy when you aren't the one holding all the cards, is it?"

Digging deep into whatever reservoir of energy he had long learned to hold on to, Alijah managed to lunge at her from the floor. It would have been an easy attack to counter, his bare hands unable to stand up to the edge of the Crissalith blade, but he had a blade of his own. At the last second, Inara saw the glow of the Moonblade in his grip. She didn't have time to chastise herself for losing sight of it - she could only defend herself.

Each cut the other with their chosen weapon, their attacks intricate and deadly. Inara's spells, however, had taken their toll on Alijah, adding to his growing injuries. Taking advantage of his sluggish movements, the Guardian shifted her stance and locked his arm in place. She knew the exact amount of pressure to apply and forced him to drop the Moonblade. As he yelled out and released the dagger, Inara twisted the Crissalith blade in her hand and thrust it up between two layers of scales in his armour. It missed his heart and rammed up through his shoulder until the hilt became lodged. His cry of pain was instantly amplified before she let him fall back to the edge of the platform again.

Inara... Athis's voice called to her in that moment. She could sense the great effort her companion required to speak to her while locked in battle. *Inara,* he said again. *What you do now will define you. Don't meet wickedness with more wickedness. You love him. Set him free.* Their bond was severed when the red dragon retracted his mind and recommitted to the fight in front of him.

Focusing on Alijah again, Inara recalled Gideon's advice. She had to feel it, one way or another. Only by acknowledging her true emotions could she make that killing blow. Standing over him now, Inara looked down at her brother. He was utterly broken. And, through that broken exterior, she wondered if she was glimpsing something of that scared boy he had once been, before all the wars.

It brought tears to her eyes.

He was still the little boy she had dreamt of grand adventures with. He was still her best friend who knew what she was thinking, who knew when to comfort her. Under it all, there was something left of him in there - she had to believe that. The Alijah Galfrey she had known was strong... and *good*.

Feeling it all, at last, Inara crouched down beside him. Her emotions had, indeed, given her the strength needed to deliver that killing blow. But it also gave her the strength not to deliver that killing blow.

"This... isn't over yet," Alijah croaked. "I *will*... beat you."

Inara met his eyes. "The Crow wasn't the only one to lie to you," she told him. "Malliath has fooled you."

Through his pain, Alijah managed to direct his scowl at her. "You... don't know what... you're talking about."

"Your bond was never altered, Alijah. Malliath just made you believe it was. You have to trust me," she pleaded. "He's had you under his thrall from the beginning. Day after day, his mind has poisoned yours. And now, he has you so enclosed in his grip that you can't see the damage being done to you. Can't you feel it? Your magic might flow from within now, but the Crissalith will still untether you. Soon, his influence will be all but gone."

"Liar," he seethed.

With tears streaking down her face, lost to the rain, Inara replied, "See for yourself, while you still can. Go into your sanctuary. Take the passage, the one that changes everything - you'll see. You *must* go through." Alijah didn't look convinced, though he also looked like he might be losing consciousness. "Quickly," she urged. "Our sanctuaries are places of deep magic. You don't have long before the Crissalith prevents you."

~

Alijah closed his eyes and let his mind fall into that deep place Inara spoke of. When he next opened his eyes, he was whole again. There was no Crissalith blade in his chest and no wounds from either his father or his sister.

He breathed in the sea air as the waves of The Adean collided rhythmically with Korkanath's rocky foundations. Turning on the spot, he noticed the darkness encroaching on the cave, a living shadow that erased the sanctuary's details inch by inch. It wouldn't be long before the Crissalith dissolved it all and banished him from the ethereal space and back to the pain of the real world.

Moving away from the spreading darkness, towards the craggy entrance, he realised he was alone in the sanctuary. Malliath was too occupied with Athis to allow his mind to inhabit the cave.

What was he even doing here? he asked himself. Inara was wrong. Yet here he was, having heeded her words. Alijah shook his head and growled in frustration. His mind felt as if it was unravelling.

As the Crissalith encroached on his bond with Malliath, severing the strands of their tether, flashes of memory assaulted him, each one a physical blow. They blinded him, showing him things he had done over the last two decades, things that made him feel sick.

"NO!" he screamed in a bid to reject the images and sounds of so much death. But there was no escaping the truth of what he had become: a necromancer.

The half-elf fell to his knees in the dirt. The darkness was beginning to lick at him from all sides except one: the jagged entrance to the cave, where the ocean washed up again and again. Instinctively, he moved away from the creeping abyss and towards the water.

He had done this before, he knew. He had walked through those waves, sunk beneath the surface, and emerged with a bond in keeping with the Dragon Riders of old, free of the way of the Dragorn.

Hadn't he?

Try as he might, he struggled to recall that memory with any clarity. He remembered Gideon telling him of the bond, of the potential influence dragons could exert on their companions, as Nylla had once done with the great Elandril, centuries ago. It had deeply offended him that Gideon would think Malliath capable of controlling him in such a way. To overcome his nagging doubt, however, Malliath had encouraged him to leave the sanctuary via the water and see for himself. He had emerged in the real world feeling no different, confident that Malliath had never attempted any kind of control to begin with.

But here he was, standing with his feet in the surf and unable to recall his actual steps into the water years earlier. More images flowed through his mind, causing him to stagger forward into deeper water. He saw himself, full of conviction, aiming his Vi'tari blade at his father's heart. If it hadn't been for Inara's intervention, he would surely have killed him.

Then he saw his grandmother, Adilandra. His actions had sealed her fate and sent her to the watery grave in which she now rested. Heartbreaking as it was, to see the disappointment on her face at the end, it was even worse to see the men, elves, and dwarves he had condemned to death. There were so many of them. He fell to his knees and yelled at the storm before hammering the waves with his fists.

Malliath had been behind it all...

That singular thought began to sharpen as new memories came back to him, memories that had been scrubbed from his mind by the dragon. His every emotion had been manipulated to direct him down a particular path, a path of destruction. Malliath hated magic with every fibre of his being. He had been the victim of it time and time again throughout a history that was so long he had earned the title of *ancient*. But it didn't excuse the dragon for using him as a tool to meet his ends.

Alijah's shoulders sagged and his head turned to the sky. He had been used. Powerful forces had turned him into a weapon and handed him to the oldest being in the world, to be used however he saw fit. And what evil things he had done. Alijah looked at his hands, hands that Malliath had used to craft the darkest of magic and turn it upon the realm.

He had been tainted to his very soul.

It was all so painful to comprehend. There could be no redemption for him - he had become the embodiment of evil. There was a part of him that wanted to return to the real world and allow Malliath to maintain his influence, to erase these memories and feelings for good. But ignorance wasn't bliss, it was dereliction of duty, a duty he had sworn to many years earlier when he had been in the company of good men like Hadavad... and Vighon. He had sworn to protect the people of the realm, not break them.

Alijah looked down at the water and took a breath. He was going to plunge deep and emerge a free man, whatever that might be. And he would accept the consequences.

Inches above the water, his head stopped before submerging. A single thought occurred to him. It was, perhaps, the clearest thought he had conjured in nearly twenty years. He thought of the battle raging in the sky above The Bastion. Athis was a powerful dragon, but Alijah knew what was in Malliath's heart, in his iron will. Inevitably, Athis would fall to Malliath, as so many before him had fallen. And then Ilargo would take his place and find only the volcanic fury of the black dragon, his death assured. And without Alijah as his weapon, he would surely resort to burning all of Verda to the ground. There were simply none who could best him.

Except one.

The effects of the Crissalith were almost absolute, the sanctuary closing in on him. Yes, he thought. There was one who could beat Malliath the voiceless.

All he had to do was let himself go and take a single step. To take a step was a simple thing, a small thing even. He had been in this moment before, in the hammering rain at the top of the world. He knew now, as he knew then, that it would take such a simple and small thing to change his destiny. He had tried that once before and failed.

He would not fail again.

~

Blasted by the rain, Inara watched Alijah closely. He had taken an extended blink, but now he looked back at her with some focus behind his eyes.

"Inara," he uttered, saying her name as if it was the first time.

A smile dared to push at her cheeks. "Alijah?" she questioned delicately. "Is that you?" More tears ran down her face. "You did it. You walked through, you changed the bond."

Alijah's expression didn't change. Instead of replying, he raised one hand and cupped her cheek, his gaze boring into her. "It's like... I can breathe again," he whispered. "I've missed you."

Inara didn't know what to say, her emotions battling with the rage and love she felt towards him. She put her hand over his and offered a warm smile. "I've missed you too," she finally replied.

Multiple roars echoed across the skies, adding to the thunder. *He knows!* Athis warned. *Malliath knows something is wrong! He's coming!*

Inara's eyes flitted from the dark sky to her brother. "We don't have long. We need to get inside."

"I'm so... sorry," Alijah said, remaining where he lay.

"There will be time for that," Inara told him with a great deal of urgency in her voice. She heaved him from the floor and took some of his weight. "We need to go, *now*. Malliath knows you've altered your bond."

Alijah didn't move, halting their departure from the platform. "There's so much... I want to say. But there are no words... that can undo what I've done."

"We need to go!" Inara insisted, sparing a brief glance at the sky.

He turned his head up to look her in the eyes, his expression that of a contented man. "There's only one thing... I have left to give."

Inara finally stopped trying to drag him towards the archway. "What are you talking about?" she asked.

"I'm sorry," Alijah repeated.

Then, in an explosion of action, he slipped his hand from hers and found the finger with the Hastion gem. A strong tug snapped the bones, rendering her entire hand useless with agony. In the same moment, he pulled the ring free, shoved Inara back, and yanked the Crissalith blade free from his chest. The gem in his possession, he had only to hold out his hand and Inara was swept away with the crystal dagger.

The platform greeted her with its unyielding embrace before she skidded across the wet stone. She heard the Crissalith clatter beside her, not far from where her father still lay. She fought against the new variety of pain and sat up to find others around her now. Her mother was crouching beside Nathaniel while Vighon and Asher stood sentinel in the rain, the four of them staring out across the open space.

The realisation of what was really happening came all too late to the Guardian. "No!" she cried, seeing Alijah's plan laid bare. "He didn't change their bond!"

Alijah paused by the very edge of the platform and turned back to face them all. "He would have me be a monster!" he yelled over the storm, his grim determination stealing his features. "I won't let him hurt anyone else!"

Inara scrambled to her feet but it was too late and Alijah was too far away. Without taking his eyes away, he stepped off the edge.

"NO!" Inara screamed, her hand reaching out to grab him in a spell, but without the Hastion gem to combat the Crissalith beside her, she was powerless. She kicked the blade away, sending it careering off the platform. In its absence, Athis's voice returned to her with clarity.

Malliath's going to save him! he warned.

Through Athis's mind, she could see the black dragon swooping low to catch Alijah, thereby saving both of their lives. A moment existed between Inara and Athis, a moment so profound and urgent that only feelings were capable of crossing their bond.

Athis knew he could stop Malliath from reaching Alijah before he crashed into the rocks. Stopping him would ensure Alijah's death and bring an end to the overwhelming threat of Malliath. But everything in Inara wanted to save her brother, her desperate need providing Athis with a choice.

Saving Alijah, however, meant saving Malliath. That in itself put the entire realm at risk. Without the Crissalith, Alijah would be subsumed by the dragon once more and they might never get the opportunity to separate them again.

There was, it seemed, only one way to end it all: they had to honour Alijah's sacrifice.

It broke Inara's heart but, for the sake of the realm and, perhaps, any kind of redemption for her brother, she said the words anyway. ***Stop him.***

Athis continued on his flight path, his wings tucked in to let him spear down at just the right angle. Only seconds had gone by since Alijah began his final journey, but his moment between life and death was about to come to an end. It was only then, a heartbeat from impact, that Inara saw the true calamity of what was about to happen.

Athis hadn't told her *how* he was going to stop Malliath...

"No." The protest could hardly be heard as she broke into the fastest run her injured hip would allow.

Athis intercepted Malliath head to head, ramming into the behemoth from the side with all the weight of his fall behind him. The pair were immediately taken from their differing flight paths and set on a new one together.

It all happened at the same time.

Alijah met his sudden end on the rocks as Athis and Malliath slammed into the mountain side. Alijah's instantaneous death crossed his bond with Malliath and stopped the dragon's heart, their reign and companionship having reached its inevitable and tragic end.

On her hands and knees, Inara had watched it all. And now she watched as the cliff gave way, its exterior shattered by the combined impact of both dragons. Athis had predicted the disaster from the moment he had set himself on course.

"ATHIS!" she bellowed, refusing to believe what she was seeing.

Sheet upon sheet of rock broke free of the mountain and rained down on Athis, burying him ton by ton. Soon, she couldn't see him at all, the entire area clouded with debris.

Inara gasped as her lungs seemed to forget how to breathe. She reached out to him again and again but there was no response in her mind, not even a feeling. Her immediate desolation sucked her in. She didn't care that massive wings were beating the rain as Ilargo found purchase on The Bastion's stone.

"Inara."

The Guardian had no idea who was calling her name. It wasn't Athis and his was the only voice she wanted to hear. And so she stayed where she was, hanging over the world, her gaze fixed on the shifting rocks far below.

"Inara."

The voice was followed by a hand on her shoulder, though many hands were required to heave her away from the edge. She was eventually faced by Gideon, who gripped her by the arms. Beside him were Asher and Vighon, but her eyes were taken beyond them, to her parents. Nathaniel was holding Reyna tightly in his arms, the pair seated on the wet stone with their faces buried in each other's shoulder.

"We will go to him," Gideon said, snapping her attention back. "Come."

Inara and Gideon alone were flown down the mountain by Ilargo. Avandriell passed them by on their way, her wings frayed and ripped in places. Inara could only give the bronze dragon a glance, her focus drawn to Athis.

Ilargo's landing disturbed more of the loose rocks but his claws were secure, rooting him to the slope. Inara didn't wait for Gideon to tell her it was safe. Within seconds of touching down, she was scrambling over the broken mountain side, the pain of her hip and broken finger long forgotten in the face of her breaking heart.

She came across Malliath's body first. Like a god thrown from the heavens, his corpse lay crumpled on the rocks. His body was severely battle damaged, marred from tail to snout with Athis's claw marks. His mouth remained ajar, his tongue hanging between his jaws and over a large stone. The black dragon had lost the life behind his purple eyes. His death, it seemed, had also ended the supernatural storm that had brought ruin to the starry night.

Scaling Malliath, Inara continued a little further up, ignoring Gideon's distant warnings about the potential dangers.

There he was.

"Athis!" Inara called his name again and again as she approached. His head and half of his neck protruded from the rockslide, allowing her to come right up alongside his face. Like Malliath, what she could see of his body revealed a savage battle with his kin. One of his crowning horns was gone completely while the other had been snapped in half.

The only eye she could see began to slowly open. Small veins, a brighter red than his scales, wormed their way into the rich blue that surrounded his sharp pupil.

Wingless one... His mind was weak, the words distant and lacking their usual edge.

It's me, she replied through their bond. *I'm here.*

Is it... over? he asked.

Yes, Inara answered, her tears flowing with abandon. **You sacrificed...** She stopped, her mind refusing to form the words. **You sacrificed yourself,** she finally managed. **Why did you have to do that?** the Guardian demanded, her grief and anger running parallel.

I was not... the only one, Athis said. *There was still... good in him... at the end.*

Inara nodded along as she knelt beside her companion, her hand pressed to his scales. **I don't want you to go. I can't lose you too. I don't know how to be without you.**

Ah... but that time... is upon us. You must feel it too. The eternal shores... call to me.

No, Inara wept, willing him to overcome Death itself. **I love you too much. You can't leave me.**

I have done... all that I was meant to... in this life. And what a life... you have given me. Know this... Inara Galfrey... I await you in the next life... where the sky is endless... and the dawn is everlasting...

With that final word, Athis the ironheart closed his eyes, never to open them again.

An indescribable sound escaped Inara's lips, a sound that carried all of her sorrow, grief, and agony. And there she remained, trapped by her misery until the sun once again graced The Vrost Mountains.

Eventually, the sound of footsteps broke her trance, pulling her from the memories she had spent the rest of the night dwelling on. Memories of Athis, memories of Alijah. That was all she had now.

Gideon stood before Athis, his hand resting against the red dragon's snout. "Rest well old friend. You were the best of us."

"I don't want to leave him," Inara said.

"Even when you were apart, you were always together. That will never change."

Inara looked up at her old mentor with bloodshot eyes and flushed skin. "What am I without him?"

"Together you made each other so much more," Gideon told her, "but it wasn't Athis the ironheart that forged Inara Galfrey into a *warrior*, into a *hero*. You are still that person. You will go on to do everything you were going to. Only now you will take Athis in your heart... and in your soul."

Gideon's hand extended towards her but Inara paused before taking it, her eyes catching a glint of red on the ground. She scooped it up and examined the dragon scale, her thumb wiping some of the dirt away. It fitted easily in the palm of her hand and she clasped her fingers around it, holding it so tightly it nearly cut into her skin.

Leaving Athis to the mountain was one of the hardest things she had ever done, but her feet managed one step at a time until they returned to Ilargo. Inara didn't miss the body wrapped in Gideon's cloak and nestled between the dragon's spinal horns. She didn't say anything, though she was grateful Gideon had recovered her brother.

As Ilargo leapt from the mountain side, his wings taking them high into the air, Inara looked out and took her last look at Athis. No, she told herself, it wasn't the last time. She would see him again, some day.

CHAPTER 58
KEEPING THE HOPE ALIVE

A sher watched from The Bastion's main entrance as Inara was enveloped by her parents. Their grief was palpable. The ranger couldn't know the loss of a son, a brother, or even a dragon, all of which he was deeply thankful for. But his eyes filled with tears seeing those he loved in such pain.

He had already offered his condolences and embraced them all individually, but they needed each other now. Together, the Galfreys were always stronger.

Inara eventually broke away from her parents and was taken in by Vighon's arms. No one disturbed them, nor the Galfreys. Instead, Asher turned around and walked outside, hardly pausing as he clapped a hand on Galanör's shoulder and offered a polite bow of the head to Aenwyn.

Among the mountain tops, a clear blue sky had welcomed the sun over the world. Without thinking, the ranger made for his companion - Avandriell felt like home. She bowed her head, already aware that he intended to stroke the smoother scales between her eyes.

In the light, he got a better look at the fierce young dragon. Her wings were ragged at the ends and some of the larger membranes were marred by narrow slits. Her claws were chipped and bloody, a price any as young as her would pay when challenging one so ancient as Malliath. Some of her bronze scales were missing, though she appeared to have avoided any direct bite from her foe. One of the tusks, just to the side of her jaw, had snapped off, leaving a red stump in its place.

I will heal, Avandriell reassured him, sensing his distress. *They will all heal,* she added, looking beyond the ranger, *given time.*

I don't think some of them want to, Asher replied, looking directly at Inara.

"I didn't think it would feel like this," Gideon said, approaching from the other side of Avandriell. "Victory," the old master elaborated. "I didn't think it would be so... *painful.*"

Asher regarded Avandriell, his hand running down her jaw, as he moved to face Gideon. "Victory is rarely anything but bittersweet," he said. "Especially in our world. There's always blood in our world."

"Our pain is shared across the realm," Gideon continued. "Everyone has lost someone. We need to help them push through this," he added, gesturing to the grieving. "The people need to start healing."

Asher frowned. "They need *time,* Gideon."

"They don't have the luxury of time," the old master said softly, hurt by his own words. "The entire realm, both humans and elves, will look to them now. They, and they alone, will lead the people into a brighter future... a future of *hope,* not grief."

Asher wanted to argue for the sake of his friends, but Gideon's pragmatism was flawless - they were all kings and queens now.

"What do you suggest?" the ranger enquired.

"We must return to Namdhor," Gideon told him. "It is still the seat of power in Illian. News will travel fast from there. The people need to *see* them."

Asher agreed, if reluctantly. "Just give them a little more time," he implored. "I will go down into the valley and speak with the others. We will need to take stock of the dead and see to the wounded before making preparations to leave."

Gideon nodded his understanding and patted Asher on the arm before walking away.

He's right, Avandriell said. *If they wallow in their grief and pain, so too will the realm. Hope has ever been Inara's message, be it in her words or in her actions. She must continue in her duty, especially now.*

Asher agreed with his companion, but he wasn't going to pass on her words to Inara. **She'll get there on her own. She always does.**

The mountains rushed past and eventually fell away as Avandriell soared into the valley. What had once been a white strip through the mountains was now a dark stain, dotted with what looked like scurrying ants from their position in the sky.

The bronze dragon glided down, moving from east to west, rather than diving. She told Asher it was to give him a rest after a hellish night, but the ranger could sense the pain in the joints of her wings and knew the truth. Rather than offend the proud dragon, he accepted her reason with gratitude.

Taking in the battlefield below, the ranger was pleased to see every Reaver lying flat in the snow and mud. He would have liked to witness the moment they fell, their end in time with Alijah and Malliath's. There were none, however, who could have been so pleased as The Rebellion forces fighting for their lives. From above, Asher could already see the wounded and the dead being taken aside.

Avandriell's sharp eyes didn't require any more than a single flyby to find Doran Heavybelly. She came to hover in the air above the king, her wings fanning until space was made for her.

"Good to see yer, lad!" the son of Dorain called. "It's been hours since the wretches gave up the fight. I was beginnin' to worry none o' ye would return."

Asher climbed down from his saddle as Faylen and Nemir appeared from the gathering crowd. Like Doran, Faylen had clearly been through all the hells to have survived the battle, her fresh wounds there to be seen at only a glance. Nemir had suffered worse, it seemed, his left arm strapped across his chest and a bandage wrapped around his head. Asher greeted them all with his usual stoical nod.

"It is done then?" The question turned Asher to Kassian Kantaris, who had found his way between a group of elves with an obvious limp in his stride. "Alijah and Malliath," he continued, gesturing to the fallen Reavers, "they're... *dead?*"

Asher took a breath and raised his chin an inch. "They are," he confirmed.

Doran eyed him a moment longer, his heavy brow twitching in contemplation. "They're not the only ones, are they?"

With great sorrow, the ranger shook his head.

In the hours, days, and even weeks that followed The Rebellion's victory in The Vrost Mountains, there was little celebration to be had as they made the slow and arduous journey north. Those who had been hiding in The Black Wood emerged to join them in navigating across The White Vale, including Doran's mother, Drelda.

Their only enemy now was winter itself.

Asher was no stranger to the harshness of the elements, especially so far north that The Vengoran Mountains dominated the horizon. For the first time in his life, however, he faced this winter from the comfort of the air, accompanied by a warming spell and Avandriell's dreams for their future.

The pair would touch down every evening and enjoy the company of others over a meal. Sometimes they assisted in hunting down food to be dispersed through the camp. Mostly, Asher enjoyed being above the grief that permeated the once rebel forces. They all felt the sting of losing Athis and the rulers among them had yet to rise above their sorrow.

Reyna and Nathaniel were recovering quicker than Inara but, having spoken to them many times since leaving the mountains, Asher knew that they had started mourning the loss of their son long before his death. For Inara, her loss was still so raw.

A celebration is needed, Avandriell had opined several times along their journey. *A great victory has been won,* she would say. *Evil has been vanquished. The efforts of the brave should not be idly put aside in favour of the keen loss felt by the few.*

Time, Asher had replied. **Something you haven't had much of. But you'll see. Take it from the man with a thousand years behind him. Time heals all.**

I have no doubt, Avandriell had agreed. *But the thousands of people beneath us require something to remind them.*

Asher had tilted his head to catch one of her golden eyes. **Remind them of what?**

That they won, Avandriell had answered.

After a long journey, nearing three weeks, it seemed the people of Namdhor had heard the dragon. Avandriell took to the ground and walked alongside the horses and Warhogs to get in the middle of it. Having seen the large force approaching from some way, the people had gathered in the lower town and lined the main road that ran all the way up the centre of the city, ending at The Dragon Keep.

Trumpets blared, drums beat rhythmically, shakers filled with grain were rattled high in the air, and the music of three dozen lutes had their tunes carried in the breeze. The crowds cheered the victorious return of their king and their loved ones. Vighon, and even Inara, waved and smiled at the people as they rode up on their horses. Beyond the lower town, rising into the city proper, confetti seeds were thrown over them all in celebration.

Within the royal party, though slightly behind Vighon and Inara, Reyna and Nathaniel rode side by side with a small entourage of elves, including Faylen. The remaining elves marched in tight formation behind the human army, a spectacle for the humans of Namdhor. Further still were the dwarves of Dhenaheim, though their king and his mother journeyed through the city beside the Galfreys.

Wait until the dwarves make camp, Avandriell said. *Then the party will really start!*

Asher had to laugh at the thought - she was absolutely right. A group of children dashing between the parade caught the ranger's eyes and he followed them to the side of the road. There, he noticed a great throng who simply stood staring at Avandriell, captured by her beauty.

My ferocity, the dragon corrected, picking up on his observation.

I don't think they've ever seen a dragon as small as you, Asher quipped, careful to guard his amusement.

I am not small! Avandriell protested.

Only then did Asher laugh to himself and bring her in to the joke. **You shall be mighty in both size and strength, young one!**

Avandriell exhaled a sharp breath via her nostrils, displeased with the connotations that accompanied being *young. I will not be young forever,* she promised.

No, Asher agreed. **But you'll always be young to me,** he added with an affectionate pat to her neck.

Ilargo's shadow came over them both. The green dragon flew on ahead, his magnificent wings blowing snow from the rooftops.

A welcoming party greeted them all outside the main gates. It was only then, at the top of the capital city, that Asher realised the banner of the flaming sword was displayed throughout Namdhor, wiping away any trace of the black dragon sigil. It brought a rare smile to Asher's face, one that spoke of hope for a future he didn't often consider.

The afternoon, and what remained of the light, was taken up by the finer details of where everyone was sleeping and, thankfully, what celebrations were to be had. It was a moment for the dwarves to come into their own, a people who knew how to celebrate. The elves contributed, and even Reyna, who was slowly emerging from her shell, was able to advise on a few elements. Kegs of ale, beer, and wine were located throughout the city and distributed to places in need of good drink. Food had been sourced from other towns and cities after news of victory had spread, though much of it was directed to those in the lower town and the poorer districts in the city's fringes.

As nightfall crept over Namdhor, it brought with it an ocean of stars to mark the occasion. Having avoided the various meetings taking place, and kept very much to the fringes of the keep, Asher found himself wandering out onto the northern ramparts. The King's Lake, the largest body of water in all of Illian, was a slab of ice below. Its furthest edges met the curving mountain range of Vengora, which stood as no more than a black silhouette against a starry backdrop.

Movement drew his eyes to the pointed plateau of rock that extended beyond the keep and hung over the lake. He soon recognised the red cloak of Inara Galfrey gently blowing in the wind as she stood by the jagged edge. Swiftly, if quietly, the ranger made his way down and left the keep behind to meet her on the plateau.

"Inara?" he called softly.

The Guardian briefly regarded him over her shoulder before returning her gaze to the horizon. "It's a strange feeling," she said, as he joined her by the edge, "to know that I can fall and he won't catch me." Inara peered down at the drop. "It suddenly feels like such a long way."

"Perhaps you don't need to be caught," Asher posed.

"I have heard this speech," she interjected. "I know my own strength. I still command a level of magic many would envy and my skill with a blade puts me above most. I'm set to become the ruler of the biggest kingdom in Verda. My words will carry across the realm and it will be reshaped because of it. I know I don't *need* to be caught," she echoed. "But that doesn't mean I wouldn't like to be."

Asher's gaze lingered over her sharp features a moment longer. She had come a long way in a few weeks; even the timbre of her voice was a display of her inner strength, a strength Athis had helped her to build through the years.

"I think it's you who will need to do the catching now," Asher replied. "Only it isn't a single person relying on you to be there." He half turned over his shoulder, a gesture to the rest of the realm behind them.

"Then it's a good thing I will have help," Inara said, giving him a glance.

The ranger responded with a light shrug. "Avandriell and I will always be around. As will Gideon and Ilargo, I'm sure."

Inara bit her lip. "I wouldn't count on them being around too much. I have a feeling Gideon and Ilargo are destined for the west."

Asher nodded his understanding. It didn't surprise him either to think of the pair returning to Drakanan or even Erador having spent years in that land.

"You don't need reminding of your allies," he said. "Nor the troubles that still lie ahead of you," he added, referring to the colossal task of putting the realm back together. "Your name, your deeds, your *loss*... history will note them all. And ever will Athis the ironheart be regarded as the greatest hero of the Fourth Age. But, again, you know all that."

"What is it I *don't* know?" Inara asked with a hint of irritation.

Asher turned to face her. He could see the cavernous hollow that Athis had left in her, a place where his love had once burned with abandon. It was the same kind of love Asher could feel every second of the day emanating from Avandriell. It was like air for his lungs.

"You are still *fiercely* loved," he told her, turning the half-elf's blue eyes on him. "And not just by Vighon, but by so many more... including me," he added before the lump in his throat prevented him. "Nothing will ever replace Athis's love, but there is so much more love you have yet to experience."

Inara wrapped her arms around him before any tears could streak down her face. "I couldn't save either of them," she wept in his embrace.

Asher held her close. "You weren't meant to," he whispered. "The choice was theirs. You only did what had to be done. What no other could."

Inara squeezed him, reminding the ranger the elf in her was much stronger than him. "Thank you," she uttered.

It wasn't long before Vighon arrived, as if a sixth sense had told the northman his love was in need of him. Asher took his arm back and happily accepted a kiss on the cheek from Inara. He left them there, high above the world and returned to the warmth of The Dragon Keep.

The ranger passed the early hours of the evening with the hottest and most satisfying bath of his life. He informed Avandriell that she had seen the last of him, for he was never leaving the bath nor the comforts of the keep. That was until a knock graced his door with a message from the king of Illian.

Now, walking through the halls of the keep, Asher came across Galanör and Aenwyn as they exited their room.

"Summoned to the throne room?" Galanör enquired, falling in beside the ranger.

"You too?" Asher replied.

The elf nodded his response and glanced out of the passing window. "Where is Avandriell?"

"She wanted to go down and see the dwarves," Asher told him. "She's grown fond of their... *culture*," he added with some amusement and a shrug. "I'm never going to get used to seeing you with only one blade," he remarked, as they turned down the next passage.

"Imagine how I feel," Galanör agonised, his hand reaching for his belt. "I feel like I've forgotten something all the time."

Never one for idle chat, Asher was glad to reach the throne room only a minute later. The chamber looked to be in the middle of decoration, but the servants had all left before completing the job. Instead, the throne room was occupied by only a few, if a powerful few.

The ranger met Gideon and Faylen with a nod, but he hesitated when faced with Reyna, Nathaniel, and Doran, all of whom now inhabited stations that required more respect than a simple nod of the head. Rather than look like a dithering fool, Asher gave them all a bow.

"Asher." Reyna said his name lightly and bowed her head in return, though Nathaniel looked somewhat awkward about the whole affair.

The same could not be said of Doran, who accepted Asher's

bow with a broad grin. "Maybe I *could* get used to this kingly business."

Asher narrowed his eyes at the dwarf before returning his grin. "And maybe you will suit it, *Heavybelly*."

"Am I late?" Kassian asked as he entered the throne room, his limp long gone thanks to his fellow Keepers and some additional spells from elven healers.

"You're right on time," Vighon announced, emerging from a side door with Inara and Sir Ruban Dardaris. "Soon, this hall will be filled and the revelry will begin in earnest." The king paused and shared a brief moment with Inara. "Before that happens," he continued, "we wanted to make an announcement—"

"To our family," Inara expanded, with a quick look in Asher's direction. The ranger was just happy to see something of a genuine smile on her face.

"Yes," Vighon agreed, taking Inara by the hand. "We are engaged to be married!" he exclaimed.

There were cheers and applause in response, including a, "Finally!" from Doran. The couple descended the steps from the throne and accepted hugs from all. Reyna and Nathaniel embraced their daughter and soon-to-be son-in-law with tears in their eyes. It was a joyous moment they had all been in much need of.

And, as Vighon had promised, revels were soon upon them. After their private celebration, servants of the keep welcomed everyone from lords to decorated soldiers who had fought in The Rebellion. Under one roof, dwarves, elves, and humans joined in merriment for the first time since victory had been claimed. Asher couldn't remember the last time he had drunk anything from a goblet. Doran had brought his own goblet of sorts, though it was more comparable to a bucket with a handle on the side.

Before volume and potency left every member of the party inebriated, Vighon stood above all on the podium, before his throne. "Victory," he declared simply, drawing every set of eyes to him. "It is not given. It is *earned*. It's earned with blood... and sacrifice. This chamber, if not the realm itself, should be filled to bursting with glorious heroes who fought for what was in their hearts. But without their blood, without their sacrifice, we would not be here to celebrate this moment. This *victory*. So raise your drinks," he said, lifting his cup. "Raise them to those who cannot stand with us. To absent friends!"

The latter was echoed throughout as the chamber drank to the fallen. Asher's goblet touched his lips but he paused before consuming the beer. He thought of Russell Maybury, Adan'Karth, Athis the ironheart, and... Alijah Galfrey. They and so many more had been taken by a fated war.

After the king's speech, the celebration was renewed and the hall was alive with chatter and laughter. Asher drifted through, allowing himself to be pulled into various conversations and debates, until he found himself alone on the dragon platform over-looking the city. From top to bottom it was awash with a multitude of overlapping parties. Every inn, tavern, and house was brimming with people and cheer. Beyond the lower town, illuminated by thousands of torches and sporadic fires, was the combined dwarven and elven camp, whose merriment carried all the way up to The Dragon Keep.

A great gust of wind battered the ranger, throwing his hair and cloak out. He turned to see Ilargo land on the platform, his golden speckles glistening in the moonlight. Gideon climbed down from his saddle having left the throne room shortly after Vighon's speech.

"It's ready," he said to Asher on his way inside.

Asher acknowledged the news with merely a look. *I'm almost with you,* Avandriell spoke into his mind.

The ranger watched as Gideon discreetly informed the selected few of the same thing he had told him moments ago. One by one, they excused themselves from their conversations and quietly made for the main doors.

Jump! Avandriell insisted.

Asher could feel her presence and knew she was close. **I'm not doing that,** he replied with a light chuckle and a glance over the edge. **And besides, you've had way too much dwarven ale.**

Accompanying the others, Asher took the traditional route out of The Dragon Keep, if on this occasion a more secretive one. Cloaked, hooded, and unchaperoned by guards, the kings and queens of the world made their way down through the city and back on themselves to reach the lake. Galanör, Aenwyn, and Faylen made their own journey together, separate from the monarchs so as to move in smaller, less noticeable groups. Kassian, however, had declined to accompany them, choosing, instead, to remain in the keep. Only Asher, after meeting up with Avandriell outside the keep, and Gideon made their way by dragon flight.

Now, under the King's Hollow, between Namdhor's rising slope and the rocky pillar that supported its weight, those few gathered around a pyre. It was a space traditionally reserved for the crowning of Namdhor's kings and queens but, tonight, it was a place to say farewell to one.

Before the fire grew and consumed the pyre, Asher looked upon the body that rested there. A few elves, those Faylen had assured Reyna were their most loyal, had placed a stasis spell over Alijah before they had set off from The Vrost Mountains. And so, weeks later, he looked just as he had the day he died. Gideon stood before the pyre and made a snatching motion with his hand, bringing an end to the spell and leaving Alijah's body to the flames.

"Here lies Alijah Galfrey," Gideon announced, "a prince of Elandril, a Dragon Rider in his heart, and a *good* man. May it be, that one day, the realm comes to learn the truth of his life, the truth of the light that lived in him, even when the darkness claimed him as its own. For now, his sacrifice will remain with us, those who loved him, who knew him as that good man." After receiving a nod from Reyna and Nathaniel, Gideon waved his hand across the pyre and increased the flames.

Standing next to Avandriell, Asher watched the fire rise from the back of the group. Inara and Vighon remained close, wrapped in each other's arms - as did Reyna and Nathaniel. Gideon stepped away from the fire and returned to Ilargo's side, where Galanör and Aenwyn stood quietly together.

A hand sneaked between Asher's arm and chest as Faylen linked herself to him, her head coming to rest on his shoulder. The ranger had seen her coming but her actions still surprised him. Rather than question the affection, he squeezed her hand and lightly kissed the top of her head. Her friendship, he knew, was a comfort he had purposefully avoided. An immortal now, Asher was pleased to know that he had a very long time to work on their friendship and, perhaps, even give Nemir a chance.

For now, he simply enjoyed their closeness and let his thoughts drift across the memories he retained from his brief bond with Alijah. Thankfully, Avandriell had pushed almost all of Malliath's memories into the abyss, leaving only Alijah's earlier life to recall. He had, indeed, been a good man.

As the fire consumed his body, Asher dwelled on an image of the young half-elf from his time on the road with Vighon. He saw him wearing a green cloak, taken from Asher's locker beneath The Pick-Axe, and a familiar silvyr short-sword and folded bow on his back, taken from the Galfreys' home.

Once upon a time, Alijah Galfrey had wanted to be just like him, a ranger doing his part for the world. That was the man Asher would remember.

CHAPTER 59
NEW BEGINNINGS

I t had been three weeks since the start of the victory celebrations, three weeks since The Rebellion had nothing to rebel against. In that time, winter had unleashed its full force, an unwelcome shield against the warmth of the sun. Namdhor was struck daily by blasting winds and the snow came day and night.

Nothing, however, could stop the Namdhorians, nor the dwarves, from enjoying their freedom from the fear and the violence that had dominated their lives for so long. Nor did the prevailing cold prevent a wedding, especially when it was the wedding of the Age.

Every soul in the city had gathered in the streets, filling the main road from top to bottom until the numbers spread throughout the lower town and beyond. With bated breath, they looked up to The Dragon Keep, their eyes fixed on the ramparts above the main gate.

Reserved a space on those ramparts, Galanör Reveeri had one of the best views in all of Namdhor. He was also freezing to his bones. He adjusted the fur collar draped over his shoulders before quickly returning his hands to the inside of his navy cloak.

"Only in the north," he muttered under his breath.

Beside him, Aenwyn contained her amusement behind a tight smile. "I think it's a beautiful tradition," she whispered.

"Tradition isn't going to keep my toes attached to my feet," Galanör complained.

"I thought you were a ranger of the *wilds*," Aenwyn said innocently.

Galanör had a witty retort on the edge of his lips when Aenwyn's comment lodged itself in his mind and brought up a very important question: what was he now? He had once been a soldier in the elven army, but his skills with a blade had caught the eye of King Elym before long. Thankfully, his time as an assassin for the king had been cut short after meeting Gideon Thorn. Being a ranger had been easy, a job the elf had discovered he was more than capable of. But now his allegiance had been pledged to Reyna and Nathaniel and, to date, his role remained undefined.

Perhaps, he mused, he would be given a high-ranking position in the army. Just thinking about returning to life in Ayda brought a dark cloud over Galanör. Despite his centuries in Ayda, he had only learned to be his true self while living in Illian and, in the process, it had become his home.

In the absence of a response from him, Aenwyn leaned in. "Sir Ruban told me royal weddings are typically planned for the summer for just this reason."

Galanör considered the bride and the groom. "I don't think there will be anything *typical* about Vighon and Inara's reign," he said wistfully.

Aenwyn agreed with a contented smile. "I don't think the people could have waited until the summer," she remarked. "The excitement has been building since news spread of their union."

And what a strong union it was, Galanör thought. Both were heroes of their time, warriors in their own right. Together, they would steer the world of man into its strongest age yet. Their obvious pairing aside, Galanör was overjoyed to see them brought together by a love they had held in their hearts since childhood.

That was worth the cold.

"They're coming," Asher said, his voice loud enough to be heard by Vighon.

The king straightened up and turned to the city. Galanör narrowed his eyes down Namdhor's slope but even his powerful eyes failed to find the approaching bride. A moment later, bells rang out, starting in the lowest tier of the city and rising higher until finally joined by the great church outside the keep. In their wake, musicians and choirs heralded Inara's arrival from various balconies up and down the main road.

In due course, the bride came into view for all on the ramparts to see. The dense crowds parted, creating enough space for Avandriell. The bronze dragon led the bridal party with Inara seated astride her. Side by side, Reyna and Nathaniel trailed her on horseback with Faylen and Captain Nemir close behind them. Elves, three abreast and twenty deep, followed them all, their melodic voices slowly but surely replacing the human choirs that overlooked the affair.

Galanör peered over the edge to watch Inara dismount and enter the keep via the decorated gates. Her parents filed in behind her until Nathaniel offered his daughter an arm to see her through the courtyard and up the steps. The remaining elves took up positions on the steps and continued to sing as they made their way across the ramparts. Like the others before him, Galanör gave a deep bow as Inara, Nathaniel, and eventually Reyna passed him by.

Galanör took a moment to admire the bride's flowing blue dress that parted at her waist, revealing her dark leather trousers and tall boots. It was the perfect blend of elven princess and hardened warrior, with a variety of soft and harsh materials. A delicate silver circlet adorned her head, ringing the half-elf's black hair.

It wasn't her clothing, however, that put her apart from the average bride. On her hip rested Firefly, the powerful Vi'tari blade. Its crystal pommel twinkled in the light with the promise of great power inside. Of course, it was the carrying of the weapon that was truly powerful. It was a symbol to the people that their king wasn't acquiring a pretty bride or a stand-in queen to agree with his every word. They were getting a ruler who had already proven she could stand between the light and the dark.

"Beautiful *and* fierce," Aenwyn commented in his ear.

Galanör smiled, entranced by Inara. "Indeed," he said, noticing the small red dragon scale that hung from her necklace.

Nathaniel kissed Inara's hand before she moved to stand beside Vighon. The couple exchanged broad smiles and resisted the obvious temptation to kiss. As Ilargo's head arched over the pair, his bulk taking up much of the courtyard, Gideon Thorn stepped in, his travelling leathers replaced with a long flowing coat that hugged his figure.

Galanör had been there when they asked the old master to perform the wedding rites. The priests of Atilan had naturally opposed, pointing out that their order had always performed royal weddings. Inara and Vighon had politely, if firmly, told the priests that it was an elven custom and that there would be no further discussion on the matter.

Minutes went by as Gideon read through the marriage liturgy, words he had been rehearsing for days in the keep's garden. From his pocket, he eventually removed a single strap of leather that he wrapped around Inara's forearm and then around Vighon's.

"You are bound!" he announced. "Never to be broken! Never to fade! Never to fear! For together, you are, now and forever... *one.*" Gideon beamed with happiness. "I believe this is the part where you kiss," he said quietly.

Neither required more encouragement than that. The entire city shook with an almighty cheer that rippled from top to bottom as the news spread. Ilargo and Avandriell lifted their heads to the sky and added a roar to the resounding glee.

Vighon stepped towards the edge of the rampart and held up his hand, calling for silence. When, at last, the city knew of their king's wishes and grew silent once more, the northman gave a subtle nod to Sir Ruban, who approached with a wooden box in his hand.

Inara shot her new husband an inquisitive look but he maintained his calm, yet serious, demeanour. "As Inara and I are bond-ed," he called out, "so too is Inara bound to you, the people, and you to her, your queen!"

Without another word, Vighon turned to Sir Ruban, who opened the lid for him, and removed a crown for all to see. Thankful for his elven eyes, Galanör was able to examine it in great detail from where he stood, and what a crown it was. He had seen the crowns of queens before, often delicate sculptures designed to reflect their beauty rather than identify them as a ruling monarch.

Inara's crown was adorned with a variety of horns and small claws, all in differing sizes. They sloped back, reminding Galanör of a dragon's head. Befitting, he thought.

Vighon stepped forward and replaced Inara's circlet with the crown, careful not to interfere with any of the delicate braids. Then he did what no king before him had ever done.

He bowed the knee.

With the exception of Inara's parents and King Doran, every soul in Namdhor followed Vighon's example and knelt in reverence to the new queen of Illian. Only when Vighon resumed his height did the rest of the city stand again. The next round of cheers was just as deafening as the first and Galanör happily added his own voice to the jubilation.

As their last act of the ceremony, both Vighon and Inara freed their blades and held them high. The sword of the north came alive with flames and Firefly shone from the glow inside its pommel. Galanör was sure the responding cheer was powerful enough to be felt by the rest of the realm. *He* would certainly never forget it.

By late afternoon, as winter's sun bade its farewell, the wedding feast had been consumed and the party began in earnest. Elves sang merrily, dwarves bellowed their laughter, and the men and women of Namdhor filled The Dragon Keep with a warmth it had long been lacking.

Galanör moved from group to group, enjoying the stories they told as well as sharing a few of his own. He cheered Asher on as the ranger sat at a table, challenged by Thraal to an arm wrestle. It seemed, for a time, that neither would claim victory but, rather inevitably, Thraal slammed Asher's hand down. There were few, even among the elves, who could best a dwarf in such a focused contest, their arms more akin to coiled steel.

More than once, Galanör had offered his congratulations to the happy couple, never missing an opportunity to talk to them, but they were much in demand. Defying the winter conditions, lords and ladies had come from every region with gifts for them, but they also expected some face to face time with their king and queen.

After a brief conversation with Kassian about the day's affairs, Galanör found himself gravitating towards Gideon, who was often on the periphery of most social gatherings. They embraced as old friends and knocked their cups together.

"Before the rumours begin," Gideon said, "you should know that I am leaving soon."

"Your companion has long been a dragon," Galanör replied. "It would be more of a surprise if you told me you were staying in Namdhor." The elf took a sip of his wine. "Do I even need to ask where you're going?"

"Drakanan will have to wait," Gideon told him. "Though Erador is my destination."

Galanör raised an eyebrow. "What business do you have there if not in Drakanan?"

"The king and queen's business," Gideon answered, after waiting for a guest to pass them by. "Vighon and Inara have fears for Erador and I share them."

"Fears?"

Gideon nodded gravely. "It was with fear that Alijah and Malliath held sway in the west. They killed anyone who opposed them and maintained order with an unnatural army. I can only imagine what's happened there since the Reavers fell. There are good people in Erador, people just like those who call Illian home. They may need our help."

"Then I would be the first to bid you safe travels," Galanör offered, clasping his friend's shoulder. "I would love to see Erador myself some day."

Gideon laughed to himself. "You're immortal, Galanör. *Some day* will come. It always does."

Movement caught Galanör's eye and turned him to Aenwyn and Reyna, both a vision to behold. "Forgive me, Gideon," Reyna beseeched, "but might I steal Galanör away?"

Gideon gave a short bow of the head. "Who am I to protest so fair a queen?"

Reyna flashed him a smile before planting a light kiss on his cheek. Then, rather playfully, she linked her arms with Galanör and Aenwyn, placing herself between them, and made for the side door of the throne room.

"Are you enjoying yourselves?" she asked, as they weaved through the party.

"How could we not, your Grace?" Aenwyn replied. "'Tis such a happy day for all."

"Quite," Reyna agreed. "And the company?" she enquired.

"We are among the best," Galanör declared. "We are surrounded by friends and friends who feel like family, your Grace."

"And have you met any of the dignitaries from the other regions?" the queen went on, pausing while a servant opened the door for them.

"I have spoken with a few, your Grace," Galanör admitted. "Though I am not the one they clamour to meet."

"Indeed," Reyna said knowingly, ushering them into the next chamber, where Nathaniel was already waiting for them. "Wealth and standing will always turn the heads of those who already have wealth and standing. For them politics can become something of a game. It is not a game for the masses, however. Reminding the powerful people of the world that peace is better for all requires..." The queen looked to her husband for assistance.

"The occasional smack around the head," Nathaniel finished with a confident smile.

"Fortitude of character," Reyna corrected, before joining the king. "And a tremendous amount of patience."

"And stamina," Nathaniel added.

Galanör took it all in and shared the same look of confusion with Aenwyn. "Your Grace?" he began inquisitively.

"We are old friends - you don't need to call us that in here," Reyna told him with an inviting smile. "Only in company."

Galanör bowed his head in an effort to contain his own smile.

"It is an honour," Aenwyn replied.

"Yes," Galanör concurred. "And, in the spirit of friendship, I have to ask: what are we doing in here?" He gestured to the empty chamber, where the party could only be heard, not enjoyed.

"And," Aenwyn added, "why the speech?"

Reyna and Nathaniel had the same excited expression. "We were going to do this earlier," the king said, "but wedding plans and general meetings of every kind kept getting in the way."

Reyna opened the lid of a small box, resting on the side table, and removed two items no bigger than her palm. "We have had these made for you both."

Galanör accepted the token, as did Aenwyn, and inspected it nearer to the torchlight on the wall. The queen had handed them both an identical metallic pin that fastened to the join on the front of a cloak, just beneath the shoulder. Engraved on the pin was the sigil of house Sevari, an elven shield covered in the roots of a tree. Galanör ran his finger over the image, impressed with the craftsmanship but still none the wiser as to why he now possessed it.

"We have already informed Vighon and Inara," Reyna explained. "We have only to tell them you accept."

"Accept what?" Galanör asked.

Reyna beamed. "Your new positions as Ayda's ambassadors."

Galanör was stunned into silence.

Aenwyn gripped the ambassadorial pin with both hands. "Truly?"

"We could not take you from Illian," Reyna said. "This is your home. But you did pledge your allegiance to us, and what folly it would be to miss the opportunity to have such skilled elves represent our interests in Illian."

Galanör looked to Aenwyn as a growing and contented smile expanded across his face. He could see the answer in her eyes and knew it to be the same as his. As one, they said, "We accept."

Reyna threw her hands up in joy and quickly embraced them both. Nathaniel hung back and repositioned a long box on the table. "That's not all," he informed, though he seemed to be speaking to his wife more than the new ambassadors.

"Of course," Reyna responded quietly, moving to the large chest at the head of the chamber.

Nathaniel opened the thin box on the table. "We also had this made for you, Galanör."

From the box, an exquisite scimitar was removed by the experienced hands of the old Graycoat. Its forging was in the style of the elves, making it a close replica to Stormweaver, though its pommel appeared to be that of an eagle's head.

Nathaniel held it out with two hands. "For you."

Galanör wrapped his fingers around the hilt and lifted the blade free. It was lighter than Stormweaver, lighter even than Guardian had been. Its edge was just as sharp though, and its balance was so fine that it could only have been made by elves.

"This is the work of my kin," he observed.

"Yes," Nathaniel said. "And, more so, the elven smith told us the name came to her in the last moments of her work."

Galanör looked to his king with immeasurable anticipation. "Rarely do elven hammersmiths know the name of the steel they work."

"Quite so," Nathaniel agreed, marvelling at the scimitar. "Yet we already know this blade is called... *Swiftling*."

Galanör's eyes roamed up the length of the weapon. "Swiftling," he uttered. Gathering himself, he continued, "Thank you. I don't know what to say. I haven't received a gift like this since Queen Adilandra gave me Stormweaver and Guardian."

"Well, you don't need to say anything," Reyna insisted. "I only hope you never have need of it." The queen turned from Galanör and faced Aenwyn. "For you, I have something a little older." Having retrieved it from the chest, the queen presented Aenwyn with her own bow. "I claimed this as my own after defeating Adellum Bövö at the battle of West Fellion. I have spent decades trying to rewrite its destiny, to give it a future in the light."

Aenwyn was shaking her head. "I cannot accept this."

Reyna thrust the weapon into her hands. "Yes you can. Today is a day of new beginnings," she continued, with a look at her husband. "And goodness knows we could all do with it. I have given this bow all that I can. Were I to take it to Elandril with me, it would collect dust; a shame when it has the potential - in the right hands - to be a force for good. I want you to have it."

"You honour me again," Aenwyn replied with a bow of the head.

Galanör looked from Reyna to Nathaniel. "You are returning to Ayda?"

"Inevitably," Nathaniel said dryly.

"Elandril is still the heart of our nation," Reyna interjected with a cutting glance at her husband. "That is where we belong. Though, we will remain in Illian for a while longer, perhaps the year. Our two realms are to be strong allies and there is much work to do here, most of which can't even be attempted until the spring."

The king and queen didn't need it, and so he didn't say it, but Galanör certainly approved, happy to have them remain in the country for another year.

"Oh," Reyna added, a thought just occurring to her. "I should say, if the day ever comes that you wish to return to Ayda, you have more than earned a place on my council, Galanör. If you would accept *that* position, I would happily remove your father in a heartbeat."

Galanör was tempted to ask for that position right now, if only to watch his father be publicly humiliated. But, for now, he was more than content to pursue his life in Illian, where he finally felt a sense of belonging.

"Perhaps one day," he replied with a mischievous grin.

"Right then!" Nathaniel clapped a hand on Galanör's shoulder. "Let us find something good to drink. We have new beginnings to toast!"

CHAPTER 60
THROUGH SHADOW

In the blistering cold of Dhenaheim's freezing wastes, Doran Heavybelly at last stood before the entrance of his home. Grimwhal.

He stared into the main passage, an abyss that did not welcome the light. Both doors, built to withstand any dwarven war machine, still resided on the stone floor, twisted and bent out of shape by the undead dragon, Morgorth. Beyond lay a labyrinth of dwarven design, a place of great halls and cathedral-like temples to the Mother and Father.

It was also home to monsters.

It felt an age to Doran since he had last stepped foot inside the walls of his ancestors but, when he had, the son of Dorain had seen with his own eye the terrible beasts that had claimed Grimwhal as their own.

But it wasn't theirs. It was *his*. And now, with the entire dwarven army at his back, he was going to reclaim Grimwhal and declare it the new capital of Dhenaheim. Such a declaration would be better made if there happened to be a Clacker's head on the end of his axe. Everything sounded better when there was a monster's severed head on an axe.

"*My Lord,*" came Thraal's voice as his Warhog came up alongside the king's. "*We wait only on your word to attack.*"

Doran heard every word but he didn't take his eye from that forbidding tunnel. He chewed over the command to attack. It felt like only yesterday he was in good company, enjoying the finest food and drink Namdhor had to offer. But it had, in fact, been just over two weeks since Vighon and Inara were wed. Now, here he was, on the verge of battle once more, his words destined to send dwarves to their death. For their home, though, for their birthright, they would happily pay the price with blood.

"*What would you do, Thraal?*" he asked his War Mason.

Thraal didn't require much time to think it over. "*I would flood Grimwhal with the toughest warriors in all of Verda and crush anything foolish enough to challenge us... my Lord.*"

"*Would you now,*" Doran replied lightly, aware that Thraal was still harbouring some violent tendencies since the death of Thaligg. "*You know, as my War Mason, you're going to have to be more than a strong arm on the battlefield. I need you to think before you lift your axe and especially before you command others into the fight.*" The king sighed. "*Use this before this,*" he said, gesturing from his head to his arm, "*and you'll save lives.*"

"*As you say, my Lord.*"

"*Well, do you know what I say?*" Doran replied. "*I say we need eyes and ears in there first. We need to know what we're dealing with before we go blundering through.*"

Thraal clicked his fingers as if an idea had just occurred to him. "*I will gather our best scouts!*"

"*Don't bother,*" the king instructed him, spurring Pig onwards.

"*My Lord!*" Thraal called after him. "*You can't go in there alone!*"

"*I'm not!*" he yelled back, only a second before Avandriell dropped out of the sky.

The bronze dragon created a cloud of snow as her wings fanned out to slow her descent. Astride her back, seated in his saddle, was Doran's oldest friend, the first human he had ever come to trust with his life.

Asher glanced over his shoulder, looking back at the expectant army of dwarves. "You might be forgetting something," he quipped.

"Still sharp as ever then," Doran replied with his usual dry wit. "The way I see it, Avandriell is still small enough to fit through our passages."

Avandriell responded with a sudden exhalation from her nostrils.

"She really doesn't like the *S* word," Asher warned.

"It'll be bit o' a squeeze in places," Doran added, hoping to appease the dragon. "But once we get into the city proper, you'll 'ave enough room to even fly!"

Again, Asher quickly regarded the thousands of dwarven warriors they were leaving behind. "You know, when we agreed to accompany you back to Dhenaheim, I assumed we would be *aiding* in the effort to rid your cities of monsters. I didn't realise it was going to be just *us*."

Doran laughed as they approached Grimwhal's entrance. "Jus' like old times, eh?"

"I've faced Clackers before," the ranger said, "but never a nest the size you described."

"We'll be lucky if that's all we face in there, lad. In The Whisperin' Mountains, Clackers are way down the old food chain. We might even snag ourselves a Stonemaw!" Doran turned his head to spy Asher's reaction. Seeing his less-than-impressed expression, the king broke out in a deep belly laugh. "I'm not so daft as to think we can clear out Grimwhal alone. Though I bet Avandriell would give it a good go."

The dragon shook her whole body, a gesture the dwarf had come to learn was one of pride and confidence.

"Flattery will get you everywhere," Asher muttered.

"With a handful o' words," Doran continued on a serious note, "I could command every dwarf into this tunnel an' they wouldn' come out until the city is ours again. But I wouldn' throw so many lives away with such a brash plan o' action. I know Grimwhal. If we're smart, we can infiltrate the city, set up stagin' posts an' clear it out district by district."

"That makes sense," Asher replied. "So you need to scout the city first. See what you're dealing with."

"Ye know," Doran remarked, "if ye ever change yer mind abou' this ranger business, I'd make a good War Mason out o' ye."

Journeying through Grimwhal's outer-most passages, Avandriell kept her head lowered and Asher walked by her side, while Doran remained comfortable astride his trusty Warhog. They stepped over the frozen corpses of both dwarves and Reavers, their bodies undisturbed since the first invasion.

The king guided them one way then the next, his memory recalling every turn in his ancient home. They eventually passed through the grand throne room and then into the cavernous city itself. It should have been a spectacle, a marvel of dwarven architecture and engineering, but it was draped in darkness and the foul odour of decay. Disappointed, Doran raised his torch, hoping the firelight would make a difference. It didn't. The shadows grew longer and dashed about in the light, tricking his eye into thinking there were creatures lurking.

"We need better light," he commented.

"I think I can help with that," Asher said.

Doran raised an eyebrow as the ranger birthed a ball of light from his palm. It flickered for a moment, threatening to extinguish, before floating above them with increasing intensity. It didn't bring out Grimwhal's beauty, but it did remind the son of Dorain how much work was needed beyond the slaying of a few monsters.

"So ye're a mage now," he whispered, as they pressed on through the streets.

"Gideon and Inara have taught me some spells," Asher replied modestly. "Nothing I can kill myself with," he added.

"Or me, I hope," Doran said with amusement.

As quietly as they could, with dragon claws and Warhog hooves, the group cautiously penetrated the heart of the city. Asher's orb followed them from overhead and revealed very little but empty streets and skeletons that had been picked clean. When they reached the crossroads at the centre of the city, Doran looked to the east. If he followed that road he would eventually come to the spot where Dakmund had been wounded by Lord Kraiden.

"We should have come across something by now," Asher reasoned, his voice low. "Light always attracts the dark," he uttered, with a glance up at his orb.

Doran dismounted from Pig and pulled free a large flask as he did. "I say we take advantage o' the peace an' quiet," he suggested, shaking the flask so Asher could hear the cider within.

Asher looked at his reptilian companion, who lay down in the street, while they found an empty barrel and a bench to sit on. Pig naturally began to investigate every nook and cranny for potential food but, since he was doing it quietly, Doran didn't disturb the animal.

"I know I've said it before," Doran began, "but I'm glad ye came. It feels like I've brought a little bit o' Illian with me."

"You think I had a choice?" Asher responded, accepting the flask from the dwarf. "As soon as Avandriell heard the word *monster* we weren't going anywhere else."

Doran flashed a proud smile at the dragon. He had never been particularly fond of any of her kind, though that had never stopped him from respecting them and their inherent wisdom. But he had come to enjoy Avandriell's company, his fondness growing the more her personality shone through. And, of course, he intended to reward them with coin and more when their campaign was at an end. They were still rangers, after all.

"So what's next for the pair o' ye?" Doran asked. "After ye've helped me, o' course. Return to Illian an' look for a contract? Pocket coin wherever ye can."

"That's the plan," Asher replied. "Though we might not be so desperate for coin."

Doran eyed him over the flask. "How so?" he enquired.

Asher took a moment to consider his words. "I'm going to reopen The Pick-Axe," he declared simply.

The king's face froze in confusion. "How's that?"

"Russell loved that bar," Asher explained "He's in its bones. I couldn't leave it to sit idle and rot in his absence. And it always made good coin—"

Doran held up a hand, his confusion lingering. "I wholly agree with yer, lad," he began earnestly. "But how is it that *ye* are openin' The Axe? Rus left ye the deed?"

"The deed was always mine," Asher told him, rocking the dwarf back in surprise.

"It was always yers?"

"I had no real use for the place," Asher said casually, "and Russell saw its potential. I gave it to him in all but deed."

The dwarf quickly shook his head. "How did I never know this? An' how did ye come to own The Axe in the first place?"

"It wasn't always a tavern," Asher replied cryptically.

"Ah," the king said with some understanding. "Would this 'ave somethin' to do with 'em mysterious lot that brought *ye* into the life o' the ranger?"

"Perhaps," Asher said.

Doran waited a moment longer but it appeared the ranger had nothing to add. "Fine," he huffed. "Keep yer secrets. Givin' The Axe some new life is a damn good idea," he added, content to leave Asher's past where it belonged.

"I noticed you still have his pick-axe." Asher glanced briefly at Pig's saddle.

"Aye. It's broken, but it was *his*. I 'aven' found meself able to part with it yet." The dwarf gave the old weapon a moment's thought. "I know where it belongs though," he continued. "If ye puttin' The Axe back into business, it's only right that its namesake hangs over the bar." He licked his lips, still unsure, even in the moment, if he could really give it up. "Ye should take it," he finally said.

"Only if you promise to meet me there for a drink one day," Asher countered.

Doran smiled at the thought. "Ye try an' stop me."

After an exchange of light-hearted banter, Asher's tone turned serious. "Will you send for your mother once Grimwhal is liberated?" he asked.

Doran nodded. "Aye. Once I know this place is safe, I'll 'ave word sent back to Namdhor. I don' want her campin' on the wastes while she waits for her home to be cleared out. I'd never hear the end o' that one."

"She seemed in good spirits before we left," Asher observed.

"She has her good days," the king told him. "She also has her bad days. On the worst o' those days, I think she blames me for Dak's death."

"I'm sure she doesn't," Asher offered, his gruff voice the softest it had ever been. "You did everything you could to save him."

Doran nodded absently, as if he couldn't wholly agree with the ranger's statement. "I'll always be tormented by things I could 'ave done differently, but that's *my* burden to live with. Me mother jus' needs *time*. That's all I can give her."

"Well, for what it's worth, your brother would be proud of what you're doing here."

Doran managed a brief smile while the ranger took a big swig of cider. "Ye're a good friend, Asher. It's a comfort to know that it'll be *ye* who attends *my* funeral an' not the other way around, as I long feared."

"We have centuries of getting it all wrong before that fateful day, my friend." Asher raised the flask. "To getting it all wrong." He took a swig and passed it to the dwarf.

Doran mimicked the ranger and his toast before tasting the drink. "Do ye think I'm doin' the right thing?" The son of Dorain had wanted to ask that question since setting off from Namdhor, but he dared not voice it to any other.

"You are the king of Dhenaheim now," Asher replied. "Everything you do is the *right* thing."

Doran chuckled to himself. "If only that were true."

Asher held his hand out for the flask. "You're referring to your decision to rule from Grimwhal in place of Silvyr Hall."

The dwarf eyed the ranger. "Ye've heard the grumblin's then, among me kin."

"There will always be grumblings," Asher told him. "There will always be those who wish for things to return to the way they were. Some will want their clan identity back. Others will want a clear hierarchy so they know who their lessers are. And then there will be a few who believe their bloodline belongs on a throne. It's been thousands of years since the children of the mountain knew a reign like yours."

Doran sighed. "Reclaimin' the cities o' Dhenaheim will put more supporters in me camp," he reasoned. "But rulin' from Grimwhal has the potential to make me look weak. Silvyr Hall has stood tall over the clans since we abandoned Vengora. Not to mention the silvyr mine it overlooks."

"Could you not claim Silvyr Hall as your own?"

The king shrugged. "I've considered it... a *lot*. But it wouldn' feel like mine. It wouldn' feel like home. Silvyr Hall has ever been in the Battleborn bloodline. If I moved in there an' took that as me throne, I'd be makin' more enemies than allies, an' I need allies everywhere if I'm goin' to figure out *how* I rule Dhenaheim. I'm thinkin' o' appointin' marshals to oversee each city."

"Like lords," Asher compared.

"Aye. Only without such a grand title. Don' want 'em gettin' too big for their boots."

"How would you choose them?" the ranger enquired.

"I'd be foolish to appoint anyone without the *appropriate* bloodline. I'll need a Battleborn for Silvyr Hall, that's for sure. Commander Rolgoth would do fine. Then I jus' need to find the highest rankin' Goldhorn, Hammerkeg..." Doran waved it all away. "Bah! Listen to me! Talkin' about kingly politics. It's a web I tell ye. I'm already missin' the simplicity o' a full saddlebag, an open road, an' naught but a big beastie on the other end."

"If you could," Asher posed, "would you give all this up for that life?"

Doran didn't answer straight away, yet he had given the question as much thought as his Silvyr Hall conundrum. "No," he finally answered, and honestly. "I ran away from all this once before. They deserve better o' me. An' I only ran away because I didn' like what we were becomin'. Now I 'ave a real opportunity to change things for the better. The clans get to remain, their heritage intact, but the feudin' will never return. Our cultures can mix an' learn from each other. *An'*," he added with emphasis, "we can stop wettin' our blades with the blood o' our kin." Doran slowly shook his head and took a long breath. "I can' walk away from that. Not for anythin'."

"Has that crown actually made a good dwarf of you?" Asher jested.

Doran looked up, though he couldn't see it resting on his head. "Somethin' had to, I suppose," he agreed with a laugh.

Asher's head turned to his left as Avandriell slowly rose from the street with a low growl in her throat. "I think that did it."

"Finally," Doran grumbled, rising to his feet beside the ranger. "I was beginnin' to wonder if all this talkin' was for nothin'."

Asher drew his broadsword, the rising steel enough to home the Clackers in on his location. "Perhaps now would be a good time to retreat and plan our infiltration."

Doran looked up at the ranger's face and discovered the same hungry expression that ruled his own. They shared a hearty laugh before the dwarf separated Andaljor, taking axe and hammer in hand.

"Ye take the hundred on the left. I'll take the hundred on the right."

Asher raised his sword in both hands while Avandriell bared her fangs. "Seems fair," he remarked.

"Aye!" King Doran hefted his legendary weapons and braced himself. "May the best dwarf win!"

CHAPTER 61
LEGACY

Seated comfortably on a smooth rock, his wand spinning endlessly between his fingers, Kassian Kantaris let his head loll back while he basked in the summer sun. South of The Evermoore, the Keeper had found the climate he felt suited to. He had longed for it after a freezing winter in the north and a spring that still felt like an extension of winter to him.

But it wasn't the climate that had brought him to The Moonlit Plains. Ever since he had passed through the region on the way to the battle, Kassian had come across something he hadn't been able to get off his mind.

Returning to a level gaze, he narrowed his eyes through the light and looked upon West Fellion. It was a ramshackle of a ruin. Long abandoned, its upkeep had been neglected and none had tried to piece it all back together. The stone was crumbling in places and utterly shattered in others. Anything made from wood was in the process of rotting and the surrounding moat was better described as a swamp.

It was perfect.

Approaching from the ancient fortress, Aphira cut a fierce figure with her wand holstered to her thigh and her sword tight to her hip, the hilt poking out of her Keeper's coat. Beyond her, Kassian caught sight of a few other Keepers as they inspected various parts of West Fellion's ramparts.

"Well?" he called out to Aphira.

"It's a dump," she told him plainly.

Kassian grinned. "But it could be our dump."

Aphira raised a sceptical eyebrow. "The required work aside - and it is considerable - it's very exposed. Even with a moat, which needs clearing," she caveated, "we could be approached from all sides. At least in Valatos we had Velia's high walls around us."

"It needs to be here," Kassian stated. "If this is truly going to be a sanctuary for people who are conduits - as well as a place to learn - it needs its privacy." The Keeper opened his arms to take in the plains. "The closest *anything* is miles from here."

"What about something like Korkanath?" Aphira put forward. "That had privacy and security."

Kassian shook his head. "We can't be an island. We need to be seen as part of the country, part of the *people*. Here, in the middle of Illian, there is no disputing that we live on land owned and governed by the house of Draqaro. We need to be making laws *with* the king and queen, not trying to live outside of them."

Aphira chewed over his answer and offered no protest. "The middle of Illian," she echoed. "Why would it ever be called *West* Fellion?"

Kassian gave a short laugh. "Back when Gal Tion was the king of Illian, it was a much *smaller* Illian. Where we stand was the most western border of his realm. This is where Tyberius Gray founded the Graycoats, on the edge of the wilds."

Aphira's eyes ran over the old stone. "And this is where they fell."

"More or less," he agreed.

Aphira turned to him. "We aren't keeping the name, are we?"

Kassian smiled knowingly but his response was drowned out by a loud call from the top of the ramparts. Following Ayden's direction, he turned on the rock and looked to the north where a hundred or more horses trotted down The Selk Road.

Aphira squinted at the distance. "Is that..."

"Our king and queen," Kassian finished. His spinning wand slipped through his grasp and he promised himself he would continue to practise the trick until his hand adapted to having only three fingers and a thumb.

"What are they doing here?" Aphira asked.

"I invited them," Kassian informed her. "They had business in Lirian," he added, gesturing to the north, where The Evermoore lay just out of sight.

"You just *invited* the king and queen of Illian!" Aphira said, her voice suggesting she was somewhere between disbelief and amusement.

"It's like you said: I'm uniquely positioned." Kassian rose from his perch and prepared himself to greet the royals.

Leading the long procession, Vighon and Inara approached the fortress on horseback, both wearing a warm smile for the Keepers.

"Kassian!" Vighon called out as he climbed down from his horse.

"Your Graces!" Kassian bowed to the king before the northman embraced him.

Inara refrained from anything so physical, though she did respond with a polite bow of her head. "It is good to see you again," she beamed. "And it has been a long time since I have stopped to look upon West Fellion."

"Of course," Kassian replied, his memory catching up with him, "your father would have trained here."

"Once upon a time," Inara said wistfully.

Vighon pulled off his riding gloves and walked towards the fortress. "I can guess why you invited us here."

Kassian stood back so he could better see both Draqaros. "Good. That saves me a long-winded speech. Though you should know it would have been eloquently put, my various points irrefutable. There was a line or two in there that would have brought a tear to your eye."

The king wasn't beyond amusement. "You can have it," he said, referring to the ruins. "Inara and I have already discussed it. West Fellion is yours, a reward for your efforts during the war."

Kassian bowed his head again. "I humbly accept your reward," he replied, with just a hint of the usual sarcasm in his voice.

Vighon grinned. "Of course you do."

"Unfortunately," Inara added, "this is the extent of our gift. You have the stone and the land, but we do not have the resources right now to help you rebuild. Coin and labour are needed in a hundred other places and they all have families living there."

Kassian held out his hands. "This is gift enough," he reassured. "And besides, we do not require coin and labour to move a few rocks around." He gave Aphira a subtle nod to demonstrate his words. With her wand in hand, she lifted one of the fortress's loose boulders with a flick of her wrist.

Vighon nodded his head approvingly. "Before you left Namdhor, we spent many a late night talking about this and about what it could be. Are we still in agreement?"

Kassian gestured for the king and queen to follow him into the ruins. "We will work together," he articulated. "But it will be for the good of the people who need a place like this, not for the realm itself."

"Yes," Inara echoed. "We will never call upon your mages to fight for our banner. This is to be a place of learning before all else."

"A place of *safety*," Kassian specified. "In these walls, anyone who is a conduit to the realm of magic will be safe to practice their abilities."

"It will have the same protection as everywhere else in Illian," Vighon assured. "And, should anyone from here seek a job, they will have the same opportunities as everyone else. Any prejudice against them will be treated as a crime."

The latter was of the utmost importance to Kassian, for they could only reintegrate with the rest of the world if they were protected by the laws of the realm. "Though our ethos will be to harness control and learn valuable spells, we will always be guiding people to use their magic to benefit others."

"What of forbidden magic?" Inara questioned.

Kassian was getting a headache just thinking of the numerous conversations he had weathered on the matter, and not just with Vighon but also his fellow Keepers. "That which is forbidden brings only temptation. Rather than draw a line through magic and punish those who are curious, I believe we should be open about the extremes magic can be pushed to. It's only by teaching of what came before us that we will learn how to tread the future."

"Very wise," Inara said. "And I actually agree. But the magic I speak of has the power to upturn the world."

Kassian held his hands up. "I'm not suggesting we teach people to raise the dead or walk through time. We need to teach people to be *responsible.*"

"There will always be those who view their sense of responsibility differently to the rest of us," Inara countered. "My brother was a prime example of that."

"That's where the importance of teaching comes in," Kassian told her. "We shouldn't shy away from the horrors we're capable of when magic is at our disposal. And it puts emphasis on us to identify those who might be at risk of taking a darker path. That's where the trust between *us* plays its part."

"Trust you've more than earned," Vighon pointed out, cooling the atmosphere.

"I would test the extent of that trust," Kassian replied, pushing the limits of his *unique position.* "I intend for this place to be one of truth and learning, but it must also be a safe place to experiment with magic so that we might advance our knowledge of it."

"Experiment?" Vighon repeated dubiously. "You never brought this up before."

Kassian made an apologetic gesture with his hands. "I know such practices were done in Valatos and never with your knowledge or permission. Unfortunately, it's a natural reflex when your life revolves around magic. We *want* to learn more. We *want* to see where the limits are and break through them. We want to know... everything. There's no getting away from that curiosity, and if we put restrictions in place, they will just be done anyway, in *secret.* That's how your *Crows* are made."

"Kassian is right," Inara said, her argument shifting. "If it's going to happen anyway, transparency will breed a healthy caution where experimentation is concerned. And, I can think of no other who could see this through," she added with a touch of warmth.

"You're sure you're up to the task?" the king enquired. "Even Korkanath and Valatos didn't have a vision so broad as this. It's quite the venture, Kassian."

"*Duty*, your Grace," Kassian corrected. "This is my duty. Seven-hundred and thirteen Drakes gave their lives so magic could endure. This place will be a monument to their sacrifice. And there are surely many in your kingdom who desperately need a place like this to call home."

Inara responded with a genuine smile. "You are not the man I once met. You are truly free from your chains of grief."

"The chains remain," Kassian replied honestly, Clara's image never far from his mind. "They're just lighter now."

"That is good to know," Inara said quietly. "And your wife would be most proud of what you've accomplished. This is a dream worthy of anyone's legacy."

Kassian agreed with a humble nod. "I only wish she were here to help me."

Vighon circled on the spot, taking the fortress in. "And what are we to call this place? West Fellion might confuse most as to what your purpose is."

"This will be a place where magic abounds," Kassian replied, looking up at the battlements. "A safe haven for the lost. There was another place like this," he said, turning back to face the Draqaros. "Welcome to *Ikirith*."

CHAPTER 62
THE BLOOD OF ERADOR

Almost a year to the day since Vighon and Inara's wedding celebration, Gideon Thorn dropped out of the sky to find that Namdhor was again in the grasp of winter, as if it had never changed in his absence. Thick sheets of snow clung to the rooftops and smoke rose from the numerous chimneys as life continued in the north of the world.

Ilargo banked and began his descent towards the city, deliberately angling himself to come in line with The Dragon Keep at the top of the slope. Gideon was sure to keep the bundle of blankets close to his chest.

Fly once more around the city, he said to his companion. *Let them know we're here.*

Ilargo beat his wings and soared past the keep, his speed enough to force a gust of wind through the open windows. After circling Namdhor and casting his shadow over the lower town, the green dragon made for the large platform that extended from the throne room. By the time he was touching down, the iron portcullis was lifting into its resting place above the arch.

Seeing Vighon and Inara brought a much-needed smile to the old master's face. The king and queen greeted Ilargo as an old friend while Gideon climbed down from his saddle and navigated the dragon's bulk and the platform's edge.

Inara's head pressed into Ilargo's scales, just below his eyes, and lingered there. "I miss the sound of your voice," she said to him.

Gideon felt a pang of great sadness shoot through Ilargo as he inhaled the lingering scent of Athis from Inara's necklace. Not only did his companion miss talking to Inara, he also missed his long talks with Athis. Gideon had often discovered Ilargo reliving memories with the red dragon.

"Ilargo is glad he does not have to miss yours," Gideon said by way of announcing himself.

Inara held out her arms. "Gideon!" she exclaimed before stopping in her tracks. Like Vighon, she was instantly drawn to the bundle of blankets in her old mentor's arms. Of course, it was the small legs poking out of the bottom that really caught their attention. "I was starting to fear the worst," she uttered absently.

"Yes," Vighon agreed, his head tilting to better see the shape within the blankets. "We didn't think you would be gone so long.... Is that a child?" he simply asked.

"Apologies, your Grace," Gideon replied as he pulled back a small hood from within the blankets. "This is Gwenyfer," he introduced, revealing the young girl and her copper ringlets. "Forgive me," he continued before more questions could follow, "but our journey has been long for one so young."

"Of course," Inara replied, obviously perplexed by the situation. "You both shall have a hot meal by the fire."

See that she is safe, Ilargo insisted as he pointed his head to the sky. *I'm going to sleep. Wake me when summer is here.*

Gideon kept his amusement to himself and wished his companion good rest. He also happily accepted a place at the Draqaros' table, by the fire. He unravelled Gwenyfer, leaving her with a single blanket and a fur over her shoulders, compliments of Inara. He quietly explained to her, in the language of her homeland, that she could eat and drink as much as she wanted, and that she was safe in the keep. Seeing some fear in her eyes, he explained it twice and even put some chicken on her fork in the hope of coaxing the girl.

What followed was a very awkward and silent meal. Vighon and Inara didn't even touch their food, so intent were they on watching the curious girl in their hall. Despite the strange tension in the chamber, Gideon gave in to his own hunger and helped himself to the food and drink on offer.

"You have been well?" he finally asked the royals.

Hesitant to begin with, both Inara and Vighon informed him on a year of travelling around the regions of Illian. As the once Master Dragorn, Gideon sympathised with the tedious affair of having to meet with dignitaries and pompous lords. Still, it had given them a chance to meet the realm as king and queen.

Spotting a group of servants moving through the chamber, each with a different task involving some form of decoration, Gideon cast a questioning look at his former student.

"We're having a *small* celebration tomorrow night," Inara explained, her blue eyes only shifting from Gwenyfer for a second.

"Of course," Gideon replied, feeling embarrassed for failing to mention it. "Tomorrow is your first anniversary. Congratulations!"

"Thank you," Vighon said politely and in spite of his clear confusion. "Though, it's supposed to be more of a celebration to one year of peace." The king observed an elaborate ice sculpture as it passed the open door. "Things seem to have got a little out of hand, I'll admit."

Inara let out a small laugh. "Who knew my husband had such a flair for party planning?"

"We northmen know how to celebrate, my love," Vighon boasted, continuing the brief merriment.

"You are, of course, welcome," Inara added quickly. "And... your friend."

Gideon bowed his head in thanks. "Have I missed your parents?" he asked, recalling their intentions to leave this very winter.

"No," Inara answered, as if that was obvious. "They were to set sail for Ayda a few weeks ago, but their vow of support for Illian has kept them here a little longer. You will see them soon though. They are due to return from Grey Stone tomorrow morning."

"I look forward to it," the old master admitted, pausing to pour Gwenyfer another cup of water. "Has there been any news from Dhenaheim?"

"Not of late," Vighon said, as he finally began to relax in the company of the girl. "The last we heard, King Doran had taken back all but Nimduhn from the terrors of The Whispering Mountains. As far as we know, Asher and Avandriell are still aiding them."

"It is a harsh realm to traverse," Gideon stated. "I can only imagine the difficulties in marching an army through it only to battle monsters on the other end."

Inara paused before sipping her wine. "I imagine Asher and Doran are loving it."

Gideon and Vighon agreed with an unreserved laugh. But when the moment ended, they were once again left in the strange situation. Gideon could practically see the numerous questions floating around their heads.

"If someone could watch over Gwenyfer," Gideon suggested, drawing the girl's attention with her name, "then perhaps we could retire to some privacy and discuss matters?"

Inara rose from her seat first and walked around the table to Gwenyfer. She crouched down and introduced herself, "My name is Inara," she said with a hand to her chest.

Gwenyfer turned back to face Gideon with an obvious question on her face. "*You can trust these people,*" he told her in the language of Erador.

Gwenyfer returned her attention to Inara and mimicked her hand to the chest. "Gwenyfer," she said simply.

Inara offered the girl a kind smile. "Seriah," the queen called, ushering one of the servants to her side. "Take Gwenyfer..." She trailed off and looked to Gideon. "Does she like animals?"

"Very much so," Gideon answered.

"Seriah, take Gwenyfer to the stables. Show her the horses."

Gwenyfer dashed to Gideon's legs when the servant tried to

take her by the hand. "She has only seen three summers," he explained with a comforting hand on her head. "We might be asking too much of her."

"I know where we can go," Vighon announced, rising from his chair. "And Gwenyfer can accompany us if she wishes to."

The king led the way, a short distance, to what had long been referred to as The Dragon Keep's war room. The majority of the floor was taken up by a three-dimensional map of Illian, a place where long-dead kings and queens had only dreamed of ruling over a realm so large as Vighon and Inara's. To Gwenyfer, it was somewhere to play.

As she jumped over mountains, the trio walked around the giant map and made for the long table that rested between the pillars and the eastern wall. Strewn across it were several maps of varying sizes and places. Inara rolled her hand and released an orb of light to shine over them in the gloom. At the same time, Vighon rifled through the maps until he was able to display a detailed drawing of Erador.

"You can speak freely in here," Vighon told Gideon. "Though we would appreciate it if you started by explaining the new company you keep."

"You've been gone for a year," Inara pointed out. "So she can't be yours."

"Quite," Gideon agreed. "I cannot boast of such a beautiful creation. But she is very important to me... and to *Erador*."

Inara eyed the girl between the pillars. "Gideon, who is she?"

"Gwenyfer, daughter of Princess Lilyander and Bloodlord Tyvan."

"They sound important," Vighon remarked.

"Her father was more rich than he was important. Her mother, however, was Princess Lilyander of Valayan Blood. The Valayans were once cousins of Etragon Blood - they, that is to say, Gwenyfer, is all that remains of either family line."

"Etragon," Vighon repeated. "I've heard that name before."

"Those of the Etragon Blood ruled Erador for most of its history," Gideon explained.

"*Atilan* was of Etragon Blood," Inara specified.

Vighon looked straight at Gwenyfer. "She is a descendant of Atilan?"

"*Very* distant," Gideon quickly pointed out. "When the Etragon line ended with Atilan, the Valayans took control of the realm. Gwenyfer's mother, Lilyander, was the daughter of the king who Alijah slew when he assumed the throne. Alijah let Lilyander live, but she was never to return to Valgala and he was never to hear her name."

Vighon folded his arms. "That's all very interesting, Gideon, but none of that explains why her daughter is with you, in *Illian*."

Gideon looked down at the map. "When the Reavers fell in the streets, Erador fell into chaos. In the absence of a monarch and a supporting army, the only law is lawlessness itself. Warlords have arisen from north to south and brought bloodshed to every town and city in their bid for dominance. I have encountered many of them myself. They have only one belief: the throne of Erador is for the taking."

"Such a prize was always going to incite violence," Inara reasoned gravely.

"Inevitably," Gideon continued, "it is a prize that will be claimed by the strongest. That is to say, the *worst*. And it was the worst who tracked down Gwenyfer's parents. The whole country knew that Alijah had spared them, the *rightful heirs*."

"How did a little girl survive that?" Vighon asked.

"Lilyander wasn't without her loyal supporters," Gideon went on. "People of position, some more powerful than others, who believe she should be on the throne. Unfortunately, their support drew the attention of the warlords. They came for Gwenyfer's parents, but not before I was able whisk Gwenyfer away. For months now she's been passed around and hidden from those who hunt her."

"No one so young should have to go through that," Inara lamented.

"And what of the people caught in the middle of all this?" Vighon enquired.

"The death toll rises every day. That is why my return was so delayed. We tried to help wherever we could and as often as we could, but the guilds and warlords fighting for the throne don't know the meaning of mercy."

"These supporters of Valayan Blood," Inara began, "they are opposing the warlords?"

"They have formed something of a *rebellion*," Gideon said. "And their numbers increase, but some of the guilds and warlords have responded in kind and forged alliances. Erador is on course for all-out war."

Inara folded her arms and rested one hand over her mouth in contemplation. "You mean to fight for them," she concluded, leading Vighon to stare at the old master expectantly.

"I do," he admitted. "There is a part of me that calls Erador home. I will not leave the people to the tyranny of monsters who would be men. If Ilargo and I don't do something, Erador *is* going to be taken by someone. And whether that be a guild master or a warlord they will have taken it with *blood* and *fear* and *steel*. And that is all the people of Erador can expect from their new ruler."

Inara regarded her old mentor with a familiar smile. "Here you are again, placing yourself between the light and the dark. It seems there is no other way for you to live."

Vighon leaned forward and rested both of his hands on the table. "You've brought Gwenyfer here to hide," he said with revelation.

"To be safe," Gideon replied. "There is nowhere in Erador where she cannot be found. I would keep her with me, but if we are to truly root out those who would kill her for the throne, Ilargo and I will need to be able to move swiftly."

Vighon pushed off from the table. "This is not to be taken lightly. None of it, be it you fighting in another war or us taking in a child." The king met his wife's eyes and he took a breath before running his hand through his beard. "Yet we will do it," he finally said.

Gideon felt a wave of relief wash over him. "Thank you." He put all of his hope into those two words.

"She will be more than safe here," Inara assured. "We will treat her as our own."

Gideon looked from Gwenyfer to Inara. "I would advise caution. You will not be able to stop yourself from loving her, but always know that she is not yours. She is *Erador's*. Gwenyfer must know this also. Call her your ward or whatever you prefer, but I beg you not to call her your daughter. 'Tis a trap of the heart, for I *will* return when Erador is made safe again. On that day, I will see that she is seated on her throne, far from here."

"I see a great alliance in our future," Vighon remarked, eyeing the girl.

"I see great heartbreak," Inara replied.

Gideon reached out and placed a tender hand on the queen's arm. "I know I am asking a lot of you. I would have considered sparing you the inevitable pain and requested safe haven for her in Ayda, with your parents, but she must learn the ways of ruling from those who reign over man's world. I know, with you, she will return to Erador all the stronger."

"You were right to bring her to us," Inara said, squeezing his hand. "Helping her frees you to help the people of Erador. It seems the least we can do to aid our neighbours."

"I cannot stay long," Gideon declared, stepping away from Inara to lean against one of the pillars and watch Gwenyfer play. "While I am here, though, I will try and help you *and* her with the language."

"This is quite the campaign you're setting out on," Inara mused. "What of your plans for Drakanan and the eggs?"

"They have waited for thousands of years," Gideon replied. "They can wait a little longer. Besides, I would prefer any dragons be hatched outside of a war. And whoever bonds with them will need committed time to training - I can't do that while I'm fighting a war."

"So you *do* intend to restart the order of Dragon Riders?" Vighon quizzed.

Gideon continued to watch Gwenyfer, his arms folded, while

he contemplated the king's words. "In time, yes. Though the time I speak of will sadly exceed your own."

"Truly?" Inara questioned.

"If it takes me a hundred years to find a suitable Rider for just one egg then it takes a hundred years. I'm not going to rush it as I did with the Dragorn. I need time myself to understand what I want the order to be. All I know is... a time of dragons *will* come again."

CHAPTER 63
CREED

From the battlements of the Namdhorian barracks, nestled at the base of The Vengoran Mountains, Vighon Draqaro looked out, to the south, and saw his city, his home. It was a monument of natural rock and dressed stone that rose from the plains and stood proud over the wild land. It was a magnificent view, yet his eyes were so easily drawn to the young girl at his side.

It had only been a few months since Gideon had unceremoniously brought her into their lives, but the northman could feel his love deepening for Gwenyfer every day. She was sweet and kind while also being bold and sure of mind. The latter frequently led to daily tantrums, but Vighon had come to adore the comfort she sought upon calming down.

Vighon lowered his hand and ran his fingers through her copper hair. Gwenyfer turned her green eyes up to him and he saw the blanket she held in her hands. It was in desperate need of a wash but taking it away from the girl had proved to be about as hard as bringing down a Mountain Giant.

Footsteps on the wooden walkway turned the northman's attention away. "Your Grace," Seriah greeted with a bow. "Queen Gwenyfer's lunch is ready."

It still didn't sound right to Vighon, but Inara had insisted on using the girl's official title around others. She had argued that it was the only way to show the people who the strange girl living in The Dragon Keep truly was. It was also meant to be a way for Vighon and Inara to protect themselves to some extent. Publicly and regularly acknowledging that Gwenyfer was the queen of Erador kept them from adopting her in their hearts.

Such a plan, he knew, was useless.

Using a mix of both languages, Vighon ushered Gwenyfer to Seriah's side. The small girl held her hands up at the familiar servant and clenched her fists repeatedly until she was picked up and carried away.

"She shows great resilience for a child, your Grace," Sir Ruban commented beside the king. "She is quite remarkable."

"That she is," Vighon agreed, reaching out to grip the railing.

"Ah," the captain continued, "here they are."

Ruban's remark drew the king's eyes down into the barracks' courtyard where twenty men and women filed out of a side door and lined up in four neat rows. They didn't appear any more remarkable than the soldiers who patrolled the ramparts or the knights that formed the king's guard. But it was not their appearance that was meant to set them apart. It was *who* had chosen them to stand in this very courtyard.

Inara strode out of a different door and placed herself squarely before them all. "Form one!" she barked.

The candidates reacted immediately, each drawing their sword from their back and falling into the first stance of the Mag'dereth in one smooth motion.

"Form two!" Inara yelled.

As one, the candidates flowed into the next stance, their blades rising over their heads.

"Face your partners in form three!" the queen commanded.

Without hesitation, the men and women turned to their pre-determined partner, the person they had been sparring with for over a month, and assumed the stance of form three.

"Begin!"

That command created a flurry of activity in the courtyard. Men and women, pitted against each other, met in a clash of steel and iron will, spreading into every corner.

"We always used training swords," Sir Ruban said with a hint of concern.

Vighon chuckled. "Inara tells me it's more about control than aggression. They have to learn when to strike and when to hold back at a moment's notice, lest they make a mistake and—"

One of the candidates cried out in pain when their partner cut a gash down his arm. Vighon gestured to the pair as they had demonstrated his explanation with perfect timing.

"Stop!" Inara called, bringing a sudden end to the lesson. She walked across the courtyard and examined the young man's arm. "This will need stitches," she informed him. "Can you stitch yourself?"

"No, Commander."

"Then you will learn," Inara instructed. "Outside of these walls, you will have only each other and you will roam in pairs. Your partner is your greatest resource. You must learn to take care of each other." The queen turned on the candidate who had failed to hold back. "That includes not hitting them with your sword, Daganar."

"Yes, Commander," he quickly replied.

Turning back to the injured candidate, Inara said, "You can still fight."

"Yes, Commander," the injured man replied, squeezing the hand of his wounded arm.

"That wasn't a question," the queen stated, before resuming her place outside the square. "Form four! Begin!"

Sir Ruban leaned in to the king's ear. "I'm glad the queen wasn't the commander here when I was training."

Vighon agreed with a nod of the head and a wry smile. "And I thought The Ironsworn were brutal," he said so only his old friend could hear him.

"You must be adaptable!" Inara continued. "Your enemy will not always come at you head on, or alone!"

Putting action behind her words, the queen freed Firefly of its scabbard and set upon the nearest candidate. They evaded her blow with just inches to spare. Their counter attack, swift and precise, caused Vighon to grip the railing until his knuckles whitened. Inara, however, met the counter attack with a sudden flourish of her blade and planted a strong kick into the candidate's gut, launching her from her feet.

Unfortunately for Vighon's nerves, it didn't end there.

Inara pivoted on her heel and lashed out at not one, but two other candidates, drawing them in to battle. The queen moved deftly between them only to strike at others, increasing the number of opponents she faced. It wasn't long before Inara was engaged in a reckless conflict with all of them.

Sir Ruban clearly shared the king's concern and even moved to potentially intervene. "Wait," Vighon ordered. "If you interfere now even I won't be able to keep you safe."

Inara danced around her opponents, always moving. More often than not, she tied the candidates up in knots, forcing them in to each other before they could attack.

"Your Grace, if even one of them—"

"I know," Vighon interjected, his jaw tense.

One by one, Inara began to force candidates from the fight by either knocking them down or finding their opening with her blade. She was careful never to draw blood, but after weeks of sparring like this, they all knew when they were bested.

Only minutes after instigating the fight, Inara was the only one left standing in the middle of the courtyard, her chest heaving from the exertion. At last, Vighon was able to take a breath.

"From every corner of Illian," Inara said, "hundreds of men and women like you made the journey, heeding my call for *warriors*. You are all that remain. But this is not the end. You still have a long way to go before you can call yourselves *Guardians of the Realm*. And make no mistake, only those I deem fit will carry the mantle of Guardian." The queen glanced over them all. "Positions!"

The candidates ignored their new injuries and returned to their original formation in the square.

"Natharei! What is a Guardian's first creed?"

Natharei raised her chin proudly. "A Guardian of the Realm holds back the darkness, Commander!"

Inara paced up and down the front row. "Givain! What is a Guardian's second creed?"

Givain squared his shoulders. "A Guardian is to be the hope that carries the light, Commander!"

"Qirinn! What is a Guardian's third creed?"

"A Guardian stands for those who cannot, Commander!"

Inara's features softened. "Very good," she praised. "Know that I have faith in all of you. If you keep true to yourself, you *will* be the first in a new order. Guardians of the Realm will be a symbol of peace and justice unlike anything that has come before, including the Graycoats of old. I will personally oversee your mandates and you will always have access to me." The queen took a breath and sheathed her Vi'tari blade. "Now go and eat some lunch," she said in a lighter tone. "Rollo, see to your arm!" she added sternly.

As the last candidate disappeared into the barracks, Inara turned on the spot and looked up at Vighon and Sir Ruban. "What do you think?"

"I think you are *beyond* reckless," the king replied, making his way down the steps to join her.

"You doubt my skill, husband?" Inara challenged with a coy smile.

"I would never be so bold," Vighon assured. "But it is not just you who could be hurt," he said softly, his hand pressing against his wife's stomach.

"There is no safer place for them," Inara promised, clasping her fingers with his.

"There are safer places for *you*," Vighon felt he needed to point out. "Places where our unborn child isn't at risk of Daganar's careless swing."

"I was never at risk," Inara said, before planting a light kiss on the northman's cheek. "You must let me do this without your constant fretting. What I'm doing here is important. It's part of *his* legacy."

Vighon nodded with a sombre expression. He knew well that Athis was rooted in the Guardians of the Realm. After all, it was the dragon's own words that echoed in their creed.

"I trust you," he uttered, returning her kiss with one of his own. "But you can't blame a husband for worrying when his wife faces twenty of the best warriors in the whole country."

Inara laughed and squeezed his hand as she stepped away, her gaze catching Sir Ruban on his way down the steps. "You haven't told him yet?" she quietly enquired of the king.

"I wanted to do it together," Vighon replied.

Inara flashed him an appreciative smile. "It should come from you though. You mean an awful lot to him."

"I know." The northman turned to regard his approaching captain. "Sir Ruban, since the queen is still in one piece, we will continue with our travel plans. Are we set for The Shining Coast tomorrow?"

"Of course, your Grace. I've already coordinated with the master of servants; we can leave at first light."

The king nodded along, already aware of the schedule. "Excellent, though I'm afraid we will have to adjust some of our plans for the return journey."

Sir Ruban's face creased in confusion, bringing some of his scars together. "Your Grace?"

Vighon glanced at Inara. "After we've said our farewells to the queen's parents, we're going to stop in Velia."

"Velia is most splendid in the spring," the captain opined, oblivious to what was coming. "Queen Gwenyfer will love it."

"We won't be staying long," the king continued. "Just long enough to inform Lord Gydon that his stewardship of Alborn is at an end."

Sir Ruban offered an approving grin. "Most wise, your Graces. Who will be replacing him?"

It was Vighon's turn to give an approving grin. "That would be *Lord* Ruban, of house Dardaris."

The captain was already agreeing with a nodding smile before his own name caught up with him. "I... beg your pardon... your Grace?"

The king laughed. "It's *you*, Ruban! You have more than earned it."

"I'm to be the lord of... Velia?"

"Yes" Vighon cheered. "You're going to have to appoint your successor, of course."

"Your Grace... I don't know how to be a—"

Vighon reached out and gripped him by the arms. "Ruban. When I met you, all those years ago, you were barely a man, yet you had already found your way from living on the streets to a captain's squire. You followed me into peril and faced things most men would run from. As the captain of my king's guard, you rose into the role of general and kept The Rebellion alive."

"It would have died five times over without you," Inara added.

"You were the backbone of the entire campaign," Vighon continued. "Alborn is the richest region in the entire kingdom. I have no greater reward to give you. Though I warn you the title of lord comes with more burdens than that of captain. You may not thank us for it."

"I would thank you right now!" The captain embraced the king before sharing the same moment with the queen. "I don't know what to say."

"Say yes," Inara replied, "and tomorrow you ride out to a new life."

Sir Ruban stood up a little straighter. "It would be my honour."

"No," Vighon corrected. "The honour has been mine, old friend."

CHAPTER 64
A NEW WORLD

The sea air blasted Reyna's golden hair out and snatched at her pale cloak. The lapping waves of The Adean and the distant calls of her kin filled her ears, though it wasn't enough to conceal the playful giggles of a small girl. Reyna leapt over the top of the grassy sand dune and pounced on Gwenyfer. The girl squealed in surprise before tickling fingers made her howl with laughter.

"Gwenyfer!" Inara yelled from the beach.

Reyna poked her head over the dune. "She's with me!" the elven queen reassured.

"There you are," Inara said with a knowing smile. "Gwenyfer is not the only queen to have disappeared on this beach. Father is looking for you."

Reyna narrowed her eyes, searching down the line of boats that rested in the surf. Despite the hundreds of elves carrying the last of their supplies, Nathaniel was easily found by the one who had loved him for nearly fifty years. Her husband was clearly scanning the white cliffs that rose up beyond the beach.

Gwenyfer burst from the grasses and rolled down the sand dune, laughing all the way. Her joy only increased when Inara scooped her up at the bottom and held her high, a broad grin welcoming the girl.

"Go and find Galanör," Inara coaxed, putting her down again.

Gwenyfer's understanding of their language still had a long way to progress, but she certainly understood the name *Galanör*. She repeated it again and again as she ran off down the beach.

"She's adorable," Reyna observed, making her way down to join her daughter. "How are you not going to fall utterly in love with her?"

"I know," Inara replied with understanding. "I'm already failing miserably."

Reyna linked her arm with her daughter. "Your father and I were the same when Vighon lived with us as a child. It was a little easier - his mother was around... most of the time," she added quietly. "But we're *meant* to love. There's no getting around it."

"A part of me hopes Gideon never returns," Inara confessed. "And another part of me hopes he will return this very day, before it's too late."

"What will be will be," Reyna said softly. "All you can do is raise her, keep her safe, and teach her. If she grows to be even half the queen you are then Erador will come to know true prosperity again."

Inara smiled and squeezed her mother's hand affectionately. "How are you feeling about... all this?"

Reyna didn't need to follow her daughter's gesture to know she was referring to the numerous ships. "I'm dreading the voyage," she said dryly. "I get terribly sea sick. Hopefully, Faylen's potion work hasn't diminished since last we made the trip across The Adean."

Inara gave a light-hearted laugh. "I wasn't talking about the journey, Mother."

"I know what you were talking about," Reyna admitted. "I would be lying if I said I hadn't been putting it off. Though I would never have left before helping wherever I could. It's just been easier to stay busy and not have to think about everything."

Inara turned her blue eyes on her mother. "It's not wrong to miss him."

Reyna wiped her tears away before they streaked down her face. "I've been holding so tightly to my memories of him - of all of us. I think that's why I wanted to do this here," she said, looking up at the cliffs. "I wanted this to be the last thing I saw before we left, before we closed this chapter on our life. I don't want any of it to fade."

"How could it fade?" Inara questioned. "Even now I can still see that young boy running over these very dunes, believing he was a Graycoat."

Reyna couldn't help but smile at the memory. "That's the world I've been clinging to." She turned to the sea. "Beyond that horizon is a new world for me and your father."

"It's a new world for us all," Inara said comfortingly. "Ayda is not so far that we can't find a way through it without each other. You only have to pick up a diviner to see me."

"You're right," Reyna replied with some confidence. "And we will, of course, return to meet our grandchild," she added excitedly. "Do you have a name yet?"

Inara continued to walk a few steps, her gaze as distant as the horizon. "Yes."

Arm in arm, mother and daughter continued down the beach. Reyna wanted to give Inara as much advice as she could on motherhood, but her better judgment told her not to. For all the advice in the world, Inara and Vighon would have to find their way through it all. And she knew they would.

"I was beginning to think you'd run away to The Arid Lands," Nathaniel jested.

Reyna met his wit with some of her own. "I would not leave my kin to suffer you as their king alone, my love."

Nathaniel laughed as he held out his arms to take in his daughter. "Let me take a look at you," he said with a cheeky grin, his eyes running critically over Inara.

Reyna stifled her laugh. How many times had he done exactly

that to her over the years? Inara put up only the slightest of protests before she simply pulled her father in to a tight embrace.

"I've never had to run a kingdom without you," Vighon acknowledged, drawing Reyna into his waiting arms.

"You never needed me," Reyna told him as they parted. "But should you seek some sage advice, I leave you with the best of company." The king followed her gaze to Galanör, who had Gwenyfer in his arms, and Aenwyn who pretended to admire the girl's stick collected from the beach.

"You couldn't have chosen better successors," Vighon complimented. "Though I will still miss you greatly."

"We will be back before you know it," Reyna reminded.

"It feels different knowing how far away you will be," Vighon decided.

"I know what you mean," Reyna said with a gentle kiss to his cheek. "But you still have much work to do in Illian. I look forward to seeing your progress upon our return."

"The next time we set foot on Illian soil," Nathaniel chimed in, "there will be more Draqaros in the world!" The old Graycoat grasped Vighon's forearm with a prideful grin before pulling the northman in to his hug.

Reyna left them to their moment and walked over to her new ambassadors. Gwenyfer was already on her feet again and dashing across the sand to Vighon's side. The elven queen watched her go, envious of the boundless energy that accompanied youth.

"It looks good on you," Reyna commented, seeing a familiar black bow slung over Aenwyn's back.

"Thank you, your Grace," Aenwyn replied humbly. "Though its power is taking some adjusting to."

Reyna gave a light chuckle. "Yes, it certainly demands practise, even in hands as experienced as yours. I'm sure it will soon come to know its master's will." The queen turned to Galanör, her emerald eyes glancing over the blades on his hip. "Are you sure you can resist the path of the ranger long enough to see your duty through?"

"If my time as ambassador is anything like yours, your Grace, Stormweaver and Swiftling will never know rest."

Reyna couldn't argue with that. "I hope for your sake your ambassadorship is nothing like mine. Though I am certainly glad Illian has the two of you here to keep an eye on it."

With that, she embraced them both and returned to her husband's side. With expression alone, Faylen informed them that they were ready to set sail. Reyna took a breath and looked up at the white cliffs before her eyes continued up and into the sky. After saying their final farewells and taking their seats in the row boat, the queen continued to look up at the sky. It was empty.

"I thought he would come," she uttered.

Nathaniel joined her with a skyward gaze of his own. "As did I," he replied. "Vighon said he only returned from Dhenaheim last month. He's probably still resting somewhere, Avandriell too."

Reyna was gently shaking her head. "They don't strike me as a pair who *rest*," she said with a sad smile.

Nathaniel laughed to himself. "You're right. They're probably slaying some beast in the wilds or accepting coin for having done so." The old knight wrapped an arm around his wife. "We'll see him again. Even if it's a hundred years from now."

Reyna climbed onto her ship hoping that would not be the case. Trying to put Asher aside, or at least her disappointment, the queen stood by the stern and watched Illian shrink away. Vighon, Inara, and the others remained on the beach, waving until they were mere dots on each other's horizon.

Only when the white cliffs were a dark line in the west did Reyna turn away. Only feet away, another elf directed his hands at the ship's sails and threw his magic into the wind, pushing the ship further into the east.

Nathaniel approached with his comforting smile and an outstretched hand. "Come with me."

Accompanying her husband, they made their way to the bow of the ship. A glassy ocean awaited Reyna and, beyond it, The Opal Coast of Ayda, her kingdom.

"It's time to stop looking back," Nathaniel averred.

Reyna looked up at him, his jaw set and eyes fixed on the future. She knew exactly what he was really talking about. Had there been a day since that fateful night on the highest ruins of The Bastion that Nathaniel hadn't wept for his boy? Reyna had comforted him again and again, just as he had done for her in those dark moments of reflection.

As ever, they would get through it together.

"A new world," she whispered to herself.

A sharp gust of wind cut by the side of the ship, turning every head to starboard. Before any could rush to the rail and investigate, Avandriell skimmed the water in front of the ship and launched up into the blue of the sky. She was bigger than the last time Reyna had seen her, but she was yet to match Ilargo's size. Nathaniel shielded his eyes from the sun as he tracked the dragon.

"Looking for me?" came a familiar gruff voice.

Reyna and Nathaniel turned around to see Asher leaning against the mast as if he had always been there. The queen shot him a smile that broadened her face and leapt into his open arms. Within his embrace, the elf was sure the ranger's strength had increased, just as Gideon's had after bonding with Ilargo.

Asher looked down at her. "You didn't think I'd let you leave so easily, did you?"

Nathaniel came at him with his arm rising up. "You're becoming a smooth son of a—"

Asher crashed into his old friend, taking his breath away with a bear-like hug. Nathaniel patted the ranger on the back and flashed his teeth with a genuine smile.

"How was Dhenaheim?" he asked.

"Cold," Asher replied. "But it had its moments. Doran sends his apologies by the way. He wanted to be here for your voyage, to say farewell. But, monsters or not, Dhenaheim needs him now more than ever."

"Of course," Reyna said understandingly.

"Is that a *new* sword?" Nathaniel asked, pointing at the blade on Asher's hip.

Reyna had never been one for swords, but even she noticed

that the ranger's broadsword was not one of the replicas he had been sporting for decades. The leather around the hilt was the same shade of green as his cloak and the rounded pommel was now fashioned with hammer-like nodules instead of spikes.

"A gift from *King* Doran," Asher explained, gripping the hilt. The ranger lifted the broadsword just enough to reveal a few inches of the blade. "Pure silvyr," he stated, with only the hint of a boast in his voice.

Nathaniel looked genuinely impressed. "Who would have thought you'd be good friends with every king and queen in the realm?"

Asher shook his head. "Who would have thought all the kings and queens in the realm would be good friends with a ranger of the wilds?"

The trio laughed together as Faylen and Nemir emerged from below decks. Reyna maintained her joyous smile while welcoming them into the sunshine.

"Asher," Faylen greeted with a friendly nod. "Drop out of the sky, did we?"

"Something like that," Asher replied.

"You must stay for lunch," Faylen insisted.

"We have more than enough," Nemir assured.

"That would be lovely," Reyna added, taking the ranger by the arm. "I would hear more of your exploits in Dhenaheim."

Nathaniel walked past them and slapped a hand on Asher's shoulder. "And I might have stashed a keg of Velia's Golden Ale on board," he said with a wink.

Asher held his arms out. "How could I say no to such hospitality?"

"Excellent!" Reyna beamed.

"I can stay no longer than that, I'm afraid," the ranger warned. "There's word of a job in Ameeraska and Avandriell is eager to test her strength against Sandstalkers."

Reyna laughed as she caught sight of the bronze dragon, gliding overhead. "Of course she does."

Asher's company, however brief, brought a swiftness to the day that made the remaining days of her voyage to Ayda all the more bearable. After watching the ranger fly away astride Avandriell, the elven fleet sailed eastward until The Opal Coast and a land of great forests welcomed them home. Thousands of elves were awaiting them on the beach and even further beyond the tree line.

Nathaniel squeezed her hand as they finished the journey in a small rowing boat. Reyna squeezed his hand in return, aware that he was about to embark on a way of life that was wholly out of his comfort zone. It was just another thing, she decided, that her incredible husband would overcome and, hopefully, come to love.

As they stepped foot on the beach, every elf bowed the knee and waited until their new king and queen ushered them to rise again. As one people, they passed into the woods and began the trek to the city of Elandril, a place of splendour, elegance, and serene beauty. Reyna didn't realise how much she had missed it until the towering spires, surrounded by waterfalls, were within sight. It was a place of eternal wonder, a heaven on earth. She saw all that reflected in Nathaniel's eyes. In that moment, the queen knew they could make their home here, together.

There had been much talk of celebrations upon their return, but Reyna had insisted upon a pause. Her first act as queen was to make a special request of the city's elders. Only after that, Reyna knew, could she enjoy the celebrations that marked the true beginning of their reign.

And so, later that first night, under a starlit sky, every elf who called Elandril home gathered outside the palace. At the centre of their attention was a simple stone altar, its top carved into a shallow bowl. The elders had engraved the rim of the bowl with the necessary spells to meet their queen's request.

Reyna stepped forward, into the open space around the altar. She wanted to cast that final spell herself, but the currents of magic had failed to flow through her since the Moonblade's creation. Having come to terms with her way of life, the queen was content to give one of the elders a nod. A wave of the hand brought flames to the altar, flames that would never die.

"My mother, Adilandra, was a queen of sacrifice," Reyna began.

"She was a queen with a vision - a vision for our people. It is our duty to continue her work, so that we continue to be a whole people under one banner. Like our memories of her, these flames are eternal. May this fire be a place we can come to mourn her, and a place to come to remember her."

Reyna stepped back to join Nathaniel and turned her gaze to the stars with the rest of her people. They held their silence for some time, paying their respects to one who would surely be noted as one of the greatest queens of the elven nation.

For Reyna, it was a time to seek peace and finally let her grief go. She stared into the flames of her mother's memorial. As important as it was to walk into this new world, the queen also knew how important it was to always carry a piece of the old world in her heart. Now she would always have a place to come and reflect on what had been, a place where memory could never be allowed to fade.

EPILOGUE

17 YEARS LATER...

On the cusp of summer, Namdhor was finally beginning to thaw after a long winter and a cold spring. Though most of the realm would still call it uninhabitable, Inara Galfrey called it home. After nearly twenty years, the harsh winds, relentless snows, and freezing plains were a familiar comfort.

Not that the north's brutal temperament ever stopped the queen of Illian. Freezing or cold - Namdhor's only temperatures - Inara would always find time to collect her thoughts on the south balcony.

She also enjoyed looking up at the sky, whatever the weather.

I await you in the next life... where the sky is endless... and the dawn is everlasting...

She heard those words every day. Not a single one had lost its clarity in her mind. Sometimes she even heard Athis say other things to her: whispers from down an empty passage or old conversations replayed perfectly in her dreams. Even now she could recall the feel of his warm scales beneath her hand.

Today was a good day, she decided. They weren't always good days. There were times when she felt trapped, her feet tethered to the ground when she should be soaring through the heavens. On those days, there were only one or two people in the entire world who could return joy to her heart.

But today was a good day. Her thoughts of Athis only took her back to happy times with the dragon. And, as morbid as it was, Inara knew she would, indeed, return to him on those eternal shores. Though she felt as strong as ever, there was no denying the ageing her body had undergone in the last seventeen years.

As Alijah had been before his bond with Malliath, Inara too was mortal, her fate as inevitable as any human's. Such was the coin toss of any half-elf's life. Any fear of death, however, had long been relinquished by the queen. Now she strived to find the beauty and joy in every moment she could. And what joy she had found over the years.

One of the reasons for that joy burst through her chamber door and the moment of peace Inara had found.

"Mama! Mama!" came the loud call from a very small mouth.

Inara left the balcony and closed the doors behind her, preventing her daughter from feeling the chill. Bounding over the stone, her dark hair bouncing on her little shoulders, the queen's youngest child crashed into her legs.

"Mama!" she exclaimed, before her words all blended into one unintelligible language.

"Adilandra," Inara said calmly, focusing the young girl. "A little slower," she bade.

Adilandra took a breath and held up a small green scale. "Gideon gave me it," she blurted excitedly. "It's one of Ilargo's!"

"I see that," Inara replied, mirroring some of her daughter's glee.

"Now I can wear it like yours!"

Inara unconsciously gripped the red scale hanging from her necklace. "That sounds like a great idea."

"Can we do it now?" Adilandra pleaded.

"We don't have time right now," Inara said apologetically, if firmly. "Our guests will be arriving any minute."

"Look!" Adilandra's attention had been drawn to the nearest

window, where a familiar green dragon flew around the city. "I love Ilargo!" she declared. "Can I go to Erador with him?"

Inara hesitated, her lips parted. "Where is your brother?" she asked, hoping to turn the girl's interest to something else.

"Sulking," Adilandra said simply.

"Ah." Inara stood up and took her daughter by the hand. "Come on. Let's see what needs to be done."

After leaving the chamber, it wasn't long before something else caught Adilandra's attention and saw her run off in a different direction. Inara instructed one of the servants to go after her and ensure she found her way to the banquet. Striding down the west wing, a pair of Guardians were waiting for her, easily recognised by their red cloaks and swords strapped to their back. Of course, Inara knew them by name. There wasn't a Guardian of the Realm who hadn't been personally trained by her in some way or other.

"Natharei. Givain." Inara didn't stop and so the two warriors simply fell in beside her.

"Commander," Givain began, "we have that report you asked for regarding the smugglers in Calmardra."

"Very good," Inara praised, taking the parchment from the man. She ran a cursory eye over the details. "This is excellent work, both of you. Your next move?" she enquired, her tone suggesting it was a test.

"We follow the smugglers, Commander," Natharei said confidently. "They are not the priority, but the slave traders they are providing resources for *are*."

"Agreed," Inara replied. "And once you find the slave traders?"

"We burn their world," Givain directed.

The queen raised an eyebrow. "You may bring down their enterprise any way you deem fit, Givain. But not before you have apprehended Palin Barbosi."

Now it was Givain's turn to raise an eyebrow. "The slave master?"

"The *well-connected* slave master," Inara specified. "I have it on good authority that he is in contact with the Broker."

Natharei turned a concerned expression on the queen. "The same Broker who is selling dark relics, Commander?"

"The same," Inara confirmed. "I suspect he or she is either a surviving member of The Black Hand or an old affiliate. Whoever they are, they have access to Black Hand stores and are supplying bad people with bad things. I want them found."

"We will question Palin Barbosi," Givain assured. "He *will* give us a name, Commander."

"No," the queen corrected. "Bring him to me. I wish to oversee the matter myself. I will be joining you on whatever hunt follows our investigation."

"It would be an honour," Natharei said with a short bow of the head.

Inara stopped at the next junction to face the Guardians. "I'm sure the honour will be mine. Now, if you will forgive me, today is quite the day and it's only just begun."

"Of course, Commander," the warriors said in unison. "Give our best wishes to Queen Gwenyfer," Natharei added.

"I will," Inara promised. "Safe journey."

Before the Guardians had even left the passage, the queen was faced by Isold, the master of servants, and a number of his staff.

"Your Grace," Isold greeted with a hurried bow.

"You look flustered, Isold," Inara observed, continuing her meaningful stride. "You would think we were having hundreds of guests in the keep today," she added with a touch of humour. For any who had seen a battlefield, Isold would be described as delicate.

"Very witty, your Grace," the master of servants complimented. "But, about those hundreds of guests..."

"Yes, Isold, out with it."

"They're *here*," he said with some trepidation.

"I know they're here, Isold. Our guests have been arriving for days now."

"No, your Grace," the master of servants fretted. "They're *here*, in the *throne room*! They were supposed to wait and be announced one party at a time before greeting you."

"I see," Inara replied, already bored of a problem that wasn't really a problem. "Protocol has been broken," she said drearily.

"Yes, your Grace. It was the dwarves, you see. There was no stopping King Doran - he said he could smell *pig*. Well, your Grace, once he stormed in there was no stopping the others."

Inara came to a sudden halt, causing some of the servants to bump into each other. "Where is my husband?" she asked Isold.

The master of servants paused and turned his ear to one of his staff. "The king is with Queen Gwenyfer and Master Thorn, your Grace," he quickly reported.

"When the hall is full and our guests are accounted for, announce us all together. Until then, whatever you do, don't come between King Doran and the pig."

The master of servants clearly had more he wished to discuss, but the queen had endured her fill of trivial dilemmas. She, instead, turned her attention to one whose dilemmas were never trivial in her eyes. Coming to a stop outside her son's chamber, Inara knocked lightly on the door. The response was muffled and so she made her way inside, there to determine the truth.

Her first born, and only son, was sitting on the end of the bed, his head bowed so his dark hair concealed his face. Inara perched on the bed beside him, unable to pierce the veil of his hair. Without seeing his face, he could easily have been Vighon when he was seventeen years old. They had the same hair, build, and they even sulked in the same manner.

He had celebrated his seventeenth birthday the previous week and was considered a man by most now. But, to Inara, he would always be her boy.

"Athis," she said gently, placing one hand on his back.

The young man finally lifted his head to reveal blotchy red skin around his eyes. "I don't want her to leave," he groaned.

"I know," Inara said softly, meeting her son's blue eyes with her own. "We all knew this day would come. But that doesn't make it any easier."

"Gwenyfer doesn't want to leave either," Athis blurted. "She shouldn't have to go!"

"You two have become close," Inara commented, having seen something of Vighon and herself in the young pair.

"You don't know what you're talking about," he complained.

The queen took a breath and nodded her head in memory. "Your father and I were close at your age. Very close. And then, one day, I had to leave to do something important."

"I know," Athis interrupted. "You went to The Lifeless Isles and became a Dragorn. I've heard the story a thousand times from everyone."

"You're forgetting the part where fate reunited us," Inara pointed out. "And, as the future king of Illian, you will surely have good reason to reach out to the queen of Erador. After all, there is so much good we can do for each other."

Athis was shaking his head, too stubborn and upset to hear her words. "That's *years* away! I don't want her to leave now. Why can't she stay with us? Illian is her home. Gwenyfer could do so much good here, where she is already loved by so many."

Inara sympathised with her son and pulled him towards her to plant a kiss on his forehead. "I don't want her to leave either," she confessed. "I look on her like a daughter. But Gwenyfer is important. *Erador* is important. It's a country as vast and populated as our own, and they are in need of Gwenyfer to take them into the future. One day, the people of Illian will look to you to do the same."

Athis sighed, wiped his tears away, and slumped into his mother's arms. "I will miss her so much."

"As will we all," Inara replied, her heart already beginning to suffer the strain of losing Gwenyfer. "But we don't need to miss her today. Today the whole realm will celebrate her and say farewell, while we get to keep her to ourselves for a few more days. So let's enjoy our time with her. Yes?"

Athis managed something of a smile and returned his mother's kiss. When he was ready, the queen took him by the arm and made for the throne room. Along the way, they were reunited with Adilandra, who was skipping hand in hand with one of the servants. Inara took her from there and succeeded in meeting up with Vighon, Gideon, and Gwenyfer before they were announced to their guests.

The queen of Erador was a vision to behold, her copper ringlets immaculate and full of life, while her emerald eyes glistened in the light. Much in the same fashion as Inara, all of her clothes were somewhere between a warrior's leathers and a queen's formal dress. It was her smile, however, that enchanted all around her. Inara was pulled in by that beaming grin until they were embracing.

"You're ready," Inara said quietly to her.

"Thank you," Gwenyfer replied.

While the young queen turned to greet Athis and Adilandra jumped into her father's arms, Inara came face to face with Gideon Thorn. He had been a guest in The Dragon Keep for nearly two weeks and had used that time to reacquaint himself with Gwenyfer before they made their journey back to Erador together. Though Vighon and Inara had informed her many times of the manner in which she was brought into their lives, Gwenyfer had no memory of Gideon or Ilargo.

But now he was here again, after seventeen years, to take her away. Gideon had assured them that the war in Erador was over, and that every warlord and crooked guild had been disbanded, slain, or brought to justice in a makeshift court system he had overseen himself. Indeed, both Gideon and Ilargo had the look of war about them, each sporting new scars. And though the war looked to have added years on to her old mentor's demeanour, he hadn't aged a day by his appearance.

"It's alright to hate me," Gideon said to her.

"I don't hate you, Gideon." Inara glanced at Gwenyfer. "Well, perhaps I hate you a little bit. But as much as this is going to hurt, I could only ever thank you for bringing her into our lives."

"This is to be the first stitch between your two kingdoms," Gideon began. "By blood or by bond, Illian and Erador are family now. These are to be our first steps on the road to lasting peace."

Inara put an affectionate hand against his chest. "I look forward to that future. Though, right now, it doesn't even begin to take some of the sting out. I still hate you," she added with great amusement.

Gideon laughed to himself and squeezed her with one arm. "We should probably go inside. From what I've heard, Doran has already eaten most of the boar."

"It's good to know some things never change," Vighon remarked, putting Adilandra down. "Shall we?" The king hooked his arm and Inara slotted into place beside him. Behind them, Athis did the same with Gwenyfer while Gideon happily held Adilandra's hand.

As the doors began to open, Isold announced their arrival from the other side. "Their Graces, King Vighon and Queen Inara of house Draqaro, the sword and shield of Illian, and protectors of the realm!" The master of servants waited until they were a few steps over the threshold before his next announcement. "Queen Gwenyfer of Valayan Blood, heir to the throne of Erador, and his Grace, Prince Athis of house Draqaro!"

Inara glanced over her shoulder to observe their entrance. Athis was three years younger than Gwenyfer yet he was already a full head taller.

"Master Gideon Thorn, Lord of Drakanan and Defender of Erador!" Isold continued. "And her Grace, Princess Adilandra of house Draqaro!"

Their welcome was one of great cheer that quickly continued into the party itself. Beside Vighon, Inara did the rounds first, greeting various lords, ladies, and governors who had made the long journey. In truth, the queen wanted to get that part over with so she could enjoy the company of her parents and old friends.

Indeed, she found the two together, easily located thanks to Doran's hearty laughter. They told each other of their respective kingdoms between their reminiscing. They shared both the hardships and luxuries of wearing a crown, many of which Inara and Vighon could relate to. It wasn't long before Galanör and Aenwyn, having fulfilled their ambassadorial duties, made their way over and took part in the merriment. Always on the move, the two elves had barely stopped in seventeen years. Now, there was even talk of them making the journey to Erador to speak on Reyna and Nathaniel's behalf.

Through it all, Inara spied Athis and Gwenyfer across the chamber. They were always deep in conversation about something. The queen in her wanted to instruct them on the importance of mingling at a party such as this, but the mother in her kept her rooted to the spot. Let them have whatever time they had left, she decided.

"Well if it ain' the biggest mouth in all o' Verda!" Doran bellowed upon sighting Kassian Kantaris approaching.

"King Doran," Kassian greeted with a respectful bow.

"How are ye doin', lad?" the dwarf asked.

"Busy," the mage replied honestly, his sandy blond hair beginning to show the first signs of grey. "But I wouldn't miss this," he added sincerely, looking to Inara and Vighon.

"How are the affairs of Ikirith?" Vighon enquired.

"We're in the middle of expanding the east wing," Kassian explained. "Our numbers are constantly growing - we need more room."

Vighon patted him on the back. "It's a good thing you're located on the plains then."

Kassian agreed with a smiling nod. "How have you found your new court mage to be?" he asked.

"Sathyrah's very good," Vighon praised. "You taught her well."

Gideon walked over, his presence alone cutting through their conversation. Adilandra was sitting comfortably in one of his arms, her fingers turning Ilargo's scale over and over again.

"Kassian," he greeted with a friendly nod.

"Gideon," Kassian replied politely.

Gideon took in the group that had claimed the area around the hearth. "Well look at this," he said with a delighted smile. "We're all back together again. I would never have thought it possible."

"By my count we're missin' one," Doran commented into his drink.

Gideon didn't need to look around to know who the dwarven

king was referring to. "I assume Asher and Avandriell were invited."

"They would have been," Vighon replied, "if we knew where to send the invitation to."

"There isn't a soul in all of Illian who doesn't know about today," Galanör said. "There are farewell parties in every street."

"He's a ranger," Vighon stated. "As is Avandriell. They come and go. That is their way."

Reyna's head tilted to the side, taking in the rest of the chamber. "I would say he's coming," she said with a knowing smile.

Inara turned around to discover that almost everyone in the chamber was slowly moving towards the dragon platform, their heads turned to the sky.

"Asher!" Adilandra rejoiced as she pushed her way down from Gideon's arm. The girl dashed to the platform, weaving her way through the numerous legs that gathered there.

Along with the others, Inara made her way to the platform, though being queen meant she didn't have to weave as her daughter did. Her eyes scanned the blue sky, noting a canopy of cloud coming in from the west.

There they were.

It was hard to miss an enormous bronze dragon soaring through the heavens, even from such a distance. In that moment, Inara envied Asher, for nothing beat arriving on dragon back.

~

Asher looked down on Namdhor's ancient keep. *You're showing off,* he accused.

Avandriell continued to fly, always sure to angle herself so her bronze scales caught the light of the sun perfectly. *Those are the eyes of the realm down there,* she replied. *It suits to have them remember us. Lords pay handsomely to slay the beasts of the world.*

Asher couldn't help but laugh. *Sometimes I worry there's too much of me in you.*

The dragon tucked in her gargantuan wings and dived down to

the keep. Asher remained close to his saddle, his chest to the leather, while his hands gripped the handles with a touch of magic to secure them. The rushing wind picked up his hair and green cloak, but he was sure to keep his eyes open. Nothing in the world could rival this feeling.

Avandriell spread her wings and arched her body until she was able to glide towards the dragon platform. She beat them twice to reduce her speed and bring her back legs down first. The entire keep shook beneath her landing, her front claws thundering into the stone. Her head bowed, Asher got his first look at the party between the three thick horns that protruded from Avandriell's head.

You enjoyed that, Asher remarked, climbing down from his saddle.

Not as much as you did, I sense.

The ranger flashed his companion a wry smile as he walked towards the throne room. He never quite made it, however, before being attacked by a creature so dreadful that he had never managed to best it. Adilandra yelled his name as she barrelled into his legs and Asher feigned injury in his subsequent fall. With the girl scrabbling on top of him, he pretended to succumb to her claws. Only when she thought herself the victor did he respond with a devastating counter attack. His tickling hands made her howl so much that the princess fell away, allowing him a moment to regain his feet.

"Asher!" Prince Athis was the next to greet him, his arm coming at the ranger from far away.

Asher gripped the young man's forearm. "If you grow any taller I'm going to have to start *defending* Giants instead of *slaying* them."

"Where have you been?" the prince asked eagerly, as he always did.

"Where haven't we been?" Asher put to him. "We last set down in Longdale. They were being plagued by a *King* Basilisk. Its mouth was so big it could wrap its jaws around Avandriell's neck." His every word excited the prince and even Queen Gwenyfer beside him.

"But you killed it!" Athis exclaimed.

"Of course," Asher said casually.

Who killed it? Avandriell demanded.

Asher's mouth twisted. "With some help," he finally added, thumbing over his shoulder.

Some help? the dragon echoed. *Next time, you can decapitate the snake with a head thicker than a tree!*

Asher stifled his laughter and turned to the lady of the day. "Your Grace," he said to Queen Gwenyfer with a bow. "Illian's loss will undoubtedly be Erador's gain. I have something for you."

Gwenyfer looked both intrigued and excited. "A gift from a ranger?" she said with anticipation.

From his belt, Asher produced a finely curved dagger just a little longer than his hand. "The blade is Basilisk bone," he explained. "It's easily concealed and light to carry, yet the bone is *strong*."

Gwenyfer happily accepted the gift, displaying it for Athis in both hands. "A rare blade," she uttered in wonder. "Thank you, Asher."

Inara came up behind them. "Are you giving my children weapons again, Asher?"

"Your Grace," the ranger greeted, extending his bow for Vighon. "Forgive my intrusion. I couldn't let Queen Gwenyfer leave for the west without a small token."

Athis looked from Gwenyfer's dagger to the ranger. "How do I get one of those?"

"Perhaps you should accompany us on our next—"

"No," Vighon and Inara said in unison.

Inara cleared her throat. "The sword techniques you've already taught them are... quite enough."

Asher flashed the young queen and prince a coy grin. He had, indeed, taught them a few strategies and techniques over the last few years that some - the Guardians of the Realm - would consider dishonourable. Everyone's attention shifted again when Avandriell turned her head to the sky and leapt into flight. By the time she had cleared the platform, the children had been distracted by something else and the party had resumed. Asher took the opportunity to properly greet the king and queen with a tight embrace.

"I knew you wouldn't miss saying farewell," Vighon said with a pat on Asher's arm. "And you are most welcome, as always. The drinks are on us." Before the king could say another word, a servant whispered in his ear, drawing his attention to a lord and lady in the far corner. "Ah. If you'll excuse me, Asher. Enjoy yourself!"

Asher turned to Inara who was still watching Avandriell ascend into the empty ocean above. "I would ask if you miss it, but that seems like a—"

"Every day," Inara replied, her eyes never leaving the sky. "I miss it every day." The queen took a breath and tore her gaze away until it was filled by the ranger. "Come," she bade with a genuine smile. "Have a drink with us. I've never tired of your stories."

Asher was happily led by the arm into a group of familiar faces. Warm greetings were made by all, including Doran who nearly tackled the ranger to the ground. Vighon soon returned from his kingly duties and gave Asher a tankard of Namdhor's finest beer. All the while, he could feel Avandriell flying side by side with Ilargo, the two exchanging stories of their own.

And, try as others did, none were able to separate the group over the day. They remained by the fire, drinking, eating, and laughing, blissfully unaware of the hours slipping by. Adilandra came and went, pausing only once to have a short sleep on Asher's lap. Queen Gwenyfer knelt down between Inara and Vighon with her drink and listened to their stories, tales from decades past. Athis was never far from Asher's side, hanging on his every word.

Every time he saw this particular group, especially the children, Asher was reminded why they had all fought so hard and for so long. The future they had forged was bright and Athis, Gwenyfer, and Adilandra were going to inherit that well-won peace. And who knew what they would do with the world? The ranger was just glad he would be around to find out.

"Your Grace!" came an urgent call, turning every head to the Namdhorian soldier rushing towards them.

Vighon sat forward and put his tankard down. "Captain Hawkins."

"Your Grace," the captain said again as he arrived by the fire. "Orcs!" he declared.

"Orcs?" Doran spat, his hand naturally falling onto Andaljor beside him. "Point me in the direction, lad!"

Vighon stood up and held out a hand to calm the moment. "Orcs, Captain Hawkins?"

"They've attacked from the mountains, your Grace," he reported. "They have set upon the barracks, to the north."

"In daylight?" Reyna questioned.

"It must be the Sons of Karakulak," Inara reasoned. "They have grown ever bolder over the last few years. They do not fear the sun."

Vighon gripped the sword of the north on his hip. "Ready my horse," he commanded.

As the remaining heroes of old stood up, ready to put themselves on that fateful line between the light and the dark, Asher had already slipped away and stridden most of the way back to the dragon platform. "Please, your Graces!" he called, halting their action. "Today is for Queen Gwenyfer. I would not have her day spoiled." The ranger gestured to the open air behind him. "Ava and I will take care of the orcs."

Without waiting for a word of reply, Asher leapt from the edge of the platform and plummeted down towards The King's Lake. Ice or no ice, the lake would kill any who fell from such a height. But Avandriell had no intention of letting her companion meet his gruesome end. The bronze dragon dived down until their bodies were perfectly aligned. With Asher secured in his saddle, Avandriell waited until the last second before fanning her wings and gliding over the surface of the water. So close was she that it rippled beneath her.

Without losing speed, the dragon climbed into the sky, giving them both a good view of the distant barracks, built into the base of The Vengoran Mountains. Avandriell's sharp eyes informed the ranger that orcs were scaling the walls astride their terrible six-legged Garks.

Asher hunkered down into his saddle, his eyes fixed on their prey and a hungry smile on his face. "Let's hunt some monsters."

The End.

EVERY ENDING
HAS A BEGINNING...

PHILIP C. QUAINTRELL

THE RANGER ARCHIVES

COURT OF
ASSASSINS

VOLUME I

PHILIP C. QUAINTRELL

————

Hear more from Philip C. Quaintrell including book releases and exclusive content:

 PHILIPCQUAINTRELL.COM

 FACEBOOK.COM/PHILIPCQUAINTRELL

 @PHILIPCQUAINTRELL.AUTHOR

 @PCQUAINTRELL

AUTHOR NOTES

1st April 2021

So much emotion right now. I can't really believe I'm here, writing this.

It's taken 6 years, 9 books, and 1.6 million words but I finally did it - I told the story burning a hole in my head and finished my very first fantasy series.

I hope you have all found this ending to be fitting and worthy of the journey we've all been on. It was tempting to agonise over it, aware that there are so many people invested now (very different to when I started), but I still had to approach it as I did every other book: I'm a fantasy reader.

I can only ever write what I would like to read, which I think has helped since we're all just fantasy readers at the end of the day. This was, perhaps, the most daunting of all the books to dive into but, once I did, I found it very hard to pull myself away. This world and these characters are very addictive and I just love letting them all out of my head.

I was also aware that this was my last chance to say and do

everything I wanted to do with these characters. All those little conversations and emotions that needed to be had - this was it! In that regard, I took my time and let everything play out on the page. If one character needed to talk to another, I just let it happen. The alternative was to let those moments go and move on in favour of the pace, but these characters all deserve their final moments in the spotlight.

And so here we are - The Echoes Saga is complete. I prefer that word to *over*. I've loved every minute and every word of it. It all began with a notepad and 'Run Boy Run' by Woodkid. I envisioned Asher riding on his horse at great speed. I knew he was both chasing something and being chased himself though, of course, at the time I had no idea what either of these things were. I know now, as do you, that that was the concept that formed the whole foundation of Asher's character. Interestingly, I listened to the same track while writing that last part of the epilogue, only then he was soaring with Avandriell at great speed.

Ooo, a little tidbit you might have missed; the chapter titles are repeated (echoes, if you will) through books 1-9. They would be hard to notice, even if you read one after the other, but I really like how the same word can be applied to different situations and characters. *I* thought it was cool...

So, where to begin? Perhaps the very beginning. My favourite part has to be when the Winds of Time spell actually connects two points in time and brings Alijah and Malliath together. This was unexpected for both me and Sarkas and I loved that it was the reason Malliath hatched in the first place. As a result, Malliath spent thousands of years bonded to someone who hadn't even been born - another reason his mental health was so poor. It also explains why Alijah could never bond with a dragon when Inara did and why he always felt like he was meant for something great, but could never find the right path. I suppose theirs was always a tragedy in the making.

I enjoyed pulling back the curtain with this last book. In the previous books, I deliberately left out the truth of the extent where Malliath's influence was concerned. I wanted you to see Alijah through the eyes of the other characters before seeing what was really going on. Ultimately, through various characters, Alijah was something of a grey area due to differing opinions on how he should be dealt with. I'm sure, before the end, you had a good idea of what you wanted to see happen to him, be it punishment or redemption. Either way, the end is the end and the characters pushed the story on more than I did.

So, as you might already know, I don't really plan out the story before I start writing. I have general 'beats' in my mind where I see the story landing in parts, but I have no idea how or if I'll get there. In my mind, Alijah never succeeded in harming the tree - that whole battle was going to be at the very end of the book and the heroes would save the day at the last minute.

As I started writing, though, I realised the pace of the story was carrying us to that point with all haste. This didn't really bother me as I thought the book would be as long as it needed to be. But then I had a new thought. What if he did succeed? I instantly knew that was the story I wanted to tell. It would speed up the pace and give the heroes a ticking clock. I also wanted to see what things would be like in Verda once magic began to fade.

From there, the story really took on a life of its own. I had absolutely no idea how they were going to beat Alijah and Malliath but, as always, the idea came to me in the shower. I tend to put my mind into that of the characters' and see where my thoughts go. In this instance, I thought like Gideon as he had a vast knowledge and the added wisdom of Ilargo.

So I naturally started thinking about separating Alijah from Malliath. That's when it got really interesting, because I LOVE it when the story naturally draws on events that have taken place in previous books that I never intended. If you ever re-read the series, I'm sure the events of book 3 will mean so much more to you now.

I felt a bit like that when I came to realise that Alijah would die in the exact same spot where he had tried to kill himself in book 4. The echo of it all really made me smile, despite the grim nature of it all.

If there's one thing I've learned writing this last book, it's the importance of the journey. I'm sure some of you out there predicted the end of the saga, perhaps even several books ago. I'm okay with that. I'm not here to subvert expectations. I'm just here to tell a story, however that might unfold. I don't really plan a lot of the story, so any surprises or twists just kind of happen organically. Sometimes, there are no twists, just a contest of wills and quick thinking on the characters' part.

For some characters, their journey came to an end in this book. I was a blubbering wreck when I wrote Athis's last scene. It was made all the harder because my newborn daughter was sleeping in a sling, strapped to my chest, at the time. Thankfully, I kept her asleep and completed the scene without calamity. In truth, I didn't know Athis was going to die. I suspected either he or Ilargo would perish in that last battle, but I didn't know which until I got there.

I tried to rewrite it a few times in my head so that he survived, but it never felt right. That kind of thing can happen from time to time, where I try and exert my influence over the story and I end up a little stuck. My imagination just can't conjure the right words, especially when it comes to putting words in characters' mouths. When that happens, I have to let go of whatever I was trying to wedge in and let the story flow organically.

It still hurt like hell to see Athis die though...

And then there's Russell. Oh Russell... His inevitable end began to take form in my mind when I was writing book 7. I'm glad he was able to make it through to this last one. I have plans for the old wolf, though. I intend to flesh his story out more in the third book of The Ranger Archives, back when Asher met him for the first time. I hope that relieves some of the heartache for you Russell fans, I know it does me. In fact, in The Ranger Archives, we'll get to see exactly how The Pick-Axe ended up in Asher's possession.

Getting back to this book, it just felt right, at the end there, to delve right in to Erador. It felt like the elephant in the room to me. Here's this massive kingdom, equal to Illian, that we know has been under Alijah's control of years and yet there was a chance we might never know what's going on over there. The more I thought about it, the more I thought about Gideon. Of all the surviving characters, he had the strongest link to the country. And our new king and queen, Vighon and Inara, would surely have an interest in their neighbouring country.

Gwenyfer and Erador's troubles just kind of clicked as I wrote the chapter. It felt organic and real and wholly believable. The fact that Gwenyfer and Prince Athis offered an echo of a younger Inara and Vighon was just a satisfying consequence of it all. If you're like me, you've already gone on ahead and started dreaming of what their future might look like.

And how could I ramble on like this if I didn't talk about Avandriell? Or Ava, as Asher sometimes calls her. Theirs was a union a thousand years and 9 books in the making! I must admit, I'm tempted to write more books about them after the events of The Echoes Saga, but we'll have to see. Mostly, I just loved the transformation that took place within Asher. In a couple of weeks I'm going to make a start on Asher's first prequel novel and I'm aware that he's going to be drastically different to the Asher I've had in my head for so long. I'm looking forward to the challenge of it as well as the adventure.

Speaking of challenges, I feel like I could talk and talk about this last book, if not the whole saga, for another 50,000 words. I think, instead, after everyone has had the chance to read it, I will do something like a Q&A on social media.

In terms of where I go from here, it's like I said - The Ranger Archives! The first title under the new series will be released in due course but I have planned for 4 books to chart a few of Asher's earlier stories. There might be more in the future, sprinkled throughout various larger sagas, but for now I'm just taking a couple of years to write these 4. In that time, alongside writing, I will begin planning in earnest for the next big epic series. You can expect to be transported back into Verda's most distant history to meet some Dragon Riders!

If you've enjoyed this book and the saga as a whole, please leave a review on Amazon. I'm a self-publisher so your comments really help me to get the word out to others. At the end of the day, I'm just a guy with a simple dream really: to be *invited* to Comic-con San Diego.

Until the next time...

APPENDICES

Provinces of Illian:

1. *Alborn* (eastern province) - Ruled by Lord Ruban of house Dardaris, the steward of Velia, Alborn's capital. Other Towns and Cities: Palios, Galosha, and Barossh.

2. *The Arid Lands* (southern province) - Ruled by Lord Hasta Hash-Aseem, the steward of Tregaran, the southern capital. Other Towns and Cities: Ameeraska, Calmardra.

3. *The Ice Vales* (western province) - Ruled by Lord Barnish of house Yendyl, steward of Grey Stone, the capital of the western vales. Other Towns and Cities: Bleak, Kelp Town, and Snowfell.

4. *Orith* (northern province) - Ruled by King Vighon and Queen Inara of house Draqaro from the city of Namdhor, the capital of Illian. Other towns and cities: Skystead, Dunwich, Darkwell, and Longdale.

5. *Felgarn* (central province) - Ruled by Lord Harlan of house Stride, steward of Lirian, the heart of The Evermoore. Other Towns and Cities: Vangarth, Wood Vale, and Whistle Town.

~

Dwarven Hierarchy:

1. *Heavybellys* - Ruled by King Doran, son of Dorain. Domain: All of Dhenaheim. Rules from *Grimwhal*.

2. *Brightbeards* - Governed by Marshal Bainish, son of Bailor. Domain: *Bhan Doral*.

3. *Battleborns* - Governed by Marshal Rolgoth, son of Bolgayne. Domain: *Silvyr Hall*.

4. *Hammerkegs* - Governed by Marshal Norn, son of Volstad. Domain: *Nimduhn*.

5. *Goldhorns* - Governed by Marshal Kelagah, son of Krom. Domain: *Khaldarim*.

~

Undead Dragon Riders and their mounts

Lord Kraiden, bonded with the dragon *Morgorth.*

Vilyra, bonded with the dragon *Godrad.*

Gondrith, bonded with the dragon *Yillir.*

Rengyr, bonded with the dragon *Karsak.*

~

Orcish Tribes:

1. *The Sons of Karakulak* - Ruled by Chieftain Targ.

2. *The Berserkers* - Ruled by Chieftain Wuglaf.

3. *The Big Bastards* - Ruled by Chieftain Gargandor.

4. *The Mountain Fist* - Ruled by Chieftain Mezeg.

Other significant locations:

Valatos (within the city of Velia) - School for magic - destroyed by Malliath.

Ikirith (inside The Evermoore) - Forest home of the Drakes - destroyed by Malliath.

Elandril (northern Ayda) - Ruled by Queen Reyna and King Nathaniel of house Galfrey. The heart of the elven nation.

The Lifeless Isles - An archipelago in The Adean and home to the Dragorn.

Korkanath (on an island east of Velia) - The ruins of the once prestigious school for magic.

Stowhold (an island north of Korkanath) - The headquarters of Illian's largest bank.

Syla's Pass (south of The Arid Lands) - Entrance to The Undying Mountains.

The Tower of Dragons' Reach (south of Velia) - The abandoned tower where once the rulers of the realm would meet with Gideon Thorn and the Dragorn.

Ilythyra (in The Moonlit Plains) - Was governed by the late Lady Ellöria of house Sevari - destroyed by Malliath.

Paldora's Fall (inside The Undying Mountains) - The impact site of Paldora's Star, a well of powerful magic.

Qamnaran (an island off the west coast of Illian) - Largest known source of Demetrium.

~

Significant Wars: Chronologically

The First War - Fought during The Pre-Dawn (before the elves began recording history). King Atilan started a war with the first Dragon Riders in the hopes of uncovering their source of immortality. The war brought an end to Atilan's reign and his entire kingdom.

The Great War - Fought during the First Age, around 5,000 years ago. The only recorded time in history that elves and dwarves have united. They fought against the orcs with the help of the Dragorn, the first elvish dragon riders. This war ended the First Age.

The Dark War - Fought during the Second Age, around 1,000 years ago. Considered the elven civil war. Valanis, the dark elf, tried to take over Illian in the name of the gods. This war ended the Second Age.

The Dragon War - Fought at the beginning of the Third Age, only a few years after The Dark War. The surviving elves left Illian for Ayda's shores, fleeing any more violence. Having emerged from

The Wild Moores, the humans, under King Gal Tion's rule, went to war with the dragons over their treasure. This saw the exile of the surviving dragons and the beginning of human dominance over Illian.

The War for the Realm - Fought 47 years ago. The return of Valanis saw the world plunged back into war and the re-emergence of the Dragorn. Gideon Thorn became the first human to bond with a dragon in recorded history. Valanis was killed by the ranger, Asher, who died in their final battle.

The Northern Civil War - In the wake of The War for the Realm, the north, under the ruling city of Namdhor, was left without its king, Merkaris Tion. In the vacuum that followed, the lords and great families fell into civil war over the throne. The war lasted nearly twenty years and ended with Yelifer, of house Skalaf, seated on the throne.

The Ash War - Fought 17 years ago. The last war of the Third Age saw Illian transition into the Fourth Age. The orcs return to the surface brought with them war and blood on a scale Verda hadn't seen in ten thousand years. Resulted in the destruction of the Dragornian population and island, as well as the restructuring of Illian's kingdoms. The orcs were defeated and from the ashes rose a new species: Drakes - half-dragon, half-elf.

The Fated War - Though it cannot be said when this war truly began, the people of Illian would mark its beginning when Alijah Galfrey led an army of undead knights through The Iron Valley and took Namdhor's throne for himself. Many dwarven bloodlines were brought to an end and the elven nation lost their beloved queen, but the entire realm came together in a unity never seen before. Vighon Draqaro returned to the throne with Inara Galfrey beside him as queen and commander of the Guardians of the Realm, their line to be continued by Prince Athis.

Printed in the USA
CPSIA information can be obtained
at www.ICGtesting.com
LVHW052340220823
756019LV00018BA/56/J